Prai

HEBBROS

"[A] tale brim full of adventure, mystery, intrigue, laughter, discovery, friendship, betrayal, loyalty, and peace. Friends and foes alike will be made on this epic journey. [C]hildren and adults alike will enjoy this clean Christian fantasy…that holds a powerful message for each and every one of us to be encouraged, convicted, and inspired by."

Alice, *Reading With Alice*

THE HEART OF ARCREA

"I was more than pleasantly surprised with this action-packed, inspiring novel and Nicole's amazing storytelling talent! A humble blacksmith makes for an endearing hero as he embarks on a perilous journey (in Lord of the Rings fashion) …Nicole Sager is a bright, new talent who I believe will go far in the world of Christian fiction. Great read!"

~Lisa Norato, Author of *Prize of My Heart*

"It is a wonderful Christian adventure…with Nicole's book they walk away challenged to improve their character, spiritually uplifted, and feeling not only entertained, but encouraged and inspired to live a better Christian life!"

~Mirren Martin, *Biblical Discipleship Ministries*

THE FATE OF ARCREA

"[J]ust as good as the first! Spies, lies, double-crosses, pretenses, and treachery abound in this story of choosing to realize God's full potential for one's life. Epic! [A]n entirely satisfying sequel!"

~Goodreads—5-Star Review

"A fast moving book, with many surprises and twists. I like that it has a good sprinkling of humor, along with the more serious parts. A great book that strengthens your trust in God."

~Amazon—5-Star Review

THE ISLE OF ARCREA

"Fast-paced, epic and amazing! This book was one of the best books I have ever read!"

~Amazon—5-Star Review

Hebbros

A Companions of Arcrea Novel

Nicole Sager

Books written by Nicole Sager

<u>The Arcrean Conquest</u>
1. The Heart of Arcrea
2. The Fate of Arcrea
3. The Isle of Arcrea

<u>Companions of Arcrea</u>
Hebbros

Front Cover Photo: ©Stockfresh
Back Cover Photo: ©Emily Nelson, Somewhat Photography
Author Photo: ©Amy Hale

Printed in the United States of America

ISBN-10: 1499253605
ISBN-13: 978-1499253603

For every child of God, young or old, who is striving to live a godly life in a dark world.

And for Julia, who waited (im)patiently. Thank you for your encouraging anticipation.

"Let GOD be magnified."
From Psalm 70:4

Table of Contents

	Acknowledgments	
	Introduction	
Prologue	A Gift, a City, & a Mountain	1
	PART ONE – OUTCAST	
1	Sedgwick	7
2	Changing Times	14
3	The Faithful	22
4	Affecting the Future	28
5	An Open Door	33
6	Cause for Celebration	40
7	Suspicions	46
8	Battle in the Schoolroom	50
9	Confidence & Confusion	59

10 Order of Terror 67

11 Raid in the Night 71

12 The Weight of Words 81

13 Banished 89

14 Window of Opportunity 98

15 Daughter of a Nobleman 108

PART TWO – FUGITIVE

16 Terror, Hope, & Candles 115

17 Of Bouts & Bitterness 130

18 Observations of a Lady 142

19 Day of Judgment 154

20 The Girl at the Chandler's 165

21 Troubling Repercussions 174

22 Daughter of a Tyrant 188

23 Attack from the Skies 191

24 Shadow & Light 201

25 Seeds of Dissension 211

26 All in a Day's Work 216

27 A Cap, a Door, & an Apple 226

28 Lord Roland's Day 234

29	Outwitting the Mordecais	241
30	Rooftop Council	253
31	A Fragile Bond	258
32	Together Again	266
33	Loose Ends	278
34	Directionally Challenged	291
35	Reason & Rebellion	300
36	Dawn of Disturbance	312
37	My Way	321
38	On the Streets	330
39	Witnessed by a Mule	339
40	What Happened at the Judgment Square	350
	PART THREE – EXILE	
41	Daughter of a Peasant	371
42	Caught by Surprise	380
43	Crooked Gateway - Golden Tankard	386
44	The Master Slaver	392
45	With the Passage of Time	399
46	Unexpected	406
47	A Mouse & a Mordecai	410

48	The Beginning of the End	418
49	Parting Company	424
50	To Keep a Promise	433
51	Courses of Action	439
52	Daughter of a King	450
53	Lord Bradley	461
54	The Fueller's Plight	474
55	To the Temple	483
56	Signs of a Storm	491
57	Sacrifice	497
58	In His Hands	504
59	Battle for Exile	512
60	Shores of Refuge	523
Epilogue	Home Again	531
*	About the Author	537

# *Acknowledgments*

This book has been such a journey for me. I feel as if I've spent the last year making new friends and having the pleasure of visiting a few of the old. With these friends I have laughed, cried, and stared at my computer screen in the frustration of writer's block! But through it all, one *Friend* in particular has proven over and over that He is *faithful* and *able*, and to Him I wish to give my first and most heartfelt thanks:

Thank you, Lord Jesus!

As always, I also want to thank my *family*, my *friends*, and *others*, who have encouraged me with sweet words and positive feedback.

You cannot know how much I appreciate you!

Lastly, I want to include a special thanks to *Caleb & Caroline*, who endured the first reading of Hebbros with a *patience* that would have baffled Luke, and an *enthusiasm* that would have made Bradley proud.

Keep walking in the strength of the Lord!

An Introduction to Arcrea & her Companions

Greetings to you, my friend! I am Blunt the Minstrel! Many of you, preparing to unroll this ancient parchment and read the account recorded upon its aged lengths, are familiar with both my name and the realm called Arcrea. Lost from your era to a forgotten age of kings & queens, nobles & peasants, quests & battles of valor, this kingdom of old was once a prominent beacon of virtuous light surrounded by other realms, dark with the shadows of evil. For those of you who are yet unacquainted with the stories told in those previous volumes, entitled The Arcrean Conquest, I will not endeavor to offer a retelling. "How uncouth!" you say, "Such ill manners this yellow-headed bard has!" Think what you will, then, of my forthright behavior, I will yet firmly believe that you must experience those other stories in full if you would better understand some characters and situations in this following account. You must discover them for yourself. So then, go first to unravel the prior history of this realm, and then return to read these further narratives of Arcrea and her neighbors. One might call them companion novels of a kingdom's companions! Ha! How witty, would you not say? Oh…ahem… What? You are already familiar with the stories of The Arcrean Conquest? How fortunate! Come then—pull up a stool and sip slowly from a mug of hot cider while you examine the following tale of the children of Hebbros and a people in Exile.

Join the Arcrean Conquest! Start with the trilogy:

1. The Heart of Arcrea
2. The Fate of Arcrea
3. The Isle of Arcrea

*"But Jesus called them unto him, and said,
Suffer little children to come unto me, and forbid them not: for of
such is the kingdom of God."
Luke 18:16*

Prologue
A Gift, a City, & a Mountain

They called it a gift. Most who knew of his remarkable ability inevitably responded by telling him that he had a gift. Others—those whose evil deeds were exposed by the gift—called it a blight. He himself wasn't sure what to call it.

The gifted young man positioned himself in a low crouch. Perched as he was on a ledge of stone several thousand feet in the air, the view was magnificent. His slate-blue eyes shifted downward and memories assailed him.

The fact that he could read men's faces as if their features were one of Master Paul's books, opened to a full description of the individual's character, had certainly served him as a gift. He could easily spot an enemy, a liar, a fool; he knew when he was addressing a man of anger, pride, integrity, or humility. But the gift had also seemed to him a bane at times. While it could bring joy, it also brought great sorrow. So many faces reflected pain, agony, bitterness, fear, doubt…and betrayal.

And he was forced to witness it all with a single glance.

There was nothing magical—nothing mystical about this gift, of that he was certain. He had long ago realized that his natural perception had merely been heightened by God to an uncanny strength and for a purpose yet unknown.

Straightening from his crouch he continued to stare down on

the point where he knew a darkened gate blended with the wall of a city. Would his "gift" prove to be a help or hindrance in the days ahead? Thousands of faces to be read. One goal in mind. His right thumb and forefinger moved habitually to toy with his bowstring as he shifted his gaze to survey the rest of the city.

Hebbros. The city dominated a valley in the northwestern region of Mizgalia, a vast realm known for its fierce population and constant habits of war. It was recognized that this kingdom harbored particular hatred for the land of Arcrea, located south of Mizgalia and beyond the vast expanse of Brikbone Mountains.

It was said that Hebbros was one of the largest and most populated Mizgalian cities, surpassed only by the royal capital of Mockmor. Massive walls protected the city from attacks and wild creatures alike, and, as some secretly thought, also served to keep the multitude of citizens from leaving. There were many who had come to Hebbros from the outside, but during the young man's lifetime it had become unheard-of for someone to relocate to a point beyond the walls.

Thirteen heavily guarded gates barred the entryways of Hebbros, twelve of which were located in the northern, southern, and eastern walls of the city. A single gate to the west, known simply as the Thirteenth, opened to the steep base of Mount Desterrar. Climbing up and away at a precipitous angle, the mountain rose from the Thirteenth until the cliffs along its summit seemed to meet the clouds. Beyond the mountain, crashing against the sheer face of her western cliffs, lay the Delfron Sea.

Thus flanked by the Delfron on one side and Hebbros on the other, Mount Desterrar remained a wilderness, accessible only through the lone western gate and festering with the wild creatures and plants that had bred there since the building of the city's wall and their resulting confinement to the mount's slopes. The sounds of vicious catawyld beasts clicking their tongues in warning filled the night air with a familiar sense of threat. Dragons, a more recent addition to the wildlife, dwelt in the caves that riddled the sea-facing cliffs, and fires were lit on the city walls each night to discourage them from descending to inflict horror on the Mizgalians.

The young man instinctively scanned the starry sky and turned from his vantage point. Deserting the stone ledge, he began to move through the shadows toward his destination.

Legends told of the Mizgalian ancients who had built Hebbros. After leaving Mount Desterrar to the beasts, the sloped wilderness had purposely been left uninhabited by humans. The city's rulers had always used the knowledge of these wilds for their own sinister pleasure, threatening to cast upon its base any who dared rebel against the Mizgalian crown. Generations later no man had yet been cast out, and still the constant looming of Desterrar's heights over the walls of Hebbros maintained a measure of caution in the hearts of the city's inhabitants.

Rebellion towards the king was unknown, at least in public.

Political uprisings had never been realized, if considered at all.

Outcasts were unheard of and Mount Desterrar remained void of humanity.

Until one day…

Part One

Outcast

"Wherefore Jesus also, that he might sanctify the people with his own blood, suffered without the gate."

Hebrews 13:12

1

Sedgwick

Ten-year-old Luke raced through the cobble and dirt streets of Hebbros as swiftly as his small feet could carry him. Dust motes swirled in a frantic dance through the air as the boy's arms pumped in time to the rhythm of his legs. His slate-blue eyes darted to search the shadows ahead for any signs of trouble or hindrance. All was clear. Of course Luke figured the majority of Hebbros's citizens would now be gathering in the city's western region rather than correcting roving children. Luke's schoolmaster, Master Paul, certainly would not come chasing after him.

At least, he hoped not.

Rounding the bend of one circular street, Luke dodged a rattling poulter's cart and ducked beneath the arm of a ropemaker giving directions to an aged tenter. Luke's eyes scanned the small stir of workmen—proof that not all of Hebbros held interest for the scene where he himself was bound.

Fear. Hopelessness. Conceit. Resignation.

Luke paused at a street corner and breathed deeply. Looking left and right, he then darted across the way to another alley heading west. Traversing along stone stairways, tilted lanes, and arched cloisters, Luke's rapid steps sounded back to him in a clattering echo as the late-summer sun dropped golden rays to warm the uneven streets at his feet.

Tilting his head, Luke caught the sounds of a multitude and urged his pace to a greater speed. Finally catching up to the fringes of a westbound crowd, he glanced at the faces around him and was pleased to see that all were intent on the business ahead. No one was interested in apprehending another boy who had escaped his schoolmaster for the day.

Anger. Curiosity. Fear. Arrogance. Disbelief.

Glancing up as he passed by the palace of Hebbros's ruling lord, Luke wrinkled his nose in confusion. What he heard from Master Paul about the Mizgalian city's leader differed greatly from what his mother told him when he returned home from school each night. He loved those secret lessons that took place once darkness had fallen and the cottage's single window had been shuttered. A lone candle always sputtered on the table before them as his mother earnestly told her children of "truth" and warned them to tell no one of the secret lessons. But what was truth? His mother's secret words contradicted everything that the schoolmasters said. Luke was not yet ready to commit his life to those words; nevertheless he reveled in the knowledge that he harbored a secret, feeling much like the spies who worked for the Mizgalian noblemen.

Luke reached up to run a hand through his sweaty brown hair. Glancing over his shoulder he cast one more look at the palace as it disappeared from his line of vision.

Sir Roland of Aylesworth, a Mizgalian knight in favor with the king, had lived in Hebbros for only three years. Upon the death of the city's Lord Aatrias, just one month ago, Sir Roland had claimed the title of Lord of Hebbros to the great wonder of many. No one knew exactly how the man had come to power, though it was suspected that King Cronin had managed the sudden promotion. Some had questioned Roland's right to the title, but no one dared argue with the man or his strict regime for fear of being punished with imprisonment, death, or banishment to Mount Desterrar.

Today's events would be proof that those fears were well grounded.

The noises of shouts and angry chants grew in volume until Luke's ears throbbed and his heart thudded with the pulsing cries. He moved steadily forward with the masses until the streets became congested with thousands, and then squeezed his way through to the front. Finally he crawled between the legs of three men in a heated discussion and found himself on the edge of a cleared area that fronted the gate Thirteenth.

Luke's small chest heaved with each excited breath as his gaze quickly honed in on a middle-aged man standing quietly before the barred gate.

Here was the reason behind the mayhem in Hebbros.

The stranger's hands were bound before him with a leather thong, and a rope around his ankle constrained him to a sturdy pole anchored in the ground. A scattering of rotting vegetables gave proof that the prisoner had suffered these humiliating conditions for several days. His calm but probing eyes surveyed the jeering crowds until they landed on the little boy across the way and he offered a quiet smile.

Peace.

The serenity in those gray eyes jarred Luke's senses, a foreign emotion combating the surrounding chaos.

Suddenly, a boisterous man from behind Luke shouted for a speech and the rest of the crowd joined in his jeering chant, requesting to hear the stranger speak. They quieted when he lifted his bound hands and closed his eyes. Luke's own eyes widened in fearful awe when the prisoner's lips moved in the forbidden act of public prayer. Would someone rush forward to strike him for the deed? No one moved to do so, contenting themselves to scorn him from a distance, and after a moment the man's eyes opened and he spoke in a rich voice that resounded through the quieting streets.

"My friends…"

"You are no friend of ours!" Someone bellowed.

The prisoner continued as if he had not heard the interruption, "A number of you have heard me speak before, and know that I oppose the system of Hebbros that has recently grown worse. We are prisoners in our own homes here! We are no longer permitted to live as we desire, but instead must live according to our foolish lord's wishes. We buy only the food and clothing that he and the Peers choose to bring to our ports. Our native tradesmen are told what they may and may not sell. We are forbidden to worship God…"

"We worship our own gods, you fool! Lord Roland himself prays to nine different deities every day!"

The stranger leveled a steady gaze on the man who had shouted, "But not the one true God."

One of the men behind Luke spat at the ground, barely missing the boy's foot. Luke shot a disgusted look at the man and moved several yards to the right.

The prisoner's gray-eyed gaze moved across the numerous faces, "Our children are being indoctrinated by Roland's regime. They are taught to revere him, honor him, obey him—love him! Even if this loyalty directly defies the wishes of their parents. They are taught that what is right is truly wrong, and that wrong is preferred over that which is good."

His words brought to Luke's mind an image of his mother leaning forward in a sincere desire to teach the love and service of a man called Jesus, while his thoughts reverberated with Master Paul's words of the day before, *"You should rise in the morning and go to sleep at night to the consideration of our great Roland's fine qualities. Show your gratefulness to him by living in accordance with his laws and restraining from any act of rebellion."*

Now Luke pondered the words, wondering why it was so important to think well of this man who had taken over Hebbros and restricted their order of life in a single month. His father and mother did not care for the new leader, but the rest of Hebbros seemed to be in favor of his rule. Was he to believe his mother's truth? Or were the masters correct when they said that many mothers and fathers in Mizgalia did not know today's truth? Had truth changed? If so, when? And how? Who had changed it? What would he do if he learned today's truth and then someone changed it to be tomorrow's truth?

Luke shook his head to clear the cobwebs of confused thought.

The prisoner was still speaking, "Do you not see the danger? He will destroy us! He *is* destroying us! Will no one step forward and join me in my cause?"

The crowd erupted with derisive laughter and the man's gaze found Luke's once more.

Grief.

The boy searched the saddened eyes across the way. He felt a strange sensation like invisible strings pulling at his small frame, trying to draw him away from the boisterous crowd and into the peaceful proximity of this stranger. A sudden longing filled him, a revolutionary urge to answer the man's call and step forward. The stranger might be a traitor to the city, but he didn't seem like a bad man. Luke's innocent heart did not want him to suffer alone.

Before Luke could take a fateful step forward, a hand clamped over his shoulder and he turned with a start to see his twin brother standing behind him. They were nearly identical with wavy brown hair, short forehead, straight nose, sturdy young frames; only Luke's blue eyes did not match the hazel of his brother's.

Anxiety.

"Luke, what are doing here?"

"You scared me, Christopher! I thought you were Warin or Wulf." Luke tried to shrug away from his brother's grip, "What are *you* doing here?"

"Master Paul sent me to find you after you escaped him in the schoolroom."

Luke scoffed, "Master Paul and his lesson in the Arcrean language can wait. Why is he making us learn that heathen tongue, anyway?"

"Come and ask him yourself."

"I have. All he ever says is, 'we will be prepared for anything.' Rubbish!" Luke swept his hand through the air, "History will be made in Hebbros today! Master Paul should have brought the whole class out to see. The very first banish—"

Christopher's hold tightened on his twin's shoulder, "Luke, I heard that the traitor will be beaten before the eyes of Hebbros. Mother would not want us to see—"

"SH! Here comes his lordship!"

Luke finally moved out from under his brother's hand and shifted for a better view as Lord Roland entered the clearing on horseback along with four mounted guards. The powerful man looked splendid in a rich purple robe and the golden signet chain hanging from his neck. The morning sun etched his regal features in bright light and burnished his dark-blond hair to gold. His controlled demeanor commanded respect. The glittering sword at his side defied any opposition. His eyes scanned the gathered thousands and landed on the prisoner before the gate.

Confidence. Hatred.

The crowd became quiet again as they waited for him to speak.

"People of Hebbros," Roland's steely gaze resumed its sweep

over the throng, "let it be known that this man, Sedgwick, has been given a fair trial by the House of Peers and was offered a chance to recant his seditious ways. He has refused our mercy and will therefore be cast out of Hebbros this day to live on Mount Desterrar alone, away from you and your children," he motioned with one arm to indicate the steep mountainside that rose on the other side of the walls, and then nodded to one of his soldiers, "Begin."

The guard dismounted and unfurled a whip as he crossed to where Sedgwick stood in bonds. Forcing the prisoner to kneel, the soldier pulled back and then returned the long cord in a practiced arc of pain.

Luke and Christopher watched in awestruck silence, wincing with every blow. A single tear crawled down Luke's face when the man Sedgwick cried out in agonized pain.

When the beating was done, the soldier removed the bonds from Sedgwick's hands and ankle and pulled him up to stand on shaking legs. Sedgwick turned to face Roland with his head held high.

The ruler narrowed his eyes and shouted, "You are banished, Sedgwick, from our fair city. You will make your own way in the wilderness of our mountain and die in obscurity. Go forth now into exile!"

The portcullis had already been raised. The gate Thirteenth creaked heavily as it swung inward for the first time in many years. Sedgwick turned to step toward the yawning threshold and the people began to taunt and jeer once again, but not before the outcast's final words met Luke's ears and struck his heart like a gong.

"I will go, Roland. I will pave the way with my own sweat, blood, and tears, that others may one day see the truth and have courage to follow me. Only know this; I do not consider this banishment a burden. I go not only to exile, but to *freedom*!"

Luke felt another tear slip unbidden down his cheek to drip from his chin. He didn't understand all that he was seeing and hearing, but something stirred deep within him, whispering that these events would alter the course of his thinking—of his life.

A moment later, Sedgwick had disappeared and the Thirteenth was closed with a groaning thud of finality. Christopher pulled at Luke's shoulder with renewed urgency and the twins turned away from the western wall. Luke looked back once, but could not see the gate through the shifting throng of Mizgalians.

A woman pushed past, shoving Christopher against his brother. Her voice trailed back to them as she shouted to a friend over the clamor, "I say he'll not last a day! The catawyld beasts have bred on the mount for generations now and it's not likely he'll survive an attack."

The second woman nodded in answer, "He'll be prey to the wilds for certain."

The boys turned onto a street heading east and climbed a set of stone steps as the predictions continued to swirl around them like a blinding fog.

Concern.

"Shelter will be scarce."

Indifference.

"He won't last a heavy storm."

Bitterness.

"The traitor deserved to be cast out. He was a threat to our innocent children."

Overwhelmed by the onslaught of surrounding emotions Luke dropped his gaze to his shuffling feet. As he followed his brother through the streets he found himself disturbed by one thought more than any other: Sedgwick had been sent into the wilderness with nothing but the bloody whip-shredded tunic on his back.

2

Changing Times

Lord Roland entered his palace in a silent rage. Slapping his leather gloves into the hands of a waiting slave, he stormed through the halls and up a circular staircase to his private study in the west turret. No one would bother him there. The guard at the base of the stairs had been employed for the sole task of ensuring that Roland was the only person who ever climbed the stairs.

Closing the oak door and crossing to one of the tall narrow windows, Roland leaned against the stone sill and stared in the general direction of the Thirteenth. His gaze darkened as he crossed his arms and thought about the day's events. He was pleased that the traitorous Sedgwick had at last been cast out of Hebbros, but the man's last words still rankled in Roland's mind.

"I go not only to exile, but to freedom!"

Freedom! The gall of the man! How dare he shout before the masses of the great Hebbros that it was freedom to be removed from Roland's power? That to be banished from the influence of the House of Peers was to be liberated!

Roland snorted incredulously and ran an agitated hand through his thick blond hair. At nine-and-twenty he was not a man of aged knowledge, yet even he could see the wisdom in King

Cronin's desires to subdue the people of Mizgalia. A king deserved the loyalty of his subjects. He had the right to assert his power and see to it that every citizen understood his or her place in society. If the king chose to enforce laws that would organize and commandeer every detail of the realm, then the people should accept his provision and thoughtfulness with grateful hearts. And silence.

Roland rubbed his jaw when he thought again of Sedgwick's shouted words.

He glanced down at the throng of people bustling by the palace gate, returning to their work after witnessing the traitor's banishment. Two brown-haired little boys, very similar to one another in appearance, hurried by, casting anxious glances over their shoulders. Roland smirked at the sight. The two children had undoubtedly escaped their schoolmaster in order to witness the exile. Clever boys.

Turning from the window, the man of power crossed to the table that dominated the center of the round turret room. He lit several thick candles, situated them to cast light where he required, and then unrolled a parchment. Taking up a quill-pen and dipping it in ink he sat in his high-backed chair and scratched several names onto the parchment, adding to the list of Hebbros citizens that required careful attention.

Sedgwick may have thought himself alone, but the House of Peers, the city's power-holding group of knights and scholars, was well aware that there were others within Hebbros who opposed Roland's new order.

Roland made several other notes and recorded an account of the day in his personal log. He remembered his private interview with King Cronin at the royal castle in Mockmor and thought of the monarch's strong urging and advice.

"It will take time, Sir Roland, for the people to adjust. Let the elderly die off and their influence will vanish as a vapor. The middle-aged and those in the prime of life will need some pruning; their influence will be harder to ignore. It is the children, Sir Roland, the children who will be most malleable in your hands. Train them up in the way you would have them to go, and the next generation of Mizgalians will be the first of many to reach that state of perfection that I seek."

Lord Roland set his quill aside and blew on the fresh ink, urging it to dry. Rising from his chair he extinguished the candles and left the room. He descended the stairs and acknowledged the guard's curt nod as he mentally reviewed the plans that were in store for Hebbros.

Training children was not a particular skill of his. He was unmarried—had no children of his own—and his own adolescence had been one of rebellion. The House of Peers, however, had offered sound advice on the matter and many regulations had been put in place since the beginning of his rule. Already it had been decreed that Peer-appointed schoolmasters would teach every boy in the city ages six to twelve, before the lads began their apprenticeships at age thirteen. Girls of the same ages would attend a weekly class of instruction taught by Peer-appointed matrons.

Roland smiled at the clever tact. This law would prevent the old-fashioned parents from instructing the next generation in the distasteful art of sedition. He thought of the two boys who had passed by on the street only moments before. No doubt, thanks to him, those lads would grow to be faithful citizens of Mizgalia. They would be men whom King Cronin took pride in.

Yes. There were great plans in store for the children of Hebbros.

Altering his course toward the palace temple, Roland decided that this day of both frustration and hope called for a time of prayer to one or all of his favorite deities. Surely they would approve of his campaign and grant him success in the days to come.

Mariah peered through the window and searched the darkened street for any sign of her sons. Their small hovel was one of many similar cottages wedged together in side-by-side formation to create a narrow street in one of the poorer sections of central Hebbros.

When it was clear that Christopher and Luke had not yet arrived Mariah pulled away and drew the shutter over the window. Her blue eyes clouded briefly with worry as she tucked a strand of brown hair behind her ear. The boys were never this late in coming home, and the streets were sure to be wound tight with tension. Today had brought the exile of Sedgwick, the leader of those in Hebbros who were swiftly coming to be known as the Faithful, an ironic label used with bitterness and sarcasm by the majority that followed Lord Roland.

"Is Father coming yet?"

Mariah turned when the sweet voice sounded from behind her, where five-year-old Charlotte sat playing with a few wooden blocks on the floor. The mother smiled, "Soon, little one."

Charlotte mirrored the smile and nodded, content to believe that all was as it should be. Mariah watched the child stack another block on her tower and prayed that the same childlike faith would fill her own heart.

Oh, but it was hard to trust God when she knew that boys like Warin and Wulf of western Hebbros—whom Luke had dubbed the Evil Twins—roamed the streets with mischief in their hearts. Her own set of twins had been warring with the other set for a year now, ever since Warin and Wulf had come to Master Paul's schoolroom after being banned from their own. There had been some trivial argument over who could claim "walking rights" on a particular street. Ridiculous!

Mariah shook her head and crossed to the crude table, where she pulled the bread and cheese from her market basket and unwrapped the thick cloth that covered them.

At the age of ten children should be making friends, not enemies. Yet how could the children of Hebbros not make enemies when the act was all but encouraged by their schoolmasters? Mariah told her sons to follow the example of Christ, turning the other cheek, but Master Paul told them to defend their reputation as victorious Mizgalians.

Mariah cut a thick slice of bread. Whether or not her sons listened to and followed her instructions, their playmates were sure to follow Paul's. This would make it harder for Christopher and Luke to stand for truth. She longed to keep her sons home each day, sparing them the hours of false teaching, but their father had already dared to approach Master Paul on the subject and had been soundly refused. Lord Roland and the House of Peers would make no exceptions to their plans. All of Hebbros would progress together, leaving no one to make their own way whether they desired such regression or not.

Mariah took the wedge of cheese and began to slice it. She glanced at little Charlotte and felt tears pool in her eyes when she thought on the following year, when the innocent girl would be required to attend a weekly hour of instruction under the tutelage of a wheedling smooth-tongued disciple of Lord Roland. Girls were not allowed to attend classes with the boys but were still expected to hear the new laws of Hebbros and take them diligently to heart.

Mariah brushed at the tears. If only she could teach Charlotte herself. She wanted to ensure that her trusting daughter heard only truth.

The door groaned and Mariah whirled to see Christopher ushering his brother inside. The relief she felt on seeing them quickly evaporated with a closer inspection. Luke's face and hands were awash in mud, except for the streaks where tears had cleared tracks down his cheeks. His eyes were bloodshot and his chin trembled as he shuddered with a heavy sob.

"Luke, what happened?" Mariah was at his side in an instant, gently leading him to a bench at the table where he promptly collapsed and covered his dirty face with filthy hands. "Luke?" When he lifted a stricken gaze to hers, unable to utter a word, Mariah turned with an authoritative tone, "Chris, shut the door and tell me what happened."

Christopher obeyed, leaning against the door after it had closed. Mariah studied his face as he regarded his sobbing twin. For many years no one outside of their family had been able to tell the two boys apart. Now that the twins were growing older, however, it was becoming easier. Christopher was growing broad and his face fuller; his demeanor was steady and loyal. Luke on the other hand was slender and wiry, and his behavior was predictably rash and spirited. Master Paul feared he was quickly becoming a firebrand, but Mariah knew that it was something deeper that made her son fearless. The gift.

Luke's uncanny ability to "read" the faces around him made it easier for him to choose friends and make decisions based on the emotions or character traits that he saw around him. It came naturally to him. The traits found in the people he glanced at simply flashed through his awareness without him putting any effort into the search. More often than not Luke didn't even realize that he was reading faces until there were too many for him to take in at once. He would then escape by lowering his gaze to the ever-blank countenance of the floor.

Mariah had once marveled that he could pay any heed to his

lessons at school with so many boys on the benches around him; but perhaps he didn't, really, and that was why Master Paul was growing concerned.

Little Charlotte grew nervous as Luke's sobs filled the air and she moved to stand by Christopher. The hazel-eyed boy laid a hand on her dark brown hair and shifted his gaze to his mother.

"It started this morning. Luke escaped Master Paul and went to see the exile."

Mariah's eyes slid shut. Had she not warned the boys that the scene would be terrible? How many faces had been read in that crowd?

Christopher continued, "I was sent to find him, and…" he looked down at his modestly-shod feet, "we…we saw him. Sedgwick. Beaten and cast out. When we—"

Luke's head shot up and he suddenly found his tongue, "It was awful! He had nothing when they sent him away! They didn't care!"

Mariah started at his passionate outburst and laid a calming hand on his small shoulder, "What happened after the banishment?"

Luke's eyes were ablaze with clear disgust for what he had witnessed. "Chris took me back to our studies. Master Paul was furious with me for running off and forced me to stand before the whole class to give an account of *all* I had seen," he winced with the words, and Mariah wondered what that *all* had included. "He made me guess how many times Sedgwick had been whipped, and then I had to describe the marks made on his back."

Luke's face crumpled again as fresh tears filled his eyes. Mariah wrapped an arm around his shoulders and remained silent. What could she say? It had been wrong of Luke to run from his authority, but shouldn't Master Paul consider this the behavior of "a victorious Mizgalian"? And it had been wrong of Paul to force a child to describe such awful scenes in detail, to other children no less, but if she spoke out the Peers would surely say that Luke should not have run away to witness the events in the first place.

Mariah reached for the thick cloth in her basket and began wiping the mud from Luke's face, "Your story does not explain away this mess." She cast an inquisitive glance at Christopher.

"Master Paul made us stay late after class. Warin and Wulf were waiting when we came out."

Luke made a bitter face, "The mottled rats! They were jealous because they didn't get to see the beating themselves. They threw mud at me, and Wulf knocked me down, the dirty old—"

"Luke!" Mariah's voice was sharp and Luke ducked his head in shame over the words that had nearly escaped his lips. Silence filled the cottage in a palpable layer of tension. The mother's eyes moved from one child to another and then closed in silent prayer.

God, it is so hard! How can we live this way? How long will the wicked prevail?

"Mother?" Luke laid a hand over hers until Mariah looked down at him. She could tell he was searching her face as he said, "I'm sorry."

Mariah nodded and tears filled her eyes as she beseeched her children, "We must be strong. God will not forsake us, even when our lives look darkest. Even when life seems unfair." She looked at Luke again, "Jesus spoke of loving our enemies, and He lived out that example for us to follow. We shouldn't call them wicked names that we would be ashamed to speak in God's presence."

"We are always in His presence!" Charlotte beamed with pleasure at her ability to add to the discussion.

Mariah smiled back, "Yes, Charlotte, we are."

The door groaned again and Christopher jumped away to let it open. Mariah looked up to see her husband, Althar, standing on the threshold. His weary expression deepened into concern as he scanned the huddled group inside.

"Has something happened?"

Mariah stood to greet him with a kiss and take his cap, and then returned to the table, "The boys will explain while I finish supper."

Long after they had been sent to their pallet to sleep Luke lay on his back beside Christopher and listened to the whispers coming from the opposite corner of the cottage. His father had been grim and silent after hearing of the day's events, and now it seemed he was discussing it with their mother.

Luke couldn't hear everything that was said, but the usual snatches of words fell on his attuned ears until he knew it was more of the usual discussion. His father spoke of hardships at the cooperage, dangerous visitors, and aiding the faithful. His mother spoke of escape, discovery, and trying not to fear.

Luke's eyelids drooped. He didn't understand half of what he was hearing, but then he didn't think he was supposed to. He didn't think he wanted to. He already saw far more than he really wanted to, reading the faces of Hebbros. Mother and Father called it a gift. They said that God had given him keen insight in a time when discernment was invaluable.

Finally Luke fell asleep to the memory of tonight's candlelit lesson at the table. His mother had smiled at them in a reassuring way and told them, "God is faithful."

3
The Faithful

Althar dusted off his hands and then crossed his arms to watch as his first customer of the day checked the repairs he had made on their barrel. The cooper's small workshop was tidy and peaceful, even with Althar's assistant, Guy, hustling to unload a costermonger's cargo of damaged tubs.

"My fruits don't sell well when I've need to store them in cracked barrels." The merchant watched as Guy lifted the last tub from his cart, "I'd near made up my mind to seek another trade, what with his lordship charging higher prices per bushel for the fruits brought in on the Delfron. However, my wife suggested I first try repairing the tubs to please the customers who grace my fine stand each day."

Guy caught Althar's glance and rolled his eyes at the fruit merchant's incessant chatter.

The man continued as he scanned his surroundings with a dubious eye, "And so I've come here as it was the least costly. I say, the place hasn't many creature comforts. Nothing to catch the eye of a passerby."

Althar's other customer heaved a longsuffering sigh—apparently as put out by the merchant's chattering as Guy was—and the cooper cleared his throat to prevent another rush of words from the costermonger, "Excessive creature comforts are not needed when a good reputation is to be had. My shop is certainly not the most successful or sought-after business in Hebbros, but I pride myself in claiming to be the most forthright and honest of my kind."

The costermonger fiddled absently with his cuff. Wispy white hair peeked from beneath his cap and seemed to float about whenever he moved his head. "But surely you have a family to support! How can an honest reputation put food in their mouths?"

Althar's hazel eyes hardened with a glint of determination, "My family may live in poverty, but our situation is no different from any number in Hebbros these days."

"These days?" The merchant's voice rose with a curious note, "Do you complain about the times, sir cooper?"

The shop was silent for a moment. Guy watched knowingly as Althar's jaw tightened and then relaxed. To speak against Lord Roland was to place your feet on the pathway to death, but to speak in favor of the ruler would be hypocritical as far as Althar was concerned. He had already touted his honesty.

Althar returned the costermonger's gaze, "My shop and my family are my business, sir, as the selling of fruit is yours. If I have a complaint against his lordship, then it is between him and myself…alone."

The merchant raised his brow a fraction and turned for the door, "I have settled a price with your man here and informed him of the day I will return for my property." He turned on the wide threshold and gave a curt nod to the young proprietor, "Until then, sir. Good day."

"Good day," Althar tipped his head in return and then shifted as his other customer rose from examining their barrel.

"Thought he'd never leave, I did." The aged man plucked the cap from his white head and dusted off the limp covering, simultaneously drawing from it a worn piece of parchment. Replacing the cap he stretched his arm toward Althar and the cooper shook the offered hand, successfully transferring the retrieved parchment to his own palm.

"I'll take the barrel now and see that—" the old man's words were cut off when a woman entered the shop carrying a small crock in need of repair. Guy moved to assist her and Althar's aged visitor spoke again, suddenly changing the direction of his earlier speech, "I've no need for a cask so large. See if naught can be done for it, and when you've looked it over feel free to dispose of it or pass it on for a price, as you see fit."

"Thank you, sir." Althar quickly tucked the parchment out of sight and turned to stand by the perfectly renewed barrel. It had been the topic of several such conversations with this same visitor, whenever a suitable subject was needed to cover the true and hidden meaning of their words. Their eyes met and Althar nodded his understanding of the older man's message.

Read the note, decide upon a course of action, and destroy the parchment.

Or forward the secret correspondence at the price of possible discovery.

The old man left the shop and the woman followed shortly after, when Guy had settled upon a price for her needed repair. The cooper's assistant set the crock aside and turned to search Althar's face. The two men had known each other all their lives. They had been neighbors as children, schoolmates as youth, and now coworkers as grown men. Each had excelled in his own way, Althar growing in knowledge while Guy developed greater physical strength and brawn. Their relationship was like that of brothers, and their similarities and differences alike reminded Althar of his own twin sons.

Guy took a step closer and lowered his voice, "The message?"

Althar glanced at the door to ensure their privacy. His hand shook slightly as he retrieved the parchment and glanced over the words. His heart hammered as he considered his options. The work offered to him through the old man's message was dangerous, treacherous, and even foolhardy. But it was good work. Honest work.

What would his Mariah have him do?

What would God have him do?

God, set my heart on the course you would have me to follow.

He took a deep breath. Decision filled Althar, and he purposefully folded the parchment and strode to the shop's hearth. Outside, a traveling minstrel passed by plying for pennies and the cooper used the noise to shield his next words from prying ears.

"The small opening in the western wall has been completed without discovery, hard by the gate Thirteenth. A load of provisions will be sent through to Sedgwick in three days' time, and

I have been asked to secret the supplies to the shop where the opening is concealed."

The two regarded one another in silence as the bard outside finished his song and received a smattering of applause from several citizens. The entertainer bowed low and then moved out of hearing down the street.

Finally Guy whispered, "If you agree and are caught, you will be—"

"Executed. Or exiled."

Guy's voice was hoarse, "You know that I support Sedgwick, Althar, but I beg you to consider the consequences. What of your family? What will become of them if you are cast out?"

Althar sighed, "The question is, my friend, what will become of them, of all of us, if I remain silent and do nothing? Lord Roland's regime must be stopped, and for now the most attainable way to begin the fight against him is to support Sedgwick. To see that he does not perish on the mountain as his lordship intends."

Guy took a deep breath and released it as he searched his friend's face, wishing for the thousandth time that he had young Luke's uncanny perception. "Then you are decided?"

Althar nodded and dropped the parchment into the fire, eliminating the option to forward the task to another.

Guy watched the parchment curl and burn and then lifted a steady gaze to Althar's, "You can count me as an aide to your plans." He turned to observe the pile of wooden tubs along the far wall and grinned wryly, "Perhaps I should arrange for our chatty costermonger's bins to be delivered. Sedgwick's load might be disguised within the merchant's property, and we will save the merchant a trip to our shop."

Althar returned the grin and shook his head, "I believe he already suspects sedition on our part. We'll make our own barrels."

The House of Peers' meeting hall was cast in the cold shadows of morning. Lord Roland pressed his seal into the puddle of blue wax at the bottom of a fresh document. He glanced up at Sir Kenrick, his closest friend and a loyal member of the House of Peers, and handed over the parchment with a satisfied grin.

"See that a copy is posted in all of the city's principal

thoroughfares and marketplaces. We've not known such a wave of dissension since the founding of our fair city, and I will not tolerate this air of rebellion that I know simmers just beneath the surface of Hebbros. Any man or woman who continues to resent my judgment on Sedgwick will follow him into the wilderness without even a chance to recant their devotion to him."

Sir Kenrick's eyes roved the document, "And their children, my lord? If the parents are exiled, you cannot expect the brats of Hebbros to continue their training with the masters. They will roam the streets and grow to be a generation more dangerous and seditious than that of their fathers."

Roland exhaled a brief laugh. He turned and lifted another parchment from the table before him, "Here is a list, carefully comprised, of those faithful to me in Hebbros. It is extensive, as you see. When a rebel is exiled, his wife will be cast out with him and his children will be placed in the care of one of these upstanding families. There they will be raised and encouraged to flourish under the care of the masters."

"A sound theory, my lord." Kenrick rolled the sealed parchment and secured it with ribbon, "However, I must naturally wonder whether the citizens listed there will agree to having one or more of the rebels' offspring thrust upon them to be treated as one of their own."

"They will agree because I will command that they do so." Lord Roland placed the list back on the table and looked at Sir Kenrick with a raised brow, "I did not name them as my faithful without cause to believe they were worthy of being listed as such. They will have no choice when it comes to my judgment," he turned and motioned for a waiting slave to bring his gloves, "and furthermore, they will be grateful that I have made the decisions for them. It is a help, not a hindrance, when a wiser man takes control of a situation and leads others forward to their betterment." Roland turned for the door, "See that my instructions are followed without delay."

"Yes, my lord."

"And inform the other Peers that their signatures were not needed for today's order of business. I have taken the matter in hand."

Sir Kenrick paused briefly at his friend's confidence in shrugging off the House of Peers so early in his rule, but thought better of voicing his doubts aloud. Offering a sharp salute, the knight met Roland's gaze and replied, "Yes, my lord. I'm certain the Peers will be…grateful that you have made the decision for them."

Roland's amused laugh echoed back across the empty stone hall as the Mizgalian lord exited the vaulted room. Sir Kenrick watched him go and then looked down at the parchment in his grasp. Incurring the good favor of a man like Roland was invaluable for someone such as he. Roland had the power to set him up for promotion within Hebbros and beyond, and could even keep Kenrick in the good graces of the Mizgalian royalty. It was sustaining this good favor that kept Kenrick in a constant state of caution and even fear. Every word, every action, must be examined before it was produced. Every thought must be contained until it had been analyzed.

Sir Kenrick exhaled slowly. Grasping the sealed parchment in one hand he turned to leave the room. After seeing that copies of Roland's proclamation were made and distributed throughout Hebbros, he would spend the rest of the day in solemn prayer to as many deities as he could think of—or perhaps he should pray only to the nine that were favored by his lordship—in hopes of their favor for his success.

In the corridor outside the large hall the knight turned left and made his way to a small chamber still within the building, where a number of scribes carefully copied all documents produced by the Peers. Lifting his head, Kenrick strode with confidence. He would play this insufferable game of politics. He would claw his way to the pinnacle of influence and control. He would be promoted, perhaps even to the seat of Chief Peer. He would do whatever he thought necessary, befriend anyone he saw as a means to his desired end and crush anyone he saw as a hindrance. In the end he would have his own way, in spite of Roland, in spite of Hebbros, in spite of Mizgalia, and he would live with no regrets.

4

Affecting the Future

Mariah stared up at the parchment in dismay. Her mouth opened in mute shock and her heart pounded an erratic beat as her eyes searched the official proclamation for what few words she could read in order to understand. Lord Roland's signature scrawled angrily across the bottom of the page, accompanied by the unmistakable seals of Mizgalia's nobility and the House of Peers. The black ink dripped in several places, as if the parchment wept for those who would suffer at its command. When she did understand the harsh meaning of the flowery notice, Mariah shifted to make sure Luke had not read it from where he stood beside her. Thankfully, his knowing gaze was locked on something else across the square.

Mariah took a deep breath and prayed that God would give her family grace in the coming days. For years faith in God had been frowned upon by the majority of Mizgalians, but generally tolerated in Hebbros until the beginning of Roland's rule as lord. Now Mariah's faith in Christ was all but forbidden, only whispered of in private. In the earlier times of limited freedom Mariah had first met Althar in a secret meeting held in the home of another believer. Now those meetings were few and far between, wrapped in the tense quiet produced by the fear of discovery.

Sedgwick's banishment to Mount Desterrar had changed everything.

With their foremost leader cast out for openly resisting Roland's oppression, the remnant of the Faithful in Hebbros were now preparing to fight back in a small way. Supplies would be sent to Sedgwick through the wall and every effort made to ensure that his exile was not his death sentence. Once Althar had decided to join the Faithful's small number of active insurgents, Mariah had somehow known that their days in the massive city were numbered. Her gaze darted over the proclamation once more. Perhaps numbered fewer than she had expected.

What would become of her children if she and Althar were cast out for supporting Sedgwick?

Tightening her hold on Luke's small hand, Mariah turned from where the condemning parchment clung to a post at the edge of the square and resumed her quick tread toward the market stalls. The basket on her arm still needed to be filled with provisions for her family.

Luke tugged on her hand and she looked down to see him shifting his gaze from the spot across the square. He looked up into her face and pointed at the object of his focus, "We shouldn't buy our meat from that butcher. He's a liar."

Two days had passed since the trip to the market square with his mother. She had been solemn and mournful after stopping to read an official parchment, and he had failed to return later to read it for himself.

Luke jolted upright and glanced to see if anyone had caught him dozing. *Disinterest. Concentration. Boredom. Zeal.* His place on the bench at the front of Master Paul's class was a most inconvenient situation on days such as this, when he was bone-weary. He had lain awake long into the night trying to sort out all that his mother had taught during their secret lessons at the table. Last night she had told them the story of Jesus, the story called Gospel, and told the three children that He alone could save them from their sins and be their strength and closest friend.

Luke's chin bounced against his chest and he jerked his head upward again. Master Paul sent him an unsympathetic glare and continued with the lecture after a meaningful clearing of his throat. The schoolmaster's voice droned on. The repetitive words swam circles in Luke's head until he was sure he'd heard the speech before and even memorized several variations of it.

Serve Lord Roland with gratefulness.

Follow the laws heralded by his lordship and the House of Peers.

Show support by purchasing the goods brought in by the Peers.

Wear the garments ordered by the Peers.

Eat the foods favored by Lord Roland.

Worship as Lord Roland directed.

It sounded as if the House of Peers, whose wisdom was preached by men such as Master Paul, wanted the citizens of Hebbros to look to Lord Roland for salvation, strength, and friendship. Never once had Master Paul spoken of Jesus. Of course, praying to Jesus was against the law in Hebbros, so it wasn't to be expected that the Son of God would be a very popular subject in the Peer-appointed schoolrooms. That is, if Jesus was indeed God's son as Luke's mother claimed.

Luke's body suddenly collided with a solid object and he jerked awake to find that sleep had pitched him to the floor at the front of his class. Laughter resounded through the room as Master Paul turned with a startled expression and Luke scrambled to regain his place on the bench. Warin and Wulf, the evil twins, howled louder than the others in their amusement over Luke's embarrassment. Lowering his gaze to the safety of the floor Luke waited until two leather shoes, brushed by the hem of a lengthy scholar's robe, appeared before him. Slowly he looked up to meet the schoolmaster's gaze. *Intolerance. Prejudice. Bitterness. Insecurity.* He waited for the man to speak.

"Have I failed to entertain you this morning, Luke?"

The boy's eyes dropped again. Why was Master Paul insecure?

"Do you feel you must entertain yourself by disrupting my entire class?"

"I didn't mean to, sir. I fell asleep."

A ripple of suppressed laughter filled the room and the evil twins openly guffawed.

Master Paul's jaw tightened, "Stand forward, boy."

The schoolmaster turned and crossed to his chair at the front of the class. Luke followed and stood before him, on the opposite side of Master Paul's scroll-laden table. The master leaned his elbows on the edge of the table and glared at the student, "You have caused me more trouble than the rest of my class put together. Is it possible you consider yourself above the House of Peers, above Lord Roland, that you would ignore my teaching of their doctrines?"

Luke lifted his head and returned Master Paul's challenging stare, "I can't help it if your speeches don't hold my interest, sir. I've heard it all before. You talk in circles and say the same things every day, over and over again."

Master Paul sniffed indignantly and straightened in his chair, "My method of teaching is no concern of yours. You will sit on that bench and listen because that is what the House of Peers has declared suitable for a child of your age."

At mention of the Peers something flickered in the schoolmaster's eyes and understanding dawned in Luke's mind. As the rest of the class began to murmur behind him, he placed his palms on the edge of the table and leaned forward to speak confidentially, "You're afraid of them."

Master Paul stilled. He met Luke's gaze and the boy saw unintentional confirmation reflected in the older man's face. Luke continued to speak his thoughts aloud.

"The Peers will question your loyalty if your pupils remain unruly and disinterested. You fear being exile—"

"Silence!" Master Paul rose so quickly his chair toppled and the table shifted, shoving Luke back a step. The murmuring ceased and the room fell silent, except for the slight sound of Warin and Wulf clicking their tongues in censure. Luke watched as a veil of anger shrouded Master Paul's gaze, shielding his vulnerability. He frowned at the boy and hissed, "Return to your seat, child, and remain there in silence until the conclusion of today's lessons."

On any other day Luke would have offered a brash salute before moving to obey. But not today. The stunning realization that a child's behavior could so deeply influence a man's future had subdued him. Luke's mind whirled with a thousand new thoughts. If Lord Roland was indeed threatening the schoolmasters in order to ensure their success in casting the young minds of Hebbros in his favor, then his lordship must fear the children's influence on the city should they refuse to conform.

Luke returned to his place on the foremost bench and sat very still, hoping to appear interested in the progressing lesson while his quick mind continued to explore possibilities.

Could a child such as he truly influence the course and future of an entire city? In what way would Hebbros best be influenced? And how did a young boy go about such an intriguing, if daunting, mission?

5

An Open Door

Althar's thin boots slapped flat against the cobblestones as he headed west. The wheelbarrow that he pushed bumped noisily through the streets as he hurried toward his destination. Turning left at the end of a major east-west thoroughfare, the cooper moved south along the row of shops that sat huddled with their backs to the city's western wall. Spying an elaborate sign hanging over the door of a mercer's shop, Althar steered the wheelbarrow to stop in front of the establishment. Casting a furtive glance in all directions he lifted out a small custom-made barrel and stepped across the threshold.

Fancy clothing made of silks, furs, and other costly materials he could not name, met the cooper's eye as he set the small barrel on the floor. Returning to his wheelbarrow for a second cask he soon placed it by the first and wiped his sweating palms on a cloth plucked from his belt. The mercer was nowhere to be seen.

Althar cleared his throat and received an answering "I'll be with you in a moment!" from the back room. Waiting by the door, the cooper's hazel eyes roamed where his meager purse never would. This shop, tucked against the western wall of Hebbros, was where the wealthy had their outrageous apparel tailored. Velvet caps and lush capes spilled from crates and shelves alongside beads, feathers, and bejeweled clasps.

The mercer finally appeared. A short man, the top of his head barely reached Althar's chest. Graying hair circled from temple to temple, leaving a bald pate. Two large eyes peered at Althar from either side of a stubby nose, and his mouth quirked as he considered the two barrels.

"You are the cooper."

Althar gave a small bow of affirmation, "I am called Althar." He reached out his hand and the mercer clasped his wrist in greeting.

"Ye*th*, I know. I am Liam the mer*th*er." He spoke from the side of his mouth with a heavy lisp and continued to peer up at Althar, as if expecting the taller man to show disgust for his impediment.

Althar gave him none, only nodded, "I've brought the barrels you ordered three days ago, sir." Liam's gaze dropped to the items in question and Althar continued, "The hoops are of beaten gold, the rivets strong, and the staves are of the finest wood I could manage in these…restricted times."

Liam ran a hand over one barrel's glossy head, "They are very fine. I *th*u*th*pect it i*th* hard for an unknown cooper to gain co*th*tly wood from Lord Roland'*th* merchant*th*." The mercer's large eyes shifted upward again to peer at Althar's face, "You have come late. I am about to clo*th*e my shop for the night."

Althar's heartbeat quickened unexpectedly at the anticipated words. Forcing his expression to remain passive even as his excitement mounted, he tucked his hand-cloth back into his belt and gave the coded reply with a steady voice.

"The door has not yet been closed."

A faint glimmer of approval flashed across Liam's gaze as he moved to shut and bolt the front door. Extinguishing all but one of the candles scattered about for light, he motioned for Althar to bring the barrels before lifting the last candle from a shelf and silently leading the way into the back room. Drawing a curtain across the doorway, he turned and whispered.

"Your wheelbarrow?"

Althar matched his quiet tone, "My assistant, Guy, is waiting nearby until the street clears and will then return it to my shop."

"Ex*th*ellent. We do not want it known that you were here *th*o late. When your cart i*th* gone, it will appear that I have clo*th*ed a*th* usual. Now, to work!"

Liam led the way to the back corner and pushed aside a worktable and several crates piled high with richly colored silks. He motioned for Althar to draw nearer, and together the two pulled a good-sized stone from a low spot in the wall. Liam lifted his candle to show Althar the small cavity that had been made behind the ejected stone.

"The *th*tone on the other *th*ide ha*th* been loo*th*ened and will be removed by *Th*edgwick from the out*th*ide. The *th*upplies you have brought will be waiting for him in the cavity."

Althar peered into the blackness of the hollow space. Too small for a grown man to pass through, it was yet large enough to conceal the supplies he had brought.

"How does Sedgwick know that we will leave him supplies? How do we know he is not already dead?"

Liam sighed, nearly snuffing out the candle, "He know*th* of the cavity for *th*omeone found a way to communicate with him before the banishment. We will know if he i*th* dead or alive only when we have *th*een whether the *th*upplies remain after a day or two." The two men exchanged a solemn glance and then Liam waved Althar forward, "Open the barrel*th*."

Althar pried both barrels open and the two men quickly transferred the goods within to the hollow space in the wall. A heavy cloak and thick tunic, a skin for water, a sharpened dagger, shoes made over by a cobbler, a warm hat, and food, including a clove of garlic that Mariah had insisted would flavor anything Sedgwick ate. Placing the last of the items into the cavity Althar helped the little mercer to replace the stone.

Liam gave a wry smile, "*Th*edgwick mu*th*t take the *th*upplies quickly before the *th*mell of that garlic bring*th* every bea*th*t on the mountain to our hollow."

Althar chuckled as he gave the stone a final shove, "I think it ironic that his supplies will be passing through a shop where only his enemies are wealthy enough to purchase goods."

Liam grunted as he pushed himself to his feet, "It i*th* true that only the wealthy can afford to purcha*th*e my good*th*," he plucked the candle from where it sat on the floor and then straightened to look up at the cooper, "but not all of the wealthy are *Th*edgwick'*th* enemie*th*."

Althar's brow creased in thought, "The wealthy can afford to follow Lord Roland, copy his habits, buy what he offers at an outrageous price… I thought it only a matter of course that they would all naturally follow after him."

"One would think," Liam gave a vague nod and started for the door, "but prai*th*e God it i*th* not *th*o."

Mariah glanced through the window at the darkening sky and prayed that Althar would return home in safety. She sat down at the small table and laid her head on her crossed arms.

"Mother?"

"What is it, Charlotte?"

Delicate fingers stroked Mariah's shoulder, "I believed it! And Chris too!"

Mariah spoke wearily, "What did you believe, my love?"

"Gospel!"

The single word was shouted, pulling Mariah's head up with a start. Her instinctive fear of the shout being overheard by someone outside vanished when her eyes met those of her daughter. Unquenchable joy spilled from the child's heart and into her young face. Standing behind Charlotte, Christopher's newfound faith echoed from his heart in a way that differed from his little sister's. Tears spilled down his cheeks as he placed one arm on Charlotte's shoulder and wiped his nose on the other sleeve. Mariah finally broke from her stare and reached out to embrace the two with a sob that bespoke her happiness.

Charlotte pulled back and pushed dark hair from her excited face, "We sat down in the corner while you were cleaning after supper and Chris told us he wanted to trust Jesus like you taught us in the quiet classes," Mariah smiled at the term used to describe their lessons of faith around the table each night. "I asked him to tell it again so I would know too, and I heard Jesus tell my heart that He loves me!" Charlotte's face pulled long with reverence, "I love Jesus now."

Tears filled Mariah's eyes as she shifted her gaze to Christopher. He felt her eyes on him and lowered his head with a sob.

"Chris?" Mariah stroked his hair in concern, "What is it?"

Another sob shook his broad frame, "I…I feel…forgiven! My

heart is new."

The three sat for a moment in tears and smiles of gratefulness until Charlotte suddenly called, "Come sit with us, Luke!"

Mariah's breath caught in her throat as she turned her head to search the room for her other son. In rejoicing over the salvation of two of her children, she had momentarily neglected to think of the third. Still sitting in the corner Luke watched the scene with his intense eyes fixed upon first Charlotte and then his twin. Mariah met his gaze when it collided with her own, and she wondered what he read in her face. Joy? Disappointment? Entreaty?

"Luke?" At a loss for words, Mariah stared at her second son. Why did he hesitate to claim faith in Christ? Always before he had been her adventurer, her revolutionary. He had dared to be different, to be first, to be right. Why not now?

Christopher moved to sit on the floor beside Luke. "He wants to influence the city of Hebbros and fears that if he becomes a believer in Christ, the One despised by our rulers, there will be no way for him to make a difference."

Mariah's head began to shake, "But Luke, this is *the* way to make a difference in Hebbros."

"No!" Luke lurched forward, "There's another way. They fear us. They fear the children of Hebbros! Children like me. I've seen their fear." Luke scrambled to his feet and panted as his excitement grew, "I'm going to lead an army! An army of children." He turned as if to reason with Christopher, "If we stand together and tell Lord Roland that we refuse to sit before the masters and watch as people like Sedgwick are cast out, then he will surely hear us and answer!"

"Of course he'll answer, Luke," Christopher shook his head, "He'll find a way to scatter your army and send you into hiding or exile yourself!"

"No!" Luke's small foot stamped the dirt floor.

"Luke, that's enough," Mariah tried to stop his next rush of words.

"Mother, I know it will work! But if I become a believer I won't be able to hide my faith like the rest of you do. I won't be able to keep from speaking of it, and then I'll be beaten! We'll all be cast out on the mountain to die and none of us will ever be able to make a difference here!"

"Luke!" Mariah's sad tone brought the boy back to his senses.

He glanced around and ducked his head in shame.

Charlotte, oblivious to the reality of her brother's bleak premonitions, leaned into her mother's side and spoke in a matter-of-fact tone, "Maybe living on the mountain is better."

The small cottage was silent for a moment until finally Mariah felt she could control her tearful voice enough to speak.

"Luke, it is true that being a believer is dangerous; but it is still the best way to resist Lord Roland's oppression. He fears the little children of Hebbros because he knows that faith in Jesus could grow in their hearts and make them strong against his evil wishes. That is why you sit before the masters and learn to love Roland and to doubt your father and me. Roland wants to control what you are being taught and prescribe what you think. He does not want us to have our secret classes around the table. He does not want you to trust that God is a gracious redeemer, for once someone possesses that knowledge and holds it close to their heart, God can do mighty things through that person. Even a child."

Once again Luke studied her face and Mariah prayed that his discerning gaze would see love, honesty, and sincerity there. Finally, his head dipped in a slow nod and Mariah dared to hope in the moment that lapsed before he spoke.

"I'll think about it."

That night, Luke tossed and turned on the pallet in the darkened cottage. Beneath him the straw rustled softly, while beside him Christopher sleepily murmured for him to be still. The image of his mother's face as she had looked during their earlier discussion invaded Luke's thoughts, begging to be studied again. *Sincerity. Hope. Anguish. Faith.* She truly believed in this Jesus and spoke of Him as she would a personal friend. She longed to see her children come to faith in Him as well.

It sounded so simple.

Luke flopped onto his back and ran an agitated hand over his sweaty little brow. Simple. Then why did he not accept his parents' God as his own? He had seen the honesty in his mother's gaze, the depth of her faith. It strengthened her, as she had said. Why then did he still doubt?

Luke had heard of fine ladies and noblemen who possessed looking glasses that reflected their image back at them. He had never understood why someone would want to stare at an image of themself, but now he wondered what it would be like. What would he see in the reflection of his own gaze? Fear? Anger? Confusion? Rebellion? Defiance?

Or was it courage? And strength?

Luke rolled over with a moan and listened to the noises that seeped in through the cracks around the single shuttered window. A lone bird whistled softly to the moon. A dog barked somewhere down the row. Several crickets chirped a steady rhythm. Inside, a mouse scurried from corner to corner. Charlotte sighed in her sleep. It should have been a night like any other.

Only it wasn't.

Beneath the shadows of a springtime eve, war had been waged on the frontier of one boy's mind. The prize: the allegiance of a child's soul.

6

Cause for Celebration

Candlelight played with morning's shadows on the rounded walls of Roland's west turret study. The lord of Hebbros stood before the central table and stared in silence at a missive that had just been delivered by courier from the king. For the third time already, his gray eyes scanned the last few words and touched on the royal seal. Finally the young noble dropped the parchment onto the table's surface and turned to gaze through one of the narrow windows. For a moment his tense jaw moved from side to side, and then he released a sigh of resignation and ran a hand through his dark-blond hair.

There was nothing he could say or do to annul King Cronin's directive. Truth be told, he didn't think he would if he could, as this turn of events would serve to further Roland's connections and the reach of his power. However, he did wish the king had used better judgment in regard to his timing.

In all Mizgalia, the city of Hebbros seemed to conceal the largest pocket of those traitors who believed in one God and preferred their Jesus to Roland himself. Roland's gaze sought the table and his eyes skipped over the king's missive to another parchment unrolled beside it. The first batch of these traitors had been narrowed down to the twenty most hotheaded and daring.

Twenty men and women had been marked for sure banishment in return for their stalwart faithfulness to the rebel Sedgwick—Roland's eyes shifted back to the king's letter—and now this. This inconvenience. This interruption to his plans.

Roland huffed impatiently and moved to retrieve the missive again. He quickly scanned it for the fourth time since its delivery. There was no doubting the clarity of the words.

King Cronin had chosen a bride for the lord of Hebbros.

And he had all of three weeks to prepare for her arrival and the wedding.

The lady Rosalynn of Villenfeld, in northern Mizgalia, had fallen upon hard times when her lord father died suddenly several months before, leaving his lands and holdings in desperate disrepair. Lady Rosalynn had been left without a dowry and her twelve-year-old brother, Lord Bradley, had quickly been declared by the king as "unable to shoulder the sudden responsibilities left upon his father's title." Lord Roland would agree to marry Lady Rosalynn and consequentially be given the lands and titles of her deceased father, to care for and restore them to glory. Lord Bradley, whose title was the only inheritance not stripped from his name by this sudden fancy of King Cronin's, would accompany his sister to Hebbros and dwell in the palace as Roland's ward.

Roland cared little that his gain would be young Bradley's loss. This was simply the wisdom of the king at work for the good of all. He only hoped the boy would be a pleasant addition to his home. There was no room for hindrances within these walls.

Rosalynn herself would undoubtedly be a suitable wife. Roland had never met the woman in person, nevertheless he had heard of the promising young beauty before her father's downfall had turned away the attentions of other suitors. He remembered hearing that she had red hair. Roland didn't know what to think of that. He had never been partial to the sight of red hair; then again, he supposed he didn't exactly loathe the color either.

Roland's hold on the parchment relaxed and the letter fluttered once more to the table's surface. He knew it was an honor to be singled out by the king for the furthering of lands and vassals. For his sovereign to choose his bride was a sign of great favor indeed. Roland recognized this fact and felt great pleasure in his king's show of approval.

If only the wedding preparations would not interrupt his plans for the rebels!

A thought struck Roland and he froze. A slow smile crept across his face and he finally chuckled to himself. Perhaps his plans need not be interrupted after all. They would simply become a part of the upcoming festivities. The wedding of a great noble such as himself was cause for celebration. A time to praise the higher powers who would bring such an event to pass.

Roland sat in the high-backed chair and quickly began to set forth an order. He murmured to himself over the newly outlined plans, "For this blessing, undoubtedly bestowed upon me by the gods, I will offer a sacrifice. The banishment will still take place, and Mount Desterrar will know twenty more renegades before the sun has set on my wedding day."

"You are being ridiculous. You will be the first to settle and be perfectly at ease before the sun has set on my wedding day. I'm sure you… Oh! Where is that fan?"

Lady Rosalynn glided regally about her chambers, directing slaves in the packing of her belongings. With her departure from Villenfeld only two weeks away, to be followed by a week of travel before she reached her new home in Hebbros, the peaceful life in her late father's castle had changed to one of bedlam. Pausing in her search for a fan of peacock feathers, Rosalynn turned to face her brother, who was ten years her junior and looking the picture of utter dejection. Lord Bradley leaned against the chamber's threshold, plucking at the long-sought feathered fan in his hands.

"Bradley! You know how long I've been searching for that!" Rosalynn crossed to the doorway and laid a hand on the fan. Her brother's grip tightened, refusing to relinquish the feathery trifle and forcing Rosalynn to pause before him. Dark eyes so like their father's—the color somewhere between inky black and rich indigo—searched her own distracted gaze with desperation.

"How will I settle in a strange place when everything has been taken from me? Even Hugh! As if my inheritance and home weren't enough, the king's man took a liking to my only friend and personal companion and took him away to serve at Mockmor. I'm no better than a peasant in our king's eyes."

"That's not true," Rosalynn brushed a patch of dust from

Bradley's red-brown hair, not daring to ask how on earth it had come to be there. "My dear brother, I know these changes are difficult to grow accustomed to, but they are the king's decree and we cannot argue our sovereign's word. When we arrive in Hebbros I will see that Lord Roland acquires a new companion for you."

Bradley scowled, "But it won't be Hugh."

Rosalynn gave an exasperated sigh, "No, it will not be Hugh." She jerked the fan from his grasp and flipped it open to shield their conversation from the ever-observant slaves, "Do not think that you are the only person affected by the prospect of being uprooted from Villenfeld. Do you think it easy for me to travel so far from everything I hold dear, to marry a man I have never met—have heard so little about? You are truly selfish, Bradley. Think beyond yourself in this matter, for we must both make the best of our troubles. Forget Hugh and prepare to make a new life and new friends in Hebbros."

She snapped the fan shut and turned with a flourish, moving away in a cloud of dark blue silk and bright red curls. They had never been close, brother and sister. Rosalynn had often wondered if they might have been better friends had Bradley been closer to her in age. She often wished he had been a sister instead.

Bradley watched Rosalynn take command of the chaos that was her personal chambers and knew that he should be doing the same in his own quarters. His own private rooms that no longer belonged to him, but to a stranger in the vast city called Hebbros; to a man who had never set foot in Castle Villenfeld, and who probably never would.

Shoving away from the threshold, Bradley suddenly turned to leave and collided with one of Rosalynn's young slaves, approaching from the opposite direction. The young girl took a step back to keep from falling over and tried to balance a pail of water in each hand.

Bradley quickly reached for the pails and set them inside his sister's chamber door. He turned back to see the young girl watching his actions with wide eyes, no doubt frightened that she would be punished for letting him share her work. Her gaze dropped to the floor and she fiddled with her leather collar, evidence of her station as a slave. Then, as if suddenly remembering her error, she dropped in a respectful curtsy, "Thank you, m'lord."

Never call a slave by its name. Rosalynn's nagging reminder flashed across Bradley's mind, but he chose to ignore it, "You're welcome, Sarah."

Her head lifted slightly from its bowed position and she peered up at him with a look of surprise. Bradley wondered briefly where she had come from. Arcrea or Belruse? Gulgthar? Dolthe? Or had she been born right here in Mizgalia? Had she been kidnapped or sold by her own people into slavery?

Bradley blinked to clear his thoughts and realized he'd been staring. His face flushed with childish embarrassment and he cleared his throat before moving past her and on toward his personal chambers. Sarah's quiet voice stopped him before he had gone three paces.

"I'm sorry, m'lord."

Bradley turned to look at her over his shoulder, "What did you say?"

"I'm sorry…for what they've done t' you." Her eyes dropped to the floor at his feet once again, "They've taken so much from you, and right after you lost your lord father. I'm sorry."

Bradley blinked in shock. This girl who had undoubtedly lost so much, who had so little, felt sorry for *him*! His gaze moved to the door behind Sarah and he thought of Rosalynn's lack of sympathy for him, consumed as she was with thoughts of her own situation. His eyes focused again on the little slave girl. She felt sorry for him. She understood that the knowledge of his father's death was still new and painful, doubled by his other more recent losses.

Bradley blinked again, "Then you are the first, Sarah."

He turned to walk away before she could see his tears.

Liam the mercer shoved the worktable aside and set a flickering candle on its surface. Motioning for the room's only other occupant to help him, he then began moving the pile of crates out of his way. At last he knelt on the floor in the back corner and with the help of Guy, the cooper's assistant, removed the loose stone from the wall.

"The candle, Guy," Liam fluttered a hand toward the light and Guy reached out a long arm to retrieve the candlestick from the table. The flame cast a glow over the two men as they leaned forward to peer into the cavity behind the stone. A moment was sufficient to take in the sight before them. Liam and Guy exchanged glances and then looked back at the wall.

The hollow space was empty.

Sedgwick's supplies had been claimed.

The exiled leader was alive.

7

Suspicions

Althar glanced up when a shadow blocked the morning light spilling across his shop's threshold. He felt his spine stiffen when he recognized the skeptical costermonger of the week before. Tossing his tools onto a worktable with a clang and a clunk, Althar dusted his hands off and watched as the merchant scanned the room with a curious, searching expression.

"May I help you, good sir?" Althar took a step closer, "Have you any complaints with the work done on your barrels?"

The costermonger's roving gaze finally met Althar's, "No. No complaints…good cooper. On the contrary, I've come to offer you more work. My wife has taken an idea into her head and begs me to see it through! She has drawn a simple sketch of several casks, which she fancies will make good flowerpots. You will do well with the task, I'm sure." The merchant held out a wrinkled piece of parchment with a simple diagram sketched in the center, and his eyes left Althar's face to scan the shop's interior once again, "I will return for them as soon as you send a man with word of their completion."

Althar cleared his throat to regain the other man's attention, "Perhaps you would like to have them delivered direct to your door, merchant?"

"No." The man spoke so quickly, so decidedly, that Althar could only stare at him in mute surprise. The costermonger turned his lips up in a thin smile, apparently meant to soften the sudden tension. It did not.

"Send your man. I will come for the casks. Good day to you, cooper." The merchant turned and left the shop before Althar had a chance to reply.

The momentary silence was broken by another voice, "Do you think he's a spy?"

Althar spun on his heel to see Guy emerging from the storage room at the back of the shop. For a moment the cooper simply stared, considering the irony of Guy's query when the assistant himself had just been eavesdropping on Althar's conversation with the merchant. Why would Guy remain hidden until the costermonger had gone? Althar shook his head to clear his thoughts. The danger of these last days had made him suspicious of everyone, even his closest friend.

"Althar?"

"I thought I was alone. After the late delivery last night, I didn't expect you to be here first thing this morning."

"It wasn't so late," Guy shrugged his broad shoulders. "What do you think, then? Is the merchant a spy for his lordship? Does he suspect us of rebellion?"

Althar glanced down at the diagram in his hand, "I don't know what to think. He seems suspicious, but perhaps he simply needs honest work done at an honest price."

Guy heard the doubt in Althar's voice, "And yet…?"

The cooper held up the diagram for his assistant to see, "These casks are so simple, even a child could make them. Why should the merchant pay for their construction when he could easily produce them himself? What continues to draw him to our shop?"

Guy took the diagram and nodded thoughtfully, "It certainly seems amiss, but what can we do? Our work for Sedgwick cannot stop now. There are scores of the Faithful in Hebbros who are willing to join our cause now that a door has been opened and a way to help our leader made clear."

Althar's gaze dropped to the floor where several scattered rivets reminded him of the days before Roland's rule. Children had not been kept in the Peer-appointed schools all day, and

Christopher and Luke had come to the shop to watch him and Guy build barrels. The two boys had laughed as they made a contest of plucking stray rivets from the floor, challenging one another to gather the greater number.

The cooper's thoughts were then moved to several nights back, when Mariah had told him of her conversation with their three children. Hearing that Christopher and Charlotte had committed their lives to Christ had filled his heart with joy, even as the same heart twisted in pain over Luke's rejection of the Gospel.

Mariah had lamented over what could be keeping their revolutionary son from embracing the truth. She had reasoned that Luke's gift of reading faces should make it all the easier for him to see the deeply rooted faith that was certainly in the hearts of the followers that surrounded him daily. And yet, Althar had countered, the influence of the Faithful was not the only force that sought to lay claim on their son. Lord Roland's lies were spoken freely from the lips of men such as Master Paul and delivered directly into the ears of impressionable youth throughout Hebbros.

Mariah had maintained that Luke had always been rash, the first to be different. Althar had agreed, pointing out that Luke's choice had been consistent with those traits. He was different in that he was the first of their children to reject the truth; rash in that he was the first to try forging his own way. Their spirited little boy would need more prayers than ever lifted on his behalf, for when Luke dedicated himself to a cause it was done wholeheartedly, and for that reason he would not commit to anything or anyone until he had searched the matter out to its core.

Althar sighed. His work with the Faithful must continue. If men like Sedgwick were allowed to die on Mount Desterrar for their faith, then children such as Luke would never know a desire to live for that same cause. But if Sedgwick lived—if he defied the logic of Mizgalia's evil rulers and made a life for himself outside the city, supported by those faithful within—then some day their voice, their faith, would be impossible to ignore, and good men would no longer live in fear of exile.

If men like the wary costermonger sought to ruin their cause, so be it. Althar would fight even harder for the good of Hebbros.

For his faith.

For his children.

Althar bent to pluck a stray rivet from the floor. He tossed the bit up into the air and caught it again when it came back down. Dropping it absently into his pocket, he turned his gaze to his assistant. "Come, Guy, we have work to do. There are flowerpots to be made, and the door has not yet been closed."

8

Battle in the Schoolroom

Luke slipped inside and leaned against the back wall. The schoolroom was empty and cool, gray in the lifting shadows of morning that played on the walls of stone. He was alone.

Master Paul would arrive soon to remove the shutters from the two windows behind his table and to air out the room for the day, but for now Luke reveled in the silence.

He had run ahead of Christopher and his twin's constant chatter about Jesus. Something had happened to his brother. Something good, Luke had to admit to himself. He saw it in Christopher's eyes when he read his brother's face. But the war still raged in Luke's mind, and he refused to give in to the pressure brought on by his enthusiastic brother as well as little Charlotte.

If he were going to take a leap of faith and believe in the Son of God for the salvation of his soul, then Luke would make the decision on his own. His mother had often said that such a choice must not be influenced by the words and decisions of others, and Luke was intent upon seeing that it was so.

The young boy leaned away from the wall and walked slowly up the middle of the room toward Master Paul's table. The cold of the stone floor seeped through his thin shoes until he shivered involuntarily. Rows of benches to either side of his path waited for

Luke and his schoolmates to fill them for the day. They would sit and squirm and long for the outdoors while Master Paul gave speeches on the goodness of Lord Roland and his House of Peers, all under the pretence of preparing the boys for their futures as Mizgalian men.

The door slammed shut behind him and Luke froze when an icy chuckle echoed across the space to fill his ears. Another mirthless laugh joined in and Luke felt the hairs on the back of his neck stand on end. He kept his eyes forward.

"Look who's here, Wulf. Our very own toppling schoolmate!"

Wulf snorted and Luke heard him take a step closer. "First to fall out of his chair, and then first to come to class. What's your game, then, Luke? You haven't taken a fancy to studying have you?"

Luke's hands balled into fists and he clenched his jaw.

Wulf's twin, Warin, spoke from behind him and to the right, "'Course not, Wulf! I'm sure he just came early to set a prank for old Paul."

"That's not true," Luke forced his voice to remain calm and quiet.

"Of course it is. What did you do this time? Put one of your father's barrel rivets on Paul's chair?"

"I didn't—"

"Spill hot tar onto his table?"

"Or loosen the legs of his chair?"

The evil twins moved closer with every word until Warin's hand suddenly gripped Luke's shoulder, "Tell us why you're here so early, pig."

Luke ducked and twisted away from Warin's grasp. *Hatred. Mischief.* "I don't have to tell you, Warin."

Wulf made a face. *Defiance. Rebellion.* "Then we'll come up with our own conclusions and tell Master Paul what you've done."

Luke forced himself to return Wulf's stare as he rose to the challenge, "You don't have proof that I've done anything wrong."

Warin chuckled and shook his head of shaggy black hair, "We'll make proof, Luk-Luk, and be sure you get the blame."

"Don't call me that!" Luke's eyes bounced back and forth between the identical green-eyed faces. They differed only where an ugly scar traced just above Wulf's left eyebrow, proof of his more impetuous nature. Both boys were broad in the shoulders and promised to be bigger even than Christopher when they were grown.

The three boys stood staring at each other in heavy silence, each waiting for another lad to make the first move. *Hatred. Vice. Pleasure in sin.* Luke dropped his gaze to the floor.

"What's the matter, Luke?" Warin's voice jeered, "Can't you handle a bit of a confrontation? Or did your mother tell you to play nice? Does she teach you to ignore old Paul's lessons?"

"Luk-Luk, Luk-Luk," Wulf quietly taunted, sounding like a chicken.

"Doesn't your mother know that we must learn to defend ourselves as Mizgalian warriors?"

"Luk-Luk, good boy Luk-Luk."

Luke's jaw tightened and he tilted a gaze of anger in Wulf's direction. His mother's admonition to love one's enemies passed through his mind the instant before an insult fell as a murmur from his own lips.

"Scar-face."

The words were barely a whisper, but enough to set Wulf in motion. *Humiliation. Bitterness.* The older boy's face creased with rage and he made a flying leap in Luke's direction. Immediately, Luke dodged to his right and Wulf toppled to the floor. Jumping onto the nearest bench, Luke hopped from one to the next toward the door until a loud bang sounded. He looked up to see that Warin had beat him to the exit and shoved a bench across the closed threshold, making escape more difficult. Warin stacked another bench on top of the first and turned to smirk at Luke just as Wulf grabbed his wrist from behind.

"Caught you, worm."

Wulf gave Luke's arm a quick jerk and the younger boy lost his balance, along with the bench that he had been standing on. The bench tipped over with a loud slap and Luke landed on top of it with a sharp hiss, certain he had just bruised his hindquarters. Luke rolled away and kicked the overturned bench into Wulf's shins, causing the twin to fall forward and land on top of him. The evil twin pinned Luke's arms to the floor and glared down at him. *Anger. Pain.*

Luke glared back, "Get off me, fright!"

"No." Wulf ground the words between clenched teeth, "Not until you apologize for what you called me."

"But it's true," Luke taunted, "and you were calling me names too."

"Apologize, Luke!"

"No!" Luke finally freed one leg and kicked at Wulf's stomach just as Warin dove into the bedlam. Soon they were a tangle of arms and legs, shouting at each other amidst the crash of benches and the shuffling and thudding of their scuffle.

"Enough!" The fourth voice was lost in the mayhem.

Luke grunted and grimaced against the pain of knees and elbows meeting his stomach, sides, and arms. Someone pulled his hair and he howled a curse in Warin's ear.

"*Enough!!*"

The tussling ceased in an instant when the fourth voice bellowed over them. Luke's ears rang and he cringed at the volume of the man's shout. Breathing heavily, he shifted his head and peered up between Wulf's leg and Warin's arm from where he lay at the bottom of the pile.

Standing there, glaring down at them, was Lord Roland.

Sunlight washed his dark-blond hair in white light and winked off of the golden signet chain hanging from his neck. A glittering sword tapped the floor when he shifted his weight, reminding Luke of the man's great power. Luke gulped as he looked up into the ruler's angry face. *Disgust. Fury.* Their eyes met and Luke gasped when a multitude of traits instantly overwhelmed his perception. *Pride. Vanity. Conceit. Love of power. Love of gain. Corruption. Immoral. Indifferent. Selfishness. Confusion…* Luke squeezed his eyes shut to escape the onslaught, unable, in his current position, to lower his gaze to the floor.

"Get up." Lord Roland's command echoed across the schoolroom and the three boys scrambled to obey.

Luke shifted his gaze to look beyond his lordship, where two soldiers stood guard by the door. On the threshold, Master Paul stood watching the scene with a pale face. *Fear.* Around him stood a crowd of Luke's schoolmates. *Surprise. Amusement. Suspense.* And Christopher. *Shock. Disappointment.* One look at his brother's face and Luke knew that his twin had not only seen him fighting, but had also heard him swear. Luke's face flushed with shame and he bowed his head, escaping to the never-changing face of the floor. Only then did he realize Warin and Wulf were speaking.

"…his fault, my lord. Wulf and I were waiting for Master

Paul, practicing the daily exercises, when Luke surprised us from behind."

"He pushed Warin off the bench and pinned my arms behind me!"

"Calling us terrible names…"

"And threatening to blame us for trouble with the master!"

Roland's eyes bounced back and forth between the identical faces, one of them scarred above the left eyebrow. The third boy appeared ashamed of his behavior one moment, and the next he glared at the twins in shock, as if they spoke fluent in falsehoods. Finally Roland heaved an impatient sigh and lifted his hand in a plea for silence, which he received.

He turned, "Master Paul, I was informed—no, *assured* that all was well in the schoolrooms of our fair city. How is it, then, that I arrive to observe yours this morning and find the room in terrible disarray, and with children fighting like common mongrels on the floor?"

Paul's face went whiter still and his wide gaze darted to and fro, taking in anew the sights of overturned benches, scattered parchments, tilted table, and spilt ink.

"My…my lord, I…I can only say that," his eyes shifted beyond Roland and turned cold when they fell on one of the three boys, "this child has caused me no small trouble. He is the only lad among all my students who brings me great grief. I have taught these boys according to the standards of the great House of Peers, I swear it! Only this…this child seeks to disrupt the peace of our schoolroom. I know not what is to be done with him. He will not learn."

Roland pivoted again and his eyes landed on the accused. The boy called Luke. Beside him, the dark-haired twins failed to hide their smirks of satisfaction. The younger boy's face was a mask of obvious disbelief as he stared up at Paul, causing Roland's brow to crease with curiosity.

"Why do you stare at your master with such an expression, lad?"

The boy's gaze shifted to collide with his and then dropped to the floor, "I'm confused, sir. He blames me for doing exactly what he taught me to do."

Roland stared at Luke, rendered speechless both by the child's wisdom and his audacity to speak it. The boy continued, warming to his subject, but keeping his eyes on the floor.

"I sit on the front bench in this room every day and listen to Master Paul's speeches about honoring you, honoring the House of Peers, and honoring myself as a Mizgalian. He tells me to fight for what I want, to defend my kingdom's reputation by defending my own, and then grows angry with me when I've done just that."

Roland's jaw worked back and forth as he stared down at the top of Luke's head. A thousand thoughts raced through his mind, but one in particular won the battle for preeminence. He turned to face the door, "Paul, you and this boy will remain here. The rest of you leave us immediately."

The mischievous twins moved for the door with a triumphant gait, shoving Luke as they passed him by. The crowd of boys behind Paul clambered away from the scene as quickly as they could. Only one who bore a remarkable resemblance to Luke hesitated before turning to leave. Roland signaled for his soldiers to wait outside with the rest of his mounted guard and then nodded for Paul to shut the door. When they were finally alone, he turned to face Luke again.

"Tell me who your father is."

Luke lifted his head and for the second time his slate-blue eyes met Roland's with a look that seemed to pierce through to his soul. The boy's eyes then widened and he dropped his head again in silence.

"Luke," Paul's voice shook as he tried to sound stern, "answer his lordship now."

The small head of sun-washed brown hair shook back and forth in a blatant refusal.

Roland took a step closer to the boy, trying a different approach, "You have nothing to fear from me, Luke. I seek only your betterment and protection. Now tell me, who is your father?"

Silence.

Roland took a deep breath of impatience, willing himself to keep control.

Suddenly, Paul's voice sounded again, "His father is Althar the cooper. He lives here in central Hebbros."

The ruler rolled his eyes in disgust at the schoolmaster's easy surrender to Luke's play of silence. He shot the man a look that spoke his displeasure and then snapped his fingers at Luke. "You will leave us now."

Luke moved obediently to the door, pausing on the threshold to look back at Roland with an expression of what could only be called defiance. His mouth quirked in an odd smile and he spoke quietly, but with sudden confidence, "'Til we meet again, my lord."

The strange words unnerved Roland. He swallowed once and then shouted, "Leave us!" before the boy disappeared outside. Breathing deeply, Roland turned to face Paul. The schoolmaster immediately began to sputter.

"You should not have let him go, my lord, without being punished for his misbehavior. He is a firebrand, my lord. A troublemaker! I tried to tell you, he is—"

"Enough, Paul." Roland stalked closer until he had backed the scholar against the wall, "Stop making excuses and listen to me. That boy speaks with the foolishness and boldness of a rebel—of those who call themselves the Faithful," he spat the words as if they were poison on his tongue. "Such a failure in his training could only be the result of the teaching in your schoolroom," Paul gulped and his face paled again, "or in his own home."

Paul opened his mouth to speak, but Roland held up a hand to stop the rush of excuses before it could begin. His pulse pounded with the excitement of apprehending another rebel. "I will look into the matter, you may be sure. If the fault is with this Althar, he will pay for his crime."

"But, my lord, the cooper is an honest man."

Roland was unsure whether Paul suddenly felt sympathy for someone other than himself, or if he knew the cooper would be blameless and so feared retribution on his own head. Roland leaned closer and hissed in Paul's face, "I do not trust honest people. More often than not, they are the secret-keepers." He backed away and moved toward the door, "However, if I do find that the failure is yours, you will regret the day you first donned your scholarly robes."

The door opened and then closed with a thud that left the room shuddering and Lord Roland was gone, leaving Master Paul alone in the overturned schoolroom.

Warin and Wulf scampered from the schoolroom, pushing their way to the front of the crowd of boys who were spilling into the street. Their schoolmates dodged from their path, casting dark scowls at their backs and muttering ugly threats that they would never dare to voice aloud within the twins' hearing.

The two boys headed west toward home, making a game of knocking the caps off of all those they passed and darting out of reach of the punishing hands that followed their actions. They ducked into alleys and clattered up and down stone stairways, laughing at the chaos left in their wake until Wulf suddenly stopped in his tracks several corners from the place they called home.

Warin sensed his brother's halt and turned with an inquisitive look, "What is it, Wulf?"

Wulf swallowed, his breathing suddenly shallow, "Do we have to go…there?"

Warin glanced in the direction of home and then returned a look of understanding to his brother's pale face, "I came this way out of habit when we left the schoolroom. We don't have to go home yet. Old Monty can't know that we left school early today, so he won't expect us 'til the usual time tonight."

Wulf nodded and unconsciously lifted a hand to finger the scar above his left eyebrow. His face darkened when he remembered Luke's taunts about the marred flesh. No one teased him about that mark and escaped his revenge.

Warin watched his twin's finger trace the long white line. "You might as well do what he asks, Wulf, and then you won't risk—"

"No. I won't call him Father, Warin." Wulf's face turned red and he spoke with a snarl worthy of any catawyld, "He's no blood relation of ours, and only wants us to call him that so we'll feel indebted to him for taking us in when our real parents died of the sickness. He lets us live in that dirty hole of a room with him 'cause some day we'll earn handsome wages as soldiers, and he wants to ensure his 'kindness' is rewarded with gold from our pockets."

"I know it, Wulf." Warin took his brother's shoulder and steered him north, "If I didn't think he'd find us and drag us back like last time, I'd suggest we find another place to live. But he knows how to make other folks believe we're his sons…"

"And pick their pockets at the same time," Wulf interjected.

"…and he's strong enough to see us brought back," Warin rubbed a hand over his own arm, where old bruises evidenced Monty's iron-like grip. "Listen. This is our last year of Peer-classes and then we'll be apprenticed. When that happens we'll find a way to escape Monty." He paused and turned to face his brother, "Until then, do whatever it takes to keep him peaceable. We'll find our way out."

Wulf curled his hands into fists and hissed through clenched teeth, "If he *ever* strikes me again, he'll be sorry."

Warin answered with a grim nod, "We'll stick together, and one day Monty will pay for what he's done to us." He playfully punched his brother's shoulder and quickened his pace up the street, "I'm hungry. Let's filch something for our midday meal."

9
Confidence & Confusion

Sir Kenrick turned with a start, as did the other Peers, when Lord Roland burst into the vaulted meeting hall. Sir Monotun stood frozen in place at the center of the room, one arm lifted and mouth open in mid-word position, clearly surprised that his boring speech had been interrupted.

"My lord Roland," the Chief Peer rose from his cushioned seat at the head of the hall and watched with a furrowed brow as the ruler marched purposefully across the open space, "you have interrupted an important session of the Peers."

Kenrick doubted that this session's importance was truly great. Sir Monotun had been droning about pigs and turkeys for an hour at the very least. However, a single glance left no room for doubt that the Chief Peer was not alone in frowning on Roland's presumption to interrupt.

Roland paused and glanced at the faces that surrounded him, "So I have, and you will continue after I have seen to a most urgent matter of my own. Kenrick!"

Sir Kenrick straightened when the room's focus shifted to center upon him.

Lord Roland approached and held his hand out expectantly, "I need to see the list of twenty."

Kenrick's fingers crawled through a stack of parchments on the table before him until finally he located the one requested, "Here you are, my lord."

Roland took the document, unrolled it, and scanned it with a furtive eye. Searching. His gaze was caught by something halfway down, and Kenrick heard him release a huff of satisfaction. Roland rolled the parchment and extended it to Kenrick in one fluid motion. The knight accepted the parchment and then watched with the other Peers as Roland turned to leave the hall.

"Was there something you needed, my lord?"

Roland turned with a strange smile, "Surprise will be our greatest asset."

Kenrick's brow quirked in confusion, "My lord?"

"Carry on, my friends. All is well. And remember: little by little."

The doors closed on Roland and the hall was silent as some wondered and others seethed over their new lord's audacity. Sir Kenrick felt more than one glance directed his way, and he relished the feeling of jealousy inspired by his close friendship with Roland. The knight turned from staring at the door to look down at the parchment in his hand. The list of twenty. What had Roland been looking for? Suddenly curious to review the list, Kenrick's fingers moved to unroll the parchment, but in the next instant all questions of etiquette and opinions of his lordship were forced aside when Sir Monotun was given permission to resume his speech.

"…great many swine in the northern region, while the opposite is true of the eastern quarters. Meanwhile, the trade of fowl in the south overruns all thoughts of swine, and the balance of our city's trade is lost…"

Luke raced through the cobble and dirt streets of Hebbros as swiftly as his small feet could carry him. Dust motes swirled in a frantic dance through the air as the boy's arms pumped in time to the rhythm of his legs. The city passed by in a wild blur of stone archways and steps, dust-colored homes and shops, shadows and patches of light. He didn't know where he was going. His slate-blue eyes sought only where to place his next step, never once lifting to scan the faces that surrounded him.

He thought again of Lord Roland's face in the schoolroom, and the wickedness that had been revealed in his gaze. He shuddered. Lord Roland was the man whose praises were sung all across the city. The man whom Luke had been taught deserved his honor and respect.

Yet how could he respect such evil?

"Luke!" Christopher's voice beckoned from somewhere behind him, but Luke ignored his twin's call. Racing into a narrow alley, he sank into the shadows with his back against the wall and his head pressed to his knees.

Tell me who your father is.

Roland's command echoed across the chambers of Luke's mind. Why would he ask such a thing? Why did his father's identity matter to his lordship? Luke dug his fingers into his hair and tried to think beyond the eagerness he had seen in Roland's eyes when he had pressed for an answer to his strange query.

I seek only your betterment and protection. Now tell me, who is your father?

"Luke, what happened?" Christopher came panting to a stop before his brother, "After I left, what did he say to you? Did he hurt you?"

"No," Luke spoke and then thought better of his answer. There had been no physical pain, but there had been anguish, a pain in his heart, when he had read Lord Roland's face. Never before had he been faced with so deep a perception into a man's character.

Christopher's silence brought Luke's head up to see his twin searching the ground with an unseeing gaze. *Distress.* When their eyes met Luke knew that his brother had accepted the answer to his last question and moved on to another.

"How could you do that, Luke? Mother has taught us to be kind to our enemies."

"It was the evil twins' fault!"

"You shouted a curse in front of everyone! What would father say?"

Luke turned his face away, "I know he'd be grieved by what I've done, and I'm sorry for that."

Tell me who your father is. Luke winced and a tear squeezed out from his eye. Was it possible that his father would be punished in some way for Luke's actions? That was unjust.

"Luke, can't you see that you've done wrong?" Christopher sank to sit beside his brother and laid a gentle hand on his twin's shoulder, "Why won't you trust in Jesus? I don't understand…"

"No, Chris!" Luke shot forward to escape his brother's touch. Jumping to his feet, he whirled to look down at his twin, "I don't want to hear any more. You believe in a God who punished his son for everyone else's sins. That is injustice."

Christopher's head was already shaking in denial as he rose to look his brother in the eye, "No, Luke. It is mercy."

Luke's young face twisted in confused disbelief, "Do you hear your own words, Chris? It's madness!"

Christopher held his hands out in a simple plea, "Let me explain it to you."

Luke shook his head as his feet began to back their way out of the alley, "You have." His voice took on a bitter note, "You've explained it over and over, and I still don't understand."

"But, Luke… Wait!"

"No." Luke's small frame shook with weary rage, "I'm tired of hearing the same stories every day. From Master Paul, from mother, from you. Everyone repeats their words, and it's all a jumble in my head. I don't understand. Everything I hear confuses me. Everything I see is overwhelming. I don't want to hear any more. I'm tired of seeing so much. Leave me alone!"

Luke turned to run again, but Christopher caught his hand before he could leave the alley.

"You're my brother, Luke. I can't leave you alone. I won't."

Tears ran freely down Luke's face as Christopher threw one arm around his shoulders. The elder twin led the younger on a slow walk toward home, sheltering Luke from the curious stares of others and guiding their steps in the right direction. As they walked together, forced to mature before their time through fears and the unknown, Christopher saw the situation through new eyes.

Luke was like a fragile butterfly, vibrant and wanting to fly to incredible heights before he was ready. A gentle pressure on his wings would hold him down until the time was right, and this would be a kindness; however, too much of that kind pressure would crush a butterfly's wings and prevent him from ever taking flight.

Christopher glanced at his anguished twin and tightened his

protective hold on the boy's shoulder. Telling Luke about Jesus was a kindness, but if Luke was unprepared to accept the truth, then too much pressure would surely turn him away from God instead of closer. Christopher would have to be patient, always ready to share truth with his brother, but using wisdom to discern when the time was right.

"I love you, Luke." Christopher gave the smaller boy's shoulder a gentle pat, "I'll pray for you."

Luke shook with a sob, "I'm scared, Chris. Everything confuses me and I'm scared."

"I know." Christopher sighed, sounding wiser than their ten years, "Just remember, no matter what happens I'll always be your brother. No matter what choice you make we'll always be a family. And I'll keep praying that you'll know the peace of God."

The twins continued on their way home, where they told their mother of the morning's occurrences. Sitting on the bench at the table, Mariah's face grew taut as she listened and her eyes slid shut when Luke mentioned Lord Roland's strange request to know Althar's name.

She cleared her throat, nevertheless her voice still sounded ragged as she asked, "Did you tell him?"

Luke shook his bowed head. His eyes had not left the floor since he'd walked through the door, and Mariah guessed that he was trying to escape from what he'd seen that morning. Now he lifted a tearful gaze to hers and spoke around a sob. "Master Paul did. He was eager to know, mother. There was so much evil in his gaze."

"Master Paul's?"

"No. Lord Roland. I've never been so overwhelmed by a face before." Luke tried to take a deep breath and shuddered, "He frightened me."

Mariah was silent for a moment. She glanced at Christopher, leaning against the wall by the door, and then shifted to watch as Charlotte played with a small piece of bread dough across the table. Finally, caressing Luke's hair with a gentle hand, she began to speak slowly.

"Perhaps you will understand now that it would be unwise for you to start a revolt against Lord Roland on your own."

Luke tensed. His eyes were studying the floor again as he spoke carefully, "I would not be on my own. I want to gather an army. An army of children like me."

"Oh, Luke," Mariah framed his face with her hands, "there are no children like you."

Luke stared at his mother. *Compassion. Pleading. Affection.* She gently rubbed her thumbs over his cheeks as she continued to speak.

"No one else sees what you see. Yes, there are others who dislike his lordship, but there are no other children in Hebbros who can look at Roland and see the depths of his wickedness with a glance."

"But I can tell them," Luke's whisper was intense. Charlotte glanced up from her dough, listening, "The people who know that I can read faces call it a gift. If I tell more people, then they'll believe me and follow me in a revolt against Lord Roland. I know they will."

Mariah's hands dropped to her lap. Luke's innocence and simplicity of thought could not be argued when he was unwilling to listen to common sense. She glanced up and saw Christopher roll his lips together and nod his head with an expression of understanding. Apparently this day had brought the same conclusions to Luke's twin.

Mariah stood, "Luke, I know this is important to you, but as your mother I refuse to let you create more trouble in Master Paul's schoolroom." Luke's head shot up and his mouth opened in protest, but Mariah continued, "You may not see it now, but you have no cause to fight for. It would be rebellion, not revolution. I will not let you start such a business."

Luke's eyes pleaded with her, "But there *is* a cause, Mother! You know that Master Paul teaches us lies, and tells us to live for a man who is wicked. If we refuse to listen to him, we can stop his lies!"

Mariah's gaze sought the view through the lone window, and her voice sounded weary, "How can I make you understand, Luke? You want to fight for the fall of evil, but when evil falls it must be replaced by righteousness if it is to be truly conquered." She turned to look down at her slender firebrand of a son. Her voice was quiet but firm as she went on, "Luke, my son, righteousness is found in Christ alone…and you have not yet found it."

He looked shocked by her blunt speech, and Mariah's eyes filled with tears at the pain she knew she inflicted. She heard a shuffling noise as Christopher took Charlotte's hand and led the little girl outside, but her gaze remained on the boy seated at the table.

"Luke, I don't want to sound cruel, but if I love you I must try to make you see the greatness of this matter. Even if it pains you to hear it." Her son's gaze continued to pierce hers and she swallowed, "You have greatness about you. You were born to lead. But you are so young, and you are not ready. You cannot fight against a force when you refuse to sever ties with its leader."

Luke's eyes widened as he sought to understand, "What do you mean?"

Mariah retook her seat beside him, "I mean that there are two sides to this battle: darkness and light. Lord Roland is of the darkness and is an enemy of Jesus Christ, who is the King of light. You have said that you are an enemy of Roland, and yet you refuse to join the army of Christ. Luke," she gently laid her hands on his shoulders and searched his face with desperation, "where, then, is your allegiance?"

"I…" Luke paused and then took a deep breath, "I don't know."

His gaze dropped to the floor and Mariah laid her forehead against his. She closed her eyes and prayed silently before speaking again. "I suggest you seek out the answer to that question, my son. When you have found it, then you will have found your purpose. For in our city, each man must choose between light and darkness, and his choice will surely decide his fate."

Luke sniffed as tears filled his eyes, and he buried his face in his mother's shoulder, "Will they punish father for what I did?"

Mariah swallowed against tears of her own. What could she say? How could she put her concerns into words without instilling fear in the heart of this lost child? How could she answer his question when she herself did not know the answer? Would Althar be punished? Would she? Not for what Luke had done, but for what they had done themselves and taught to their children. For they—Althar and she—had made their choice long ago. And they had chosen light.

The rising sun warmed his calloused fingers as he worked to

clear the narrow path of weeds. Coming to a steep slope of rock, he took out hammer and chisel and began to chip away at the stone, slowly forming a crude stairway. Sweat dripped into his eyes as the sun climbed high and then dropped low, but still he worked on. Pausing to rest only when he grew too weary to think, and concealing himself only when the tongue-clicking catawylds drew near, he passed each day in the same routine.

Clear the path and march upward. Ever upward.

While he worked, his lips moved in prayer. Praying to the God who had been outlawed from the walled city below him, yet who still chose to work in the lives of a faithful few. It was on behalf of these Faithful that his prayers were spoken now, as the sweat of his brow and the blood of his hands mingled with the dirt at his feet.

Step after step, he prayed for them by name.

Inch by inch, he prayed for their children.

And then, one morning, a terrible sense of foreboding gripped his heart with urgency. His gray eyes were drawn to the city he had left behind, and his gaze took in the sight of a thousand bright banners fluttering from the pinnacle of every tower and high structure. The city was draped in a cloak of festivity. A celebration would soon be held in Hebbros.

On the rocky ledge where he had been working, Sedgwick fell to his knees and bowed his head in fervent prayer. His anguished heart was heavy with the knowledge of their coming trials, yet he did not ask that they might be spared the sentence that had fallen on his own head. Instead, the plea that arose from his lips that day was simply, "God, strengthen them and give them grace."

His prayer ended, Sedgwick turned and began his work once again, preparing a path that led upward to the summit of Mount Desterrar.

10
Order of Terror

Lord Roland traversed the halls of the Peers' meetinghouse, his sword clicking against the floor with each purposeful step. Behind him, a scribe scurried to keep up with his pace.

Beside him, the Chief Peer cast furtive glances in his direction. Finally, as the door to the meeting hall came into view, the notable Peer voiced his uncertainty.

"My lord, do you not think that this matter should be postponed until after your marriage?" Roland's steady tread did not slacken and the Chief Peer hurried his words as they neared the door, "Matters concerning the Faithful have been in constant review by the House, and none of the Peers believe they pose any danger for the near future. Would it not be wise to have the full support of all Hebbros during the celebration of your wedding, just two days away? Let them think they are secure for now."

Roland finally stopped walking, so suddenly that the Chief Peer had gone two steps further before he also stood still. His robes swirled around him and he worked to calm his quick breathing as he waited for the lord of Hebbros to answer his query.

"Most honorable sir," Roland's voice held a steely calm as he met the older man's questioning gaze, "they have thought themselves secure long enough. They have plotted rebellion since the day of Sedgwick's banishment. If you and the Peers believe that to be inconsequential, then perhaps you are not fit for the chairs you hold in this hall. One might think that you yourself supported this rabble."

The Chief Peer stiffened indignantly, yet fear shone in his eyes. "My lord, I only thought that you might wish to postpone this event until after your day of joy."

A sinister smile appeared on Roland's face and he gave a short chuckle of amusement, "Have no fears, Peer. This event will bring me great joy."

They started forward again and entered the meeting hall to the cry of a herald. The members of the House turned as one to watch them enter and then moved to sit. The Chief Peer took his seat at the top of the hall and motioned for Roland to join the venerable House for their special session. Roland nodded and moved to his own chair beside the Chief. When all were seated, a trumpeter sounded the beginning of their meeting and the Chief Peer nodded to the herald, whose tinny voice then echoed across the vaulted room.

"The House of Peers calls forward Sir Kenrick of Hebbros."

Sir Kenrick rose and walked to the center of the room, facing the top of the hall. His eyes flickered briefly to the lord of Hebbros before the Chief Peer nodded to Roland, who stood and addressed the selected knight.

"Sir Kenrick, as a faithful member of the House of Peers and a loyal knight in the command of King Cronin, you are selected this day and set apart for a new purpose in our midst. As lord of Hebbros, I initiate this day a new order of knights called the Mordecai Order, for the protection of the city of Hebbros." Roland saw Kenrick's mouth twist in a brief smile, and he mirrored the expression with anticipation of seeing his plans come to pass. "Sir Kenrick, I hereby name you Chief of the Mordecai Order. I place in your hands the supervision of all things pertaining to those rebels who call themselves the Faithful—those following in the steps of Sedgwick—and to their children, who will be resettled in homes belonging to those loyal to me and to the House of Peers. Look well to the task, sir. If your name should come to bring terror to the hearts of Hebbros, then you will have done your duty well, for only when the people fear the consequences of rebellion will they cease to partake in it."

Sir Kenrick saluted, "I am honored by your confidence, my lord, and trust that my services in the Mordecai Order will please you." Drawing his sword, the knight held the blade out on open palms as a symbol of his offered service, "My sword is yours, my lord. I would now request that my lord give me the choice of the Order's first knight, for I have the ideal man in mind."

Roland sat back in his seat and motioned with one hand for Kenrick to go on, "Who would you have, sir?"

Kenrick sheathed his sword with a sharp snap and stood at perfect attention, "An acquaintance of mine from the east, whom I knew when training in the royal capital of Mockmor. Sir Valden of Lork."

The Chief Peer motioned for the record of knights to be brought forth, but Roland held up a hand to stay the action. The Chief Peer looked annoyed, but Roland ignored him and shifted his gray eyes back to Kenrick.

"Do you vouch for his character and loyalty?"

"On my honor, my lord. He will not disappoint the Order."

"Then I will prove my faith in you by trusting your choice in this Valden. Bring him to me when he has been summoned to Hebbros, and I will personally welcome him to our fair city." Roland took up a small wooden box and, removing the lid, revealed a ring with the newly-fashioned seal of the Mordecai Order, "This ring will give you all authority in matters pertaining to the Order. Use it wisely. Use it well."

Kenrick accepted the ring and slipped it onto the middle finger of his right hand. He studied the simple design of the coin-shaped golden seal, decorated with a raised letter M and an arrow laid horizontally across the middle. He raised his eyes to meet Roland's gaze and gave another salute, pounding his right fist over his heart. Lord Roland acknowledged the gesture and then turned to address the Peers.

"In the history of the rebels, the legend is told of a queen who saved her people from destruction. Her cousin bore the name of our new order. Mordecai. He himself was a rebel, refusing to bow before his rulers and daring to lift his voice against the king's man. In the legend, their Mordecai was lifted up in greatness. Now, in this time of great power, the Mordecais of Hebbros will also be exalted. However, they will bring an end to the rebels who would resist our ruling and stamp out the name of the Faithful from our midst."

The gathered Peers united in a shout of consent and Roland lifted his hands for renewed silence. His lips curved in a smile as his eyes scanned the group, and his heart reveled in the feeling of power that this place brought him.

"My friends and noble Peers, the knights of our great Order will surely live up to their name. For in the language of the ancients, Mordecai was the word used to express our very goal. Annihilation!"

Kenrick drew his sword again and lifted it with the shout of "Cast out the rebels! Exile the Faithful!" and soon the hall reverberated with the echo of his impassioned cry. Roland listened in silence as the infectious noise of support grew, and finally left his chair to leave the hall. Turning to the Chief Peer, he spoke over the din.

"See that the other matter is tended to. I have agreed to lower the age of squires from fourteen to thirteen so that boys may begin their training as soon as they leave the schoolrooms."

"Yes, my lord," the Peer bowed low.

Roland nodded and turned to go. Stopping beside Kenrick on his way out, the ruler spoke at a volume heard only by the knight, "Gather a force large enough to secure the twenty, and have them ready by sundown tomorrow."

Kenrick's eyes gleamed, "Yes, my lord."

11
Raid in the Night

Luke sat on the floor in the corner of his family's simple cottage. Knees drawn up to his chest, his fingers played absently with a twig while his eyes cast covert glances in the direction of the table. Christopher and Charlotte sat listening to their mother tell the story of the boy David, who had killed a giant named Goliath. Their father sat at the head of the table, also listening and adding to the story's telling as his hands moved skillfully over a bit of work that he had brought from the shop. Althar glanced in his direction and Luke averted his eyes to focus on the twig before he could read his father's face.

The day had been busy, but strangely quiet. Luke and his classmates had been released from the schoolroom at an early hour and ordered to decorate the outside of the building with flowered garlands and laurels in honor of the wedding that would take place the following day. The evil twins had been at their usual work of mischief, tripping and shoving Luke with every opportunity that presented itself, until Luke finally gathered a small group of boys who helped him bind the troublemakers with a length of garland and tie them to the door-latch. Warin and Wulf had roared and howled until Master Paul came to see the trouble, opening the door and toppling the twins in the process. Luke had been singled out for a reprimand and the evil twins given leave to go home. And so the decorating had been accomplished amidst much laughter and shouting from the boys who were left, and at last the front of the schoolroom looked like a solid wall of blooming greenery.

And yet, with all the laughter and shouting, with all the singing and merrymaking that had taken place throughout Hebbros, Luke's day had been shrouded in a strange stillness. He had felt as though he looked on from a dream.

Luke glanced at the table again and caught Christopher's gaze. *Sorrow.* His brother had taken no part in tying the evil twins to the schoolroom door, and had even cautioned Luke against the action. Ever since he had made the choice—decided to take on the burden of being one of the Faithful—Christopher had been different. He no longer supported Luke's pranks and always watched his brother's antics with an expression of sadness.

Luke too had changed. He no longer sat at the table for their mother's secret lessons and the beautiful stories that had so captivated him. He saw now that the meetings were meant to share teachings of the Faithful, and he could not bring himself to join them openly when he had not yet made his choice of allegiance. He had tried, had come so close to accepting the truth in his heart, but always the fingers of doubt would wrap their dangerous hold on his thoughts, and he would again shrink back from making the decision.

Perhaps tomorrow. Tomorrow he would choose. Always tomorrow.

"Luke?"

Luke looked up to see his mother kneeling before him with a sweet smile on her lips. *Concern. Compassion.* She reached out a hand and caressed the right side of his face. "You know you are still welcome to join our secret lessons, if only to hear the stories you love."

He nodded, "Yes, I know. I still listen."

Her smile deepened, "I love you, Luke."

"I love you, Mother."

Mariah began to rise, but Luke placed a hand on her arm and spoke with an earnest whisper, "David was a boy; he did great things for his people, and he was only a boy like me." She nodded and he continued, "I want to do great things like David did, but you said that I'm not ready. How did he do it? How was David ready?"

Mariah silently prayed for wisdom before answering in a quiet tone that matched her son's, "He knew from Whom his strength came." Luke watched her face, waiting for her to continue, "David fought for our God, and God gave Him the strength he needed to complete the work prepared for him. When we live for Christ He gives us work to do, and there is nothing that can stop that work from being accomplished. No power on earth, not Lord Roland or even King Cronin, can stand against the power of Jesus. There is no power or force that can overcome God."

Luke stood to his feet and Mariah rose with him. She took his hand in hers and Luke let her lead him to the table, where they sat side-by-side. Luke ignored the watchful gazes of his siblings and studied the table instead, his thoughts churning.

His forehead creased, "But…how can God be so wonderful in the stories you tell, and then so awful to make His son die for everyone else's sins? That's injustice."

Althar set his work aside and folded his hands on the table's rough surface. His voice was gentle as he smiled at his son, "It is not injustice, Luke. It is mercy."

Luke's head lifted and turned at the words. *Patience. Love.* He remembered hearing the same thing from Christopher. Beside him, Mariah gently clutched his hand. She could see in the strained lines of his face that Luke was trying hard not to reject the truth, but to understand it. She closed her eyes in earnest prayer for her son and a tear slipped out from beneath her lashes.

Finally Luke spoke in a voice barely above a whisper, "How is it mercy?"

Althar met his wife's gaze over Luke's head. Hearing their son's question was like throwing the crossbar from a locked door and opening it wide. He wanted to hear more. Althar swallowed as he searched for the right words.

"Man's *injustice* punishes the innocent. God's *mercy* redeems the guilty. Yes, God did offer His son to die, to accept the penalty of sin in our stead, but it was not unjust. Jesus is the only One who could thoroughly satisfy the debt of sin, for He is perfect, and so He came freely to take our chastisement. Jesus was a *willing* sacrifice, and so the act was not one of gross injustice, but of loving mercy. When He arose from the dead three days later, Jesus conquered death so that we might live now with the promise of spending eternity in His presence."

The small cottage fell silent for several minutes. Althar, Mariah, and Christopher waited prayerfully for Luke to speak. They had done all they knew to do, said all they knew to say. It was God alone who could soften his heart now.

Charlotte sat with her small arms folded on the table in front of her, chin resting on her arms and dark hair framing her innocent face. Her eyes swiveled back and forth like a pendulum, resting first on one face and then another. She realized that these moments were important, but was having trouble understanding why the atmosphere had suddenly grown tense.

Luke sat utterly still. While listening to his father's words he had lowered his gaze to the table and he kept it there now, studying the crude surface instead of the faces around him. He knew that if he looked up he would see hope, eagerness, and tears wrought by emotions too deep for him to examine alongside his own thoughts. He longed to finish this fight, to end this battle, knowing he had not made a decision based on the expectations of others.

Was it true? Had God's decision to sacrifice His son been not only one of justice, due to Christ's willingness to die, but also one of mercy? Mercy extended to Luke. Could it be that if Luke joined the army of Christ as his mother had suggested, that God would still be able to use him in Hebbros? To put a stop to Lord Roland's evil? Regardless of the danger that such a faith would put him in.

Luke took a deep breath and felt the fingers of doubt beginning to tear at the edges of his thoughts. A small cry of affliction escaped his lips as he brought his elbows to rest on the table and cradled his troubled head in his hands. Was he foolish to think that following Christ could open any possibilities for greatness? Lord Roland hated the Faithful, had banished their leader to the side of a beast-laden mountain to die. Why would he spare others who followed the same God, giving them the chance to rise against him?

The atmosphere around the table grew thick with conflict. In Luke's ears came the rushing sound of a shrill wind, and a heavy groan shook his thin frame as the battle for his allegiance raged hot within him.

Charlotte lifted her head from her arms and stared with wide eyes. Christopher's chin trembled and Mariah cried openly, while Althar gripped Luke's shoulder with a strong hand and cried out in a voice raw with emotion, "Oh God, help my son! Please show him truth and remove the veil of darkness from his eyes."

Luke gripped the hair at his temples and sucked in a deep breath, "Help me, God!"

The fingers of doubt suddenly lost their grip as a hand stronger and gentler moved to rescue his tormented thoughts. The shrill noise left his ears and was replaced by a quiet whisper, like the soft lap of waves against the northwestern docks, or like the reassuring breath of a mother hushing her baby for the night. Luke exhaled slowly as a deep peace enveloped him and the seeds of faith, planted for so many years, finally sprouted as he reached out to take hold of God's truth.

The cottage became silent once again, Luke's heavy breathing the only sound that penetrated the stillness. Charlotte studied the other faces at the table, trying to grasp the significance of the moment, until her gaze rested on the boy across the table.

"Luke? You all right?"

Head still cradled in his hands, Luke nodded. A moment later he lifted his face to reveal tear-filled eyes. Taking a shuddering breath, he turned to look at his father. *Hope. Expectation.*

"I understand now." Althar lay a hand over his son's and Luke continued, "God's mercy redeems the guilty," his voice cracked as he reached the end of his statement. His face split with a grin. His heart felt light, relieved by the knowledge that he had finally grasped truth. With a sigh of release, he turned to his mother, "Now I know where my allegiance lies. God sent Jesus to die for my sins, and pursued me even when I fought against Him. The least I can do is serve Him."

Mariah smiled through her tears and held her son close. "I know God has a special purpose for you, Luke. Always seek His face." She turned to include her other children with her words, "God has great plans for each of you, and united together by the bond of Christ I know you will be strong."

Beyond their snug cottage a wail suddenly rent the night air. The cooper and his family turned as one to look toward the shuttered window. Other cries sounded, followed by the sound of many feet, some scampering while others marched, until the raucous happenings seemed to surround them.

Charlotte ran to her mother's side and Mariah turned wide eyes to Althar, "Is it the revelers? Celebrating his lordship's marriage?"

Luke watched as his father seemed to listen a moment longer, his gaze changing with various emotions. *Confusion. Realization. Disbelief.* Althar met Mariah's gaze and tried to convey his thoughts through a stricken look, for his mouth would not form the words. The mother's eyes widened and her arm tightened around Charlotte just as the door burst open with a resounding slap against the wall.

Screams filled the air, but Luke was unsure of who cried out. He watched in mute shock as a tall dark-haired knight ducked through the door and glanced at the family surrounding the table. *Reveling in power. Self-centered. Proud.* His cold gaze settled on Luke's father.

"Cooper Althar, you and your wife are hereby condemned for rebellion against the crown of Mizgalia, dissention in the city of Hebbros, and revolt against his lordship, Roland of Aylesworth, through aiding the banished Sedgwick and continuing to unite with those called the Faithful."

Althar rose quickly to his feet, "Please, sir knight. I will go with you, only let my wife remain here to care for our children."

The knight glanced at the cooper and smirked before turning to leave the cottage, "Your children will be cared for, rebel." He motioned to several soldiers outside, who were all clad in black armor similar to his own, "Take them, and bring the three brats."

"No!" Luke shouted after the tall knight. Fear constricted his lungs as he watched his father move to block the door only to be pulled outside by two of the soldiers. Another armored pair entered the cottage and one quickly grabbed his mother by the arm. The other circled to herd the children from behind the table.

"No, please! Don't touch them! Althar!" Mariah fought against the soldier's grip as she clung to her sobbing daughter, "Christopher, you must take Charlotte. Hold on to her, do you hear? Luke! Luke, stay with your brother!" With a final jerk, the soldier pulled her across the threshold and she disappeared from sight.

"No!" Luke roared against the pain that pierced his heart as he escaped the last soldier and raced through the open door. On the other side of the threshold he froze.

Outside on the narrow torch-lit street were two caged carts, one with several men and women inside and the other carrying their children. Terrible wails sounded from both of these carts as mothers and fathers reached through the bars of their cage in a last futile attempt to hold their sons and daughters. Cries of agony and whimpers of fear filled Luke's ears.

Beyond the street, nervous shouts could be heard spreading like water through Hebbros as people scrambled to see what was happening and then ran for cover, afraid that they would be the next man or woman tossed into the knight's cart. Confusion reigned on this night.

"Mother!" Luke caught a glimpse of her being lifted unceremoniously to join his father in the first cart, and then he felt a shove from behind as the child-catching soldier exited the cottage, shepherding a bewildered Christopher and a wailing Charlotte before him. Ducking away from the massive hand that reached for him, Luke bolted toward the cart that bore his parents.

"Let them go!" Luke took a flying leap that perched him on the back of the cart. Clinging to the bars of the cage until his small knuckles turned white, he searched the occupants' faces—*Fear. Confusion. Anguish. Bitterness*—until his gaze rested on the two he sought. "Mother! Father!" His shout was drowned by the noise of the confused city around him, nevertheless Althar and Mariah turned at his voice and moved toward the back of the cage, pushing their way through the crowd of other desperate parents.

Before they could reach him, a thin-faced woman grasped Luke's wrist through the bars and cried into his face, "Tell my son I love him! Tell him to be strong in the Lord!" Luke's eyes widened as he stared at her. *Strength. Faith. Sorrow for another.* "Please tell him!" Luke responded with several quick nods and forgot to ask who or where her son was.

"Luke!" Althar finally came close enough to reach a hand toward his son. Luke stretched a hand through the bars and his father's fingers brushed across his, passing a small object into his smaller grasp. Suddenly, Luke was grabbed from behind and shoved away from the cart.

"Back away, brat." A massive soldier, clad in black armor like the others, towered over him and pointed a thick arm to the left, "To your own cart with the other children!"

A pair of large hands lifted him kicking and screaming from behind, and a moment later Luke found himself huddled with his brother and sister in the back of the second cart. Tears flowed freely from every eye, and each gaze shouted a message of fear to the perceptive lad who had just joined them.

Luke's breath came in short gasps. Closing his own eyes against the faces, tears, torches, and soldiers, and shutting his ears to the screams, wails, shouts, and curses, he thought back to the peace he had known just moments before the raid had begun. Chest heaving, he tightened his hold on Christopher's shoulder and wrapped his other arm around Charlotte, who sat between them. Bowing his head, he sought the One who had brought that blissful quiet to his soul, "Help us, Jesus. Please help us, Jesus."

A young boy sitting across from them watched Luke and then leaned closer, causing a thatch of black hair to fall over his right eye. He pointed at Luke, "You're praying."

Another boy, several years older than the first and sporting a head of blond hair, shook his head at the other's words, "That's rather obvious, Elbert. Of course he's praying." He brushed a hand over his doublet, the filth of which proved he had not been an easy catch for the soldiers. His mottled red face showed that he had shed some tears, but was now trying to show a bold face.

The group swayed as the cart started forward with a jolt. Christopher, trying to sooth Charlotte by creating conversation, asked the blonde, "Are you brothers?"

The other boy shook his head and jabbed a thumb in Elbert's direction, "Never seen him before this night. He was picked up in southern Hebbros. I come from the city's eastern quarters, as does Joel there," he motioned with his head to yet another boy, about seven years of age, cowering in the corner. "I'm Ned. Who are you?"

Christopher introduced himself and his two siblings, while Luke continued to repeat his simple prayer in a furious grasp for peace.

Elbert eyed the two brothers and then leaned forward again, "You're twins."

Ned rolled his eyes, "Obvious, Elbert. They've got the same face." He glanced at Christopher and then indicated the dark-haired boy with another tilt of his yellow head, "I think he's still in shock. This is terrible business."

Elbert kept his eyes glued to Luke's tear-stained frantic face as he spoke to the cart in general, "They took us because our parents are of the Faithful."

A groan, "Obvious again, Elbert. I think we've all come to that conclusion by now, as all of our parents are of the Faithful. Would you please stop pointing out the painfully apparent?" Ned's gaze shone indigo in the torchlight as his eyes shifted to Christopher again, "They're going to split us up to live in the homes of those who are faithful to Roland," he spat against the side of the cart as if mentioning the city's ruler had tarnished his tongue.

Luke's head shot up at Ned's words. *Fear. Anger. Shock. Defiance.* His gaze swept over the group and he shook his head, "They can't split us up!"

"They will."

Luke turned to look his brother in the eye. *Helplessness* fought with *Courage.* He thought of their mother's final words before a wail had rent the night outside their home: *United together by the bond of Christ I know you will be strong.*

"Chris, we have to promise we'll stay together."

"We can't promise, Luke," Christopher shook his head even as his arm tightened around Charlotte, who was still crying and shouting for their mother. "They're stronger than we are. We can't fight them."

Luke thought of his plans to overthrow Roland's evil rule. His mother had said he was not ready to fight, for he had no cause to fight for. He had one now. He spoke to the cartload of children, "We will some day. We can promise to join together when the time is right. When we're stronger and have more followers. Even if they split us up now, we can remain faithful to what our parents have taught us. And one day we'll fight back."

Ned grinned, "I like your manner, friend." He held out a fist, "Promise."

Bracing against the pitching of the cart, each child reached out and added their fist to the group in the center. Even little Charlotte, tearful and whimpering, added her small fist to the others when Ned grinned and gave her a nod of encouragement.

With his heart throbbing a painful tempo, and unaware of the extent of endeavors he was about to begin, Luke added his own fist and tightened his fingers, "We'll find others like ourselves and grow our society until the day we're ready to strike back. To save our good parents and to keep ourselves from the same fate…whatever that fate is." Casting a glance over his shoulder to the other cart, Luke swallowed against another rush of tears, "Agreed?"

The others nodded and then shrank against the sides of the cart when the cage came to a halt before another unsuspecting home. Screams once again filled the air and Luke closed his eyes and tightened his fists until his hands ached.

Ached unbearably.

As if something were cutting into his palm.

Luke's eyes popped open. He looked down and opened his right fist, revealing the small object that his father had passed through the bars. A rivet. From the floor of the cooper's shop, no doubt. His hand closed again around the inch-long piece and another fountain of tears filled his eyes as the bit of steel inspired memories of happier times. Leaning his head back against the cart, Luke's eyes lifted to reach beyond the torchlight, the towers, and the misery, to search the dark sky that stretched beyond. He wondered what it would be like to sit high above the city like one of the stars, having not a care or worry and feeling the peace of God as he watched in trusting silence what happened in Hebbros below.

God, I barely know You. Help me to trust you now. Help us to overcome evil.

12
The Weight of Words

Rosalynn's horse rounded the last bend in the forest road and the lady looked up to get her first view of Hebbros. She reined her horse to a stop and the entourage came to a slow halt behind her. Here where the forest ended the ground gave way to a small slope before leveling out into a vast valley that stretched before Lord Roland's equally vast city. Rosalynn's brown eyes widened as she took in the breadth of it and lifted her gaze to study the mountain that rose beyond Hebbros and loomed over the walls in a show of unyielding power.

From the city's towers and spires thousands of brightly colored banners floated in the early morning breeze, a festive reminder of why she had come. Rosalynn swallowed at the thought and wondered again whether she had been sufficiently prepared to be the wife of King Cronin's favorite. The banners continued to wave a welcome to her, but theirs was not the approval she sought. Would the city's populace of thousands greet her just as warmly as the flags? Would Lord Roland? After all, he had not been given the choice of his bride.

Tucking a springy curl of fiery red hair behind her ear, Lady Rosalynn nudged her horse forward once again.

Riding a short distance behind his sister and thoroughly

omitted from her thoughts, Lord Bradley stared in grim silence at the city of Hebbros. The place was massive. One could easily lose himself just taking a stroll within the boundaries of those walls. Bradley straightened at the thought. Perhaps he could manage getting lost in Hebbros and then find a way to escape the life that King Cronin had forced upon him, as his brother-in-law's ward. His shoulders slumped with immediate defeat. Once he rode through the gates as a member of the wedding entourage wearing this ridiculously embroidered doublet and ermine-trimmed cloak, there would be no anonymity for him.

Bradley scowled and muttered to himself, "I may as well carry a great banner with painted words that say 'How do you do? I'm Lord Bradley, her ladyship's brother. Please don't let me leave the palace, and take me back there if I run away.'"

"Beg pardon, my lord?"

Bradley turned to see the captain of the Villenfeld garrison riding nearby. His horse nickered pleasantly at the close company of the man's animal, while the boy's shoulders slumped even more with the reminder that nothing he did or said went unnoticed.

"It's nothing, Captain."

The boy cast a sidelong glance at the soldier, briefly wondering if the captain would listen should Bradley tell him of the heavy thoughts that weighed on his young mind. Every day his future grew more dismal and blank. Every night he went to sleep feeling more unloved and forgotten than he had the night before. Of course his sister had been busy with preparations for her wedding, but they had still dined together and seen each other at various times throughout the day. Not once since the death of their father had Rosalynn asked how he was coping with the loss. Not once had she offered regrets that Hugh had been stolen away. Not once had she invited him to share his thoughts about relocating to Hebbros.

She simply didn't care.

Bradley's gaze slid back to the captain. The idea of releasing his burden to this man quickly passed as he watched the soldier scan their surroundings for danger. The captain had come along with a contingent from Villenfeld to see after Rosalynn and Bradley's safe arrival in Hebbros and to swear a new allegiance to Lord Roland. The soldier was preoccupied with his current mission. He was too busy to hear the cares and woes of a child.

Bradley glanced over his shoulder and caught sight of a slave cart near the back of the entourage. An appealing idea sprang to life in his mind and he turned back to the captain, trying to fill his voice with a measure of the authority he had been born with, "If my sister asks after me, and I highly doubt that she will, tell her I'm still riding within the train, but I've grown tired of keeping to my place here."

Before the captain had a chance to respond, Bradley turned his horse's head and urged it into a trot heading back the way they had come. Grateful that his late father had taught him to sit a horse well, Bradley trusted his animal to keep a good footing while his eyes once again searched out the slave cart. Spotting the wagon and heading in that direction, the boy soon rode alongside and hailed the crowded load of Rosalynn's slaves. The travel-worn women mustered smiles for the young lord and offered him the usual blessings for the happy day. Bradley shrugged these off and continued to scan the dusty group until his dark gaze rested on another young face.

"Sarah," his face split with a wide grin, "I want you to ride with me."

The slave women looked shocked by his announcement, as did the soldier who drove the cart. Sarah's eyes widened and her pert-nosed face turned one way and then the other, searching the others' expressions for what answer she ought to give. Her calloused fingers moved to touch her leather collar and she shook her head, "Can't. Not allowed."

Tired of being cast off, Bradley huffed a sigh and nudged his horse closer, "Of course you're allowed. I say so."

The driver turned on his seat to quirk an uncertain brow at the little lord, "Hold there, young sir, I must refuse your request. The slaves have been placed under my watch, and her ladyship would certainly be displeased with me if I allowed one of them to leave the cart to join her noble brother on horseback."

Bradley's brow quirked in turn, "She will be even more displeased when you allow me to ride with the slaves in the cart, which I most certainly shall if you don't give Sarah leave to ride with me." The soldier paused, unsure of what to say, and Bradley continued in a slightly desperate tone, "I have spent the last few weeks of preparation and travel alone. I have no friends left to me and I face the possibility of being friendless still in my new home.

My life has changed too quickly over the past few months and is about to change further still. Everything else has been taken from me." His voice shook slightly as he met the soldier's gaze, "I would like to have a friend 'til I reach the gates of Hebbros."

The soldier was silent for a moment before he leaned into a nod and then faced forward to slow the cart's horses, "Very well, sir. Quickly now, before everyone looks this way."

The driver hopped to the ground and lifted the brown-haired little slave from the cart. Placing her on the horse behind Lord Bradley, he then turned to climb back to his own seat before his face stretched to mirror the girl's broad smile. The cartload of slaves behind him watched in stunned silence as the young lord kicked his horse into a trot and moved ahead with one of their own kind. Immediately after the children had moved away, the women began to whisper amongst themselves. The driver slapped the reins over his own animals' backs and began the slow walk forward once again. He watched the two children on horseback disappear into the crowd and shook his head with a grin, "Now there is a boy bound for trouble, and no mistaking."

Clinging desperately to Bradley's middle, Sarah watched as the gates of Hebbros drew nearer and felt a pang of regret that her ride would soon be over. She had never ridden a horse before, and was surprised to find she liked it. They had been crossing the wide valley at a leisurely pace, along the outer fringe of Lady Rosalynn's entourage and to the sound of Lord Bradley's constant chatter. Sarah listened as best she could to the endless flow of words that rushed from his mouth, and wondered if he had spoken to no one since his father's death. It seemed he was now releasing several months worth of dialogue into her ears.

"…don't know what to think of that. Do you?"

He paused and Sarah realized she'd missed a question. "Beg pardon, m'lord?" She raised her voice to a near shout to be heard above the surrounding noise.

"Never mind. Am I talking too much? I know I am. I usually do when there's someone nearby who will listen. I used to talk to Hugh all the time. Hugh was my personal companion before King Cronin's man took him away to serve in the city of Mockmor. I used to talk to Hugh until my face grew tired, and then I would go to sleep until I could talk some more the next day. Do you ever talk until you're tired and have nothing left to say?" Lord Bradley craned his neck to look her in the eye and Sarah returned the look in silence. Bradley shook his head and answered his own question as he faced forward again, "No. No, I don't think you do."

His matter-of-fact tone produced a giggle from Sarah, and Bradley echoed the sound. Their sense of amusement seemed to escalate uncontrollably as they then searched for and found other things to laugh at in their surroundings. Bradley's horse seemed to catch the spirit of hilarity as well, adding a prance to his steps that tossed the children up and down. Bradley threw his head back in a rare burst of carefree laughter. The ermine trim on his cloak tickled Sarah's nose and she laughed again, marveling at the strange sensation of joy that bubbled up inside of her. She couldn't remember the last time she had indulged in laughter. Life as a slave did not encourage very much mirth.

Bradley turned to glance at her, suddenly serious, "Where are you from? What kingdom were you taken from?"

Sarah's smile disappeared and her eyes clouded with painful memories, "Dolthe. Eight years ago the Mizgalian army crossed the border and destroyed thirteen Dolthian villages in four days. They took many captives."

"How old were you?"

"Three years." Sarah bowed her head and a tear slipped out beneath her lashes, "M' mother and father were sold t' a Gulgish slaver."

"Does your collar hurt?"

"Sometimes. Other times I forget it's there." Her fingers unconsciously moved to grip the leather strip. She remembered the day when it had first been made to circle her neck and then fastened permanently. The following days and nights had been miserable hours of pain as the leather rubbed her skin raw.

Lord Bradley was silent for a long while. Finally, he turned a steady gaze over his shoulder, "I'm going to—"

"Bradley!"

Lady Rosalynn's exclamation of surprise ended on a squeak of horror. Sarah jumped at the sudden shriek and Bradley's head whipped around to face his sister. Apparently, they had ridden too close to the front of the entourage and Lady Rosalynn had spotted them. Her expression now changed from one of shock to one of anger, and her red curls fairly quivered with rage.

"What on earth do you think you are doing?"

Bradley offered a smug grin, "Following you to Hebbros."

Rosalynn's jaw clenched, "With a slave?"

"With a friend."

"A friend!?"

There was that squeak again. Sarah peeked around Bradley's shoulder, which had suddenly grown tense, and saw her mistress flash a glare of wrath in her direction. She shrank behind his lordship seeking a measure of security, if only for a moment.

"Slaves are not friends, Bradley."

He lurched forward and growled through clenched teeth, "How would you know?"

Sarah now shrank from his lordship as well, suddenly afraid of the angry boy, and nearly toppled backwards off the horse. Lord Bradley's face had turned bright red and he was shaking with a rage of his own as he glared at his sister. The crowd around them had fallen silent. Uncomfortable. Sarah glanced up at the walls of Hebbros and thought she should have stayed in the cart.

"Bradley," Lady Rosalynn's voice was a steely calm; more dangerous, Sarah had learned, than an angry shout, "you will return the slave to her proper place at once…"

"She's going to ride with me, Rosalynn."

"Or I will have her sold from the ports of Hebbros as soon as we pass through the gates today."

Bradley tensed even further before his shoulders drooped and he lowered his head in defeat, "I'll take her back. Only please don't send her away, she's my friend."

Rosalynn's thin face beamed with a smug satisfaction over her victory and she motioned for her entourage to continue, "When you have left her with her kind you will return to ride with me at the front. We've nearly reached the eastern gates and I'll not have you enter Hebbros at my side covered in dust from riding with the rear guard."

She turned her horse's head and resumed her place in line while Lord Bradley turned his mount toward the back. Sarah's young heart ached for the little boy. She understood his need for a friend. His father had died, his companion had been taken away, and his sister didn't seem very fond of him. He was frightened by the prospect of living in a strange place, and wanted someone nearby who would experience the first moments of trepidation with him.

Bradley glanced over his shoulder to gaze after his sister, and Sarah saw his indigo-black eyes glisten with fresh anger. He reined in beside the slave cart and turned to look at her. "You'll still be my friend."

Sarah didn't think it was a question, but she gave a mute nod of obedience anyway. Lord Bradley continued to speak as the driver lifted her down and placed her back in the cart.

"I'll find a way to help you, Sarah. I'll find a way to get your collar off so you won't hurt any more. One day you'll be free. I'll help you, I promise."

The driver grunted as he climbed onto his seat once again. The other slave women hid mocking laughter behind their hands and whispered to one another about "his poor lordship" and "the silly lad, to have such a fanciful idea." Sarah ignored them all. Fingering her collar of leather, she returned Lord Bradley's woeful stare of determination. And believed every word he said.

Lord Roland stood beside Lady Rosalynn as the priest from the palace temple performed their marriage before the throng that had gathered in the Peers' meeting hall. Rumors of her beauty had been well grounded and Roland found himself casting frequent glances at his new bride. Her red hair was actually quite lovely; he couldn't imagine why he had assumed it would be otherwise.

The priest droned on and Roland grew restless. He glanced at Rosalynn again and she looked up at him with a timid smile. He smiled in return, only to have the grin slip from his face when his gaze moved beyond Rosalynn to her brother. Bradley's scowl turned to a glare before the boy shifted his focus back to the ceremony and his face became a picture of dejection.

The insolent brat. Did he think Roland had had any more control in taking away his lands and vassals than Bradley had?

The priest finally motioned for them to join hands and a strong cord was wrapped around their fingers, the symbol of a lasting bond. A moment later Roland sealed the union with a kiss and then turned to face the cheering crowd as lord and lady of

Hebbros. Roland tucked his wife's arm in his and led her through the congratulatory masses toward the door, where fresh horses and a contingent of soldiers would be waiting to begin their wedding parade through the city streets.

Passing by Sir Kenrick on the way out, Lord Roland caught the knight's eye and gave a quick nod. Kenrick nodded in return and gave a small salute before disappearing through the crowd to obey the unspoken command. Roland watched him go and smiled to himself, redirecting his look of pleasure to grin at Rosalynn when she glanced his way. Yes, he thought to himself, his wife was quite lovely, and he was glad after all that King Cronin had arranged for them to marry. It had removed from his shoulders the burden of finding a bride on his own, and also provided an opportunity to celebrate with the banishment of twenty rebels.

He glanced in the direction Kenrick had gone.

His wait was nearly over.

The time had come.

13
Banished

The time had come. The time for what, none of them knew. Luke sensed a shift in the atmosphere when the city beyond the small window grew loud with celebratory joy. Lord Roland's wedding had taken place and now all of Hebbros would show their delight through several days of merriment and revelry. Luke turned from the narrow view to scan the room above the Hebbros garrison. Well, not *all* of Hebbros would celebrate.

By the end of the previous night's raid Luke's quick gaze had counted twenty men and women, including his parents, who had been dragged from their homes by the dark-armored soldiers and tossed into the first cart. Their twenty-eight children had been stuffed into the second.

Luke was unsure where exactly the elder prisoners were now, but he assumed they had been taken to a prison cell beneath the garrison. The children, while they had not spent the night in lush surroundings, had fared better. The guarded room over the garrison was small and bare, but it was also dry and warm. The twenty-eight young occupants had huddled together, bound by the invisible cords of shared affliction. Some had managed to catch a few moments of blessed slumber, while others stared wide-eyed and afraid into the dark, wondering if the light of day would bring terrors more fearsome than those witnessed in the shadows.

Luke sank against the wall beside Christopher. On his twin's other side, little Charlotte lay with her head resting in Christopher's lap. She had dropped into a fitful sleep sometime during the night. Beyond Charlotte, Ned sat with his yellow head leaning against the wall and stared blankly across the room. Waiting. Elbert, who, oddly enough seemed drawn to the company of the brash blonde, lay curled in a ball before them, by all appearances asleep.

A shuddering sob drew Luke's attention to the far corner, where several young girls sat with their arms around each other. *Fear. Weariness. Loyalty.*

From the floor, Elbert blew the thatch of black hair from his face. *Annoyance. Disbelief.* He groaned to no one in particular, "She's still crying."

"Obvious, Elbert," Ned closed his eyes and shifted for a more comfortable position against the stones at his back, "We can all hear her sobbing. In fact, we've all been listening to her cry since the moment she was tossed into the cart last night."

Elbert sighed and covered the ear not pressed to the floor with one hand.

Luke exhaled his own sigh and looked toward the group of girls. The small one in the middle—his mother would have called her a "petite thing"—was the only one in the room who had any tears left to cry. *Agony. Pain. Helpless. Confused.* Her redheaded friend, whose name was Pavia, had called her Lillian, and Luke thought that Elbert had been correct when he said she looked as delicate as one of the flowers whose name she bore.

Lillian's had been the largest home visited by the tall knight and his minions, and the girl's pale skin evidenced an indoor life of wealth and ease. Long white-blond hair had escaped her intricate braid to fall in a curtain around her thin face, which had turned as red as any cherry after hours of hysterical tears. The moment she had been "tossed into the cart" Lillian had let out a shriek worthy of shaking the city to its core. The soldier responsible for depositing her in the wagon had roughly clapped a hand over her mouth and growled a threat in her face that only managed to change her shrieks to heavy sobs.

The sobbing had not yet ceased.

Luke cast a sidelong glance at his twin. Christopher absently stroked Charlotte's hair while keeping a concerned gaze on the far corner. He had been watching Lillian and Pavia since the moment the two girls had joined them…when Lillian had shrieked in Christopher's ear.

Without thinking, Luke leaned forward for a better angle to read his brother's face, but his twin's eyes dropped to Charlotte. *Loyalty. Care. Sympathetic.* Luke sat back and drew his knees to his chest with a sigh. Christopher had always had a protective and compassionate nature about him that Luke admired, but could never seem to grasp for himself. He just wanted Lillian to stop crying.

Defensive. Lillian's redheaded friend glared at him, and Luke realized he had been scowling.

"Leave her alone," Pavia snapped. "You had your turn to cry."

"I didn't mean to frown." Luke's scowl deepened, "I'm tired."

"Aren't we all?" Ned yawned and Pavia turned her green-eyed wrath on him.

"Then go to sleep!"

Another girl called across the small space, "Who could sleep with all that noise Lillian's making?"

"I could!" Little Joel sat up, rubbing his sleep-fogged eyes and sporting a fan of dark brown hair that stood on end all over his head.

Pavia narrowed her eyes like a cat about to pounce on its prey, "That's because you're a baby, Joel. Babies can sleep anywhere."

"I am not!"

"If he's a baby, then so is Lillian."

"I am not!"

"She cried all night long!"

"She's frightened, can't you see?"

"I want mother!"

"I have to—"

"Great turnips, I've got a bruise!"

"Everyone's shouting…"

"Obvious, Elbert."

"*Enough!*" Christopher raised his voice over the din just as the guard outside pounded a fist on the door. Twenty-eight pairs of eyes shifted to stare at the door in fear—even Lillian stopped short with a hiccup. When Christopher spoke again, it was with a quiet steady tone.

"We can't fight with each other. We have to remember why we're here. Our parents are members of the Faithful, and if they are the ones who were chosen for arrest they must have been actively fighting for their faith. I'm sure many of us are members of the faith as well. I know I am. Our parents would want to know that when they left us we remembered what they taught us and remained strong in Christ. Don't you see? We're not enemies here. We're comrades."

Luke jumped to his feet, "He's right! I'm a new believer, but I do know that we can grow in our faith and make sure Lord Roland doesn't destroy it with our parents."

Joel's arch of hair swayed wildly when he turned a sharp look at Luke. *Shock*. "He's going to destroy them?"

"I don't know what he's going to do to them, Joel. We do know that Roland wants to split us up, and he'll try to force us to be like him."

Luke glanced at the few who had first been in the cart. *Support. Excitement. Encouragement. Determination.* He glanced at the door and lowered his steady young voice. His eyes glittered with hope and the other children drew closer, captivated by the boy's spirit and authority.

"Some of us have decided that we won't give in. We're not strong enough to fight back now, but we'll grow in number like our parents. We'll find others in the city who think as we do—their parents might be arrested next—and we'll become an army of sorts."

Fascination. Awe. Trepidation. Devotion. Honor. Humility. Criticism. Caution. Loyalty. Trustworthiness. Doubt. Luke read a wide array of emotions in the group before him. He took note of those who appeared negative and filed away their names for future consideration. He couldn't force them to join him, but he also wouldn't risk discovery by including someone he couldn't trust. Most were ready to begin, to carry on the faith that Lord Roland wished to wipe out through the brutal annihilation of its teachers.

The group began to whisper excitedly, forming plans and talking through ideas that were childish in their simplicity, but inspiring in their creativity. As the chattering progressed, Luke assumed the role of authority and kept things organized as best as a child knew how. He proved himself capable and insightful, due to his special gift, until he was inherently branded their leader.

A hushed cheer of camaraderie went up in honor of the boy's quick promotion. Luke saw Lillian's crystal-blue eyes fill with admiration and he promptly sent her a look of disgust. He shifted to see Christopher watching him—*Affection*—and Charlotte watching Christopher. *Trusting*. Luke grinned. His little sister would certainly follow his lead in matters concerning this pact, but she would do so by taking her cues from the levelheaded Christopher. Perhaps his twin would be a better choice for their leader.

The door suddenly swung inward and the group of children fell silent, each aware that what they had planned in this room could be considered dissention by their city's ruler. So they stared quietly at the man standing on the threshold; the tall knight who had led the raid. His black hair was curly and a short beard framed his full face. He was clad in the black armor they had seen the night before, and a golden seal on his right hand flashed in the light spilling through the window.

Luke studied the knight's face and once again saw evidence of pride and power. Then their eyes met briefly and the boy was overwhelmed by a wave of evil much like the one surrounding Lord Roland. *Corruption. Dishonest. Inconstant. Dishonorable. Crafty. Insecure. Hypocritical. Unashamed.*

Luke dropped his gaze to the floor.

Sir Kenrick let his cold gaze touch on each little face in the room and then offered a chilly smile as he adjusted his leather gloves, "Form a line, children. It is time."

"*ACHOO!*" Bradley reared back and delivered another monstrous sneeze. The entire city was covered and draped in greenery and frivolous flowers, perfuming the warm air and inspiring this terrible reaction in the young lord's swollen sinuses.

"*ACHOO!*" Bradley scowled at the woman who had just thrown a small posy in his face and then faced forward again with a heavy sigh. Roland and Rosalynn, apparently oblivious to all but each other, had been blessed by the masses in the name of every deity, not to mention several that Bradley firmly believed had been invented on the spot. Of course he had been included in these blessings as the bride's brother, but instead of feeling refreshed he found himself wishing the parade would conclude so that he could return to the palace and hide away in his chambers for a day or two. Or four.

With every blessing, the air became more oppressive.

With every cry of adoration, the streets became more congested. Like his head.

With every clop of the horses' hooves, it became apparent that there was some other event looming ahead. The celebration was not yet over. Expectancy hung like a cloud over Hebbros.

Finally they came to a junction where several major thoroughfares intersected before the city's western wall. Bradley's gaze was immediately drawn upward to Mount Desterrar, looming over them, and then down to a gate tucked within the wall and with the number 13 etched in a great stone arch overhead. He drew his horse to a halt beside Rosalynn and Roland, directly across the square from the gate, and watched as the surrounding alleyways and streets filled with a tight crowd of spectators.

But spectators of what?

The crowd grew silent as Roland prepared to speak. Bradley shifted to listen and promptly sneezed into the sudden stillness.

"People of Hebbros," Roland's powerful voice carried easily over the square and echoed through the streets, "Our gods have seen fit to bless me this day with a bride, the Lady Rosalynn," he offered her a fond smile and Bradley nearly gagged at the open show of affection. "I intend to present a ceremony today in honor of our marriage and in thanks to the deities who have blessed us. A band of twenty rebels have been caught within our walls, to be cast upon Mount Desterrar as was their leader before them. Their children, precious souls, will be well provided for by the more loyal citizens of Hebbros."

The whispering that had begun with Roland's first words grew to a murmur. Speculations and tittle-tattle flew from every mouth and filled every ear until Bradley was unsure whether "twenty rebels were being banished" or "forty camels were being famished."

A gleam of satisfaction glinted in Roland's eye, but his face was a picture of apparent regret as he continued, "Let their fate be a warning to all, and a favorable offering to the gods." He looked to the left and gave a solemn nod, "You may commence."

Bradley craned his neck to see two carts driven into the square. In the first were a number of bedraggled men and women whose hands were bound. The twenty rebels, Bradley guessed. His gaze switched to the second cart and all of his petty complaints of moments before vanished at the sight of so many dirty children crammed inside the cage and straining for a glimpse of those who must be their doomed parents.

The crowd began to taunt and shout, spitting at the ground and hurling some poor merchant's produce with the same hands that had tossed flowers just minutes before. Bradley watched as the twenty were pulled from the first cart and set in a line before the gate. The noise from the children's cart grew louder, desperate. Several of the bound women cried openly, looking back toward the second cart, while the men clenched their jaws against tears. One woman looked up to Mount Desterrar and fell forward in a faint, only to be jerked back to her feet by a dark-armored soldier.

Bradley stared in stunned silence, hearing the words Dissention, Rebellion, Traitors, and Guilty screamed from every side, but unable to link such harsh language with the peaceful-looking row of condemned before him.

A man to his right shook a fist in the air and bellowed, "This is what comes to you Faithful!"

The man spat at the ground and Bradley's brow creased with confusion.

Faithful? Faithful to what?

"What have they done wrong?" Bradley's question was lost in the escalating noise of the crowd.

A soldier stepped toward the rebels, bearing a whip, and Bradley's gaze sought the cartload of children. A number of small hands stretched through the bars toward the line of condemned. Most were younger than Bradley.

Suddenly the young lord's focus was snagged by a wiry, brown-haired boy who clutched the bars and stared at Roland from within the cart. The boy's gaze was intense, boring into Bradley's brother-in-law and refusing to let go. Bradley shifted to glance beyond his sister and saw that Roland had seen the boy and was staring back. An unseen feud seemed to pass between the two and then Roland sharply turned to give the expected order.

"Begin!"

The brown-haired boy wilted against the bars.

The soldier who bore the whip bowed and then turned to face the prisoners. Bradley's eyes widened as the man's arm pulled back and then flew forward in a practiced arc. With the first crack of the whip the crowd's jeering intensified, blending in a muddle of unidentifiable noises and receding from his senses until Bradley heard nothing but the cries coming from the second cart.

The children watched and cried. Bradley saw himself weeping at his father's deathbed.

The children reached and strained. Bradley saw himself racing after the king's messenger, as the man had taken Hugh away.

Turning away from the painful scene with a gasp, Bradley looked at his sister. Rosalynn looked shaken and pale, but resigned and detached. As far as she was concerned, these twenty were no better than troublesome slaves who deserved these afflictions. Bradley's gaze shifted beyond her to peer at Roland. What kind of man forced young children to watch their parents suffer?

"What have they done wrong?"

This time, Rosalynn heard Bradley's question and turned to look at him with troubled brown eyes. For a moment he wondered if she would raise an objection, but then she shook her head.

"This does not concern us, Bradley."

His eyes widened in disbelief, "Yes. It does. We live here now and these are our people."

Rosalynn turned away from his glare and watched as the portcullis was raised and the gate Thirteenth swung inward with a groan. Through the opening Bradley could see the slanted grounds of Mount Desterrar tilting away from the walls. He gazed up at the summit and wondered what creatures and perils these twenty would be forced to face on the mountain. Was it possible to survive such a wilderness? Bradley found that he hoped it was.

The crowd quieted to a low murmur as a herald cried the names of the men and women who were condemned to exile. Lord Roland then straightened in his saddle to shout at the miserable prisoners.

"For your offences against the crown of Mizgalia and the power of Hebbros, you are hereby banished from our fair city to die in obscurity. Go forth now into exile!"

Their hands loosed from their bonds, the twenty lifted their heads and straightened as much as their sore backs would allow. One man—a cooper, if Bradley remembered the herald's cry—met Roland's gaze, and the crowd's murmuring stilled when he opened his mouth to speak.

"We will go, Roland. We will pave the way with our sweat, blood, and tears, that our children may one day see the truth and have courage to follow. We go not to exile, but to *freedom*."

A sense of wonder seemed to constrain those who would have spoken, and the twenty were marched through the gate before a silent crowd. Bradley glanced from one face to another. Each seemed awed by the cooper's words, as if they couldn't believe he had made such a declaration. Even Roland appeared momentarily stunned. The moment had been drained of its former sensation of victory.

The gate closed with a heavy thud and the crowd began to cheer once again, tentatively this time. Gradually the noise regained its thunderous volume and once again Bradley found himself wishing to escape to his private chambers. He watched as the cartload of quiet children was driven from the square, and he wondered what would become of them. There were a great many. Bradley swallowed and shook his head against the images that had been seared upon his mind. He doubted he would ever forget the events of this day.

Perhaps he would hide away in his chambers longer than a day or two. Or four. Perhaps he would lock himself away from Hebbros for a whole week.

Or maybe a month.

Bradley pressed his heels to his horse's flanks and followed Roland and Rosalynn from the square, heading toward the palace at last. The crowd made way for them, cheering and chanting their pleasure over the banishment. Bradley cast a single glance back at the gate and then took in the reveling of the flower-pelting masses.

Facing forward again he sneezed three times in a row.

Perhaps he would extend the length of his hiding to a year.

14

Window of Opportunity

A pair of strong hands lifted Luke down from the cart and set him on the street before a small and unassuming cottage. Waiting for the soldier to turn and lift out his brother and sister, Luke peered at the sagging structure and unconsciously tilted his head to balance his view of the slanted façade. The place looked terribly miserable. His gaze shifted to the darkening sky, visible beyond the roofs of Hebbros. They had been riding through the city all day, watching as the other children of yesterday's exiled were parceled out to new homes. Now it was their turn. Luke and Christopher and Charlotte had been kept until the last.

The cage door closed with the now familiar protest of rusty hinges and Luke spun in panic when he realized he was the only one standing on the street with the soldier.

Christopher and Charlotte stared back at him from inside the cart. *Shock. Fear. Alarm.*

"No, wait!" Christopher lurched for the bars of the cage, "Bring him back!"

"Take me too!" Charlotte shrieked at the thought of being separated from another person she loved.

"Stop! They're coming with me. You can't separate us!" Luke

jumped for the back of the cart, but the soldier caught him mid-leap and gruffly turned him back toward the leaning cottage of misery.

Sir Kenrick appeared from around the side of the wagon. Ignoring the distressed cries of all three children, he nodded his head, "Let's take him inside."

"No," Luke growled and dug his heels into the dirt and cobblestones. The soldier jerked him forward and Luke made himself limp, dangling obstinately from the man's grip and making it necessary to drag him across the road.

Charlotte shrieked his name and Luke squeezed his eyes shut. He could hear Christopher trying to comfort their sister, but his twin's voice sounded more like a whimper, proving that he himself needed to be consoled as well.

The realization that he would be alone suddenly struck Luke like a blow to his midsection and he felt strangely hollow inside. His face took on a blank mask and his mind refused to process what was happening around him. Somewhere along the edge of his awareness he knew he was being led into the crooked cottage and placed on his numb legs before a beefy man and his rail-thin wife. Sir Kenrick spoke to them and the man replied, but Luke could not have repeated what they said if his life had depended on it. To him their words were a garble of muffled noise.

Feeling more than seeing someone's gaze on him, the boy lifted his head and met the stare of the housewife. *Hardness. Disgust.* Luke glanced away. He wanted his mother. As he shifted his eyes, his attention was immediately drawn to a precious sight beyond the woman's head.

A window.

His eyes widened and he dropped his gaze to the floor as his mind set to work on a plan. The other children may be resigned to this change in their lives, but he wasn't. The others might accept these new families as their own, but he wouldn't. He would fight this injustice if he spent his last breath in the struggle.

"Luke," the sound of his name suddenly cut through his reverie and Luke stiffened when Sir Kenrick continued in a haughty tone, "these are your new parents." He motioned to the couple with his arm, "Your father is a blacksmith, and when you have finished your schooling you will be apprenticed to him and learn an honorable trade. Your mother will see that you get to the schoolroom each day, and you will obey her in all things. Do you understand this?"

Luke clenched his jaw and stared at the floor between them.

"Luke." The knight's voice was hard, threatening, "Answer me!"

"Let him be." Startled, Luke flinched when a shrill voice interceded on his behalf. He slid a glance at the rail-thin housewife as she pressed her bony hands to her hips and nodded respectfully to Sir Kenrick, "He's frightened now but he'll do well with us, I'm sure. Just don't press him to speak tonight. He's had a shock and isn't likely to answer you, and I'd like to set down to supper before the food gets cold."

Sir Kenrick's jaw twitched and his head lifted as he observed the woman, wondering whether taking heed to her speech would be considered degrading to his position. The blacksmith spared him the decision.

"I'll see to him, sir." The man nodded and his beefy jowls quivered, "You can leave the boy to my care."

Luke's gaze moved to the window once more as Sir Kenrick turned with a flourish and left the cottage with the soldier in tow. The door squealed shut and a moment later the sound of the cart reached Luke's ears, growing fainter as it carried his brother and sister farther away from him to an unknown point in the city.

He was alone.

Gritting his teeth, he stared at the window.

"Set yourself at the table, boy. Supper is ready."

Luke ignored the blacksmith's caustic tone. Now that Sir Kenrick was gone, the man's attitude of acceptance toward him had shifted, along with the crooked cottage's atmosphere.

"I said set yourself at the table, boy!"

Luke's slender fingers balled into tight fists. How he longed to lash out at this man, this blacksmith who would presume to act in place of Luke's own gentle father. How he longed to meet the man's glare with one just as hard and shout that he would never consent to Sir Kenrick's orders. He would never consider this warped excuse of a cottage as his home, nor would he treat these people as his family.

"I'll not tell you again, boy," the blacksmith growled impatiently. "Sit now or starve."

"Let him be," the housewife's shrill voice called from where she stood by the table. "He'll come to when his stomach starts complaining."

The blacksmith grunted and crossed to the table, where he dropped his bulky weight into a chair that was almost as unbalanced as his cottage. His wife set a mug of ale on the small table's surface and then sat herself in the other chair. Warm smells wafted across the room to fill Luke's nostrils and his stomach growled in hungry protest at his refusal to join the couple for supper. His eyes slid closed momentarily as he forced his thoughts back to his plan.

The window. *Focus on the window.*

And he did.

For two hours.

Luke's body felt heavy with weariness and stiff from inactivity. His face remained an unaffected mask and his eyes continued their constant study of the window…and of the view beyond it. He hoped that his unchanging and defeated posture would give his hosts the impression that he would remain with them quietly, causing no trouble. At the end of two hours, he was rewarded with the knowledge that his plan had worked.

The blacksmith rose from his seat by the fire, where he had been bent over a piece of work. He glanced at Luke and scowled as he spoke to his wife, "The gods of Hebbros know that I'd do anything to please them, but if I had my way such devotion would not require that I open my home to the tarnished child of a rebel." He spat into the flames on the hearth, "Lord Roland will not make friends with this new edict."

"The boy won't be trouble. Look at him." The woman stretched her arms over her head and twisted the stiff kinks from her back, "He's a right quiet one, and quiet ones are easy to handle. Soon enough he'll be apprenticed in your shop and you'll be glad that Sir Kenrick brought him to our door. I'm off to sleep now."

"What do we do with him?" The blacksmith nodded toward Luke as he turned to follow his wife's example and retire for the evening, "We can't just leave him standing there."

The rail-thin housewife sat on the edge of the pallet in the far corner—by the window—and cast a glance between the room's two other occupants, "Why not? He hasn't moved for hours and he won't be going anywhere now that night's fallen." Her eyes narrowed as if warning Luke for good measure, "The streets of

Hebbros are a cruel place to be, especially at night."

The blacksmith turned, "You hear that, boy? The darkened streets of Hebbros are no friends to a wanderer."

Luke continued to stare straight ahead.

"Bah!" Waving an irritated hand at Luke's silence, the large man banked the fire and moved to the shadowy corner where the pallet lay.

Luke blinked in the darkness, waiting for his eyes to adjust, and remained motionless. Within minutes the cottage was filled with the sound of snoring—both the blacksmith's and his wife's. A small smile tilted Luke's mouth and he took a step toward the window in the far wall. His body instantly roused from its lengthy period of idleness and his weariness slipped away as he moved carefully across the floor and lifted himself to perch on the open sill. With a single glance over his shoulder to ensure that the man and his wife were still sound asleep, Luke slipped through the casement and dropped to the narrow dirt track that ran behind the cottage and its neighbors. Jumping to his feet, he took off at a run with one destination in mind and the blacksmith's warnings of the cruel streets nipping dangerously at his heels.

Some time later, crouching in the shadows of his father's cooper shop, Luke drew his knees to his chest and buried his face against them to cry. He cried for his parents, his brother, his sister. He wept for the friends he had known so briefly, who had bonded with his cause so thoroughly, yet were now scattered throughout the city. He had to keep them unified. Somehow.

A loud cackle of a laugh sounded as someone passed by the shop's window and Luke pressed himself further against the wall. His round eyes grew larger with renewed fear and a sob escaped his throat as he thought of his frightening dash through the city, only recently concluded here. The blacksmith's wife had been correct, and her description of Hebbros mild. The streets were not only cruel at night, they were terrifying. The darkened thoroughfares had created a strange maze as he tried to collect his bearings and find the cooper shop. Suspicious and unsavory characters had lurked in every shadow; homeless or unwilling to take shelter in the home they had, they sought to find pleasure in some mischief or other. Luke had been relieved to slip unnoticed through the door of his father's shop, but now worried that he might be discovered if someone remembered that the cooper had been exiled and his shop abandoned.

Abandoned. Luke's brow furrowed at the thought. It was true his father would be unable to return to the shop, but where was his assistant, Guy? Luke hadn't seen the burly man since…he didn't know when.

Swiping a hand across his face, sticky with sweat and drying tears, Luke shifted his attention to the cloth belt at his waist. Twisting the piece around so that the knot was within easy reach, he put his fingers to work untying it just enough to slip an inch-long bit of steel from the bond. Holding the small object on his open palm, Luke stared at the rivet that his father had passed to him through the bars of Kenrick's cage. Here in the shop, the floor was comfortably littered with bits of wood and a few rivets like the one in his hand, evidence of the work his father had done. Luke closed his fingers over the steel bit that had come to hold special meaning to him. His father's last gift. A rivet representing memories of a happier time.

Luke took the rivet between his thumb and forefinger and studied it as best he could in the shadows. This small object, when joined by others just like it, could hold together a barrel. The barrel, when held together by these rivets, could hold anything.

Luke blinked.

"Amazing," his softly spoken exclamation sounded loud in his ears. "We, the children of the Faithful, are like rivets. If we keep our promise to band together, then one day we'll be built up like a barrel, holding and preserving our faith."

Luke's gaze shifted to the floor, spying a number of rivets along the wall where they caught the pale light of the moon through the window. Tying his own rivet back into the knot of his belt, he grabbed a small crock from a worktable and began filling it with a number of the steel pieces from the floor.

"Everyone will get one," Luke murmured to himself as he bent to his task. "I'll find the other children and give each boy and girl one of father's rivets. We'll keep them as a symbol of our pact."

A shuffling to his left startled Luke and sent him backing into a corner. A shadow emerged from the storage room and Luke sucked in a gasp when a pillar of moonlight filtered through a break in the thatched roof and illuminated his face for the newcomer to see. The shadowed figure stiffened and the two stared at one another across the dark room for an instant before Luke suddenly lurched for the door. Tightening his arm about the crock of rivets, he scrambled to lift the crossbar from its cradle. A hand suddenly clamped over his shoulder and Luke swallowed a shriek as he was turned about to face the stranger.

"Let go of me!"

"Luke!"

The boy froze and lifted his head to search the face of the man before him. Hugging the crock to his chest, he swallowed and then frowned, "Guy?"

The massive cooper nodded and slowly released his hold on Luke's shoulder, as if fearful that the boy would resume his escape and vanish. Luke studied the man, wishing he could read Guy's face, but unable to see his gaze in the darkness of the shop.

"You are well?" Guy kept his voice low.

The crease of a frown remained imprinted in Luke's forehead, "No, I am not well. My father and mother have been exiled to Desterrar, my brother and sister were separated from me, and now I'm alone in a city that hates me and hates people like me."

Guy dipped his head and Luke caught a glimpse of his face in a shaft of moonlight. *Shame.* "But you are unharmed?"

Luke ignored the question and asked one of his own, "Where were you?"

"What?"

"These last few days; the raid, the exile, the celebrations. Where were you?"

Silence.

Luke's frown deepened into a look of confusion as another thought pressed his mind for release, "You're a member of the Faithful, aren't you?"

The question hung in the air between them, along with its implication. Why had Luke's father been singled out for banishment as one of the Faithful, when Guy had seemingly escaped notice in the matter? Had Althar been banished because of Luke's reckless behavior in the schoolroom after all? Or…

Closing his eyes and taking a deep breath, Guy crouched before the ten-year-old so that they were eye-level. At this height his face was lit by soft light from outside and Luke would be able to see, to read, his face. Opening his eyes, Guy met the probing gaze of the child before him. He knew of Luke's gift and what this child's intense search would reveal, but it could not be helped. No matter how much regret filled a man, time could not be turned back. Deeds could not be undone.

He knew the instant Luke's discovery had been made.

Betrayal. Regret. Fear. Luke's head bumped against the door as he recoiled from Guy's telling gaze. The crock of rivets slipped from his hands and the cooper caught it before it smashed against the floor. Guy peered at the number of rivets inside and then looked again at Luke. The boy's eyes filled with tears and his face crumbled with a wounded look.

"You?" Luke's whisper of disbelief became a cry of rage with his next words, "You betrayed them! You were father's closest friend! He trusted you, and you…you…"

Luke's small fists pounded against Guy's shoulders only once before the cooper gathered the boy's wrists in his free hand.

"Please," Guy pressed the boy's hands in a pleading gesture, "I have already rebuked myself and called *Guy the cooper* every shameful and disgusting name that I could without further dishonoring myself before God."

"Is He really your God?" Luke scoffed.

Guy looked away and he released Luke's wrists, "He is. Luke, you cannot yet know the pressure that comes when… Or know the fear that takes hold of a man when he is…" Guy's gaze collided with Luke's once again and the child shrank from the raw emotion he saw there. *Terror.* "I was afraid, Luke. I warned your father of the consequences that would come from his decision. People of great power and influence in Hebbros suspected Althar's actions as an active member of the Faithful and I was contacted as one closely connected to his work. They threatened me, child. I cannot convey to you the force of such threats. I was convinced to give them the names of several Faithful and ordered to confess Althar's association with them. They threatened me with immediate death."

"So you sent my father *and my mother* to theirs?"

Guy bowed his head, "Luke, we cannot change the past no matter how ashamed we are of it. I have asked God's pardon for my fear and for the actions that it produced, and I pray that you too will one day be able to forgive me."

A conflict waged in Luke's chest as he fought the urge to

knock the shameful man backwards. His mother had taught him to forgive as Christ forgave, but she hadn't known of Guy's deception!

God's mercy redeems the guilty.

Luke's head bowed at the memory of those words. Who was he to refuse the extension of mercy when a man's sin was truly an offense against his Creator, and God had already offered him pardon?

"Rivets?" Guy's voice brought Luke's head up to see the look of question in the man's eyes. Guy held out the crock and Luke took it with a nod.

"I'm going to give one to each of the other children, the others whose parents were exiled." He paused, unsure whether he could trust Guy with the information. Suddenly he straightened, thinking that this was as good an opportunity as any other to stand for his faith, "We made a pact to stand together and to keep our faith. These rivets will remind us of our purpose in holding together."

The cooper nodded his understanding and rose to his feet, hiding his face in the shadows once again. He was quiet for a moment and Luke wondered if Guy was considering telling his friends of "great power and influence" about the children's pact. When the man spoke next, his words sounded through the stillness of the shop like a clap of thunder.

"I'm going to take you back."

Luke's chest felt constricted, "What?"

"You were taken to a new home today, yes? And you've run away. I'm going to take you back."

"No!" Luke ducked away from the cooper and the door but Guy caught him and swung him back around, placing a silencing finger to his lips. Luke readied himself for a bellow that would rouse the city from slumber when he suddenly heard the sounds of raucous laughter passing by outside the shop. The crude remarks that accompanied the laughter reminded Luke that if he shouted, the only people he could count on coming to his rescue were those in the streets whose reputations were more disreputable than Guy's. A glance told the boy that the cooper too was wary of the passersby.

"Luke, listen to me," Guys whispered words were sharp. Luke turned to face him fully—*Daring. Determination. Decision*—and his tension eased slightly. "I'm going to help you."

"By taking me back?" His face compressed with an incredulous look.

"Luke, you cannot wander the streets until the day comes when you are strong enough to avenge your parents' banishment."

"You mean their death."

Guy shook his head, "I have reason to believe they will survive. Sedgwick is alive still, and will be able to aid the newly exiled members." Hope flared within Luke's chest and questions filled his eyes, but Guy stopped their surfacing with a wave of his hand, "I'll say no more. The less you know the safer you'll be."

Luke scowled but chose a safer question, "How can you help me?"

"First, I will take you back to your new home."

Luke stiffened with uncertainty but kept his eyes glued to Guy's, reading the commitment evidenced there, "I won't stay there. I'll just run away again."

Guy sighed, "Be that as it may, if I take you back it will provide a place for you to stay and also give the leaders of Hebbros less cause to suspect me of aiding the Faithful. They will cease from watching me so closely."

"That will help you, not me," Luke crossed his arms over the crock of rivets.

Guy ignored the comment. "Once the knights of this new Mordecai Order are no longer concerned with me and the activities I participate in, I will send word for you to meet me here in secret. That is when I'll offer you the greatest help I can."

"Do you truly believe my parents are alive?" Luke tilted his head, intrigued, and repeated his earlier question, "What help can you give me?" His eyes roved the shop, giving voice to his unspoken thoughts. He didn't see how a cooper could aid his cause.

"Luke." When the boy's eyes returned to focus on his face, the corners of Guy's mouth lifted with a conspiratorial smile, "Making barrels is not the only talent I possess."

15

Daughter of a Nobleman

Kingdom of Arcrea, Lord's Castle in Frederick's Region

Lord Frederick finished a turn and gently brought his sword around to meet the one held by his seven-year-old daughter, Elaina. She flashed him a dimpled smile that emanated confidence and then returned her focus to the weapons held carefully in the space between them. The two continued the intricate pattern of steps that comprised the Arcrean Sword Reel, a dance introduced by their land's ancient natives and passed down to subsequent generations. Lord Frederick offered quiet instructions whenever the girl faltered.

Pausing briefly after an overzealous turn, Elaina brushed dark loose curls from her face and then adjusted her grip on the hilt of her child-sized sword.

"Take the steps gently, daughter," Frederick gave her an amused smile. "We'll go faster when you know them so well you could dance it in your sleep."

Her dark eyes, close-set in her juvenile face, glittered with humor, "I'd like that." She copied the downward slant of her father's sword and they made a full turn around one another before she grinned mischievously, "Wouldn't Mother make a fuss about that?"

Frederick caught a laugh before it escaped, trying and failing to give her a stern look, "Tut tut, child. You mustn't take delight in vexing your poor mother."

Elaina ignored his mild rebuke, "Here comes the box step. Then my favorite part where our swords meet at the cross-guard."

The box step was performed in graceful movements. When the swords locked as Elaina had anticipated, the dancers paused long enough for Frederick to tap a finger against his daughter's nose. She rewarded him with an impish grin and backed away to continue the reel. When the last step had been completed the two sheathed their swords and Lord Frederick made a low bow.

"Beautifully done."

Elaina offered a curtsy that would have pleased her mother had the woman been present to see it. Straightening again, she seemed to sense another presence and turned to look toward the hall's heavy oak door. Frederick followed her gaze and spotted the shadowy figure leaning casually against the wall, obviously waiting for them to finish their dance. Frederick cleared his throat, unnerved and yet pleased by the young man's uncanny ability to enter a room without the occupant's knowledge.

"Elaina, take the swords and lay them out on the side table."

Elaina reached for her father's sword and crossed to the designated table, offering a shy smile to the newcomer as he offered her a nod of respect and moved to converse with her father. Leaving the weapons side-by-side on the smooth surface, the young girl turned to watch the two men. Her father's eyes narrowed and widened by turn, changing with his emotions as the young man calmly relayed whatever his news was. Intrigued as always, Elaina plucked at the purple folds of her skirt and took a step closer.

"Your lordship asked that I investigate the rumors concerning Lord Quinton. I penetrated his private quarters and discovered that he has indeed been conducting searches for the heart of Arcrea by sending out companies of soldiers disguised as common peddlers, and in some cases as sailors."

Frederick's head lifted thoughtfully, "Sailors. He searches in the southern regions, then? By the sea."

Elaina caught the young man's nod. She licked her lips, her excitement mounting as she listened to them discussing the kingdom's ancient riddle about a heart. The first man to discover the mysterious object would be crowned as Arcrea's first king. Her father intended to be that man.

"I will send word to lords Geoffrey and Stephen. They will help me put a stop to Quinton's searches if only to keep his men out of their regions. The other lords will aid us if Quinton proves to be obstinate." Frederick nodded to the other man, a smile of pleasure easing the lines of his face, "Well done, Falconer. Sir Malcolm served me well when he presented you to be my chief informant. I swear there is not a wall built that you could not find a finger-hold in its stones or a footpath ascending its smooth surface."

Young Falconer's jaw stiffened and he cast a sidelong glance in Elaina's direction. Frederick turned and studied his daughter as if seeing her for the first time. Elaina studied his distant expression and released a sigh. He had forgotten her presence when faced with matters of the region. Again.

She glanced from one man to the other, sensing their discomfort over the fact that Lord Frederick had just unveiled before a child the clandestine position that Falconer maintained. Straightening her posture as her mother had taught her from the age of three, Elaina took another step forward and offered the dimpled smile her father loved. If she could not keep his company for long outside of these political matters, then she simply must join in his web of intrigue.

"I like hearing about your work. I promise not to tell." She placed a slender bejeweled finger against her lips in a show of silence and then glanced at the man called Falconer with a whispered query of awe, "You are a spy?"

His sharp features, obviously schooled for secrecy, remained an unaffected mask as his gaze moved from her to her father. Frederick's eyes narrowed as he studied Elaina, and then his features broke with a laugh.

"Ah, child! If only your mother showed the curiosity for my work that you do, and not merely for the wealth that it gives her. Our region might soon be the greatest in Arcrea through the support of two such determined women!"

"It is already the greatest region in the land. And you, my father, will be the first king."

"Indeed. I shall do my best to give credence to your words." His expression grew suddenly dark and serious, "Elaina of

Frederick, in order to protect our homeland and spare lives from death, do you now swear by the heart of Arcrea that you will keep the confidences you have heard today and may yet hear in the future?"

Breathless at the thought of being included in his work, and therefore not easily forgotten, Elaina laid a small hand of over her heart in a solemn pledge, "I do swear, Father."

"Good." Frederick took her hand and turned to Falconer, who stood eyeing them both as a silent witness, "I can trust her to protect matters of the region." Her father's gaze dropped to meet hers again, "She is a girl after my own heart and loves this land as I do. She will do great things in her lifetime, I am sure of it. I see a bright future when I look into her face. Now then, Falconer," Frederick turned, "my knights along the border of Mizgalia have sent complaints regarding a Mizgalian assassin who has appeared at various locations along the Brikbone Mountains. I wish to speak with you regarding your next assignment…"

Elaina watched as her father crossed to sit before the hall's massive hearth, Falconer following to stand at attention beside him. The young girl slowly trailed behind, smiling to herself as Lord Frederick's words of confidence in his daughter echoed within her very soul.

Part Two

Fugitive

Four Years Later

"Let us go forth therefore unto him without the camp, bearing his reproach."

Hebrews 13:13

16
Terror, Hope, & Candles

It was an oppressive summer day. Heat rolled in shimmering waves over Hebbros, leaving the banners and flags strung from a sea of towers and turrets to hang limp and lifeless in the palpable warmth. In the stifling streets below, the dusty city's inhabitants did their best to traverse the crowded thoroughfares while occupying the cool shadows that clung to the faces of many structures.

Along one street, ignoring the sweat that glistened and dripped from his rotund face, a locksmith marched purposefully toward the heart of the city. One fist swung in time to his steps while the other kept a firm hold on the arm of a wiry youth behind him.

"This'll teach ye t' be runnin' from me shop, ye scalawag." The locksmith gave the boy's arm a tug and nearly fell backward when his own arm was jerked in return. He whirled with a fierce scowl, "Stop that! I've kept me patience for nigh on a month now, and what've ye repaid me for me kindness? Naught but trouble and terror."

"You were never kind to me," the youth retorted.

"Ye were never deservin' o' the kindness!"

"Ha! So you admit it." The tall boy planted his feet on the

cobbled street and fought the locksmith's every step. Setting his jaw, he finally relaxed his stubborn stance and jumped forward a pace, causing the older man to topple onto his hindquarters in the street. Several passersby laughed openly at the sight.

The locksmith jumped up with a growl and cuffed the youth before continuing to drag him through the streets. "It's to the temple I'll be goin' after I've left ye with the Order."

He was answered with a mocking snort, "You, turning religious?"

A grunt. "'Tis known through Hebbros that Luke the Terror could drive a man nigh t' drink and madness, let alone t' religion. Aye. To the temple wi' me today and I'll be beggin' to understand what my sins were that caused me t' deserve a month o' such troubles as ye've brought on me head."

"Luke the Terror" scowled but fell silent as he cast a sidelong glance at the locksmith and then focused on keeping up with the man's uneven stride. He'd known where they were headed even before the locksmith made mention of the Order. During the four years since his parents' exile to Mount Desterrar he had made the same trip numerous times with other guardians, and he doubted this would be the last.

Four years had done much to change Luke's outward appearance. His young frame had grown tall and lean. Strength had begun to harden his limbs due to many apprenticeships and in addition to his secret classes tutored by Guy. His gift of deep perception had grown keener, exposing the false affection and indifference of his many caretakers, and his mind had continued to sharpen, using his newly acquired skills to calculate and plan to the disadvantage of his enemies.

Now following the locksmith, Luke opened his mouth to speak and then paused to clear his throat. In recent days, to his great mortification, his confused voice always sounded as if it couldn't decide whether to speak in the higher or lower registers. He was beginning to despair of ever sounding normal again.

"You know I'll run away again."

"Little I care," the locksmith exhaled heavily, "for next time it won't be from me."

Their steps finally brought them to a vast shadow that darkened the cobbles. The shade created a refuge from the heat for a good-sized crowd of commoners who were buying, selling, and trading a multitude of goods in the street. Luke scanned the lot of faces, greedy and miserable every one, and then lifted his eyes to the source of the welcome shadow; the intimidating garrison that now stood beside the House of Peers' meeting hall.

The three-year-old structure had been built entirely of black stone and housed the dark-armored knights of the Mordecai Order. The arrow-pierced M of their insignia had been emblazoned on a golden shield of impressive size and mounted over the public entrance. Luke remembered seeing the emblem on a ring worn by Sir Kenrick, the knight responsible for arresting his parents. Kenrick had come to be known and feared as chief of this vicious order. Lord Roland had entrusted him with all details concerning the Faithful, and Kenrick had performed his new duties with zeal.

A shove from the locksmith propelled Luke through the archway leading to the garrison's public courtyard. Immediately his slate-blue eyes darted corner-to-corner and shadow-to-shadow, searching for the one Mordecai whose presence always unnerved him.

Feared even more than Kenrick was his first knight, Sir Valden of Lork. The man was cold and unfeeling. Sly as an Arcrean ignispat and fierce as a catawyld beast, he had been responsible for unearthing and exposing the names of many Faithful since his arrival two months after Lord Roland's marriage. As a result, Mount Desterrar had been the recipient of many more lives, claiming the exiled of Hebbros one banishment at a time. Some had perished within sight of the city walls. Others had disappeared from view to an unknown fate.

Luke sighed with relief when his search of the courtyard produced no sign of Sir Valden. He had met the knight's gaze once, on his second "visit" to the Order, and the level of capable evil that had been revealed left Luke feeling tarnished. Sir Valden was indifferent and desensitized, and the depths of his wickedness had surpassed that which Luke had seen in Lord Roland and Sir Kenrick both.

The courtyard teemed with knights and squires intent on one task or another, all shouting commands or good-natured jibes at their fellows. The sounds of clashing swords and resulting cheers rose from beyond the wall opposite the public entrance, where the Order's practice yard offered the Mordecais exercise and entertainment.

Approaching a door to the left of the courtyard, beneath a wooden placard bearing the word Reestablishment, the locksmith applied a heavy fist to the panel. An armored guard quickly answered his knock. The soldier's gaze moved to Luke and he smirked knowingly before stepping aside to let them enter. Crossing the threshold, Luke's eyes were immediately drawn to the man seated at a stone-topped table in the center of the room. Sir Kenrick drank deeply from a goblet and then swallowed as he set the chalice aside.

"Sir Kenrick…sir," the locksmith, suddenly nervous, doffed his cap and dipped his head respectfully, "I must beg yer pardon and return the boy." He jerked his balding head to indicate the tall youth beside him, "He's been naught but trouble for me fro' the very start. I tried t' be kind and patient"—Luke snorted at this—"but 'twere no use. Why, he's run fro' me shop two times this week alone!"

"Three times," Luke muttered the correction.

The locksmith cast him a dark scowl and then turned to face Kenrick again, "I've got a shop to be runnin', sir. Me work, and thereby the good of our fair city, suffers on account o' this lad."

Sir Kenrick's cold eyes slid to observe Luke and the boy boldly met his stare, reading the multiple layers of emotions and traits reflected there. At length the knight waved a dismissive hand toward the door behind them.

"You may go, good locksmith. Hebbros and the Mordecai Order acknowledge your dutiful…attempts. Rest assured, I will see that the boy is reestablished before the week is out."

Luke's jaw clenched with familiar rage at the word *reestablished.* The leaders of Hebbros spoke about the children of the Faithful as if they were no more than a herd of cattle or a litter of unwanted pups. If the "calf" happened to bawl for its mother, or the "pup" growled when threatened, it was quickly returned to this room in the Mordecai garrison to be reestablished in a new home or in the very least reminded of its "obligation to conform to its new life." It had been the same for four years.

Of course, most of the children had grown acclimated to their new situations in a matter of weeks. During his regular forays through the city, when running away from one caretaker or another, Luke had managed to locate many of his comrades from the night of that terrible first raid. Only the locations of his two siblings had been successfully withheld from his knowledge.

To each of his friends he had distributed a rivet from the collection gathered in his father's former shop, and encouraged them not to give up hope. By all appearances his friends had remembered their pact to remain true to the faith, but a measure of resignation had settled over them. They would bide their time in silence. Most had finished their years in the Peer-appointed schoolrooms and were excelling in various apprenticeships throughout the city.

Luke on the other hand could not be content to acclimate himself even for a season. The very thought drove him to distraction and balled his hands into determined fists. He had to fight injustice and make a stand for truth, even if it was done impulsively.

His mother's many lessons of godliness had been buried in his heart. Unfortunately, they had remained that way. Buried. Having rested four years without proper cultivation, the seeds of his budding faith had grown very little, and so he lived by his established inclinations of rashness, revolution, and oftentimes rebellion.

The soldier closed the door behind the satisfied locksmith and Sir Kenrick rose from his padded chair. Stepping to the far wall, sectioned off into small scroll-filled compartments, he selected one of the documents and turned to unroll it across his table. He scanned the parchment and then quirked one brow as he reclaimed his seat. Luke remained motionless, following the knight's movements with a studious gaze.

"So then, Luke," Kenrick plucked a quill-pen from its stand on his table, "during the four years of your reestablishment the Mordecai Order has placed you with twenty-six different families. Each has returned you after an average length of two months spent in their care. One family, after only a day."

Luke shifted his stance and exhaled half-a-laugh at the recollection. His grin quickly evaporated when Sir Kenrick's glare never wavered.

"For two years you ran from your caretakers and schoolmasters, and for another two years you have run from and inconvenienced those overseeing your apprenticeships." Slowly, Kenrick moved to dip his pen in a well of black ink while his eyes roved the parchment before him, "You ran from the blacksmiths, the fuellers, the ropemakers, the masons and carpenters, the taverners, the wheelwrights, and now," the quill scratched a quick note, "the locksmith."

Luke wet his lips with a swipe of his tongue, "You left out a few."

Kenrick surged to his feet and planted his fists on the table, "I know it, you insolent brat!" His face stretched taut as he tried to control his breathing, "You have defied me at every turn, and resisted all efforts to help you create a new life. Apparently you remember every apprenticeship you entered. Did you think so little of those men that you could not endure to learn their trade?"

Luke's nostrils flared with indignation and his young voice cracked as furious words spilled from his mouth, "You're right, I do remember. I remember the night you tore my family apart, and the events that took place the next day. I remember every cruel look and the words of hatred I've received since then. I remember every bit of mistreatment and every gaze that's fallen on me. I was not cared for in those homes. I was not wanted in those shops. Those people gave me no reason to stay, and only wanted me back when they needed to earn your approval. The people of Hebbros are afraid to fail. They're afraid of you and they're afraid of Lord Roland."

Kenrick's eyes narrowed, "They should be."

Luke's wiry frame straightened, "But I'm not." His head slowly began to shake from side to side, "I'm not afraid of you. I'm not afraid of your Mordecais or of Lord Roland. I'm not afraid of the House of Peers and their puppet schoolmasters. I've seen your fears and weaknesses. I'll always be bold enough to run from you. No matter how many times you try to break me, I'll always survive," Luke clapped a hand to his chest, holding it over his heart, "because I have faith in Jesus Christ, and there is nothing you can do to take that from me."

Kenrick's gaze darkened. Four years, and still this boy clung to the influence of his rebel parents. What would it take to fracture his resolve? The knight reclaimed his seat, "Your faith cannot be one of virtue and honor if you hold to it so dearly and yet feel free to disrespect your elders."

Kenrick saw Luke flinch at his acute observation. A brief cringe creased the skin around the boy's eyes, evidence that the barbed words had had some effect. Luke continued to hold the knight's stare, but his eyes glazed over with a distant look as his gaze turned inward. The room was silent for a moment and then the young dissenter opened his mouth to speak again.

"There were only two people who ever taught me to be respectful…and you banished them."

"Lord Roland banished them, and he did so for your own good." Kenrick aimed a condemning finger at Luke's chest and sneered, "And you are wrong; many people have attempted to teach you respect. The schoolmasters alone delivered several years worth of lessons to your ears, trying to teach you to respect your leaders."

Luke shook his head, "They taught me to respect myself."

The guard at the door guffawed softly at the boy's quick and countering replies. Kenrick scowled and the man resumed his silence, staring with a blank expression at some point beyond Luke's head. Sir Kenrick's gaze shifted back to Luke.

"You will not win, boy. You cannot win, don't you see? You will always be placed in another home, another apprenticeship, until the day you are old enough to be cast to a certain death on the mountain as your parents were before you. Unless, of course, you come to your senses and adjust to your new life as a man of Hebbros."

A steady knock sounded at the door behind Luke and his senses were immediately heightened. The soldier moved to open the door and then stepped back to give Kenrick a view of their visitor. Suddenly stiff, Luke did not turn. Instead his eyes dropped to where sunlight spilled over the threshold and the shadow of a man stretched across the floor and between his feet. His heart pounded.

"You may enter, Valden." Kenrick motioned to the newcomer and then glanced at Luke, "My business here is nearly concluded and then I will hear your report."

A soft grunt was the only answer Kenrick received as the guard closed the door and Sir Valden stepped to the side of the room. Luke felt the man's presence like a heavy cloud, making the space feel small and confined. Instinctively, he took a deep breath to curb the tightness in his chest. Out of the corner of his eye he watched the black-armored figure lean casually against the wall and felt the man's sharp gaze scan his lowered face.

"Again?" Valden's gravelly voice broke the sudden silence that had fallen upon his arrival.

Kenrick glanced from his first knight to the boy and back again. He reached once more for his quill-pen and gave a single nod, "Again. Though no surprise."

Valden grunted and leaned away from the wall. Covering the distance in two long strides, he crooked a finger under Luke's chin and tipped the boy's face up for examination. Luke's eyes resisted the upward motion and remained lowered, traveling no further than the knight's chin. When Valden spoke again his breath washed over Luke's face in a gut-wrenching wave of filth, and Luke fought the urge to vomit.

"Everyone insists he's a spirited firebrand, but I've never witnessed any signs of such behavior in him." He dropped Luke's chin and turned to Kenrick, "He seems no more harmful than any of the others."

Kenrick froze with his wet pen poised over Luke's records and stared at the two across the stone table, obviously questioning Luke's rare sedateness in connection to Valden's presence.

Luke resisted the natural impulse to meet Valden's gaze, and instead glanced at Kenrick. He saw the knight's consideration of Valden's effect and winced. How he wished he could reverse his reaction to the man beside him and show the brute exactly what Kenrick meant by "spirited firebrand." He was just another man, another Mordecai. Nevertheless, Sir Valden's arrival upon any scene always fell like a restricting grip on Luke's lungs, deflating his attitude of bravado and laying a cloak of oppression over the boy's heart. Now Luke waited anxiously for Sir Kenrick to decide his fate and send him away—anywhere, as long as it was away from Valden.

The scratch of the quill-pen echoed in Luke's ears. Sir Kenrick was silent as he finished with a flourish, set aside the pen, and stood to return the record to its compartment in the far wall. He turned and reached for his goblet, swallowing the last of its contents before restoring his focus to the others in the room.

"Growell, take the boy to the holding room." His eyes met Luke's, "You will remain there until I am able to escort you to your new home."

At the prospect of leaving Sir Valden behind a measure of Luke's boldness returned. As the guard called Growell took his arm and started toward the door, Luke turned to walk backwards and scoffed at the words just spoken by the Order's chief.

"Holding room? You may as well call it a prison cell. You treat us no better than common criminals, and care for us even less. And as to a new home?" Luke spat at the ludicrous thought and saw Valden's brow quirk just before the door closed with a thud.

"Come along, boy," Growell gave Luke's arm a jerk, forcing him to face forward.

Luke spun away from the door marked Reestablishment and caught sight of Sir Valden's horse being tended outside the stables. At the sound of Growell's impatient words, Valden's young squire turned from brushing the animal.

Luke froze.

The squire stared back with a slack jaw and then suddenly started forward with a shout, "Luke!" He abandoned the brush to the dirt and raced across the courtyard.

"Chris!" Luke tugged free of Growell's grip and sprinted toward his brother.

"Come back here!" Growell's shout was lost to Luke as his heart hammered in his ears. Tears blurred his vision as he watched his twin draw closer. For four long years they had been separated, and only now, at the sight of Christopher's face, did he realize the true depth of his longing to see family again.

A stableman appeared and after a quick glance at the scene gave chase to Christopher's fleet form. Behind Luke, Growell's feet pounded across the courtyard in hot pursuit. Luke felt an icy gaze lock on the back of his head and knew instinctively that Sirs Kenrick and Valden had come to the door to see the commotion. The two boys locked eyes and surged forward in a desperate effort to cross the last few yards that separated them. Suddenly the stableman managed to snake an arm around Christopher's waist, jerking him to a halt.

"No!" Luke shouted as a hand clamped down on his own shoulder and pulled him in the opposite direction. His arms thrashed wildly. Catching hold of his brother's hand, his grip tightened. Christopher's hold strengthened in return and a thrill jolted through Luke at the contact.

"Enough of that," the stableman attempted to pry their fingers apart, but desperation lent force to their clasped hands.

"No, please! He's my brother." Chris strained to keep his

hold.

"Let go of me!" Luke bellowed as he tried to elbow Growell in the stomach. Tears born of rage spilled down his face, mingling with the perspiration that dripped freely from his hairline.

"Enough!" Sir Kenrick's shout echoed across the courtyard and stilled the four struggling at its center. Breathing hard, Luke glanced to see that everyone in the yard had stopped to watch the scene, and several curious knights had appeared at the gate leading to the practice yard. Taking advantage of the pause, Luke readjusted his hold on Christopher's hand and then glanced back at the Reestablishment room. Kenrick and Valden looked on from the threshold as he had suspected.

"You're struggling with children one-third your ages, you fools." Sir Kenrick flicked his wrist at the two grown men, "Give them a brief moment." His mouth twisted in a wry smile, "It is highly doubtful they will see each other again, and perhaps the wise young squire will encourage his brother to accept his fate."

Growell relinquished his hold reluctantly, as did the stableman, and the two brothers stumbled into each other's arms. Luke crushed his twin in a powerful embrace, squeezing his eyes shut as he relished the protective hold of his brother's arms, digging painfully into his own shoulders and back.

A sob shook Christopher's brawny frame and he pulled back to study his twin. He grinned, "You're taller."

"You're twice as tall," Luke mirrored the look of joyful wonder as he tried to grasp the reality of his brother's presence. Taller, broader, bronzed by the sun and muscular from activity, Christopher was his twin's physical opposite. Luke's grin stretched and his voice cracked when he spoke, "And your voice is deep."

"Yours will settle too." Christopher glanced at Kenrick and lowered his voice to a murmur, "Why are you here?"

"I'm here every couple of months…or weeks. I won't settle for a life they choose for me. I can't. One day we'll be strong enough to fight back, and it won't help our cause if we're comfortable with the very injustices we're resisting."

"I wouldn't ask you to become like them, only don't forsake your testimony for Christ. God speaks loudest through a life lived for Him, even if it means humbling ourselves before our enemies. Don't you remember Mother's lessons?"

Luke shifted uncomfortably at this second reminder that his

behavior was not honoring to his Lord. Unwilling to admit that their mother's teachings had grown cold from neglect, he glanced up and changed the direction of their conversation, "You are Sir Valden's squire? Why have I never seen you here before? I'm here often enough."

"I'm training as a squire at the palace garrison. I've been serving Sir Valden for three days now, since his other boy died during a raid in the north of the city. I don't think he'll keep me, though, because of my past connection to the Faithful. He wouldn't trust me in his service, and for good reason."

Luke quickly reached beneath the laces of one shoe and withdrew the rivet he had kept there in hopes of one day meeting up with his siblings. Pressing the bit of steel into Christopher's hand he gave him a small smile, "To remember."

Christopher glanced at the rivet and a sad smile crossed his face. With a glance, he saw Kenrick nod toward the stableman and he quickened his speech, "Have you seen Charlotte?"

Luke shook his head, "Not once. Have you?"

The stableman grasped Christopher's arm and the boy gave a quick nod, "Twice, a year ago." The two boys were pulled apart and led in opposite directions. Christopher called out before the distance between them became too great, "Candles."

"Candles?"

"One for you, another for Charlotte," Christopher gave Luke a meaningful look, willing his brother to read his gaze. He swallowed, "I love you, Luke."

Tears burned behind Luke's eyes and clogged his throat in a great lump. He nodded and spoke with a croak, "I love you, too."

Christopher disappeared inside the stable, no doubt receiving a harsh reprimand for abandoning his task. Luke's gaze remained fixed on the wide doorway where he had last seen his twin, longing for one more glance and hoping against hope for another opportunity to speak with his twin. His gaze shifted to the two knights watching from the Reestablishment room and all vestiges of hope disintegrated, replaced by a firm resolve.

Sir Kenrick believed this had been the twins' last meeting.

Luke would see to it that the knight was wrong.

"You were right," Valden watched as Growell led Luke away, "The boy has some spirit in him."

Kenrick grunted, "More than is good for him." He sank into his padded chair and looked up with an expectant expression, "Had you finished with your report, or is there more?"

One corner of Valden's mouth lifted in a cruel grin, "One thing more." He tilted his head toward the door, indicating the scene that had just been witnessed in the courtyard, "I'll need a new boy, one that has no connection to the rebels, before tonight."

Kenrick's gaze sharpened, "Another raid? So soon?"

"I've discovered the meeting place of the few Faithful who have been gathering these last months. Our raid three nights ago, besides being the death of my last squire, was not what I had hoped for. Since then I have learned all I needed. They'll be finished tonight."

Sir Kenrick moved to dip his quill in ink, "Then I shall inform Lord Roland he is to expect another banishment."

"Not this time." Valden spoke firmly, softening his tone as he continued, "The people of Hebbros already believe Roland spends too much time dealing with the Faithful, and not enough time seeing to their needs. You have been given charge of all matters concerning this rabble." He took a step closer, "Grant me permission to bring an end to this faction. My way."

Kenrick did not blink, "How many?"

"Fifteen rebels."

"If Roland sees this as a breach of command…"

"Tell him they were responsible for the death of my squire. He cannot argue justice."

Sir Kenrick tapped one finger against the tabletop and then returned the quill to its stand, "Permission granted. Finish them off."

Growell led the young prisoner up a flight of steps to a turret room and shoved Luke inside. Luke sank against the wall of the bare room and listened as the lock slid into place. New purpose filled him. He would see his brother again and he would find his sister. Luke leaned his head back against the black stone wall of his prison cell and stared at the ceiling with a thoughtful gaze.

Candles. *One for you, another for Charlotte.* Luke thought back to his brother's gaze and reviewed what he had read there. Christopher's parting words had clearly held a hidden meaning.

One candle for Luke. Christopher's earlier advice regarding the faith had been given with clear concern and honesty. He wanted Luke to reevaluate the way he lived and behaved before others, to realign his conduct to match the godly example he had witnessed in his parents' lives. He wanted Luke to be a candle, a light of example in a dark city.

Luke squirmed. It was true he had lost his Faithful teachers and was no longer able to sit beneath their tutelage, for though he still met with Guy for lessons in another skill, the cooper was never inclined to speak freely of the faith. Still, Luke could have been using these past four years to practice the lessons he had learned before the banishment. Kindness. Humility. Meekness. Honor. Obedience. Respect. *Always seek His face.* His mother had encouraged her children to seek their heavenly Father in all things.

Of course Christopher would follow such words of guidance, and he would do so admirably. Luke's twin had never struggled when it came to following the rules. Luke, on the other hand…

Well, no harm in trying. Wiping the sweat from his brow, Luke closed his eyes against the heavy air of the turret and heaved a sigh.

"God, I think perhaps I may have been some sort of, maybe…foolish," he cracked one eye open and glanced heavenward with a sheepish grin. His father would have been appalled to hear such a lack of sincerity in his son's prayer. Luke sighed. He couldn't help it! Twice today it had been suggested that his life was not a reflection of his faith, and yet he had thought that his constant efforts to battle injustice had been just that. An expression of his commitment to Christ. Of his personal vow to fight for the Faithful.

"I know Christopher wants me to act as our mother taught us, but really he listened closer to those lessons than I did." Luke ran a finger along the floor beside him, "I enjoyed the stories more than the teaching, and then when I joined the Faithful as a follower of Christ and was ready to know more my mother was taken away. So many thoughts and ideas have been presented as truth, forced into my head by just as many people. Some of those thoughts I know are lies. Others…it's hard to tell." Luke shook his head, brow furrowed, "How can Chris and the others justify a life of humility before men like Kenrick and Valden, when in their hearts they're preparing to fight against them?"

Aware that his one-sided conversation had gotten him nowhere, Luke decided to label it as an attempt to follow his brother's advice anyway. Sitting motionless for several minutes, he considered with miserable curiosity the way his skin crawled with perspiration and humidity. As the day dragged on, Growell returned once to leave a mug of water and then left without a word. Shadows traversed the holding room as the afternoon waned and Luke wondered if he would spend the night here in the dark.

Luke stiffened as his thoughts shifted.

Dark… Light… Candles.

Rising to his feet, he peered out through the narrow slit window to the courtyard below. Christopher had said *another* for Charlotte. Charlotte's "candle" held another meaning. One that differed from Luke's.

Luke paced the turret room and pressed his calloused palms to his temples in deep thought, "Think…think…candle…can—Aha!! Simple!" He tensed with excitement and smiled when he realized how obvious Christopher's hint had been.

Charlotte had been reestablished with a candle-making chandler.

Hours passed. Darkness fell and a noise drew him once more to one of the windows. Through the narrow slit he looked down on the yard and saw a band of Mordecais mounting their steeds outside the stables. Torchlight illuminated the group, glinting off of swords and bridles with sickening clarity.

Sir Valden watched the preparations of his men from where he sat atop a great black horse of his own. The Order's first knight barked an order to his squire—Christopher's replacement—and then glanced up at Luke's window in the holding room. It was too dark inside for Valden to catch sight of him, nevertheless Luke pulled away from the sill. The moment passed and the knight turned his mount's head for the gates, issuing a firm command to his men. The Mordecai knights followed their leader through the gates and out of sight, the sounds of their galloping horses growing distant as they rode further north.

Luke sank against the wall and stared into the shadows.

Another raid. More lives disrupted. Fewer Faithful left to

make a stand.

Let it be soon, God. He clenched his fists and leaned his head back. *I'm ready.*

17
Of Bouts & Bitterness

Christopher gave his sword-arm a shove and spun away from his opponent, whisking the sweat from his eyes with a fierce shake of his head. His light brown hair had turned black under the weight of perspiration, and now stuck to his face and neck in soaked strands. His sharp blue gaze followed his competitor as the two boys circled one another and prepared for another bout. Surrounding the training arena, fellow squires shouted encouragement or advice and goaded their comrades to enhance their performance. Christopher blocked out the noise and focused solely on the contest at hand. He doubted anyone was cheering for him anyway.

He readjusted his hold on the grip of his practice sword. His opponent, Titus, advanced with a heavy combination and Christopher stood his ground to beat off the attack. Groans went up from their adolescent audience and someone shouted for Titus to "squash the quiet one." Titus glared at the taunting lad and then turned a look of frustration on Christopher, who met his stare with a practiced calm. How he wished he could read gazes the way his twin did.

Christopher the Silent. The epithet had been whispered behind his back until it echoed through the corridors of the palace garrison, the place that had been his home for the past four years of reestablishment. The other Faithful children had been sent to live with families, finishing out their years in the schoolrooms before serving apprenticeships under their new caretakers or with nearby tradesmen. Christopher had been tested by a master swordsman and then offered as a prodigy to the army of Mizgalia at the age of ten. Sir Kenrick had made his case an exception, permitting him to forgo the last two years of his schooling.

Titus advanced again and Christopher retreated two steps as he studied his competitor's form and style. The other boy relied heavily upon his offensive attacks, but seemed less adept in his defensive stances. Christopher gave a mental nod. He would let Titus tire himself out with advances for a while longer before finishing the fight with an onslaught of his own. His mind remained engaged in the competition while his thoughts drifted to his recent past.

After being tested, the master swordsman had declared Christopher a brilliant natural and Sir Kenrick immediately enrolled him in training as a squire for future knighthood. Christopher had quickly discovered that he was indeed a natural in the skills required of him. Every lesson was followed easily, every effort felt instinctive. For four years he ate, slept, lived, breathed, and absorbed lessons in horsemanship, swordsmanship, marksmanship, strength, speed, dexterity, climbing, swimming, chivalry, heraldry, and even dancing.

The past few days had been spent in the service of Sir Valden, gaining new insight and knowledge of what was expected of him as a squire. The Mordecai Order's first knight had been a hard and precise master, expecting his temporary squire to learn quickly and foresee the fulfillment of his needs. Christopher had been relieved shortly after their visit to the Order the previous afternoon. The new squire had arrived to replace him, and Chris rejoiced that God had placed him in the brief situation that had crossed paths with his brother. Seeing Luke at the Mordecai garrison had refreshed him like a cooling drink of water on a hot day.

Hot like today. Christopher released a breath that sounded like a pant and quickly wiped his sleeve across his eyes, leaving a track of perspiration on the cloth. Heat danced in waves atop the garrison walls. Christopher eyed the limp banners on the tower and longed for water to relieve his discomfort.

"Come, Titus. He's tired, can't you see? Give it your all, man, and conquer Sir Silent!"

There it was again. Christopher the Silent. Of course, it was true. He had accepted his new life in silence. Silent, he listened and learned and trained. Silent, he watched and waited and prayed. Waited for the day when his twin would call the children of the exiled together, and prayed that the day would be soon.

There must be some way they could fight back. But not in the way that Luke was hoping for. Not with swords and clubs and a desperate assault against the garrisons of Hebbros.

Meanwhile he used his time wisely, perfecting every skill he could. His protective nature thrived in the arena and his instructors assumed he was admirably dedicated to the defense of Hebbros's citizens. In truth he eagerly awaited the city's downfall.

Life in the garrison had made him quiet and observant, earning him the oft-repeated name. His comrades thought him odd. They envied his advantage and skill and assumed his silence to be arrogance, while in fact he utilized the solitude to strengthen his faith through prayer and the recollection of his parents' biblical teachings. The isolation also provided further training by letting him study the other boys to deduct the best way to trounce them in the arena.

As he had done with Titus.

His current opponent finally brought his latest advance to an end and retreated for a brief respite. Christopher caught the slight signs of weariness that were beginning to show in the other boy's demeanor. Immediately he surged forward with a combination that disarmed Titus and toppled the boy onto his hindquarters in the dust. Another victory added to Christopher's impressive record. The crowd of squires released a collective sigh of disappointment and then began to applaud their expected appreciation for a good performance.

Christopher stepped forward and offered a hand to Titus, "It was a good match."

Titus scowled and rose to his feet, brushing aside the offered assistance with a look of disgust, "It was an unfair match, that's what it was. You've had a whole year more of training than I have, though I'm a year older, and the instructors have advanced you in every possible way. How do they expect the rest of us to grow confident when they insist on matching us against their pet squire?"

He spoke the words with a sneer as he bent to retrieve his practice sword. Christopher—true to form—remained silent, unsure of what he could say that would not further anger the older boy. He was sure Titus too would excel in lessons such as swordsmanship if only he would commit himself to the training rather than visiting so often with one of the young laundresses. Titus straightened and met Christopher's gaze, and then turned to leave the arena with a shake of his head. Two other boys approached the center of the practice yard for a bout and Christopher moved to follow Titus. He was eager to leave the arena to this next set of opponents before they could cause a scene.

"Well done, O silent one!"

Too late.

Christopher came to a halt when the two approaching combatants blocked his path. He looked up into the two identical faces, each framed by shaggy black hair tied back in a club, and then met the gaze of the one whose left eyebrow was framed by a scar.

"Thank you, Wulf."

"He speaks!" Wulf feigned amazement.

Standing beside his twin, Warin smirked, "Of course he does, brother. He's just not as vocal as his twin, Luke the Idiot." His smirk expanded into a grin when Christopher stiffened, "Don't care to hear anyone speak ill of your brother, do you? You should hear the names he's earned for himself of late. People all over Hebbros know of your brother by terms that would color your mother's face with shame."

Warin's face split with a smile of triumph when he saw a spark of fury ignite in the usually placid face before him. He knew that loyalty to his scattered family ran deep in Christopher's veins, and the boy was taking the bait as planned. With a sidelong glance Warin caught sight of Titus, who had turned with his friends to watch their exchange. He chuckled to himself. It was known throughout the garrison that a long-lasting feud existed between the two sets of twins, and everyone had been expecting the storm to break for four years now.

No need to disappoint them.

"Titus is right, you know," Wulf nodded his head at the other youth. "The masters keep setting you against the boys that have less experience than you. That doesn't seem fair for either party involved."

"It's not my choice."

"If you're as good as they say, you should be practicing against boys who've had the same amount of training or more."

"I follow orders," Christopher clenched his jaw, waiting for an opportunity to excuse himself. Sweat dripped an annoying path down his face and back, making him long anew for a bucket of water to pour over his head.

"I'll give you a fight right now." Wulf's fingers twitched, as if itching for the spat, "Let's have a go at it."

Christopher frowned at Wulf, "My training is always arranged and approved by the instructors."

Warin smirked, "It doesn't have to be. Favored darling that you are, you should be allowed to train on your own if you've a mind to. It's only for a little fun."

Wulf quirked his eyebrows in a dare, "What do you say, friend?"

Christopher shook his head and moved past them, "You're not my friend and I don't want to fight you."

The twins watched him cross the arena with their arms folded and mirthless laughter on their lips.

"Coddled babe!" Wulf called after him.

Christopher ignored the taunt and had nearly made it to the outskirts of the yard when Warin threw a soft-spoken barb that finally shattered his outward calm.

"Coward. Just like the rest of his dissenting family."

Christopher's feet fumbled to a halt and refused to carry him any further. One fist closed in a white-knuckled grip over the hilt of his practice sword while the other moved to touch the rivet from Luke, which hung from a cord about his neck. His spine stiffened and his eyes closed in a brief prayer. *God, help me…and don't let me hurt them.*

With an enraged cry that echoed across the surrounding walls of the garrison, Christopher turned and sprinted back across the yard. Warin and Wulf waited with their practice swords ready and amused smiles twisting their faces into knowing looks. As he drew nearer two thoughts suddenly filtered through Christopher's mind: First, he could not engage them in anger, for they would feed on his fury and bring the fight to a swift and humiliating end. Second, they would not be having Wulf enter the conflict alone, as suggested before, but were planning on encountering him together. Two against one.

Christopher did not slow as he approached their position at the center of the arena, but instead used the momentum to take a flying leap that would land him on top of them unless they moved. The side-by-side twins took a single step back and lifted their swords to create an X that would block his descent. Christopher swung his own weapon in an overhead arc and brought the dull blade down on the crossed swords with a resounding crack. The twins recoiled from the force of the blow and then quickly swung their swords outward in unison. Christopher ducked clear of the dangerous cuts and immediately moved in for another advance.

On the outskirts of the yard, the squires who had scattered at the conclusion of the last fight now gathered again to witness this long-awaited contest. At last the twins would fight Christopher, and Christopher would fight not only one squire who was his equal, but two! As their shouts grew in volume and fervor, others from within the surrounding structures emerged by window and door to inquire about the excitement and were soon watching in fascination as well. One of these was Sir Fraser, captain of the palace garrison, who appeared with a baffled expression on his weathered face. He was followed from his official quarters by Lord Roland.

"What is the meaning of this outrage?" Sir Fraser's bellow was muted by the excited shouts.

One nearby youth turned and gave a sharp, fisted salute over his heart, "'Tis the twins, sir; Wulf and Warin. They finally convinced Christopher the Silent to meet them in a challenge. Called him a coward, they did!"

Roland strained to hear the young squire's explanation over the bedlam and then turned his focus back to the fight in the yard. The blurred movement of lightly armored figures accompanied by the crashing of swords represented a fight between two boys of identical appearance and another squire, slightly younger and half-a-head shorter than his opponents. Roland squinted and studied them. The three faces seemed familiar to him, which was surprising. In recent days alone he had witnessed so many faces that all had begun to look the same in his eyes.

"Who are they?" He addressed the knight beside him, but

kept his eyes on the fight.

"The twins are Warin and Wulf of western Hebbros. Sixteen years of age, they are in their fourth year of training. I've suggested them as candidates for the Mordecai Order. The other lad is Christopher of central Hebbros. Fourteen years of age, he is also in his fourth year of training." Sir Fraser nodded when Roland turned a look of surprise on him, "A brilliant young man, obviously a natural and highly favored by our instructors. He'll prove to be a great knight of Mizgalia, I'm sure."

"But not for the Mordecai Order?"

Fraser shook his head, "His birthparents were some of those first Faithful, banished four years back. Sir Kenrick refuses to take any of them into the Order. Too great a risk, he says. They're more likely to betray the Order and aid the rebels. Just as well, I say. If all of our finest knights join your esteemed Order, my lord, then we'll have naught to offer to the armies of our great kingdom."

Roland lifted his head in a silent nod as he contemplated the man's words and shifted his gaze back to the fight.

Christopher brought his sword down to deflect Warin's uppercut and then lifted it again as he swung to meet Wulf's slice. His left shoulder throbbed from a hit that had landed there, and the stinging at the back of his hand foretold of a bruise. The twins had separated and were doing their best to overwhelm him from both sides. They had not been fighting in this heat for as long as he had and would not grow weary very soon. Christopher would need to end this quickly, and not by strength. He would have to outsmart them.

Feigning a thrust in Warin's direction, he quickly doubled back and swung low at Wulf. Caught by surprise and with his sword in no position to defend his legs, Wulf took a knock to the knees and dropped to the dusty ground with a heavy thud. As the one twin toppled, Christopher turned back to face the other, delivering a swift combination that took him in close. Ducking low, he landed a sideways shove to Warin's waist. Warin flipped over Christopher's back and landed with a thump beside his brother. Sputtering in the dirt, the stunned twins quickly brought their weapons up as before to deflect an overhead slice from their standing opponent. Christopher's sword shoved the tips of the others to the dirt, where he quickly planted his boot to keep them in place.

The practice yard fell silent, except for Wulf's groan of mild pain. Heads turned and glances were exchanged as each marveled over Christopher's unexpected victory against two equals. Breathing heavily and sweating profusely, Christopher held his sword out and pointed the rounded tip at the two on the ground. He regarded them with a hard gaze and spoke between breaths.

"Do not…speak ill of my family…again."

A smattering of applause began to multiply as Christopher turned and strode to the edge of the yard. Ignoring the respectful acknowledgement, he stored his sword with the others of its kind and then found a bucket of cool water, which he promptly emptied over his head. Clearing the gathered moisture from his eyes, he plodded to the stable doors and quietly disappeared inside. The amazed crowd began to disperse, snickering at the evil twins and offering narratives to the clueless few who had just arrived on the scene.

"Agh!" Wulf rolled to his feet and flung his sword away from him. He swore mightily as he kicked a cloud of dust after Christopher and then spat at the ground, "Devious little rat! He hasn't heard the last of this."

"Shut up, Wulf." Warin shoved his brother out of the way and retrieved the discarded sword to put away with his own, "Keep shouting your obvious threats and we'll have the whole garrison against us. We might have beat him if you hadn't grown cocky."

"Me?" Wulf sputtered, "I'm not the one who flipped over his back! You might have at least landed on your feet."

"I told you to shut up! And you're the one who fell first."

"Why you sniveling—"

"Wulf! Warin!" Another squire approached, interrupting Wulf's growl, "Sir Fraser sends orders for you to make haste to the gate. Your father has been granted permission to see you."

After a moment of stunned silence, Wulf's face darkened like the sky before a sudden storm. A volley of oaths escaped his mouth in quick succession and the other squire eyed him curiously until Warin stepped up to him with a glare plastered on his face.

"You've delivered your message, runt, now disappear."

The squire made a face and scrambled away, casting a disgruntled look over his shoulder. Warin watched the boy's retreat until his brother's irate voice spoke behind him.

"You said he'd leave us be, Warin. You said our

apprenticeship would be our escape."

Warin turned to meet his brother's venomous gaze, and his jaw tensed. "I know I did, and it will be."

"Apparently not! What is he seeking to gain from an interview with us if not a portion of our pay?" Wulf's hand lifted unconsciously to finger the scar over his left eyebrow, "We make a paltry sum as it is, serving the knights. Why does he expect us to share with him when he's done *nothing* to deserve our support?"

Warin cast a glance around the yard and then gave his brother's arm a guiding shove, "Start moving." Matching his twin's agitated pace, Warin waited to speak again until he had tossed their practice swords on a matching pile and turned toward the gate, "No one has said that we're to split our meager profits with a man who gave us little more than a roof over our heads and a thorough knowledge of profanity. We owe him nothing but disgust."

Wulf smirked and then lifted his green eyes to the garrison's gate ahead. His gaze locked on the broad-shouldered man who stood just inside the entry, chatting pleasantly with the guard while awaiting their approach.

Warin too studied the man. From his grizzly scowl-marked face to his thick padded shoes, Monty was the personification of a snarl. Cruel, heartless, and possessive of any possible gain, Monty had choked out every last trace of the twins' adolescence and forced them to mature as men after the deaths of their parents. There had been no affection, no praise, and no escape. He hated them as much as they hated him, nevertheless he clung to their potential prosperity as Mizgalian knights, determined to drain their success to his advantage.

Monty caught sight of the identical twosome and a snakelike smile took over his face. His eyes bounced back and forth between them, unable to tell them apart until he distinguished Wulf's scar. Warin grimaced with the realization that hiding the marred flesh on his brother's face might have been proof enough that this man was not their father. Any man should be able to tell his own twins apart without such aid. Too late to hide the difference now, Warin hoped there would be no future opportunity to put Monty to the test. He would be pleased if they never saw this man again.

"There ye are, my boys," Monty extended two thick arms in what should have been a welcoming and fatherly gesture. The beefy limbs dropped to his sides again when the twins halted several yards away and eyed him with distaste. A sneer crossed his face and his square-tipped fingers, adept at thievery, clenched in agitation.

Wulf's tense frame stiffened further, "Why are you here?"

Monty's chuckle was mirthless, "T' see you, a'course." His voice rasped with every syllable, an effect produced by years of angry shouting, "A father misses the sight o' his sons when they're no longer t' home. I came t' see how ye're farin'."

Warin's eyes narrowed, "If you're here to see your sons, I wonder that you asked to see me and Wulf. We're not your sons."

The guard's expression became one of confusion while, obviously prepared for such resistance, Monty bowed his head in mock remorse, "T' think ye'd disown me now, with yer poor mother in the grave and me feelin' so poorly most days." He delivered a timely and well-rehearsed cough and then released a heavy sigh, "'Tis a cruelty, boys, and a blight on yer blessed mother's good training."

Warin shook his head with disgust, "What do you want, Monty?"

A strange gleam lit the pickpocket's eyes and Warin suddenly felt a pang of wariness. Monty shifted to glance beyond the twins and they turned to see Sir Fraser emerging from his quarters and marching their way with a sealed parchment in one hand. Monty's rasp brought both of the boys' dark heads back around to face him.

"I told ye I came t' see how ye're farin'. B'sides that, I already got what I came for."

Sir Fraser approached and held out the sealed parchment, which quickly disappeared within the folds of Monty's tunic. The garrison's captain then turned to include Warin and Wulf in his explanation, "I was not aware these fine lads had a father living or I would have seen to the details before now."

"What details?" Wulf's suspicion was obvious in his sharp tone.

Sir Fraser quirked a brow and spoke with patience, probably thinking that the oversight had been a mere matter of ignorance, "During the years of your apprenticeships, you are obliged to provide your parents with a portion of your wages so long as they are in need of such recompense."

"He's not our—"

"Monty doesn't need any—"

"Boys," Monty growled, "don't interrupt yer s'perior."

"But the wages are *ours*," Wulf's countenance grew darker by the minute.

"The knowledge which you are receiving in our care is considered the greater portion of your wages."

"He has no right to them because he's not our father," Warin spat the words.

Sir Fraser cast a forbearing glance from one to the other and continued as if Warin had not spoken, "This understanding is approved and bound by the laws of Hebbros, to be annulled only upon the conclusion of your apprenticeships or the death of a member of this agreement, whichever comes first."

The twins stared at Sir Fraser as if the knight had just pledged his allegiance to the heathen kingdom of Arcrea. Surely the man had lost his hearing. Or had been bribed.

Seeing a chance for escape, Monty gave a quick salute and turned for the gate, "I'll be on my way, then, sir. I thank ye for yer aid and the time spent wi' my sons. G'day to ye."

"A good day to you, sir. Warin, Wulf, back to your exercises. I expect your next match to be an improvement on today's bout with young Christopher." Sir Fraser nodded to the guard who had let Monty out and turned to cross the yard with a long stride.

Wulf eyed the knight's retreating back and ground his teeth together, "The dirty rotten traitor. I'd wager a whole year's pay Monty bribed him."

"My thoughts exactly." Warin nudged his brother away from the gate and the alert guard, "Neither one of them has heard the last of this."

Wulf turned to study his brother, "You have a plan?"

Warin turned to meet his twin's gaze, "Old Fraser himself suggested our only escape from Monty's chains and this ridiculous contract."

A shrewd smile spread across Wulf's face as understanding dawned in his mind, "That he did." Rubbing his jaw and casting a swift glance around the yard, he lowered his voice, "What do you say to discussing said escape over a pint at the Squire's Tavern?" He chuckled, "I daresay Lord Roland made many friends with his decree that taverns ought to sell penny-ales to boys of all ages."

Warin paused and briefly considered Sir Fraser's directive to return to their exercises. Heading to the tavern now would not be the first time he and Wulf had delayed their superior's orders, and the matter of escaping Monty seemed more dire at the moment than their need to wield a sword correctly. Warin gave his brother a nod and together the twins slipped away to escape the garrison walls for the nearby tavern.

18

Observations of a Lady

Rosalynn smiled when she finally spotted her husband, followed by his stoic-faced guard, striding purposefully along the private path below from the garrison to the palace. When he had disappeared from view, her ladyship let the heavy drapes slip from her fingers to fall back into place across the window. Roland would stop in to see her soon, as he had promised.

"You know, the only thing he does well is love you and your children."

Rosalynn sighed and turned to face the speaker, who lounged on a divan before her hearth. Forcing her voice to sound sweet, she nevertheless added the bite of sarcasm to her tone, "And the only thing you do well, my brother, is laze from room to room accomplishing absolutely nothing."

Lord Bradley shrugged carelessly, tossing his sister an untroubled grin, "I wouldn't say absolutely nothing. Why, just yesterday I managed a stroll to the stables, where I selected a new horse for myself in honor of our…mother's cousin's brother-in-law's third nephew's birthday." The grin turned impish, "The irony comes in that I forgot the honored lad's name. Pity, too, for I had planned to name the horse after him."

Rosalynn shook her head in disgust, "And to think that my husband's money shelters, clothes, and feeds your pathetic lifestyle. It really is boorish of you, Bradley."

"Well then," Bradley swung his legs over the side of the divan and sat forward, "you'll be pleased to know that my 'pathetic lifestyle' leaves me with little appetite to satisfy." His tone remained light, but a hard glint flitted through his dark eyes, "And if you and your husband did not require the nobility to pattern your ever-changing style of dress, I would not need so many changes of garment."

"It stimulates our increasing economy." Rosalynn sank into the seat opposite the divan and regarded her brother with superiority, "When Roland and I lead a change in the styles of Hebbros it creates an influx of business for the city's numerous mercers and tailors. The people spend money to dress well. The same concept applies to many aspects of our lives, as well as those of our children. By the time the styles have changed, an impressive amount of gold has been spread throughout the shops of Hebbros only to circulate through our purses again in the forms of taxes and fines."

"Yes, yes," Bradley threw himself back against the divan and waved his hands in illustration, "and you use that money to build the new outer wall as the city grows to accommodate the scores of people who seek to live in Hebbros, that they too might follow after the great Lord Roland like a line of submissive ducklings. Scores of new citizens means additional buckets of gold, and that money is then used to pay the Peers' commission as well as the soldiers who live to terrorize the commoners when they are not encamped along our war-fraught borders. You see? I've been paying attention."

Rosalynn turned her face to the fire, lit to discourage the cool shadows within the shelter of the stone walls. Covertly eyeing her brother, she added, "The added monies are also used for the purchase of more slaves for the building of the outer wall."

The brother stiffened, clenching his jaw, and the sister hid a smirk of condescension. Sixteen years of age and Bradley still refused to cooperate with her view of the slaves. It was the one subject on which neither was willing to bend. All other topics were negotiable and open for playful bantering. And Bradley did love to banter with her.

Aware of the awkward silence, Rosalynn shifted and cast another sidelong glance at her handsome brother. He had grown into a young man of wit and charm, spending his unproductive days in the useless practice of wandering about, learning and relearning everything one could about the palace and those in the service of its lord. He knew every slave by name and always received from them warm smiles of respect or a chorus of twitters when he passed by. Rosalynn rolled her eyes at this thought. Yes, her brother was a favorite among the indentured, and he showed great interest in them in return. And Rosalynn knew why.

Turning to face him fully, Rosalynn studied her brother's pensive profile and dark red-brown hair as he stared at some unseen point across the room. In spite of their time spent together since arriving in Hebbros, they were still not very close. Instead, Rosalynn had grown wary of Bradley. He had changed—was no longer the angry little boy often given to rebellious outbursts against Roland. Instead he was cheerful, carefree, and careless.

In a word, he was indifferent.

Rosalynn was aware that Bradley still disliked Roland. He still resisted the idea of slavery. He still wanted more for his life than constant dependence on the man who had inherited his own rightful title. Yet, at the same time, he seemed resigned to his place in the palace at Hebbros. Could the old anger and bitterness still be boiling just below the surface of a lighthearted façade? Was the anger still there, only contained?

Seeming to sense her scrutiny, Bradley shifted his head to return her gaze. Conflicting emotions plagued the indigo depths of his eyes, and Rosalynn felt the briefest pinch of sympathy before recalling their point of conversation. Glancing at the collar-wearing attendant in the corner, she lowered her voice to a soft murmur, "Bradley, you know you cannot free all the slaves."

"I never said that that was my aim." His voice was bland, neither angry nor merry.

"Perhaps not in so many words, yet I know you do seek their liberation."

Bradley perched himself on one elbow and stared intently at his sister, "Can you not hear what you're saying? '*Free* the slaves' and 'liberation'…your own words suggest that they are in bondage."

Rosalynn stiffened her already straight posture, "It is their lot in life."

"Yes," Bradley nodded his sarcasm, "just as it yours to forbid their happiness. Come, Rosalynn, would it really be so terrible to pay them a small wage for their labor?"

Cornered by his calmly-spoken argument, Rosalynn exhaled sharply and cast about for a reply, "It is good that you have no money of your own to spend, lest the city fail through your silly efforts to buy her downfall with the destruction of her workforce."

"There are *thousands* of Mizgalians within this city who would gladly build the wall and serve at your table in return for a small sum that would feed their families more than a stolen crust of bread."

"If they are stealing bread they should be carted to the stocks and the pillory."

Bradley chuckled, "My dear sister, the peasants are stealing bread because the slaves have been forced into every respectable position and they are left hungry, with no way of gaining food otherwise."

Rosalynn stared at her brother in mute surprise. He had thought this through until his arguments were almost sensible. She must learn not to underestimate him by assuming that his indifference toward life affected his every thought.

Bradley drummed his hands on the divan and smiled at the ceiling, "Speaking of ducklings, can you imagine Kenrick or Valden waddling on webbed feet and possessing a little black bill for their mouth? Ha! The idea strikes me as thunderously humorous."

"Really, Bradley," Rosalynn tilted her head in admonition as her brother lost himself to a wave of merriment. In a mere moment the tension had melted from his inky gaze, replaced by a charming glimmer of wit. Once again he was indifferent.

Knowing that Roland would soon appear, and not wanting him to find her in a heated argument with her brother, Rosalynn determined to produce a certain balm.

"You there," she turned to the attendant, ignoring Bradley when he corrected her with the slave's name, "send word to the nurse and have her bring Lord Jerem and Lady Celia to my chambers at once."

The attendant left with a bow and Bradley shifted his position on the divan, "You are expecting Roland?"

She lifted a brow, "Perhaps."

He chuckled, "Rosalynn, your attempts at peace are painfully transparent."

"Then take heed and encourage the peace you know I seek. Play with the children and do not attempt to irritate my husband with your frivolous speeches."

Bradley's eyebrows lifted, "First I'm boorish, now I'm frivolous? Rosalynn, you wound me."

Within another moment the heavy oak door swung inward and Roland entered the room with a smile for his wife. She rose to meet him with an expression that rivaled the sun for brilliance and Bradley rolled his eyes when they exchanged an affectionate embrace.

"By the seats of your nine deities, Roland, must you always greet her in that way when I'm present?"

"Must you always be present?" Rosalynn shot him an annoyed glare.

Roland kept an arm about his wife as he offered his brother-in-law a brief nod, "Bradley."

The boy returned the greeting with a careless flap of one hand, "Afternoon. Or is it still morning? By my ridiculously-feathered cap, if I haven't lost track of the time!"

"You are not wearing a cap, and I wouldn't know." Roland's pleasant tone belied his annoyed words, "I, too, have lost track of the time, but only because I've spent the hours in constructive behavior." He moved to sit beside his wife, "How have you spent your day, sir?"

Bradley extended both arms to indicate his current posture, "As I was expected to."

Rosalynn heard Roland's inhale of frustration, "You might exert yourself with the masters and learn the use of a weapon."

Bradley gave a lighthearted groan that ended as a brief laugh, "The bow is such a taxing of one's perception, best left to those with keener abilities than my own. The staff seems so childish, like boys playing with sticks before they're permitted to use the sharper tools of a man. I already know enough of the sword to make me dangerous when one is in my possession, and the dagger appears to be so self-explanatory." He gave a reassuring pat to the small sheath at his waist and smiled at the unimpressed pair seated across from him, "And I'm sure you'll both be delighted to know that I no longer practice with the bed curtains for an imaginary foe."

"Bradley!"

Rosalynn's rebuke was interrupted before it could begin when a knock sounded and the door opened once again. The collared attendant reentered and bowed low before opening the door further to admit three other arrivals.

"Father!" Three-year-old Jerem cried with delight as he leapt across the threshold and raced to Roland's side, where he received a manly clap on the shoulder and was invited to describe the events of his morning. Rosalynn beamed at her golden-haired son and then glanced to observe her brother.

Sitting straight on the divan now, Bradley smiled briefly at Jerem and then lifted his gaze to the doorway, where one-year-old Celia sat cradled in her nurse's arms. Rosalynn's eyes shifted there as well and she snapped her fingers to acquire the girl's attention.

"Bring Lady Celia to me."

"I'll hold her for a while," Bradley stood. "Perhaps I'll earn your favor if I follow your advice and do something useful." He reached to take his niece from the nurse, who received a pleasant smile over the baby's auburn head, "Good afternoon, Sarah."

The slave girl caught her smile before it had fully formed and then lowered her gaze as she transferred Celia to Bradley's arms. Fiddling briefly with her leather collar, she turned and moved to stand by the silent attendant in the corner.

Rosalynn rolled her eyes, a common reoccurrence when her brother was present, "Bradley, we do not address them by name. For the thousandth time, she's a slave."

"And I'm a noble nobody. Perhaps thinking of that will resign you to letting me greet my friends." He flashed her a wide-eyed look, "But don't think on it for too long. You may consider sending me to work in the kitchens."

"Bradley, you're impossible."

"I know." He tossed Celia up in the air and caught her in a burst of squeals, and then sat her on his shoulders and spun in a circle.

"My turn! Spin me around, Uncle Bradley!" Little Jerem left his father's side and jumped from one foot to the other, clapping his hands.

"Not this time, son." Roland's voice brought Jerem's dance to a sudden halt. The boy, very like a miniature of his father in appearance, shifted his large brown eyes to study Roland's face, as if weighing the wisdom or folly of resistance.

When Jerem bowed his head in resignation, wisely forsaking the idea of an argument, Rosalynn shifted guiltily with the knowledge that any praise for his early training in good behavior could only be laid at the feet of his young nurse. Rosalynn's gaze moved to where Sarah stood against the far wall. The slave girl's head was bowed in familiar obeisance, but her eyes shifted now and then with the practiced art of following the actions of her young charges.

Three years ago, on the night of Jerem's birth, Rosalynn had thought it folly to leave her newborn in the care of a girl barely twelve years of age. However, when morning had come and the sun's rays slanted through the window over the precious sight of a careful Sarah singing softly over Jerem's sleeping form, Rosaylnn had declared to Roland that the girl was exactly what she desired in a nurse for her child. She had laughed when he presented her arguments of the night before, and stated with assurance that the girl would learn quickly. And she had.

Rosalynn's eyes now moved to take in the sight of her auburn-haired Celia cradled in Bradley's arms. The babe had taken to the slave nurse so quickly that Rosalynn had feared Celia would think of Sarah as her mother. Rosalynn had begun sending for her children more often, spending more time listening to their prattling tales and bestowing more smiles on their antics. She had tried to balance the new concept of motherhood with her position as the first lady of Hebbros, and always felt herself lacking in both titles. The balancing act left her in a constant state of exhaustion and worry.

Of course, Roland said she was perfect. Her fears of being a terrible mother and inadequate noblewoman were always eased when she laid them out for her husband's examination. He would quirk an eyebrow, laugh a little, and give her that favorite smile that always made her grin in return. "You're perfect as you are, my love," were always the words he used to calm her fears. And she believed him.

Rosalynn blinked and realized that while she'd been musing she had missed an exchange between Roland and Bradley. Her powerful husband had at some point claimed his daughter from Bradley and now stood beside Rosalynn's chair, cradling the docile Celia on one arm. Jerem's feet were visible beneath the drapes, proof that he had run for cover at the first signs of conflict. Rosalynn's gaze shifted nervously to her brother. The air was alive with a tension that desired to dominate the room; nevertheless Bradley appeared indifferent.

Roland was the first to speak, clearly annoyed, "Some day, Bradley, you will learn not to take my position in this city for granted."

"What an awful day that will be!" Unaffected, Bradley perched himself on the arm of the divan and crossed his arms, "Who would you have, then, to remind you of your mere humanity? Someone has to remind you that you are not a god."

"Bradley, don't." Rosalynn murmured a warning, but it was lost beneath Roland's next words.

"I have borne your presence in my home with a fair amount of tolerance because you are my wife's brother, and have nowhere else to go."

"That is a bleak picture, isn't it?"

"But I am also your ruler, and as such I deserve your respect."

Bradley picked at a loose thread on the divan and Rosalynn made a mental note to have the less-than-perfect seat replaced.

Roland shifted Celia's weight, "Do I make myself clear?"

Bradley crossed his arms again and looked up at Roland with an expression that came close to boredom, "I live in your city, Roland, but that does not make you my ultimate authority. As a Mizgalian, I'll answer to King Cronin. As a man, I must answer to whatever higher power cares enough upon my death to inquire about how I lived my life."

Roland's nostrils flared with rage and Rosalynn stood to take Celia from his arms, "Roland, please, think of the children."

Ignoring her, Roland pointed a strong finger at the boy across the hearth, "King Cronin appointed me as your guardian. Therefore, as my ward you are expected to honor me as you would your father."

Rosalynn's eyes slid shut. Of all the things for Roland to say, that had been the worst possible option.

Bradley remained calm, outwardly indifferent, but his sister did not miss the stiffening of his shoulders or the spark of fury that finally churned in his hard eyes. His hands were clenched beneath his crossed arms, and when he spoke it was with an eerie tranquility that bespoke false composure.

"You are not my father, Roland. You are not *like* my father. You are not deserving of the same respect that my father had, and you will certainly never receive it from me." Bradley turned to Rosalynn and offered his ever-ready smile, "Until next time, dear sister."

Bradley moved toward the door and Roland glared after him, "Learn to show your authorities their due respect or I will be forced to give you cause to regret your defiance."

"Will you?" Bradley turned on the threshold with a careless expression on his face. He pursed his lips in thought, "What will you do to me, Roland? What could you possibly take from me that isn't already in your possession?"

Roland's gaze flickered briefly to the two slaves in the corner beyond Bradley, and then returned to rest on the boy's face, "I have the power to take from you what you do not know you have, as well as the ability to give you what you do not want. Tread carefully, Bradley. Choose wisely."

The youth returned the leader's stare for a long moment before turning and slowly strolling from the room. The door met its frame with a light click that sounded loud in the silence following his exit. Jerem peeked from his hiding place behind the curtains, Sarah glanced from the fearful boy to the door, and Rosalynn felt her breath release on a sigh she had not realized she had been holding.

"We have not argued for some time now, Bradley and I." Roland resumed his seat and Rosalynn, still holding Celia, tentatively followed suit. He gave her a troubled look and gently caressed his daughter's auburn hair, "I hate to think of the danger he will find himself in if he does not submit himself to my authority. You must see what you can do for him, my love, and soon."

Rosalynn smiled at the endearment, ready to believe that her brother was at fault, "I have tried, Roland, but he has changed so that I never know whether he is being serious or teasing me. He seems to live in a constant state of apathy."

Roland tucked a red curl behind her ear, "We'll think of something."

Jerem crept carefully around to his mother's side just as another knock sounded and Rosalynn's attendant opened the door to reveal a young squire. The boy gulped nervously and then saluted Roland before voicing the reason for his presence.

"Greetings from Sir Kenrick, my lord, who begs an audience and awaits your company in the Great Hall."

Lord Roland nodded and rose to his feet, "I will see him directly."

In another moment the ruler had bid his wife farewell, the children had been led away by their nurse, the silent attendant had stoked the fire to a comfortable height, and Rosalynn found herself seated alone in her chambers. She stared at the dancing flames on the hearth and tried to review all that had just occurred within these walls. With a bitter sigh, she finally threw her hands up in confusion and admitted to herself that she must be an ignorant woman.

Sarah balanced a weary Lady Celia on one arm and clutched Lord Jerem's trusting hand with the other as she led the way through several corridors and toward the rooms belonging to her charges. Little Jerem chattered excitedly about a new wooden sword, and Celia laid her soft head on Sarah's shoulder. Torches perched in several wall sconces provided some light for their journey through the palace but offered little of the heat that marked the summer season out-of-doors. Sarah shivered as she considered the chill of the palace's interior, grateful at least for the scarlet-colored runner that lined the halls connecting the private chambers of the nobility.

Finally coming to the recess of a large doorway and passing beneath its decorative oak frame, Sarah released Jerem's hand in order to return the groaning door to its cradle with a shove. Turning from this task she found that Jerem had fallen silent and was staring at something across the room. Looking up to see what had captured his focus, she came to an abrupt halt.

Lord Bradley leaned against the sill of the far window, waiting for their return from Lady Rosalynn's chambers.

"You shouldn't be here." The forthright words slipped out before Sarah could bite them back. They seemed to go unheeded anyway. His lordship continued to stare out at the city as if he had heard neither they're noisy entry nor the words falling from her quick tongue.

Sarah's heart hammered in her chest, prodded by the thought that his presence here, seeking refuge after an argument with Lord Roland, could very well bring retribution on her own head. Yet as a slave she was in no position to send the young nobleman away from his sister's children.

Jerem tucked his hand back into Sarah's palm as they stood staring at their visitor.

"My father was angry with you."

Lord Bradley finally turned from the window to glance at his nephew with a smirk, "Your father is always angry with me, Jerem. In fact, I think it would be safe to say that he—"

"M'lord." Sarah's interjection brought a swift end to his words, which would surely have been demeaning. The young slave felt Celia's head loll to the side and she quickly adjusted the sleeping baby's weight. "Jerem, run and see if Cook left you a basket of sweet rolls by the hearth while I put your sister t' bed." The little lord scampered to obey and Sarah turned back to regard Bradley with a mild reproof, "You can't be speaking ill of them in front of their children. Word will surely wing its way back t' their ears that you've poisoned the young minds in your favor."

"I know it. Sometimes, though, I wish Roland would find something to accuse me of and toss me out on the streets rather than trying to turn me into one of his ducklings."

A small smile played about Sarah's mouth, "Toss you out? You wouldn't last a day." She turned toward Celia's canopied bed but stopped when Lord Bradley spoke quietly.

"I won't stay. I only came because I find it so peaceful in here, like a safe haven after a storm. And I don't have to pretend when I'm with you."

Sarah breathed in the scent of Celia's auburn hair, wishing that the same carefree existence that belonged to this child might also be available for her own pleasure. She felt pulled in two different directions, each with a rightful claim on her life. One side demanded her allegiance as a slave to her mistress, the other craved loyalty to this young noble who steadfastly remained her friend against all odds.

Sarah looked up and met the turmoil in Lord Bradley's gaze. Since his arrival in Hebbros, he had wandered from one hobby to another, one place to the next, searching for purpose within the walls of another man's home and finding none. She considered suggesting he might find solace in faithfully attending the temple ceremonies, but knew that her own mandatory audience before Lord Roland's deities had done nothing to quiet the questions of her own searching soul.

Casting a quick glance in Jerem's direction and finding the boy utterly absorbed with a sweet roll in each fist, the young slave whispered, "M'lord, I don't think…" her words tapered off to silence again as she reminded herself that Lord Bradley was not one of her charges, to be corrected like a child.

"What is it, Sarah? Tell me, please."

She swallowed to moisten her dry throat, "I think you ought t' be more careful."

Bradley's lighthearted smile returned and he cocked his head to one side, "I'm always careful. Roland is all pomp and pretty words, but he really can't bring any more harm on my head." He glanced at her collar and his eyes grew sad and then optimistic, "I haven't forgotten my promise to you."

Sarah nodded as her own expression saddened, "I know."

Lord Bradley turned with a nod and quietly left the room, leaving Sarah to stare at the door as it groaned to a close. When the latch had clicked, she turned with a heavy sigh and lowered Celia to her down feather bed.

She lifted a hand to trace the close boundary of her leather collar. She knew he had not forgotten. She herself still remembered his words of four years ago, promising freedom from pain and slavery. But Sarah also knew that this young lord who sought a slave's liberation was yet himself shackled by the chains of a dangerous master.

Lord Bradley was a slave to bitterness. And until the day his own fetters were loosened, he would be unable to see clearly the way to free another.

19

Day of Judgment

Luke paced the short distance across the holding room, one of the few places he had been unable to escape from during four years of bondage. He reached the rounded wall and pivoted on one heel to pace the other way, practicing his mathematics by counting and multiplying the number of steps in every way he could.

For three days he had occupied this room, waiting for Sir Kenrick to decide upon his next fate, and thinking on Christopher's admonition to retain a testimony for the Lord. Luke already had a reputation in Hebbros as the most spirited and resistant child that Sir Kenrick sought a home for. It would be a humbling experience to break that pattern of defiance, and then where would he be? What would become of the stand he had made for justice? Those he resisted would consider him defeated, and his fight would have been a waste.

Luke wasn't yet willing to live a façade of peace in order to surprise the enemy with a war later. He thrived on sustaining even the smallest fight now.

Luke swung his arms in methodical circles, and then led his limbs through the familiar motions of pulling a bowstring taut and releasing an invisible arrow. He thought of the powerful physique presented by his brother several days before and a smile bloomed on his face. Thanks to Guy's secret lessons in the art of the bow, Luke had come to recognize the strength of his arms as his own greatest physical asset. Christopher, on the other hand, had by all appearances developed the same amount of strength in his little finger! At fourteen, his twin was already becoming a solid mass of strength and power.

Luke dropped his arms to his sides and closed his eyes to reminisce. It had been so good to see his brother. He must find his sister soon and be reunited with her as well.

The lock on the door suddenly grated a complaint against its key, and the panel swung open to reveal a man on the other side of the threshold. He stood still for a moment, studying the young prisoner who stared back from the middle of the holding room.

Luke's eyes widened in confusion and then dropped to the floor.

Sir Valden stepped into the room and spoke without ceremony, "You're to come with me."

Luke flinched beneath the gravelly voice. In the next instant, fingers of iron closed around his bicep and seemed to lock in place, immovable as they pulled their prisoner through the door and down the circular stairway to the courtyard. As they neared the door to the reestablishment room Luke leaned in that direction, anticipating their steps to end before Sir Kenrick's stone-topped table. Sir Valden corrected Luke's course with a stiff jerk.

"Not this time. They're waiting for you next door."

Luke shot a look of surprise at the dark-armored Mordecai and then twisted to peer over the rooftops and towers of the Order's garrison to the spires of the meeting hall beyond. Sir Valden ignored the boy's confusion as they passed through the public gate and turned to walk from one structure to the next. The din of the crowded street lulled briefly when they appeared, and Luke found himself in the tunnel of a hundred gazes as Sir Valden easily cleared a way through.

When they had climbed the gray stone steps to the entrance of the House of Peers' meeting hall, Valden nodded to the guards for admittance and then spoke again.

"You've caused quite a stir with this last failed reestablishment." He kept his eyes on the corridor ahead and his hold tightened on Luke's arm, "It surprises me that one so young is not afraid of the powers that control his destiny."

A chill crept over Luke as the man's rasping tone echoed back from the stone walls and wrapped around him like an uncomfortable and oppressive wet blanket. Pushing past his fear of Valden, he turned his mind to the conversation and compelled his mouth to speak the words that surged to his tongue. Inspired by his mother's teachings of years before, they were words that would make Christopher proud.

"There is only one Power that controls my destiny, sir, and that Power is Jesus Christ, the essence of love. Why should I be afraid?"

Sir Valden grunted, "You speak of your God, the deity who took your parents from you and left you to struggle alone for a useless cause."

"Lord Roland took my parents from me, and Sir Kenrick left me alone by taking my brother and sister away. God has not left me. His presence in my life is the only reason I continue to fight these four years after the raid, and He is the foundation of my hope for justice."

Sir Valden chuckled and the terrible sound reverberated through the echoing passages, "I had thought a boy with such quick use of his brains could be brought to see the folly of his parents' dead faith and make his own way in the world apart from their influence." Another short bark of laughter, "But I find you even more daft than I had thought, to put all your trust in this God of the Faithful."

"And you are dafter still, for you put all your trust in yourself."

Luke snapped his mouth shut with a click of his uneven teeth. Sir Valden came to a halt in the middle of the corridor, forcing his prisoner to pause beside him. The boy cringed. His rashness had caused him to momentarily forget his fear of this man and loosened his tongue to speak without thought or respect. Spoken to any other man, the brash observation would not have cost Luke a second thought. But to Valden…

Luke slowly looked up and forced his gaze to return the one of awful weight above him.

Sir Valden glared back. "Where did you hear such insolent talk?" The knight's voice sounded ominous in the shadowy hall.

Luke's gaze dropped to the stone floor, "Nowhere."

Valden's grip tightened and Luke flinched when experienced fingers dug into his flesh. "I wish to know who is spouting such disrespect for my person to the youths of Hebbros, and especially to the likes of you. Now, *answer me*!"

The last words were emphasized with a shake that would have sent Luke toppling off balance had his arm not been a captive of the Mordecai's iron grip. With his heart beating faster than a catawyld's clicking tongue, Luke swallowed a lump of returning fear and shook his head.

"No one told me. I didn't—" His words were interrupted by a cuff to the side of his head.

Fury ignited in Luke's belly. The long-ago counsel of his father and the more recent admonitions of Guy, to withhold knowledge of his gift of perception—to tell as few people as possible and never the enemy—slipped from his mind with that last blow. Knowledge of his gift, in the wrong hands, could be destructive. Nevertheless, indignation sparked bright in his slate-blue eyes, fueling once more his ability to look up and speak, or shout, his mind.

"*I knew it on my own!*" The youthful roar vibrated in his ears. Sir Valden's eyes narrowed and the boy continued before the knight had a chance to speak, his words spilling out without thought, "No one had to tell me and I didn't have to ask. I can read it for myself, just like I can see that you're evil." Luke moved as far from the knight as his arm-held-hostage would allow, "You've done so many wicked things, adding one more sin to your soul doesn't bother you. You've silenced your conscience, and that is why you're the only man in Hebbros who causes me any fear. Only I do not fear *you*, only what you might do without a second thought or regret."

"You *read* it…for yourself?"

Luke saw Valden processing all that he had just heard and suddenly the boy swallowed. He had said too much. Far too much.

He shivered and his skin crawled with apprehension as his common sense returned and he observed his current position, alone in a darkened hall with a man who made the evil twins sound like the mildest of threats, and whom he had just censured. He glanced toward the doors of the inner meeting hall and wished to move in that direction, to forget this scene in the corridor, the words exchanged with this terrifying man. But Valden remained motionless and his next thoughts were produced in a low voice, thoughtful and conspiratorial.

"You give this reason for fearing me and yet you do not fear Sir Kenrick for the same. Why is that?"

Feeling like a mouse before a hawk, Luke spoke quietly before Valden could force the words from his mouth, "It's true Sir Kenrick does not regret what he does, but you are impulsive while his actions are thought out and planned before they are carried out. His greatest fear is that he will slip on his own path to greatness if he does not thoroughly examine each step."

"Interesting," the single word was drawn out on a raspy breath and Luke shrank from it. "And you can know this by merely…"

"Sir Valden." Another voice boomed through the corridor and Luke inwardly sagged with relief when he saw the Chief Peer emerge from the door to the inner hall, "Come along man, we haven't all day to settle this issue. We've matters of greater import to attend to."

"Yes sir," Valden set his jaw and glared at the man's retreating back. Shifting his gaze to Luke, his eyes narrowed again before he tugged on the boy's arm and led him the last few yards to the door where the Chief Peer had disappeared.

The muffled sound of someone shouting echoed from the corridor outside the door and a moment later fell silent. The gathered Peers exchanged glances and then set their eyes on the far panel, waiting for it to swing open and reveal the troublemaker.

Lord Roland sat beside the Chief Peer in the meeting hall, waiting for Kenrick's friend, Sir Valden, to appear with a boy who had proven himself a nuisance. On a small table before him lay documents pertaining to matters of trade and updates on the building of the new outer wall. Slave counts, tax feuds, orders to send help to the Brikbone border wars, a swineherd's complaint, and even the report of a nearby dragon-sighting, all sat awaiting his perusal.

Yet he must set them all aside to rebuke a mere youth.

"Ridiculous," Roland muttered under his breath. He glanced at Kenrick across the hall and continued his private commentary, "Can he not subdue one child as he does all the others?" Adding volume to his tone of annoyance, Roland asked, "What is taking so long? The walk from the garrison is not one of great length, am I correct?"

The Chief Peer swayed forward and rose from his chair, and a moment later the older man's voice echoed down the outer passage. Shaking his head, the Chief Peer strode back to his seat and settled on the cushion just as Sir Valden entered with the accused.

The boy was tall and slim, but had a sinewy build and sharp eyes beneath brown hair in desperate need of a trim. Sharp eyes that met and held Roland's gaze until the ruler was sure his very thoughts had been discerned. Only once before had he felt so vulnerable.

Roland surged to his feet and pointed, "You're the boy from the schoolroom!" His eyes widened as recognition fanned the memory to life like a flame, "Some years ago you fought with two others and then spoke to me with insolence, and you…" the recent familiarity of a similar face suddenly made sense. He turned to no one in particular, "He has a twin."

Kenrick nodded and unrolled a parchment. "Luke's twin, Christopher, has been in service as a squire at the palace garrison for four years, my lord."

"Remarkable," Roland murmured the exclamation to himself as he reclaimed his seat. He did not often remember a random face twice. Then again, this boy was more peculiar than he was random. His eyes returned to Luke and he found that a smirk now lit the youth's face.

"I said we'd meet again, didn't I?"

Roland stiffened at the reminder of those last unsettling words, spoken by an imp of a child before he had slipped away to adolescent freedom on the streets.

Sir Valden grabbed the boy by a handful of hair and hissed in his ear, "Do not address his lordship with such disrespect, and do not speak unless given permission to do so."

Luke's eyes quickly lowered, but one corner of his mouth still harbored a grin and his tone still bore a hint of brazenness when he spoke up yet again. "He gave me permission when he addressed me as an old acquaintance."

Forestalling a backhanded slap to the youth's cocky face, Roland plucked a document from the top of his stack and raised his voice over Valden's growl, "Enough of this foolishness. I have far more important matters to discuss with the Peers, and wish to conclude this business with all haste. Luke," Roland leveled his gaze on the lad, "your conduct of the past four years, following the banishment of your rebel parents, has been irresponsible and reprehensible."

"Repre-*what*?"

"Guilty." The single word filled the vaulted space in an instant. In the rumbling aftermath Roland rose to his feet, too agitated by this boy's uncanny gaze and calm façade to remain seated.

"The citizens of Hebbros have endeavored to shelter, feed, clothe, and teach you, since the day you were delivered from your former life of confusion. You have turned your back on these offers of mercy and scorned all attempts to lead you in a path of honorable living. The people of our fair city should not bear the burden of your survival, and so they are henceforth released from their duty to care for you. You will receive no further offers of food, shelter, clothing, or instruction from anyone within the walls of Hebbros until that day you repent of your actions and commit to reforming your life to one of obedience and perfection in Mizgalian society. Do you understand?"

The accused mumbled a response that was lengthier than a mere yes or no.

Roland grit his teeth, "What did you say?"

Luke lifted his head and held it at a daring angle, "I said no one is perfect, my lord. You are asking me to live in a manner that pleases your ideals, but your ideals are corrupt. Are you asking me to be corrupt, then?" His piercing gaze wandered to other faces in the rounded rows of seats, "Every man here harbors secrets. You're liars, thieves, hypocrites, cowards, confused…"

"Silence!" Roland stiffened with rage, but Luke pressed on.

"Your own teaching is faulty. Your schoolmasters told me in one breath that I ought never lie to the city's ruling lord or to a member of the House of Peers, and in the next breath said that children should twist the truth when speaking to their mother or father if a falsehood suited the occasion better."

"I said—"

"Are these same lessons being taught to your own children?"

"*Silence!*" Roland's bellow sounded loud enough to shake the foundation of the hall. Several of the Peers laid a hand to their ear and shrank away from his fury as far as their chairs would allow. Served them right, Roland thought; the no-good, silent, observing, pack of sniveling grumblers.

A shove from Valden sent Luke sprawling to the floor and Roland took momentary pleasure in the boy's subservient posture, even if it was forced. Roland's gaze flickered briefly to Valden and found the Mordecai watching Luke with a look of grim pleasure and an expression that suggested he had just made a revelation. Roland thought back over Luke's words and wondered at the boy's acute knowledge of the corrupted Peers. It must be common knowledge.

"Stand him on his feet and keep him quiet. You, boy, have no respect for your authorities. This is the second time you have dared to correct me in my method of ruling, and I will not allow it to go unpunished. My verdict stands. Bring the collar."

Luke watched with widening eyes as a large, barrel-chested man emerged from the shadows along the hall's outer edge. A second man followed a step behind, carrying objects that Luke could not identify.

"What are they—?"

"Quiet, brat," Valden rasped.

"My lord," another voice interjected, "I think perhaps…"

"You should not think." Roland cut the man off with a tone of finality and then nodded for the two newcomers to carry out some preconceived plan, "Proceed."

Luke stiffened and then dropped to his knees beneath a sound shove.

I should have held my tongue. Someone tilted his head forward. *I should have been silent. Didn't Mother say Christ was silent before His crucifixion?*

A thick strap of leather, one inch wide and dyed the color red, was wrapped around his neck for measurement and then removed with a rough brush against his skin. Over the sounds of his own inner panic and the shuffling and murmuring among the Peers, Luke heard Lord Roland's voice pounding a rhythm of condemnation and judgment.

"Luke of Hebbros, also known as Luke the Terror"—a sharp blade sliced the leather in two, cutting one side down to make a perfect fit—"you are hereby ordered to wander the streets of our city, friendless and alone,"—a metal plate was pinched to either end of the red strap—"until the day you repent of your rebellious actions against the authority represented in myself…"—the leather embraced his neck once again; Luke arched his back and tried to pull away, but was held in place by an iron-like grip that could only be Sir Valden's—"and in the House of Peers…"—something hot flashed by his face in a flare of orange and red heat. Luke froze and held his breath to keep from running into the fiery object—"and in the knights of the Mordecai Order."

The soft tap of metal against metal sounded at the back of his neck, and Luke's chest constricted with the knowledge that the strap's metal-plated ends were being fused together with intense heat.

Roland's voice droned on, "As the slaves of Mizgalia wear a leather collar to signify there lowly position among us, so you also will wear a collar to represent your slavery to the old-fashioned and dangerous ideals so abhorred within the walls of Hebbros."

The fiery rod was pulled away and a tankard of cold water poured over the melted plates, solidifying the attachment and soaking Luke in the process.

A moment of silence settled over the hall, punctured only by the sound of dripping water.

"You may release him."

Roland's command was followed by the sudden liberation of Luke's limbs. Already on his knees, Luke fell forward with his hands to the floor and promptly heaved what little food he had been served that morning. Sounds of disgust rippled through the hall, but Luke ignored them. Closing his eyes, he concentrated on taking several deep breaths despite the uncomfortable new addition to his apparel.

The collar.

It chafed. It choked. It hurt.

Clenching his jaw, Luke wiped his mouth on his sleeve and then forced himself upward from the floor and to his feet. Trembling from the sheer adrenaline and then weakness of the last few moments, he stood and let his gaze scan the other faces in the room.

"If you—" Luke stopped when he choked on the words. Closing his eyes, he continued in a quiet murmur that reached every ear due to the utter silence of every other throat. "If you meant what you said, that I'm to wander the streets…" he took a slow breath, "I'd like to leave now."

Lord Roland's chest heaved with the thrill of a satisfied command. Pointing one arm toward the door, he silently granted Luke's request and then lowered himself onto his cushioned chair. Luke turned to go, taking slow steps and working on steadying each breath. Behind him, Roland's voice echoed threatening across the room.

"You will be watched, boy. Choose carefully where you go, to whom you speak. Honored Peer, have a notice written and posted throughout the city. I want no confusion regarding this boy's sentence. He is henceforth a fugitive in Hebbros."

Outside the meeting hall Luke crept down the stone steps and around the corner of the impressive structure. Sinking down against the wall, he slipped a finger inside the close boundary of his red collar and took another deep breath. He tried to pry the leather off by force, but the melded plates held faster than the clasp of Sir Valden's hand. A heavy sob of helplessness shook Luke's frame and a single tear slipped between his closed lashes. With his mind's eye he reviewed the jarring and terrible scene he had left behind, the tangible sights as well as the hidden revelations of his gift.

To his left and around the corner the noisy street sounded much the same as when he had passed by with Sir Valden—the haggling merchants and oblivious peasants whose lives had not just been altered.

At least he would be permitted to roam the streets unhindered.

Luke's eyes shot open. A smile split his face. He was free! How could he have overlooked this joyous fact? His friends, the other Faithful children, would surely offer him food and other necessities in spite of Lord Roland's directive. He could find Charlotte, visit Christopher, and spend his time encouraging the others to remain strong in the faith. Lord Roland had said that he would be watched, but if Luke could find a way to evade the man's spies then perhaps he could change Lord Roland's curse to a blessing.

Feeling hope build within him, Luke rose to his feet and suddenly remembered his final glance around the meeting hall, and what he had then discovered through his gift. Each face had contained a myriad of traits and emotions, but only one had revealed what he had been searching for.

Compassion. Sympathy. Pity.

Luke turned where he stood and stared up at the outer wall of the Peers' magnificent structure. His eyes peered at the stones as if he could see through them to the surprising realization made only moments before.

The Chief Peer did not support Lord Roland's regime.

Not everything in Hebbros was as it seemed.

20
The Girl at the Chandler's

Charlotte set aside another candle of rolled beeswax and reached for the implements to make another. She enjoyed this process more than the slower work of dipping in hot wax and hanging the candles to dry. Beeswax was easier, in her opinion, and dipping them mindlessly gave her too much time to think.

As she lifted one edge of a new sheet of beeswax and folded it closely around the long wick, Charlotte tuned her ear to the strains of voices on the other side of the workroom.

"She is a pretty bit of a thing." The visitor's voice sounded like warm honey, oozing pleasantries and then sticking with discomfort, "A pity she came from one of those renegade families, but a great credit to you now, I imagine. How old did you say she is?"

"Our Charlotte is nine years old now and every bit our own regardless of her unfortunate past." Mother Chandler sounded every bit the proud mama, despite the fact that she and her husband still insisted Charlotte address them by the titles of their trade. Visiting with a woman from across the square, Mother Chandler mindlessly dipped candle after candle in a pot of melted wax as she eyed Charlotte with her controlling gaze.

Charlotte's nimble fingers continued to roll the wax into a tight wand. Her gaze watched to make sure the ends remained even. Her cheeks flamed self-consciously as the two women commented on her beautiful hair and large eyes of hazel brown, her slender fingers and delicate features.

"Of course, it's to be expected that a girl of mine will grow up to be a great beauty," Mother Chandler preened at her own unfounded compliment. "I always said she would. And now we've taken in my husband's nephew—"

"Young Marley?"

"Aye, the very boy. His parents died when the fever swept through the lower part of the city. Now he's apprenticed with my husband and I've set my heart on having the two children wed when the boy's apprenticeship is done with."

Charlotte's eyes closed with a sigh and her face crowded into a wince at the familiar words regarding her fate.

"So young?" The visitor breathed the query with a gossip's aura of wonder. The bit of news was sure to be known throughout all of Hebbros within an hour of the woman's departure. This had undoubtedly been Mother Chandler's design in mentioning it to the woman.

"No, no," Mother Chandler waved one hand dismissively as she reached for another candle with the other. "Not any time soon. By Lord Roland's beard! The girl is only nine, as I have said before. They'll have to wait some years yet."

"Does Lord Roland have a beard? I hadn't noticed."

"Aye, a close-cropped beard, but a beard all the same. Now that is a fine man, if ever I saw one."

The gossip nodded in ready agreement, "So commanding in his presence. And Lady Rosalynn! So regal and gentile."

Both ladies released a sigh of pleasure and approval. A voice called from outside and Mother Chandler directed Charlotte with a jerk of her head, "Get out there, girl, and see to the customer. Father and Marley won't be back from the palace for some time." She turned to her friend as Charlotte rose to obey, "My husband is selling a batch of our candles to the man at the palace in hopes of gaining a new alliance."

Charlotte stepped through the workroom doorway and into the bright sunlight. Beneath an awning meant to shade the stall's wares, candles filled a number of crates stacked to either side of the door and filled two barrels that flanked the small space. A tall youth with dirty-blond hair stood inspecting one of the beeswax wands.

Charlotte stared at him for a moment before venturing a timid, "Ned?"

He turned with a start and his brow creased with confusion for a moment before recognition dawned, "Charlotte?"

"Shh," Charlotte put a finger to her lips and peered over her shoulder into the workroom. The noise of the street seemed to be covering any noise in the stall. "They don't want me to remember anything or anyone from before the banishment. If they hear you, they'll send you away."

Still wearing an expression of amazement, Ned pointed to a crate on the ground at their feet, "The chandler ordered this piece of work from my master's shop, and I was instructed to deliver it." They knelt by the crate and Ned shifted through a wad of straw for the order. Taking longer than necessary, he glanced up and whispered, "I've passed this shop countless times before and never seen you."

Charlotte matched his hushed tone, "They keep me in the workroom, making candles. The beeswax kind."

He grinned at the bit of irrelevant information, "I prefer beeswax too. Have you seen your brothers?"

Charlotte nodded, "I saw Chris twice, a year ago."

"Luke?"

She shook her head and tears stung her eyes, "Not ever since they split us up."

Ned lifted a small sign from the crate, engraved with Father Chandler's name and several fancy swirls and pictures. Charlotte ran her fingers over the smooth wood.

"It's very pretty."

"It ought to be after three years of misery in that stuffy carpenter's shop, once I finally left the Peers' schoolroom."

"You made this?" It seemed odd that someone so brash could fashion something so delicate.

Ned nodded and rose to his feet, handing the sign to Charlotte, "Luke has spent these four years running from every master and searching out the children of the Faithful. Last I saw him, he'd found everyone but you and Chris. If I see him again, I'll tell him where to find you."

"Thank you." Charlotte smiled and then her sweet face grew serious again, too serious for a child of her age, "Do you think my brothers and I will ever be together again? Or will they keep us apart forever?"

Ned swallowed as the little one's large eyes filled with tears. Forcing a grin to shape his face, he pat her on the head and then bent to retrieve the crate, "Keep your chin up, Charlotte. Luke will think of something, especially now that he's been set loose on the streets."

"What do you…?"

"Who is this, Charlotte?"

The little girl started and turned to see Father Chandler approaching with a crate still filled with candles. Following close behind him was the contemptible Marley, a greedy, selfish, lazy, sneering, lad of fourteen, who was already fond of ale. Both chandlers eyed Ned with suspicion, and Father Chandler quickly set about dismissing the tall youth.

"Be off with you. We do not wish to buy your wares, young man."

"But you already have, sir," Ned replied.

"I what?"

"I'm here to deliver the sign you ordered," he motioned to the strong piece of wood in Charlotte's arms. "I was just about to settle on the payment with your assistant."

"Well then, I'll just set this crate down and retrieve my purse. Marley, stay here with the lad. Charlotte, return to the workroom."

With a final glance at her friend, the brown-haired girl disappeared through the door from whence she'd come, followed by the master chandler. Ned shifted the straw-filled crate in one arm and glanced up to see Marley studying him with eyes so cold they could freeze a summer day. The boy looked to be slightly younger than Ned, but had the aged look of one who had seen and lived through too much. A sickly aroma clung to the air about him, evidence that Marley already made a habit of frequenting the taverns for a penny-ale.

Ned cleared his throat and shifted again, taking a moment to watch the activity on the street. When Marley continued to stare at him with hostility, Ned finally offered a glare of his own.

The chandler reappeared, "Here you are, young sir. Payment in full. You will thank your master for me. The work is beautiful."

"I'll tell him so." Ned nodded to the older man and turned to leave, ignoring the icy look of contempt that seemed rooted to Marley's flushed face.

As he traversed the too-crowded streets of Hebbros, Ned thought of his surprise at finding little Charlotte. He remembered with a pang of sadness her hopeless words, and her unspoken fear that the enemy might have won.

Will they keep us apart forever?

"God, don't let it be so." Ned paused before the door to the carpenter's shop, scanning the milling crowd with a weary gaze. He thought of the raid four years back and remembered the look of shattered agony that had shaped his mother's face. His father had been dead for several years already, and his mother had raised her only son with a firm resolve to follow truth. That he had been forced to watch as she was carted off to exile had torn at her loving heart.

Now Ned was alone. There was no one left to whom he truly belonged, no matter what Sir Kenrick said of his reestablishment. But little Charlotte hadn't been left alone; she had brothers who could care for her if only they were able. Ned lifted his gaze heavenward, "God, strengthen our scattered band and bring us all back together again."

Turning to enter the shop, he was hailed by another young voice from across the street. Ned looked over his shoulder and found the ropemaker's apprentice watching him from where he sat perched on a stool outside his own place of work, hands absently clutching a bit of unfinished rope. The boy nodded to Ned and a thatch of black hair fell over his right eye.

"Something's bothering you."

Some things had not changed in four years. Ned exhaled half-a-laugh and pushed the carpenter's door open. Glancing back, he met the young roper's eye, "Obvious, Elbert."

After Ned had disappeared from sight, Father Chandler and Marley entered the workroom. Marley cast a scowl in Charlotte's direction, "You shouldn't be talking to strangers."

"Leave her alone, Marley," Father Chandler removed his cap.

Charlotte frowned, "All the customers are strangers, and you weren't here to answer his call."

"Whose call?" This from Mother Chandler.

"Charlotte, soften your tone and be respectful to Marley."

"What stranger?" Mother Chandler tried again to press her query into the fray. The gossip still sat beside her, drinking in the scene of conflict with a relish that bespoke her favorite pastime of retelling the story to a captivated audience.

"Never mind who he was," Father Chandler waved his hands in a dismissive gesture. "I must return to the palace with my candles on another day." He forestalled his wife's questions with a ready answer, "Lord Roland was at the meeting hall and the slaves were frantic to prepare a large banquet to be set out on his lordship's return. They had no time to see me."

Marley spoke up with a sneer, obviously delighted with a bit of unpleasant news, "That boy, one of the rebel children, has finally been punished for his constant defiance of Lord Roland."

Charlotte bristled at his description of those like her who had been carted and scattered like cattle because of their faith.

"The boy has been collared like a slave and sentenced to roam the streets without aid or kindness until he repents."

The gossip leaned forward, eager, "Do you speak of the rebel boy who refuses to be sheltered by our people? The one called Luke the Terror?"

A gasp followed the woman's words and all eyes turned to Charlotte. The little girl's mouth had dropped open in shock. Ned's reference to Luke being set loose on the streets suddenly rang clear in her mind.

"Luke? Of the Faithful? He's my brother!"

As soon as the words had fallen from her lips, Charlotte felt the atmosphere in the room shift to one of discomfort. The air was suddenly thick and stifling. Charged with tension.

Mother Chandler moved like a flash of lightning, one minute on the other side of the room and the next standing over Charlotte with a dangerous glint in her eyes. "Stop with that nonsense, girl. I'll hear no more of it."

Charlotte swallowed a lump of cold fear, "But it's true. He's my brother."

"He's not!" Mother Chandler snapped and Charlotte flinched. "That boy can't be your brother."

"But he is." Tears sprang to Charlotte's eyes as she clung

desperately to the truth. Marley's words filtered through her mind again and she sought his face for answers, "What do you mean 'collared'? What did they do to him? Is he hurt?"

"Quiet! You don't have a brother."

"I do! I have two brothers!" Charlotte wailed helplessly at this woman's attempt to make her forget, "They're twins."

"That's a lie! You never had any brothers. I'm your mother, and there's your father and your cousin. This is your home, and you live with us making candles."

Beyond Mother Chandler, the two men of the house stood silent by the door, leaving Charlotte to the woman's cutting words. The gossip watched with wide eyes, eager to catch every detail. Mother Chandler continued to shout against Charlotte's memories, beating against the girl's hope with an arsenal of sharp lies.

"You have no brothers, and no sisters. I'm your mother. You're being ungrateful and foolish. Now finish that candle before I urge you to do so with a switch."

Charlotte bowed her head over the familiar beeswax and began to roll it evenly, straining to see her work through the veil of tears that blinded her. *How much longer, God? When will this end?* Her heart formed the silent plea, repeating the cry so often heard from her birth mother's lips.

Father Chandler and Marley left to care for another customer. The gossip slipped out the back door, closing the panel of woven reeds with little more than a whisper of noise. Mother Chandler went back to the task of dipping candles, monotonous in its endless repetitions. Her scowl remained fastened to Charlotte's pale face, daring the girl to reintroduce the argument of moments before. Charlotte's tentative gaze lifted to meet the woman's eyes and then darted away, flickering about the room and trying to find somewhere, anywhere to rest other than Mother Chandler's frowning face.

Suddenly, another face appeared in the window beyond Mother Chandler's broad shoulder. A face shaped not by an intimidating glower, but by an impish grin. A face that Charlotte knew well. In fact, she was also well acquainted with its double. The slate-blue eyes belonging to this face twinkled with daring as they glanced at Mother Chandler's back and then returned to wink at Charlotte.

"Luke," Charlotte breathed the name and then stiffened when

the room's other occupant paused and narrowed her eyes. Luke disappeared when he ducked below the windowsill.

"No more of that," Mother Chandler hissed through her teeth, "or you'll wish you'd complied long before now."

Charlotte dipped her head in a nod and for a moment dared not look anywhere but at the beeswax beneath her fingers. When she finally risked another glance at the window, she saw Luke reappearing over the sill an inch at a time. His eyes were bright with an excitement that she and Christopher had never fully understood, relishing the danger of the moment. When his head and neck became visible Charlotte caught sight of the collar that Marley had mentioned, circling her brother's neck. Her heart ached for Luke, sharing his pain.

Luke glanced at Mother Chandler and the tip of his tongue appeared, clutched between his front teeth in a look of determination. He shifted his head to smile at Charlotte and offered her a small wave, as if they had only been separated for a few days. Charlotte fought back the urge to return the gesture and watched as Luke deliberately placed a small object on the sill. He gave her a significant glance and then nodded silently at his present. Obviously, he was leaving it for her to retrieve later and wanted to ensure she was aware of the fact. Charlotte offered a slight nod and glanced at Mother Chandler, hanging another candle up to dry.

Luke's expression became serious. His mouth formed a grim line as he stood gazing at her from outside. His eyes studied her face, her situation, her work. He pointed at her and lifted one hand to make it level with his shoulder. *You're taller.* Charlotte smiled and lifted her eyebrows, tilting her head toward him. She hoped he would understand that she was returning the observation. He was much taller than when she'd last seen him. He looked broader, though not as broad as Chris, and stronger. His gaze was sharper and clear, still a visual echo of the fire that drove him to action.

His smile was tinged with sadness as he offered her a silent salute, and then he was gone.

Charlotte blinked against another wave of tears. She seemed to cry a lot these days.

"Stop your sniveling."

And Mother Chandler always seemed to notice when she did.

Charlotte sniffed and bent over her work. Another two candles had been added to her basket of work before Mother

Chandler finally stepped away from her own task and stepped outside to ask her husband a question. As soon as she had gone, Charlotte jumped from her stool and raced quietly to the window. Her slender fingers closed around whatever Luke had left on the sill and she darted back to her seat just as the chandler's wife returned through the street-side entrance. Charlotte dropped Luke's gift into her basket and began to roll another candle, waiting for her heart to stop racing.

It was another hour before Mother Chandler left the workroom once again to prepare the evening meal. Once she was alone, Charlotte hopped up and sifted through her basket to find the small bit of steel at the bottom. Lifting it out and placing it on her palm, she sank to her stool and stared with a mixture of sadness and hope at the reminder Luke had left behind.

A steel rivet from the floor of their father's cooperage.

21
Troubling Repercussions

Like a shadow detaching itself from the night, Luke slipped through the cooperage window and dropped silently to the floor. "Guy? Are you here?" His whispered words reached for the dark corners, searching for the cooper, "I had to come later than usual to be sure I wasn't followed."

"I thought that might be your reasoning," the bulky shadow that was Guy emerged from the storeroom and stood with arms crossed over his wide chest.

"I saw Charlotte today. I couldn't speak with her, but I left her the rivet. She's grown so much." Luke smiled at the memory of her seated wide-eyed in the chandler's workroom and admitted, "She's pretty, like mother."

"You can't stay." The sudden statement fell across the space like a clap of thunder on a cloudless day. Luke stiffened and a thread of unease traveled up his spine.

"What do you mean?"

"I know of Lord Roland's ruling; of his orders that no one is to offer any aid to the collared boy." In the darkness, Guy's head lowered, "I'm sorry."

Fury ignited like a ready blaze in Luke's core. Tension curled his fingers into fists. "You've been helping me for four years. What makes this time different?"

Guy took a step closer, "I've done all I can, Luke. I taught you to make a fine bow and matching arrows. I've taught you to use the weapon with skill. All that's left is for you to sharpen those skills with practice."

The cooper was still masked by shadows, but Luke could feel the man's fear without needing to read his gaze.

"I promise I'll be careful, Guy. I'll make sure no one follows me here. I'll wait until after dark." Guy's head began to shake in denial and Luke's whispering took on a desperate edge, "Just leave me some food. Scraps. Anything you can spare. I'm free to wander the streets now, and I plan to use this as my chance to organize the others who are waiting to fight for justice."

"You cannot fight against the nobility of Hebbros any more than you could storm King Cronin's castle at Mockmor."

Luke clenched his jaw and shifted with agitation, "You've trained me all this time, preparing me for the very fight that you now say is impossible and without hope. If you did not believe in the cause, then why did you help—"

Guy cut him off with an impatient sweep of his arm, "I was not preparing you to fight. I was preparing you to survive."

He reached into the storeroom and then tossed a long object across the small space. Luke caught his well-crafted bow, as well as the full quiver that followed close behind. The boy stared at the tools for a moment and then lifted a confused gaze to his traitorous trainer.

"Survive? You expect me to use these skills on the streets of Hebbros? I can't carry a bow and quiver through the city without raising suspicion, especially now!"

"Not *in* the city. Outside of it."

Guy's answer stopped Luke's response before it could fall from his lips. The boy's brow creased and he shook his head, "What are you talking about?"

"I'd hoped you would come to this conclusion on your own, but I see you haven't," Guy reached for Luke's arm and drew him away from the door. His voice dropped until it was barely audible, "Luke, your position in this city changed the moment your parents were marked as rebels. In spite of Sir Kenrick's efforts to reestablish you, he and every other citizen know that you and the other Faithful children no longer belong here. You are in this city,

Luke, but you are not of it."

Luke's heart lurched with a sudden suspicion of Guy's meaning. It was not what he wanted, not what he had intended, but a pang in his conscience suggested that perhaps it should have been his goal.

"You want me to leave Hebbros."

Guy's massive hand squeezed Luke's shoulder, "I don't *want* you to leave, but I do think you *must.* A life of resistance within the walls of Hebbros will either bring you to your knees in surrender or have you cast out for rebellion. You know nothing of the outside world, and knowing of your ignorance, Roland would pursue you anywhere in order to assert his authority. Except one place."

Luke tightened his grip on the bow as new thoughts found room to grow in his mind, "You mean Mount Desterrar."

"I do."

"You want me to banish myself? Cast myself into exile?"

"You are already in exile. You're a fugitive within these walls."

Luke flinched at the truth of those words.

"But not just you," Guy added. He led Luke into the further privacy of the storeroom and closed the door. Not risking a lamp, he leaned against the closed panel and spoke into the thick blackness that stretched between them, "I believe your parents, or at least some of those who have been cast out, are still alive. I have seen signs of life, human life. Find your friends, plan your escape, and make your way to the top of the mount."

Luke's jaw dropped, "All of us? How would we—"

"That is for you to plan. I can help you no longer."

"But," Luke paused, unable to keep up with his racing thoughts. "If you've thought this through, if you think it's wise…why don't you go too?"

"It will be far easier to get a child out of Hebbros, which is why you must do this soon, before you're the size of a full-grown man. I've made a comfortable life for myself, and as long as I don't cause trouble I'll remain as I am. I practice my faith in silence and no one knows the difference. No one can judge me."

Luke's stomach knotted with a measure of scorn when he heard Guy's tone of resignation. In the next instant he was overwhelmed by a wave of sadness. How terrible for a man to lose faith in the safekeeping of his all-powerful God.

Guy opened the storeroom door and the darkness eased only

slightly, "You must go now. I wish you Godspeed. And Luke…the door has not yet been closed."

Luke felt the weight of those strange words settle in his mind. He secured his quiver of arrows over one shoulder and chased it with his bow. He adjusted the quiver's strap across his chest and stepped through the door and out into the shop. Pausing before the window where he had made his entrance, he turned to look back at the large shadow he had left behind.

"Thank you for all you've done. My father would have been grateful." He saw Guy lower his head again, a sign of his constant shame, "May God grant you strength to live for Him."

The familiar action of leaving through the window found Luke on the street a moment later. Tears burned in his eyes as he strode away, realizing he would never return to his father's shop. The man there now had kept the cooperage alive, but at the cost of his former life. Guy's vibrancy, his inner strength, his boldness, had shriveled and died in the shadow of Sir Kenrick and his Mordecai knights.

Luke could not let that happen in his own life. He could not let the powers in Hebbros do such a thing to Chris and Charlotte, or to the other Faithful children.

He would get them out.

Luke paused at a corner that would move him out of sight of the cooperage. He glanced over his shoulder at the dark shop and released a slow breath.

"Is he right?" Luke's gaze lifted to search beyond the rooftops, "Should I be preparing to run rather than stay and fight?"

What would you be fighting for?

The question flitted through his mind, gentle as a spring breeze. Luke turned and started walking again, away from Guy, away from the cooperage, away from questions he did not want to answer. To answer honestly would be to admit four years of foolish thinking. He moved stealthily through the streets, avoiding alleys and byways that were alive with revelers and ne'er-do-wells. But the thought persisted. It pressed and prodded at his need for logic.

What would he be fighting for if he continued with his personal plans?

Justice? For himself and the many parents who had been exiled? Guy's suspicions of life on the mountain caused Luke to cast a glance at the hulking shadow to the west. Either his parents were dead or they had carved out a life for themselves on Mount Desterrar. No matter the outcome, they would no longer desire Luke's definition of justice. They would not wish for him to start a war on their behalf, nor would they want permission to return to Hebbros.

They would rather have their children returned to them.

Luke thought back to the night of the raid and an observation that Charlotte had made. *Maybe living on the mountain is better!* Luke had never considered the possible truth to those words. The mountain had always represented terror, banishment, death, and shame. Yet to those who were members of the Faithful—Sedgwick, his father and mother, and even Guy—the mountain had come to mean something far different.

Refuge.

Luke's steps faltered and he came to a halt in the middle of a street that glowed with the odd light of several taverns. His eyes stared straight ahead, seeing nothing but his thoughts. What had his father's words been? So similar to the thoughts spoken by Sedgwick…

"We will pave the way with our sweat, blood, and tears, that our children may one day see the truth and have courage to follow. We go not to exile, but to freedom."

Pave the way. See the truth.

Going to freedom. Courage to *follow.*

Why had he not seen it this way before?

Luke swept a hand across his forehead and into his hair. But what if Guy's guess was wrong? What if the exiled had all perished on Mount Desterrar? What if there was no one left and he attempted to extricate a band of children from the city, only to bring them to a wilderness inhabited by catawyld beasts?

"Well, well, well, if it isn't the famous rebel of Hebbros. Luk-Luk the Great."

Luke blinked and his focused thoughts evaporated on a wave of discord. Standing on the street before him, a brawny silhouette in the light of Squire's Tavern, was Wulf. Taller, broader, fiercer than he had been four years ago, the older boy held himself with an air of confidence. The pommel of a dagger glistened at his waist in the dim light.

"What are you doing in this lane?" Warin's voice sounded from the tavern door, where the other twin leaned casually in the entrance, "Are you lost, little one?"

Luke returned his attention to Wulf and saw the familiar multitude of faulty emotions and defective character traits, all laid bare within the youth's emerald gaze and amplified by the influence of ale. Nothing had changed for the better since their last meeting.

On the contrary. Everything had grown worse.

"No, I'm not lost. I'm…out for a stroll. If you'll excuse me," Luke moved to bypass Wulf, "I don't have time to talk with a drunkard."

Wulf's high-pitched laugh took Luke by surprise and he turned to cast a look of shock at the taller boy. In the same instant, Wulf's hand snaked out to grab hold of Luke's arm. Luke tried to jerk away, but the grip was tight and unrelenting.

Warin leaned away from the supporting doorframe and spread his feet for a wider stance, "You've got nowhere to go, you pig, and even if you did it wouldn't matter a jot." A sickly smile spread across his face, "Join us for a drink."

"Certainly not. I don't drink ale."

Wulf laughed again and his breath washed over Luke's face, making him gag. He became aware of Wulf's free hand removing his bow and quiver and tossing them into the shadows of an adjoining alley.

"Don't feel bad on account you're penniless. Wulf and I will treat you, and you can return the favor another day. Get him in here," Warin turned on his heel and disappeared inside.

Wulf followed, stumbling once and all but dragging Luke into the establishment. A crowd of boys, both older and younger than he, sat on benches that lined long tables. Did their mothers know they frequented these hovels, wasting their time and money on ruinous ale? Luke flushed with shame and anger when he thought of his own mother's likely response if she should learn of his presence here, forced or not.

Wulf shoved his prisoner onto the end of a bench and Luke winced at the sudden impact. The evil twin's fingers continued to dig into his shoulder as Warin took a seat beside him and slid a tankard across the boards.

"Drink up."

Luke became aware of a number of stares being directed his way. Snatches of whispered commentaries reached his ears—twins, Christopher, fight, revenge. Words that implied a common knowledge of his relationship with the evil twins. They were all watching, waiting to see if a fight would break out. Luke's eyes swiveled back to the tankard before him. Their hopes for a scrap may be rewarded before the night was over.

"I won't drink it. Now let me go." He tried again to twist away from Wulf's grip, but years of disappointed efforts had apparently lent strength to the youth's fingers, drunk or no.

"Not so fast," Warin gripped his other shoulder and squeezed painfully. "We can't let you leave without making sure you've got a full belly. That wouldn't be very polite of us, especially seeing you're an old friend and all."

Luke's heart began to beat loud in his ears. If only he had paid closer attention to his surroundings. Now things were looking a little on the helpless side. He would not willingly consume even a drop of ale; the twins would not let him go until he'd drained the mug.

Turning a steely glare on Warin, he ground out a refusal through clenched teeth, "Let go of me, you insolent dog. I'm not going to touch you're filthy ale."

A boy across the table weaved slightly to the left as he laughed and pointed an unsteady finger in Luke's face, "Coward! What's the matter wi' you? Scared o' what your mother'll say?"

Wulf spat at the table, "He hasn't got a mother."

Luke's eyes narrowed, "I know what my mother *would* say and I'd deserve her rebuke, sitting here and wasting time with the whole drunken lot of you."

"That sounds like an insult," the boy across the table scowled.

"Then you may take it as such," Luke replied.

"I don't tell my mother," another boy across the table leaned over the crude surface as if to whisper conspiratorially, though his words were loud enough to be heard from the distant Arcrean coast. "She thinks I work long hours under my new master's orders, and I decided not to correct her. My old schoolmaster said that letting them believe a falsehood was alright if it brought them less worry."

"That's shameful of you," Luke decided not to elaborate on his sharply spoken words, as the inebriated lad wouldn't remember a word of it.

"Quiet." Warin slammed his fist onto the table, "You're stalling. Drain the tankard on your own, or Wulf and I will help you."

"I told you I won't touch it. I'd rather keep my wits about me."

In the next instant, bedlam erupted in the already boisterous tavern.

Luke saw Warin spring from his seat at the same time Wulf pinched a nerve in his shoulder and forced Luke to sprawl on the bench. His head cracked against the wooden seat and laughter echoed in his ears as firm pressure was applied to his collarbone, pinning him in place. Growling and kicking, Luke felt the futility of his resistance as more and more boys crowded in to assist the evil twins. They stilled his flailing limbs and chanted for the ale until Luke wondered where on earth the taverner had run off to. Had the man left his establishment to be overrun by this mob? Or was he there, watching the event unfold and refusing, or not caring, to lend a hand? If he recognized Luke by the bright red collar, the latter may very well be the case.

Warin grabbed the tankard and held it over Luke's face. Luke squeezed his eyes shut and pressed his lips together. The mug tipped and brown liquid splashed over Luke's face and up his nose, forcing Luke to open his mouth and choke. He twisted away from any more liquid with a sharp lurch and landed on the floor by the bench.

"Stop it! Leave me alone!" Luke felt degraded, diminished, and small. He was helpless against this horde, when he should have been able to fight. Two tears escaped beneath his lashes, tracing a path through the ale's residue on his cheeks, and a cry surfaced from his heart in a final attempt to regain his dignity. "God, save me!"

Wulf turned Luke onto his back and held his head while Warin prepared to pour the rest of the tankard's contents into Luke's mouth or face, whichever was available. Suddenly, another voice was raised over the chaos and the room became still.

"I say, who's the poor soul at the bottom of that heap?"

The tavern's occupants turned as one to regard a young man by the door. His garments served as proof of a lavish lifestyle, and the rakish angle of his hat proved he didn't care. About anything.

Everyone stood there, staring at the newcomer with interest and surprise. Using the distraction to make his escape, Luke slapped the disastrous tankard from Warin's grasp and scrambled to his feet, spitting to rid his mouth of any vestiges of ale. He too turned to face the door and froze with surprise when he saw what had been hidden from his angle on the floor. Standing beside the wealthy youth, half over the threshold and half still outside, was a black horse.

After a moment the young man seemed to notice the animal's presence and offered a casual explanation, "Ah yes, my horse." He presented the reins with one hand, "I dismounted to find that no one had heard my arrival and therefore no one came out to attend us. So I brought him along."

There was a brief pause before the taverner—cowardly man to leave Luke to the mob—rushed forward to offer his newest patron a drink. One boy was commandeered to care for the horse. Outside.

Luke edged away from the table as the room slowly began to fill with noise again, only this time it was not directed at him. Seats were resumed and tankards cradled in youthful palms. Staying close to the wall, Luke moved toward the door, feeling the glares of Wulf and Warin on his back.

"Hold up, Luke!" A hand clamped over his shoulder, already throbbing from the last round of rough treatment, and Luke's eyes slid shut. He could not lose this time.

"Release him."

Luke opened his eyes to see the wealthy young man staring at him. Luke stared back. They were about the same height, he and this stranger, though the other young man appeared to be several years older. Dark red-brown hair framed a face that looked comfortable wearing an expression of indifference. Eyes that looked black in the light of the tavern studied first Luke's face and then his collar. Their gazes collided and Luke read a number of emotions that contradicted his casual demeanor and that were overshadowed by one trait in particular. *Bitterness.*

Wulf's hand fell away from Luke's shoulder even as Warin piped up from farther behind, "My lord, you don't know this boy. He's a troublemaker."

"Oh, I know very well who he is," the red-headed lord replied. "He was the boy at the bottom of the pile." His gaze shifted to Luke once again, "Care to take a stroll? The weather is lovely this evening, very conducive for walking through dangerous streets and all."

Turning on his heel, the young man left the taverner and his customers to watch as Luke followed silently several paces behind. Once outside he retrieved his bow and quiver, breathing a sigh of relief when he found they had not been stolen. Slipping strap and bowstring over his shoulder he swiped a hand over his dampened face and hair, wiped his sticky nose on his sleeve, and rejoined his rescuer.

The young lord had taken his horse's reins from the serving boy, and turned at Luke's approach, "We'll find a well in one of the local squares and you can draw water to rid your person of that ale."

Luke made a short bow before the young man, "Thank you, sir. You were an answer to my prayer."

A short laugh, "And which deity did you pray to, Luke the Terror? Yes, I know who you are, and that collar will give you away to every ill-meaning citizen in Hebbros as well." He held out a hand, "I am Lord Bradley, noble nobody if you must know, and greatest source of annoyance to his lordship, Roland. My brother-in-law."

Luke clasped the proffered hand, "I've heard of you."

"Heard nothing good, I imagine." Bradley laughed and offered the debonair smile of a nobleman, "But don't believe everything they tell you. I've heard myself say that I'm quite charming and not at all a bad sort of fellow, so you can be absolutely certain it's true. Now tell me, which deity condescended to use me as an answer to your prayer?"

"I pray to the God of heaven and earth. The Creator. The Lord Jesus."

"Ah yes, I had heard that you were one of those fanatics who prays to another God."

"Not *another* God. He's the *only* God."

Bradley opened his mouth and then snapped it shut. Finally he chuckled, "I find myself with so many arguments and witty replies begging to be used in response to your statement, that I simply cannot choose which would serve my purpose best. Therefore, I'll use none of them and instead ask how you came to be pinned beneath the rubble of thirty bent on your destruction."

He turned and started walking up the street and Luke fell in step beside him, thankful that the lane where they walked was fairly quiet and not crowded with numerous kinds of danger.

"Two of them are old enemies, my lord. It's a long story."

"I haven't had a story since my father's great aunt, the Lady Rathcum, put me to bed with a terrible tale of flying rodents, singing goats, and a little boy punished for boorish behavior. I had the strangest notion the little boy was meant to be me, but I couldn't say for certain because I missed half of the narrative wondering if the wart on Lady Rathcum's nose was painful and if her face continued to scowl when she slept. I was tempted to sneak into her chamber that night to see for myself, but couldn't gather the courage to approach her, even fast asleep. My, but she was an ancient woman."

Luke answered with silence, unsure that there was a proper reply to such a ramble.

They reached the well and Luke drew a bucket of water and splashed the fresh liquid over his face and into his hair. He scrubbed his features with calloused hands and rubbed his eyes clear before tossing the bucket's remaining contents into the street. The square was bright with lantern light spilling from every structure along its border. A number of people moved about in groups or alone, exchanging dark glances and completing matters of a dishonest nature. They ignored the two youths at the well in return for their own desired privacy, unlike other sections of the city where wandering the streets at night was a sure way to be robbed of any valuables or worse.

Luke turned to Bradley, "You should go. I'm grateful for your help, but you'll be in trouble with Lord Roland if you keep company with me."

"I'm always in trouble with my sister's husband." In the lantern light Luke saw the wave of resentment rise up in Bradley's gaze, even as the young man's face stretched with a grin over his last words.

"Is Lord Roland the source of your bitterness, then?" The question forced itself from Luke's mouth, propelled by the deep perception that had become first nature to him, as well as by his need to attack a problem directly.

Lord Bradley's expression turned to one of astonishment, "What do you know of my bitterness?"

Luke shrugged and continued to study Bradley's gaze, "I simply noticed that you use the art of indifference as a shield to hide your bitterness and pain from others."

Bradley sputtered, "You *simply noticed?*" His outward calm had slipped and Luke recognized the fear of vulnerability, "One does not *simply notice* another person's deepest secrets and trials. They have to be looking for them."

Luke lowered his head to stare at the cobbled street. He had already revealed too much about his gift to Sir Valden, of all people. Would it be wise to tell someone else whom he barely knew? Besides, Bradley's sudden change of countenance proved that his "secrets and trials" were things that he protected against prying eyes for the safety of his very existence. His lordship did not wish to discuss them.

"It was nothing, my lord."

Bradley's eyes narrowed, "Are you some sort of spy or prophet? Are you here to tell me that I'm doomed to an unthinkable death for holding a man's dishonorable actions against him?"

The idea brought a smile to Luke's face and his chest heaved with a chuckle, "No sir, not a prophet. I'm only a Mizgalian peasant, but I do…see things."

"See things?"

"Yes, deeper than the average man's perception can reach."

Bradley's jaw worked back and forth for a moment until his voice finally caught up with the action, "Ahhhh…I see. I think. Perhaps I don't. It may be easier to grasp if you presented it in a musical format. A lyrical song or two, accompanied by a whimsical dance to interpret the words."

Luke stared, taken aback by the sudden return of Lord Bradley's casual air, and then realized that the young nobleman was trying to reinstate the walls of indifference that protected him. Luke complied and followed the shift in conversation.

"I'm not a singing man, sir, or I would do my best with your suggestion."

"Really? Hmm, I'm having difficulty picturing you in the throes of an expressive dance." Bradley took up his horse's reins from where he'd tied them at the well, "Here is where I must bid you farewell."

"Goodbye, my lord, and thank you again for your help." They nodded to one another, refraining from drawing unwanted attention with a series of polite bows, and Bradley turned to leave. Luke called softly after him, "I'll pray for you."

Bradley paused only three paces away and pivoted on his heel. He glanced at the disreputable folk who shared the square and then strode back to stand before Luke. His mask of indifference had once again fled, and his voice was low when he spoke.

"As the likelihood of my seeing you again is all but nonexistent, I'm going to take a chance and be entirely honest with you; something I've been with only one other person on the face of this earth." A deep pain filled his eyes, "The only way your God can possibly help me is by sending me back where I came from, restoring my inheritance, and bringing my father back from the grave. As not one of those desires is actually attainable, I must conclude that my situation is hopeless. You'd be better off praying for the redemption of every other man in this square."

"But you're the only man in this square who actually wants it. Redemption, I mean. I know because I can see."

Bradley stared at Luke, speechless.

Setting aside etiquette, Luke reached out to place one hand firmly on the nobleman's shoulder, "As for your three desires; if that were truly the only way my God could possibly help you, then that would make Him a very limited God. I don't believe He is limited. I believe He could answer every one of your prayers."

"They're not *my* prayers! By my never-whiskered chin, I don't pray for those things," Bradley flapped one hand in a careless gesture, striving for his habitual nonchalance once again. "Besides, my father is dead. Your God certainly won't bring him back to life."

"Probably not," Luke conceded. "But as He raised Himself from the dead I don't think it's a matter of His inability to do so, but rather His desire to lead you on a better path."

"*A better path*?" Bradley sounded incredulous and then amused, "You know, you really do sound like a little prophet. You should consider standing on the street corners and foretelling the futures of every man who walks by. Marvelous amounts of money to be made there."

Luke was not impressed. For the first time in four years, he had spoken from the heart about his God, and in return had received an off-hand bit of mockery. He turned from the well and walked from the square in whatever direction he happened to be facing. The clopping sound of hooves soon told him that Lord Bradley was following.

"Hold up a moment, friend," Bradley's voice held the hint of a grin. "I meant no offense. Though, by my shoe strap, I do seem to offend people every which way I turn. Shake hands, will you? I'd like to know I parted ways with such a conscientious lad on good terms."

Luke paused in the darkened side street and spoke as if he had not heard the other young man, "My lord, if your father was still alive where would you be now?"

Lord Bradley blinked and then shrugged, "Back home at Villenfeld, roaming the grounds with my former companion Hugh and utterly annoying Cook."

"So you wouldn't have been here to rescue me from the boys in Squire's Tavern."

"Pardon my heartless take on the matter, but I find it little consolation that the events of my life heretofore were set in place so that I might drag you from beneath a pile of drunken adolescents."

Luke smirked but persisted, "What if God brought you to Hebbros for a greater purpose? What if He plans to grant your desires, but in a way you had not expected?"

Lord Bradley let out a slight laugh, "I declare, you sound more like a prophet by the minute. Grant my desires you say? Very well, suppose your God should restore me to home again and with my inheritance intact; are you saying you believe He could also restore my father to me?"

Luke's grin spread into a full smile, every fiber of his being leaping to the nobleman's challenge, "Are you prepared to find out?"

Bradley's face lost all traces of humor as he stared at Luke with the beginnings of uncertainty. Luke took a step closer, excitement lightening his features. He could feel his long-dormant faith strengthening with his need to share it.

"I believe God could provide each of the things you mentioned in more ways than you think possible, and that is what I'm going to pray for. Not that you will get what you want, but that you will understand what it is you are truly seeking for, and that God will provide it in such a way that you can no longer deny His existence."

22
Daughter of a Tyrant

Kingdom of Arcrea, Village of Oak's Branch in Frederick's Region

From the height of his black steed, Lord Frederick looked down on the inhabitants of Oak's Branch as they bowed their submission and acknowledged his authority. He spared a brief glance over his shoulder to check the proximity of his mounted guards, and his gaze fell on the girl riding just behind him. His eleven-year-old daughter could not have been more proud of him had he flown to the moon. Frederick faced forward again with a slight smile.

Elaina straightened her back and adjusted the costly material of her skirt as her pony entered the outskirts of the village several miles from her father's castle. The peasants bowed as the noble entourage passed by and Elaina responded by lifting her nose into the air. The haughty demeanor learned from her mother came in handy when she found herself surrounded by the kingdom's lower populace.

"They are beneath us in every way." Her mother had drilled the knowledge into Elaina from an early age. "It is our duty to see that they are aware of their status, and that they maintain their position in society. Their very presence on this earth is for the promotion of their betters and the provision of our comfort."

Lord Frederick reined in before a blacksmith's shop and Elaina followed suit. A man of large stature emerged from within and eyed her father warily as he wiped his hands on a leather apron. He dipped forward in a bow just as a youth some years older than Elaina stepped from the shop and bowed as well. Obviously father and son, the two smiths stood side-by-side and waited for their ruler to speak.

"Gregory," Lord Frederick addressed the elder of the two, "a good report has reached my ears concerning the quality of your work here. My own smith at the castle has not pleased me of late, and so I bring the work to you."

Elaina's father motioned to his left as a soldier appeared driving a wagon of arms to stop beside the shop. Gregory and his son eyed the cart's load, a mountain of dulled weaponry and rusting equipment, and then returned their gazes to Frederick when he spoke again.

"Your payment will be the good standing found in serving your lord"—the blacksmith's son cast a swift glance at his father, obviously displeased with the offer—"as well as the satisfaction of knowing your services render aid to our men fighting in the Brikbones. I will send a man to collect the cart at week's end."

"Week's end?" Gregory's voice was deep and tinged with astonishment, "My lord, this load will take some time to complete, and there are yet others waiting for their own orders to be finished."

"The other orders can wait." Frederick's tone took on a note of steel, "Finish the work by week's end or the blame for our next loss against the Mizgalians will be laid at your door. Rest assured, if word gets out that Gregory the blacksmith refused to promote our border wars, no Arcrean of good account would condescend to visit your shop."

Elaina saw the blacksmith's eyes narrow and his son's jaw clenched in anger. The other villagers had come close enough to hear and now stood in silence, waiting to hear Gregory's answer.

The blacksmith released a long breath and offered a curt nod, "We'll do all we can to complete the task before the given time, my lord."

Frederick leaned over until he towered above the blacksmith, "See that you do all that you can and more. I will settle for all or nothing, and should it be nothing you will regret the day you first struck iron to anvil."

Gregory took a steadying breath and spoke to his son as he returned Lord Frederick's gaze, "Come Druet, we've work to do."

The village seemed to release a collective sigh as the two smiths moved toward the wagon left standing by their shop. Lord Frederick turned his horse's head to return home.

Elaina pressed her heels to her pony's flanks and fell into place behind her father. She cast a glance over her shoulder and watched as several villagers approached Gregory and his son, offering their assistance in unloading the cart. Elaina faced forward again. She was glad her father had threatened the blacksmith. How dare the man suggest that the order of his superior was not attainable? It was that man's job to see that he *made* it attainable.

Elaina tossed her plaited hair over her shoulder and tilted her nose higher as she rode past a girl her own age. The other girl was filthy, ragged, and dressed with poor taste. Elaina would be ashamed to step outside her chambers in such a state, let alone out-of-doors. The commoners always complained and blamed their harsh conditions on the taxes, which her father introduced for the betterment of the land. They didn't have the money, they said. Elaina would suggest they work harder to earn more.

When they had reached the castle and dismounted in the courtyard Elaina turned to watch as the portcullis was lowered and the massive gate swung back into its cradle, shutting out the rest of the world from her haven of safety within. Elaina turned toward the Great Hall, where her mother would be waiting for a report on her improved riding skills. She smiled to herself.

Peasants. What a pitiful lot of shamefully necessary people.

What a relief that she was not one of them.

23

Attack from the Skies

Roland rose from his chair in the west turret and extinguished the candles. Retrieving a sealed parchment from the table before him, he pinched the document in his fingers and left the room. At the bottom of the circular staircase he met the guard's stoic gaze and acknowledged the man's salute, and then turned to face the courier at post. He extended the sealed document for the young man to tuck away in his doublet.

"Ride tonight and see that this is delivered with all haste."

A firm salute and the courier was gone. Roland turned as Sir Kenrick approached from the other direction.

The knight saluted, his fist still bearing the golden coin-shaped seal of his order, "Lord Bradley is in the Great Hall as you requested, my lord."

"Very good, Kenrick."

The chief Mordecai nodded, "With your permission, sir, I must return to the garrison now and attend a conference with Sir Valden."

Roland waved a hand of dismissal and turned away. Traveling through the torch-lit corridors of his palatial home, the lord of Hebbros saw naught of his surroundings. His thoughts pulled his focus inward.

Entering the Great Hall, Roland's gaze was instantly grabbed by the young man sitting before the hearth. Nearby, the castle chamberlain strolled the length of several tables overseeing the cleaning work of a handful of slaves. With a sharp snap of his fingers and a jerk of his head, Roland sent them all scurrying from the room. A moment later, when the muffled thudding of closed doors had grown quiet, he moved slowly across the rush-covered floor. Like a hawk watched a mouse before diving from the sky for the kill, he studied the hall's one other occupant.

The hall was deeply shadowed. Outside, the light of day was giving way to the darker shades of evening, and only a few candles and the fire on the hearth had been lit for the benefit of the slaves.

Before the fire, Bradley sat casually with one leg propped over the arm of his chair and arms crossed loosely over his chest. His eyes, locked on the dancing flames, held none of the usual humor, rebellion, or indifference, and he seemed oblivious to the fact that he had been left alone with Roland. His demeanor was one of brooding reflection.

Roland's jaw grew stiff as he came to stand so that his face was masked by shadows while Bradley's was illuminated by the fire's blaze. Bradley's pensive expression disappeared the instant he blinked and looked up to find Roland standing over him. Roland was instantly aware of the audacity building within the younger man's bearing.

"You sent for me, dear brother? Time for my monthly lecture, or have you finally discovered what I've been telling little Jerem?"

Roland froze, caught off guard, "What have you said to my son?"

Bradley laughed, "Nothing. Lord Jerem is a model worshipper of your…outstanding character. I simply wanted to see your face when I suggested something of the kind." His eyes swept the room behind Roland, "No entourage today? I take it, then, that you haven't come to arrest me?"

Roland folded his arms across his broad chest, "Then you are aware that you have done wrong?"

"Of course! By my father's favorite scowl, I've done so many things worthy of arrest I'm amazed my sorry hide hasn't been carted away a dozen times over."

Roland's fists clenched until the ring on one finger cut into his palm, "Do not toy with me, Bradley."

"I'm not toying." Bradley swung his lower leg up to cross over the other's raised ankle, "Everyone does something wrong at one time or another, some more than others. For instance, haven't you ordered the arrests, deaths, and banishment of many innocent people?"

Roland surged forward and tipped Bradley's chair so the younger man had to drop his feet to the floor for balance. With one hand planted on the chair-back beside Bradley's head and the other clutching the hilt of his sword, the hawk stared down at his mouse with a glare that said he would soon make his dive from the sky.

"Those people have all been rebels, not innocents," spittle flew from Roland's mouth and Bradley forced himself not to flinch. "Rebels against me, rebels against Hebbros, and rebels against the very fibers of Mizgalia and the king himself. They deserve punishment and they receive punishment. And now it has come to my attention that you are consorting with these very rebels. Perhaps you are one of them yourself."

Bradley made a show of slowly removing Roland's hand and lowering the chair legs back to the floor. Rising from his seat he met Roland's fiery gaze, now accentuated by the orange light from the hearth.

"I haven't the slightest idea what you're talking about." He turned to go but Roland grabbed the front of his doublet and whirled him around again. Bradley's arm quickly shot up, knocking the other man's grip away, and he fought to keep his voice calm, "Do not touch me again, Roland."

Roland ignored him, pointing a condemning finger in his face, "You know very well what I am speaking of. Did you think I would not carry through with my threat to that boy, that I would not have him followed to ensure that my orders concerning him were carried out? You deliberately went out last night, the very day of his sentence before the House of Peers, and sought to keep company with the boy, Luke."

"Oh come, Roland, I didn't seek him out."

"But you befriended him."

"I merely saved a Mizgalian boy from the torment of others."

"A torment he deserved."

Roland's tone of steel gave Bradley a moment of pause. He took one step back toward the hearth, "You would say that of a child?

"It is because of his age that he was not given a harsher sentence."

"He was—"

"Do not change the subject!" Roland's words echoed against the rafters high overhead, "You were seen last night aiding that boy and then accompanying him to a less-than-savory part of the city, carrying on in conversation all the while. Every one of your actions was in direct opposition to my orders concerning the rebel."

Bradley emitted half-a-laugh and moved to lean one shoulder against the stones beside the large hearth. Crossing one ankle over the other, he shrugged, "I've heard you accuse me of nothing more than being neighborly."

Roland's eyes narrowed, "Were you aware of his identity?"

For a moment the only sound was the crackling fire.

Bradley worked his jaw back and forth and finally tilted his head up with a careless, "I was."

A snakelike smile appeared briefly on Roland's face and Bradley's insides tightened with sudden apprehension. His brother-in-law had been hoping for that reply. He had expected it.

The hawk took the dive and started in for the kill.

"You understand, don't you, that you must be punished for defying my orders?" Roland slowly turned and sat in the chair vacated by Bradley. The younger man's gut twisted into a tighter knot, though he kept his worry concealed behind the familiar mask of indifference. He remained silent.

Talons extended, the hawk fell closer to clutching his prey.

"I am sending you back to Villenfeld, where you will be forced to remain on the premises of the castle until further notice."

Bradley's jaw dropped in spite of himself. He was going home? And so soon after Luke had begun to pray to his God! Never mind Roland's directive to remain on the castle grounds. He would be more than satisfied to stay at home, and would eventually find a way to evade his brother-in-law's interference altogether. His thoughts paused momentarily over the thought that he would be leaving poor Sarah behind, but immediately he resolved to find a way to keep his promise to her in spite of the distance.

Trying to hide a smirk, Bradley dipped his head in the semblance of a bow and leaned away from the hearth. His easy stride carried him across the space lit by the fire's glow, "Send a page to tell me when I should be ready to depart."

"Day after tomorrow." Roland studied the far wall. The hawk's talons closed in a death-grip over the mouse, "We must ensure you reach Villenfeld in time for your wedding."

Bradley froze. His mouth opened and then closed, but no words would come. This was not what he had asked for. This was not what Luke had promised.

Roland filled the silence with further explanation, smiling to himself over Bradley's shock, "I learned from Rosalynn that you have been pledged since birth to the Lady Agatha of Burdney Hall."

Bradley finally spoke, his tongue thick and his words heavy, "I never agreed to such a pledge."

"Infants rarely do." Roland rose and faced Bradley, who stood at the edge of the firelight with his back to the ruler, "The Lord of Burdney is a great power in Northern Mizgalia. A worthy connection to make and an enviable ally."

Bradley slowly turned to face Roland, "He broke off the arrangement when my father died and Villenfeld fell into disrepair," a hint of his smirk resurfaced, "and I was glad to see the end of it."

Roland's face was like stone, "I have been in correspondence with his lordship, and have corrected the error. The Lord of Burdney has agreed to give you the hand of his daughter, Lady Agatha, in two weeks' time…"

"Two weeks!?"

"And I have agreed to his terms. You and your bride will live and stay at Villenfeld, which I will continue to repair, and I will grant you a reasonable yearly sum to see to the more domestic matters required on a daily basis. The castle and its immediate grounds will be returned to your name. However, all other vassals and assets left by your father will remain in mine, as they were the dowry of my own wife."

Bradley's head had begun to shake, and as Roland finished speaking he shouted, "The Lady Agatha cannot yet have fourteen years to her name!"

"She is exactly fourteen. Girls marry quite young these days," Roland's grin bespoke his pleasure at finally being the one to rile his brother-in-law.

Bradley's upper lip curled in disgust, "And what did his

lordship promise *you* through this agreement?"

Roland answered with cold silence.

Bradley spoke again, in clipped tones, "I do not want to marry Lady Agatha. The marriage would be nothing more than the alliance of two power-hungry lords—neither one of them being me! The only reason you want this marriage to take place is to expand your own holdings in Mizgalia." Bradley drew himself up to his full height, which was still shorter than Roland, "I will not allow you to choose my bride."

"I already have." Roland's face looked carved from granite, "The courier has been dispatched with a full agreement to Lord Burdney's terms and conditions."

Bradley's gaze darted towards the front entrance and then returned to Roland's face. There would be no sense in trying to stop the courier. Roland would have ensured the man was beyond reach by the time Bradley heard of it.

"Whatever is the matter, dear brother? Where is that charming wit that has served you until now?" Roland chuckled, and then his expression darkened, "I told you I would not let you make a fool of me. I warned you to take better care of your actions. I told you to grant me respect."

I hate you. The words stuck in Bradley's throat, but spewed freely through his angry gaze. Trembling with wrath, he pivoted on his heel and strode from the Great Hall.

Sarah looked both ways and then led little Jerem into the corridor. She should not feel guilty, as she had not been denied permission to be here, but their secret forays out to the kitchens had not been sanctioned either. She shifted Celia in her arms and checked to be sure the baby had not lost her warm sweet roll. Jerem smiled up at her and slipped his small hand into hers.

"Finish your roll, m'lord, before we get t' your rooms." She smiled and Jerem nodded as he tucked a bite into his mouth.

They still had quite a distance to go. The entrance used by the slaves to travel between the palace kitchens and the Great Hall was on the opposite side of the structure from the noble family's quarters. Only Lord Bradley's chambers were in this portion of the castle, as far from his annoyed brother-in-law as possible while still offering him a place to stay.

As they passed by the Great Hall the doors suddenly burst open and Bradley himself exploded into the corridor from within. Sarah jumped back and Jerem choked on his bite of sweet roll, while Celia started and then laughed when she spotted her uncle. Sarah gently clapped Jerem on the back to dislodge the bit of food. She cast a curious look at Bradley, "M'lord?"

Without even a glance in their direction Lord Bradley stormed off in the direction of his personal quarters, footsteps pounding a path of rage until the distant sound of a door slamming echoed back to them through the halls and stairwells.

Eyes wide, Sarah turned to continue toward the children's chambers. She stopped again when a fierce roar, like the cry of an injured animal, reverberated through the castle. Catching her breath, Sarah glanced over her shoulder to where Bradley had disappeared from sight. His anguished cry filled her ears until she winced and Lord Jerem did the same. Lady Celia whimpered and laid her head on Sarah's shoulder, bringing the slave back to the present need and starting her feet forward again.

But her thoughts drifted back. Never had she seen Lord Bradley so angry. Livid. What had happened to make him relinquish his easygoing demeanor and lose control of his temper?

The doors to the Great Hall opened again and Sarah looked back to see Lord Roland emerge. She stopped to offer a curtsy as he approached them, looking very satisfied and pleasant.

He rested a hand on Jerem's blond head, "And where is your small party off to?"

Sarah waited to speak, giving Jerem a chance to answer. When it became apparent he was either still shaken by the sight of his infuriated uncle or utterly absorbed in his sweet roll, Sarah quietly answered, "I'm taking them up t' put them t' bed, m'lord." A sense of honesty forced her to add, "We've just been t' the kitchens for a treat."

Celia silently held forth her sweet roll to illustrate the word *treat* for her father. Lord Roland laughed and caressed his daughter's face, "Very well. I will not keep you from such important business, and with such a fine treat in hand." And with that he strode away in the direction of the west turret.

Sarah watched him go and then turned once again toward their destination. She swallowed against a feeling of uncertainty, ill at ease to learn that for once it was Lord Bradley who had been angered by his brother-in-law, and that that same brother was indifferent to the matter.

Suddenly, an unearthly shriek—certainly not Lord Bradley—sounded from somewhere beyond the castle walls. A shiver of fear raced up Sarah's spine and she tightened her hold on Jerem's hand, pulling him away from the mysterious sounds and toward the safety of their chambers as quickly as his little legs would allow.

"Hurry, Jerem. Run!"

Bradley slammed open the door to his personal chambers, prepared to slam it shut again when he spotted two slaves preparing his fire and bedding for the night. "Leave me!" His growl sent them scurrying out as quickly as possible before he satisfied his need to slam the oak panel back against its frame.

Standing in the silence that followed, Bradley's face crumpled and a roar of sheer pain and anger drained from somewhere deep inside of him. For the past few years he had managed to control his temper in front of others. He had built a fortress of bitterness around his heart and maintained its security by mastering the art of indifference. He had met anger with charm and battled sarcasm with wit. But tonight his fortress had been compromised and his arsenal of apathy had retreated from the fight, leaving him vulnerable.

Bradley grit his teeth and crossed to the small table beside his bed, where a sword rested in its sheath. Slapping his hand over the weapon, Bradley tore the sheath away and tossed it behind him. He stood for a moment staring at the polished blade. His words to Rosalynn and Roland drifted through his memory. *I know enough of the sword to make me dangerous when one is in my possession.*

Perhaps he had been a bit modest.

Turning, he lifted his eyes to the curtains that hung around his bed. More boundaries. His life under Roland's thumb was unlimited in its boundaries and restrictions. With a growl of unleashed wrath, Bradley swung his sword and fell to the attack.

Luke had promised to ask his God to grant what Bradley truly wanted. In answer, Bradley had received a command to return to Villenfeld for an *un*wanted bride.

Pieces of the heavy curtains dropped to the floor in bits and chunks.

Where was his restored inheritance? Where was the return of his father?

In minutes what was left of the curtains hung from the bed frame in ragged strips. Bradley was breathing heavily, oblivious or uncaring of the tears that wet his face. He eyed the damage before him with approval and then his gaze landed on a tapestry hanging by the far window. Rosalynn had selected the piece from a local merchant back home.

Rosalynn. His sister had told Roland about Lady Agatha.

Traitor.

Spinning the hilt of his sword in the palm of his hand, Bradley stepped around the bed and crossed to stand before the large decorative hanging. He studied the embroidered picture of a country estate and then lifted his sword to pass judgment on the piece.

Suddenly the image of Luke's face swam before his mind's eye. *Not that you will get what you want, but that you will understand what it is you are truly seeking for, and that God will provide it in such a way that you can no longer deny His existence.*

Bradley heaved an audible sigh of frustration. He hung his head and lowered his sword. He didn't understand, he couldn't understand. Why would a divine being show concern for his awareness of their existence? Didn't the priests teach that the gods were merely concerned with those who already believed in them? Anyone else was of no importance as long as the deities received adoration from a few. And they certainly did not care for the events that took place in any particular mortal's life. Did they?

An unearthly shriek suddenly rent the night air.

Bradley's head shot up and he turned to the view beyond the window. Eyes wide as a shiver of fear raced up his spine, he moved to lean on the sill and peer out over the shadowy city of Hebbros. He adjusted his grip on the sword's hilt and waited.

The entire city seemed to be holding its breath with him.

A shadow floated in and out of sight, hovering over the city. It was quickly joined by another and another, weaving through the spires and towers of Hebbros like children playing a game of chase.

Bradley shoved away from the window and raced out of his chambers. Dashing down a corridor and up a stairwell, the young lord rushed outside to join the lookout on the castle's eastern tower. The two men stood and stared in shock at the massive shadows flitting about with effortless ease over the safe haven of their city. Giant bodies were kept afloat by leathery wings, and long necks dipped for a more thorough search of the streets below. Bradley swallowed a lump of apprehension, knowing they searched for food.

As they watched, one of the beasts came to rest on a stone tower belonging to the Peers' meeting hall, a short distance from the castle. Stones crumbled beneath its clumsy landing. Stretching its neck toward the street below and snorting a fine white powder that Bradley could see even from this distance, the creature let out another shriek. The eerie sound crawled through the city and up the tower wall, lending a tremor to the lookout's voice as he spoke the terrible truth that neither wished to acknowledge.

"Dragons."

24
Shadow & Light

Obvious, Elbert! That creature nearly landed on my head! I could see that it was a dragon, you didn't have to tell me." Ned ducked into a narrow alley and Elbert slipped in behind him. The two leaned against the sandstone wall of a two-story structure and panted for breath, "The question is," Ned swallowed, "what are said dragons doing here in Hebbros? I thought they nested in the cliffs of western Arcrea."

"Obviously…not," Elbert gave his friend a wry grin.

Ned rolled his eyes and wiped his sleeve across his face. The sun had set and daylight was fast fading. There should have been children scampering through the streets, relishing the cooler air and shadows after a day of oppressive heat. There should have been peddlers rolling their carts away for the night, and little girls hawking flowers or bits of string.

But the streets were empty.

The city was quiet.

Hebbros was holding its breath, and had been since the first shriek of the dragons.

Ned cast a glance at his companion. Two years younger than he, Elbert was in his first year of apprenticeship while Ned was in his third. The younger boy possessed a broad face that culminated in a square jaw, framing a mouth that was always set in a grim line. His black hair fell in half-curls to his eyebrows, except for the portion that was fond of reaching further to cover his right eye. The boy was always dressed in the same neat garments, an off-white tunic with a black vest and trousers.

The numerous raids of the Mordecai Knights and the following banishments had affected each of the suffering children in a different way. Some had grown timid, others more daring. Elbert had been thrown into an initial state of shock, and as far as Ned could tell, had never fully recovered from it. He thrived best in conditions of peace and handled stressful situations by focusing on the simple basics. The obvious. The boy was sharp as any tack and very observant. Unlike Luke, whose observations seemed like a natural reflex, Elbert's were results of a finely honed skill, worked for and studied.

Ned was absolutely certain that he would one day be driven to lunacy by the agonizing clarity of Elbert's words. Nevertheless, much as he thought an older brother might feel, Ned couldn't imagine life without young Elbert's reminders that the sun was shining, the breeze blowing, the day stifling…or that dragons were flying overhead.

"Are you all right, Elbert?" Ned whispered into the eerie stillness of the alley.

Elbert nodded and shifted his gaze to the slit of sky visible overhead.

The two boys had been kneeling in the street, cleaning up the spilt contents of Ned's toolbox after a large scowl-faced man had rudely knocked him down in passing. The shriek of dragons in the sky had frozen the street in a brief picture of shock, and then pandemonium had broken loose in the city. In the span of mere seconds men, women, and children had vanished behind doors and through windows. Every entrance had been closed and locked, and the eerie silence had begun its reign. Ned and Elbert had found it impossible to rise from the street in the bedlam, and had nearly been crushed in the press. Covering their heads until the thunder of retreat had died away, the boys had then looked up to find themselves alone and with no shelter left unbarred.

They had tried to force the latch on several doors when suddenly a shadow had blocked the light of dusk and Ned had looked up to see a dragon eyeing him from above. All thoughts of shelter had vanished, replaced by the pressing need to survive, and the two boys had bolted further down the street and out of sight.

Now Elbert chuckled, the sound rusty from little use and rising from deep in his chest, "Ned, you scream like a little girl."

Now that was most definitely *not* obvious.

"I do not!" Ned drew back, affronted, "In fact, I considered my natural yelp to be quite masculine." He shook his head, "What a couple of yellow-bellied chickens we are. We should have stayed and fought them off, the ugly monsters."

Elbert cast him an incredulous glance, "With what? Your shoe?"

Ned looked down to where he still clutched the toolbox in his arms, "There's a hammer somewhere in here. I might have thrown that in his face."

Elbert grunted, "And like a dog with a stick, he would have spat it right back at you."

Ned cocked his jaw in aggravation, "Let's move on."

"We have nowhere safe to move to."

"Obvious, Elbert. The entire city is a maze of peril at the moment, but we're in just as much danger here as we would be anywhere else." Ned strode to one end of the alley to peer up and down the street. Suddenly, he stiffened, "Elbert, look."

Elbert stepped quietly along the wall until he was standing beside his friend. His eyes scanned the street, seeing nothing, and then lifted to follow Ned's gaze upward. His jaw went slack with shock, "There's a fire."

"Obvious, Elbert. There's a massive orange glow atop Mount Desterrar. But what kind of fire?"

"Fire is fire, Ned."

"That's not what I meant, and you know it. Look at it. It's stationary, not moving or spreading. It's being contained by something."

"Or by some*one*." Elbert added, eyes still locked on the strange light at the top of the mountain, "Dragons are afraid of fire. Many people use it to keep them away."

The two boys turned to look at one another as a possibility sprouted in both of their minds.

"You don't suppose…?"

Elbert nodded, "They're still alive."

"Some of them, at least." Ned studied Desterrar's peak with a look of wonder. The part of his soul that had thought he was alone in the world suddenly warmed with the beginnings of hope. Was his mother still alive?

The light of day had finally faded, amplifying the impressive glow against the darkened western sky. A number of dragons still hovered over the shadows of Hebbros, instilling fear in the hearts of the Mizgalian people. The terror had abated, however, in the hearts of the two young boys who stood gazing at the beacon of hope, beckoning from a wilderness of exile.

Ned took a deep breath as the twin shrieks of several dragons echoed from various parts of the city. Elbert blew that thatch of hair from his eye and turned with a silent query in his gaze. Ned's face stretched to return Elbert's rare grin and he felt their friendship solidify. A silent pact was made. From this point on they were brothers. They were comrades. They were fugitives.

Hebbros could no longer be their home as long as their true people lived elsewhere.

Elbert thrust his hand into the space between them and Ned grasped the proffered arm by the wrist, clapping Elbert on the shoulder with his other palm. Elbert's blue eyes studied the older boy's face, seeking simplicity in the sudden tension, and he tilted his head in the general direction of their masters' homes.

"We're not going back."

"Obvious, Elbert." Ned's grin broadened, "We need to find Luke."

Luke raced around the corner and was brought up short when he collided with a cart sitting abandoned in the street. Grunting, he shoved away and moved to the closest door. No one answered the pounding of his fists and he moved further down the street, trying every shop and receiving the same response, or rather the lack thereof.

"Help me, please! Let me in." Luke set his fists to another door, aware that whatever noise he made in the silent streets of Hebbros would be heard by the vicious horde of dragons that eyed the city from above. His gaze roved the front of the shop and landed on the door latch. He had been apprenticed to a locksmith…once. Perhaps he could force the latch to comply.

Before he could put one his many sets of limited skills to the test, Luke was surprised and relieved to hear the latch click on a door across the street. The door opened just a sliver and a man's eye appeared in the gap.

"Please," Luke bolted across the way and all but hugged the door in his attempt to gain entrance, "I need refuge, sir. Just a corner of your shop to sit in while I wait the monsters out. Please let me in, I won't be any trouble."

The eye bounced from Luke's panicked face to the red collar and back again, and Luke knew he would be denied.

"No trouble you say? You've been trouble since the day of your birth, boy. I can't let you in, on account I'll suffer the wrath of every power in Hebbros if I do."

"Please!"

"Be gone with you, lad. Everyone knows you're fond of a fight, so go fight the beasts off and earn yourself some good favor for a change."

The eye disappeared and the door slammed shut. Luke turned his back to it and sank to the stoop. He fingered his bowstring and eyed the darkened sky, straining to hear any sign that might indicate the current position of the dragons. Guy had said his skill with the bow merely lacked practice. Luke had not counted on that practice being against a skyful of hungry beasts five times his size. Alone. He wasn't ready for such a feat, and he knew it. Even his usual tendency toward recklessness had fled.

A massive shadow, outlined by the starry sky beyond, flew by overhead and emitted a satisfied shriek. Another dragon echoed the sound from across the city.

Luke had to find shelter.

Vaulting from the stoop, Luke took off in the direction opposite the dragons—at least the two he had heard. Losing himself in the twists and turns of Hebbros's streets, he paid little heed to where he was going. His thoughts cried out in anxious prayers to his heavenly Father.

Where should I go? What should I do?

Luke flew up a set of stone steps, skipping every other one, and raced through a small square. He thought he might be heading west and glanced up to check his position by Mount Desterrar. He froze, nearly tripping over his faltering steps. With his eyes riveted to the looming shadow of the mountain, Luke stood in the middle of a narrow street and gaped at the sight above him.

A light! The peak of Mount Desterrar was aglow with the light of a fire! From this angle Luke could not see the fire itself or the cause of it, but the unmistakable hue of a giant flame cut a sphere through the darkness and warmed the small clouds that hovered comfortably around Desterrar's heights. Luke stared at the light, taking note of the fact that none of the dragons were venturing anywhere near the obvious sign of life.

"Dragons are afraid of fire," Luke murmured to himself in the empty street. "The fire was started on purpose to keep them away, which means…"

They were alive. Guy had been correct and Luke's parents were alive! Luke couldn't explain why he was so certain that his father and mother were among those taking shelter in the warmth of that flame, nevertheless he was confident in the assumption.

And that meant the time had indeed come to plan an escape from Hebbros. It would not be the war that he had been hoping for, and yet the thought of supervising an exodus from this restricting city did hold an element of danger. Perhaps it would be more of a battle than he had thought; a battle of wits, evading the watch of the Mordecais.

Luke turned in a slow circle. He was still in need of immediate shelter, and if no one would let him into their homes then he would have to find refuge elsewhere. Luke's eyes lifted to the rooftops and then darted to the flame on Mount Desterrar. He grinned. Getting closer to the dragons might be considered foolish, but if he could copy down here the plan that was obviously effective up there, then sitting on a roof could be the safest option he had. But first he needed something with which to start a fire.

A noise startled him and Luke spun around, afraid he had missed the approach of a dragon. Voices seeped from a nearby side street, sounding strange in the former stillness. Luke's brow furrowed and he quietly trotted to the corner and prepared to peer around it. And then one of the voices grew louder and Luke froze with recognition.

"Warin, every time one of those monsters shrieks it scares me halfway to the grave."

"Shut up, Wulf." Warin's voice was quieter, and Luke strained to hear, "It's because of the dragons we're able to put our plan into action so soon. If we ever want to be free from him, then tonight's the night. The scare from the dragons will create a cover for us. Stop being such a yellow-livered ignispat and let's get this done with."

Luke heard Wulf mutter as the evil twins moved several steps closer to his end of the street. He prepared to dart out of sight should they appear, but the twins stopped short of the corner and remained within the close confines of the lane. Luke dared a quick peek to see that they had stopped halfway down a line of sagging doors, and were now flanking one threshold in particular. He remembered they had once lived in the western portion of the city. Had this been their home?

With a glance at his brother, Warin lifted a hand and delivered a knock to the sorry looking doorframe. Wulf cast a furtive glance up and down the street and Luke backed out of sight. Regardless of the deep shadows, Luke thought it highly possible that the twins were accustomed to seeing in the dark. They were rarely up to any good, and favored darkness over light any day.

I shouldn't be here. The thought passed through Luke's mind an instant before Warin spoke again.

"M*aaah*-nty," the name was dragged out in a soft taunt. Wulf chuckled and the sound crept around the corner to where Luke stood, gripping his lungs in a sudden state of dread.

Something was not right here.

Another knock and Warin's voice sounded louder, "Monty, let us in. We've been caught without shelter and need a place to hide until the dragons have gone."

The plea sounded so similar to the one Luke had offered half-an-hour before, and yet somehow something didn't ring true. Wulf and Warin were squires; they had been dressed as such when Luke had last seen them at the tavern. Sir Fraser at the palace garrison would have granted his men admittance had they asked for it.

Luke told his feet to move, to walk away, but his legs refused to budge. His lungs felt tight, constricted by the atmosphere of tension that radiated from the side street.

A gruff voice suddenly joined Wulf and Warin's pleas for help, sounding muffled through the closed door, "Get back t' the garrison, ye nitwits, 'fore they cut yer pay and toss ye t' the streets."

"The dragons have been circling that part of the city, Monty. Let us in."

"Ask yer friends at the taverns for 'elp."

"We can't be sure we'd make it back there. We'll pay you for the shelter."

There was a moment of silence and Luke risked another peek around the corner. The evil twins stared at one another as they waited for a response to their offer of compensation. Luke's brow furrowed. They were too calm for boys seeking refuge from hungry beasts.

A dragon's shriek sounded somewhere to the south, quickly joined by the cries of others. They had found food. Luke shivered at the thought and turned his attention back to the matter at hand.

The sagging door opened a fraction, revealing a face permanently marked by a scowl. The face shifted in the darkness, peering at one twin and then the other. Finally the man opened the door a little wider and stuck out a beefy hand, palm up.

"Pay up first, both of ye, and then ye'll get yer shelter," greed colored the man's words and spurred his actions.

Luke felt the tension escalate as the twins glanced at one another and Warin gave a fraction of a nod. Each of the identical youths reached about his person and Wulf quickly produced a small pouch that clinked with the weight of coins. Were they truly seeking a place to stay? Luke's gaze shifted to follow Warin's movements and his eyes widened with realization when he saw the youth's hand close on the hilt of a dagger tucked into the back of his belt.

Luke tried to say something, to stop the twins from murdering this man, but his throat would not cooperate any more than his legs would. A thought struck him and he lifted the bow from his shoulder.

The door opened further. Monty's arm shot out and his fingers closed over the pouch that dangled like bait from Wulf's fingers. He turned to face Warin, "Yer turn. Pay up."

Luke's slender fingers drew the bowstring taut.

Warin freed the dagger from his belt, "Here's your payment you old fool, and long overdo."

Luke's arrow zipped across the short space and dug into the mortar over Monty's doorframe. Warin and Wulf started at the sight of the shaft and then whirled in his direction, catching sight of his shadowy figure in an instant.

"*Luke!*" Wulf's enraged growl echoed through the streets.

Monty caught sight of Warin's blade. The scowl of his face

deepened and he launched himself from the doorway.

Luke quickly turned and bolted from the scene. He did not know who that man was or how he had come to be associated with the evil twins, but Luke had no desire to make either introduction or inquiry. This was not his fight, and for once he no longer wished to make it so. Breathing heavily, the young fugitive continued to put distance between himself and his enemies, not daring to pause and look back.

Wulf drew his dagger to match Warin and the twins backed away, remaining side-by-side as they suddenly found themselves facing a beast more intimidating than any number of dragons.

Monty's chuckle rattled in his throat, "Did ye think ye could catch me by surprise?" He stalked toward them, a dagger of his own held loosely in his hand, "Did ye think ye could best me?"

Warin's voice sounded venomous in the dark street, "We would have if that brat hadn't stopped us. Rest assured, we'll take care of him when we're done with you."

Monty laughed, "Ye think ye'll be able t' take me now that I know?"

"We should have come for you sooner, you lowly dog."

Monty sneered, "After all I done for ye."

"After all you've done *to* us, you mean." Wulf drew a second dagger from his belt and locked eyes with the man before them, "I hate you."

Monty leaned forward to scoff, "And I hate the very sight o' yer scarred hide, so that puts us at even odds."

With a flash of movement that seemed to contradict his bulky frame, Monty suddenly lashed out with one arm. The twins jerked away from the path of his dagger and in the same instant were knocked off balance by a blow aimed at the legs. Wulf toppled into Warin and the two slammed against a wall on the opposite side of the street.

"Agh!" Warin slid to the ground and cradled his head with both hands. The familiar feeling of defeat pulled at the edges of his mind. He and Wulf had never won a fight against Monty. He looked up to see the brute looming closer and he cringed, waiting for another blow. If only his head would stop throbbing, he could get to his feet. Wulf sank to the ground beside him.

"Ye fools!" Monty raged, "Ye stupid, brainless, spineless, weaklings! I'll teach ye to—"

An arm suddenly caught Monty from behind, jerking him backwards and forcing him down to the cobbled street. Grunts of pain and exertion sounded, and the struggle had scarcely begun before it ended with the flash of a dagger.

Wulf and Warin sat in shock. Monty was dead.

In the silence, their rescuer rose and turned to face the twins. Warin's eyes widened and he scrambled to his feet despite the pain thundering in his head. Wulf did likewise, staring at the black-clad man before them.

"Sir Valden?"

The knight stepped closer, his gravelly voice grating on the stillness around them and cutting directly to the point, "You have waited long for this freedom, have you not?" He nodded toward Monty's motionless form.

Wulf nodded, still surprised by the sudden turn of events, "You have no idea."

"Oh," Valden grunted, "I think I do."

Slowly, Warin replaced his dagger to his belt, "We are in your debt, sir. How can we ever thank you?"

Valden was ready with an answer, "You can offer me your allegiance."

"Sir?"

"I have many matters that require my careful attention in this city, and so I cannot always pursue the issues that I would most desire. I will speak with Sir Kenrick tomorrow, and he will gain your documents of transfer to the Mordecai Order. You will serve me personally and no else, is that clear?"

Wulf and Warin both offered quick nods of agreement. This man had just ended their years of bondage to a cruel man. They would deny him nothing.

"What do you want us to do first?" Wulf asked.

Sir Valden turned to glance at the traitorous arrow stuck in the wall over Monty's door, "I want you to bring me the rebel boy, Luke."

Warin exchanged a glance with his twin and a slow smile spread across his face at the prospect of revenge, "With pleasure."

25
Seeds of Dissention

Sir Valden walked a pace behind Sir Kenrick as their steps led them to the Peers' meetinghouse. To any observing eye it would appear the first knight of the Mordecai Order was seeing to the safety of his chief on the streets. In reality, Valden was busy planting the first seeds of a seditious movement.

"You must convince them before his lordship arrives," the knight's voice rasped in a low undertone, propelling Kenrick up the steps of the hall and through the corridors. "Suggest to the House that last night's raid might have been prevented had Lord Roland paid closer heed to the warnings and sightings laid before him by the Peers themselves."

Sir Kenrick paused and turned to scrutinize the other man's face, "How do you know of those warnings?"

Sir Valden answered without pause, "Everything spoken of within the walls of this place eventually leaks out into the streets. Talk is heard everywhere, and it is a part of my occupation to seek out which rumors have a solid foundation."

Sir Kenrick studied him a moment longer and then turned to continue down the corridor. Sir Valden fell in step behind him, wishing he had the same ability that the boy Luke possessed. It had not taken him long to understand what Luke meant when he had said that he "knew it on his own." Valden had been further convinced of his suspicion when the boy had later glanced around the hall and offered an accurate description of the Peers' many faults.

The boy possessed a keen ability of perception.

Very keen.

Valden glanced at Kenrick. What thoughts and fears were running through the other man's head? Did he wonder—correctly, but that was beside the point—if Valden had been spying on the Peers and Lord Roland, thereby gaining knowledge of the early warnings of dragon sightings? Was he afraid that Roland had favored Valden by offering the information voluntarily? Valden smirked. If he could have Luke accompany him under the guise of a personal slave, then discerning these things would be much easier.

Valden chafed at the knowledge that only two days before, Luke had been imprisoned at the Mordecai garrison awaiting his sentence. Valden might have taken charge of him then. Now it would be more difficult.

He had lost track of Luke the night before, during the city's mad dash to escape the dragons. When he had come upon the scene between Monty and the twins, and witnessed Luke's interference, he had realized the advantage of gaining two assistants to do personal work for him. Consequentially, he had stepped in to put an end to matters in the dark lane. Now, while Valden tended to issues on a broader scale, Wulf and Warin would track down the little rebel. When it became necessary, Valden would create a convincing story as proof that Luke should be entrusted to his care.

They came to the circular hall's doors and Valden spoke again, "I'm honored that you saw fit to grant my request for the two assistants. I'm sure they will do well in furthering the Order's service by serving me."

"Of course," Kenrick offered a slight nod of his curly head. "Your work in Hebbros has been admirable. Anyone would see fit to reward your loyalty."

Valden's head lifted in acknowledgement of the praise even as he wondered if Kenrick was seeking to threaten him with a reminder of where his duty rested.

Sir Kenrick went on in a low tone, "I see the wisdom of your suggestion. I will seek to gain the Peers' favor by pointing out

Roland's failure to protect the city against an attack such as we had last night. Lives were lost because of his oversight."

Sir Valden offered a smart salute and lied, "You have my allegiance and support, sir."

Kenrick nodded and Valden followed him into the hall. The gathered Peers were a sight similar to a flock of flustered chickens. With a knowing glance Valden parted from Kenrick and weaved through the crowded room like a snake, seeking out the most vulnerable of the prey.

He spotted Sir Monotun and grinned. The man was dull, longwinded, and apt to cling to the smallest of details. Just what Valden needed. Moving to stand behind Monotun as the bearded bore added his opinion to the rest of the room's din, Valden waited until Kenrick had gained most of the Peers' attention and then spoke quietly over the man's shoulder.

"As a personal friend of his lordship's, Sir Kenrick has great insight into Roland's affairs."

Valden moved on to his next target and spoke in the ear of another half-distracted Peer, "Sir Kenrick has great skill as a leader. See how well he has handled the rule of the Mordecai Order."

The next man tilted his head to hear Valden's words better, "Do you not wonder if our own Sir Kenrick might make a better leader for our city than Roland, who was chosen *for* us, and not *by* us? Does not the king trust our judgment in deciding on a ruler?"

The Mordecai knight retreated to the farthest corner of the room as tension and opinions alike escalated in the vaulted chamber. Sir Valden watched and listened as several Peers praised Kenrick for his care of the city and noted aloud that Roland should be threatened with a replacement. Kenrick wisely quieted those thoughts for the time being and went on to suggest the erection of fire towers throughout Hebbros, to keep the dragons from attacking again.

The Peers exchanged looks of pleasure.

Sir Valden leaned away from the wall and slipped out into the corridor just as Lord Roland arrived at the meetinghouse. Valden offered the ruler a salute and then affected a shrewd look as he glanced back at the doors he had just exited.

"You'd best hurry, my lord, Sir Kenrick is already there."

The distracted nobleman cast him a swift glance, as if trying to determine the meaning of Valden's words, but the knight was already turning away. Surging ahead, Roland entered the hall to take his seat as numerous scowls were aimed his way. The council was begun with a shuffling of feet and a mass occupying of the rounded formation of chairs.

Sir Valden left the Peers' hall with a satisfied smile. Seeds had been planted today. Thoughts would be considered. Actions would be taken. Valden would see to it that Sir Kenrick was promoted in the thoughts of every man who mattered, and one day Kenrick would be considered for lordship over the city of Hebbros. In the thrill of promotion and the wave of popularity, Kenrick would believe that his time had come. He would not consider that Valden had been pressing another scheme in the shadows.

Kenrick would present ideas to the Peers, but the ideas would really be Valden's.

Kenrick would preach wisdom to the House, but the wisdom would really be Valden's.

Kenrick would forge a path for the city, but the leading steps would really be Valden's.

Kenrick would strive for the seat of lord, but the seat would really be Valden's.

Valden made his way back to the Mordecai garrison, his sharp eyes studying the crowds on the street. The power of Hebbros, the second largest city in the kingdom of Mizgalia, would one day be his. A former peasant from the village of Lork, he would rise to make his mark in the realm. He had guessed that this was also Kenrick's aim, but Kenrick was not crafty enough. Kenrick was afraid of his superiors when he should have feared his subordinates. Valden was afraid of no one.

But Valden needed to know more. He needed to be sure that Sir Kenrick did not become aware of his deception. He needed to know if any of his own men planned to double-cross him. He needed to know when he had struck the right amount of fear into someone's heart, making them more useful to his cause. He needed to know when someone needed to quietly disappear, as Monty had. He needed the ability to accurately discern a man's character.

He needed Luke.

Valden climbed a circular stairway to his chamber in one of the garrison towers and drew his sword from its sheath to examine the blade.

Valden was by far a man with little religious conviction.

Nevertheless, he might call it a gift from the gods that he had discovered a boy who possessed the very talents he was in need of and more. Rebel or no, the collared boy would be of great use to him as he sought to overthrow the powers of Hebbros, both existing and potential.

Luke had already admitted his fear of Valden's brutality, and so Valden would know how to enforce Luke's submission and cooperation. Only a few nights before, a band of fifteen Faithful had perished at Valden's hands. He was not afraid to threaten this young rebel.

Luke would serve him, and when Valden was satisfied with as much power as he could gain, Luke would disappear just as many others had vanished before. Luke's death would be necessary. As much as Valden knew he could forever find use for Luke's remarkable gift, he also knew that if ever there was someone to fear it would be the young rebel. Dissension and mutiny would always be possibilities so long as Luke was in Valden's service. The boy's uncanny perception, coupled with his fierce loyalty to justice and a dogged willingness to fight for morality, had the potential to be funneled into an unstoppable force.

In his ascension, the vital key to Valden's greatness would be to ensure that Luke never discovered the true potential of his own power.

Satisfied with the fitness of his blade, Valden returned the sword to its sheath with a snap. He folded his arms across his chest and leaned against the room's small table, thinking of the identical squires who would be arriving soon from the garrison to enter his service. He would need to learn how to tell them apart without looking for Wulf's scar. Voices, speech patterns, and mannerisms would all need to be studied.

"They had best come prepared for a challenge," the knight interrupted his own silence, "for that is precisely what I have in store."

26

All in a Day's Work

Thirteen-year-old Pavia heard the rattling of a latch and immediately she stiffened. Turning from where she knelt scrubbing the floor, the redheaded girl watched as one of the locked doors was shoved against its moorings from the inside. As the action was repeated again and again, Pavia could see that the weakened iron fastener was ready to give way. The beast would soon escape for the second time this week.

Pavia's green eyes darted around the simple stone structure, known simply as "The Row." The doors would be locked, just as they always were. The front entrance was only opened to admit or release one of the workers after a recognized signal had been given and acknowledged from the outside. The only windows were four slits, three inches high and two feet wide, at the top of the wall. The loft above the door would provide no shelter from the current danger.

Pavia shifted to study the numerous cages that lined the walls to the left and right of a central walkway. It looked much like a stable, only the box-shaped stalls climbed the walls in four rows and contained creatures far less desirable than a horse.

The latch clattered again. This one refused to be held.

Pavia's cleaning brush struck the wall with a bang as she

tossed it and raced for the door. She pounded the signal with one fist and waited for some sign that the guard had heard her.

"What's amiss?" The man's voice was muffled through the thick wooden panel.

"Let me out! Catawyld Five is trying to get loose again."

"Sorry, lass," he didn't sound apologetic in the least, only bored. "I'm not allowed to unlock The Row when there's possible danger."

The last few words took on a note of antagonism, and Pavia knew he was refusing her plea on purpose. The rat! She pounded both fists against the door to release some of her fury, "If I die in here you'll still have to open the door to catch Five again!"

No reply. Pavia whirled and put her back to the door. Her eyes fell on the cage with the loose latch.

The Number Five crate was on the left side of the center walkway, where newborn catawyld beasts were kept until the day they were ready to "cross the aisle." Her eyes moved to the right side of the walkway where the cages of mature catawylds were moved into place before a network of doors in the outer wall. When a cage was opened from inside The Row, the corresponding door could be opened from outside the structure, releasing a specific creature into a covered arena for one-on-one combat against a knight. Sir Fraser used this exercise, adopted from the king's garrison at Mockmor, to further train his most skillful knights. So far not one of the liberated catawylds had returned to its cage alive, and the conquered beasts had been replaced by those lately grown to maturity.

The clattering became more insistent as Catawyld Five worked the latch out of place. The other beasts hissed and growled at the commotion, clicking their tongues in warning and confusion. Pavia shivered at the sound. Even as newborns, the catawylds of the Hebbros garrison were kept apart, one to a cage. Between their natural vicious natures and the starving conditions that kept them ready for a fight, it would be disastrous to pen them together.

Pavia's heart pounded to the erratic beat of the yielding latch and the clicking tongues of a few dozen beasts. Her eyes shifted to land on a sword, hanging on pegs in the wall for this purpose. She had not been given any formal training during this first year of her apprenticeship at The Row, but perhaps desperation would lend her a fair amount of skill.

She could only hope…and pray.

Desperately.

Shoving away from the door and the help that would not come, Pavia quickly raced to the wall and grasped the hilt of the sword. The metal latch gave way to the incessant beating and fell to the floor with a clang of iron against stone. Pavia clutched the sword to herself and watched as Five leapt from its crate and dropped two layers to the floor.

The catawyld was young, not yet fully-grown to the usual dog-sized build. However, its large feet, webbed between the toes, seemed to have reached a mature size. Its head could only be described as pointed, with a sharp-looking snout and large ears that could have heard a mouse running across the floor of the faraway kitchens. A tail similar to that of a cat's whipped the air as Catawyld Five studied its surroundings and bared its double set of dirk-teeth.

Pavia swallowed at the sight of those fangs and Five whipped its head around to stare at her.

In another instant Five had crossed the center aisle and climbed the right-side crates, much to the aggravation of the beasts inside. Standing on top of the wall of cages, the escaped catawyld moved to the end looming over Pavia and clacked its tongue in a warning of its impending attack.

Keeping her eyes glued to the creature above, Pavia slid along the wall and then the door in an attempt to put some distance between them.

"No need to be chummy," she murmured.

Five responded with another baring of its teeth.

Chummy indeed.

Pavia swallowed again, working up her courage and waiting for the pounce. Had this beast been born in the wild, it would have attacked on sight.

"You know I've practically raised you?" Pavia glared at Five, "I know its not much of a life, but if you stop and think, you'll see I'm in the same condition. I get locked in this building every day to clean every corner, feed you a pittance, and see to the pack's breeding. Do you think I'm looking forward to spending the rest of my life with you and your descendants? Well, I'm not!"

Five gave a wrathful shriek and crouched on top of the crates. Pavia heard a male voice on the other side of the door, in conversation with the guard. After a moment both voices grew in volume. Pavia snapped her attention back to Five. She couldn't let herself get distracted. It could be the difference between life and death.

"I don't know how Mame got you back in your crate the last time you escaped," she spoke of another woman who worked on The Row, "but I don't intend to show mercy if you won't cooperate." Five suddenly became motionless, highlighting the voices outside. "I intend to live through this ordeal," Pavia whispered across the room and then directed a plea heavenward, "God, help me."

The young catawyld pounced from the top right-side crates to the floor along the left wall, making the leap look effortless. Timing herself to react when the beast landed, Pavia swung her sword from side-to-side and succeeded in sending Five in momentary retreat.

"*God, help me please!*" The words escaped Pavia's lips again, only this time as a terrified shriek.

Over the past four years she had not ceased to believe in the God introduced to her by her parents, but she had gradually fallen away from the habit of prayer. She had continued to believe that one day she and the others would make a stand or be delivered from injustice, and yet she had slowly come to accept her fate as an unwanted child of the Faithful movement. A movement that had become all but nonexistent thanks to the Mordecai Order.

Again and again, Five pounced and Pavia swung her sword in defense. The girl's arms quickly grew weary beneath the weapon's weight and she sought another avenue of retaliation. Her gaze fell briefly on the feed barrel at the other end of the aisle and an idea struck her in all of its uncertainty.

Watching Five for any signs of another attack, Pavia moved along the rows of crates to the barrel. Prying the lid away with one hand, she reached inside and grabbed a handful of the smelly contents. Five clicked its tongue as it eyed the treat hungrily, and Pavia threw the meat over the beast's head. The meat landed in a heap halfway up the aisle and Five yielded to the hunger in its belly and dove after it.

Immediately, Pavia dropped her sword and scrambled up to the catawyld's deserted cage. Crawling inside, she gripped the handle and pulled the cage door shut just as Five leapt after her with a shriek. Pavia echoed the scream as she held the door shut and listened to the perturbed beasts in the crates that surrounded her. She tried to take a deep breath, but the pungent air choked her and threatened to make her gag.

Clicking its tongue in an angry cadence, Five clawed at the cage door and the loosened panel threatened to give way. Pavia clung to the handle, putting all her strength to maintaining the closure of the door.

"God, save me!"

A loud thud suddenly echoed over the bedlam and the catawylds fell silent. Pavia swallowed a sob as she waited breathlessly for a sign of what had made the noise. Had another crate fallen and a second catawyld escaped? Oddly, the noise had sounded more like a door slamming than a crate falling, but that couldn't be.

With a hiss, Catawyld Five deserted Pavia's cage. The young girl could hear the beast moving across the floor, over crates, and along the walls toward the front of The Row. What had captured its attention?

Several minutes of uncertainty followed. The catawylds resumed their shrieking and tongue clicking, and Pavia backed further into the filthy crate. She listened as Five chased a new object of prey around The Row and the hunted responded with grunts that sounded distinctly human. The whisper and thump of Five's padded steps were followed by the metallic sound of a sword slicing through the air. Finally there came a pounce that was followed by a catawyld's shriek, and then the drive of a blade was accompanied by silence.

Every beast on The Row went instinctively quiet.

Pavia placed a hand over her racing heart and waited. She could hear the steady tempo of someone's heavy breathing as they moved closer, and then suddenly the hapless door of crate number five was thrown open to reveal a face that Pavia had seen only twice before.

"Christopher!" Pavia sagged with relief at the sight of someone she could trust. She had not seen this boy since the day Sir Kenrick had brought her to begin her apprenticeship on the palace grounds, and then only in passing. Nevertheless, she had seen and heard enough of his character to understand that his was a friendship worth relying on.

Hazel eyes studied her for signs of injury as Christopher

helped her down from the elevated cage, "You all right?"

Pavia glanced up the aisle and spotted the lifeless form of the terrible Five, and then nodded in answer to Christopher's query. She brushed straw and worse from the skirt of her brown dress and then straightened. At a height of five feet, the top of her head barely reached Christopher's shoulder, but she had come to expect no different. Her mother had been a small woman, and Pavia knew that she favored the wonderful diminutive spitfire in every other way. Why should her lack of impressive stature be any different?

Craning her neck to look Christopher in the eye, Pavia gave an awkward nod, "Thank you. I don't know how you talked the guard into letting you in, but it was an answer to my prayers that you arrived when you did."

One corner of his mouth lifted in a grin and he led her toward the door. Pavia turned her face away from the grotesque sight of Christopher's victory as they passed by the motionless catawyld. The other beasts were beginning to click their tongues over the smell of a fresh kill.

Pavia quickened her pace to keep up with Christopher as they neared the door, "I don't remember seeing you in the arena before. When did Sir Fraser make you fight a catawyld?"

"This was my first one," he answered casually. "I've watched others do it, though, so I learned the different patterns and techniques and practiced them on my own." Christopher wiped his sword clean and returned it to its sheath. He gripped the handle on the door and glanced over his shoulder, "The guard didn't let me in."

Pavia met his gaze with a question in her own. He sounded as if he were preparing her for something. Christopher opened the door for them to slip outside and Pavia froze at the sight before her.

A crowd of thirty or more squires stood in a semicircle around The Row's entrance, each with his mouth hanging open in shock. Pavia had a strong desire to snap each jaw shut with a strong pop beneath the chin. Off to one side, the guard sat with his back to the wall and his hands and feet bound. An unhappy scowl marred his face, and upon seeing Christopher emerge from the building he instantly sent up a furious cry.

"Untie me at once, you mongrel! How dare the rest of you stand there idly watching? I will inform Sir Fraser before the day is through!"

Christopher calmly moved to the guard's side and crouched low, "And I will tell him that you shirked your duty by leaving a young girl to the jaws of a catawyld when you might have released her before it escaped. The least you could have done was let me in to do your work without having to tie you up first."

The guard spat in Christopher's face and Pavia's fingers itched to wipe it off when Christopher did not. Her stomach churned at the thought of all the blood, spittle, and refuse she had seen within the last five minutes alone. On a normal day she might have handled it well, but apparently her limits had shifted when her life was on the line.

The guard was speaking again. "My duty is to see that that door stays locked on all accounts when danger is imminent, and danger was apparently imminent. Sir Fraser will see the wisdom of my choice and have you expelled from his garrison."

"I will do nothing of the kind," Sir Fraser's voice rose from the back of the crowd and the squires saluted as they parted to make way for him. Christopher untied the guard and stood, finally wiping the side of his face on the shoulder of his light armor. Sir Fraser glanced from the guard to Christopher to Pavia, and then back to the youth in the middle. "Am I mistaken, or did you enter The Row to save this girl from death at the risk of…everything?"

Christopher nodded once, "I did, sir."

The guard sputtered, "I told him I'm under orders to keep it locked, sir, but he overpowered me and…"

Sir Fraser quirked a brow and the man fell silent. The garrison's captain looked again at Christopher, "You succeeded, I presume, for I can smell the aftereffects."

"I did, sir."

Sir Fraser gave an amused grin, "Did you not think that the beast may escape The Row entirely and reek havoc in the garrison?"

"I did, sir. That's why I waited only a moment to listen and ensure that the beast was not near the door when I entered. But I couldn't stay out. It would be dishonorable to throw away even one life, especially a woman's, when the chance of success is just as great or greater then the chance of failure."

Sir Fraser regarded his favorite squire in silence for a moment, and then lifted a curious brow, "Where did you learn such a concept?"

Pavia felt dwarfed beside Christopher when his rigid posture grew straighter, "My mother, sir."

A cautious look passed through Sir Fraser's eyes. He blinked and turned away to face the group of squires, "Three of you will enter The Row to remove the dead beast. The rest of you will return to your training immediately." He glanced back at Christopher, "You have earned some respite. Take the remainder of the day to rest."

"Thank you, sir." Christopher watched as the crowd dispersed and then sidestepped out of the way as the guard moved to open the door for the three squires who had remained behind. The man muttered and cursed at the turn of events, and Christopher glanced down to see Pavia's reaction to the crude language. She was watching Sir Fraser's retreat across the yard.

"He didn't even offer you a 'well done' when he heard that you defeated your first catawyld. He must know it's your first. Doesn't he care?"

Christopher shrugged, "Will they make you return to your work today?"

She wrinkled her nose as she glanced through the door at the fight's leavings, "I suppose I should first report the broken crate to the man at the stables. Perhaps he'll make one of the others clean up what's left when he knows what I've been through."

She didn't sound very hopeful. Christopher turned and fell in step beside her. He had never earned himself a day free of work, and wasn't quite certain how he ought to go about resting as Sir Fraser had suggested. What did one in his position do for leisure? Sit in a chair? Read? Stare at the sky? Eat? How very tedious and uninspiring. Stepping into the stables, they were greeted by the wonderful aroma of horses and fresh straw. Perhaps Christopher could lounge in the loft all day.

The peace of the moment was shattered when a voice suddenly called from a nearby stall.

"Pavia, my pocket-sized pet! How does the day treat you? And Chris. How unfortunate to see you. I was hoping to leave the garrison without having to see your face again."

Christopher bristled at the sight of Warin leaning against the corner post of a horse's stall. Further down the aisle, Wulf glanced in their direction and leapt over the half-door of another booth. He remained at a distance however, watching as Warin took command of the scene. Christopher longed to offer a quick-witted reply, but he kept his tongue in check and remained silent.

Pavia had no such qualms.

"Don't call me that, you oaf, and be kind to him. He just rescued me from death by catawyld and deserves a little praise from someone."

Warin snorted, "Well it certainly won't be from me." He opened the stall to lead the horse out into the aisle, "Wulf and I have had a promotion. We're off to the Mordecai garrison to be accepted into the Order as personal assistants to Sir Valden himself—something that Chris failed at during his recent attempts as the man's squire." He flashed a charming grin at the little redheaded girl, "Say you'll miss me, pet."

Pavia frowned in disgust, "I'd rather be back in that box, hunted by a catawyld than tell such an outright lie." She marched off to locate the stable master, calling over her shoulder, "Good riddance!"

Warin laughed and Christopher turned to climb the ladder to the loft. He turned back when Wulf called out to him, pausing on his way out the door with a horse of his own in tow.

"So long, O Silent One. Remember us once in a while," his grin made Christopher's gut twist with apprehension, "and think of us when you hear about your brother."

"What do you mean?" Christopher was off the ladder's bottom rung in an instant, standing with his face an inch from Wulf's. Warin suddenly swept his brother out the door with a muttered command to close his mouth before Warin closed it for him. Christopher watched them go, praying silently for Luke's safety and feeling helpless. He had been able to rescue Pavia from a terrible death, but he would be useless here at the garrison if something were to happen to his brother.

Standing in the stable's large doorway, Christopher lifted his gaze to the peak of Mount Desterrar. He had seen the light during the dragons' raid. He had wondered about its source and knew that the time had come for the children of the Faithful to take action. To leave. To escape.

"Where are you, Luke?" The question hung unanswered in the shadow of the stable door. Christopher blinked. Why should he wait for his twin to come and find him? Perhaps he should go and find his twin.

"That man is a dirty thief and a rotten scoundrel." Pavia approached behind him, "He's going to take the repair funds from my pay, and he's also sending me back to clean up the…mess."

Christopher's gaze was still locked on Desterrar's peak, "I have a better idea."

Oblivious to his preoccupation, Pavia crossed her arms and slouched against the doorframe, "Well I have a thousand ideas that are better than his, but not one of them can be accomplished without me getting whipped for disregarding an order."

The longer Christopher stood in thought, the more he warmed to his plan. He had never been the impulsive one in his family, Luke had always been the one to act in a rash and reckless manner. However, the urge to forge ahead to something new and better burned unmistakable and insistent in his heart, especially with Warin and Wulf now on the loose. Today would be perfect, as he was expected to be out of sight, resting, for the entire day!

Christopher spoke suddenly, interrupting Pavia's running monologue about the infuriating stable master, "We need to leave. We're going to find Luke."

Pavia stared at him for a moment, as if trying to comprehend what he had said and why it was more important than what she had been saying. She blinked, "What?"

Before Christopher could respond, another voice called out and a young girl of fifteen or so appeared in the doorway. She wore the collar of a slave though her garments were fine, evidence that she served within the palace walls.

Pavia leaned away from the threshold to greet the girl, and Christopher was reminded of her gentle care of Lillian after the raid. Pavia was accustomed to serving ladies.

"What's wrong, Sarah? You're trembling," Pavia took the girl's hands in her own. "Where are Lord Jerem and Lady Celia?"

Lord Roland's children. This must be their nurse.

Sarah swallowed, "I haven't time t' explain. Pavia, I'm about t' do something very foolish and I need your help."

27
A Cap, a Door, & an Apple

"I'm going to run away." Lord Bradley spoke matter-of-factly as he shifted his hat and peered at his reflection in the mercer's clouded looking glass, "That's all there is to it. I simply must uproot myself from the cushioned life in Roland's palace and remove myself to another more private existence."

The mercer tried to apply a feather to the cap but Bradley waved him away.

"No no, my good man. No feathers. I beseech you, no feathers! Do you have anything simpler? A tunic of dirt-brown perhaps? Come, come, I must blend into my new choice of society so well that one would question whether I was a part of the pavement itself. Really, sir, I do not think you are taking my plight seriously."

"Forgive me, my lord." Liam the mercer eyed Bradley with confusion as he returned a robe of bright green to a chest by the window, "I did not think that a noble *th*uch a*th* your*th*elf would truly throw away a life of ea*th*e."

Bradley pressed his lips together in concentration as he struggled to keep up with the merchant's lisping dialogue.

"Yes…well! You supposed wrong, good mercer. If anyone asks—Hand me that plain cap there, will you?—you may tell them that Lord Bradley ran away, and with good reason. No, I don't like this cap, hand me the other one. Though I think it highly unlikely anyone will think to ask you about my whereabouts, sir. No offense intended. Perhaps I'll migrate south and join the army of an Arcrean lord. Ha! Let's see Roland convince my unwanted bride to join me there!"

Liam's large eyes popped with further confusion as Bradley's words sped to a stop, "You are married, *th*ir?"

"No, of course not." Bradley tilted the peasant cap low over one eye and grinned at the mirrored likeness, "Rather roguish, don't you think? No, I am not married, but I've been pledged since birth to the Lady Agatha of somesuch hall or other. It's the thing to do in the nobility, you know. Hand me those shoes, would you mercer? Imagine! Being pawned off and traded like a piglet on market day. Not very flattering for either party involved, eh? Perhaps I should complete the charade by oinking and squealing the vows on my wedding day. Don't you think that would bring a heartwarming effect to the ceremony?"

Liam helped Bradley into the requested shoes and then stood back while the nobleman rifled through more wares. The mercer scratched uncertainly at his bald crown, "To be hone*th*t, my lord, I do not think that your bride would appreciate *th*uch a *th*ene."

Bradley spoke reassuringly from the depths of an overflowing chest as he tossed unwanted merchandise hither and yon, "Oh, nonsense! Have you never met the Lady Agatha!? She'll be grunting and squealing right along with me." He smiled to himself as he emerged from the chest with several articles in hand and his cap hanging haphazardly from his head, "I say, our vows will be quite singular. You know, I'm really warming to the idea!"

Liam heaved a slight sigh of forbearance as he helped Bradley don the chosen garments. The young lord grinned to himself and speculated on what his sister's reaction would have been to see him dressed as a commoner, "She would undoubtedly spit at me for lack of a better rebuke. I'm surprised you have such a good stock of peasants' attire, mercer. Your shop seems to cater more to the upper classes."

"Ca*th*toff*th*."

"What?"

"Ca*th*toff*th*."

"Oh, of course. Castoffs. Naturally." Bradley withdrew a

handful of coins he had taken from Roland's chambers and held them out to Liam. When the mercer did not accept them, Bradley looked to find the little dwarf of a man studying him with an intense look in his enormous eyes. Bradley's gaze bounced from proffered money to mercer several times before he asked, "Is it not enough? Do I owe you more?"

Something in the mercer's expression told Bradley the man had not even noticed the coins. When Liam spoke, the young lord's suspicion proved to be true.

"My lord, i*th* it truly an arranged marriage you are running from?" His eyes narrowed a bit as he continued to study the youth, "Or do you e*th*cape a life without purpo*th*e?"

Heart pounding, Bradley retreated a step. It was one thing to have his physical appearance mirrored before his eyes. It was another matter entirely to be presented with a reflection of his heart. His conversation with Luke had been the same way.

"Excuse me, mercer. I'm late for an appointment." Bradley grabbed Liam's hand and dumped the coins into the mercer's palm. He sidestepped for to the door, but was stopped when Liam touched his sleeve. The mercer cast a furtive glance around the shop and out the window, and then leaned closer to Bradley.

"The door ha*th* not yet been clo*th*ed."

Bradley's glance flitted to the door, "Clothed?"

"Clo*th*ed."

"Ah, yes…closed. The door has not yet been closed." Bradley glanced again at the dark panel, his gaze one of utter confusion, "Good sir, the door is most certainly shut."

Liam smirked, "Not that door."

Bradley was unsure whether he should be exasperated or amused, "Which door are you speaking of?"

Liam turned and began cleaning up the merchandise that Bradley had littered across his shop, "There i*th* only one, and if you *th*eek for it you will find it."

Bradley was decided. He should be exasperated. However, all he felt was a deep curiosity that was growing by the minute, "And where should I seek for this door?"

Another customer entered the shop and Bradley pulled the ragged cap over his red-brown hair to avoid recognition. The newcomer glanced about, a tall man with a mane of white hair that stood on end all over. Liam graciously lisped that he would see to the man's needs momentarily, and then turned to walk Bradley to the door. In a quiet voice, but loud enough not to sound suspicious, the little mercer sent the young lord off with the answer to his last question.

"Apparently, you will find it by *th*eeking where you would not look before."

In another moment Liam had turned and disappeared inside his shop, greeting the customer in a warm tone. Bradley was left standing on the front stoop, wondering over the little man's words until he remembered he would be late for his next appointment. The young lord started up the street, trying to mimic the undignified manner of walking that he had observed in the lower classes.

A hot breeze floated lazily through the streets, stirring the hem of Bradley's shabby tunic. He glanced down at the rough garments he wore and grinned when he thought of his destination. Thought up and planned that very morning, his next move would be the very essence of irony; and preoccupied as he was for the time being, Roland would never see it coming.

Luke ducked and dodged around a corner just as an apple flew past his ear and splattered against the opposite wall. Breathing heavily, Luke leaned with his quiver against the stones behind him and fingered his leather collar. The costermonger in the square continued to shout demeaning threats after the young fugitive who had dared to ask for a pail of decayed goods. The merchant was going to toss them in the streets unless some swineherd offered to purchase them for a penny. Nevertheless, Luke's request for something to fill his belly had not been received well.

The boy's slate-blue gaze dropped and he eyed the fruit so recently used as a weapon, rotten to the core and lying in a soft mess at the base of the wall. His stomach growled, threatening to go after the food on its own, and Luke sunk to his knees and quickly crawled the short distance to scoop the apple into his palm. Juice dripped between his fingers and he quickly licked at the droplets to moisten his tongue and throat.

Cradling his lumpy puddle of breakfast, Luke scurried from one alley to another until he was a safe distance from the square with its angry fruit-seller. Leaning against another wall and alert to movement from either direction, he lifted the soft apple to his face and devoured the fruit in two bites and a slurp. Luke gave a sigh of satisfaction and then grimaced when the too-sweet mouthful landed in his belly as a souring mass.

Wiping his sleeve across his mouth, Luke turned to leave the temporary hiding place. He came to a halt when two boys suddenly blocked his path of escape. Luke's hand went instinctively to the bowstring across his chest, but he paused before drawing the weapon. The three stood staring at one another for a moment before one of the newcomers broke the silence between them.

"We found him."

The other inhaled deeply as his eyes rolled heavenward, "Obvious, Elbert. Tens of thousands in Hebbros and all we had to do was follow the trail of people who were shouting after the 'collared rebel.' We knew it was only a matter of time before we caught up to him."

Elbert brushed a thatch of black hair from his right eye and grinned at Luke as he nodded in Ned's direction, "He's in a bad mood."

Luke copied the other boy's grin, "Still?"

Ned cleared his throat, "I'm standing right here, no need to talk as if I weren't." He glanced up and down the crowded thoroughfare behind him, "Let's find someplace sheltered. No offense, Luke, but if we're caught talking to you in the open, we'll be thoroughly flogged and sent back to our masters."

"Have you run away, then?" Luke waited for their answering nods and then motioned with one hand, "I know the perfect place."

Walking on either side of their collared friend, Ned and Elbert shielded Luke from the eyes of the pressing crowd as Luke pointed which direction they should go. Heading east, they wove their way through a maze of shadowed steps and sandstone archways. Merchants hawking their wares sang to the people in hopes of gaining a sale, while little girls sold bits of cloth and shiny rocks to the more compassionate passersby.

Ned watched as one child managed to earn two pennies for a pebble with a bird painted on it. He shook his head, "Those sad-faced little thieves could sell a man the cap off his own head."

Luke nodded and then pointed to a narrow space between

two buildings, "There."

They entered the space in single file and Luke led the others to the back of the alley, where a stone stairway led up the rear-facing wall of the building to their right. At the top of the steps Luke checked to ensure the roof was deserted, and then motioned for his friends to join him. Elbert produced a potato from a pocket hidden in his garments and used a dagger to divide it three ways. Luke devoured his portion and then lowered himself to sit with his legs crossed and his bow placed on the roof beside him. The three sat huddled together, keeping their voices low in spite of the unlikelihood of discovery.

"I found this spot last night." Luke cast about a furtive glance, "It appears no one's been up here for some time."

"And I doubt they'll be anxious to come up here now with the threat of dragons," Ned added, and then nodded toward Mount Desterrar, "But apparently higher up is the safest place to be, as long as one has a fire going."

Luke's eyes brightened, "You saw the light too? I copied the idea, using that clay bowl over there as the base for a makeshift torch."

"That was smart," Elbert eyed the bowl and its smoldering contents.

Ned leaned in with an intense whisper, "We'll use this spot as our hideout until the time comes for our escape. Now tell us what to do, Luke."

He and Elbert both watched Luke's face, waiting for him to speak. Luke studied their expectant gazes and knew that they had come prepared to take action. They too had seen the evidence of life on the mountain and felt that the time had come to act. Excitement sparked in the air around them and coursed through Luke's veins. Unable to keep a passive expression, his face broke into a smile.

"I've spoken with Guy, my father's former assistant at the cooperage."

"Will he help us?"

"No." A flicker of emotion passed through Luke's eyes, "He's given me knowledge of the bow, but beyond that he refuses to risk his comfortable life for the dangers of the Faithful."

Ned's face was a mask of disbelief, "That's what our faith is—dangerous! What did he expect, if not scorn, when he accepted

Christ and joined the Faithful?"

Luke shook his head and held up a hand, "Whatever his reasons or fears, he is the one who first suggested to me that our parents are still alive and making a life on Desterrar. He thinks we ought to escape the city while we still can and join them. Children can conceal themselves in more places than a grown man can."

Ned studied the floor of the roof in concentration, "They can also fit through smaller spaces. My mother once spoke of a hole somewhere in the western wall. It sounded as if the Faithful used it to pass supplies through to Sedgwick."

"In secret."

"Obvious, Elbert," Ned spoke the familiar phrase, but without the usual note of sarcasm. He glanced from one lad to the other, "Just as those before us were bold in their faith while secret in their work, we must ensure that our escape remains hidden from the knowledge of our enemies. The moment they learn of our plans, we'll be hunted down and carted back to our masters, or worse."

"Which means we need to get out soon," Elbert's finger tapped an impatient rhythm on his knee, as though he wanted to quit the city that very moment. "It won't be long before they realize we're not coming back."

"Our plans will surely be suspected," Luke spoke solemnly. "We must prepare to be persecuted as our parents were. Our hope will be to escape the city, but there is no guarantee that we'll succeed. Lord Roland has ordered that I am to be followed while I wear this collar, and it's only because of the dragons that the Mordecais' watch has been interrupted. As Elbert said, we won't be able to hide the fact that the reestablished children will suddenly leave their apprenticeships and band together for an exodus."

"We can keep apart, smaller bands in various parts of the city," Ned's eyes sparked with inspiration. "As our leader, you can assign captains to lead groups of five to ten children. Each captain will be responsible for finding and retrieving certain members from their new homes, and then maintaining order over their group until you send word to move."

Luke nodded as he listened, trying to ignore the irritation that surfaced with the idea of sharing the command with others. He wanted to see this work through to success, and in order to do so he would keep all matters concerning the escape in his own hands.

Suddenly a thought struck him, and Luke looked up with an expression that was nearly startled, "How many children are there, anyway?"

Ned opened his mouth to reply and then snapped it shut with uncertainty.

Elbert scratched his head, "There were twenty-eight of us in that small room after the first raid, but…"

His words tapered off and Ned finished the thought, "But there have been other raids since."

"Other children," Luke murmured. He fingered the red collar and one side of his mouth lifted in a small smile.

"What are you thinking, Luke?"

"After dark tonight everyone will lock themselves indoors, afraid of another attack. We'll use the night hours to further our plans." Reluctantly admitting to himself that he would have to let the other boys do something, he glanced from one to the other, "You two will try to find some of the others, including Christopher as one of the first, and return here by dawn. Build a low shelter that won't be seen from the street below and keep out of sight."

"Where will you be?" Ned asked.

Luke's grin broadened, "I'm going to pay a visit to Sir Kenrick."

28

Lord Roland's Day

Disastrous. It was the only word he could use to describe the events of the day. Well, he supposed he could also use the word *infuriating*. Or unbelievable, or maddening, or confusing, or progressively worse and increasingly dangerous! He was about to lose every vestige of control.

"Oh Roland, what will I do?"

Roland cursed and shoved away from the hearth to glare at his wife. They were standing before the fire in the Great Hall, and Rosalynn had approached to be near him. She swallowed a sob and bit her lower lip, straining to keep her tears in check. Roland knew that none of this could possibly be her fault, and yet no one else was close enough to bear the brunt of his fury. And she had been the one to bring him the latest addition to his troubles.

"What will *you* do?" His voice rose in pitch to a near shout and Rosalynn shrank away from him as he stalked toward her, "What am *I* going to do, Rosalynn? Do you have any idea how many problems I've been presented with today? How many people have brought their troubles for me to make right? And you ask me what *you're* to do?"

Rosalynn's legs bumped into one of the high-backed chairs and she promptly sank onto the cushioned seat and gave in to a wave of tears.

"You don't…understand!" Her words were separated by gasps and sobs, "I need her! I…trusted her, and I need…need her now more than ever." Rosalynn lifted a gaze of agony to his, "I'm going to have another child."

Roland's eyes slid shut. Disastrous.

The night before, dragons had attacked his unsuspecting city, and as a result fourteen citizens had lost their lives. The morning had begun with a layer of oppressive heat that had grown heavier by midday. His son had decided to cry when Roland told Jerem he could not accompany his father to the meetinghouse. Rosalynn had been sick. Roland had been detained by a thousand petty matters and had arrived late to meet with the House of Peers, only to be unsettled by Sir Valden's words at the door. The Peers had been in an abominable frame of mind, unhappy with everything he had said and even daring to hint that he should be replaced. After only one crisis in Hebbros!

Roland had returned to the castle to find that the nervous cook had burnt the main course. He had quickly retreated to his study in the west turret only to have his sanctum invaded for the very first time since his rule in Hebbros had begun.

Rosalynn had somehow managed to climb the stairs while the guard had tried to drag her back down. She had fallen into Roland's arms weeping, and only when he had led her back down and seated her in a chair in the Great Hall had he managed to learn that the hysterics had been caused by the disappearance of the children's nurse. Roland had known his wife was deeply unsettled when she actually referred to the slave by name.

"Sarah has disappeared and no one knows where she has gone! She asked another slave to see to the children while they slept a while this afternoon, and she never came back!"

With sudden suspicion, Roland had immediately turned to address one of his guards, "Find Lord Bradley and bring him to me at once."

Rosalynn's eyes had widened, but she had remained silent.

Until a moment before.

Another child.

He did not wish to seem callous. He loved his wife and two children, but weren't two enough? He had a son to claim his title, and a daughter to marry off to some wealthy nobleman. What would he do with more? Second sons became possible threats to the heir, always dissatisfied with their own inheritance. Additional daughters grew up like a flock of emotional geese, squawking and fluttering about until an advantageous marriage had been arranged and they were sent away. At least Celia was a docile child, not given to the unsettling habits of nervous fowl.

The guard finally returned and saluted as he bowed before Roland, "Lord Bradley was not in his chambers, my lord, but as I was returning here he was being brought in through the outer gate."

"Outer gate?" Rosalynn stood to her feet, "Where has he been?"

The soldier kept his attention on Roland, "The slave, Sarah, was also being brought in."

"What!?" Rosalynn gave a confused squeak.

Roland motioned for his wife to make no further comment. He nodded to a soldier by the door, "Have Lord Bradley brought in. Keep the slave nearby."

The door opened and four soldiers ushered in a youth that looked like Bradley. Roland stared. Rosalynn made a slight cry that sounded like a mewling cat and dropped back into her seat. The young man lifted his chin and there was no mistaking his indifferent manner. It was Bradley. Covered in dirt and other filth, sporting a black eye, and wearing the course garb of a peasant, but it was Bradley all the same.

What on earth had his brother-in-law been up to? Roland had a sinking feeling he knew.

Disastrous.

Rosalynn interrupted before Roland could get straight to the point, "Bradley, where have you been?"

"Out." The imp had the nerve to cock a grin.

Rosalynn frowned and stood to her feet again, "Where on earth did you get those rags?"

"They are called clothes, dear sister, and I bought them from a lovely little shop with the help of Roland's money—you know, circulating funds and all that."

Roland grit his teeth, but refrained from commenting on the stolen coins. Instead he lifted his chin and spoke with a strange calm, daring Bradley to oppose him with a full confession.

"Bradley, you will have your belongings packed before the day is out. You leave tomorrow for Villenfeld."

The spark of triumph that Roland had been fearing suddenly sparked in Bradley's indigo eyes. The young man tilted his head, looking for all the world like a common rogue beneath the angle of his dirty cap. He met Roland's gaze steadily, and the ruler knew he had been trounced.

"You can't send me back to Villenfeld for a bride, Roland."

Roland's jaw grew stiff and he ground out the single word, "Why?"

"I'm already married."

Rosalynn returned to her chair in a faint and several female attendants quickly sprang forward to revive her. Whispers quickly circulated through the hall. Glances of astonishment were exchanged. Roland continued to glare at Bradley, and the youth returned his stare.

Roland snapped at a guard, "Bring the slave in."

Rosalynn regained consciousness just as Sarah was led into the hall. The kitten's whine that escaped Roland's wife at the sight of her favorite slave quickly became the equivalent of a catawyld's scream as the girl was brought closer. When Sarah was brought to a halt before them, Rosalynn jumped from her chair and delivered a hard slap to the slave's face.

"Don't do that!" Bradley lurched forward, straining against the soldiers' hold on his arms.

"*How could you!?*" Rosalynn screamed over a cowering Sarah and then dissolved into another batch of tears. Retreating behind Roland she paced before the hearth, wringing her hands and moaning pathetically.

Roland continued to stare at Bradley, unable to comprehend the young man's desire to thwart him at every turn, and enraged at his ability to do so.

Four of the soldiers who had brought the two young people into the hall had retreated several paces, leaving two men to hold Bradley and two to hold the slave. Along the peripheral of the large room, Roland was aware that a number of slaves and hired attendants were watching in breathless silence, afraid to move and yet afraid to stay.

The ruler's gaze finally slid away from Bradley to land on the girl several yards away. He had never paid much attention to his children's nurse, other than to note his brother-in-law's singular interest in her welfare. He supposed she was a pretty girl, but barely more than a child. Roland smirked when he recalled Bradley's complaint over Lady Agatha's age. This slave was no more than a year older than Lord Burdney's daughter.

The lord of Hebbros strode across the space to stand before the slave. He sensed Bradley stiffen and took some pleasure in the younger man's fear. Sarah stood with her head bowed in silence. Roland snapped his fingers in front of her face and she lifted her head, though her eyes remained lowered. Roland forced his stiff jaw to form the first words he had spoken in some minutes.

"Bradley, you will remain silent. You girl, did you marry this *boy*?" He spoke the last word with emphasis, clearly conveying his opinion that they were foolish children.

Sarah nodded. A quiet twitter of amusement swept through the gathered crowd, but was quickly hushed by the overseer. It seemed Roland was not the only one who saw the folly of these two. Everyone could see the absurdity in this situation. Everyone except for Bradley and Sarah. Roland took a steadying breath, willing himself to remain calm even as his mind screamed at the mountain of troubles he must yet see to.

"What did Lord Bradley promise you, girl?" He clasped his hands behind his back and took several steps to the right, stopping before Bradley. He met the youth's defiant stare as he continued to address the girl, "Did he promise you would become one of us?"

Bradley hissed an objection but Roland silenced him with a swift cuff to his ear. He glanced back in time to see Sarah shaking her head in denial of his assumption. Roland paced back to the left, "Did he promise you freedom?"

She moved as if to shake her head, but paused, her eyes shifting back and forth. Roland held back a grin, amused by her confusion. Casting another look at Bradley, Roland leaned closer and spoke in an ominous tone, "Tell me what he promised you, that a young slave would forget her place."

"Nothing," the word was spoken in barely a whisper. Sarah lifted her brown eyes to meet his for an instant before thorough training demanded that she lower them to the floor again, "He offered me nothing, m'lord, simply asked."

Roland chuckled. The overwhelming events of the day finally lent him a sense of hilarity and he laughed outright, "He simply *asked*?" He turned to jeer at Bradley, "What did you do, stride into the children's rooms and unceremoniously ask their nurse to marry you?"

"Yes," Bradley and Sarah answered together.

Behind him, Rosalynn gave a humorless bark of laughter.

All hilarity gone, Roland stalked over to Bradley and grabbed a handful of the boy's dirty tunic, "Did you forget that you were already pledged to another?"

Bradley's gaze was like steel, hard and unmoving, and his voice was toned to match, "I never asked another, and now the deed is done."

Roland shoved Bradley back, the guards' hold alone keeping the youth on his feet, "Do you think I cannot reverse your foolishness? Don't you realize I have the power to annul this ridiculous excuse of a marriage? I can convince anyone who hears of it that it never happened, or silence them for good," he cast a meaningful glance at the slaves around the room. "When will you learn, Bradley? I hold the power. I decide."

"And when will you learn, Roland, that you are not a god?"

The hall was silent as everyone held their breath.

Roland turned away before he did something rash and stood for a long while staring into the hearth. An idea suddenly struck him and his smile turned snakelike. "You are right, Bradley," he turned to face the accused again, "I am not a god, and I will leave your ultimate punishment up to those higher powers. You will keep your vows to this girl."

A sense of shock coursed through the air. Rosalynn froze. Whispers hummed along the line of slaves like a swarm of bees.

Roland continued, enjoying the sensation he was creating, "However, your alliance with a slave will not elevate her status to one of nobility, but will rather lower your status to one that is equal with hers."

Silence settled over the hall again. Rosalynn gasped and sank back into her chair. Sarah closed her eyes and a single tear fell free. Roland held Bradley's steady gaze, disappointed that Bradley did not appear more daunted than a slight furrowing of the brow would allow.

The lord of Hebbros nodded to the guards, "See that the girl returns to the care of her charges." He grabbed Sarah's chin and hissed in her face, "You will attend to your duties in this palace without fault or complaint if you do not wish to see harm come to your husband."

With a single sob, Sarah nodded and was dragged away before she could so much as glance at Bradley.

"As for you," Roland turned to face his wife's brother, and he spoke to the guards, "Take him to the Mordecai garrison and inform Sir Kenrick that he is to keep Bradley as a…guest, until I've decided where to put him to work." He smirked, "He has no friends in the Order who will let him leave prematurely."

The guards turned to obey, dragging Bradley toward the exit.

Rosalynn whimpered, "I should have sold her. I should have sold her the day we came to Hebbros. I should have sold her the very first moment I became suspicious of his interest. I should have sold her!"

Roland turned for the door, leaving his frantic wife to her shrieking and raging. He tried to shove aside the reminder that there was another child on the way as he stormed across the hall and out the door. The slaves scampered back to their work, whispering and speculating and hoping to be the first to spread this incredible bit of gossip beyond the Great Hall.

Drawing closer to his west turret, Roland caught sight of a man dressed in the royal livery. He groaned inwardly. Could anything else unexpected happen this day? Approaching the royal courier, he extended his hand and received the king's message, which proved to be an order for Roland to host a Lord Brock and his entourage. The man was apparently traveling to take up his post as King Cronin's ambassador to a distant island, and was expected to pass through Hebbros on his way there.

The courier asked permission to speak and it was granted.

"My lord, I'm sorry to say that foul weather and other troubles along the route have delayed this message. I should have arrived to deliver it some time ago, so you might have had two weeks to prepare for Lord Brock's arrival. He is now to be expected in only two days' time."

For a moment, Roland merely stared at the messenger. Face blank. Expressionless.

Finally, he turned without a word and climbed the stairs to his private study.

Disastrous. Simply…disastrous.

29
Outwitting the Mordecais

The late afternoon sunlight waned until it was at last replaced by the gray blanket of evening. Small lights began to appear throughout the city of Hebbros, like sparkling stars in a sea of inky shadows. Within minutes the first lights were joined by others, blinking into existence and multiplying until they were a hundred and then a thousand. Candles. The miniature flames flickered and danced to the eerie cadence of a city's anxious prayers.

Lord Roland had put forth a decree. The House of Peers had seen to the drawing up and distribution of many copies throughout the city. The people of Hebbros had listened to the public reading of this order, and some had read the posted words themselves.

Fire towers would be erected for the safety of Hebbros, to ward off any further attacks by the dragons. In the meantime, at sundown each household was to offer up a prayer for their safety, showing faith in the fire's protection and the mercy of their gods by unbarring their windows to display the lighted candles displayed on every sill. Any house that remained dark would be at the mercy of the Mordecai knights.

Luke was uncertain whether the prayers of safety were being directed to the candles or to the dragons; however, he was certain that something evil lurked in the streets of Hebbros that night. As he carefully made his way through the empty thoroughfares toward the Mordecai garrison, the murmurs and whisperings of his fellow Mizgalians praying to some false deity or other seeped from every window like a constant hissing in his ears. A chill crept up his spine and his skin turned clammy, defying the warmth of the summer night.

Overhead, the silhouette of a dragon appeared. Luke froze and watched as the monstrous beast floated noiselessly by, contemplating the wisdom of descending on a city that sported several thousand bits of flame.

Taking a deep breath, Luke continued on his way. Ned and Elbert would be seeking out several others from their original group, encouraging them to leave their places of reestablishment and join him at the rooftop hideout tonight. Luke was anxious to have Chris in their number, and to remove Charlotte from the chandler's home.

Luke climbed a set of stone steps two at a time and turned onto the city's major east-west thoroughfare. During the last four years, he had managed to locate each of the twenty-seven other children who had been a part of the Mordecai's first raid. His task for this night would be to discover how many other children had been torn from their homes in the Order's additional raids among the Faithful.

The Mordecai garrison soon loomed ahead, towering over the surrounding structures and even vying for preeminence with the Peers' grand meetinghouse, which stood beside it. Luke studied the garrison of black stone and thought that it was correctly situated here at the center of Hebbros, as it was indeed an accurate picture of the city's darkened heart.

The public gate had been left ajar in the event some window was found devoid of a prayer candle and the knights needed to return to their black fortress with the faithless prisoners in tow.

Without warning, a woman's frightened wail sounded from inside a nearby cottage. A baby began to cry. The murmurs continued. The whispers became urgent. Suddenly, an unseen force pressed upon Luke like a heavy hand, concentrating in his temples with a confusing pain. Luke clutched his brow and thought of the day four years earlier, when he had accepted Christ as his savior. The shrill noise of Christ's enemy in combat for his soul had been very like the pressure he was feeling now.

"Help me God, for only You can dispel this darkness." The prayer escaped his lips, a single beacon of righteousness glowing faint in the surrounding shadows and gaining strength as the hand of Almighty God interceded to push back the evil that would try to stamp it out.

Feeling the pressure pull away from his temples, Luke breathed deeply and lifted his eyes heavenward, "Thank you, Jesus." The powerful name, whispered in simple gratitude, chased the powers of darkness further away.

Luke breathed deeply as the air cleared. The magnitude of what he was trying to do suddenly presented itself before his mind's eye. No matter how many children were in need of an escape, he would have an enormous task on his hands. Deep in his heart a voice whispered that he could not do it alone. He must humble himself and give the work to his Lord, the God who had come to Luke's aid so efficiently only moments before.

Luke clamped down on these thoughts and clenched his teeth in determination, "I will fight for Him. I will bring honor to His name and justice to the Faithful."

Luke focused once more on the garrison across the way. Several sentries stood watch atop the wall, but their stances proved they were clearly not expecting anything unusual to occur. The young boy managed to slip closer when they had turned to pace, and soon crept silently through the outer gate and into the public courtyard.

The Reestablishment room was locked as expected, but Luke made quick work of the fastener and then opened the door just wide enough to slip his bow through and lift the inside crossbar free from its cradle. Stepping inside, he quietly closed and re-barred the door. He checked to ensure the shutters were closed and then stepped to the stone-topped table and lit several candles. As the low flames flickered and settled into spheres of warm light, Luke's eyes lifted to the opposite wall, where numerous compartments contained the records of every child brought through this garrison.

One scroll for every child. One record for every compartment.

Luke circled the table and came to stand in front of the niche-covered wall. Using his finger to point at each scroll, he quickly moved down one line and then another. His lips moved as he silently counted. He grinned when he recognized the compartment where his own lengthy document resided, and then continued until he had reached the last scroll. His eyes shifted to the right, past several empty compartments, and landed on a document in the corner that appeared thicker than the others. Pulling the parchment from its place, Luke turned and unrolled it across the table.

A list of names met his gaze and Luke smiled. This must be the master record. Running his finger down the neat rows, he counted once again and confirmed that he had come to the correct number the first time.

One hundred twenty-three.

Luke slowly took a deep breath. There were more than his exaggerated guesses had planned for. He ran one hand through his hair and then nodded to himself and went to work.

A quick search produced a blank sheet of parchment, and ink was available on the table at his elbow. Luke dipped Sir Kenrick's quill pen into the inkwell and began to scratch a rather messy but legible copy of the master list. After two hours of jotting down names and checking the appropriate record for the child's current location, Luke was finally satisfied with the results of his work.

He began rolling up the master scroll, but paused when an idea came to him. Christopher would call it rash, he knew. Ned would ask why on earth he had given them away so easily, and Elbert would stare at him and say…something obvious. Luke's fingers itched, urging him to resist the impulse and return the parchment. Smiling, he took up the pen once more and scrawled a line of words at the bottom of the page.

When the list had been restored to its compartment and his copy folded and stuffed into his tunic, Luke extinguished the diminished candles and moved to the door. Slipping out of the room and into the shadows of the courtyard, he grinned to think of Kenrick discovering that someone had managed to break into his center of power.

Luke glanced back at the darkened doorway and noted the sign that hung overhead. He placed a hand over the list hidden in his tunic and smiled ironically. It was time for Sir Kenrick's goal to be well and truly accomplished: The children of the Faithful were soon to be utterly and truly reestablished.

Luke turned toward the gate but stilled when a strange sight caught his eye. A single candle glowed in one of the narrow windows of the familiar holding room. It was odd to think of anyone but himself occupying that small space in the turret, and the fact that the current resident had been given a prayer candle was terribly intriguing. Casting a sharp look about the courtyard, Luke disappeared among the shadows that lined the walls and silently made his way toward the tower's stairwell.

Lord Bradley had not cried in three years, two months, seventeen days, nine hours, and thirteen minutes. It had been a memorable bout of tears, shed with abandon and witnessed by a great many nobles present for a grand banquet in the Great Hall. Lord Roland had insisted his brother-in-law be seated at the lowest table in order to give precedence to the honored guests, and Bradley had responded with an unstoppable fountain of enraged tears. The invited noblemen had looked aghast. Roland had smirked and then ordered Bradley from the room. It was only then that Bradley had realized his removal from the banquet had been the plan all along. Roland had bested him in a battle of wits.

That day had marked a turning point in Bradley's young life. He had decided then that he would no longer give Roland the pleasure of humiliating him, and the only way to accomplish that was to pretend he did not care. He had not cried since. Not even when Roland had announced his plans for an arranged marriage had Bradley given way to tears.

Every trace of anger and bitterness had been bottled up and stopped by a firm lid of indifference. Each thought of frustration and anguish had been well concealed, only vented in private to a patient and forbearing Sarah.

Bradley leaned his head back against the curved wall of the Mordecai's holding room. Sarah had been so kind to him, returning his friendship when every ounce of her training must have been screaming against the wisdom of such a choice. She would have been right to ignore his pleas for camaraderie. Noblemen simply did not befriend their slaves. Nevertheless, she had always offered a listening ear and whatever encouragement she could. She had even believed him capable of one day fulfilling his promise to free her from slavery.

And he had repaid her with shackles heavier and more

oppressive than a leather collar.

How had he convinced himself that marrying Sarah might solve all of their problems? If anything, the marriage had added to their troubles tenfold.

Bradley drew his knees up to his chest and draped his arms over them. He turned his head to stare at the stubby candle on a narrow windowsill. The candle he had refused to pray over. The gods of Hebbros were certainly not interested in his welfare, and so he would show no interest in them. The low flame flickered and danced in the night air.

Bradley's gaze grew distant. The harebrained notion of marrying himself off had occurred to him only that morning. It was a sure way to trump Roland as well as escape a marriage of convenience to Lady Agatha. He had known without deliberation that Sarah would be his only choice for such a scheme, being the one female he held in high regard, and he had immediately set out to find and ask the girl for her hand.

Bradley grinned briefly when he remembered his explosive entrance into the children's rooms, and the distinct look of shock that had remained planted on Sarah's face for a full minute after his hastily put question. And then a marvelous thing had happened. Sarah's expression had undergone a strange transformation, passing through numerous emotions so quickly he hadn't had time to identify a single one, until finally her features had come to rest upon a look of pure joy and immense pleasure.

Bradley was well aware, as was Sarah, that he was not what the bards would call "in love" with the dear girl. Nevertheless, in that moment, facing Sarah's obvious delight over his impulsive—not to mention selfish—proposal, Bradley had admitted to himself that such a state of the heart must be possible. And not merely in the minstrels' sonnets. Given time, he might be able to offer Sarah his heart as well as his hand. Given time.

Bradley scoffed at his own nonsense and turned away from the thought of caring.

The candle began to sputter. Bradley watched the blinking reflection on the walls and sighed. The press for time had caused him to act rashly, and he had been far too impetuous. Of course Roland would retaliate by reducing Bradley to the status of a slave! His quickly shaped marriage would remain intact, but Bradley knew that slaves rarely married publicly for fear of being sold apart. He may not have another chance to speak with Sarah—his wife!—let alone have time for learning to love her as she deserved. He may never see her again except in passing, if he saw her at all.

Bradley's shoulders slumped in defeat. Roland was sure to be thorough in manufacturing a misery-fraught punishment for the two young people who had defied him so efficiently.

The candle blinked out and the room was left in total darkness.

A single tear fell unhindered from Bradley's eye. His own solution had left him worse off than the burden of the original troubles, and had brought hardship to others in the process.

The door suddenly opened and closed, the action so fluid Bradley would have missed it altogether in the dark if not for the quick puff of air that the movement sent across the room.

"Who's there?" He called out.

"Who's asking?"

Strange. The Mordecai Knights were aware of Bradley's presence. They had made fun of his unfortunate turn of affairs upon his arrival. But this was not a Mordecai.

"I am Lord Bradley, if you must know, which I dare say you do not."

"Lord Bradley?" The voice sounded young, surprised, and in the midst of that mysterious change that ultimately decided every man's intonation. The newcomer drew closer and crouched down a mere pace away, "It's me, Luke. The collared boy."

Bradley's brow quirked as he tried to make sense of this lad's presence, "Did your brother tell you to come find me?"

"My brother? You know Christopher?"

Bradley's eyes were beginning to adjust to the lack of a candle, and he made out the faint outline of Luke's trim figure against the backdrop of a window in the far wall, "I met him only today. He was one of the witnesses at my wedding."

A pause.

"Your wedding?"

Bradley felt his sense of humor returning with the presence of a friend, "It was very impromptu, or I would have sent you an invitation."

"But how did my brother come to be there? And why are you here?"

Bradley started to answer, but paused after a glance at the

door, "First, how did you get in here? I thought I was being guarded."

Luke's silhouette shrugged, "The Mordecais are lax tonight because they're expecting the city to be quiet, due to the dragons. There was no guard in the stairway just now. He must have left you for pleasure elsewhere when he thought no one would notice." Luke suddenly stepped forward and offered Bradley a hand up from where he sat on the floor, "Come to think of it, we could get you out of here if we go while the watchman is gone. You can hide away with my friends and I."

"Friends?" Bradley accepted the proffered hand and rose to his feet.

"We're the children of the Faithful. I'll trust you not to speak of us to anyone."

"If I show my face anywhere in the streets I'll be taken back to Roland. My secrecy will be enforced, though you have my word I would hold my tongue regardless of this fact."

The two moved to the door and stepped out after listening for the guard. In the dim light that cut through a window, Bradley grinned at the compromised padlock, "How did you manage it?"

Luke spared a glance over his shoulder, "I was apprenticed to a locksmith. Once."

They closed the holding room door and made their way down the circular stairway, pausing on the bottom step. Luke motioned with his hands for Bradley to wait while he checked the courtyard for any signs of life. With a sharp movement, Luke suddenly pushed Bradley into the shadows and then ducked behind a stack of crates outside the door. The firm tread of a Mordecai's boots grew louder as Bradley's guard passed within a yard of each boy and climbed the stairs. Before the sound of his tread had disappeared, Bradley felt Luke's grip on his arm and immediately fell in step behind his young rescuer.

"Call me ridiculous," Bradley whispered, "but I'm strangely put out by the fact that my guard so obviously considered the watch of my cell door to be insignificant. Why does no one take me seriously? I might have been a dangerous threat to the garrison!"

Luke decided to ignore the tirade, "I pray he decides to keep the cell door closed until morning, but in case he doesn't..." his voice was barely more than a whisper, but Bradley understood the command to hurry. Luke pointed toward the public gate and they followed the shadows around to that point as quickly as they could. Timing their exit to occur when the watchmen had their backs turned, they slipped out into the streets of Hebbros undetected.

The nervous prayers of the city's inhabitants had ceased for the night, and the innumerable candles had begun to extinguish one by one. No cry of alarm rent the night air, and for a moment Bradley felt at ease. Silently they traveled up streets, down alleys, around corners, and through empty squares, before Luke suddenly halted in a nondescript lane and pivoted in alarm.

"You're married!"

For the life of him, Bradley couldn't understand why his companion sounded panicked, "That is correct."

"Where is your wife? Did we leave her behind?"

Bradley's eyes widened, "By my clumsy shoes, I forgot all about her! I say, I'm not good at this marriage business at all."

"Where is she?" Luke urged, clearly afraid they had left her at the garrison.

"She's still inside Roland's palace, caring for my niece and nephew. I dare say that's the safest place for her until I contrive a way to get us both out of Hebbros."

Luke crossed his arms, "Will they harm her when they learn of your escape?"

Bradley paused to consider that possibility, "I think not. My sister is unarguably attached to her, and would be desolate for a suitable nurse if Sarah were unable to perform her duties."

Luke nodded, "Then we'll carry on and discuss a rescue when we've met up with my friends."

A dragon flew by overhead, silencing the two youths until the massive form had moved on to scout other parts of the dark city. Luke pressed on in the opposite direction as the beast and questioned Bradley about Christopher's presence at the wedding.

"It's simple, really," Bradley whispered. "While I was out purchasing a disguise," he motioned with one hand to his current choice of garb, "Sarah was responsible for finding one or two people who would agree to witness the wedding without speaking of it to anyone. She is acquainted with a young girl who breeds catawylds for the palace garrison, and so went to recruit her for the task. This young girl was apparently in the company of your twin—remarkable likeness you share, I must say. I knew you were related the moment I caught sight of him. Sarah begged his assistance as he was handy and quickly obtained it."

"Do you remember the other girl's name, my lord?"

Bradley thought for a moment, and then spoke with a single nod, "It was Pavia."

Luke paused in his trek through the byways and turned to study Bradley by a shaft of moonlight, as if he sought assurance that the nobleman was trustworthy. After a moment, Luke nodded and moved forward again. Bradley remained silent as they crossed an open square, and then resumed his monologue when they had passed into the shadows on the other side.

"I met up with the trio outside a small temple that caters to the religious needs of the lower classes. We had planned to perform the ceremony there, but Christopher suggested we go before a—how did he call it? A 'man of God'. The God who, your brother was certain, had created the marriage relationship at the beginning of time. Naturally I couldn't argue with that assurance, and so soon we found ourselves standing before some balding chap in a lonely little shop that I honestly don't recall the true purpose of. A few moments more and I was a married man!" Bradley's quick smile fell into a scowl, "As we left the shop, Sarah and I were discovered and recognized by Roland's men. They quickly hauled us back to the palace for judgment. Most unceremonious."

Luke grunted his acknowledgement of the tale as his eyes scanned the path ahead. Bradley watched the boy and then quirked a brow, "How did you find me if Christopher did not hear of my plight and tell you? What were you doing at the Mordecai garrison?"

Luke spoke through a grin, "Working for our cause."

Bradley gave a halfhearted shrug and followed Luke around a sharp corner and up a flight of stone steps, "Other than allegiance to the 'only God', I don't even know what your cause is for, my friend."

"You will." Luke peered around another bend in the road, "I'll explain it to you myself, as I began to three nights ago. My faith grows stronger with the need to share it with you."

"Glad to be of service. And speaking of three nights ago, your prayers for me have been an utter failure. I haven't had my home, inheritance, or father restored to me, and yet I have gained numerous other troubles since our last meeting. Care to explain this catastrophe?" Bradley's voice sounded pleasant enough, but it carried a note of exasperation.

Luke chuckled and turned to face Bradley as he spoke, "I didn't say I would pray for those specific things, because I know they are not what you truly want."

"How could you possibly know what my desires are?"

"I told you. I see things."

"Ah, yes. The deeper insight, or somesuch drivel."

Luke only smiled again, "I can't see your desires, it's true, but desires are formed by the empty places in our hearts. When I look at you, I can see your emptiness and understand the needs you're trying to fill. From that knowledge I can determine what you truly seek and desire." When it appeared Bradley would comment, Luke held up a hand and continued before the other youth could speak, "You may look at the events that occurred today as further troubles on your head, but I see them as the first steps toward answered prayer."

Bradley's brow furrowed, "But how?"

"I believe my God has the power to make building materials out of stumbling blocks. You won't see God's grace in your trials unless you start looking for it."

Looking for it. The words jarred Bradley's memory and he saw before his mind's eye the lisping mercer from western Hebbros. What had he told Bradley to look for?

"Can you explain, Luke, why a merchant would tell me to seek out a door in a place I haven't yet searched? The idea was most confusing when presented to me earlier today, and then I forgot about it entirely what with my wedding, which was followed by an arrest, trial, and imprisonment."

Luke turned to check the next street for ensured secrecy, "What kind of door?"

"An open door, apparently, though his was decidedly shut." Bradley ran a hand through his red-brown hair, "Nevertheless, the mercer insisted that the door has not yet been closed."

Luke came to a sudden halt and Bradley crashed into his quiver and bow from behind. Luke whirled and caught Bradley's shoulders against his palms, scanning the older boy's face with wide eyes, "What did you say?"

Bradley's expression was startled, "I was merely stating that the little mercer's door was already—"

"No, not that! The last thing you said, that the door…"

"Has not yet been closed," Bradley finished the phrase and peered into Luke's face, suddenly aware that his young guide was no longer looking directly at him. Luke's unfocused gaze had shifted to stare over Bradley's shoulder.

"It's a watchword."

"I beg your pardon?" Bradley turned to ensure that Luke was not speaking to someone who had appeared behind him. No one else stood on the street.

"Those words," Luke's eyes focused once again on Bradley, "I heard them before from another…friend." His hands dropped from Bradley's shoulders and his face split with a slow grin, "Of course."

Bradley remained silent, uncertain whether he was being addressed or forgotten.

"The door has not yet been closed." Luke murmured the words to himself, as if tasting their worth on his tongue.

A shriek suddenly rent the air and the two boys started as one, lifting their gazes to the starry sky. Instinctively they pressed themselves against the shadows of a nearby wall beneath overhanging eaves, and waited for the dragon to pass by. When all was silent again, Bradley fell in step beside Luke.

"That beast must have come to investigate when it heard our less-than-graceful collision a few moments ago."

Luke's response was a distracted grunt. A grin still shaped his face when he turned to peer at Bradley, "Do you think you could find that mercer again? The one with the door?"

"I should hope so. I had planned to return someday for a delightful cap I spotted in my mad dash for this disguise."

"Good. Let's hurry back to the hideout and meet up with my friends." A barely suppressed excitement carried Luke's words and stirred the air, "There's much to be done, and apparently the door has not yet been closed."

Bradley heaved a dramatic sigh, "That is the second time today I've been told those exact words, and both times were with extreme conviction and by very odd people. I'm sure the phrase holds some great significance or other, but I must admit…it has most certainly been lost on me."

30
Rooftop Council

Charlotte leaned against Luke's side as they sat on the rooftop around a clay bowl that held a small fire. The scaly hunters that glided overhead hissed their annoyance at the flame, but dared not come any closer for fear of entangling themselves in the light. Taking shelter in the sphere of the bowl's warmth were Ned and Elbert, along with Luke and a young man who had been introduced as "Bradley, without the *lord*—and both implications are true."

Charlotte had smiled at that. Apparently this Bradley was a castoff nobleman who was also not a member of the Faithful. Without the Lord. That would not be true for long if Luke's look of determination proved Charlotte's suspicions. Her brother had taken a particular interest in Bradley's faith, or lack thereof, and had already begun to lead the young man to his Savior.

A mask of indifference shaped Bradley's face. His eyes, an undecided shade between black and indigo, sparked with interest as he studied the faces of those around him, and his reddish-brown hair glowed like embers in the firelight. He appeared at ease wearing a costume that belonged to men of lower rank, however his rigid posture showed a slight insecurity over his surroundings.

Charlotte's eyes moved to study the others. Like her brother,

Elbert and Ned had both grown taller and stronger, though their strengths lay in different areas of capability.

Luke's arms had become appendages of iron, girded with knowledge of the bow. His eyes were constantly alight with spirit and resolution. His passion for the cause of the Faithful drove his every thought, and his mind was sharpened by his special gift.

Ned's apprenticeship as a carpenter had developed his physical form and sharpened his eye in the creative method of his master's trade. The air of confidence that Charlotte remembered from four years back still clung to Ned like a favored cloak. His smile was easy and his manner outgoing.

Elbert had learned the trade of a roper, the oft-monotonous task callusing his hands and providing ample time to hone his skills of observation. Hiding behind a floppy thatch of black hair, his blue eyes darted from face to face, seeking answers and insight. Simplicity.

The four boys spoke in hushed tones about the events of the night thus far. Charlotte heard her name spoken and glanced up as Ned told the others how he had practically plucked her from her pallet in the chandler's workroom, "Right out from under their noses. And then Elbert and I whisked her away through the night to meet you back here." Ned's smile cocked his face at a brash angle, "I wish I could see the look on that Marley's face when they discover she's gone."

"Who's Marley?" Luke asked.

Ned wrinkled his nose in disgust, "The selfish no-good lad who was intended to be Charlotte's betrothed."

Luke met the other youth's gaze with a look of disbelief, "She's only nine years old!"

Charlotte squirmed uncomfortably and tilted her head to look up at Luke, "Me leaving won't bother Marley but for a pinch to his pride. He'll probably drown his sorrows in a penny-ale first thing tomorrow."

Luke was horrified, "Charlotte, where did you learn such language?"

Ned coughed behind his fist, "Chandler."

"By my diamond-studded doublet," Bradley chuckled, "I haven't been so amused since my nephew, Jerem, took a grave disliking to his little shoes and pelted one across the room, where it landed on Roland's head as he was giving orders to the garrison's captain."

The other four stared at him in silence until Luke finally took a breath and said, "My lord—"

"Please, call me Bradley. We're obviously such good friends now."

"Bradley, then," Luke conceded as he continued to observe the noblemen with an odd expression. "Since making your acquaintance, I've been left speechless far too often for good manners. That said, because your noble station begs a reply, yet the oddity of your conversation often leaves no room for response…I must ask you to forgive my frequent silence."

Bradley's eyes sparkled mischievously and he seemed at a loss for words himself. Finally he offered a solemn nod and spoke as if passing judgment in the House of Peers, "You have my full pardon, good sir."

Charlotte covered a giggle with her small hand. Elbert's shoulders shook with suppressed laughter. Ned, forsaking all etiquette, laughed outright and toppled over backwards. Bradley grinned at Luke and the two joined in the merriment, induced by a heavy measure of exhaustion on all sides.

As the laughter abated, Charlotte lowered her head to Luke's shoulder and lifted his arm to place it around her, thankful when he tightened his hold in reassurance. Luke had never mastered the art of comforting others and offering solace in the midst of anxiety; it was more like him to jump into the fray than look after those who had escaped it. Christopher on the other hand had always remembered Charlotte's more delicate nature, offering a brotherly embrace or word of comfort when she most needed it.

"We have to work swiftly," Luke's voice broke into her thoughts. "We need to find out if the mercer who spoke to Bradley is a member of the Faithful."

Ned nodded, "Perhaps he can tell us where to find that hole in the western wall, the one they used for passing supplies to Sedgwick."

Bradley's head shook and his face held a hint of wonder, "This story grows more marvelous by the minute! Supplies were being secreted to the exiled, and Roland was never the wiser?"

Elbert glanced at Luke as he nodded toward the young lord, "You sure he'll keep our secret? He does have friends in high places."

"Obvious, Elbert. He's a nobleman."

Charlotte grinned, "We have a Friend in higher places Who will protect us."

Ned nodded and grinned at Charlotte before turning to hear Luke's thoughts on the matter. Luke studied Bradley for a long moment and Charlotte knew he was reading the young man's face. It seemed Bradley too was aware of the fact, for he suddenly smiled and asked, "What do you see, my friend?"

Luke blinked, "Nothing that threatens our cause."

"I'll take Luke's word for it," Ned added several scraps of wood to their fire.

Elbert's gaze swung back and forth before he conceded, "You know what you see, Luke, so I'll trust you too."

Luke must have told the other boys about his gift. Charlotte took note of this as her eyelids drooped heavily and snatches of conversation drifted through her awareness…

"One hundred twenty three children…"

"Hole in the west wall…"

"Guy the cooper…"

"Watchword…"

"Bradley's new wife…"

"Christopher."

Charlotte's eyes slid open at that name. How she longed to see Chris again. It was not that she loved one twin more than the other, but she had certainly been closer to Christopher. They two had more in common with one another than with Luke, whose life they had always watched with great interest and some trepidation. His reputation as an impetuous firebrand was something Luke's siblings admired, but it was also something they would never dream of striving for themselves. Christopher preferred to weigh his decisions with care, considering everyone involved. Charlotte preferred to learn by watching others, and to be led by someone she trusted.

"We should wait for Christopher," Charlotte's words brought every eye to rest on her. She straightened from Luke's shoulder and glanced at her brother, "You'll lead well, but Chris will help keep us calm and make us think before we act. He'll bring our group…" she twisted her face in an effort to think of the right word, "stableness."

"Stability," Ned corrected in agreement, and he, Luke, and

Elbert exchanged glances.

Bradley looked on for a moment and then spoke, "Do you think your brother and that girl, Pavia, would have returned to the garrison? When we left the shop after my wedding it seemed the other two were intent on heading in the opposite direction."

Luke's eyes darted back and forth across the space between them, his thoughts almost visible in the firelight, "They may be looking for us. Ned and Elbert, you two came to find me when you saw the light on Desterrar. We still have hours left before sunrise. We'll scout a bit more to see if we can locate them, and meet back here before dawn. If we can't find them soon we'll push on and trust God to cross our paths before it's too late."

The others nodded and Charlotte's eyes drooped once more. It had been a long time since she'd been with a member of her real family, and she felt undeniably safe now that she had one of her brothers beside her. She thought of her mother and father, hopefully alive and well on Mount Desterrar, and prayed that she and the other children would soon be reunited with their parents. She believed that God was able to do the impossible, and she clung to the faith that He would answer her plea.

And God, wherever Chris is, please keep him safe and help him to find us soon. The prayer drifted upward from Charlotte's thoughts as she finally gave in to the warmth of the fire and the irresistible weight of slumber.

31
A Fragile Bond

In the early hours of morning, the Chief Peer glanced about the dimly lit hall as several other Peers entered and took their places in stony silence. The slight whisper of the scholars' robes against the stone floor sounded loud in the apprehensive stillness. The windows had been shuttered against the prying ears and eyes of a thousand possible spies, and a minimum of candles lit the space with a secretive flush. Finally, the last Peer entered and nodded, indicating that all were present.

All, that is, except Lord Roland and Sir Kenrick.

The Chief Peer rose from his chair and raised his arms into the air, pausing as all eyes shifted to observe him. Expectancy hung like a fog in the atmosphere. He lowered his arms and spoke with a calm passion, meeting every man's gaze in turn.

"I have called you here this morning to discuss a matter of great importance. Our great city has been strengthened during the rule of Lord Roland, however I fear for our future. In his quest to make Hebbros great, Lord Roland would let Mizgalia fall. In his desire to make this city the greatest, he would let the kingdom falter to her knees. His purpose is too narrow, his objective too limited."

The honored Peer paused to retrieve a parchment from the

small table beside his chair, "I have here in my hand orders for Hebbros to send reinforcements to aid in the Brikbone border wars. His lordship has ignored the king's mandate for several weeks now, choosing instead to honor progress reports on the new wall and requests from the Mordecai Order with his time and attention. Roland is a favorite with the king and is therefore forgiven much. Nevertheless, his apathy toward matters of the realm at large will lead our city to be scorned and despised by our neighbors. I fear that if we do not return our efforts to a full support of the king's business, we will be in danger of finding ourselves without allies should future conflicts arise."

A general murmur of agreement arose as the Peers considered the Chief's concerns. One scholar stood and addressed the hall.

"I think it unwise to continue seeking retribution on the minority known as the Faithful. Our time would be better spent strengthening the majority who are followers of Mizgalia's preferred deities."

"Indeed," a knight rose and joined the scholar. "If the majority stands firm in their views, the minority will soon fall into line and join the ranks of true religion or disappear altogether. We have far greater matters to concern ourselves with than a mere handful of confused citizens."

"In my opinion, to put it briefly…" Sir Monotun hefted himself to his feet and promptly spent a good fifteen minutes sharing his view on the subject.

The Chief Peer listened as tensions released and fears were revealed. Many Peers spoke openly and all seemed to be in agreement.

The lord of Hebbros needed to rethink his nearsighted goals for the city.

Or be replaced.

The Chief Peer demanded the former silence of the hall and it was quickly granted. Everyone waited with bated breath for him to speak, to instruct, to lead.

"We must proceed with care. Many have thought to honor Sir Kenrick with the opportunity to assume the seat of lord. However, we cannot be certain that even he can be trusted. He is a close friend of Lord Roland and already favored with the rule of the Mordecai Order. You will have noticed that he was not invited to join us this morning. Indeed, no one outside of our number can become aware of our gathering."

The Peers nodded their agreement even as some eyed one another with suspicion.

"During our next council we will voice our concerns to Lord Roland in a peaceful but unarguable manner. If he refuses to acknowledge our apprehensions," the Chief Peer lowered himself into his chair, "then we will take matters into our own hands."

The Peers' voices drifted upward to swirl like fanciful ribbons beneath the hall's vaulted ceiling. Tied together by unity of thought, the ribbons created a strong cord of purpose and decision. Seated in the rafters supporting the domed roof, a dark figure smirked as he watched the council from his lofty perch high above their heads. Concealed by shadows, the interloper listened as the Peers hardened their resolve and strengthened the cord that drew them together.

It was an invisible cord, touching the heart and mind.

It was a progressive cord, growing ever stronger.

It was a deadly cord, fashioned as a noose to snare an unsuspecting party.

The shadowy figure propped one foot on the beam where he sat and draped an arm over his knee. His self-satisfied smile proved that the events below had not come as a surprise. They had been expected. This meeting, this agreement, this bonding together of the Peers had been part of a greater plan. The silent interloper knew that he was witnessing the beginning of the end. The end of the House of Peers, at least as this council knew it.

As for their clever cord, braided together in a moment of generosity and affability toward their fellow councilmen, it would indeed be fashioned into a noose.

But it would be the Peers themselves who were hanged by it.

"*Where is he?*"

Sarah jumped when the heavy door flew open to smack the wall with a sharp clap. Lord Roland stood framed by the decorative oak casing, an angry scowl marring his features as he glared at her across the room.

"Where is he?" He asked again.

Sarah blinked and stared. After being dragged from the Great Hall the evening before, she had spent the rest of the night caring for Jerem and Celia—now her nephew and niece by marriage. She had controlled her emotions and presented her charges with a cheerful face. The untroubled façade had disappeared, however, the moment the two children had fallen asleep and Sarah had been left alone with her thoughts.

She should have refused Lord Bradley's proposal. It was as simple as that. She should have said no and yet she had agreed, foolish girl that she was, and brought a thousand new troubles on them both. Lord Bradley, who had lost so much and sought desperately for true freedom, would now be forced to endure the ultimate humiliation and live as a slave to his brother-in-law.

Unless he was sold…

Oh, why had she not tried to convince him of his plan's foolishness?

The tears had been unstoppable, and Sarah had done her best to mute the sounds of her anguish by crying into the depths of a pillow from Celia's bed. She had awakened this morning to find that she had fallen asleep on the floor before the hearth. Her face felt stiff and swollen.

Now she stared at Lord Roland in confusion. Where is he, he had asked. Was he speaking of Jerem? Certainly the man had seen his son make a dash to hide behind the drapes.

"I don't know what you're talking about, m'lord." Sarah handed Celia a wooden ring to play with and then rose to stand with bowed head in respect for the baby's father.

Roland towered over her, fury emanating from his person, "Where is Bradley?"

Sarah's head shot upward of its own accord, "Where is… He's gone?" The shock of Roland's words coursed through her like a bolt of lightning.

Celia waved her arms in the air and chanted her own version of her uncle's name, "Bally! Bally!"

"Quiet!" Roland shouted at his daughter and she dissolved into tears. The other nurse who had stayed to keep watch when Sarah had left came forward to pluck the child from the floor, and then moved to the far side of the room.

Sarah watched as the other woman performed the tasks that had been hers for so long. Pushing this thought aside, she blinked and stared at Lord Roland in obvious distress as she repeated, "He's gone?"

Roland snarled, "If he was still where I put him last night, then I would not be asking you where he is, would I?" He grabbed her arm and hissed, "Where did he plan to go? What friends did he have who would be able to secret him away?"

Exhaustion numbed Sarah's mind and furrowed her brow, "How could he have told me, m'lord? I was dragged away without speaking t' him, and I wasn't told where you put him. I've been here watching over your children all night."

Roland shoved her away and turned with an enraged growl to pound a fist against the stones over the hearth. Jerem whimpered from behind the drapes.

"Roland! You're frightening the children," Lady Rosalynn appeared in a flurry of red hair and billowing robes. She avoided looking in Sarah's direction as she moved to touch her husband's arm, "If you need to question one of the slaves, have them sent to the Great Hall. Your children's private chambers are no place to hold an inquisition."

"There is no inquisition, Rosalynn." Roland moved toward the door with an impatient tread, "She knows nothing."

Roland disappeared as suddenly as he had arrived. Little Celia reached for her mother, and Rosalynn took the child from the second nurse. She spared the older woman a single glance and addressed her in a haughty tone, "You will remain here for several days yet, to keep watch."

The nurse curtsied and retreated to the corner.

Jerem poked his blond head out from behind the drapes, "Can I come out now?"

Rosalynn offered him a smile as she fussed over Celia, "Yes, my love."

The little lord hopped from his hiding place and proceeded to test his balancing skills on first one foot and then the other, "Father was very angry at Sarah."

Rosalynn stiffened, "You will address her as Nurse, Jerem." She passed Celia back to the older woman, obviously refusing to come any closer to Sarah's position by the window, "And in truth your father is angry with Uncle Bradley," her eyes met Sarah's, "as he should be."

Sarah shivered beneath the woman's cold gaze. To think that she was now Lady Rosalynn's sister-in-law! Certainly she would never tout that knowledge outside of her own head, but it was still an unsettling thought. Once again the frantic thoughts of the night before assaulted her. What had she been thinking?

In another moment Sarah was left alone with the two children and the silent guardian nurse. She found Jerem's toy sword and helped him to build a fort, and then took Celia from the older woman and cradled the baby in her arms. Breathing in the scent of the baby's soft hair, Sarah closed her eyes as two tears fell from beneath her lashes. She felt again the pain brought on by Lord Roland's query.

Where is he? Where was Bradley?

It was true their marriage had been a thoughtless undertaking. Nevertheless it had taken place. They were bound together by vows spoken before a man acquainted with a mysterious God, supposedly the creator of marriage Himself. Bradley always kept his promises. Sarah had thought that his sense of loyalty and his practiced indifference would make him unwilling to back down in the face of Roland's threats. She had been so certain he would fight for what was right.

But Roland's words left no doubt that Bradley had escaped.

And he had left her behind.

Roland stormed through the halls of his palatial home, blind to the finery that surrounded him as he inwardly cursed his infuriating brother-in-law. He had been so pleased with himself the night before. Enslaving Bradley had been the best idea to ever occur to him! And then the young dog had somehow slipped the Mordecais' watch *and* entered Kenrick's Reestablishment room for who-knew-what dastardly purpose.

He thought back to his brief interview with the slave, Sarah. He was convinced she knew nothing of Bradley's whereabouts. The shock on her face had been transparent and genuine. If she had known of Bradley's escape, she would have attempted to go with him.

"My lord," Kenrick's voice echoed in the corridor, drawing

Roland from his thoughts. The knight appeared urgent as he stepped forward, "May I speak with you in private, my lord?"

Roland gave a vague nod and led the way to a small bare room in the base of a tower. As he closed the door on their discussion, he noticed Sir Valden standing watch across the hall.

"What is it, Kenrick?" Roland drew a weary breath, "Aside from my…family troubles, Lord Brock arrives tomorrow and I must see that my orders regarding his stay in Hebbros are being carried out with all speed."

Kenrick bowed, "I understand, my lord, but this news could not wait. I have just heard from a trusted source"—his eyes shifted briefly to the door and Sir Valden beyond—"that the Chief Peer has called a council this morning and purposely excluded your lordship and myself."

Roland's interest mounted, along with a flash of anger, "What was the council for?"

"They gathered to find fault with your ruling of Hebbros and to discuss a replacement for your seat. They say your purpose for the city is narrow-minded and shallow, and even dared to suggest that your judgment of the Faithful is a pointless endeavor. They would remove you from power."

Roland clenched his jaw until his teeth began to hurt, "Come with me." He marched to the door and tore the panel open, emerging into the hall on a wave of rage. He called to Sir Valden as he started down the corridor, "I will use your horse, sir."

"Of course, my lord," Valden fell in step behind Roland and Kenrick.

Roland motioned for a page to race alongside him, spewing orders as fast as the boy could take them, "Take Sir Valden to the stables and have a horse saddled for him as quickly as possible, and then run to Sir Fraser and have him bring a contingent to the Peers' meeting hall. After that, see that Lady Rosalynn is informed of my quick departure. I will see to the matter of her brother on my return."

"Yes, my lord." The page offered the best bow he could while running to keep up and then raced to fill each command with Valden following for a fresh horse.

Outside, Roland mounted the Mordecai's waiting horse while Kenrick claimed his own, and the two were soon galloping through the crowded streets toward the grand structure at the heart of the city. Dismounting before the hall, Roland tossed his reins to a liveried slave, climbed the steps, and paused to listen. In the distance he could hear the quick march of Sir Fraser's contingent, coming to reinforce his every word.

He would not need to speak many.

Entering the building Roland immediately sensed the charge of excitement that filled the air. Rebellion. Sedition. Followed by Kenrick and driven by the voices of the gathered Peers, he advanced on the inner hall and opened the doors with a mighty shove.

The silence was sudden. Every eye turned toward him. Every mouth dropped open in surprise. Every heart pounded in time to the steady beat of fear that pulsed through the room.

The silence was exhilarating. Roland's gaze locked on the Chief Peer, standing before his honored seat. The lord of Hebbros started across the room, his footsteps muted by the deafening stillness. Still no one spoke.

Finally, Roland halted before the Chief Peer. Behind him he heard the arrival of Sir Fraser and his company of soldiers, and he felt empowered. Grabbing the honored Peer by the arm and shoving him into the middle of the room, Roland turned with a glare.

"Kenrick, this man has questioned my dealings with a certain party of rebels. See that he is delivered to the Mordecai garrison for inquisition regarding his support of the rabble known as the Faithful and sedition against his ruling lord."

The element of fear heightened as Sir Kenrick, joined by Valden, moved to lay hold on the Chief Peer. Roland watched them with a hard gaze and then lifted his voice in a mighty bellow.

"There is *no more* House of Peers!"

32
Together Again

The city of Hebbros held its breath like a child brought before a parent who is displeased. The streets were wrapped in an air of uncertainty.

Lord Roland had put an end to the House of Peers. The gathering of honored scholars and knights had been questioned like common criminals, and then some had been sent home with a warning to watch their step. Others had been led away to die. The Chief Peer sat in chains in the dungeon below the Mordecai garrison, accused of sympathizing with the rebel band called Faithful. The Peers' meetinghouse had been acquisitioned by Roland to be used as his personal court of judgment.

The former system of local leadership was no more.

Lord Roland would be their leader, their judge…their government.

Luke had spent the majority of this day traveling through the city, trying to learn all he could about the seditious council and its catastrophic end. Instead of facts, however, he had quickly gathered that he—the collared boy—was unwelcome in any and all circles, and so he had set about finding another way to go unnoticed. His quick mind had not been long in making a suggestion.

Now, as the late afternoon sun slanted across the sky and Mount Desterrar cast its vast shadow over the great city, Luke raced along one rooftop and then another, leaping across the narrow spaces between each building and descending to the streets when any gap was too wide to manage. Always returning to the roofs, Luke watched the city from his elevated vantage point, hearing much talk and seeing the many emotions that passed through the gazes of Hebbros.

Pausing at the corner of one rooftop in southern Hebbros, Luke peeked over the edge to the lane below. A group of priests ambled by like a flock of solemn birds, droning and chanting as their leader swung a lighted lantern back and forth in the street. Luke shook his head. They believed the passing of the flame accompanied by their prayers to a strange god would incur protection against the dragons' nightly visits.

Pulling back from the edge of the roof, Luke drew the folded parchment from his tunic and scanned it for several minutes. It was time to begin calling the other Faithful children to action. There had still been no sign of Chris or Pavia, but in a city this size it was no surprise. Luke trusted they would find each other soon. Until then, he would do his best to begin gathering the members whose location he was aware of.

But they couldn't all stay at the rooftop hideout. If Luke was nervous that five of them would be discovered, how could he even think of concealing one hundred twenty-three? It was unthinkable. And yet, why shouldn't he call the Faithful together now and consider the problem of concealment later?

Luke pressed his fists to his head, trying to remind himself to be reasonable…and failing.

"What would Chris say to do?"

"Well, for starters I would tell you to stop running like a madman over the roofs of Hebbros. Mother would faint straight away if she saw you risking your neck like that."

Luke jerked his head up to see a broad silhouette crouched before him, "Chris!" He launched himself at his brother and the two exchanged a firm embrace.

Chris clapped Luke on the shoulder and then pulled back to smile down at his twin, "I can't tell you how good it is to see you again."

"I feel the same." Luke grinned, and his brows rose in

question, "You saw the light on Mount Desterrar?"

"I did," Chris glanced up to the indicated peak, "and though it goes against every rule of honor to leave my command at the garrison without any explanation, my duty to my family and to my faith is greater. It's time, Luke. We must join our parents in exile."

"That's what I think too. We need to gather the others who are still willing," Luke leaned forward excitedly and then paused. "How did you find me?"

Chris lifted one brow and gave his brother a telling look.

Luke sat back, deflated, "My rooftop escapades were not as subtle as I had thought."

"Subtle!?" Chris shook with a laugh, "Far from it, brother. Such a word could never be used to describe you." He tousled Luke's hair and grinned, "Your flying leaps were rather…obvious."

Luke made a face, "You sound like Ned." He rose to his feet, "I'll have to work on my timing next time I decide to fly. It really is the most convenient way to travel the streets, Chris."

Christopher shook his head, "If you say so. I've been stuck inside a garrison for four years, so I wouldn't know. Come on," he motioned to the stairway that led to the street, "Pavia is waiting below. We're anxious to join the rest of the group, for we assume that others have gathered, and we want to hear what plans have been formed."

Luke followed his brother down the crooked set of stairs and came to an abrupt halt when Chris suddenly stopped on the step below. Chris looked both ways and then pivoted to search the alley beside the stairway. Luke studied his twin's gaze.

"Where did you leave her, Chris?"

Chris left the steps and peered into the shaded alley, "Pavia?"

No answer.

"Pavia, where are you?" When silence was once again his only response, Chris marched to the alley's entrance to search the bustling street. "She's gone. I should have let her come with me to the roof when I went to fetch you. Careless… I should have known someone from the garrison might recognize her and take her back. What if they give her the whip? Or worse." Chris turned a tight gaze to Luke's pensive face, "The other catawyld breeders know she's afraid of the beasts. What if they toss her into the arena for sport?"

Luke skipped the last few stairs and descended to the earth

with a single bound, "Surely they wouldn't do that to a girl."

"There are many at the garrison who are cruel enough for any evil." Chris ran a hand through his hair, "Why didn't I think to prepare for a situation like this?"

Luke's head began to shake from side to side, "Chris, it's not your fault. We'll find her. We can head for the garrison now and cut off whoever took her before they reach the gates. I've got my bow and you've got a sword." He shrugged as if the matter was clear and simple, "We'll just rescue her."

Chris pressed his mouth into a firm line and nodded once, "We have to try." He turned toward the street but paused when Luke called him back.

"Not that way. We'll go by way of the roofs and make it in half the time."

Chris cast a wary glance at the looming rooftops and looked ready to argue with his overconfident brother when a small figure slipped into the alley behind him and released a heavy sigh.

"Foolish girl!" The petite newcomer scoffed, "I can't believe I once thought her a gracious child."

In a flash, Chris spun on his heel and gripped the speaker by her shoulders, pulling her further into the alley and placing her back against the wall, "Where were you? I told you to stay behind the stairs."

Already halfway to the roof, Luke dropped to sit on the steps and watched the interesting proceedings below with an amused expression. He could tell by the strain in his twin's voice that losing track of Pavia had wreaked great havoc on Chris's purely honorable sensibilities. Chris obviously considered Pavia under his protection, and the thought of harm befalling anyone in his charge, and particularly a female, was unbearable.

Luke's gaze shifted. Pinned beneath Chris's firm grip as well as his steady glare, Pavia's eyes widened and her mouth dropped open in shock at the quiet youth's sudden outburst. In an instant, however, her shock turned to irritation, "If we're all going to work together in order to escape Hebbros, you need to learn to trust me."

"How can I trust you when you do the exact opposite of what you're told? Where were you?" Chris repeated the question in a tone of steel.

Pavia returned his stare for a moment and finally motioned to the street with a nod of her red head, "I saw Lillian pass by and wanted to invite her to join us."

With a quick sweep of his gaze, Luke took note of the fact that Lillian was nowhere to be seen.

"I thought you'd been kidnapped or taken back to the garrison." Chris's tone left no room for excuses, even as it conveyed his fear of several moments before, "Don't do that again."

The irritation drained from Pavia and she lowered her gaze, "I'm sorry. I thought you would guess that I'd come back, and I only went because I knew you wouldn't leave without me."

Luke laughed, "We were about to go rescue you from your captors. Pity you had to turn up so soon. I was hoping to storm the garrison gates and sally forth on horseback to carry you to safety."

Chris released Pavia's shoulders and the girl turned to study Luke with her arms crossed, "You haven't changed at all."

"I'm glad to hear it," Luke rose and descended the stairs. "I take it Lillian was not excited to hear of our band joining together?"

Pavia's face wrinkled with disgust, "She looked me up and down as if I were a filthy rat and then turned her nose up to say that she was waiting for you to call us together."

It was Luke's turn to wrinkle his nose, "Me?"

Pavia nodded, "You're our leader. I tried to tell her that some of us are gathering on our own, but she insisted you would come for her." Pavia rolled her eyes, "She's probably spent these four years dreaming up her own version of our escape, complete with heroic deeds and glory, and now she won't have it any other way."

Chris crossed his arms and leaned against the wall, his broad frame shielding their conversation from the eyes of any passersby, "You seem to understand her pretty well. How long have you known Lillian?"

"I knew her for five years before the Mordecais' raid. Lillian was three and I was four when we met. My mother was hired as a companion to Lillian's mother, and soon after I was taken on as Lillian's."

Luke nodded thoughtfully, "I remember that her home was the largest one visited by Sir Kenrick and his knights during that raid. Her family was wealthy."

Pavia nodded, "Her father was an honored scholar, on his way to earning a seat in the House of Peers. Both of Lillian's parents joined the Faithful after hearing the Gospel from my mother."

Luke frowned, "What about Lillian? Isn't she a member of the Faithful too?"

"I don't know." Pavia leaned back against the coolness of the shaded wall, "She seemed to support the faith, and loved hearing stories of its heroes, but…" Her brow furrowed and she shook her head, "Sometimes I wondered if she truly was a follower of Christ or if she was following her own fantasized version of Him." Pavia's gaze grew distant, clouded by memories. "I think she believed she would never have to choose between a life of comfort and a life for Christ. In her mind they were one and the same."

Luke's expression was one of confusion, "But when her parents… The raid! I assumed that she was also…"

Chris shook his head, "Luke, just because the parents were members of the Faithful doesn't mean that all of their children have made the same decision to follow Christ. That's why Lord Roland didn't banish us with our elders, and Sir Kenrick took the time to reestablish us. They wanted to remove us from the influence of the Faithful and place us under the false teachings of Mizgalia. They're trying to destroy our faith."

Luke stared at his brother. Christopher was right. Why had he never considered the possibility that any number of children on his list may not be members of the Faithful? Perhaps they had not even known that their parents were. How many had forsaken their knowledge of Jesus to embrace the lies of men such as Master Paul and Lord Roland? How many of these friends, whom Luke had been planning to rescue, were actually his enemies? Luke thought back to the night when he had seen the betrayal in Guy's gaze, and winced when he envisioned reading the same in the eyes of those whose parents were waiting on Mount Desterrar.

"Luke?" Chris laid a large hand on his twin's shoulder, "Are you all right?"

Luke blinked to clear his thoughts. His two companions watched him with uncertainty and concern. "I should take you to the hideout now." He glanced at Chris, "Charlotte is anxious to see you and I'm sure she'll enjoy having another girl in our midst."

Luke moved to step past them and Pavia grabbed hold of his sleeve, "What about Lillian? She wants you to take the call to her. If you talk with her she might see the importance of what we're doing. Maybe she really is a member of the Faithful, but she needs someone to remind her that God is greater than her fears and stronger than our enemies."

What if she is *our enemy?* The question teased the edges of Luke's mind, but he kept his thoughts to himself. Looking down at Pavia, he read the turmoil in the redhead's gaze. Raised as a loyal friend to Lillian, she wanted to believe the best until proven wrong.

"We'll discuss it with the others." Luke turned away again and this time ignored the slight tug that Pavia gave to his sleeve, "Let's go."

Bradley watched from across the rooftop as reunions were had, old friendships rekindled, the nightly fire built, and stories exchanged among the six other children. Several times Luke had beckoned for Bradley to join them, but after greeting Chris and Pavia and answering their questions regarding recent events, the young lord had retreated to observe from a distance and declined all further attempts to include him.

They were different, this group of children. Instinctively he knew that the difference was a result of their faith, as members of the Faithful.

But faithful to what? He had asked the question years before, as a witness to the banishment of their parents, and once again that very morning. Luke had responded without pause, "Not faithful to what, but to whom. We strive to be faithful to God."

Now Bradley turned and focused his gaze on the first fire tower completed for the safety of the city. Erected in the courtyard of Roland's palace. Bradley shook his head over the evident selfishness of his brother-in-law. At least Sarah would be safe there.

Bradley's thoughts returned to the Faithful. Luke had told him the story of Jesus' sacrificial death and resurrection for the benefit of all mankind. He'd had trouble keeping up with Luke's fervent method of narration. He could tell that the boy was focused on repeating the story properly, and that Luke believed his own words to be true, and yet something seemed out of joint. Why did Luke address these depths of his faith only when asked about them? Bradley had thought that a religious man's faith would drive every aspect of his life, and yet whenever Luke spoke of the Faithful it was not about their God, but rather their fight for justice.

Luke's story was a beautiful tale, Bradley admitted, but not one that he could accept as anything more than legend. Nevertheless, he would not ridicule those who did.

He turned to observe the six seated around Luke's fire. Apparently the Faithful simply desired to worship their God without persecution. It seemed a small matter. Many other gods were worshiped in the kingdom of Mizgalia without question or harassment. Why these people? Why this faith? Why this God?

Luke's fiery persistence made it obvious that Luke wanted Bradley to join them, to become a member of the Faithful. But from what Bradley had seen, their faith was one that resulted in banishments, loneliness, and hiding in fear for one's life. The Mordecais had taken everything from these children. Why should he join himself to such a cause? He had already had everything taken from him. By all appearances, Bradley's condition was no different from theirs.

If there truly was something more, something deeper to their faith, then Bradley wanted to see proof. Something remarkable. Something so incredible it would leave him speechless. Something like his desires being granted in response to Luke's prayers.

Bradley's heart quickened at the thought. What if Luke's prayers were indeed answered? What if this legend regarding the God of the Faithful was true? What if Bradley discovered that there *was* something more to this faith and it answered every need that had long burdened his heart? What if this faith was like the door spoken of by the little mercer—the only place where he had not searched for answers and purpose?

He watched as the silhouette of a dragon dipped low over the south quarter of the city, still seeking food beyond the fire tower's reach.

Bradley suddenly found himself hoping. Could it be? Would the Faithful's God care enough for his troubled soul to drop a miracle—or three—in Hebbros? He thought back to the three desires he had listed as a challenge to Luke's God: his home, his inheritance, and his father. Bradley sighed.

Impossible.

A firm hand gripped his shoulder and then released its hold as Bradley turned to see Christopher standing beside him. The tall youth, still so young, smiled at Bradley and pointed toward

Roland's fire tower, "Are you wishing you were back in the safety of the palace?"

Bradley felt his customary grin steal over his face, "I'm sure Roland would love to see me crawling back for mercy about now, but I can't say I would find safety beyond those gates." Bradley's light tone belied his heavy heart, "Nothing but my brother-in-law's revenge awaits our next meeting, and so I've determined that must never be."

Chris was silent for a moment, "What about your sister, the Lady Rosalynn? Will you never try to see her again?"

Bradley shrugged, "Her love for Roland overrules any devotion to me. She does whatever he tells her to, which includes trying to remold me into something I'm not." His voice dropped to a murmur, "She'll be glad to be rid of me."

Chris cast him a sidelong glance full of pity, "And Sarah?"

Bradley's face flushed red, "Shameful as it sounds, I must admit I keep forgetting about her." He turned to face Chris, forcing himself to smile, "Not entirely, you understand. She's been my greatest friend for years and I remember her as such, but my mind has not yet grasped the concept that she's my wife. To make matters worse, she was taken away only an hour after our wedding and I haven't seen her since."

Christopher's steady gaze was full of sympathy and understanding, and Bradley forsook all pretense of indifference. The smile slipped from his face, replaced by a look of pain, "I wasn't ready for marriage, Christopher; but I was so enraged by Roland's tyranny, I was prepared to enter such a union in order to escape. I risked my own life of opulence to upset Roland's plans, and worse still, I risked Sarah's life and happiness for my selfish purposes."

Chris lowered himself to sit on the edge of the roof, "And everything about your situation grew worse, despite your best efforts to make things better."

"Indeed," Bradley sank to sit beside his friend. "Things have never been worse."

Chris offered a nod, "My mother used to say that when we try to untangle the knots of life on our own instead of asking God to do it for us, we'll only make a greater mess of things. She said God understands the very path that each thread takes, so why wouldn't we seek to place the whole lot in His hands?"

They were silent for a long moment, staring out at the darkened city.

Bradley finally shifted and spoke in a quiet voice, "I don't know how to give my problems to an invisible God. Truth be told, I'm not sure I want to."

Chris nodded without turning and answered with wisdom beyond his years, "I understand. You see trusting in God as an admission that He's in control, and if He's in control then that means He allowed the troubles that have shaped your life. Placing your trust in the One responsible for your very need to trust doesn't make sense to you."

"It doesn't," Bradley agreed, and his posture relaxed. "For a moment I thought you were going to ramble on about the finer points of your faith and insist as Luke does that I must join your cause."

Chris glanced over his shoulder and then grinned at Bradley, "Luke is very spirited and determined. He's always been passionate about his purpose and wants everyone to agree with him immediately." His gaze returned to the city, "There was a time when Luke himself refused to listen to any talk of our faith. I came to understand that my job was to love him anyway and wait until Christ had softened his heart."

"And how did you know that I was not ready?"

"You remind me of my brother. You know, he didn't join the faith until the very night of the Mordecais' raid. Our parents were taken away right when Luke needed them most, and because he waited so long to accept the truth, in the end he missed out on hiding much of it in his heart. He's still learning some of the basics."

"That explains a few a things," Bradley grinned.

Chris paused before speaking again, "My lord, there is something I'd like to say. If I may." He waited for Bradley's nod and then continued, "It may sound harsh, but God is more interested in your response to trouble than in your deliverance from it. As your redeemer, He seeks to draw you to Himself, and He knows how hot the fire must be in order to refine the gold." Chris stood and offered Bradley a hand up, "The beauty of these truths is that God won't give us any trials we can't survive as long as we have His help. So the question is, will you accept that help?"

Bradley bowed his head for a moment and then looked out

over the city once again, "Thank you, Chris. I appreciate your sincerity."

Chris nodded, "I hope after we rescue Sarah you'll both agree to climb Mount Desterrar with us."

Bradley chuckled, "I do want to escape the city, but I hadn't thought about doing so with a multitude of children whose faith I cannot claim." His gaze sharpened, "Chris, my heart is ready to believe almost anything for the promise of peace in my soul, but my mind refuses to look beyond common sense. I need proof if I'm to believe in something invisible."

"Good," Chris offered a good-natured grin, "because the proof of our faith is the part that is visible. Come with us, and if you still refuse to see the light," his smile broadened, "then you could descend the mount another way and find passage across the Delfron Sea to any place you might choose. Even another Mizgalian port."

Bradley considered this and had to acknowledge that it seemed more sensible than setting out with no plan and no destination in mind. However, his pride would not let him commit to such a plan just yet. "I'll think about it." He offered a grin, "I wouldn't want to make any plans before discussing them with my wife."

"Very well. Now I must return to the fire and try to convince my brother that calling the Faithful before deciding on the night of escape is foolhardy. I think we should form a plan, choose a night to carry it out, and *then* send out the message for all the others to join us at the right time and place. It will be impossible to hide over one hundred children and keep Sir Kenrick from rounding us all up again for reestablishment. In fact, I think the wisest course would be for those of us who are here to leave immediately."

Bradley cocked an eyebrow, "Am I to understand that your brother is struggling to see the wisdom in your words?"

Christopher gave a wry smile, "Like you, my brother is still learning how to hand his troubles over to God. Rashly, he wants every plan put into immediate effect and doesn't see the need to wait until all the knots are untied and smooth. He also has a confused perspective on how to serve God and it's called, *Do Everything Yourself.* Which of course is impossible."

That would explain Luke's fight-focused faith.

Bradley shook his head in amusement, "For twins, you and

your brother are nothing alike. I used to wonder what it would be like to have a twin, but now… No offense, but I'm rather glad I came by myself."

The two laughed and then turned when Ned exclaimed, "Obvious, Elbert!"

Christopher clapped Bradley on the shoulder and motioned toward the fire, "Let's see if they have any ideas for rescuing Sarah. We must pray the Lord returns your bride to you before you forget her altogether." They turned, but he paused to speak once more, "Remember this, Bradley. Faith is the substance of things hoped for and the evidence of things not seen."

33
Loose Ends

Sarah stretched her arm to its limit and just missed catching Lord Jerem as he raced by. His mischievous giggle floated back to her as she sank before the hearth in exhaustion. It was midnight and still his lordship refused to be put to bed. Knocking a chair over on his way past, Jerem released a loud laugh and then moved to toss the pillows from his bed.

It had been like this all day. The second nurse had been called away to help with preparations for the arrival of a Lord Brock, and little Jerem had immediately rebelled. Gone was the sweet boy who had held her hand and rescued her from imaginary villains. In his place was a lad who screamed in her face, slapped her hand, kicked her shins, and called her Nurse with a sneer.

Finally, after hours of torment, Sarah realized what had brought about the change.

"My mother doesn't like you anymore," Jerem had made a face at her and then scrambled away to knock his toy horses down with vicious slaps.

She had lost his respect. When Lady Rosalynn had all but blamed Sarah for Bradley's actions the day before, Jerem had taken note of his mother's scorn and used it as an excuse to disregard Sarah himself. Only after the second nurse had disappeared had he been bold enough to show his contempt.

From her place by the fire, Sarah watched Jerem run in circles around the room. Celia sat in her bed and laughed at her brother's antics, kept awake by his shrieks of defiance. Suddenly Jerem came to a stop by his sister's bed. Slanting a look at Sarah over his shoulder, he quickly turned and spat in Celia's face. The little girl's wail rent the air as Jerem scurried away in delight over his success. Halfway across the room he turned to see what Sarah's reaction would be.

The young nurse could only stare. Every ounce of fight had been drained from her weary body hours earlier. What could she do? Giving a command had not worked. Pleading had been pointless. Rebukes and frustrated sighs fell on deaf ears. Lady Rosalynn did not allow her to use a switch.

Celia's cries at last penetrated Sarah's thoughts and pulled her to her feet. Crossing the room in confounded silence, Sarah scooped the baby up in her arms and wiped away the offending spittle. Jerem's brow puckered at the lack of response.

"You can't catch me, N*uuu*rse!"

Sarah ignored the little terror and gently bounced Celia in her arms. Moving back to the hearth, she sat in one of the padded chairs that faced away from Jerem and watched the baby's eyelids grow heavy with sleep.

"Come and get me," Jerem taunted from somewhere behind her.

Sarah ignored him.

"I'm getting away, Nurse!"

Celia's eyelashes fluttered at her brother's call, but her small frame finally relaxed in slumber.

"I'm going to spit again," Jerem's voice grew uncertain.

"Go ahead," Sarah spoke softly to keep from waking Celia, and Jerem was silent for a moment.

"You want me to spit on the floor?"

Sarah watched the flames on the hearth and spoke without turning to look at him, "Do whatever you like, m'lord. I'm going to put Lady Celia t' bed and then get some sleep m'self. You stay awake all night if you like."

There was another pause before Jerem spoke again, "I'll…make lots of noise and keep you awake."

"I've slept through terrible noise before m'lord."

"I'll march in circles around you and wake Celia up again."

"Good. Marching will make you tired."

The pause lasted longer this time as Jerem considered his options. Sarah heard the three-year-old deliver a colossal yawn, and then listened as he shuffled away.

"Goodnight, Sarah. I'm going to bed."

Sarah's eyes slid shut in blessed relief. Jerem had been exhausted, and so her ploy of indifference had worked this time. But what about next time? The more Lady Rosalynn scorned her, the more Lord Jerem would follow in his mother's footsteps. Sarah would not last long as the children's nurse if she could not obtain their respect, and yet Lord Roland and his wife had taught through example that slaves were not to be respected, but despised.

Which was Sarah supposed to be, an authority figure or a subordinate?

Within minutes, Jerem's soft breathing sounded evenly from across the room. Sarah stood and returned Celia to her bed before resuming her seat by the fire.

Tomorrow Lord Brock would arrive and Lord Roland would be busy seeing that his important guest was satisfied with his stay in Hebbros. His lordship would have no time or desire to hear the request of a slave. Sarah would wait until after Lord Brock had gone, and then she would seek an audience with Lord Roland and beg him to send her away. Perhaps he would remove her to another part of Hebbros, perhaps to another city or even another kingdom. Sarah didn't care. She simply wanted to dwell in a place where those around her had no reason to despise her, and where she would not be daily reminded of Lord Bradley and his breach of promise.

Sarah rose and moved to the open window, where the night's prayer candle had long ago burnt itself to flat nothingness. Leaning against the sill, the young slave rested her chin on top of her folded arms and searched the dark night beyond with saddened eyes.

"Where are you, Bradley? And why didn't you take me with you?"

Kenrick stood before his stone table and studied the map of Hebbros spread out before him. Sir Valden's rusty voice grated on his ears from across the room.

"Something is afoot, sir. Five rebel children, formerly reestablished by yourself, have disappeared within several days of one another, all since the night of the dragons' first attack. Two were from the garrison and three from the homes of tradesmen."

"You're sure they were not carried off by the dragons?"

"I find it hard to believe that the beasts would only carry off those whose parents have been banished, sir. Also, a fire has been lit on Mount Desterrar's peak every night since the dragons' arrival. A controlled fire. There is life, human life, on the mountain."

Kenrick straightened and gave a Valden a long look before speaking, "Five children. Besides Lord Bradley?"

"Yes, sir," the dark-armored knight nodded, "and there is reason to believe Lord Bradley's escape was assisted. The lock on the holding room door appears to have been tampered with from the outside. My guess is that he has joined himself to the rebels. What better way to show revenge toward his brother-in-law?"

Kenrick's eyes swept the Reestablishment room. He had gone into a rage the morning before when he discovered that Lord Bradley had escaped and entered his private sanctum. Now Sir Valden's words caused him to reconsider. Had Bradley been the one to enter this room after all?

A lock had been tampered with. Which of the children had been apprenticed to…?

Kenrick's gaze sharpened, "Where is the boy, Luke?"

"My assistants are tracking him as we speak."

"You lost him."

Sir Valden stiffened, "The entire Mordecai garrison suffered a delay when the dragons attacked the city. Everyone went into hiding that night."

"Everyone except Luke." Kenrick returned his focus to the map, "Apparently he managed to slip away from your able grasp that night."

Sir Valden's eyes sparked angrily, "I understand the importance of keeping a watch over this boy and seeing that Lord Roland's orders are carried out. However, I am not so foolish that I would throw my life away in pursuit of a single scamp who lives by a code of rash behavior. I wouldn't be surprised to learn that he is responsible for luring the five other children away from their homes."

"Indeed," Sir Kenrick's tone was distracted as he traced a finger over the mapped streets, "the five other children…"

Suddenly, Kenrick shoved away from the table and turned to stare at the wall of compartments. His eyes widened as his thoughts raced in a thousand directions. Life on Mount Desterrar. Luke's slip of Valden's watch, followed by Bradley's escape, followed by the disappearance of five other children. The Reestablishment room had been unlocked and rummaged—candles burnt low, quill pen left carelessly in the ink, documents sitting at the wrong angle. What if…?

Kenrick's gaze slid to the parchment in the lower right-hand corner. The master list. He reached for the thick document and unrolled it across the surface of the map.

"Kenrick?" Sir Valden eyed him curiously.

Kenrick's eyes roved the list, the names of all the children who had been reestablished by the Mordecai Order. Such a register would be of great help to anyone seeking to contact any or all of the rebels' offspring.

"Look there," Valden stepped up to the table's opposite edge and planted a finger at the bottom of the page. Kenrick's eyes followed the motion and fell on a line of nearly unreadable script along the parchment's lower border.

I'll finish from here. Catch us if you can.

Kenrick's eyes widened and narrowed in turn. How dare that young firebrand say he would "finish" as if Kenrick's work these four years had been a part of some greater plan? How dare the little rebel enter this room and make use of the Order's private records? How dare he…?

Kenrick's growl of frustration grew until it became an enraged roar that shook the very walls. With an angry sweep of his arm, the chief Mordecai shoved the contents of his table to the floor and then pounded the stone surface with both fists.

"*Brat!!*"

Outside the Reestablishment room, a shadowy figure blended with the dark walls of the garrison as he listened to the conversation taking place within. The interloper—the same who had secretly witnessed the House of Peers' ruin the day before—smirked when Sir Kenrick bellowed a string of curses. Apparently the Mordecais' chief did not have total control of his dealings, as he wanted everyone to believe.

"He's planning an exodus, I would bet my life on it! He's had his heart set on some sort of uprising from the very first day." Kenrick growled, "Find him, Valden, or you'll find yourself wearing a collar to match his. After four years of keeping them in line, the escape of any number of those children would be a disgrace to the Order."

The interloper sank deeper into the shadows as the door opened and the Mordecai's first knight appeared and stalked across the courtyard to retrieve his horse from the stables. Another smile crept over the eavesdropper's face as he watched Valden stride away. There went another man who believed that he had everything under control.

He could never be more wrong.

The interloper's eyes shifted to Kenrick's window once more.

An exodus. How interesting.

Lillian stared at the door until it closed with a dull thud, and then the twelve-year-old made a face of disappointment. She'd expected the oak panel to yield a louder and more dramatic crash when it shut. That certainly would have made her visitor's exit more threatening, which would have been exciting. Alas, nothing about this house was loud or exciting, and here she had had proof. Even the doors dared not make an excessive amount of noise when they had been slammed shut by an angry youth.

Lillian's gaze drifted over her lush surroundings. The front receiving room had a window that overlooked the busy cobbled street near the harbor, and was decorated in rich blues accented by soft gold. It was her favorite room in this house, where she had spent four happy, if uneventful, years with her parents.

Her new parents.

A familiar pinch of discomfort followed that thought, but Lillian brushed it aside as she moved to look out the window. Her crystal-blue eyes darted from side to side until they landed on her recent visitor, who was just disappearing around the corner at the end of the street. Whirling from the sight of the crowded lane, Lillian turned and collapsed onto her blue divan in a flurry of soft lavender skirts and white-blond hair. She released a dramatic sigh.

She remembered the day she had been brought to this quiet, unexciting home. Sir Kenrick of the Mordecai Order had brought her into this very room where she had met the portly man and his wife who were to care for her after her birthparents' banishment.

"This is your father, girl," Kenrick had motioned to the man, a prominent merchant in Hebbros, and then shifted to include the woman, "and this is your mother."

Lillian had begun to cry and the merchant's wife had reacted swiftly, moving forward to envelope the child in a sympathetic embrace. Tender nothings, intended to soothe, had been whispered in her ear until Lillian felt safe and protected. These people would care for her and not force her to choose between a life of comfort and a life of exile.

When she had next looked up, Sir Kenrick was nowhere in sight and her new parents had begun to shower her with presents from the merchant's latest shipment of goods. Her favorite gifts had been the story parchments, translated from foreign scripts to her native Mizgalian tongue.

Before long, Mother had insisted that her "Flower" was too delicate to venture out to the schoolrooms every day, and so for four years Lillian had been kept at home, completing her schooling under the watch of a private tutor approved by the House of Peers. This would be her last year of lessons.

And then what? Lillian wondered if she would be forced to sit quietly all day long when she had no more lessons to study. She knew her father and mother preferred a quiet home with no unnecessary commotion, and though Lillian had become accustomed to this undisturbed manner of living, she also longed for a bit of adventure.

Her eyes moved to the small trunk beneath the window, where she kept the parchments that bore the stories she most preferred. A smile lifted the corners of her mouth. There, within the lengths of rolled parchment, Lillian had first been introduced to a life that could be thrilling, daring, and romantic. Mother often encouraged her reading, a skill unknown by many, and as a result Lillian was most often to be found here on her divan with a parchment unrolled over her drawn-up knees.

She had almost come to believe that any real excitement would forever pass her by.

Almost.

Lillian straightened on the divan and sat perched on the edge, staring at the closed door once again. She may have learned to be ashamed of her connection to the group called Faithful, but that association had certainly come in handy during the last few days. She had been sitting in just such a position several mornings before when two young men had entered and asked to speak with her.

Lillian sighed as if it had been the knight from her favorite story who had appeared and not two youths in light armor bearing the arrow-pierced M of the Mordecai Order. They were mysterious and dark-headed—much like she pictured Sir Farewell from *The Dragon of Penloc*—and both were exceptionally tall. And very obviously twins.

"Warin is by far the more handsome of the two," Lillian murmured to herself and plucked absently at the folds of her cashmere dress, "but the scar over Wulf's eye makes him look more daring and roguish. I wonder how he got it."

They had been charged with a mission, Warin had said, to track down a rebel who was even now roaming the streets of Hebbros unhindered. A dissenter who had been collared by Lord Roland because of his resistance against the laws of Mizgalia. A firebrand who had once known Lillian. The young knights had spoken their assurance of her loyalty to the cause of the Order and Lord Roland himself, and had asked her to inform them should the boy Luke contact her in the name of his forbidden faith.

Flattered, Lillian had agreed to their request. After all, she had given up all pretence of following her parents' faith and was now living comfortably. The other reestablished children should learn to be content as well.

"When the first twenty Faithful were banished there was talk of one day rising against those who had sent them into exile," Lillian had spoken with an eagerness to please. "Luke was announced the leader and later he brought everyone a rivet from the cooper's shop to remind us of our bond."

Warin's sharp eyes had narrowed on her, "Why didn't you tell someone he was stirring dissention?"

Lillian had shrugged and quickly shaken her blond head, "I

never tell anything that might make my parents worry. You see, they like things to stay quiet. Besides, I haven't seen Luke since he brought me a rivet, and I don't even know where that little bit of iron got off to anyway."

That had been several days ago.

Today, just moments ago, Lillian had received another visit from the Mordecai garrison in answer to her summons. Warin had come alone, Wulf choosing to remain in search of Luke. Lillian had spoken of seeing Pavia, and the former friend's invitation to join their small band, which was now beginning to assemble. She had been so pleased to have a bit of news to pass on, and felt just like a character in one of her stories. Bold and brave, uncovering the secrets of an unlawful mob.

And then Warin had scowled.

"You didn't ask where they're gathering? You already told me Luke's planning an uprising, I need to know where he's hiding!"

"I thought he would come in secret last night and ask me to join them, but he never did."

"Don't wait for him to be a hero, Lillian. He's a callous rebel who thinks only of himself."

Lillian frowned at the memory of his anger, though he had still not grown very loud. Had his mother never taught him any manners? Of course, she was just a child, and Warin no doubt thought her yet unworthy of a lady's respect.

Gradually, he had gathered himself enough to suggest in a calm monotone that it was her duty to discover where Luke was hiding his troupe. It would be simple. Allow herself to be seen on the streets again and agree to visit her former friends when they approached her. Then return home and send word to the garrison of their whereabouts.

"Do you think you can do that?" Warin's question had been laced with doubt.

"Of course I can," Lillian had lifted her chin in opposition to his skepticism, "if you stop chastising me and start treating me like a lady."

His brief smirk had quickly been erased and he had stepped forward to take her hand and kiss her fingers like a courtier. Lillian was sure she had blushed with embarrassment even as her thoughts started whirling in panic. What if her mother had entered the room and seen a stranger bowing over her hand?

The gesture had been sweet, but his green eyes had flashed with something dangerous just before he had left with a final caution, "This is important work I'm entrusting you with. See that you do it right…my lady."

Lillian leaned back on her couch and took a deep breath as Warin's visit continued to replay in her mind. The thought occurred to her that he had been far too familiar and at ease with such actions toward a lady. Yet he had behaved in just the same way Sir Farewell would toward the noble ladies of Penloc. It must be the proper thing to do. Lillian simply wasn't familiar with the ways of the court.

The door opened without a sound and Mother entered on a whisper of fabric as her hem brushed across the floor. The portly woman glanced about and then smiled at Lillian. When she spoke, her soft voice matched the serene atmosphere of the house.

"I was just coming to check on you, Flower." She caressed the side of Lillian's head, "I thought I heard a stranger's voice. Did we have a visitor?"

Lillian dropped her gaze to study the floor. There was no need to deny that her mother had heard someone, but there was also no need to divulge the truth about Warin's visit. He had entrusted her with a secret mission, and that would cause her mother to worry. Lillian's schoolmaster had taught her it was wrong to cause unnecessary anxiety when silence or a half-truth could provide a balm of peace instead.

"Yes, someone was here," Lillian looked up to smile at the woman beside her, "but he was looking for someone who does not live here, and so I sent him on his way."

"Ah," Mother nodded. "This city is so large, one can easily become confused by the many streets. I hope he finds whoever he is looking for."

Lillian's smile tilted mischievously as her mother turned her back to leave the room, "So do I."

Warin stepped across the threshold of Squire's Tavern and paused briefly before marching across the boisterous establishment and hauling one patron up by the neck of his tunic.

"What are you doing here?"

Wulf jerked away from his brother's hold and reclaimed his seat. He grinned and nodded toward the frothy tankard before him, "What does it look like I'm doing?"

Warin clenched his jaw, "We had planned for you to hunt Luke down while I checked on the summons from that petty little dreamer."

Wulf smirked, "Petty or pretty?"

"Petty." Warin gave his brother a hard glare and took a seat on the opposite side of the table, "Why aren't you out looking for Luke?"

Wulf rolled his eyes and propped one booted foot on the bench beside him, "I did look. I hunted and listened and watched until my eyes and ears became sore. Every time I catch sight of that pest, he vanishes the very next instant. I decided to wait and see if Lillian found anything."

Warin snorted, "Hardly. But soon." He swiped Wulf's tankard from the table and tipped his head back for a deep swallow. Sighing with satisfaction, he clapped the mug back onto the table and ignored his brother's glare, "Very soon, Wulf."

"That was mine, you pig," Wulf caught the tankard and pulled it back toward his side of the table, signaling the taverner for more ale.

Warin shook his head, "You drink too much anyway."

Wulf bristled, "And I suppose that's far worse than you being the greatest flirt in Mizgalia?"

"I am not," Warin propped his back against the wall behind him and watched as the taverner refilled Wulf's tankard. The man pocketed the coin offered by his twin and then moved away.

Wulf curled a possessive grasp around the mug and cocked his brow in a look of disagreement, "Warin, you spend all of eight seconds with a maid and she's suddenly convinced that she's madly in love with you."

Warin waved his hand in absent dismissal, "That's not a problem, that's a gift."

Wulf scoffed and nearly choked on a sip of ale, "Only until every girl in Hebbros believes you're pledged to her." The sound of Warin's chuckle grated on Wulf's nerves and he scowled, "Oh, I forgot. I should have said every girl except Pavia. She wouldn't have anything to do with you."

Warin smirked with a lack of interest, but Wulf could see that his comment had pinched his brother's pride.

"You know I only teased Pavia for the fun of it, and she knew it too. Besides, she's barely older than our two-faced Lillian, who's just a slip of a child. And as for the scenario you just painted, I'll never be brought to face such a catastrophe as that. I'll be far away from Hebbros before any females can get such an idea into their heads."

Wulf froze in the act of bringing his tankard to his lips. He stared at Warin over the brim, "Far away? Where are you going? What are you keeping from me?"

"Nothing yet," Warin grinned and took the mug from Wulf, taking another drink. "I've simply decided that I won't waste my whole life here in Hebbros. It may be the second largest city in Mizgalia, but that means there's one bigger. I plan to work my way to Mockmor and serve on the king's guard. Perhaps I'll travel to Arcrea some day and get a look at those heathens down there."

Wulf watched as his twin stole another sip from his tankard, "And what about me? Where am I in your plans?"

"Wherever you want to be." Warin chuckled, "I'm not exactly your keeper, am I? What do you want to do with yourself?"

Wulf gave a noncommittal shrug, "I always figured on staying here in Hebbros. Work my way up to a position of honor—"

"In the Mordecai Order?" Warin leaned forward and lowered his voice, "You know Kenrick and Valden monopolize the garrison's system of power. Our places on Valden's staff are a gift from the gods, Wulf. We've been catapulted into positions that might've taken years to earn otherwise. But we'll never be promoted unless we go elsewhere. Valden wants us right where we are, and he has the power to keep us there as long as we stay in Hebbros."

Wulf scowled, "I still think it's possible."

Warin sat back, "Suit yourself. I intend to strive for more, but first I'll stay and settle our score with Luke."

"You know Valden wants him."

"Yes," Warin took another sip of Wulf's ale, but his distracted twin didn't seem to notice, "and Valden will get him…after I'm done with him."

Wulf nodded, his thoughts churning, "I find it suspicious, this sudden interest Valden has taken in Luke. What does he want that brat around for? If what we overheard is true, and Luke possesses incredible perception, he could cause us a lot of trouble. Especially if he keeps turning up when we least expect him, like the night we planned to kill Monty."

Warin grunted in agreement and drained the mug with a final swallow.

Wulf blinked.

"Hey!" He lurched forward and grabbed the tankard. Glancing into the empty mug, he reached across and cuffed his twin on the ear, "That was mine, you oaf!"

His growl was met with a laugh as Warin dodged another blow and slipped away to head for the door. Wulf followed reluctantly.

"We'd better report to Sir Valden. We'll learn something soon, I can feel it in my bones." Warin paused on the threshold and grinned at a passing maid. Glancing at his scowling brother, he continued, "Perhaps on the way back to the garrison we'll step into a temple and ask Roland's favorite deities for a blessing on our cause."

"Our cause," Wulf murmured as he trailed behind his brother. "Your liberation *from* Hebbros, my promotion *within* Hebbros, and Luke's capture before he keeps any of it from coming to pass."

34
Directionally Challenged

Lord Roland took a bite of mutton and glanced at Lord Brock, seated to his right at the banquet's table of honor. The man was several years younger than Roland and carried himself with an air of assurance, but he also had a tendency to whine. Apparently, Brock was accustomed to having his way.

Rosalynn sat to Roland's left, sullen and quiet. They had spoken little to one another since the night of Bradley's disappearance and Rosalynn's announcement that she was with child. She seemed to believe that he was angry or disappointed with her, and Roland had been in no mood to correct her assessment. He was not disappointed, merely put out. Another child meant more work for him.

Rosalynn glanced his way and Roland tried to offer a small smile. Eventually he would get around to telling her that he was not angry. They would be able to arrange another profitable marriage for this child, as they would for his brother and sister. All would be well.

Rosalynn looked away and Roland heaved a sigh. He doubted he would ever understand the moods that his wife experienced. They were predictable as night and day, yet uncertain as a storm at sea. He looked the other way and watched Lord Brock help himself to another platter of chicken. For pity's sake, the man was as thin as a shepherd's staff! Where on earth did he put it all?

"I will not stay long." Brock swallowed a bite and licked his finger, "I really must be on my way. Gilbrenor is still some distance southwest of Arcrea, and King Cronin has great plans for the island…and for me." He smiled at Roland as if they shared a great secret, "Officially, I will take residence on the isle as the king's ambassador. However, our sovereign made several hints that he is setting me in place for future purposes."

Roland turned to study Brock and the other lord leaned in with a conspiratorial whisper, "When the time is right, there is every reason to believe that Mizgalia will expand her borders by taking possession of the island and placing it under Cronin's rule. When that day comes, be it tomorrow or ten years hence, I will be in place to rule Gilbrenor in His Majesty's absence."

Jealousy burned in Roland's chest. Who was this Brock, to be entrusted with a journey that may result in the conquest of other lands? Was not Roland the king's favorite? Why had Cronin chosen another man for this great honor?

Roland shoved these thoughts aside long enough to reply, "You seem the right man for the mission. Our king has chosen well."

"Hasn't he?" Brock leaned back with a gleam of satisfaction in his eye, "This day has been long in coming, but at last the king has decided to reward my years of steadfast service in his army and in his court. I will not disappoint him." With a dubious glance at his surroundings he decided to add, "And you too are…*greatly* favored by His Majesty. Hebbros is a grand city to say the least. I only wish I could stay longer to witness more of her marvels."

Roland pasted a smile on his face at the man's effort to eke out a compliment, "It is a pleasure you will be unfortunate to miss. Perhaps when I accompany you to the docks tomorrow we can take a more scenic route."

The next course was brought into the Great Hall and further conversation was hindered by the exclamations of the guests, the more notable citizens of Hebbros, over the fine food. Roland made a show of taking Rosalynn's hand and hoped the sign of affection would lift her spirits. Meanwhile, his thoughts spun as a new plan formed in his mind.

If King Cronin wanted to expand the borders of Mizgalia,

why limit such a conquest to one island that may take years to conquer? Roland smiled to himself. There were other lands, other provinces that might be taken. Lands such as those across the Delfron, which were an easy distance from Hebbros. Roland had a powerful army at his disposal. Why waste such power? He would pray over these thoughts the next time he entered the temple.

Roland rose to his feet, the sudden movement drawing every eye in the hall. Grabbing the goblet that sat in front of him, the lord of Hebbros lifted it in a salute.

"A toast, my friends," he smiled at Rosalynn, and then his gaze swept the room to land on Lord Brock, "to progress, expansion, and His Majesty the king."

A roar of approval followed Lord Roland's toast as Sarah passed the Great Hall on her way out to the kitchens. Little Celia had quickly fallen asleep at the end of a tiring day, but Lord Jerem refused to so much as touch his bed until Sarah returned from fetching him a sweet roll. The second nurse had remained behind with the obstinate child while Sarah raced to comply with his demands.

"How long will this go on?" Sarah spoke to herself as she stepped outside, and so was surprised when someone answered.

"Unfortunately, if you're a slave like me it will probably go on 'til the day you die."

Sarah turned to see a woman standing nearby, leaning against the palace wall. The stranger smiled at Sarah and swept a strand of blond hair behind her ear, "I didn't mean to startle you. I'm sorry."

"You didn't. I mean…it's all right."

Sarah stepped out of the way as another slave rushed by with a tray of steaming food for the banquet. She studied the woman, who looked close in age to Lady Rosalynn. She wore a leather slave's collar and her robes were embroidered with the insignia of another lord.

"I don't recognize you. Did you come t' Hebbros with Lord Brock?"

The blond woman offered a slight nod, "I did."

Sarah nodded toward the kitchens, bright and glowing with the warmth of many fires, "I'm on m'way t' fetch a treat for

Roland's little son, Lord Jerem. Come along if you'd like."

The woman smiled slightly and gave another nod, "Thank you. I've been standing outside that door smelling all the food that goes in. I'd like something to take my mind off of it."

Sarah grinned, "I doubt going t' the kitchens will take your mind off the food, but I'll welcome a friend t' talk to." She glanced at her companion as they fell in step together, "I'm Sarah."

"I'm called Tessa."

Sarah waited for the other woman to speak again, but finally broke the silence herself, "Your voice carries a bit of an accent. You're not Mizgalian?"

Tessa shook her head, "I was kidnapped from northern Arcrea during a raid thirteen years ago. Traces of my native tongue often affect my speech. You?"

"I was brought from Dolthe twelve years ago."

Tessa shook her head, "These Mizgalians think they have every right in the world to take from their neighbors. Unfortunately, no one seems capable of stopping them, and so it would seem they're right."

Sarah nodded, finding comfort in speaking freely with another slave. The two were soon conversing like old acquaintances as they retrieved Jerem's sweet roll, and then Tessa accompanied Sarah back through the palace halls to the children's rooms. With the excitement of the ongoing banquet, no one paused to question the stranger's presence in the corridors. As they neared their destination, Sarah finished telling her new friend about the events of the last three days, ending with Bradley's disappearance and Jerem's rebellion.

Tessa's brow furrowed with sympathy, "What will you do?"

"Beg Lord Roland to send me away."

Tessa's eyes widened, "But what if your Bradley plans to return for you?"

"He planned his own escape the very night he was imprisoned. If he wanted to come for me, he would've done so by now."

Tessa laid a hand on Sarah's arm, "Promise me you won't act in haste."

Sarah wrinkled her pert nose in bewilderment, "I've thought on this for several days now."

Tessa's head shook back and forth and a crease worried her

forehead, "When I was kidnapped from my homeland I left behind a mother, father, and brother whom I loved very dearly. I had no choice," her grip tightened on Sarah's arm, "but you do. Don't forsake those you love without giving them a chance to prove that your fears are ungrounded. You made a covenant, Sarah, and you should strive to keep it no matter what."

Tears blurred Sarah's vision, "But what can I do? How long must I wait for him?"

Tessa's hand fell away and she shook her head sadly, "That I cannot tell you. For months after my abduction I lived for the hope that my brother would come and find me, rescue me. Now my mind tells me that such a hope is foolish, but my heart still refuses to give it up. Maybe one day…" Tessa lifted her gaze to meet Sarah's, "Have you prayed about it?"

Sarah gave a slight shrug, "I don't know which deity is the right one t' ask."

"There are so many in Mizgalia," Tessa's brow furrowed in thought. "Surely there is a god who cares."

"I suppose I'll have t' ask them all."

A shriek suddenly rent the air, followed by Celia's high-pitched wail. Jerem. Sarah's shoulders drooped with the weighty thought of the long night ahead. Tessa quickly said goodbye and hurried back the way they had come, and Sarah turned to slowly march toward the children's quarters.

Her prayers would have to wait.

Luke grumbled and murmured as he moved through the darkened streets of Hebbros alone. How could the others side with Christopher's plan, deciding after two observations and an "Obvious, Elbert" that it was better and wiser than Luke's idea? Luke was the leader. Luke would decide. Chris's plan would take too long or result in leaving one hundred children behind. Luke needed action *now*. They could think of details later.

Be still. The thought was like a whisper in his heart, reminding Luke of those secret lessons learned at his mother's knee.

He shook his head, "I can't be still, it's not in my nature. Someone has to go and call the others, and it seems I'm the only one who's willing!"

Luke retrieved the list of names from his tunic and checked once more to see that he had the correct destination. He remembered little Joel with a smile, and was looking forward to making the eleven-year-old boy his first rescue of the night. Returning the list to its place, Luke moved to the edge of the rooftop where he had been perched for some time, waiting for the city to fall asleep. He would take Joel back to the hideout and the boy's joy over being rescued would prove to the others that they had to move quickly.

They had to do this Luke's way.

Calculating the distance to the next building, Luke backed away from the edge and then raced forward to make his leap. He landed softly and rolled to a stop, thankful he had left his bow and quiver behind tonight. Quickly jumping to his feet, Luke moved to the edge and lowered himself over the side and down to a second story window. His drop was successful and he landed with both feet on the sill.

And on the tail of a sleeping cat.

The cat's shriek was unlike any noise Luke had ever heard. With a cry of shock and dismay, he lost his balance and slipped backwards, catching hold of the sill with both hands before he tumbled in a nasty fall. Hissing with rage, the offended feline bolted from the sill and disappeared inside. Simultaneously a woman's scream sounded from within, accompanied by a man's yell and a boy's voice shouting, "Great turnips!"

Dangling from the windowsill, Luke held his breath and waited. Footsteps quickly pattered across the room above and a boy's head appeared over the sill.

"Great turnips, there's somebody out here!"

"Get back, Joel!" The woman inside shrieked, "Away from the window, you simpleton!"

Joel. In the moonlight, Luke stared helplessly at the very boy he had come to rescue, and his breath caught at what he read in the other gaze. The shaggy head vanished from sight. Heavier steps pounded across the floor and Luke knew that Joel's caretaker was coming to the window. He had to escape. Looking down, Luke judged the distance from sill to street and decided he would rather take the risk than be caught and dragged back to the Mordecais.

"You there!" An angry voice roared overhead just as Luke's fingers released their hold. Dropping from the window, he quickly plummeted toward the earth below.

It was well past midnight. Sarah glanced around the corner and was relieved to find the dark corridor empty. Slipping through the shadows, she moved toward the doors at the other end of the hall. Roland's temple. The sacred place where his lordship's nine favorite deities could be approached at once.

Sarah heard voices down another corridor and figured the guards must have stepped away. Taking advantage of the moment and a chance to forgo any questions, she slipped inside.

It was cold. Cold and dark even with candles flickering to either side of the dais across the room. The stone floor exuded a chill that traveled up Sarah's spine until she shivered and wrapped her arms around herself. Feeling eyes on her, Sarah looked up at the nine statues that lined the far wall of the temple. Unseeing eyes of stone.

Forcing her feet to carry her forward, Sarah followed two rows of pillars toward the dais; three pillars to either side of the elongated room. She stopped well away from the nine statues, fearful to appear too close, and dropped to her knees several yards from a small incense altar. A warm glow filled the altar's basin, but failed to quell Sarah's fear of this otherwise cold place.

Feeling eyes on her again, Sarah looked over her shoulder and into the shadows along the wall behind the pillars. No movement. No sound. Facing forward again, she clasped her hands together and lifted a beseeching gaze to the nine figures before her.

No words would come.

"I…I…" Sarah's eyes darted back and forth in confusion. What had she come to say? "I don't know which of you t'…ask. Or what t' ask. I…I'm so confused!" Covering her face with both hands, Sarah waited. Perhaps one of them would take pity on her and answer the unknown question that she hadn't asked.

Come unto me, all ye that labor and are heavy-laden.

The words were whispered to Sarah's heart at the same moment an image of her strange wedding appeared before her mind's eye. The boy named Christopher had spoken of the God who created marriage at the beginning of time. Could He be speaking to her now?

She lifted her head. Her eyes traveled past the nine statues and rested on the ceiling above. She thought of what lay beyond the rafters. Beyond the sky, the stars, and the clouds. Beyond the heavens.

"God," her whisper charged like a shock into the surrounding stillness. "Christopher's God. If You're really out there somewhere, please help me. He said You created marriage, and so I beg You t' save mine."

She was quiet for a moment, waiting once more. What should she expect now?

The sound of wind creeping through unseen crevices suddenly sounded like a harsh laugh that filled the temple. The candles beside the dais danced wildly, threatening to leave her in darkness. The light of the flames played shadows on the faces of the nine statues, giving them an odd look of reproach. Were they angry with her for seeking help from another?

"But you were silent," Sarah cried out as she studied the figures. "What should I do?"

The wind howled louder and swirled like dark ribbons around Sarah's head until she covered her ears and closed her eyes. Scrambling further from the dais, she retreated to one of the pillars and lifted her tear-stained face heavenward, "Oh God, help me! What should I do!?"

Immediately, the noise became still. The young slave felt as if a wall had been erected between herself and the dais, separating her from the dark presence she had felt a moment before. Instead, warmth covered her like an invisible blanket of shelter.

Run from evil.

There was her answer. It didn't address the problems regarding her marriage, but it was clearly what she should do now.

"I shouldn't be here." Sarah couldn't understand why or how, but tonight, after years of being taught otherwise, she knew that evil lurked in this temple. She quickly stood and retreated through the doors and down the passage.

Suddenly, her steps faltered and she paused in the middle of an empty corridor. A sense of awe filled her as she realized that Christopher's God had proven Himself greater than the overwhelming presence of evil. He had heard her, answered her, and protected her, when she sat in a place of worship that was not intended for Him. In a city that outlawed the very mention of His name.

"Jesus." The very magnitude of this God's abilities suddenly made His identity obvious, "You must be Jesus."

Sarah tasted the sweetness of that name on her lips and smiled. She wanted, *needed* to know more about Him, but who would tell her? She had heard of the band called Faithful, and wondered now if Christopher and Pavia were among those who worshipped the outlawed God. But how could she find out as long as she was kept inside the castle?

"Jesus, what should I do?"

The young slave, hungering after truth, waited in the corridor. What should she do? About Bradley, Jerem, and her faith, or lack thereof? What should her next step be?

And then the answer came. Strong, sure…and unexpected.

Be still.

35

Reason & Rebellion

The shadowy figure—the interloper—watched as the young slave girl raced from the temple without a backward glance. He shook his head and sneered. How Lord Roland would rage if he knew someone had prayed to the forbidden God within the sanctum of his favored deities.

The interloper drew his cloak tighter around him and moved deeper into the shadows along the wall. Situating himself in the darkest corner of the temple, he set his sights on the double doors, visible between two pillars. His thoughts returned to the scene he had just witnessed.

The girl had been very young, no older than fifteen or sixteen, yet she had come seeking a blessing on her marriage. Considering that she must work here in the palace, and judging that her distress and pain were fresh, the unseen witness quickly decided she must be Lord Bradley's new bride.

He chuckled. A slave? What had the foolish noble been thinking?

The girl's other words, whispered and shouted by turn, had indicated an influence of the Faithful. This may support suspicions regarding Bradley's affiliation with the rebels. She had said the name Christopher. Apparently, the girl's head had been stuffed with nonsense and she had a notion to heed it. She was as foolish as Bradley.

Voices in the outer passage suddenly drew near and the interloper sharpened his gaze. The doors were pushed open and torchlight wavered over the threshold, revealing four men. Two of them, soldiers bearing the torches, entered and cast a brief glance over the room, searching for danger with a casual attitude that said they expected none. Turning back with a salute, they moved to stand guard outside the temple doors. The interloper's eyes shifted to the two men who remained. One was a priest. The other was Lord Roland.

The priest's ample robes dragged on the stone floor as he crossed to a small altar that stood like a pedestal before the dais. Dipping his hand into a bag strung from his wrist, the holy man then scattered a cluster of incense over the altar's basin. Tendrils of smoke rose from the bowl as he swayed back and forth, humming a string of odd notes and chanting several indecipherable words. Roland watched in silence until the ritual had been repeated several times.

"That will do," the nobleman finally spoke, his voice thunderous in the odd stillness.

"Yes, my lord," the priest droned. He bowed before the nine deities and then moved to stand on the other side of the altar.

"You will leave me now." Roland's command caused the priest to draw up short, and a look of confusion passed over the man's face. Roland scowled, "Now."

The single word reverberated through the temple with authority. The unseen interloper waited in the shadows as the priest quickly bowed and scurried for the doors. The double panels groaned as the guards pulled them shut, and a dull clunk sounded as they met the doorframe.

Roland waited until he was supposedly alone before he stepped closer to the dais. He stared up at the nine statues, his eyes unwavering, as the candlelight burnished his hair to a fine gold and highlighted the strength in his features. The ruler of Hebbros considered himself entitled to be here, at home in the company of the gods. Many would agree with him.

The interloper did not.

The silent intruder narrowed his eyes and studied Roland closer. The nobleman blinked bleary eyes and swayed gently on his feet. Apparently his lordship had not entirely escaped the effects of the wine at tonight's banquet. His mind was not entirely clear, but it would be clear enough.

Perfect. The cloaked figure smiled to himself and slipped into place behind the nearest statue.

Roland shook his head, as if the motion could dislodge the headache that sought to overtake him. The incense filled the temple with a heady aroma. Tendrils of smoke snaked upward from the altar, reaching for the heavens in an airy dance that dissipated overhead. Roland took a deep breath, inhaling the priest's sweet-scented offering and soaking in the essence of power that permeated the room.

It was time to pray.

Roland stepped up to the altar, steadied himself against a wave of dizziness, and then moved to stand directly in front of the dais. The nine deities stared down at him, awaiting his request. Lifting his arms in petition, the city's ruler threw his head back and began.

"O mighty ones, hear and answer me with all haste. My king, the great Cronin, seeks to enlarge the boundaries of Mizgalia, and I, Roland, wish to go out from Hebbros in order to serve my king in his quest to make our realm even greater. I seek your permission and blessing on such a crusade, that I might conquer heathen lands and place them beneath the rule of Mizgalia and the power of our gods." The words of his prayer echoed back to Roland from the walls of stone and he dropped to his knees before the dais, "Show me the way, that I might conquer in your name."

Wind whistled through several unseen crevices, mocking the emptiness that met Roland's request.

"*Speak to me!* Grant me permission to cross the Delfron for the honor of Mizgalia." The echo of his words died away and Roland bowed his head, intent upon waiting until he received the answer he had come for. Suddenly, the wind died to a mere whisper and Roland froze when a strange voice crept into the stillness.

"Wh*aaa*t is th*iii*s?" Low and raspy, the airy tones lengthened each word in a lofty sound of disbelief. A moment passed before it came again, from somewhere along the dais, "Do I h*eeea*r the s*ooo*und of a requ*eee*st?"

Roland blinked in shock. Could it be true? Had the gods come to meet with him tonight? Were they speaking to him now? Was this the voice of the god of war? Or perhaps the god of justice? He eyed the nine statues and wondered briefly if this were merely some lasting effect of tonight's wine. But no, he had most certainly heard someone speak, and his guards had checked the temple for trespassers.

The voice came again, louder this time and fraught with anger, "I hear a plea for power, the plea of one who seeks to gain his fullest potential. But I see no offering. I see no gift, brought in hopes of trading for my services. You seek a blessing, but I seek a sign of your loyalty."

Roland's heart began to pound in fear. A gift. He had neglected to bring a gift for the gods! The nobleman's eyes darted back and forth, scanning the row of statues. Which was the deity who spoke to him now?

"What would you ask of me? Name your desire, O great one, and I will bow to your wishes. Only promise me victory in the crusade to come."

"I will promise nothing," the voice held a tone of iron, immovable and imperious.

"Of course," Roland lowered his head in obeisance. "I will simply follow you in hope, believing that you will reward my obedience to you."

The voice had moved to the other end of the dais, "Your claims of loyalty to the gods of Mizgalia have failed to impress me, since I yet see proof of your lenience to another."

"A…another?" Roland faltered in confusion. His vision momentarily blurred, blending shadow with smoke. One of the temple candles flickered wildly and then sputtered out, leaving one side of the dais in total darkness.

The voice hissed, dripping with malice and scorn, "The God of the Faithful still grips a remnant of your people. I cannot take first place in the hearts of Hebbros so long as He is present."

Roland's brow furrowed, "But I have tried to rid the city of this God! I banished a number of them years ago and have outlawed their faith. The founders of the Faithful are either banished or dead, and can no longer spread their words of poison to—"

"What good will you do, if you uproot a plant but neglect to pluck up the seeds it has left behind? You will be overtaken by the growth of the future more than that of the past! The collared boy alone would raise an army of children who seek to overthrow your rule against them. Even now he is drawing numbers of children away, seeking to escape your rule."

"What?" Roland's brow furrowed in disbelief and the headache he had tried to keep away grew suddenly intense, "What would you have me do?"

There was a pause before the voice spoke again, clearly taking pleasure in the words, "Purge the city of this rabble."

Roland sat back and stared up at first one and then another of the nine statues, "They will be banished."

"Have you learned nothing?" The voice lashed out with such force the smoke rising from the altar quivered on its journey upward. Roland cowered beneath the displeasure and waited for further instructions. "Banishment is too easy for them. It is rumored even now that those who were cast out before still live on Desterrar's peak. Execute the remnant that is even now gathering together, threatening the peace of Hebbros. This will be a favorable sacrifice to honor your gods so we will hear your request."

"Yes. Yes!" Roland's eyes grew wide with a half-crazed excitement as his thoughts moved to plan ahead.

The voice sounded pleased with his fervor, "When these gifts have been offered, these sacrifices made, then a blessing will be granted you. However, you will not crusade in other lands. Hebbros is enough. Hebbros is yours. Take it for your own. You deserve it."

Roland's eyes widened, gluttonous for power, "I see! Yes, I can see now!"

The interloper finished speaking from his hiding place behind the dais. He watched as Roland made a fool of himself, bowing and chanting and praising the nine deities for their favor. When he could stand it no more, the hidden figure moved around to the side of the dais where the last candle flickered and waved his cloak in an arc that extinguished the lonely flame. The temple fell into darkness and the interloper moved to assume his role as Roland's god once more.

"Go now, and prepare for the greatness to come."

"I will, O great one," Roland's voice sounded through the thick blackness as the ruler backed toward the doors. A moment later a shaft of light cut across the temple from the passage beyond. Roland staggered across the threshold, and then the panel closed with a thud and all was quiet.

The cloaked figure moved from behind the dais and along the wall to the doors. When he was sure that no one lurked in the corridor outside, he slipped from the temple and made his way through the palace and out into the night. He thought of Roland on his knees before the dais and chuckled. So many men were vying for power in this city, and each believed they were the ultimate authority. In the end they were no more than a number of puppets dangling from the strings of this interloper's ingenuity.

A dragon shrieked hungrily somewhere to the west and he glanced in that direction before quietly disappearing down a narrow side street. He moved along the labyrinth of familiar byways until finally pushing through the door of one establishment, boisterous with life despite the night's threats of beast and brigand alike.

The newcomer waited by the door while his eyes adjusted to the dim light of Squire's Tavern. The long tables were crowded with boys—squires, peasants, and apprentices. A gullible lot. They were even easier to mold and lead than Roland.

The taverner caught sight of him and nodded his head toward the storage room at the back. The interloper nodded and moved in that direction, slipping through the storage room filled with barrels and crates until he came to the opposite wall. Pressing his hand to a false panel, he slid the hidden door aside and stepped through to the landing at the top of a staircase. Descending slowly, he reached the bottom step and scanned the secret room below the tavern. Benches lined the walls and filled the space in the center, each crowded with young men and boys who looked to him for leadership and guidance.

His army. A hush fell over the room as they waited expectantly for him to speak. Most of them served the Mordecai Order as squires, knights, or mere water boys. Each bore the marks and scars of abuse, produced by a life in service to brutal men. Men pursuing the destruction of the Faithful.

The cloaked chief smiled darkly. Ironically, Roland had named his dark Order after a man found in the legends of the Faithful. He too had studied the story, and for himself and his order claimed the name of the ancient Mordecai's enemy.

"Haman, what news?" One of his followers called when he remained silent. The group's leader smiled again when he thought of the tidings he bore. They deserved this bit of encouragement.

"My friends," he held out his arms in a warm gesture, "the end of the Faithful is near, and Roland will secede!"

The room erupted in a cheer that charged the strained atmosphere, and the man called Haman was grateful that those in the tavern above would be too drunk or distracted to hear the response over their own revelry. He let his gaze sweep across the room. Their numbers were growing daily, attracting the vagabonds and brutes who wanted more from life than simply following the next order, obeying the next law. Roland's reign as lord of Hebbros was taxing the patience of every citizen, and many were ready for his rule to end.

The interloper smiled. In the Faithful's legend, Haman had failed in his mission for greatness. He had not looked at his plan from every angle and searched it for possible holes. This time everything would be different. As sure as the sun rose in the east, Hebbros would be his.

Luke winced and grit his teeth against a fresh wave of pain that was both physical and mental. He ambled blindly through the streets, hoping that he was heading in the right direction and dragging a leg that he knew was broken. He tried to forget the sight of Joel's face in the window above him. What he had seen there had been far more painful than the subsequent fall. He rolled his eyes. If only that cat had chosen a different spot to rest, he might have spoken with the boy.

A door opened and closed on the street ahead, briefly spilling light and laughter onto the cobbles outside. Luke recognized the establishment and grimaced. Squire's Tavern. Prepared to pass the place by, Luke paused when he heard the sound of someone approaching on the lane ahead. Ducking into the shadows along the tavern's outer wall, Luke watched as a cloaked figure approached and entered the establishment.

Luke sat back and leaned against the wall to catch his breath. He'd been on the move for several hours, ever since his drop from Joel's window. A loud pop had accentuated his landing, and Luke had known a moment of nothing but absolute pain. Clear, sharp, debilitating pain. The adrenaline of being pursued had propelled him away from Joel's home for several minutes before Luke had opened his eyes and found himself lying on the street, apparently waking from unconsciousness. Pulling himself to his one good foot, he had then forced himself to keep moving, not willing to be spotted by dragons or ruffians.

Pain twisted through Luke's left leg and his back arched with the torturous agony. A moment passed and the pain lessened slightly. Luke breathed heavily as sweat dripped from his brow. The bone would need to be set. Soon. He brought his hand up to his neck, and his fingers clutched the red leather collar. Thanks to Roland, no physician within the walls of Hebbros would tend to his injury.

Suddenly, Luke became aware of a humming noise. He looked to the right and saw the faintest glow of light escaping through a tiny grate at the base of the tavern wall. Using his right arm to pull himself along, he crawled on one side until he could peer through the small opening used for ventilation. From what little he could see, Luke guessed that beyond the grate was a room beneath Squire's Tavern. A crowd of men had gathered and they were speaking in hushed tones. This must have been the humming noise.

Abruptly the voices grew still and the few heads that Luke could see turned to face a common focal point. One man called out in the silence. Luke pressed closer to the grate, but to no avail. From this vantage point it was impossible to view whatever had claimed the room's attention.

"My friends…" a voice spoke from within and Luke suddenly tensed, a thread of unease crawling up his spine, "the end of the Faithful is near, and Roland will secede!"

The room erupted in a cheer that was muffled by the grate's size and the room's position underground. In the excitement, one man's eye turned toward the grate and Luke pulled away with a jerk, pressing his back against the tavern wall. The brief look into the stranger's gaze had been enough for Luke to know that danger lurked here. These men were angry, defiant, and ruthless. They would not be pleased to know that someone was privy to their secret meeting.

Breathing heavily and ignoring the intense pain of his broken leg, Luke stared at the wall of the shop next door and listened as the voice continued to speak from below.

Was the voice vaguely familiar? Or had his sense of reason been shattered with his leg?

"The tide is turning and soon the Faithful will no longer consume our lord's thoughts and energies. Those rebels will be executed in honor of Roland's revolt, and he will take Hebbros from the crown of Mizgalia. We will have war!"

Luke shivered when he heard the pleasure with which those words were spoken. Executed? War?

The voice continued, "But will the city remain his? Will he survive his own rebellion alive?"

"NO!" The crowd shouted their emphatic reply as one.

"Death to Roland!" One angry rebel cried.

Sweat dripped from Luke's hairline, defying the cold tremors that had seized him, and he blinked against a wave of dizziness.

"My friends, the time has come. Pledge your allegiance to this cause and follow me. Obey me. Heed me. Roland must fall if Hebbros will rise!"

"Down with Roland! Give us war!" Another man interjected, and soon the air inside the room reverberated with the chant.

Luke's heart pounded in time to the repeated words. He could hardly believe his ears. He was aware that many did not care for Roland, but he had not realized that the people's hatred ran so deep. What was their reasoning? Roland thought too much of destroying the Faithful? They disliked his numerous laws and taxes? Luke had thought the citizens of Hebbros would be pleased with their ruler's allowance for evil, yet here he had uncovered a plot to kill Roland. He could scarcely fathom the thought! Even he and the other Faithful children would never think of plotting such a thing, though he himself counted the ruler amongst his greatest enemies.

Luke's vision tilted and he jerked his head to compensate the unsteadiness of his brain. The break in his leg pulsed to a silent rhythm of agony.

A step paused on the street at the end of the alley and Luke tried to turn his head toward the sound. A figure approached and a man stood over him, "What have we here? Are you awake, boy?"

Luke could not reply through the fog that now shrouded his brain. Suddenly the man held out a walking stick, and thinking to rouse the sleeping or drunken lad he gently tapped the stick against Luke's foot. His left foot.

Luke felt the torturous shock course through him and heard an agonized yelp escape his lips before everything around him pulled away in a dreamlike swirl. From the dragons floating overhead and the noise beyond the grate to his failure in banding together the Faithful, Luke watched as from a distance as the world fell away and everything became dark.

There was only pain.

Nothing else mattered.

Luke gave a half-conscious laugh that sounded more like a groan. Pain. Perhaps that was all that life had to offer him. When all else was said and done, if everything else was taken from him, what would he have left if not pain? A wave of defeat settled over his anguish-wrapped mind. The Faithful were to be executed, the true rebels would kill Lord Roland, the city would continue to slip down a lawless slope of sinful mire, and there was nothing he could do to stop any of it. He would die here and everyone would forget the many failures of the collared boy. They would forget him.

A faraway thought called to him from across a great black abyss.

I know God has a special purpose for you. Mother! Luke thrashed in the darkness and searched for her beloved face, but could not find her. Where had her voice come from? *Always seek His face, and united together by the bond of Christ I know you will be strong.*

The words produced the image of a barrel that drifted on a dark sea. The barrel suddenly burst, and the rivets that had once held the cask together now floated aimlessly about. Useless. Without purpose.

Be still.

Those words again. In shame, Luke grimaced and turned his face away from this second voice. He knew it must be his Savior, his God. No one else could repeat a command the second time with as much love and patience as they'd spoken at first. But Luke did not want to heed this command. Did not want to be still. He had been born for action.

There are two sides to this battle…where then is your allegience? His mother's voice again, and with those piercing words. Who was he fighting for? Which cause was he truly serving when he fought for immediate action? When he desired to control every aspect of the combat? Luke chafed at the questions, knowing deep inside what the answers would be.

Suddenly, the vision of the rivets was swept away on a wave and the dark sea rose up like a wall before him. Instinctively, Luke turned away.

I have given you a gift. The Savior's gentle voice called to him again. *Look now. Use it for my glory, and not your own.*

Trembling, Luke turned back to the wall of water that stood before him like a noblewoman's looking glass. His reflection was clear, perfect, and unmistakable. Knowing what was expected of him, Luke lifted his eyes to the one gaze he had never read before: his own. He'd never needed to look. He knew what was in his own heart. Or did he?

Luke met his own gaze and held it, captivated and appalled by what he saw.

Pride.

Other traits vied for predominance as well—*Selfishness. Contempt. Rebellion. Arrogance*—but each was held at bay by the domineering presence of Pride. Luke squinted and peered deeper, trying to catch sight of the positive qualities that his mother had so often praised him for, but they too were lost in the ugly shadow of the negative.

Pride goeth before destruction, and an haughty spirit before a fall.

Tears streamed down Luke's face and he nodded in answer to the painful truth, "Pride cannot succeed. I have fought for my own way and through my stubbornness failed to complete my own selfish work. Lord Jesus, You called me to serve You and instead I have fought against You to please myself. I wanted to be in complete control when I should have committed everything to You and followed as Your obedient servant."

The wall of water collapsed and began to spin in a whirlpool around him. Luke felt his feet being tugged by the sea and he frantically cried out, "Save me, God! Save me from this destruction! Rescue me from falling! Teach me how to be humble."

Be still.

Now? How could he? The waters would destroy him!

Be still.

Yes, Luke decided, he could do that. It was all that his Savior asked of him for now.

Lie still, Luke. The words changed and Luke felt his body growing heavy and numb. *Lie still. All will be well. It will hurt for a moment, child, but in the end it will bring healing. The Master still calls us to His work, and the door has not yet been closed. All will be well.*

In a flash of realization, Luke knew he was regaining consciousness, and someone was indeed speaking these words to him.

Two hands pressed against his shoulders, pinning him to a flat surface beneath. Two more hands took hold of his broken left leg and a stranger's voice counted to three. His leg was quickly jerked, producing a series of loud pops, and Luke experienced another moment of absolute pain. The agony spread to encompass his entire being, and then there was nothing.

Once more, the world fell away and everything became dark.

But this time, there was only peace.

Nothing else mattered.

36

Dawn of Disturbance

Leaning on his staff of solid oak Sedgwick made his way to the lookout, a ledge of stone that protruded from the mountain several thousand feet above the walls of Hebbros. Standing there, held aloft by an appendage of stone with naught to embrace but sky and open air, he was sure it felt no different than flying might. It had been some time since his last visit to the ledge, though his prayers had daily returned to the object of the stone's vantage point. His wise gray eyes lowered to rest upon the maze of streets and sin below. It was a massive city, and yet so small and insignificant when viewed against the backdrop of an entire kingdom.

Sedgwick's eyes slid shut and a single tear dripped from beneath his short lashes. The city of Hebbros was a burden on his heart, one the Master continually brought him back to. It was a city on the road to destruction. His own last days within its walls had been torturous, chained as he was by the gate Thirteenth and forced to witness numerous crimes that were considered daily habits by the other citizens. Abductions, thefts, murder; all orchestrated or encouraged by the liars, swindlers, and cheats who freely walked those streets of grime and filth.

And the children. Sedgwick groaned and used his staff to

lower himself to his knees. He must pray for the children. So many of them were kept in ignorance of the darkness that surrounded them. Innocent until it was too late. They were taught to tolerate the lesser evils of their elders—as if sin could be measured and balanced by levels of corrosion—so that when they grew older the greater evils seemed less troubling. A sobering act of sin would hardly seem an offense if one had been taking babe-sized steps in that direction all his life.

Clutching his staff, Sedgwick lifted his hands in heavy-hearted petition. The motion put him in mind of the ancient tale of Moses, who had stretched his hands heavenward in a similar fashion. God had seen the faithful man's act and turned the raging tides of war so long as Moses had persevered to lift his arms.

This morning Sedgwick's Lord had urged him here to the lookout for a reason, laying on the simple man's heart the need to cry out for intervention. If he must, he would spend this day's every breath in prayer for those children of Hebbros who may yet be seeking a way to freedom. The God of Moses was still the same today, and on behalf of the Faithful Sedgwick would pray that the tides of war might once again be turned.

Sir Valden grabbed a fistful of Wulf's jerkin and slammed the youth against the wall, "Where is the boy, Luke?"

"How should I know?" Wulf choked the words out, affronted that the blame for Luke's disappearance should be laid on his shoulders, "Every time we catch sight of him he up and vanishes the next instant!"

"And how do you manage to catch sight of him at all when your brother tells me most of your time is spent drowning your earnings in ale?"

"That's not true." Wulf sent Warin a scathing glance and then shifted his gaze back to the knight who held him hostage, "We've both done our share of searching the streets. We even have a mite of a girl ready to lead us to his whereabouts."

Valden gave the boy one last look of disgust and then shoved away to pace the small room. Released from the knight's grasp, Wulf sagged against the wall and ran a hand over his rumpled clothing.

Valden would never admit this aloud to anyone, hardly even to himself, but his carefully formed plans were beginning to unravel from within his grasp. Recent investigations had produced proof that a secret faction was planning a rebellion. Every lead led to a dead-end, though Valden had succeeded in eliminating Sir Kenrick from his list of suspected ringleaders. Nevertheless the thought that an unknown party was gathering private information and preparing to use it against the city's ruler was unsettling. Especially if Valden himself planned to eventually become the city's ruler.

He grit his teeth in silent fury, clenching his fingers into fists until the blunt nails dug into his palms. With the House of Peers no longer existent, he had thought it would be simpler with only one seat of power to overtake. Now the number of his opponents was beginning to multiply, and figuring in new logistics was simply giving Valden a headache. He needed to eliminate any other candidates who plotted for ultimate control. One, he knew, was Kenrick. The other, this mysterious ringleader of the rebels. Well, he could only erase what he could see, and for now Kenrick was the only opponent in sight.

But the game for power was not the only thing bothering Valden. It was this fanatical movement that had suddenly overtaken Roland.

Valden paused in his pacing, shoulders rising and falling with every frustrated breath, and spoke without turning to look them in the eye, "You idiots have had three days. More than enough time to find him and bring him to me."

"Sir," Warin finally spoke up, as incensed as his brother, "we've tried, but the crowds make it difficult to keep up with him during the day, and the dragons keep us from making a thorough search at night."

"The fire towers should give you some protection now that Roland has officiated the construction of so many throughout the city. As for the crowds," Valden turned and the twins shrank from his hostile glare, "push through them, knock them down, trample them, force them out of your way, *anything!* Just find the boy and bring him to me."

"Yes, sir."

"Roland is even now passing an order that those Faithful children who are gathering together are to be arrested and put to death. I need Luke alive. Find out if he's planning an escape to Desterrar. Get this 'mite of a girl' to talk. Interrogate former members of the Faithful and find out where he spent his time. Threaten them if you must," Valden turned his glare on Wulf and stepped closer, "Get out there now and find him once and for all."

"Yes, sir."

The knight's gaze shifted to Warin, "And don't show your faces in this garrison again until you come dragging him in behind you."

"Get out there now, all of you, and don't show your faces on this roof again until you come dragging Luke behind you!" Pavia backed the four boys toward the stairs with a fire of determination in her green eyes. Christopher glanced from the pint-sized redhead to the shocked faces of Ned and Elbert on his left. He bit back a grin just as Pavia turned her sharp gaze in his direction, "He's your brother, for pitiful sake…"

"Pitiful sake? I don't think that's a—"

"…aren't you concerned that he hasn't come back from last night's foolish attempt at a rescue? Don't be such cowards!"

"I say," to Christopher's right, Bradley drew himself up and pushed his ragged pauper's cap forward. "Let's not forget to whom you're speaking. It is considered insolence to address a nobleman in such a manner."

"Oh, please." Pavia crossed her arms with a huff that sent her red mane flying in three different directions, "Last night you were just Bradley, and today it's *m'lord*?" She narrowed her eyes to mere slits, "Make up your mind."

Bradley cleared his throat, "I would merely like to point out that I may not be the wisest choice to send out in search of our friend. I may be recognized."

"Any one of us could be recognized!"

"Bradley may not wish to join us at all," Ned scratched his blond head. "He spoke last night of his plans to eventually leave us."

"He's not one of us."

"Obvious, Elbert."

"Enough," Chris held up his hands in a calming gesture.

"What Bradley chooses to do is his own decision. He certainly won't want to remain with us if our words continue to pick him apart like catawylds on a deer's carcass. Now, Pavia is right about Luke; we need to find him and soon."

"He left his bow here," Elbert pointed, "so we know he's without defense."

Ned nodded, "And he would have returned if he could. He's too fond of his role as our captain to give up the prestige."

"So where do we look first?" Pavia asked impatiently.

"We?" Christopher quirked his brow, "I thought you were staying here."

Pavia shrugged, "The longer we stand here talking about how terrible it is that he's out there alone, the clearer it is we need as many people searching as we can. I'll go north."

She started to march past, headed for the stairs, but Chris put a restraining hand on her shoulder, "You're not going out on the streets alone. None of us are. It's too dangerous. We need to think before we throw ourselves out on the streets like bait. The Mordecais have surely begun to piece together our disappearances and will be watching for us."

"So what do we do?" Pavia's increasing impatience was clear as she rocked back and forth on her toes.

Chris looked at each expectant faces and slowly took a deep breath. There was no time to plan as he would have liked, so why did he hesitate to order a citywide search for his brother? Luke had always been the one to make decisions on a moment's notice. What would he have suggested?

"Mother and Father would say we ought to pray," Charlotte's voice drew everyone's attention to where she stood behind them. Her large hazel-colored eyes were filled with a calm that had seemingly fled the roof when they'd awoken to find Luke was still gone. "God knows where Luke is and He knows how to lead us there."

Chris released a sigh and smiled at his sister. How had she maintained such faith? And why did the rest of them seem to lose sight of all they had been taught by their Faithful parents?

"You're right, Charlotte. Let's pray for guidance." Every head bowed and Christopher began, "Oh God, we don't know what to do, but we trust that You do…"

Bradley, head lowered in deference to the others, looked up as

Christopher's simple words were lifted in humble petition. Luke's twin was so certain his God was listening, so sure of receiving an answer. Why couldn't Bradley act in such faith? Why did he feel lost and foolish when he prayed? Drawn away from the group by a sense of shameful isolation, Bradley wandered to the edge of the rooftop. Taking a deep breath to steady himself, he promptly sneezed.

"Amen." Chris finished praying and turned, "Bradley?"

The young nobleman held a finger to his nose and pointed, "Look. People are starting to gather on the other rooftops—*ACHOO!*—and it looks like they're preparing for a parade. I should know. I remember the flowers all too well. *ACHOO!* We have a memorable past, those flowers and I."

Pavia appeared at his elbow, "They must be gathering to watch Lord Roland escort Lord Brock to the docks. They said at the garrison the man is sailing for a distant island, and Lord Roland has been beside himself trying to make a good impression for the king."

"There will be soldiers," Elbert eyed the gathering masses.

Ned opened his mouth to reply, but Chris spoke first, "Anyone from the palace garrison would know Pavia or myself, and nearly all of Hebbros could recognize Bradley. We need to leave before we're spotted up here." He checked for the sword at his waist and then turned and grabbed Luke's bow and quiver. Taking Charlotte's hand, he started for the stairs at the back of the building.

"Where will we go?" Ned called after him.

"Somewhere safe," Elbert answered.

"*Any*where safe," Chris amended the statement and helped Charlotte down the first few steps.

"I agree," Bradley's voice was thick. "Anywhere away from the—*ACHOO!*—flowers."

"Do you have any ideas?" Pavia raced to catch up to Christopher, "We certainly won't be welcome in any merchant's establishment."

"No," Ned followed. "Besides, most places will have their doors closed today if the excitement is so great."

Bradley froze, "Doors. Of course! I know the perfect—*ACHOO!*—place. I'll take you to the mercer who used the same watchword given by that fellow, Guy."

Chris waited until Bradley had finished four magnificent sneezes in a row, and then nodded, "Lead us there, Bradley, and hurry. We don't have much time before the streets are impossible to get through."

"These streets are impossible." Wulf cursed at an old man who had stepped in front of his horse, "How are we supposed to spot that dog, Luke, among the thousands of other faces out here? And if we do see him, how are we supposed to catch him when we can barely move an inch in any direction?"

"We'll make a way through. Now shut your mouth and open your eyes." Warin's cool gaze scanned the street as they turned another corner. All around them, the city had thrown on a festive air at a moment's notice. Flags, flowers, and streamers decorated every structure. Word of Roland's public escort for Lord Brock had leaked to the masses, suggesting that Roland would be pleased if the people of Hebbros gave his guest a farewell worth remembering.

But not everyone would enjoy the parade. As they had prepared to leave the garrison only an hour before, Sir Kenrick had brought an order from the palace and read it aloud to the Mordecais. At Roland's command, the knights were to scour the city and locate the six rebel children who had vanished during the last few days. All had been condemned to death. Any persons found harboring them would meet the same fate.

Warin ran his fingers through his black hair, "I don't know how Valden plans to get away with saving Luke alive. And I certainly can't fathom why he wants to."

"Forget him," Wulf shrugged. "Lord Roland gave an order, and his position in this city outweighs Valden's wishes. Valden can forget his own plans and accept what Roland says." Fingering his scar, Wulf scowled, "Serves him right for treating us like vile scum after we've served him so well these last days. I'm glad of Lord Roland's order. Luke has been a nuisance long enough."

"I agree with that," Warin eyed his brother and then turned to watch the street again. "I don't agree, however, that the two girls should be condemned to death."

"Of course you don't," Wulf rolled his eyes. "Don't tell me

you've gone soft."

"I didn't say they shouldn't be punished," Warin growled. "They're just as much at fault as Luke for taking up their forbidden faith. All I meant was, as ladies they deserve a lighter sentence. I, for one, respect the law of chivalry that says we ought to protect females."

"Yes, and that's about as far as your chivalry goes. For pity's sake, Warin, you're a Mordecai. We do whatever it takes to get a job done. Hasn't that always been your personal motto?"

Warin shook his head in annoyance and lifted a sarcastic brow at his brother, "You're in a fine mood today. What's made you so agreeable?"

Wulf glared at his twin, "I'm anxious to have done with these…these games. I've endured Luke's taunts and triumphs for too long, and now I've finally been ordered to give him what he deserves. Today is the day, I'm certain." His green eyes traveled from face to face in the surrounding mob as he urged his horse forward, not caring whether everyone cleared out in front of him, "I plan to find little Luk-Luk before the sun goes down, and I'm going to give him a farewell just as memorable as Lord Brock's."

"Where is father? He'll miss the parade," Lillian followed her mother from the blue and gold receiving room and out onto the street.

"Your father had business to attend to, Flower," the gentle woman replied. "He said he would watch from the window."

Lillian nodded and then lost herself in the glory of the scene before her. Already girls were throwing flower petals into the road, preparing the way for Lords Roland and Brock. Banners fluttered in the warm breeze. The air smelled of roses and lilies, heady and aromatic. Lillian breathed deeply and thought how wonderful it would be if a dashing knight approached to offer her a flower instead of casting it on the road to be trampled by Roland's horses. She sighed. Unfortunately, she wouldn't be here for anyone to offer her his rose.

"Oh my, the noise is incredible," her mother winced at the deafening crowds. "I'm grateful we do not have a parade every day."

"Indeed," Lillian agreed, "but how exciting it is!"

A neighboring woman approached to speak with her mother and Lillian saw her chance to slip away. "Mother, I'm going to stand by Lida," she tossed the words over her shoulder as she turned up the street.

"Stay out of the way of the horses, Flower."

Lillian ignored her mother's call and quickly disappeared among the bystanders. Passing the cobbler's daughter three doors down, she smiled and waved at Lida before continuing along the lane. There had been no time the day before to carry out Warin's plan, but today would be perfect. Surely Luke's band would be among those in celebration, hidden in plain sight from a thousand pairs of eyes who did not know them.

But Lillian would know them. She would recognize that patronizing young servant, Pavia, who had dared to approach her in the streets like an old friend. Lillian would find them and tell Warin and his brother of their whereabouts, and maybe, just maybe, she would earn herself a rose after all.

Lillian smirked to herself, "Time for some excitement."

37
My Way

His left leg felt stiff and constrained. Pain throbbed relentlessly through the limb, a constant reminder of the previous night's events. Luke opened his eyes and studied his surroundings in confusion. He had drifted in and out of consciousness during the night and knew that he had been carried from the alley outside of Squire's Tavern, but this was certainly not what he had expected to see when he finally awoke.

A vast canopy was draped over his massive bed, which was buried under a mountain of lush pillows and soft green coverings. Decorative tapestries adorned the sandstone walls and framed a narrow window, open to a warm breeze and the air of excitement that buzzed outside. The distant sound of lapping waves caught Luke's ear. He was close to the docks.

Across the room, a small fire was dying on the hearth after a night of keeping away the chill. Standing before the fire were two men in close conversation, obviously not wishing to be heard. They were strangers, Luke knew as he studied them both. He had never seen them before.

"Where am I?" Luke tossed the question into the space between them and it hung suspended for a moment, unanswered, as the two strangers turned to stare at him.

"And so, you're awake at last." The man on the left advanced on the bed with a wide smile, his fine wisps of white hair floating upward with the forward momentum. A wiry man full of irrepressible energy, he came to a stop beside Luke and smiled down from an impressive height.

Luke read his gaze and attempted to smile back.

The second man seemed more reluctant to approach the bedside. A portly gentleman, he seemed hardly younger than the first man, but with a head of thick dark hair that refused to gray. He took a step closer and then watched from the foot of the bed as the wispy-haired man began to question Luke.

"Do you feel any pain?"

"Yes."

"That's good, that's good. Do you remember anything about last night?"

Luke cast a glance at the second man and then replied, "I remember everything up until that man found me. After that I was unconscious."

"That's good too!" The lively man brought a cup of water to Luke's lips and helped him to drink.

The dark-haired stranger watched with sad eyes. "So young," he murmured, and then resumed his silence.

When he had had enough, Luke pulled away from the cup of water and repeated his earlier question, "Where am I?"

The first man flattened his unruly wisps, his eyes sparkling with pleasure, "On your way to freedom, my boy."

Luke's confusion was deepening by the moment.

"You're in my home," the man at the foot of the bed spoke softly, as if he feared someone might overhear. "I had business in another quarter of Hebbros last night and found you as I was returning home."

"He summoned me here in the middle of the night, as soon as he had carried you up to this spare room." The first man spoke as he mixed a poultice in a small bowl, "I have been his secret physician and good friend for many years, and so he knew he could trust me to keep your presence here confidential." He chuckled, "You're quite renowned for a lad of your age."

"So young," the other man murmured again. "So young."

The physician slowly unwrapped Luke's leg and began to spread the thick poultice on the boy's skin. Luke made a face at the mixture's foul smell and then looked up to meet his host's gaze. His brow puckered at the emotions roiling within the man's eyes, but he turned to address the wispy-haired friend instead.

"You said secret physician. Why is that?"

"Ha! You are a bright lad, bright indeed!" The man began to rewrap Luke's leg, "I used to practice the art of medicine openly, but had to forsake the occupation when Roland passed a law forbidding anyone over the age of fifty-three from receiving medicinal care. Fifty-three! It's not right. I couldn't act according to his silly rules, and so I learned to pass myself off as a merchant. A costermonger to be exact. In secret, I have continued to aid my trusted friends in any way I can. In return for my continued services, they keep my secrets as well."

"Like the fact that you're a member of the Faithful?"

The physician paused and turned to stare at Luke, his bright eyes mixed with astonishment, "Why, yes. Yes I am. How could you tell?"

A corner of Luke's mouth lifted, "I can see it in your eyes." His gaze shifted to the other man, "And you are not. So why are you trying to protect me?"

The man's eyes grew moist and he blinked away a sheen of tears, "You are so young."

"Yes, you keep saying that." Luke paused, "What is it that you regret, sir?"

The two men exchanged looks of surprise, and the physician finished tying a new wrap around Luke's leg, "Amazing, simply amazing. No wonder the Mordecais want you silenced. You can see straight through them, can't you?" He shook his head as he gathered his supplies into a bag, "I wish I had your insight, boy. Before the first banishment, I spent months trying to find any member of the Faithful who would reveal his faith to me. I wished to know more, but they were so secretive. I'm surprised Sir Kenrick has managed to flush out so many! I thought I had found a man once—a young cooper—who would let word of his alliance slip. Alas, he was too clever to fall for my tricks of conversation, and I was too afraid to ask him outright in the case he was not. In the end I learned that he had been banished."

Luke was stunned, "My father was the banished cooper!"

The physician straightened and stared at Luke, "Astonishing! Amazing, the people you'll run into when you least expect it. It was your father's bravery and steadfastness that led me to finally deciding I would join the Faithful no matter what. If a man could have that much peace when approaching his certain death, then I wanted to know his God. It has been hard to learn of this faith, what with the lack of any who can or will speak of our Lord, but I have begun little by little."

Luke felt the poultice on his leg growing stiff. An uncomfortable sensation.

He turned to the man at the end of the bed, "What is your story?"

The portly man slowly inhaled, and Luke thought he would refuse to speak. He was not obliged to explain anything to this youth. He had rescued the boy and that was enough. However, after a moment, he glanced at the physician and began, "You are correct when you say I am not a member of the Faithful. My brother was, however, and I treated him with scorn. When my brother was banished, I was among those who shouted loudest for his silence."

Luke's eyes widened with understanding, "You mean Sedgwick?"

The man's eyes filled with pain and he glanced away, "Yes. My brother was a good man, while I have always been selfish. Being a prominent merchant in Hebbros, I have many assets to protect and I have always done so at any cost. I saw allegiance to Roland as the wisest course, one that would ensure my livelihood, and so I worked against his lordship's enemies in order to gain his favor. Even when those enemies included my brother and his fellow members of the Faithful."

He paused to collect his thoughts and the physician turned a look of sympathy on his friend.

The merchant continued, "I was so loyal to Roland, his lordship chose me to bring up one of the children whose parents had been exiled. One of your friends," he nodded to Luke. "A beautiful little girl with golden hair and sad eyes."

"Lillian," Luke quietly interjected.

"She was so small and frightened. I thought myself better than those who had left her behind. How could they choose a life of rebellion over the welfare of their child?"

Regret filled the man's eyes again and Luke unconsciously winced at the overwhelming insight.

The physician quietly asked, "Shall I tell him the rest, my friend?"

The merchant shook his head, "I will finish. About a week ago, maybe two, I discovered the identity of another Faithful man. I reported the name to Sir Kenrick and the home was raided, but in the process a boy—Sir Valden's squire—was killed." He gripped one of the bed posts and clutched it until his knuckles turned white, "He was so young." He shook his head at the memory, "I blamed myself for bringing such a tragedy to pass, but there was nothing I could do to change what had happened."

Luke tilted his head to one side, "So you found me on the streets and decided to do the Faithful a good turn, hoping to wash away the stains of the past."

The physician made a slight sound that was almost a chuckle, "I told him that only God can do that, but he doesn't like to hear such things."

Luke glanced from one to the other, "If you are reporting the Faithful to Kenrick, why do you not condemn the physician here?"

"He's afraid to," the wispy-haired elder smiled. "As I mentioned before, if my patients know of my faith they will not speak of it in return for my continued services. If I am cast out, my friend here will no longer receive medicinal care from the physicians of Hebbros." He leaned closer and spoke in a loud whisper, "He's over fifty-three."

The merchant rolled his eyes, "And you are older still. Come, come, we must hurry before the parade is over and our chance is gone."

"What parade?" Luke asked.

"I'll tell you later." The physician's speech became rushed, "First, as it seems you have not noticed, I should tell you that after setting your broken leg, I removed this," he reached to a point beside the bed and retrieved a long strap of red leather.

"My collar," Luke reached up to finger the skin at his neck. Tender to the touch, he could tell it had been rubbed raw.

The physician saw him wince and nodded, "I have another salve that I will rub on your neck, and then, my boy, you must prepare yourself for a day of hardships. No, no questions. I will explain."

The merchant moved away from the footboard and crossed to the window to look out. The physician scooped a finger's worth of salve from another bowl and began to lather the ointment on Luke's neck. Luke hissed at the contact, but managed to hear every word that the man said.

"Of course, I needn't remind you that not a word of this is to be spoken beyond the walls of this fine room. My old friend and I are not nearly as brave as we ought to be, and so neither of us is prepared to reap the rewards of our defiance to Roland's orders. But hear me, a rumor has reached us that Roland will sentence a small gathering of you Faithful children to death upon your capture."

Luke gave a slight nod. The rebels beneath Squire's Tavern had alluded to the same.

"The safest thing for you to do is escape Hebbros, and escape it today. The festivities in honor of Lord Brock's departure have sprung up like a weed. No one knew there was to be a parade until early this morning! However, the Lord knew a distraction was needed this day and He provides for His own, does He not?"

The merchant grunted but said nothing and continued to stare out the window.

Luke felt his heart beginning to race with tremulous excitement. Leave the city today? The plan was so sudden, so exhilarating and yet so terrifying at the same time. He'd known they would attempt an escape at some point, but he had not been waking each morning with the thought that today may be the day. It was always tomorrow. Another day.

The physician went on, "I have sent for another friend, a Faithful man, who tells me there is life on the mountain. The fire, you saw it, yes? Your parents may yet live!"

With a glance to the window Luke saw the merchant flinch, but still he said nothing. The young boy looked up at the man whose feathery hair framed his head like a wild white halo.

"I've thought the same. There are six of us who wish to leave. I had thought to gather more, but one such mission failed last night and ended with this," he motioned toward his leg, wrapped and stiff. "I also discovered last night that my attempts to call the other children together would have been futile anyway. I saw that boy's face. He was content." An image of Joel's face swam before his mind's eye, making him cringe, "He didn't want to be rescued—doesn't even remember that he *needs* to be rescued. Four years ago I reminded them to stay true to our cause, and everyone agreed to be steadfast." Luke leaned back, sinking into a mound of pillows, "But if Joel is anything like the rest, they've forgotten."

The physician gave Luke's words a thoughtful pause before he spoke, "You said there are six of you ready to leave, did you not?"

"Yes," Luke slanted a glance at the physician.

"Then the six of you must go now."

Luke's revolutionary spirit leapt at this thought, but his sense of commitment resisted, "But what about the others? I haven't called them yet."

"Did you call the other five who are ready?"

Luke blinked, staring up at the elderly man as the truth rang in his heart, forcing him to answer, "No. They saw the fire on Mount Desterrar and knew it was time. They came to find me."

The physician's eyes lit with a warmth that touched Luke deeply, "Luke, the fire on Mount Desterrar was there for all to see. Some will choose to ignore it, others may not see it at all, but those who decide to act upon the truth that it represents must not be put in danger so you might wait for others who will not come. Perhaps our Lord did not intend for you to call, but to go. Let God be the One who speaks to their hearts, and you be an example for them to follow. Show those others that an escape from this place can be made—*should* be made. Leave the city, Luke, and go to live in freedom."

Freedom. The word sang sweetly in Luke's ears. Not the dirge of a faraway hope, but the chorus of something attainable, something within reach.

Is this what you would have me do, Lord? Did you send this man to show me the way?

Luke sat still for a moment, resting in the momentary peace of a safe haven and feeling a weight lifted from his shoulders, "Is it really that simple? I just need to go? I can be out of the city by tonight? It sounds so…easy."

The physician finished packing his bag with a light chuckle, "Life is usually simpler than we choose to make it."

The merchant finally turned from the window, "We are losing sight of the point, my friend. Finish telling him."

"Ah, yes, the plan. The Faithful friend that I spoke of will come soon to take you with him. He will conceal you in a barrel, which is where your hardships begin. The journey to your next stop will be painful, thanks to your broken leg. When you have reached another place of safety, this man will ask you where your friends are staying so that he might send them word and have them join you. When all is set and night has fallen, you will be sent through the wall to the base of Mount Desterrar. And there the rest of your hardships begin. Unfortunately you children will be on your own, but a path that will lead you to the top has been spotted north of the gate Thirteenth."

"You will not join us?" Luke's excitement was increasing.

The physician gave a sad smile, "The passage through the wall is not large enough for a grown man. A youth much bigger than yourself will have difficulty."

Luke thought of Christopher and prayed his larger twin would make it through without any trouble. He took a deep breath, relieved to sense the peace that filled his heart. He had asked that God would teach him to be humble, and today he had accepted the plans of others in place of his own. He prayed that God would continue to give him grace as he followed the path that had been chosen.

This is the way, walk ye in it. The words were whispered on his heart, prompting a distant memory of his mother's lessons.

The merchant, leaning against the window sill, now stepped away and drew closer to the bed, "There is another reason I decided to shelter you, Luke, and I must explain before it is time for you to go."

"Come, come man," the physician spoke up, "don't sound so ominous."

The merchant waved the words aside, "The thought that my daughter's true parents may yet be alive has haunted me for some time now. The idea does not sit well, and though you both will say I cannot cleanse my soul with acts of goodness, I would at least ease my conscience." He met Luke's steady gaze and the boy read a world of sorrow and confusion, "I want Lillian to go with you."

The physician's jaw dropped and for once he was speechless.

The merchant held up his hand, "However, she would not go now even if I begged her. She has been raised to resist your faith. Nevertheless, I feel it would please the gods of Hebbros if I promise to one day return her to her parents." The man shrugged, sounding as if he were trying to convince himself, "A sort of balm to cover my sins."

Luke plucked at the bed covering with his forefinger and

thumb, trying to reconcile what this man was leading up to, "How does that create a reason for you to help me?"

The merchant swallowed, "It will make no sense to you coming from me, but I see that our city is falling into degradation and lawlessness. Those children whom you spoke of, who have failed to gather together at this time, will eventually need to relearn of your faith. Their parents' faith. As will Lillian. I do not understand the Faithful and I have no wish to," his eyes hardened with defiance, and then had to soften with the concession, "but there must be a remnant that will one day be willing to leave this city."

Luke's fingers curled around the bed covering in an unconsciously firm grip as the merchant finally came to stand beside the bed. His gaze was a sea of churning emotions and traits, and Luke could not look away. The man laid a hand on the boy's shoulder and pressed it with a desperation known only to those who refused to fight their hopelessness.

"'The door has not yet been closed.' Yes, I have heard the watchword of your people, and out of kindness to my physician I swear it is safe with me." He leaned closer, willing Luke to understand the depths of his words, "The door has not *yet* been closed, but one day it will be and that is why I am saving you alive and letting you go free." The merchant met Luke's gaze with one of determination, "I want you to come back."

38
On the Streets

Roland's forefinger tapped an impatient rhythm against the pommel of his saddle. Lord Brock had taken an unaccountable amount of time preparing to leave the palace. The lord of Hebbros feared that his people would soon grow weary of waiting for their parade and leave the streets as nothing more than a deserted maze of stone and cobble.

At last Brock made an appearance and began the process of mounting his horse with assistance. Roland glanced over his shoulder and caught his wife's gaze, rolling his eyes in disgust at the other man's helplessness. Rosalynn's brown eyes warmed at his attention and a small smile lifted the corners of her lips. It was a start, Roland thought, but it wasn't the smile that usually lit up her entire face. He supposed he should find time today to reassure her regarding the new child. All would be well.

Plastering a look of composure on his face, Roland nodded to Brock—finally sitting erect atop his horse—and then lifted his hand in a signal to the gatekeeper. The impressive iron-studded panels were unbarred and slowly swung inward to reveal the street, lined with spectators who were craning their necks for a sight of the nobles' entourage.

When a guard had gone before to ensure the path was clear,

Roland led the way out of the palace courtyard with Lord Brock riding at his right. Rosalynn fell in place behind them, guarded by Sir Kenrick and followed by the children. Jerem mounted on his own pony, and Celia cradled in the arms of the young nurse atop another. Roland scowled when he thought of Bradley's wife, another matter that would need to be addressed soon.

Lord Brock's company and a large contingent of Roland's soldiers, led by Sir Fraser, brought up the rear of their lengthy parade. The people of Hebbros would be pleased with the spectacle.

Roland remembered to put a smile on his face as he waved and nodded to the masses. Flowers and garlands were tossed from a thousand quarters, speckling the street until the cobblestones were hidden from view. Behind him, Celia shrieked with delight at the aromatic display of affection.

Roland continued to wave, continued to smile, while inwardly his thoughts left the scene of noisome praise and turned to other matters entirely. Once Brock's ship had set sail, it would be time to set his sudden revolution in motion. The gods had blessed him with inspiration, given him a journey of power to embark on. Why wait to make his move?

Already he had sent soldiers to secure the thirteen gates around the walls. No spies would be able to enter or leave the city undetected. The work of the Mordecai Order would be expanded. No longer would they merely locate the few called Faithful, they would now be responsible for rooting out any who were *un*faithful to him. Hebbros would become it's own realm and King Cronin would be hard pressed to fight the act of rebellion while his armies were busy in other lands. The merchants who traded for Hebbros would be put through careful questioning in order to determine their loyalties.

Lord Brock would be allowed to leave. Roland would not think of revealing his plans before the man had gone, and it was out of the question to think of keeping the insufferable whiner as his hostage. Roland simply wouldn't have him. Therefore, Brock's ship would be the last to leave the harbor without obtaining Roland's express permission. From this day forward, all vessels and shipping routes would be subject to his lordship's total control and oversight.

Roland sighed. So much to do—smile through a parade, cheer

his wife, deal with the bothersome slave girl, execute a number of young rebels, announce his intentions to secede from the Mizgalian realm, prepare the city for inevitable war, and a thousand minor details beside.

A sadistic grin curled his lips. All in a day's work.

Sarah kept her head down as another slave led the children's ponies through the streets behind Lady Rosalynn. Cradled in her arms, Celia crowed and fluttered with delight as a shower of rose petals descended on them from an upper window. Sarah caught some of the soft bits in her hand and held them out for the babe to touch with a dainty finger. To her right, Jerem sat straight in his saddle, clutching the hilt of his toy sword and shouting orders as if he were a knight heading into battle.

Taking a deep breath, Sarah risked a glance at the crowd. Her eyes darted back and forth, searching, and then lowered again to the back of Celia's head. Be still. She reminded herself of the previous night's decision to follow those instructions. She could wait. She could be patient. She must. When a master wanted his slaves to provide excellent service, he did not remain silent and expect them to guess how he wanted things done. It was the master's privilege to set the standards in his own house. The God of the Faithful could be no different. If He truly wanted her to know Him, to serve Him, then He would make sure she received the proper training.

But how? She couldn't help but wonder. Her loyalties, once stretched in two directions, were now pledged to the bitter young man who was her husband, and who was also missing. In his absence, she must serve in Roland's palace. How could she learn of this forbidden faith when bound to people who wanted nothing to do with it?

Sarah smiled at Celia when the little girl craned her neck to babble something at her nurse. When the crowd's shouts once again captured Celia's attention, Sarah ventured another glance at the growing mob. If Bradley had remained within the walls of Hebbros and was truly a man of his word—a man who would not forsake their vows, no matter how hastily given—then today would be the day for his return. The crowds would conceal him, and the chaos would create the perfect cover.

Sarah's gaze suddenly collided with the eyes of a spectator. A young man on horseback, with shaggy black hair and the dark attire of a Mordecai knight, had caught her eye from the outer fringes of the crowd. A chill raced up her spine and she shivered in spite of the day's heat. The youth's green eyes—one framed by a long white scar—mocked her despite the distance and Sarah felt decidedly put in her place.

Before she could look away, another young man appeared, riding up beside the first. Their faces and apparel were identical. The second youth glanced at his twin and then up at her. He offered a cocky salute and a practiced grin, and then elbowed the first young man into motion. Turning their horses away from the crowd, the two disappeared down a narrow side street.

Sarah released a breath she hadn't realized she had been holding. Glancing around, she saw that no one else had sensed the same presence of evil that she just had. Every face was filled with joy and every tongue was singing praises to their ruler. Glancing back to the side street that had claimed the two young men, Sarah took a deep breath and tried to shake off the feeling of dread that had suddenly shrouded her.

"Lord God of the Faithful, protect me today, and protect Bradley wherever he is."

Sarah resumed her former posture, head bowed over Celia's. A single tear escaped her lashes and dripped into the little one's hair, but Celia did not notice. Sarah's ears ached with the deafening noise of the mob, her heart pounding in time to their chants. So many people had come to see Lord Roland through the streets, to send Lord Brock on his way. So many people.

But where was Bradley?

"*ACHOO!*" Bradley scowled and dodged another posy of flowers. Their small group had reached the city's major north-south thoroughfare and the crowd's mounting excitement indicated there was not much time before the parade would arrive, cutting them off. Chris had come to the same conclusion. The younger but larger youth looked left and right and then tugged on little Charlotte's hand.

"We've got to cross quickly. Come on." Leading the way across the street, Chris maneuvered through the mob until he was clear of the press on the other side. Pausing in a side street, he and Charlotte waited for the others to catch up. "Which way now, Bradley?"

Pinching his nose to cut off the escape of a thousand sneezes, Bradley pointed with his other hand and answered in a nasally tone, "West to the wall, my good man, and south of the east-west thoroughfare."

In spite of danger they were in, Charlotte chuckled at the nobleman's comically spoken instructions. Chris glanced at his sister and tried to bite back a grin of his own. Pavia and Ned had no such sympathy, and both stood smiling at Bradley's miserable condition.

Elbert crossed his arms and stared, "You're allergic to flowers."

A laugh burst from Ned as he leaned against a wall, "Obvious, Elbert! He's barely containing another round of sneezes and his eyes look near to swollen shut."

Charlotte giggled again and Bradley tried to smile at the little girl. Though the youngest in their group, she was maintaining her composure remarkably well.

Chris wiped the grin from his face and cleared his throat, "The roads should be clearer further away from the parade, but if we become separated remember: west to the wall, and south of the east-west thoroughfare. Find the mercer's shop and gain entrance when all is clear. Use the watchword, 'the door has not yet been closed,' and wait there for the rest of us. Once we've regrouped, we'll consider what our next step should be."

"Don't forget to look for Luke on the way," Elbert suggested, and the others nodded.

The intensity of the crowd along the main thoroughfare began to increase and Bradley glanced over his shoulder. The leading guard was passing by, clearing the way for his lordship to pass through.

"Time to go," Chris called from behind Bradley. The others started after him, away from the bedlam, but the young nobleman could not force his eyes to leave the scene on the other street. Roland and another lord rode past, followed closely by Rosalynn. His sister smiled at the crowd, but Bradley could tell her heart was not in the festivities. Had he been the cause of her melancholy?

And then—beautiful sight! Bradley's wife rode by. Bradley's hand dropped from his nose and, wonder of wonders, he did not sneeze. He stared at Sarah as she rode in the parade, cradling his niece in her arms, and realized just how much he had missed her these last three days. He missed her calming presence and words of wisdom, her smile and look of compassion.

Bradley frowned and unconsciously took a step closer. Sarah wasn't smiling or compassionate now, in fact she looked utterly terrified. Bradley set his face with determination and started moving back toward the crowd. Something was wrong.

Two men on horseback turned into the narrow lane, blocking his way, and Bradley drew up short. Instantly, he recognized their attire as that of the Mordecai knights, and his heart began to pound. The two caught sight of him and urged their horses to a faster pace.

Bradley's mind whirled. Having escaped the dark Order three nights ago, he couldn't imagine the Mordecais would treat him kindly if they caught him now. Aside from this, he was currently keeping company with a band of children who were also determined to elude the Order. Bradley spun away from the riders and was relieved to see that his friends had already gone. However, it was only a matter of time before one or more retraced their steps to see if he was catching up.

Bradley knew what he must do. He had given them directions to the mercer's shop, and it was time for him to leave them alone in order to keep them safe. His presence would only complicate matters, and he couldn't leave the city with them anyway while Sarah was still here.

"You there," one of the Mordercais called out in a voice as harsh and cold as steel, "why do you not honor our lord by partaking in the festivities?"

Bradley suddenly reared back and delivered all of his pent-up sneezes in one colossal blow. The two horses shied away from the sudden onslaught of liberated sinuses, and Bradley took that as his cue to exit the scene. Turning on his heel, he raced to the end of the narrow street and headed north, away from the mercer's. Behind him, the two Mordecais ordered him to halt and then shouted with rage when he did not. It was not long before the sound of their pursuit pounded loud in his ears.

Bradley thought of the other children on their way to the western wall and smiled. This revelation of putting others before self was new to him, but he found he rather liked it. Like a balm it began to fill a long-ignored void in his life, in the place where he had lacked purpose. Could this satisfaction be the reason those men and women of the Faithful had been willing to go into exile? Had they been filled with a purpose beyond Bradley's comprehension? Is that why Luke and Chris and the others wanted to escape Hebbros? What would be their purpose in being faithful to God beyond the walls?

Bradley turned a sharp corner and shoved against the opposite wall to keep his momentum. He glanced over his shoulder as the two horses slowed to make the turn, and then he climbed a set of stone steps, taking it two stairs at a time. Studying his surroundings as he ran, he heaved a sigh of frustration over his lack of a solid plan. Absently he touched a hand to the empty place at his side. What he wouldn't give for a sword.

Sir Valden stood at the top of the stairs, studying the rooftop that stretched before him. A makeshift shelter, recently abandoned; a clay bowl with the smoldering remnants of the previous night's fire; and footprints in the dust that caked the modest surface. Seven sets of footprints. Some were larger, but others were definitely the size of a child's shoe. Valden took note of the number and wondered whether another rebel had joined Luke's band or if his own theory regarding Bradley's escape had been true.

Valden stepped away from the roof's edge and crouched to study the prints closer. Huddled together here, separated there, six sets made a path to the far edge of the roof, which overlooked the parade route, and then marked a retreat to the stairs that he had just climbed. The individual who belonged to the seventh set of footprints had been gone far longer. Their prints were not so clear as the others, not as defined in the layer of Mizgalian dust.

Rising to his feet, Valden turned and let his eyes trace the majestic lines of Mount Desterrar, burnished by the morning sun. The beauty of the site was hindered only by the knowledge of what lurked in every shadow along those slopes.

Valden's sources said these children would seek an escape

from Hebbros in order to discover whether their exiled parents still lived. Valden could not comprehend such love.

Logic said no child would willingly seek its doom in a wilderness inhabited by beasts and uncertainty. Valden knew these children did not rely on logic. They leaned solely on their faith. Even Luke, whom Valden had once suspected was a tame lad, clung with a fierce determination to the basic principals of his faith, whether or not he had come to fully grasp them.

Fools. Valden turned from the roof, his Mordecai cloak swirling the dust in a wave that settled over the numerous footprints. Descending partway down the stairs, he leapt the remaining distance to land in the saddle of his waiting mount. Setting his heels to the black beast, Valden was soon heading away from the scene of celebration and the crowd of people who were unaware of the game of cat-and-mouse taking place behind their backs.

Setting his jaw, the knight steered his horse through the streets, heading for the one place where he thought a child in this situation might return to for their self-imposed banishment.

Beyond the reach of Lord Roland's parade Mordecais filled the streets, searching for a band of rebel children who had been the blight of Hebbros long enough. Today their foolishness would come to an end. Today Lord Roland would forget them and set his sights on more power. Today would bring war to Hebbros, a war that many hungered for simply because they longed for the thrill of battle. In the end Roland would fail, and Hebbros, restored to its rightful place in Cronin's realm, would need a new leader.

Haman—the interloper and ringleader of his own seditious Order—smirked as he thought on the happenings in Hebbros and looked forward to her bright future. Just as soon as his men had satisfied their thirst for war, be it days or years, he himself would bring Roland to a swift end. He would then see to it that the king became aware of his identity—the man who would bring an end to the Hebbros rebellion—and that he was rewarded accordingly.

Complete control of the kingdom's second largest city would do just fine. For a start. Haman grinned. Who could know? Once he had managed that much, it just might become impossible to stop any more such accomplishments.

39
Witnessed by a Mule

Which way now? Lillian looked left and right, up and down the empty street, but couldn't decide which direction would be best. She glanced up to catch her bearings by the position of Mount Desterrar. Always before she had traveled about the city in the company of her father or mother, following wherever they had led and not bothering to keep track of which way they turned. With a huff of frustration, she wished she had paid closer attention. Now she didn't know where she was.

Flicking her blond hair over her shoulder, Lillian shrugged off the feeling of insecurity that sought to overcome her. She had wanted excitement, and now she would get some. Eyeing the surrounding structures and byways with an assessing gaze, she wondered aloud, "Where would they hide?"

A noise caught her ear and Lillian turned to see a donkey cart making its way south on the road. The cart's driver was a small man dressed as a merchant, with gray hair that fringed a bald pate and large eyes flanking a stubby little nose. Lillian's eyes shifted to the back of the cart, where a large barrel had been set on its side and tied in place to keep it from rolling. Plenty of room.

"Excuse me," Lillian waved as she rushed across the street

and came along side the cart. "Would you let me ride on the back of your cart?"

The odd-looking fellow brought his donkey to a complete stop and peered down at her a moment before speaking in a voice that matched his strange appearance, "My child, the *th*treet*th* are dangerou*th* for one *th*o young. May I a*th*k why you are alone?"

Lillian bit her lower lip and glanced away for only a moment. If she told him she needed to get to the heart of the city in order to help the dark Order track down a band of rebels, he was sure to think her insane.

"You are not running away, I hope?" His eyes narrowed as he scrutinized her.

"No," Lillian quickly shook her head and a lie slipped easily from her tongue, "I was separated from my mother in the crowds, and I need to head that way," she pointed south, "so I can find my way home."

A soft thump sounded somewhere nearby, nearly drowned out by the noise along the parade route, and Lillian gave a skittish start before looking about for the source. The streets looked unchanged from their eerily quiet state, only now she noticed that here and there shadowy figures slipped in and out of dark alleys and side streets. Lillian swallowed. Perhaps she had been wrong to suspect everyone had gone to watch the festivities.

The little merchant pressed his lips together and studied her for a long moment from the seat of his cart. He seemed to take in her appearance as well as her size and apparent age, all in a swift glance. Lillian heard the soft thud once again and she opened her mouth to ask what was making the noise, when suddenly he made a decision, "Climb on."

"Thank you, sir." Lillian quickly moved to the back of the cart and hopped up to sit with her back to the barrel. Her legs dangled over the street as the cart began to bounce forward.

They rode in silence for several minutes, listening as thousands of other citizens cheered for their lord. Lillian smiled at her success in coming this far and told herself she must come up with a plan. She would begin her search near the heart of Hebbros, where she had last seen Pavia, but if the other children were no longer wandering about…

"Child." Lillian heard the soft call and looked over her shoulder. Her eyes met the troubled gaze of the merchant, who had turned on his seat to look back at her.

"Yes?" Lillian matched his quiet tone, though certainly no one would have cared if she'd chosen to yell.

"Child," he repeated, "are you Lillian?"

Lillian felt her mouth drop open in shock and her heart froze in the unfamiliar hold of fear. Who was this man? How did he know her name? Had she begged a ride from a man who was intent on kidnapping her? Inhaling to deliver a shrill scream, Lillian was suddenly stopped short when someone else's yell interrupted her attempt.

"Look out!"

Bradley rounded the corner and caught sight of blessed relief. A donkey cart! Having dodged the pursuit and unsavory words of the two frustrated Mordecais for the better part of an hour, his lungs were now beginning to burn with a pain that nearly matched the agony in his legs. The last alley he had chosen had been too narrow for a horse to pass through, leaving him with a chance to get ahead while the two shadows circled around another way.

Just a little further…

A cursory glance told Bradley that an elderly chap was driving the cart while a child, a little girl, rode perched on the back. The wide eyes of both persons followed his progress across the street, widening even further when he made a flying leap—a most excellent execution of athleticism, if he might have said so himself—that landed him on the donkey's back. The beast gave a terribly noisome protest, and Bradley had just enough time to shout over his shoulder for the others to hold on tight, before the whole lot shot forward at a maximum speed that somehow seemed to increase by the yard.

"Yes!" Bradley laughed into the dusty wind and grabbed his cap as it attempted an escape. Putting distance between himself and those dastardly flowers had freed up his sinuses, and now he breathed deeply of freedom. He glanced back to ensure both merchant and child were clinging to the cart for dear life, and then faced forward to watch the road, "Onward, my good beast, and give my aching legs a rest!"

Suddenly Bradley stiffened and a look of confusion passed

over his face. He glanced over his shoulder again, and this time took a moment longer to study the unmistakable face of the man on the seat of the cart. He faced forward again.

The mercer!

The galloping donkey took that moment to bring everything to a complete and utter halt. Maintaining his hold on the beast's bridle, Bradley managed to keep from being pitched several blocks down the road. He did, however, get tossed from the animal's back and over its head, landing on his hindquarters in front of the donkey. Scrambling away from the possibility of flailing hooves, Bradley jumped stiffly to his feet and gaped at the stubborn animal.

"Really!? You couldn't have run a bit further?" He turned to stare at the mercer, "You…you're… Why are you here and not…?"

Glancing up, Bradley took note of Desterrar's position and realized he had been heading south, closer to the other children. He pressed his palms to his forehead. This city! The number of streets alone was more than enough to drive a man to bewilderment.

A course laugh fell on his ear, and Bradley looked up to see the two Mordecais arriving on the scene. Inwardly, he sighed in defeat. Outwardly, he erected his wall of indifference and turned to face them.

"Well, well," one of the identical youths lifted his brow in recognition, "if it isn't his redheaded lordship, dressed as a pauper." He laughed, "Wulf, I do believe your preference for drab apparel has, for once, been outmatched."

Bradley quirked a brow and turned to watch as the mercer attempted to coax the donkey back into motion. *Redheaded lordship?* That was a new one.

The one called Wulf scowled, "Tie him up, Warin. I'll stay up here and see that he doesn't make a run for it. Roland will be glad to hear that his dear brother has been found."

"Brother-in-law," Bradley corrected as he brought a disinterested gaze back to the dark duo. His eyes narrowed, "I've seen you before. You were at the tavern tormenting a young boy."

"The very same," Warin made a small bow over the pommel of his saddle while his twin spat onto the street at the mention of Luke.

Behind Bradley, the donkey shook his head from side to side, refusing to budge an inch. The mercer spoke a few lisping words and the animal sank back on its haunches in the street. Traitorous creature. Bradley had never been fond of mules.

Warin dismounted and stepped toward Bradley, but his gaze was snagged by the cart and those riding it. Taking no chances, he caught Bradley's upper arm in a grip of iron before turning to face the cart, "Lillian?"

The child's white-blond head peeked over the edge of the cart and she gave a nervous wave, "Hello."

Still seated atop his horse, Wulf rolled his eyes, "What are *you* doing here?"

Lillian straightened her spine and lifted her nose, trying to look unruffled by the fact she had nearly gone careening off the back of this speeding mode of transportation only moments before, "I am trying to help *you* by following the orders I received yesterday. I had just accepted a ride on this man's cart when you came along."

Wulf groaned and Warin bit back one of his own. Of all the days for her to try and "help." Ignoring the old man and his donkey, Warin pushed Bradley against the side of the cart and swiftly tied the renegade nobleman's hands behind his back. Grinning as he tightened the rope, he spoke over Bradley's shoulder, "Roland was sad when he heard you'd left us at the garrison. I'm sure he'll be pleased to know you've returned."

Bradley endured the scent of unwashed skin and old ale until Warin had finished speaking. Turning from the cart, he met the other youth's remarkably green gaze, "You shouldn't speak of things you know nothing about, especially when those things have to do with your betters."

The smile fled Warin's face and a muscle twitched in his jaw. He narrowed his eyes to mere slits and spat a stream of venomous words that Bradley could only hope did not reach poor Lillian's ears.

"Do you know the word Justice, my lord?" The angry Mordecai brought his face within an inch of Bradley's nose, "I think you should prepare to become better acquainted with the term."

The threat rang hollow in Bradley's ears and he remained unaffected as he returned Warin's glare, "The word Justice is one that I have long been fond of spouting, but perhaps I might introduce you to its opposite. Are you familiar with the sting of *injustice*?" Something shifted in Warin's eyes and Bradley continued before the other could speak, "I say you should not speak of what you do not know, because I know you couldn't possibly understand what I have suffered behind the walls of Roland's palace. If you did know, you might sympathize with me. That, sir, is what I run from."

Warin's brow creased, "What could you possibly know of injustice, what with your life of cushions and comfort?"

"How would you know there were cushions?"

Warin answered Bradley with a slap across the face, earning a gasp from Lillian and a hoot from Wulf. "Forward, swine, before I save his lordship the trouble of passing your sentence by serving it myself."

Bradley stumbled a step when Warin shoved him from behind. They were headed for Warin's horse when Lillian jumped from the cart and ran forward, "What about me?"

"What about you?"

"I want to help. Will you let me ride with you further south? If I don't hurry, my mother will surely send someone to find me."

Warin bit back a retort and happened to glance at Wulf. His twin's gaze was riveted on something beyond his shoulder. Turning, Warin found the old merchant wiping his brow as he frowned at his uncooperative donkey.

"You there," Wulf urged his horse a few paces closer, "what is your business here, away from his lordship's festivities?"

The man looked up and offered a respectful dip of his head, "I am a mer*th*er, good *th*ir, on my way home," he motioned to the south, along the shop-lined road that crawled along the western wall. "I wa*th* called to the north quarter thi*th* morning to fetch a load of good*th* that could not wait."

Wulf's expression was clearly suspicious, "Not even until our lord's parade had passed?"

The mercer held his hands out in a helpless gesture, "I am an old man, *th*ir, and quite *th*mall. I could not have found a way through the crowd in order to view the fe*th*tive *th*ight."

"Do you know this man, Lillian?"

The girl turned to look at the merchant with an odd look of fright, "No. I only asked for a ride on his cart."

"Come on, Wulf, let's go," Warin called, and Wulf turned a

dark look in his direction.

Hoof beats announced the arrival of another Mordecai and the knight soon reined in beside them in the road. He quickly glanced over the group and offered a small nod to Wulf before focusing on Warin, "Lord Brock's ship is now departing and Lord Roland has called the people to gather at the judgment square before the Thirteenth. Sir Kenrick calls the Mordecais to obey his lordship with or without the six brats."

As the knight spoke, his black horse sidestepping as if to avoid the tension, Bradley's gaze wandered to the little mercer only to find the man staring back at him. The man's large eyes grew a bit wider before darting a glance toward the back of the cart. Bradley looked there, took note of the large barrel, and then returned his gaze to the old man. What was he supposed to see?

Bradley's mind whirled with the irony of this situation. Chris had surely led the others to the mercer's shop by now, only to find that the mercer was not at home and his shop undoubtedly locked against the immoral souls of Hebbros. They would be stranded on the street, very near the public square where Roland had just called for a gathering of thousands.

The mercer had to go away. Bradley gave the man a meaningful look and then shot a glance to the south. *Go home!*

The mercer gave a brief frown of confusion and then his eyes moved in the opposite direction. *The cart.*

Bradley's eyes moved decidedly south.

The mercer's eyes jerked back to the cart.

South.

Cart.

Home.

Barrel.

"Ugh!" Bradley heaved a sigh over their silent battle of glancing hither and yon. This was getting them nowhere.

Warin glanced over his shoulder and scowled, "Quiet, you, or I'll stuff you in the mercer's barrel and roll you to the square."

The other knights laughed and continued to speak of the morning's search.

Bradley froze as the truth dawned on him like a bolt of lightning on a clear day. The Mordecais were searching for six children and heading for the judgment square. They were searching for the Faithful! He glanced at the mercer and found the man eyeing Warin. What had the nasty knight just said? Stuff him in a barrel? A gasp rose in Bradley's throat and he choked it back. The mercer's gaze swung to collide with his and understanding passed between them.

A load of goods that could not wait. Bradley glanced once more at the barrel and then gave the man a slow nod.

The third Mordecai rode south after refusing to give Lillian a ride. The twins scowled after him and Warin turned a menacing look on Wulf, "You take her, I've got the prisoner."

Wulf cursed, "We're not obligated to give her a ride anywhere. If your laws of chivalry won't let you leave her in the street, then you take her. I'm going to inspect this merchant's wares before I leave satisfied that nothing slipped my watch."

Warin growled at his brother and turned to grab a frightened Lillian by the arm. Tossing the child up onto his horse, Warin swung into the saddle behind her, still holding tight to the rope binding Bradley's wrists. Lillian glanced down at Bradley with an expression that revealed her doubts about this morning's choice of activities.

Meanwhile, Wulf had cut the barrel's bindings and turned it so that he could pry it open. Bradley's palms began to sweat as he watched the youth work at the head.

Suddenly, the unexpected occurred. A loud crack sounded, echoing in the relatively quiet street. Time seemed to stand still as several hoop rivets deserted their moorings and the barrel's headboard shot out from its framework, crashing into Wulf and knocking him to the ground. The two horses harrumphed in protest and shied away, pulling Bradley and his bound limbs along. In the same instant, the young lord became aware of two things. First, the mercer had wisely disappeared from the scene, hopefully heading south toward the other children. Second, a figure had emerged from the barrel, bursting forth directly behind the lid and landing feet first behind the cart.

"Luke!" The name exploded from four pairs of lips at the same moment, startling the horses yet again.

Bradley gave a yelp as Warin's mount danced to the left, forcing him to follow the steps at an awkward gait. "I say," he grunted to the animal over his shoulder, "you're not the best partner I've ever taken to the floor with."

Propelled from the barrel's innards, Luke landed with his

weight shifted decidedly on his right leg. His bandaged left leg landed on the obstruction that was Wulf, lying flat on his back in the street and with the round headboard across his chest. Taking advantage of his enemy's minor setback, Luke simultaneously moved out of reach and slid Wulf's sword from its scabbard.

"Yes! Over here," Bradley turned this way and that, waving his hands behind his back and trying to steer clear of Warin's circling horse, "The sword. I can use that!"

Ignoring the pain that shot like fire through his leg, Luke hobbled across the road towards Warin's horse, sword in hand. Wulf gave an enraged cry and scrambled to his feet, searching his person for a dagger as he lunged after Luke. Warin tried to draw his sword but quickly found Lillian's presence to be a hindrance. The young girl shrank from everything around her until it became too overwhelming and she released a series of shrill screams.

"Shut up, Lil," Warin barked in the child's ear. "Wulf, come and take my sword!"

Dodging hooves and Warin's attempts to kick him, Luke circled behind Bradley and slid the edge of Wulf's blade against the nobleman's bonds. His hands liberated, Bradley immediately spun and accepted the sword that Luke thrust into his grasp. Pivoting on his heel again, his redheaded lordship lifted the blade in defense as Warin's horse danced out of the way—at last freed from its burdensome partner—and Wulf was able to advance with Warin's weapon in hand.

Beyond frustration, Warin finally managed to cease his mount's nervous circling. Lifting Lillian by the back of her dress, he roughly deposited the girl back on the ground some distance from the scuffle and forestalled her complaints by setting his heels to the flanks of his horse and riding back into the fray.

Lillian continued to scream.

Pursued by Warin, Luke circled around the donkey—placidly chewing on a piece of straw—to the side of the cart where Wulf's horse was tied to the wheel. Marveling briefly over the fact that the donkey had somehow found straw, Luke drew the physician's gift of a dagger from his belt and quickly sliced through the looped reins. The dagger was returned to his belt and in another instant, carried aloft by adrenaline and prayer, the young fugitive was in the saddle.

"Bradley," Luke called over the impressive clash of arms

coming from the other side of the street, "I need you to reach Lillian and get ready to catch a ride."

Bradley gave a small nod in reply as he parried a vicious attack from Wulf. Gathering the reins in his hands, Luke saw Warin rounding the back of the cart and finally he urged his own borrowed mount forward. Delivering a war-whoop worthy of the ancient settlers, Luke charged across the street and directly into the path of Wulf and Bradley's skirmish. Both combatants dove for cover, Wulf into a nearby alley to keep from being trampled and Bradley in the opposite direction, towards Lillian. The young girl saw him coming and renewed her shrieking.

Pulling this way and that on the reins, Luke was beginning to understand how to direct a horse, and soon had his animal doubling back toward the south. Charging across the road after him Warin pulled up short when Luke changed directions, barely preventing a collision. Growling with frustration, Warin paused briefly to collect his twin.

Setting heels to flanks, Luke moved up the street gathering speed. Up ahead, he saw Bradley scoop Lillian up with one arm, preparing to use the other to "catch a ride" as Luke had suggested.

"Get ready!" Luke tucked his right foot into its stirrup and braced the stronger limb against the oncoming weight. Shifting the reins to his right palm and using the same arm to grip the horse's neck, he leaned to the left.

Bradley ordered Lillian to hold on tight lest he drop her. The frightened girl obeyed and Bradley held out his left hand, ready to catch Luke's. He started running back toward the oncoming horse, hoping to create the needed momentum. Once again, time slowed in the nobleman's mind as Luke's horse approached and their hands found a solid clasp around the other's wrist. The moment the contact was made, Bradley leapt for all he was worth and swung through the air, landing himself and young Lillian in the saddle behind Luke.

Feeling them settle at his back, Luke roared with victory and urged the beast beneath them to greater speed. Bradley found a solid hold around Luke's middle and situated Lillian between them for safety. The girl's blond head whipped back and forth, showing an angry scowl.

"Luke, what do you think you're doing? Let me down!"

Luke glanced over his shoulder with a mischievous grin, "Be

still, little one. I'm helping your father keep a promise by framing you as a member of the Faithful."

Lillian's face grew a shade redder, "I'm not little, and my father did not promise my abduction."

"Suit yourself. Now stop shouting in my ear."

They continued south, pursued by the two Mordecais and unsure of their destination. All around them the noise of thousands grew louder, the city's populace gathering with a din that rolled through the streets like thunder. Before them lay the judgment square and a future of uncertainty.

Behind them, composed in spite of the chaos that had so recently surrounded him, the mercer's donkey finished his bit of straw, rose from his haunches, and ambled slowly down the road toward home.

40
What Happened at the Judgment Square

The renowned gate Thirteen loomed to Valden's left as he sat astride his mare and stared to the north. Waiting. Behind him, five Mordecai knights were positioned across the road, their horses nodding and jangling bridles in anticipation. The people of Hebbros were on their way from the northern docks. Valden hoped the same could be said for the last of the condemned children.

His steely gaze drifted upward to Desterrar and then dropped to land on five additional Mordecais stationed closer to the gate. Each was responsible for detaining one of the young people who had rounded the corner some time ago, halting in the middle of the street when they found their way blocked by the Order's first knight himself.

Valden smirked. These adolescents had been so unprepared. Their only weapons had been a bow—probably Luke's, for none present had been able to use it—the temper of the redheaded girl, and a sword. The boy Christopher was well equipped with skills regarding the blade, Valden had learned that much during the boy's three-day-term as his squire. But today Christopher had barely had time to draw the weapon against three men, let alone use it.

His arm now gripped by a well-muscled knight, Christopher

stood so that he could shield the two young girls in their party as well as keep watch over the entire square. His sister stood quietly behind him, while the feisty redhead continually peered around his elbow. The two other boys glared sullenly at their guards, the dark-haired lad keeping quiet and the blonde occasionally offering his opinion of the entire situation.

The sound of horses approaching at a fast pace grew louder, and Valden's senses became fully alert. A moment later the first horse appeared, carrying three young people, and close behind it came a second animal, bearing two Mordecais. Wulf and Warin.

The first horse was reined to a sharp halt at the north edge of the square and the sound of a young girl screaming pierced Valden's ears. The girl's fellow-riders cringed and then stared across the square at the blockade of dark knights. Their expressions registered surprise and a twinge of defeat.

Warin drew his horse to a standstill beside the first and Wulf dismounted, grabbing the reins from the boy who had been in control of the animal.

"Luke," Valden's rusty voice echoed within the archway of the Thirteenth, "how good of you to join us." The boy's collar was gone, Valden noticed. Of course that had only been a matter of time. The knight glanced beyond the firebrand to his companions, "And Lord Bradley! I wondered if you might cast your lot in with this rabble. What a pity I was right."

"Actually… Well, never mind," the nobleman shook his head and looked away.

Valden's eyes narrowed in concentration, "Who is the girl?"

Warin answered, "Her name is Lillian. Her parents were banished with the rest, and she was reestablished with a merchant. She recently swore to be an ally in our search for the others."

Valden grunted, "Sounds suspicious." He dismounted and nodded to his two assistants, "Put her and Bradley with the others. I'll speak with Luke privately."

"No, wait!" Lillian panicked as Wulf dragged her from the saddle, "I'm not one of them. You don't understand. I've been helping your knights! I don't believe what the others do, and I never agreed with my parents either."

With a few long strides Valden stood looming over her and Lillian's mouth snapped shut. Her eyes widened in fear as Valden leaned down and growled in her pale face, "I care little for your arguments, child. If I say your story is suspicious, then that is exactly what it is. Go and stand with the others."

She complied without further comment and was met by a scowl from the little redhead. Another knight came to escort Bradley away, and Wulf turned to pull Luke down with a rough jerk. The enforced dismount caused the boy to stumble when he reached the ground, and he reacted with a sharp hiss as he gingerly shifted his weight to his right leg. His left leg was stiff and appeared bandaged beneath his pant leg. Valden met Luke's gaze and quirked a brow in question, but the boy quickly lowered his gaze to the street.

"Come with me," the knight gave Luke no choice as he gripped his arm and led the way across the square. When they were a safe distance away and would not be overheard Valden spoke again, "There is not much time. The people of Hebbros will be gathered soon, so I will be brief with you. When Lord Roland arrives he will sentence you and your friends to death, charged with sedition, rebellion, and the support of an outlawed faith." He paused for a response, but Luke's face remained a blank mask, "I cannot help your friends, but I am willing to help you in return for your services."

A pair of slate-blue eyes slowly lifted until Luke returned Valden's stare. The knight could feel the inward searching of the boy's gaze and wondered briefly at the results.

"You have a gift," Valden spoke firmly, "and I have need of it. I will promise you your life in return for the reading of men's souls."

Luke made a scoffing sound and looked away, shaking his head, "I do not read men's souls, Sir Valden. I merely see evidence of what is really there, the results of what's inside."

"That is all I ask," Valden's tone made it sound like an easy decision. Luke would be a simpleton to turn him down.

"My God gave me this gift in order to use it for *His* glory. Not yours. It is mine to serve *Him* with. Not you."

Valden's jaw clenched and his fists trembled with suppressed anger. He grabbed the side of Luke's face and tilted his head back, forcing the boy to look him in the eye, "You are a fool if you give up this chance. You would rather die bearing the same shame that exiled your parents, than save your life to serve a greater purpose?"

Luke swallowed, the ring of raw skin at his neck looking harsh in the light of midday. His eyes attempted to dart toward the ground several times, but he finally forced them to hold Valden's glare. His head shook slightly from left to right, and when he spoke his voice was firm with conviction, "I would rather bear my parents' reproach than wear your honor, for it is not honor at all, but treachery. I will not help you."

"I could force you to serve me, and you would have no say in the matter."

An infuriating smile pulled at the corners of Luke's lips, "If you make me share other men's secrets with you, then I'll share yours with Lord Roland."

A flicker of fear raced through Valden's expression and then hardened into a hateful rage. Releasing Luke, he delivered a swift kick to the boy's injured leg, watching impassively as the lad dropped to the ground with a roar of pain. Behind him, Valden heard Christopher match his twin's bellow with one of outrage, and their sister and Lillian began to cry. The little redhead spat a furious string of words at her guard, while Bradley tried to assert his status as a lord and another boy shouted about something being obvious.

"Silence, you mongrels!" Turning away, the knight strode back across the square and motioned to Wulf, still standing by his horse, "Hold him with the others, I've changed my mind."

"With pleasure." Wulf tossed his reins to Warin and quickly obeyed, half-dragging Luke to stand with the group by the gate, "You deserve what's coming to you, Luk-Luk."

"Leave him alone, you awful excuse for a yellow-bellied ignispat!"

"Quiet, Pavia," Wulf glared at the pint-sized female, and she glared right back.

Chris tried to lean closer to his brother, "Luke, where have you been? What happened to your leg?"

"Broke." Luke spoke through clenched teeth and his nostrils flared with an attempt to withstand the pain, "Was mended…but broke."

Further conversation was brought to a halt when the first of the gathering arrived along the edges of the square. An air of excitement permeated the city as everyone waited and wondered, speculating over what Roland's speech would relate to. Thousands filled the surrounding streets and windows, pressing as far into the square as they could while still leaving space for his lordship to stop and address them.

The noise was deafening, rising and swelling like a living sea. To the eight children held captive across the way, the sights and sounds were threatening. In more ways than one. As they stared back at the crowds who studied them openly, one pair of eyes darted from one spectator to another with a sickening realization. Not only had the people brought themselves to the judgment square, they had also brought their leftover bits of greenery and flowers…

At last the parade arrived, or what was left of it since Lord Brock's entourage had departed. Roland rode into the square, casting a smug glance at the group by the gate and then nodding his approval at Sir Valden. Kenrick left the line and rode to take his place with the Mordecais, exchanging a few words with his first knight before settling into silent observation.

Roland turned his back to the gate and faced the crowd. The golden-haired ruler sat erect and eyed the people with pride. His wife and children had stopped halfway across the square, watching him and awaiting his speech along with everyone else. Hebbros was a fine city, and now it would belong entirely to him. He felt no guilt, no doubt over this decision. As the deity in the temple had said the night before, he deserved it.

Roland took a confident breath and opened his mouth to deliver the words prepared during Brock's escort, when suddenly he was cut off by three monstrous sneezes. In shock Roland whirled and scanned the group behind him, trying to locate the source of the familiar sound. His eyes landed on the party of condemned children.

"Bradley!" The children's nurse cried the name of his brother-in-law as she quickly slid from Celia's pony, handed the babe to another slave, and raced across the square before anyone could think to stop her. The crowd, still unaware of the young lord's marriage, began to whisper in shock when the slave threw herself at Rosalynn's brother and clung to his neck weeping.

Bradley's response was awkward to say the least, what with one arm in the solid grip of a Mordecai and another sneeze begging for release. Nevertheless the scene was somehow touching, as evidenced by the soft sighs and twitters of the ladies assembled, and Roland rolled his eyes. This was not how he had intended to begin his speech. How his brother-in-law had managed to disappear for three days' time and still show up to thwart him at the worst possible moment, he would never know.

"Would you like me to fetch her, my lord?" A soldier nodded at the pair.

Roland glared at the reunited couple, "No. Leave her. She's made her choice and must now bear the consequences."

Standing nose-to-nose with Sarah, Bradley stared into brown eyes that had turned liquid with tears and silently thanked the Faithful God for instituting marriage. Regardless of the underhanded manner of their vows, this sweet creature now belonged to him; a fact that still refused to fully register in his mind.

Bradley glanced over Sarah's shoulder and saw Roland glowering at them while Sir Fraser's men worked to quiet the excited mob. Rosalynn's expression was unreadable. The other children were politely pretending to ignore the scene, while the Mordecais in charge of them stared rudely.

So be it. It was now or never.

He looked at Sarah and nodded to the square she had just crossed with marvelous abandon, "I don't deserve your kindness after the suffering I've caused you. I've been miserable these last few days, knowing that I ruined your life with my selfish desire to thwart Roland."

Sarah blinked away her tears and managed a teasing smile, "I knew there were risks in marrying a scoundrel, and the only reason I've been miserable is because I thought you'd left me." She glanced back the way she'd come and her eyes widened at the sight of whispering witnesses, "Gracious, I've never behaved like that before! Was I scandalous?"

"Quite," Bradley grinned. "Though I'm glad you came, for it was impossible for me to even consider lugging my friend here all the way across the square," he tilted his head toward the beefy guard that clutched his arm and the man grunted. "If not for that predicament, I would have come to you instead."

Chris glanced over his shoulder, "Not much time, Bradley. The crowds are growing quiet and Roland is preparing to start."

Sarah searched Bradley's face, "What's happening? What are

they going t' do t' you?"

Bradley tried to erect his wall of indifference, but felt the foundations crumbling even before he began, "Well, as a matter of fact, I've been consorting with Roland's enemies and will undoubtedly be sentenced to the same fate as these others." His brow furrowed, "They're going to be sentenced to death."

Sarah gasped. In her mind she tallied the multitude of losses that had marked their brief lives, and she wondered with pain if today would be add to that terrible list. Would she lose her husband before their friendship had a chance to grow? Last night she had been hopeful that they would be reunited and able to learn more about the Faithful's God together.

Her grip on the neck of his tunic tightened, "Why?"

"Because their faith is too big for Roland to live in the same city with it." Bradley attempted a light chuckle, but his thoughts churned with the question of whether he was prepared to face an unsettled eternity. His companions seemed so calm in the face of death. He cleared his throat and produced a smile, "Anyway, as time is short, I must be quick and give you something that was forgotten in the odd commotion of our wedding day."

Sarah gave him a wobbly smile, "You don't need t' give me anything, Bradley."

"No, no, I'd like to. You see this is something that my father, rest his soul, once charged me to keep and safeguard until the day I could present it to my wife. And I have. For you."

Bradley paused long enough to lift Sarah with his free arm and turn so they were hidden behind his burly Mordecai friend, before he tenderly presented his bride with his first kiss.

Luke ignored the embarrassing dialogue between his noble friend and the slave girl, and focused on scanning the crowd. Roland was furious with Bradley; the soldiers were impatient with the people; the people were curious and suspicious; Sir Kenrick was still basking in the pride of having ridden in the parade; and Valden was plotting someone's demise. The most interesting study he found was Lady's Rosalynn's gaze, which bounced from her brother to his companions and back again.

Luke sighed, feeling very small in the vast city of strangers.

There was no familiar face to suggest a rescue might be attempted, and Wulf's grip on his arm was a constant reminder that escape would be impossible this time. Roland would condemn them, and they would die before the sun had dipped behind Desterrar.

Thou shalt heap coals of fire upon his head, and the Lord shall reward thee.

Luke's eyes darted to observe Roland. Instinctively, he knew what his Savior was asking of him, and he shook his head. *I don't want to show him kindness. He's about to sentence me to death.*

Love your enemies.

Luke thought of the night before, his broken leg, the rescue, and his decision to commit his troubles to God. He had resolved to be humble and obedient. Now he would fail the first opportunity to act upon his resolution.

Roland's voice suddenly boomed across the square, spilling his venomous words into the surrounding streets and reaching with tentacles of power to every window and shadowed lane. Criers listened and took turns carrying the proclamation to those unable to hear as clearly from where they stood in the back.

Luke listened to the words that were no surprise to him and yet came as a shock to every other citizen. Under Roland's rule, the city of Hebbros was officially seceding this day from the realm of Mizgalia. Certain laws and taxes would be enforced to support this disaffiliation, and the city would prepare for resistance against the king's army.

The people of Hebbros were stunned to silence and pandemonium in turn. Women shrieked and wept, while men shouted or cheered. After half-an-hour of reasoning, Roland finally managed to regain control with the announcement that this plan had been suggested and encouraged by the gods of Mizgalia themselves.

"We cannot but succeed with such allies," Roland's tone left no room for argument, "and in honor of their blessing on our city the gods have asked of us a sacrifice."

Do good to them that hate you. The words flashed through Luke's mind along with an image produced by the stories his mother had told, of Christ teaching a multitude who would reject Him to love those who would crucify Him.

Roland's voice grew louder and more insistent, backed by a power and authority that Luke and his friends could never conquer on their own. The ruler pointed a condemning finger their way, "These are the children of those called Faithful—faithful to a forbidden God—and they are the last of their kind who would dare stir up sedition in our midst."

"No! I'm not one of them!" Lillian shrieked, but the noise of the crowd overpowered her. Pavia sent a scathing glance her way.

Luke ignored them, his gaze still on Roland as the Master's gentle prodding became stronger.

Roland continued, "It is the wish of our favored deities that these few should die for the good of all, along with my own brother-in-law, who would cause a resistance of his own, and his new wife, a slave who would dare to think more highly of herself than she ought."

Sarah gasped and Bradley shouted in a vain attempt to gain his brother-in-law's attention.

Luke's gaze left Roland to land on the man's wife. Lady Rosalynn's face had gone pale and her lips had parted in shock. She sat in frozen silence for a moment before turning to address a soldier. A moment later the guard and several slaves left through the crowd, escorting Roland's two children from the square toward home. Rosalynn turned back to the scene before her and absently rubbed a hand over her abdomen.

The crowd had quickly forgotten their earlier surprise and fear over Roland's announcement, and now grew loud with an unnatural craze at the thought of seeing justice met before their eyes. Songs to promote their own wickedness were begun, and many chanted for the blessings of their favorite gods.

The children of the Faithful shrank from the evil that suddenly enveloped the square like a well-worn cloak. They exchanged glances of fear, and even Bradley, Sarah, and Lillian beheld the sight with expressions of horror.

Coals of fire… Love… Do good…

"My lord!"

Luke was unsure how, but his single cry reached across the deafening noise and landed in Roland's ear. The ruler turned from the sight of his raving people and his eyes immediately found Luke's stare. Roland turned his horse partway around and held up one hand toward the mob. The people along the edge of the crowd grew quiet, watching with interest, while elsewhere in the city the noise of eerie celebration continued.

Roland's gaze narrowed on the boy whose collar had somehow been removed, "Unless you wish to submit before death, there is nothing you can say that will interest me."

Luke paused briefly before replying, "I wish to submit."

Gasps of disbelief punctured the air around him, and Roland's face took on a look of surprise.

"Luke, no!" Chris grabbed his twin's shoulder with his free hand, "They can't hurt a hair on our heads unless God wills it. Be strong!"

"Bring him here," Roland motioned to Wulf and the youth pushed Luke a step closer.

"No," Luke dug his heels into the cobbles and looked up at Roland, "I need to come alone."

The ruler's eyes twitched with suspicion, but curiosity overruled and he nodded to Wulf, who reluctantly released Luke and shoved him forward. Luke grimaced, stumbling on his left leg until finally he gained his footing and limped the distance between himself and Roland, praying with every step. Roland watched him approach, staring at the young firebrand down the length of his nose. Finally, Luke stopped beside the man's horse and tilted his head back to meet the cautious gaze above him.

"Well?" Roland quipped the word in a tone of iron.

"Luke, don't do it!"

He glanced back at his friends, all watching him with dismay. Bradley wore an expression of utter confusion.

Luke returned his attention to the man on horseback, the only person within hearing distance of the words he was about to say, "I would like to submit…a bit of information."

It was Roland's turn to look confused and a bit angry, "What did you say?"

"I feel it's my duty to inform you, my lord, that there are several people in this city who covet your seat of power. Among others, there is a faction that meets below the Squire's Tavern who anticipated your decision to secede, which causes me to wonder if your plans were plotted by another to cause your ruin. I cannot swear to the identity of their leader, and so I won't name a man and condemn him to death. I just thought you should know that your life is in danger."

For a moment Roland stared at him with a face so blank even Luke had difficulty reading his gaze. Then the eyes of gray hardened in steely resolve and Roland spat a stream of words that Luke's mother would have blushed at.

"You insolent brat! If you think to bribe me with these stories in hopes of saving yourself alive, it will not work. I have made up my mind, return to the others."

Luke shook his head and kept his gaze steady, "My lord, I'm about to die in honor of your future, I didn't have to give you news that might ensure it lasts longer. I might've taken these secrets to the grave and earned myself revenge."

With that, Luke turned and with a stiff gait made his way back to the group by the Thirteenth. He held out his arm for Wulf to reclaim it in a viselike grip, and stood waiting for Roland to continue with his speeches and merriment. Those who had watched the short interview stood waiting for an explanation, while the majority of the city continued in its oblivious revelry.

Roland was speechless. His tongue felt heavier than lead, tied and unable to release a word. He stared at Luke's retreating back, and then met the boy's gaze for only a moment before tearing his focus away from those probing eyes. He stared at the people who waited for him to go on. He opened his mouth and then closed it, beginning several times to speak against the group of serene children, only to stutter back into silence.

How was he to continue? Why couldn't he? His mind was made up, but his throat simply would not produce the words, the order to proceed as planned.

He cast a withering glance at Luke. Factions planning his demise? Plotting the actions that he himself had set in motion? Ridiculous. The people loved him!

Gathering his resolve, Roland cleared his throat and opened his mouth to issue the command. Suddenly a wail rent the air, shrill enough to silence the crowd halfway back through the streets.

"Roland, no! Don't do this thing, I beg of you!"

Eyes wide, Roland whirled his horse about and stared at his wife. In the shocked stillness that followed her cry, Rosalynn's face crumpled and she leaned forward in her saddle as a sob shook her petite frame. Her red curls fell like a curtain in front of her face until she looked up again with tear-filled eyes, "Please, my lord. He is my brother, and they are *children*!" Her eyes beseeched him as her right hand moved instinctively to cover her abdomen. Their child. "Spare them."

Roland's thoughts screamed at him from a thousand different directions. *It is the children, Roland, the children who will be most malleable in your hands… Spare them… When these gifts have been offered, these sacrifices made, then a blessing will be granted you… They are children… Your life is in danger…*

"*Enough!!*" Roland's roar stilled what had been left of the celebratory noise. The city fell silent. Running an agitated hand through his hair, Roland squeezed his eyes shut. Here was his chance to rid himself of these seditious children once and for all, and yet it was also an opportunity to make his wife happy again, to show her he cared about her. But how could he, when the gods had declared this as the only acceptable sacrifice?

Or had it been the gods after all?

No. He could not go back on his word. The people would think him a fool if he gave in to every wind of conviction.

Roland lifted his head, refusing to meet his wife's gaze, "There must be a sacrifice."

A murmur spread through the crowd, some in favor of their continued festivities, others suddenly questioning the methods by which the celebration would be carried out. Before the mob could regain its former level of mayhem, another voice cut across the square and a man stepped through the crowd to stop just inside the human border.

"My lord, I will take their place."

Roland swallowed, "Who are you, sir? And what business is it of yours whether they live or die?"

The man held his head erect, "My name is Guy, and I am a cooper. I once betrayed my closest friend to the raid of your Mordecais, knowing that it may lead to his death. I cannot stand idly by now and do nothing to save his children."

Roland's eyes slid closed. It was a dream. Surely, this was only a terrible dream and he would soon wake up. One thing was certain. When he did wake up, he wanted to know that all of these problems had been dealt with. His eyes opened.

"Guards, take that man and bind him. His desire shall be granted before the sun is set." He turned his horse's head and shouted to the gatekeepers before he could question his own decision, "Open the gate Thirteenth!"

Roland's gaze lowered to find Luke staring at him. He returned the boy's gaze evenly as the portcullis groaned upward and the massive threshold yawned its way open. The crowd did not jeer as they had in times past. Instead they watched in silence, as if afraid a spoken word would change Roland's mind yet again and have them all thrown into prison or exile. They were wise.

Luke's eyes shifted to the man called Guy and a wave of emotion overtook the boy's face. His jaw quivered for a moment and he barely managed a nod of thanks before he was forced to lower his head and swipe a sleeve across his eyes. Behind him, several of the other children wiped their own tears as they all turned to stare through the gate that had swallowed their parents four years before.

Roland took a steadying breath. He was aware of a number of dark looks being cast his way, but he forced himself to keep to the path he had chosen. He would compile a list of those who disagreed with him and keep a careful watch on them.

Finally Roland could stand the strange silence no longer. He rose in his saddle and glared at the nine young people, "You have been charged with sedition, rebellion, disorder, and a number of other offences, not the least of which is your refusal to forsake the forbidden God. As ruler of this realm, Hebbros, I hereby condemn you to whatever fate the gods may consign you to, and cast you into exile." His words were with met with more silence and Roland finally lost control, "*Get out!*" He shrieked, and his horse sidestepped nervously. "You are no longer welcome here. I command you to leave this place immediately and never return."

Luke's steady voice lifted to fill the square, "We will go, and pave the way that others may one day see the truth and have courage to follow. Only remember, my lord, we go not to exile, but to freedom."

Roland leaned over his horse's head and spat each word with as much hatred as he could muster for these troublemakers, "I never want to see your faces again!"

Slowly the crowd began to join in with their own taunts. The mob released their jeers and words that were meant to shame. A thousand curses were flung at the backs of the condemned, but the nine faces remained unaffected. Turning their backs on the wave of hatred that threatened to crash down on them, they joined hands and crossed the threshold to Desterrar.

Sir Valden could hardly believe his eyes. The Thirteenth swung shut with a resounding thud of finality, and still he struggled to make sense of what had just taken place in the judgment square. He shifted in his saddle and exchanged glances with Kenrick, and then with Wulf and Warin. They appeared just as shocked and taken aback as he felt.

Roland had let them go! Luke had dared to refuse Valden's request, and in the end he had gone free! There had not even been time to convince Roland that Kenrick was guilty of secretly stirring revolt and ought to be executed with the others, because the execution had never taken place!

Barking a command to his men, Valden turned his horse and rode east, heading towards the Mordecai garrison and some peace and quiet.

He needed to think. And when he was done thinking, it would be time to act.

Haman grit his teeth and turned from the square, pounding his fist on the nearest structure. The rebel chief was anything but pleased that Roland had decided to stray from the plan. Haman had been counting on the Faithful being extinguished. The city needed to move on from the ridiculous zealots who carried the religion's banner.

At least Roland had not withdrawn his vow to secede from Mizgalia. The followers of Haman would still have their war, and Haman would still take Roland's place of power after he eventually took Roland's life. And then, Haman paused in the street to stare at a point beyond the western wall, at least he would know where to find the Faithful, that he might one day bring an official end to their insufferable lot.

Everything was green. And alive. The air itself seemed inclined to stir much cooler here than within the city's walls. The city they had left behind. Hebbros.

In spite of the danger they were still in, and the reluctance of some to be there in the first place, the nine children could not contain their grins and looks of wonder. Each had to bend and feel the unhindered grass, prickly to their down-turned palms and free of the city's dust and grime. Each had to touch the bark of a tree and tilt their head back to search for the topmost branches. They had stepped into a place of marvel and discovery. Of beauty and newness. This was the world beyond Hebbros.

They first moved further south along the wall, where Liam the mercer had secreted a load of supplies through the hole in his shop, as well as a parcel from the physician that included a clean wrap and bottle of salve for Luke's leg. Beside the stack of goods sat Christopher's sword and Luke's bow and quiver, discarded by the Mordecais and thoughtfully recovered by friends. Bowing their heads, the group thanked God for His protection and provision.

After this they traveled north, eventually coming to the base of a rugged path that led upward to the mount's summit. Though it looked like a difficult climb, and in some places utterly treacherous, it showed signs of having been traveled before. Bearing the mercer's gifts, they began the long journey upward.

Among those who expressed most outward excitement over their banishment was Sarah. While preparing Jerem and Celia for the parade that morning, she would never have guessed that she herself would not be returning to the palace. And she had been thrown together with the very people whom she longed to speak with. As the climb continued, holding tight to Bradley's hand, she asked many questions of the Faithful.

They told her of the God of mercy, who had sent His Son to die in her stead.

"Like Guy did for us t'day?"

"Yes," Chris helped Charlotte over the edge of a steep place and then reached down to help Lillian, "but Jesus did not betray us first, as Guy did."

They told her of Christ's resurrection, how He had conquered sin and death. They talked of how He waited for sinners to acknowledge their condition and come to Him for cleansing.

"He purchased us at the cost of His own life." Luke turned a rabbit on the spit and watched it sizzle over the fire, "You are familiar with the ways of masters and slaves. Masters purchase the person of a slave, and the slave serves because he must. When God purchased us, He paid the price of freedom for all mankind.

Freedom, not a life of slavery."

"And yet you still serve Him," Sarah observed.

Ned responded, "In our faith we serve Him because we love Him, and we love Him because He loved us first. Our service to Him is a gift that we choose to give out of the gratefulness in our hearts."

Chris turned to look at Sarah, "If Lady Rosalynn, in all sincerity, had offered to purchase your freedom and let you go free, would you have scoffed at her gift?" Sarah shook her head and he continued, "It is the same with Christ, only many do refuse His offer of forgiveness and eternal life, and they scoff at those of us who have."

The group fell silent for a moment, and then from where he knelt behind Sarah, Bradley broke the stillness, "Almost there. And…it's…off!" Sheathing a dagger from Liam's supplies, he moved to sit beside her, and with untamable satisfaction glowing in his eyes, gently laid a strap of brown leather across her outstretched palms, "Just as I promised."

Sarah's face was a picture of wonder as she stared down at the broken collar. Tears formed in her eyes and fell unheeded into her lap. After a moment her shoulders shook and she began to cry, and then laughter took the place of sobs.

"There aren't any words to express this happiness." Sarah took his hand and smiled through a film of tears, "Thank you." She turned to glance at the others, "I've finally shed the last of m' life of physical slavery. What better time t' accept that other offer of freedom that has been given me?"

That night, high above the walls of Hebbros, Sarah became a follower of Christ and a member of the Faithful. Seeing her faith brought Bradley one step closer to making the same decision, but still his need for logic caused him to resist the truth. Now that his problems had been taken care of, he thought he had no need for a higher power. Even the trouble with his sinuses had abated in the clear air outside the city walls.

Lillian, who had heard the words before, still resented the truth as much as she resented the people and situations that had brought her to this point. This was not the excitement she had had in mind when she left her mother on the street.

For three days they climbed the path that had been carved into the mountain. Only once did they meet a catawyld, but

Christopher was able to dispatch it quickly, putting to use the practice he'd had defending Pavia at The Row. They left the beast's carcass to distract the others that shrieked in the distance, and quickly moved on their way. When they marveled at how few troubles they had encountered, little Charlotte reported that she had been praying every step of the way, and no one doubted her.

Luke paused on the path and rubbed his hands down his stiff leg, hoping to coax the muscles into relaxing. The others had been helpful, but he had drawn the line when they suggested someone carry him. They were so close, and he desperately wanted to take the last steps on his own two feet.

The stars had emerged in the evening sky, seeming to blink with excitement over how far they had come. From different points of the mountain, dragons dropped from their caves to sweep low over the city of Hebbros.

Had that awful place been his home only three days ago? Had God truly intervened and caused Roland to let them through the gate? Luke remembered the words spoken by the physician and thought of how true they had been. Life was usually simpler than he chose to make it.

Suddenly Luke froze and behind him the others followed his lead. Up ahead, above them on the path, Desterrar's peak had begun to glow with the light of a giant flame. And then came the noise, soft at first, but building.

"People are singing," Elbert spoke into the quiet hush that had fallen over the group.

Ned laughed and let out a whoop, "Obvious, Elbert! We're almost there!"

An air of giddy excitement simmered and pushed them upward the last distance until there was only one more shelf to climb. As Luke reached to grip the ledge above him, a hand suddenly clasped his from above, pulling him up over the edge. In another instant, Luke's feet had been firmly planted on the more level ground of Desterrar's peak. Around him, the other children were quickly lifted to safety and for a moment they could only stand and stare at the sight before them.

A village had been built along the gentle lines of the peaceful summit. At the center was an enormous fire tower used to protect the inhabitants from dragons. Beneath the tower, in the warmth of the flame, people were mingling and laughing and singing praises to God. One woman caught sight of their group and slowly started forward, and then realization dawned and she began to run with her arms outstretched and ready to embrace them. Behind her, others began to turn and see and soon the entire village was headed their way.

The man who had helped the children over the last precipice moved to stand in front of them. Luke blinked back tears and recognized him as Sedgwick, the first outcast of Hebbros. Borrowing the strength of a staff, Sedgwick smiled at the nine young people, and then his gaze found Luke and the boy was overwhelmed by all that filled the older man's gaze. So much had transpired since that fateful day when they had stood on opposite sides of the judgment square. Sedgwick gave a small nod, and just moments before Luke's mother would reach them he uttered three wonderful words that stirred each one of their souls.

"Welcome to Exile."

Part Three

Exile

Eleven Years Later

"For here have we no continuing city, but we seek one to come."

Hebrews 13:14

41
Daughter of a Peasant

Kingdom of Arcrea, Village of Balgo in the Region of Ranulf

Elaina glanced over her shoulder just before a slight rise in the land hid Balgo from view. She faced forward again to watch her steps and her lip curled at the thought of her home. The smelly little village surrounded by gently sloping sheep fields had been her place of abode for the past three years, ever since a blacksmith from Oak's Branch had solved the ancient riddle of Arcrea's heart and been crowned the realm's first king. As a result, the land's seven former lords had been stripped of their titles and reduced to the lives of common peasants.

Everyone had said it was an act of mercy on King Druet's part.

Elaina called it insolence.

Throughout the entire kingdom, only one village had been willing to house the former nobility and train them in new skills. Balgo was a place of gray-stone, thatch-roofed cottages and primitive places of labor. Its southeastern border was tucked against the base of a lone mountain, commonly called the Lost Brikbone, and some of the streets were cobbled by rocks that had rolled from the summit. Others were mere tracks of dirt.

Elaina glanced down at her unattractive shoes, caked with

dust and a bit of mud, and rolled her eyes. There was no help for it. She lifted the hem of her skirt and climbed over a rotting log, and then reached a stand of trees and began pressing through the maze of twisted limbs. If only her life had not become as tangled as these branches.

Straightening after ducking beneath a hanging vine, she swept a strand of hair behind her ear. Her mother was always saying that her hair, long loose curls the color of dark molasses, was her finest feature and would surely help her to secure a good husband. Elaina gave an undignified snort. Finest feature? How was that supposed to help her as a peasant out in the middle of nowhere? And the only husbands to be had were filthy tradesmen or silent shepherds who preferred to keep their own company. Elaina would rather die an old maid.

Having already reached the wizened old age of twenty-two…she just might.

Frustration welled in Elaina's middle and burned in her lungs until she had to pause and take a deep breath of the late-summer air. How had her world crumbled so easily? She and her father had had everything planned out and in control. None of this might have happened if only she had succeeded in her mission to help bring an end to Druet before the heart's discovery. They had come so close, and her father would undoubtedly have finished the young blacksmith off had not Falconer arrived to play the part of a rotten traitor. Her father's chief informant had joined himself to Druet's cause and was even now serving the new king while her father worked his fingers to the bone as a common peasant.

Elaina grit her teeth as she wound her way along an invisible but well-memorized path through shady trees and overgrown brush. A tear slid unbidden down her cheek. Her father was far from common, and she hated to think of him as anything but the powerful ruler he had once been. If only she had done better, and considered all the angles while spying on Druet's band.

Nevertheless her father had adjusted surprisingly well to his new way of life. Since the day Druet had spared him, Lord Frederick had seemed a different man. More thoughtful. Calm. Resigned. Her mother, on the other hand, still insisted on acting like a noblewoman, regardless of the fact she must now make three meals a day, help care for their dirty animals, and wear course dresses that itched in winter and stuck to her skin in summer.

Elaina came to the top of another small rise. The view was magnificent, speckled with signs of autumn and cooled by a gentle breeze, but she ignored it. Descending to the bottom, where several large stones protruded from the hillside in a seeming pile, she circled to one in particular that leaned vertically against the slope. Placing her hand against the warm surface, Elaina glanced around to see that no one had followed, and then slipped behind the massive rock and into the hidden mouth of her favorite cave.

The temperature inside was considerably cooler than out in the sun, and Elaina suppressed a shiver as her eyes adjusted to the cave's dim interior. The short tunnel she had entered behind the rock quickly gave way to a large open space beneath the hill she had just descended. A small smile tugged at the corner of Elaina's lips. Here she would be free to think, to explore her own confusion and ire as long as she wanted. Here she would be left alone.

Well, almost.

Elaina dropped to the packed earth and rolled to the left just as the whisper of a blade swung past overhead. Using the momentum of her sudden movements, she returned to her feet with the agility of a cat and whirled to face the shadow that had snuck up behind her. The brawny shape of a man blocked the exit and stood spinning the hilt of his sword in a beefy hand.

Elaina narrowed her eyes at the brute and quickly turned to race toward the opposite wall. Behind her she heard the scuffling sound of his boots as they clapped against the dirt in pursuit. When he moved away from the short tunnel, a bit of light spilled inside and revealed the object she had been aiming for. Elaina slapped her hand over a sword that hung on pegs in the wall, and tore away the scabbard just as her attacker caught up to her.

Spinning just in time to block an overhead slice, Elaina delivered a combination of her own. Surprising the man with a feint attack, she ducked beneath his arm and made it safely away from the wall. He turned and swung back into the competition, and their swords clashed a deafening report in the underground space.

The two combatants kept their focus on the movements of the other until their weapons became locked at the cross-guards. Immediately, the image of a seven-year-old girl standing in the same position with her father flashed through Elaina's mind and she faltered.

"Stop." The word flew through the air with authority and the fight came to a halt. The brawny attacker glanced in the direction of the speaker and then shoved away from Elaina with a muttered curse.

Light bloomed in the cave as a man of average height and graying hair stepped away from the wall, where he had just mounted a lit torch in its wall-sconce. His gaze swept over the male opponent and landed on Elaina, "This is the same place we stopped last time." His gaze was questioning and commanding at once, "You must conquer this if you would progress further with your skills."

"I know, I know!" Elaina shook her head and blinked against the memories of her childhood, of dancing with her father, before the image could be completed with him tapping the end of her nose. She rubbed a hand over her eyes as if to wipe it all away, "I expect it to happen, and yet it surprises me every time." Her gaze sought the instructor's, "I can't keep my actions from triggering memories."

He nodded with assent, "What you must learn is how to keep your memories from triggering your actions."

The brawny fighter sheathed his sword and leaned against the far wall with his arms crossed, "All she has to do is keep from ever locking swords with her opponent."

Elaina's eyes sparked angrily, "You did it on purpose this time because you didn't want me to defeat you."

"That's not true." His eyes narrowed, "You'll never be good enough to defeat me."

"Enough, Talgus." The instructor lit another torch and set it in its sconce, "Your words of pride will keep you from succeeding."

Elaina retrieved her scabbard and strapped it around her waist, "At least I sensed his approach." She darted a glance in Talgus's direction, "I thought we had agreed on a slight signal to commence the fight in order to keep me from losing my head."

Talgus shrugged, "You knew I was here waiting for you. Why signal when I knew you were expecting it anyway?"

The instructor turned a piercing eye on the younger man, "An agreement is an agreement. If you cannot show honor in such a small matter, I cannot trust you in others."

"Oh come, Leo," Talgus leaned away from the wall and pointed a stiff arm at the girl in the middle of the room, "she's

Frederick's daughter! She plotted against the life of our king and you trust the wench with a blade, yet you threaten to remove your trust from me when I've assisted you for seven years!"

Elaina jumped in before Leo had a chance to reply, "It's not as if I'm planning a rebellion, Talgus. Great goose eggs, you've made it very clear that I wouldn't have a following to support me should I try. I like the sword. I like practicing the sword." She stepped closer and growled in his face, "It gives me an opportunity to relieve the tension that comes from having one's *life fall apart*!"

"The only thing that fell apart was your father's desire to keep the peasantry in servitude to his every tax and whim."

"My fath—"

"Enough." In contrast to the two young people, Leo remained calm, "Talgus, she is entitled to purchase instruction like any other peasant"—Elaina winced at the reminder of her rank—"and I am entitled to accept whatever students I see fit to instruct."

Talgus shook his head and stalked from the cave without a backward glance. Elaina watched him go and then shifted to look at Leo.

"He'll be back." The instructor signaled for her to sheath her weapon and then reached for two practice swords, "In the meantime you'll have to settle for practicing with me."

Elaina offered her dimpled grin, "I would prefer that anyway."

Leo tossed her a blunted weapon made of dense wood, "Careful. These may not have teeth, but they still bite."

She smiled, "I won't let it hit me."

He lifted a brow, clearly doubting her words, "Your skill is admirable, Elaina, but I cannot deem you entirely capable until you conquer the thoughts that rise up to cloud your judgment."

Elaina glanced away, uncomfortable beneath the weight of his reproof. Another sign that she had failed someone. Why couldn't she ignore the memories when they came? What made them impossible to resist when they called her to indulge in the reliving of happier times.

The image of her father reared up again, and the tip of her nose began to twitch. She tightened her grip on the hilt of the practice sword. When was the last time he had used that sign of affection? When had he last made time to perform the Arcrean Sword Reel with her?

"Elaina?" Leo's voice broke through the fog of confusion and she met his questioning gaze.

"I'm just tired today." She stepped back and prepared for the next bout, "I'm ready now." He set himself in a beginning stance and Elaina sent him the impish grin of her girlhood, "Prepare to meet your match."

Leo raised his brow, "Are you speaking to me, or to those distractions we've been discussing?"

"Both." Elaina's weapon swung playfully as she rolled her wrist and began the fight.

Elaina slipped through the door into her family's simple cottage and offered an innocent smile to her parents. Her father glanced up from his chair by the hearth and returned her silent greeting with a small smile of his own. Her mother turned from mixing a lumpy concoction in a wooden bowl, and scanned her with an appraising look.

"Where have you been?"

"Walking." Elaina was glad most of the perspiration from her swordplay had dried in the breeze on her walk home. Her mother would not smile on the thought of her daughter learning such a skill. "The weather is lovely today."

"Were you walking alone, or in anyone's company?" Her mother's question sounded innocent enough, but Elaina heard the familiar implication in the words.

"Alone."

Mother pursed her lips in disappointment. "It would be simple enough to convince Lord Quinton's son to join you on your rambles through the village. Young Wesley was in line to rule the region that neighbored ours, and would be a wonderful alliance should your walks about Balgo eventually lead you to the altar."

Elaina cast her father an imploring look.

Frederick smirked and then glanced at his wife, "Aurora, Quinton is no longer a lord, and therefore his son is no longer heir to a region that neighbors one that is no longer ours. Marrying young Wesley would in no way be an alliance of worth, unless you favor the idea of being connected to the house of a tanner."

Elaina bit back a smile as her mother's lips quirked into a sideways scowl, "Of course we are no longer nobility. However, it may be that Druet will one day release us from this village and restore something of our status in Arcrea." Her gaze swiveled to her daughter, "And I'm sure Wesley's mother mentioned to me just the other day that she positively adores the way you style your hair."

Elaina's expression shifted to one of confusion, "My hair?"

"Yes. I'm sure I've told you countless times that your lovely hair would play a part in securing your future. Such an unusual shade between black and brown." Aurora sighed as she renewed her stirring of the bowl's contents, "Yes, she told me directly that she has made up her mind to convince Wesley that he ought to seek your hand."

"Well, he may seek it if he wishes, but I may not be inclined to give it."

The stirring became more vigorous. "Your father will be the one to bless the union if he sees fit to do so, young lady. At your age you should be pleased by any offer."

Elaina took a slow breath and glanced at the ceiling, "Well, it's a mercy he did not inherit his father's seat before the regional names were established. 'The Region of Wesley' doesn't sound half as impressive as his father's name."

"I'm going to ignore that," her mother turned to add a few more ingredients.

Elaina crossed to the hearth and stopped beside her father's chair. Leaning down, she studied the bow he was fashioning, "It's beautiful, father."

"Thank you, daughter," he nodded, his gaze fastened on the narrow length of yew wood. "It's not quite what I want yet, but in time it will be right."

"Nothing will ever be right again," Elaina muttered as she moved to retrieve the water bucket from the corner. Louder, she said, "I'll run out to the well."

"Elaina." Her father's voice stopped her as she opened the door. "Look at me."

Gritting her teeth against the wave of bitterness that threatened to choke her, Elaina turned with her hand on the door. Her mother looked up from the bowl to glance at one and then the other. Her father studied her across the room, and Elaina knew he had heard her muttered words.

"It's been three years."

"Three years of misery."

"Druet could have had us put to death."

"He also could have stayed in his father's shop and never gone to search for the heart."

Frederick shook his head, "The heart was destined to be discovered. Better that it was by a man of integrity who saw fit to spare our lives."

"Integrity!?" Elaina slammed the door back against its frame and gripped the handle of the water bucket until it bit into her palm, "The man began his quest as an act of defiance against you, and then 'saw fit' to send his betters into a life of desolation and poverty."

"We have not lacked, and we were no longer his betters when he was crowned king. Our situations were reversed."

"*You were supposed to find it!*" Elaina's words spewed from between clenched teeth and were followed by a moment of silence as her parents stared at her, shocked by her outburst of wrath. "You were supposed to discover the heart and be king."

"Elaina, my dear," Aurora left her bowl and rounded the table, "a lady does not raise—"

"I'm not a lady!" Elaina dropped the empty bucket with a clatter. "Not anymore. I'm a peasant. A dirty, smelly, lowly peasant who feeds pigs, and gathers eggs, and collects mud on her shoes and under her nails. And I'm stuck in this place, this filthy village, until the day I die. I'm surrounded by people who were once great, but are now resigned to live in this muck and grime, and who all tell me that I should be grateful. Grateful for what? That I'm still alive to see my parents reduced to paupers? That I lived through the terrible nightmare of arriving in this place as its newest inhabitant? That the day's labor no longer hurts my hands because they're covered in calluses and scars?" She glanced at her mother, and her tone turned sarcastic, "Oh, I suppose I should be grateful I still have my hair. That will surely come in handy when I want to impress the young men, none of whom I wish to marry. But at least I'm not bald!"

"Elaina!" Her mother's tone was shocked and her expression hurt, but Elaina turned away before it could pinch her conscience.

Her eyes landed on her father, his eyes saddened and reminding her yet again of her failure to impress him. Tears stung her eyes, but she blinked them back. "I would rather I had died in my attempts to make you proud than suffer through another day of reliving my failures."

Frederick stood, his bow sliding to the floor, "How can you say such a thing when you know very well that you have always made me proud?"

"Do I know that?" Elaina shook her head and backed against the door, reaching for the latch. "What I know is that you sit in the artillator's shop all day, crafting weaponry, and then you come home at night, more often than not bringing more work with you," her eyes slid to the bow on the floor at his feet. "You sit there, day after day, quiet, brooding, indifferent. You have lost your passion to live, and I am left to be a spare piece that no longer fits in your existence. We used to do everything together, and now you barely look at me!"

"Elaina, I… I have not lost my passion to live. I have found a different method by which I must survive. I must work now, to provide for you and your mother, because— Elaina!"

His final words were whisked away by the evening breeze as Elaina threw open the door and raced outside. Away from the cramped cottage and excuses. Away from the disappointments and failures. Away from the memories.

42

Caught by Surprise

The following morning was one of stilted silence. Elaina had returned after dark and gone straight to the small pallet-room to sleep. When she awoke with the sun, her father had already left for the shop where he was apprenticed, and her mother was just coming in with a basket of eggs. Aurora glanced at Elaina as she set her burden on the small table.

"I saved you a biscuit."

She had said nothing more, and so Elaina had not offered any comments of her own. The biscuit was eaten, soaked in milk, and then Elaina had gone to fetch water from the well in the square.

Her dress of scratchy gray had suffered greatly during her walk the day before, and so she changed into one of the few gowns brought from her father's castle. The soft folds of deepest blue were the perfect balm for her sour mood. Wrinkling her nose at the worn gown of dull gray, she lifted it with two fingers and tossed in a pile to be scrubbed.

By midmorning, Elaina was beginning to feel stifled by the lack of communication. She was just about to say so when a quick rap at the door announced the arrival of none other than Lord Quinton's wife and son. Elaina suddenly found herself wishing the silence could have continued.

Wesley's mother dragged her son across the threshold and entered with a flutter of compliments for the neat cottage. The two guests were ushered to the table as Aurora swept the contents of the crude surface out of sight and all but tore Elaina's stained apron from her waist.

"Sit, sit! Elaina brought fresh water just this morning, such a dear girl. I'll bring you each a mug to cool your throats. The weather has been so hot of late, yes? Except, of course, in the evenings, when Elaina takes her walks."

Elaina stiffened and her eyes widened. She glanced at her mother just as Aurora placed a cup of water in front of the young man across the table.

Aurora blinked innocently, "Wesley, do you like to walk?"

The stunned tanner was spared a response when his mother replied in his stead.

"Oh how lovely! The dear boy loves to amble here and there quite regularly. Why, just this morning he agreed to accompany me here in order to bring a gift for darling Elaine."

"Elaina."

"Yes, of course. Laina."

"How sweet of you, Wesley, to think of our dear Laina," Elaina scowled when her mother turned the mispronunciation into a pet name. "Just last evening she was in need of some cheer."

"How fortuitous then that we came today!"

"Indeed."

The two mothers sat grinning at one another until Wesley's turned to prod him on with silent but obvious motions. The poor man looked askance at his mother until she finally grabbed a small parcel from his hands and thrust it toward Elaina with an overenthusiastic smile.

"For you."

Elaina cast a glance of sympathy at Wesley and then loosened the twine that held the wrap in place. Inside was a vest made of tanned leather, dyed a rich red and trimmed with strips of embroidery. She fingered the soft fabric in a moment of genuine pleasure, and then looked up at their guests, "Thank you."

Wesley offered a slight shrug along with the first words he had spoken since entering the cottage, "Mother made it."

"Oh, nonsense," the woman slapped his arm. "You tanned the leather!" She turned to the other women, "Of course I turned the hide into a vest and embroidered the trimming. Red is your favorite color, is it not, Laina?"

Elaina refused to offer even the slightest nod so long as her name was being distorted. Wesley's mother seemed not to notice, however, for she was immediately off on another rant about the finer qualities of her very embarrassed son.

Suddenly the woman grabbed hold of Elaina's hand and dragged her into the pallet-room, where she promptly shoved the vest on over the girl's dark blue dress and cinched the laces at the back. Elaina gasped when the fabric hugged her midsection, and then her hand was grasped again as Wesley's grinning mother led the way back into the main room.

Poor Wesley looked about to bolt.

It was time for an escape.

Her mother was just pointing out how lovely Elaina's hair was today, when the young lady interrupted the rush of complimentary words.

"I'm sure Wesley has more important things to do than sit here and listen to us chatter. So, as we are both so obviously fond of a good walk," she pinned the young man with a gaze that said he should comply, "shall I accompany you as far as the tannery?"

Wesley's stool nearly toppled over backward as he surged to his feet, offered a quick bow to her mother, and then moved to open the door. Aurora's eyes narrowed slightly, clearly questioning her daughter's true motives for taking the air.

Elaina nodded at Wesley's mother as she passed by, "Thank you for stopping in."

The door closed on the woman saying what a fine pair the two would make. Elaina glanced at the red face of the young man beside her and decided to act as if she had not heard. As they started up the street, she ran her fingers over the edge of the soft vest and glanced at Wesley again.

"The gift was a kind gesture, even if it wasn't exactly from you."

He nodded, but kept his eyes forward.

"You did fine work with the leather. Do you enjoy being a tanner?"

Wesley started to shrug, and then decided to offer a further response, "I do. I enjoy using my hands to work, honing skills that will sharpen my knowledge and add to my strength." He studied the street ahead, running a hand through his light hair, "I wouldn't have had such an opportunity if I was still heir to my father's region."

The words stung Elaina's pride. How was it that everyone else could adjust to this life among the peasantry and find a reason to thrive in it? Yet she had trouble with merely giving up her softer footwear.

They approached the tannery and Wesley turned to offer a slight bow, the habits of a nobleman still ingrained into his manners. He offered her a slight smile, "Thank you for helping me get away."

Elaina returned the grin and shifted to watch those already at work in the shop, "They mean well, and I'm sure they are both anxious to see their children happily settled."

"I know it." Wesley nodded. A brief pause ensued and then he turned to go, calling over his shoulder with another smile, "I also know that your name is E-laina."

Elaina laughed softly and waved before turning to slowly make her way back home. She paused outside the artillator's shop to watch her father at work on another bow. A stack of narrow wooden strips rested at his elbow, ready to be fashioned into arrows. He was unaware of her presence, and when eventually he looked up to rest his eyes, she was already gone.

Elaina's conscience grew heavy as she bypassed her family's cottage on the square and headed north out of Balgo. Her mother's attempts at matchmaking had been performed with good intentions and a pure heart. She truly did seek her daughter's happiness. Elaina had been rude to make a hasty exit, and now she would cause her mother undue worry if she failed to return soon.

There was that word again. Failed.

Elaina shook her head and quickened her pace. She needed to ease the tension that had arisen with last night's argument, and a lesson with Leo would accomplish just that. She would be home in time for supper, and then she could smooth over all those nasty things she had said.

As she made her way toward the cave, Elaina became aware of storm clouds gathering in the west. On the horizon to the north and west, the Brikbone Mountains could vaguely be seen crawling along the Arcrean/Mizgalian border. Not long ago, she had lived much closer to the majestic mountain range. Before Druet had taken her freedom away.

Thunder rolled in the distance as Elaina reached the mouth of the cave. She glanced over her shoulder, wondering if it would be wiser to turn back now, and then slipped behind the giant stone and into the short tunnel.

Something was wrong. Elaina knew as soon as she had taken her first step inside. On any other day she would feel Leo's presence by the far wall and sense when Talgus approached from behind to begin one of their mock skirmishes. Skirmishes that had become far more brutal during recent weeks. This day was different. Without waiting for a signal, Elaina darted across the room and grabbed her sword from the pegs in the wall. She whirled with the blade in hand just as lighting forked across the storm-darkened sky outside and silhouetted a figure in the cave's entrance.

"Talgus?"

Leo's assistant responded with a dry chuckle and then advanced on Elaina in three long strides. Their swords had met only three times before he managed to slide his blade along hers and lock them at the cross-guards. Immediately the memories assailed Elaina. She was a child again, soaking in the attention of her father and waiting for him to tap the end of her nose in the middle of their beloved dance.

Talgus waited. Leo's command to halt the bout never came, and so he continued to apply pressure to her sword until Elaina could withstand neither his strength nor the strain of her past. Dropping to her knees, Elaina felt when her sword was slapped from her grasp and her hands were quickly tied in front. She resolved to stay calm. Bound and defenseless, she would be unable to overpower him.

Talgus pulled her to her feet with a sharp jerk, "My father was killed by one of your kind, and I've waited a long time to see his death avenged. I'll be the better man by not putting you to death, but I swear, by the time you reach your destination you'll wish I hadn't been so kind."

Elaina blinked away the fragments of memories that still clung to her awareness and looked up at the man of thirty-or-so years, "Let go of me this instant," the words sounded feeble in her own ears, but she had to try. "Where's Leo?"

Talgus shoved her toward the mouth of the cave as thunder

rolled closer in the heavy sky, "I sent Leo home when it became apparent the storm would strike soon. I told him I would remain here for the night and send you back to Balgo should you be foolish enough to venture out for another lesson."

Elaina reached the cave's entrance and felt Talgus's fingers circle her arm in a grip of iron. A shiver of fear raced up her spine and she eyed the fast-approaching storm, wishing she hadn't been as foolish as he had predicted.

"You're not taking me back to Balgo."

Talgus laughed, "For a simpleton, you're quick-witted."

"Talgus, let me go."

Ignoring her, he led her away from the rocks and circled to where his horse was tied to a low shrub. Elaina offered some resistance, but her feet slipped on the grassy slope and her desperation could not break his resolve. They reached the animal and Talgus lifted Elaina onto the horse, quickly leaping into the saddle behind her. Taking the reins in one hand, he placed his other arm around her waist and turned his horse to face west.

The first raindrops began to fall and Elaina glanced at the threatening sky, ready to unleash its fury on the region of Ranulf. Talgus spurred the horse to a gallop and her gaze shifted to look ahead, where storm clouds stretched their fingers over the gently rolling landscape and hid from view the majestic range of Brikbones.

43

Crooked Gateway - Golden Tankard

Elaina woke with a start when Talgus's horse snorted and began to slow its pace. She stretched her neck from side to side, wishing her hands were free so that she might rub the stiffened muscles. They had been riding for a day and a half, stopping only to rest the horse for an hour at a time. Their meals had consisted of hard bread and dried meat stored in the saddlebags, and Elaina's stomach was beginning to make a habit of growling at her. She refused to complain, however, for fear that Talgus would stop feeding her altogether.

Elaina blinked and took in her surroundings. They were riding through a forest late in the day and evening shadows were beginning to stretch out behind them. The scenery was peaceful, untouched and hazy in the slanting rays of sunlight that fell through the green canopy overhead.

"Where are we?" Her question was answered with a sharp squeeze to her waist that halted her breath.

Talgus grunted and brought the horse to a halt. He lifted his fingers to his mouth and delivered a shrill whistle that made Elaina cringe. Shouts were heard in the distance, and soon a band of ruffians emerged from the trees to surround them. Their leader, a tanned brigand with long hair tied back in a club, approached the horse and eyed first Talgus and then Elaina.

"What would be bringin' the likes of you to my coast?"

Elaina's brow furrowed. Coast? Were they near water?

Talgus reached into his saddlebag and the leader quickly grabbed her captor's wrist, "No tricks, friend. The last man what tried didn't see the end of the day."

Talgus scowled, "Why would I attempt foul play when I've just announced my arrival? I have a document that proves I'm expected here today or tomorrow."

The leader showed a row of white teeth when he grinned, "Let's be seein' it, then."

Removing Talgus's hand from the bag, the man proceeded to reach inside himself and quickly produced a folded piece of parchment. His eyes scanned written words that Elaina could not see, and then lifted to return Talgus's impatient stare, "Yer here t' see the Mizgalian."

"I am, sir."

The brigand stretched out a hand in welcome, "Ferrand, chief o' the clan Knavesmire." He turned without waiting for Talgus to return the introductions and called to one of his men, "Help 'em dismount and take his horse t' be stabled for the night." He turned to smile down at Elaina as she was dragged from the saddle to stand in their midst, "Might the lovely lady be the promised acquisition for our northern friend?"

"She is." Talgus gripped her arm and pushed her forward a step, "Where is the man?"

Ferrand quirked his dark brow at the other man's brusque tone, and calmly took Elaina's arm in his own grasp, "I'll be escortin' the lady. Follow me."

Bone weary and without any means of escape, Elaina inhaled slowly and tried to grasp all that was happening. Talgus had brought her to Knavesmire, the clan that populated Ranulf's southwestern border and was separated from the kingdom of Mizgalia by only the width of a Brikbone. The Knavesmire encampment stretched along the northern banks of a vast bay, the waters of which also touched the regional borders of Osgood and Hugh. Situated at the crux of two kingdoms and the Arcrean Sea, the compound had been called the "Crooked Gateway" by many who were aware of the clan's corrupt nature and dealings.

Elaina glanced at the proud chief who led her by the arm.

Ferrand was a dangerous man, known for trading with or stealing from any criminal merchant or poor soul who happened across his path.

So why had Talgus brought her here?

Ferrand led her, along with Talgus and the company of brigands, into the heart of Knavesmire. A series of docks lined the bay, and from there the village crawled up the banks. Despite the danger she was surely in, Elaina marveled at the way the cottages seemed to climb over rocks here and bury themselves in the steep hillside there. The place was a tapestry of ingenuity. The paths of dirt that served as streets were busy with people hawking wares that had probably been stolen. Children raced up and down the banks, playing games with one another or running from mothers who called them to wash for supper.

At last they turned toward the docks and made their way to one of the noisier establishments that faced the water. Elaina let her gaze roam the small vessels that bobbed in the lapping tide, and then shifted to take in the scene where Ferrand had brought them to a halt.

A crowded tavern, deemed significant enough to bear the name the Golden Tankard, was a ramshackle affair of slanted beams and crumbling stones. Several tables had been moved outside and a number of patrons sought purchase on the benches, the better to enjoy both the sunshine and the presence of an outsider who sat in their midst.

The sunshine was warm. The outsider, cold.

A pair of green eyes shifted over the rim of his tankard and collided with her gaze, causing Elaina to shiver involuntarily. His expression was hard and indifferent, and somehow rebellious. Ignoring a clansman who was narrating a story for his benefit, the stranger lowered his mug and studied the newcomers. Elaina watched as he scanned their small crowd. With shaggy black hair and sharp features, he could only be a few years younger than Talgus, yet he seemed self-assured and confident beyond his age. He was a man of influence and position…and far too aware of his good looks. He caught sight of Talgus and rose to his feet, cutting off the storyteller in mid-sentence.

"The man from Balgo," his Arcrean was severely stilted, and his accent Mizgalian. His gaze landed on Elaina as he continued to address her betrayer, "You bring the lady?"

Talgus nodded, "Frederick's daughter, just as I promised. She'll make any noblewoman a fine slave."

Elaina stiffened, roused from her travel-weary state, and swiveled her head to glare at Talgus, "A slave!? How dare you!" She shifted her glare to include Ferrand, "Unhand me, you fiend! I refuse to be subjected to such outrageous behavior. Your mothers would all be appalled by your conduct."

The crowd from Knavesmire exploded in a wave of mirth, laughing and slapping each other's backs.

Elaina's temper flared, "This is not funny!"

Ferrand finished laughing and looked down at her, "Yer words about our mothers be what's funny. My own dear mother helped t' land a ship on the rocks of Hugh once, so we might pillage the vessel for valuables!"

Elaina's horrified expression brought on another gale of coarse laughter, and it was several minutes before any semblance of calm had returned.

The Mizgalian stood watching the scene with some amusement. Finally stepping forward and taking Elaina's arm from Ferrand, he drew a pouch of coins from his belt and tossed it to Talgus. Elaina watched as the surrounding clansmen eyed one another, taking note of where the bag disappeared. Talgus would surely find himself without a purse by day's end.

Serves him right, Elaina thought, *the rotten scoundrel.*

"You've done well and I'll take her." The Mizgalian turned and flipped a coin to the proprietor of the Golden Tankard, and then began moving down the docks, taking Elaina with him, "We leave now."

"What's yer hurry?" Ferrand quickly caught up and matched his pace to theirs, no small feat considering the Mizgalian's impressive height and long strides. Elaina ran to keep up, afraid he would drag her if she did not.

"No need to delay," the foreigner responded to Ferrand's query. "I have slaves enough to satisfy my lord's most recent demands. I'll return when he requests more."

"A'right then," Ferrand seemed flustered by the man's poise. He held his hand out in an unspoken pact and met the gaze of the much taller man, "A'ways a pleasure dealin' wi' you, Sir Warin."

Sir Warin. So the man was a knight. As they continued down the docks, leaving the clansmen behind, Elaina glanced at the insignia on his dark apparel, trying to be inconspicuous as she failed to make out the name of his Order.

"Mordecai." Sir Warin kept his eyes on the boardwalk ahead, but his grin said he was answering her unasked question. Elaina tilted her nose in the air and looked away, but the small golden plate with an arrow-pierced M had branded itself in her mind's eye.

They boarded a small vessel, where twenty other unfortunate persons had been chained to the deck, obviously the rest of the knight's human cargo. Sir Warin passed Elaina off to a waiting soldier and then turned to address the slaves while their newest member was chained beside them.

"We sail tonight to bypass the Brikbones. Tomorrow we head northwest by land. Prepare for hard travel. If you lag, you die." The green eyes scanned the faces with a hard glint that assured them his threat was not an idle one. "We reach our destination in one week, and you will be sold as slaves in the province of Hebbros."

Sir Warin turned and barked an order in Mizgalian, and soon the boat was heading west along the banks of the vast bay. The sun was bright on the horizon, bathing everything in a warm golden glow as it prepared to dip out of sight for the night.

Elaina huddled against the side of the vessel, staring at the chains that hung between her wrists and bound her to the deck. Was she truly destined for the heathen kingdom of Mizgalia to be sold as a slave? She tilted her head back and closed her eyes. She had let Talgus catch her unawares, falling for the ambush of those painful memories and then failing to run when escape might have been possible. Now, once her feet were returned to solid ground, escape would mean traveling by foot over the Brikbones and skirting Knavesmire without getting caught by a band of roving brigands.

Elaina clenched her hands and sighed inwardly. She had to find a way out of this absurd situation. Her, a slave to a Mizgalian noblewoman? She wanted to laugh at the mere thought of such a suggestion.

Fingering the edge of her red vest, she opened her eyes and gazed at the darkening sky. Would her parents miss her? Would they think she had run away and be glad that they were rid of her many complaints?

Perhaps this was for the best. She had wanted out of Balgo, and now she was being conveniently escorted out of the kingdom.

Certainly King Druet would deem it unnecessary to send someone after her; therefore, if she could find a way around the small issue of slavery, she would be free.

The gentle rise and fall of the boat soon began to lull Elaina to sleep. Her aching muscles relaxed and she let her eyelids droop. The thought occurred to her that she would never see her mother and father again, and then an image appeared, of Lord Frederick smiling down at her. He leaned down to tap the end of her nose, and then, before the dreamlike vision could be completed, darkness swallowed the sight and sleep finally claimed her weary mind.

44

The Master Slaver

The sky was beginning to lighten from deepest blue to gray when they disembarked from the Knavesmire vessel and stepped onto Mizgalian soil. The captain of the small craft saw his passengers safely ashore and then turned to sail back the way they had come.

Warin waited only long enough to see that his men were pushing the twenty-one slaves into some semblance of a line, before he set a brisk pace heading north. About a mile from the coast they came upon the campsite where the rest of his soldiers had been waiting with forty more slaves. The company came to attention when he appeared at the edge of camp, and he acknowledged the show of respect with a curt nod. His aide appeared at his side and he handed the slave his gloves.

"Have my horse prepared for travel, Epic, and see that the new slaves are fed a morning's rations."

"Yes, sir." The blond-haired, honest lad of sixteen bowed and turned to obey. Warin watched him scurry away and allowed the briefest grin to stretch his face. The poor lad's mother had meant to name him Eric but had misspelled it from the start, leaving everyone to believe he had been curiously titled on purpose. When everyone continued to call him Epic, even his mother had admitted it suited him better.

Warin had claimed the boy seven years ago, as part of his earnings after a slave run similar to this one. The two had somehow forged a tentative friendship. Warin treated the boy with a measure of kindness that few knew existed in the fierce Mordecai. In return Epic served him with unmatched loyalty and proved to be the brightest piece of Warin's life. Having someone to whom he could show a trace of mercy served as a balm to Warin's otherwise callous life of cruelty.

Warin ran a hand through his hair, the action reminding him of his brother. He scowled. Wulf still let his hair grow long, tying it back in a club, while Warin had decided to improve his looks by trimming the shaggy black mess just below his ears. All the better, he thought, to keep from being confused with his twin. Too many people had approached him, thinking he was Wulf, and if there was anything Warin hated, it was being treated like his irresponsible twin.

Epic approached, leading Warin's horse, and the knight quickly mounted and rode to the edge of camp. His brow creased as his thoughts continued to dwell on his twin.

While Warin had seen to his own promotion within the Order by claiming the dreaded position of Master Slaver and taking the city's slave trade to new heights, Wulf had been content to remain in the service of Sir Valden. Warin knew his brother preferred the easy work of hunting down traitors because the task left him ample time to visit the taverns. Still, he had been surprised when Wulf refused to accept a position on his staff of slavers.

"I wouldn't place myself under your thumb for half the kingdom," Wulf had laughed over his tankard of ale. "Besides, Valden's come to trust me. I think he plans to promote me sometime soon."

Warin shook his head in disgust. When had his brother decided that gaining anything positive from life was a pointless endeavor?

Turning his horse's head, Warin studied the camp. It was a sight of upheaval as soldiers directed slaves in the process of taking down tents and loading the mules' packs. His eyes scanned the teeming grounds, resting here and there on various slaves. Most were strong and accustomed to hard work, others were slight of build and would be preferred by the nobility to serve in their homes. It had been a successful run.

A hiss like that of an angry ignispat sounded off to his left and Warin glanced that way. A flash of dark blue and red preceded a slave's attempt to strike a soldier across the face. The soldier caught the slave's wrist and threw her to the ground, pointing to a load of folded canvas and ordering her to carry it across camp to the line of waiting mules. The slave's dark eyes flashed as she grit her teeth and glared up at the man. Getting to her feet, she scooped the canvas up and turned as if to obey, only to swing back around and dump the heavy load on the soldier. The man uttered a string of curses as he toppled backwards to the ground.

Warin spurred his horse forward and reined in just as the soldier delivered a harsh slap to the girl's face, "Enough, Mugg. The slaves can't be marked when we put them up for auction."

Mugg looked up with a red-faced scowl, "She can go for a penny for all I care, the little wench!"

Warin looked at the young woman, the one promised by Talgus, and frowned, "I had thought a female of noble birth would never show such a lack of propriety."

One dark brow quirked at a superior angle, "Your Arcrean is atrocious, sir, and you thought wrong. My noble birth taught me to strike with better precision. And where I come from it is considered an even greater misstep to kidnap a woman than to have her defend herself."

"Where you come from there are no slaves," Warin quipped, "so you can't possibly know how your kind are to be treated."

"My kind?" The young woman's face reddened, "First you point out my noble birth, and now you put me in my place as a slave? Your deductions are dizzying, sir, and I'll no longer be the subject of them."

With that she turned and marched away. She had only gone three steps, however, before Warin's nod to Mugg was obeyed and she was brought to a halt. The young woman squirmed, stomped, and spat, but to no avail. Warin smirked at her feminine hostility and then addressed Mugg over the noise of her protests.

"Tie her to the last mule and have the rearguard keep an eye on her. If she refuses to load the animals, let her walk in the cloud of dust and grime that trails behind them."

Her look of wide-eyed horror was the last thing Warin saw before he turned his mount and headed northwest out of camp.

Soon the entire entourage fell in line behind him, and at last they were on their way home to Hebbros.

Elaina coughed and sputtered as dust—Mizgalian dust—stung her eyes and covered her from head to toe. She had walked for half a day behind the soldiers, slaves, and mules, and now her hair was thick with dirt and her shoes heavy with the road's grime. When at last she was released from the mule and sent forward to enjoy a brief respite with the others, she made sure she didn't so much as glance in Sir Warin's direction. Hateful man.

Collapsing beside another slave at the edge of a stream, Elaina drank deeply from the swift current and then used a stick to scrape whatever was caked on the bottom of her shoes. Tears stung her eyes as she thought of the cruel remarks she had made to her mother and father. What she wouldn't give now to be back in Balgo, enjoying a quiet midday meal with her mother and looking forward to an evening of practice with Leo. She could even endure another chat with Wesley's mother if only she were safe at home.

"Would you like to wash the dirt from your hair?"

The question surprised Elaina even more than the fact anyone was paying attention to her. She glanced up and met a gaze of deep blue in the face of the slave beside her. The petite young woman appeared to be close to Elaina's age, and had strands of mouse-brown hair peeking from beneath a light blue kerchief. Her dress of pale yellow was spotted with dirt and wore nameless stains as if they were a fashionable accessory, and the sleeves of her once-white underdress were torn in several places. Chains dangled between her wrists, just like Elaina's, but her countenance was peaceful and her expression compassionate. She pointed to Elaina's head.

"If you lie back on the bank, I'll help you scrub the dirt from your hair. I'm sure it can't be comfortable to carry so much dust."

Unaccustomed to such genuine, unasked-for care, Elaina could only stare at the other girl through the tears that still filled her eyes. The young woman smiled and gently helped Elaina to lie down in the grass.

"My name is Sadie," she said. Mindful of the chains, she dipped Elaina's grimy tresses into the stream and began to work her fingers through the tangles, "I'm from the city of Filliger, in the Arcrean region of Hugh. Some of the others have said you are Elaina, the daughter of Frederick. Is that true?"

Elaina studied Sadie's face. What would she say if Elaina confessed to being the same young woman who had betrayed Druet on his quest for the heart of Arcrea—betrayed him in the region of Hugh no less—and nearly succeeded in leading him to his death? Most Arcreans despised her, and those in Balgo had put up with her out of necessity. Only Leo and the former nobles had seemed indifferent to her past.

Gathering what was left of her dignity, Elaina prepared for rejection, "It is true."

Sadie's expression remained soft as she scrubbed the dirt free with her fingertips, "I've often thought it would be nice to meet you, but I never imagined it would be in this way." She leaned a bit closer and her eyes searched Elaina's, "Are you afraid?"

Elaina could barely comprehend the fact that this stranger was treating her so kindly in spite of her identity. She blinked and tried to remember what Sadie's question had been.

"Afraid? Of the slavers? Great goose eggs, of course not! I'm not scared of what lies ahead, but I am terribly upset by it. Why, I'm mad enough to plot mutiny against that insufferable Sir Warin and his entire lot of piggish soldiers."

Sadie giggled and helped Elaina to sit up, drying the soaking strands on her own hem and then forming a braid with adept movements. She tied the braid off with a strap of leather pulled from around her arm, and then shifted to sit beside Elaina. Her voice was as gentle as her hands had been.

"If you wish ill upon Sir Warin, then you are the first in our company. The other young women think he's the handsomest man they've ever seen, and every one of them is determined she'll marry him before we reach the auction block, to free herself from a life of slavery."

Elaina snorted, "I would prefer slavery."

Sadie shrugged, "I think they're scared. They speak nonsense in order to keep their minds off of their fears. As for the slaver, no one can deny that he is a handsome man, but there is a familiarity with cruelty about him that only God could wipe away. Sir Warin is a man in need of prayer."

Elaina bristled inwardly at the words, but refused to say

anything unkind to her new friend. Prayer, if ever it was put to use, should not be wasted on the likes of a Mizgalian slave trader.

Sadie's deep blue eyes studied Elaina, "You are not afraid then, of what the future may hold?"

"I haven't let myself think of the future unless it includes an escape."

"They have guards posted at all times," Sadie plucked a piece of grass, "and the chains we wear would alert them to any movement."

Further comment was cut off when a horse snorted behind them and the two young women turned to see Sir Warin watching them from the opposite bank. Sadie quickly lowered her head to stare at the ground, but Elaina returned his stare with a fearless gaze. His expression was grim, causing Elaina to wonder how much of their conversation he had overheard. He remained silent for a moment, standing beside his horse as the animal drank from the stream, and then finally he spoke.

In Mizgalian.

Elaina rolled her eyes, "When I said your Arcrean was atrocious I didn't mean I wanted you to start speaking gibberish instead."

Sadie looked up and cast a glance between the two, "He says if you think you can refrain from any more heathenish behavior, he'll see that you walk with the other slaves during the next leg of our journey, and not behind the animals."

Elaina looked askance at the girl. How had she come to be familiar with the language of the northern heathens? And why? Elaina couldn't imagine it being pleasant, wrapping one's tongue around such a jumble of consonants and guttural throat-noises.

One corner of Sir Warin's mouth lifted in a grin as he looked down his nose at Sadie. "Very good, Little Mouse," he spoke in Arcrean. "Where did you learn?"

Sadie swallowed, obviously uncomfortable with being the center of attention…or with having the contemptible slaver call her by a pet name. "I was raised in a port city, sir, where many tongues were spoken. I learned as a matter of course."

He acknowledged her words with a sparse nod, and then his eyes shifted to take note of Elaina's wet hair and Sadie's soaked hem. His gaze flitted from Elaina's braid to the spot on Sadie's arm where the leather strap had left a faint mark where it had been tied.

Elaina scowled, ready for him to move on, "Very well, I'll refrain from slapping that ugly soldier whose name is far too odd to be the one given by his mother. Now would you kindly leave us be?"

He quirked a brow before turning to mount his horse, and spoke as if leaving had been his idea. "Line up with the others. We're heading out."

"Yes, sir." Sadie rose and pulled Elaina up with her, their chains jangling together in a terrible song of affliction.

The knight fit his feet into the stirrups and narrowed his gaze on Elaina, "See that you cause no further trouble, or I will be forced to prove that I am indeed familiar with cruelty."

Sadie flushed at the implication he had overheard her. Elaina laid her hand on the girl's shoulder and frowned at the inconsiderate brute, thinking very strongly of sticking out her tongue like an immature child.

Sir Warin smirked at Sadie's embarrassment as he turned his horse's head, spurring it away from the stream and toward the front of the entourage. When he had ridden out of earshot, Elaina muttered a sequence of angry words that would have shocked her mother. Sadie glanced at her with a bit of that shock on her own sweet face and then tried for a look of understanding.

"Come, Elaina, we'll pray for him while we walk."

"I don't pray. Even if I did, I wouldn't pray for him. He doesn't deserve compassion."

"No one does," Sadie shook her head as she pulled Elaina forward, "and yet God still gives it."

45
With the Passage of Time

Mount Desterrar, Village of Exile

Desterrar was a beautiful pallet of autumn colors, with trees of yellow, orange, and red climbing its impressive slopes in explosive expression of the season. Luke stood on the lookout rock several thousand feet above Hebbros. His eyes swept the length and breadth of the city, reviewing the pattern of snaking streets and remembering details that were indecipherable from this vantage point.

The door has not yet been closed, but one day it will be.

The merchant's words of so long ago had played constantly in Luke's mind, like a song that had no end. Instinctively, he knew the only way to halt the mantra would be to close the suggested door in its face.

I want you to come back.

Luke's gaze sharpened on the place of fermenting evil below. Soon. It would be soon.

Luke lifted his eyes and swept the eastern horizon. Somewhere out there, beyond the limits of his gaze, was the royal city of Mockmor. Since the day of Roland's rebellion, the outcast citizens in the mountain village of Exile had watched and waited for King Cronin's forces to arrive and contest the secession of

Hebbros from the Mizgalian realm. Surprisingly, when the soldiers had come, the small number had laid siege only to the city's landward side, and then returned to the east after a mere two months' time. Hebbros had been unaffected.

Luke shook his head. The king's armies were often called innumerable, yet they were forced to divide themselves amongst the many wars being fought by the realm's monarch. Ever at war with the kingdoms surrounding his borders, Cronin had found himself without the time or a sufficient number of men to retake Hebbros.

Roland, on the other hand, had been busy claiming more and more land for his self-acclaimed dynasty. Already the walls of Hebbros had been expanded, and now they were being rebuilt again. Day after day the slaves worked to push the boundaries of the city just a bit further.

Luke exhaled and spoke into the still air, "If Cronin continues to ignore the sedition of his former favorite he'll wake up one morning to find he is without a third of his kingdom."

"And the walls of Hebbros will still continue to crawl eastward."

Luke turned at the sound of another voice, "And how is the village guardian this morning?"

Chris shook his head with a grin, "Still reeling from the great honor that has befallen me." He stopped beside Luke and took in the magnificent view, "When the village elected to appoint a man as official guardian, I fully expected it to be one of the older men. I would have preferred it, and I could have served as his junior."

Luke shook his head, "How can you stand to be so humble all the time?" He laughed when his brother cast him a sidelong glance, "Eleven years ago I determined to practice humility in everything I did. Today, I'm still working on the beginning stages of the admirable trait!"

Chris smiled kindly, "And yet you are spirited and far more daring than I would ever dream of being. Each of us has skills that make us fit for our individual calling."

"Which is why you're the right man to be the leading protector of Exile. Unrest is in the air, Chris, and you are the village's most proficient swordsman."

"Bradley's skills are quite admirable."

"But Bradley still refuses to share our faith. So long as his peace is uninterrupted, he will see no need for our God. Your faith, however, has grown with the lack of conflict and the teaching of our elders."

"I'm grateful for your confidence. And I'm glad that Sedgwick saw fit to name you as the next successor in line for village elder, after himself and then father."

Luke gave a short bark of laughter, "Now that is a decision that I did not understand at last night's council. I'm hardly an elder, and everyone knows I won't take any role of honor in Exile until I've completed the business that awaits me in Hebbros. If I die in the attempt to bring out the remnant of the Faithful, then it will have been pointless to name me as the future leader of Exile."

Chris turned to look his brother in the eye, "God would not call you to fail in His work."

"But He may call me to die for it," Luke held his brother's gaze, "and for that I am prepared. The streets of Hebbros reeked of sin when we left them behind, and eleven years of sitting stagnant could only make things worse. I'm not ignorant of the danger my presence in the city could create for myself as well as others. If there comes a choice, I would rather sacrifice myself to see some other soul reach freedom." Luke's eyes shifted downward to the walled city, "I've experienced the peace of Exile for so many years now, I can no longer imagine what it must be like down there, stuck in the mire of expected corruption. Chris, they don't know what they're missing."

The twins turned from the rock ledge and climbed the short distance to the summit, where the village nestled into the gently rolling terrain of Desterrar's peak. Luke paused on the path to take in the sight, remembering that night when he and eight others had reached the safety of Exile.

Chris paused beside him, "Ned's skills in carpentry have made the cottages sturdier."

At the mention of their friend, Luke chuckled, "Did you see his face last night, when Father finally decided on a day for the wedding?"

Chris grinned, "I think he feared the day would never come, and now it's only a week away. Elbert says Ned nearly fainted on the spot."

They shared a laugh and Luke shook his head as he scanned the village, "I'm glad they'll be wed at last. He's loved her for a very long time. I must say, I didn't think he was such a patient man."

"I think that was his mother's doing."

Luke nodded as they started forward again, "Ned's mother wouldn't tolerate nonsense if it was presented by a court jester."

They walked several paces more and then looked up when someone called out. Pavia waved and trotted toward them, her red hair tamed for once by a braid that formed a crown around her head. Loping behind her was the young catawyld beast she had caught and tamed as a newborn.

The young woman came to a stop on the path before them and smiled, "I offer you both congratulations for the honors of last night's council."

"Thank you," Chris nodded. The catawyld sat beside him and leaned against his leg.

Luke eyed the beast and then squinted at Pavia, "Remind me again how you convinced the village to let you keep little Fluffy here?"

Pavia crossed her arms, "His name is Trig, and the village trusted your brother's promise to oversee my work in training the catawyld as a pet."

Luke glanced at his twin, "And you're sure you know when a catawyld is trained?"

"No. But I know when a catawyld is wild."

"Very funny."

Pavia bent to scoop the medium-sized beast into her arms. Trig dangled from her hold and studied Luke with a lazy expression. It was so unsettling.

Luke shivered, "I'll never get used to that."

Pavia nuzzled Trig's head with her chin as if it were a normal kitten, "I was taught to breed catawylds, don't forget. If that counts for nothing else, at least I can say I have an extensive knowledge of their temperaments and habits."

The three walked further into the village, talking and laughing as they enjoyed a day of peace.

Luke glanced at his brother. Unbelievably, Chris had grown taller and broader since they'd left Hebbros, the top of his head reaching some inches beyond Luke's height of just over six feet. The larger twin had become a tower of strength in the village, as well as a pillar of kindness and humility that defied his fierce size.

Luke took in his brother's neat appearance and grinned when

he thought how it differed from his own. Everything about Chris was clean and tidy, while Luke's mother and sister were constantly begging to repair his clothes and cut his hair. While Chris kept his locks trimmed decently up to his ears, Luke waited until he couldn't stand the way it itched his neck. He ran a hand through his unruly mane and then scrubbed his knuckles over the rough shadow of a dark beard, one thing he and Chris did have in common.

Luke smiled and Pavia glanced his way, "What?"

"Nothing," he shook his head, "only I think I ought to have my hair trimmed."

"It's about time." Pavia raised a fine red brow at him and then turned back to her discussion with Chris. Luke bit back another grin. Chris's additional height had only served to make Pavia's lack of it more extreme. The five-foot spitfire didn't even reach the height of his twin's shoulder. At times like this, when they all walked together, she was forced to run in order to keep up with their longer strides.

"You promised me another bout with the sword if I put my hair up and out of the way." Pavia dropped Trig onto the path and looked up at Chris, pointing a finger at her crowning braid, "As you can see…"

He grinned and studied the path ahead, "I'm returning to the head of the Banishment Path to keep watch, if you bring the practice swords we'll run a bout there."

Satisfied, Pavia gave a nod and they watched in silence as Christopher left the village road to stride toward his post. A short distance later, Pavia left Luke alone and went to fetch the swords as requested.

Luke stood still for a moment, listening to the sounds of the village. Peaceful sounds. Normal sounds. Sounds that were evidence of life being lived and enjoyed. He heard a child's laughter and glanced to the cottage on his left, where Bradley and Sarah lived with their four children. The quiver-full of young blessings, the eldest being nine and the youngest three, had been a means of enriching the lives of the couple who had been married in a state of rash uncertainty. God had been good to bless their marriage in spite of Bradley's continued resistance of the faith. Luke felt certain this was a direct result of Sarah's unfailing prayers.

Some had given up hope that Bradley would join the faith,

and had even questioned whether he should be allowed to dwell in their midst. But his family's presence and the fact that he had been banished like the rest had nullified the brief moments of doubt. God was not finished with Bradley, and as long as the Savior was able to sanctify, Luke would not give up hope for the nobleman's redemption. Bradley believed there was a God, but failed to see his personal need for salvation. His human logic kept getting in the way of simple faith. Luke sometimes shuddered to think how the young man might be brought to see the truth in the full light of reality.

Luke turned and strode back the way he had come. He would continue to pray for Bradley, that God would yet meet the nobleman's earlier challenge and fulfill those three requests. Smiling to himself, Luke thought of how at least one had already been answered.

Striding into the field that lay to the north of Exile, Luke pulled his bow from his shoulder and checked the string. He adjusted his wrist guards, fashioned from his old collar of red leather, and drew an arrow from the quiver at his back. Still his favorite pastime, archery practice gave him time to think…

About Bradley and his spiritual darkness.

About Hebbros and the remnant of Faithful who would surely be waiting in answer to his prayers.

About Exile and the peace that it offered A symbol of the free gift from Christ to all who believed.

About Lillian, who still endured this life only because she had nowhere else to go.

About Charlotte's upcoming marriage to a dear friend, and his brother's blindness to the equal happiness that could be his.

With each thought, an arrow flew across the field to lodge in whatever target he had eyed; a thick stump, a fallen log, a protruding root, and even a specific spot in the ground. When his mind eventually ground to a halt, he retrieved the darts and returned them to his quiver.

Swiping his sleeve across his forehead, Luke glanced at the sky and saw that it was time to gather a band and fetch wood from the side of the mountain, to be used as fuel for the village's fire tower. He turned toward the village and paused when he saw Sedgwick and his father watching from the edge of the field. He drew closer and his father smiled warmly.

"Your skill has been a blessing to the village, son. I'm grateful that Guy taught you before he…" Althar finished with a stiff nod and glanced away, still saddened by the knowledge of his old friend's betrayal and death.

Sedgwick placed a hand of fatherly comfort on the cooper's shoulder and then turned to Luke, "Althar tells me that you too can feel the tension rising from below."

Luke nodded, "I've been following the advice you both gave me, spending time each morning praying and reviewing as many scriptures as I can remember. God's word offers comfort and wisdom. But I also feel Him pressing a need on my heart, and I know the time is coming for me to return to Hebbros and fulfill my promise to the merchant."

Althar nodded, "The remnant in Hebbros must be called out soon. The city has been built on a foundation of corruption, and its end is surely near."

Sedgwick nodded thoughtfully, "The fall of Hebbros will bring true deliverance to the people of Exile as well. Our people will continue to grow, new families will be born and our numbers will multiply until the village can no longer hold all of us. But while Hebbros bars our way off of Desterrar there is nowhere else for us to go. One day, God willing, we will be free to return to the valley floor and tell others of our blessed faith."

Luke and Althar remained silent, nodding as the elder spoke.

"We must pray that God will make the way clear. That you will know when is the right time to descend the slopes, and whom our Lord would have to go with you."

Luke's eyes darted to the village elder, "Go with me? I had planned to go alone. It would be easier to hide and to read the gazes of Hebbros if no one else went with me. I've always enjoyed doing things myself." He ducked his head, "I would prefer to go alone."

A brief smile touched Sedgwick's lips, "I know you would. However, the Lord has pressed a need on my own heart of late, and I'm anxious to see if perhaps His plans for the remnant are different than we first suspected."

46

Unexpected

City of Hebbros

Sir Kenrick sat in the Reestablishment room, his stone-topped table littered with various documents. He had kept the room's title in honor of Roland's desire to reestablish the city of Hebbros as an entity in and of itself. However, now that the Faithful had been eradicated, the purpose of the Mordecai Order had expanded to concentrate on routing any and all enemies of Roland. Some knights had been trained as spies, others were merely a presence on the streets.

Kenrick's eyes roved the parchments before him. His greatest problem at present had arisen when Valden informed him of a faction of dissenters who met in secret and called themselves the Order of Haman. Nothing else could be discovered about the group, though it was assumed they were planning a rebellion. Kenrick took note of the Order's choice of name and cocked a haughty brow.

Putting a finger to one document, he scanned a record detailing the recent actions of one citizen. Finally he shook his head, rolled the parchment, and stood to return it to its proper nook in the wall. There was nothing to suggest this suspect was the mysterious Haman. Perhaps the next record would reveal some evidence.

Kenrick returned to his seat just as a dull thud sounded outside. He looked up as the door swung open and a cloaked figure entered the room. Beyond the newcomer, Kenrick's guard was nowhere in sight. The door closed and the Mordecai's chief lifted a startled gaze to the unexpected visitor, "Who are you?"

A humorless laugh, "Now that would be telling, Kenrick."

The hooded man approached the table and Kenrick stood, resting a hand on the pommel of his sword, "What do you want?"

The question went unanswered as the stranger glanced at the table's contents. He looked up then and let his hood fall back to reveal his face. Kenrick's eyes widened and his jaw went slack.

The newcomer grinned and motioned to the scattered parchments, "It appears you've been looking for me."

Kenrick took a step backward, repulsed and alarmed, "You? You are—"

The cloaked shadow flicked one hand and a dagger flashed, "I'm Haman."

His life had been comfortable for eleven years. The Faithful had been silenced within the city walls, the Mordecai Order had seen to the disappearance of any others who attempted to defy his rule, and King Cronin had been unable to send a sufficient army to reverse the Hebbros rebellion.

But how long could his success last? A nightly flame still glowed on Mount Desterrar, proving the Faithful were yet alive. Sir Kenrick had relayed information that suggested a secret faction was preparing for an uprising. Further still, word had reached him through a network of spies that Cronin had entered a temporary peace treaty with the Arcreans, leaving him free to center his attentions on Hebbros.

Lord Roland had almost succeeded in forgetting the premonitions of Luke the Terror. The insolent pup's warning that his life was in danger. No threats had been made, no attempts on his life. It must have been a ploy for mercy. Unfortunately, Luke's face occasionally appeared in Roland's dreams, urging him to watch his back and bringing to mind again the look of sincerity that had shone in the boy's face so long ago.

Roland studied the charts, lists, and reports that lay scattered across the table in his west turret. The raised taxes were successfully upholding the various enterprises that had become necessary in recent years. An outside source had to be paid for the fire towers' fuel. The city's merchant fleet had required constant repairs. Sir Fraser's army, as well as the Mordecais, had to be clothed and fed. Sir Warin's newly revived slave trade had to be supported if Hebbros would continue to profit from the resulting sales.

Besides all of this, Roland himself had come to require greater compensation for his services as the district's ruler. Not only had young Brone joined the family those ten-and-a-half years ago, but also four other children in the years after.

Roland pressed two fingers against his temples.

Seven children. Jerem, at fourteen, was still considered a miniature of his father, looking much like Roland had as a youth and already preparing to shoulder the responsibilities that would one day be his. Celia, now twelve, was still a quiet child, and close friends with her sister Addie, who was eight. Born several months after the rebellion and two years older than Addie, Brone enjoyed following in the footsteps of his elder brother, while Joseph and Thomas, at five and two, were like a formidable force of mischief for their nurse.

Seven children. Six of them blond- or auburn-haired, with features that reflected a combination of both parents, while little Joseph sported bright red curls, brown eyes, and a peppering of freckles. A replica of his mother.

The newest member of the family, a girl, had arrived only three months before, and a thousand memories had been resurrected when Rosalynn named her Sarah. Roland shook the thought from his head, determined to ignore the questions.

When the ruler of Hebbros finally left his west turret some hours later, the guard at the bottom of the stairs acknowledged his appearance with a sharp salute. Roland gave the man a miniscule nod, and then heard a voice calling to him from behind. He turned to see the Mordecais' first knight approaching at a swift pace.

"What is it, Valden?"

The knight's expression was grave as he drew nearer, his quick steps pounding a clipped rhythm against the stone floor. Something was wrong. He came to a halt before Roland, neglecting to bow, and spoke with direct firmness.

"Sir Kenrick is dead."

47
A Mouse & a Mordecai

Mizgalian Road, One Day's Journey From Hebbros

Elaina trudged along the road, aching from head to toe and feeling heart-sore at the thought of each step taking her further from the hope of a successful escape. Beside her, Sadie passed the time by praying and singing in turn. Her angelic voice offered gentle encouragement to those around her, and occasionally fell silent when unbidden tears filled her eyes. Elaina watched the girl in silent awe and wrapped a comforting arm around her shoulder when she cried. Sadie had shown great strength throughout the long days of travel, nevertheless each of the slaves had taken time to mourn the death of a future so abruptly altered. Sadie was no exception.

"I'm going to escape," Elaina murmured after one of her friend's rare bouts of tears. "Even if I must wait until we reach this Hebbros, and then find a way to elude the slavers until I find someone who is heading south. A cart, a boat, anything will do. I'll have them take me with them as far as the border. I'll return to Arcrea and send word to the king that I've discovered a slave-route of the Mizgalians. Perhaps then, in return for the information, Druet will free my father from his enforced stay in Balgo."

Sadie wiped the last of her tears from her eyes, "Here I am

weeping because I was taken from my life in Filliger, when I ought to be grateful that I'm alive at all."

Elaina heaved an impatient sigh, "Did you hear anything I said?"

Sadie's laugh was infectious, and Elaina found herself smiling in return.

"I'm sorry, Elaina. I did hear you," she slanted a look at her friend and grinned, "and it was the same thing you've been saying for the last five days. Perhaps you should not worry so much about running from God's plan, and start looking for ways to thrive in it."

Elaina scowled, "This is God's plan for me? You think God did this to us, and yet you still praise Him with every breath?"

Sadie inclined her head and a strand of brown hair fell from her kerchief, "I believe that God allowed these events to shape our lives because that is exactly what He plans to use them for—to shape us. It is clear there is evil in this world, and God is able to use evil for good. These terrible things that we weep about will one day be turned into something worth rejoicing over."

"How can you be sure?"

"I have faith."

Elaina shook her head in denial, "I do not share your faith."

"Regardless of that fact, whatever happens in your life is still a small piece of God's greater plan. His purpose will be fulfilled, and He is able to use anyone to see it through."

Elaina thought for a moment and then asked, "What if it is God's will that I escape?"

Sadie smiled, "Then He will provide a way for you to do so."

A sudden commotion up ahead brought their conversation to an end and halted the progress of the slave line. A woman cried out and was answered roughly by one of the soldiers. Elaina could see nothing from her position near the rear, as the slaves craned their necks, curiously seeking a glance of the trouble. Gradually they were shifted to one side and ordered to continue their march.

A lean figure trotted back along the line of slaves and stopped beside Elaina and her friend. Epic, Sir Warin's personal slave, pulled at Sadie's arm as he kept pace beside them.

"Please come." The youth spoke in accented Mizgalian, and Elaina struggled to catch any of the words she had learned along the road, "Master Warin…command…Arcrean."

Sadie nodded and stepped out of the line to follow Epic forward at a faster pace.

"What did he say?" Elaina grasped at the other young woman's sleeve.

Sadie spoke over her shoulder, "Sir Warin has ordered me present to translate for an Arcrean."

Elaina watched as Sadie joined a group huddled around the cowering figure of a slave woman. Sir Warin sat atop his horse and watched Sadie approach. His gaze shifted to Elaina and she narrowed her eyes in a hostile glare.

If hatred could be cooked and served as a meal, her loathing of the Mordecai knight would have provided the entire entourage with a satisfying banquet. The man was insufferable. He thought nothing of demeaning the slaves with harsh words or a sound cuff to the ear. His natural expression was one of haughty indifference, and he was most at ease when favoring some poor female with his well-rehearsed charms. Unfortunately, due to his "need" for her friend's bilingual abilities, Sadie was most often the recipient of Sir Warin's attentions. Elaina rolled her eyes. If he was still like that at nearly thirty, he must have been a terror in his youth.

Facing forward again, she focused on putting one foot in front of the other. Sadie had proved a faithful friend to her these last few days, and had been in high demand with others in the caravan as well. The other slaves had sought her encouragement, young Epic had been drawn to her cheerfulness, the soldiers had appreciated her compliance in the slave line, and Sir Warin had ordered her assistance with various matters of translation.

Elaina's head began to shake in bewilderment. Had Sadie's lot been hers, she would have dropped faint with exhaustion by now. She could not comprehend such strength. How did Sadie remain unaffected by the trials that beset her every step? How could she manage to stand beneath the burdens that had been forced upon her petite shoulders?

Sadie would say that the strength had come from God.

Elaina wrapped her arms around herself as a chill breeze worked its way to her bones. Whatever it was that made Sadie so different, it was certainly lacking in her own life.

Sadie stepped between the two hovering soldiers and knelt beside the slave woman. She glanced up at Sir Warin and spoke in Mizgalian, "What happened?"

The knight looked down from his horse, his brow cocked ever so slightly, "That's why you're here, Little Mouse. The woman keeps blubbering in your native tongue faster than anyone can comprehend. I've been told my Arcrean is atrocious, so you can imagine how well we're getting along."

Sadie turned her attention to the woman on the ground. She swept the slave's hair from her face and queried gently in Arcrean. The woman's wild eyes darted from the soldiers and Epic to Sir Warin, finally landing on the young woman kneeling beside her.

"Adele," Sadie repeated softly, "what happened?"

Adele's gaze slowly focused on Sadie's face and she sobbed several words of pain while motioning towards her feet. Sadie listened, simultaneously shifting to remove the other woman's poor excuse for footwear.

"Sir Warin, Adele's shoes were in a poor state when our journey began, and now they've been pulled to pieces by the road. Her feet have become blistered over the last few days and now the sores have opened. The pain is crippling her so she can't walk."

Warin's lip curled and he looked away, "Excuses."

Sadie shot him a grim look, but quickly returned her focus to Adele.

Warin barked a command and the two soldiers turned to rejoin the slave convoy.

"Wait!" Sadie called out but the soldiers did not stop. She looked at Warin, "What can we do to help her? Perhaps someone can carry her on their horse for a while, until her feet have healed."

His look of amusement broke into laughter, "She's a flawed slave. I care little whether she lives or dies, let alone whether her feet heal." He turned his horse's head, "Leave her and rejoin the others."

Adele took in the scene and clutched at Sadie's arm, babbling another stream of Arcrean words. Sadie shook her head at the woman and spoke in a soothing tone, "Shh, don't worry, Adele." She glanced up, "Epic, may I have the water from your drinking-pouch?"

Stunned, Warin watched as Sadie ignored his command to leave and took the leather water pouch offered by his aide. She smiled her thanks at Epic and then pulled the kerchief from her head, splashing the boy's drinking water onto the blue rag and gently wiping the other slave's bleeding feet. Adele's sobs subsided and she observed the gentle little mouse of a slave with grateful tears.

The sight twisted like a thorn in Warin's conscience and he rebelled against the presentation of goodness. Dismounting and tossing the reins at Epic in one fluid motion, he pulled Sadie up by her hair and jerked her around so that she would face the coming reprimand. The young woman gave a squeal of fright and pain, echoed by the startled cries of Epic and Adele, and then awaited his rebuke in anguished silence.

Sadie's eyes filled with tears, and she bit her lip as Warin's grip on her hair pinched her scalp. The knight's glare was laced with anger and something else, and Sadie wondered briefly if she had seen a trace of guilt.

Suddenly he shoved her away with a growl and she stumbled into Epic. The boy kept her from falling and she turned back just as Warin whirled to loom over Adele.

"I don't have time for defective slaves." He drew his sword to confirm the words, and Sadie's heart froze when he lifted the weapon over Adele's prone figure. The slave woman shrieked, lifting her arms to shield herself.

"No!" Sadie lurched away from Epic to throw herself down across the injured woman.

Warin's shoulders tensed, suddenly resisting the downward arc, and the blade halted in the midst of its deadly path. Breathing heavily, his nostrils flared like an angry bull's as he leaned down and gripped Sadie by the arm. Yanking her upright, he spoke through clenched teeth, "Get out of my way, slave."

"No." Sadie stiffened and met his glare in a rare show of defiance, "You're not thinking clearly. If you were, you wouldn't be threatening a woman."

Warin's frown deepened. Throughout the week's journey, this slave had been the essence of meekness and compliance. He had aptly called her Little Mouse, never observing any signs of stubbornness until today, when in defense of a helpless individual. Epic had told him the other slaves considered Sadie to be the strongest in their number, and he wondered now if they had been right.

Eyes of fascinating blue steadfastly returned his stare as the anger melted away and was replaced by the former feeling of amusement…and a touch of annoyance.

Sadie's chin quivered, proving she was not without apprehension, "I will not let you slay this woman, especially for such a petty reason. You say you have no time for someone in her condition, but I say that I do. Allow me the use of a mule and let Adele ride. Leave her in my care for the remainder of the journey and I will see to it that she is no longer 'flawed' by time we reach the slave market."

"We reach Hebbros at sundown tomorrow."

"She will at least be able to walk again, without such intense pain."

Warin considered her bargain. It would be much simpler to have done with the troublesome Adele here and now. He could leave her beside the road, toss the mouse over his shoulder, and rejoin the caravan without feeling an ounce of pity or remorse. However, with Mizgalia's king honoring a peace treaty with the Arcreans, it was very possible that Cronin would turn his focus to the west, and war would come to Hebbros. If so, then every sale made in Warin's slave market would count toward funding the resistance.

Warin let go of Sadie's arm. Slowly releasing a breath, the knight turned to find Epic watching with an expression that was half fearful and half filled with the same admiration he felt for the courage of this usually timid slave.

"Epic, take my horse and fetch a mule."

The boy was in the saddle and riding after the slave line in an instant. Warin turned back to find Sadie kneeling once more and gently cleaning Adele's feet. He crossed his arms.

"Your headscarf will be ruined."

She didn't look up, "A kerchief can be replaced. A woman's life cannot."

Warin shrugged and looked toward the point where his aide had ridden, "There are so many people in this world, some of them must be disposable." She turned a look of shock his way and he went on, "The city of Hebbros alone is crawling with more people than anyone cares to count. Everywhere one turns they're running into five people trying to pass in the opposite direction at once."

"Then let them out."

Warin looked at her and released a short laugh, "That would be foolish. Any number of people in Hebbros could be a spy. If released from the city, they would report any weaknesses to King Cronin."

Sadie rose and shielded her eyes as she searched the distance for Epic and the mule. Turning back to Warin, she wiped her hands on her skirt and spoke with her customary humility, "If that is the case, then there are only two things you can do. Ensure there are no weaknesses, or see that Cronin has no reason to spy on you in the first place." She turned as Epic rode up, leading a mule, and spoke a few words to Adele before looking back at Warin, "There is another thing you could do, but I doubt it is something you are interested in at this time."

Unable to think of a worthy response to her volley of quick-witted observations, Warin could only stare at her and raise his brow, silently asking for an explanation to her last remark.

Sadie turned a brilliant smile his way, unable to hide the depth of her peace as she said, "Sir Warin, if the city were mine I would leave it in the hands of God and pray for His watch upon it."

Warin's stomach leapt for his chest and he swallowed against a wave of nausea. Epic dismounted and the knight left the aide to look after the two slaves, spurring his horse away from the scene—and the presence of one little mouse in particular—as quickly as he could. Galloping toward the front of the entourage, he shook his head to clear his thoughts and then rubbed one hand across his eyes.

He was a Mordecai, bound by the Order's founding laws to rid the city of Hebbros of the ones called Faithful. Never had he questioned the orders of his superiors. He had always done whatever it took to ensure success, both personal and public. Now, with one slave's profession of faith, Warin's thoughts churned with inexplicable turmoil.

Sadie was undoubtedly a member of the Faithful. He should have recognized the signs sooner. Whether the Arcreans referred to them by the same name, he didn't know, but her actions and words had made it clear that she worshipped the same God followed by Luke, Chris, and the others in exile.

Warin slowed the pace of his horse. He pretended to study the line of slaves and ignored the deadly glare that Elaina was directing his way. When he had reached his place at the front, he turned in the saddle and tracked the two figures in the distance, heading this way and leading a mule with one rider.

He was escorting her to her death.

Warin grit his teeth. Why couldn't these people keep silent about their faith? Surely the Arcreans were aware of the Mizgalian forms of worship. Surely they would know that to speak of their radical beliefs in a hostile foreign territory was an act of greatest folly.

Why then did they insist on so openly following their outlawed God?

And if outlawed, how did their God keep coming back as though undefeated?

His horse sidestepped, sensing his tension, and Warin calmed the black beast before spurring it forward again, farther ahead of the group. He gripped the reins and determined to regain control of himself. He had sold hundreds, thousands of slaves, and Sadie was just another tally mark, added to his records and sold to the highest bidder. If someone took offense to her faith then it would be her master's duty, and not his, to report the issue.

To the Mordecais.

Warin pressed his lips together in thought. Perhaps in return for her services in translating, he could show a slave one act of kindness. He might tell her how the people of Hebbros viewed her kind and suggest that she keep the matter quiet, forget her God, and adopt the city's beliefs.

Mentally nodding approval of his own idea, Warin began to relax. It would be worth bending his reputation for cruelty if he could save the Arcrean maid from swift death in Hebbros. For one thing, his dedication to chivalry, which had been far too neglected of late, would not allow him to ignore the plight of an unsuspecting woman. Then also, when that woman's heart overflowed with such uncommon selflessness and sincerity, she did not deserve to die for it. Even if she accredited her character to the work of a forbidden God.

48
The Beginning of the End

Lady Rosalynn cradled her youngest daughter in her arms and gazed down at the little one's face. With the birth of each of her seven children her wonder for the miracle of life had magnified, causing her to examine her own beliefs regarding the purpose of mankind. Was her time on this earth meant to be a nameless existence? Or was her life part of a greater tapestry, woven by some divine hand?

Rosalynn touched the tip of her finger to her daughter's rosebud mouth. How Roland would rage if he knew to what lengths she had gone to find the answers to her questions.

The door to her chambers opened and she looked up as Roland entered. He smiled and leaned down to press a kiss to her head, and then took a moment to gaze at the sleeping infant.

"I still don't understand," he whispered, "why you decided to name her after your former slave."

He drew a chair nearer and sat beside her, and Rosalynn pressed her lips together before offering a soft answer. "I did not name her after my slave," her eyes sought and held his gaze, "I named her after my brother's wife."

A look of confusion crossed Roland's face, "You hated her. You despised her attachment to your brother, and now you bless her with the honor of a namesake?" He shifted as a new thought struck him, "Had our child been a boy would you have called him Bradley?"

Rosalynn placed a hand on his arm, "When my brother was exiled I did not question your decision. I begged you not to slay him, but I did not argue his banishment. Since that day I have wondered more times than I can count what I might have done differently. Had I been a better sister, perhaps he would not have rebelled against you." Rosalynn's hand slipped away and she looked down at little Sarah, "The more I thought on Bradley's indifference, the more I realized how often my own life has been shaped by that same trait."

Roland shook his head to deny her words, "My dear wife, you are the most thoughtful creature I have ever met."

Rosalynn looked up with tears in her eyes, "Thoughtful, yes, but only to please myself. I wanted so much for Bradley to be a credit to me, to lose his identity and follow my lead, that I never considered he might find true happiness on his own." Her brow furrowed in puzzlement, "Even now I cannot understand why his marriage to Sarah was such an awful thing."

"She was a slave," Roland reminded her, "and he was a nobleman."

A sad smile pulled at Rosalynn's lips. "A noble nobody," she murmured, as memories of her brother's bantering swept through her mind.

She let the matter drop as the baby started to wake and Roland reached to take their child. She leaned against the arm of the divan and watched as the lord of Hebbros comforted his infant daughter. Little Sarah closed her eyes again and Rosalynn studied Roland's pensive face.

"You are thinking of Kenrick again."

Roland exhaled and nodded, "Valden informed me that a secretive band, known as the Order of Haman, has been stirring sedition in the streets of Hebbros. It appears this Haman is responsible for Kenrick's death."

"How does Valden know this?"

"The villain had the audacity to leave a note on Kenrick's table, saying, 'I'll finish from here. Catch me if you can.' His alleged name was signed at the bottom."

Rosalynn leaned closer, "Finish what? What was Kenrick

doing that this Haman would wish to complete himself?"

Roland shook his head, pressing his thumb and forefinger to his eyes.

Rosalynn's brow furrowed, "You are worried."

Roland was silent for several moments. When he spoke again it was in a careful whisper. "Years ago, I was warned that a band of renegades had threatened my life. I put it from my mind and heard nothing more about it until a week ago, when Kenrick's death ignited a thousand questions in my mind. Was Kenrick plotting against me? Did this Haman learn of it and put an end to those plans before Kenrick beat him to it?"

"Roland, do not speak such things!" Rosalynn touched his shoulder and he placed his hand over hers.

"I must think of these things in order to stay alert. Threats are to be expected when tensions rise. What frightens me is the thought that I no longer know whom I can trust." His eyes took on a faraway look and he murmured, "Perhaps the only trustworthy citizen was the one whose kindness I scorned."

"Who was that?"

Roland blinked and looked at his wife, "It no longer matters." He placed the baby back in her arms and soon departed for a conference with Sir Fraser.

Rosalynn sat in deep thought for a while longer before rising and giving Sarah into the care of her nurse. Grabbing her cloak from its peg, she moved through the palace corridors and made her way out to the gardens, where she slipped out of view behind a tall hedge. Feeling for a hidden notch in the wall, she pushed through a well-concealed door and emerged into a narrow lane between the palace and a row of battered cottages.

Rosalynn pulled her cloak's hood over her head. A breeze filtered through the street and she turned into it, heading away from the palace at a swift pace. She kept her eyes downcast, fearful of the sordid lot with whom she shared the streets, but more afraid of what might happen if she did not act upon her instincts immediately.

When finally she reached her destination, she glanced at the sign over the door before pushing through to enter the shop. She waited a moment while her eyes adjusted to the dim interior and then stepped forward as the shopkeeper appeared in the doorway of a back room.

"Please, sir, is there any way to send a message?"

The little man blinked large eyes and shook his head as if confused, "I beg your pardon?"

"A message. There must be some way! My husband's life may be in danger, and I need the other few to pray."

The merchant glanced about his shop of fine wares and then brought his curious gaze back to the noblewoman, "And how might *I* be of any help?"

Rosalynn closed her eyes and briefly chastised herself. She had forgotten the watchword. She opened her eyes and scanned the shop before taking a step closer and whispering, "The door has not yet been closed. I need a message sent through before it is."

Liam the mercer smiled and offered a nod, "Now that i*th th*omething I can help you with."

The following morning, Haman stood atop the city's eastern wall and gazed with intense pleasure at the sight on the horizon. Highlighted by the rising sun, an army of vast size marched toward the rebellious province of Hebbros, armed and ready for war. Freed for a time from the Arcrean border wars, Cronin's forces had come west at last.

One sentry sent up the cry of alarm, and his shout was echoed along the wall until their panic had spilled into the streets below. The slaves along the new outer wall were marched inside and set to the task of reinforcing the existing boundaries. The twelve gates that faced north, south, and east were inspected and confirmed as solid and impenetrable. Citizens ran hither and thither, fetching supplies from the market and begging news of the authorities.

This was what he had been waiting for. Haman watched from his lofty vantage point and smirked at the chaos he had helped to inspire by giving voice to a god. Starting today his Order would have their war, and when their thirst for battle had been quenched, the rest would be his.

Success was closer than ever. Almost.

"The scouts are returning, Master," Epic pointed ahead to

where two riders galloped in their direction. The lightly armored scouts soon reined in and saluted, sweating in the late afternoon sun despite the cool air.

"What news of the road ahead?" Warin asked the one on the left.

The man met his gaze evenly, "Sir, the road to Hebbros is clear for now, but Cronin's forces, under the command of Sir Hugo, are approaching the city from the east at a rapid march."

The second scout spoke up, "Our pace must be doubled or the army will cut off our access to the city by nightfall."

With a curse, Warin wheeled his mount and road back along the line, shouting to the soldiers who prodded the slaves up the road, "Remove the supplies from the mules and have them carry the slaves. Each of you, lead a mule and take any leftover slaves on your horses with you. We ride hard for Hebbros or risk a confrontation with our lord's enemies. Move!"

His orders were obeyed faster than he had anticipated. The slaves cooperated, preferring to reach slavery alive than to risk this being their last day. Sir Warin scanned the progress and bellowed instructions when necessary. He searched for Epic and saw the boy catch a ride with one of the soldiers, and then turned toward the back of the line, where Sadie was leading Adele's donkey on foot.

"You there," Warin shouted at a nearby soldier as the man helped Elaina onto his horse, "take this mule's lead rope and make for the city with all haste." He lifted Sadie onto his own horse with little effort and settled her in front, continuing to address the other man, "Do not stop for anyone, and meet at the slave market."

"Yes, sir," the soldier nodded and spurred his horse forward.

Warin quickly turned his horse and pounded a trail north, barking orders at every soldier he passed, "Make for Hebbros regardless of the others! Save yourself and meet at the slave market!"

The entire company was soon racing toward their destination, spread out along the road according to their individual speed and abilities. Warin kept a trained eye on the view ahead and occasionally cast an anxious glance to the east. Only a few more miles before a rise in the land and a turn in the road would bring Hebbros into view.

A soft sound caught his ear and Warin peered over Sadie's shoulder to see her lips moving in prayer. No doubt she asked her

God for a safe arrival in Hebbros. He clenched his jaw and urged his horse to go faster. If they reached the city in safety, it would be due to his quick thinking and not the aid of an invisible God. Praying would only confuse her perception of that truth.

"Little Mouse," Warin called forward into the wind and she turned her head at the sound of his voice. "You should know that the people of Hebbros, our ruling lord in particular, do not look kindly on the people of your faith. Your God has been outlawed from the province, and to worship Him is against the laws of our land."

A short laugh lifted her shoulders, as if the idea that her God had been banned was a comical one, "And what is your opinion of my faith?"

Warin frowned at her casual acceptance of his words. She needed to understand the gravity of his warning. "I've been trained as a Mordecai knight, an Order established for the original purpose of annihilating the Faithful—the name my people have given your kind."

Sadie was silent for a moment before calling back a reply, "That was not an opinion of my faith, Sir Warin." She grinned and then became serious, "Your kindness in choosing to warn me at all is proof that God has heard my prayers for you. You have just offered me further evidence of my God's existence and power. Why, then, would I choose to deny Him?"

Warin clamped his mouth shut, speechless. Not since his mother had been alive had anyone admitted to praying for him, and his mother's prayers had been to the Mizgalian god of justice, when seeking retribution on her troublesome twins.

Warin glanced over his shoulder to check the positions of his entourage, determined to put all thoughts of matters spiritual from his mind. He simply needed to keep quiet around this slave. She had an answer for everything.

49
Parting Company

Elaina winced at the bone-jarring pace of the soldier's horse. Behind them, Adele clung to the neck of her speeding mule as though her life depended on it, which, Elaina figured, it probably did.

As far as she was concerned, it was difficult deciding which fate could be worse. Falling into the hands of the Mizgalian army as a hostage, or being trapped in a foreign city and never again permitted to venture outside the walls. Sadie had learned from Sir Warin that the only way an inhabitant of Hebbros was likely to leave the city was by death or banishment to the wild slopes of some mountain. Elaina's gaze moved to the east and she watched the horizon, suddenly longing to catch sight of the enemy.

In the next instant, the road took a sharp turn and the ground rose up before them. The horse slowed only slightly as they climbed a gentle incline, but the soldier pulled back on the reins and allowed it a moment's rest once they reached the top.

Elaina's breath left her as she gazed on the impressive sight before her. A mountain that rivaled the majesty of a Brikbone rose into the sky in a blaze of sun-kissed autumn finery. In the shadows of its eastern slopes several dragons floated on the cool air, waiting for the cover of night to scavenge the countryside. Lowering her gaze, Elaina found the base of the mountain engulfed and surpassed by a city the size of none other she had ever seen. Banners fluttered from every spire and tower, lending a carefree appearance to a place that must be in turmoil over the approaching Mizgalian swarm. Portions of the city and the vast valley they had yet to cross before reaching its gates were burnished gold by the sun, and in spite of her desire to go no closer, Elaina could not take her eyes from the beautiful display.

The soldier pointed his finger and proudly uttered a few Mizgalian words that Elaina easily understood, "Mount Desterrar. Hebbros."

He set the horse and donkey in motion once more and they descended a gentle slope into the valley. Scanning the broad expanse ahead, Elaina could see they would be the first of their party to reach the city.

She smiled. Perfect.

The walls loomed higher and higher as they drew nearer. They passed through what appeared to be a new outer wall, still under construction, and Elaina craned her neck to study the existing boundaries. Beyond the walls, her eyes followed the lilting flight of a daring dragon and then paused when she spotted a row of faint specks that might have been humans near Desterrar's peak. She couldn't be sure. Elaina's brow furrowed, but in the next instant all thoughts of the mountain were cast from her mind when they passed through one of the city's gates. The soldier reined to a halt as the portcullis was dropped behind them. Elaina heard the awful clang of iron and chains, and swallowed back a sense of dread. She felt as if a giant had just swallowed her whole.

The soldier spoke to a guard and Elaina supposed he was relaying information regarding the rest of their party's imminent arrival. The other man nodded and turned to address an armed troop while Elaina's escort turned his mount north.

The city was clearly in a state of panic, judging by the streets clogged with rushing people who were shouting at one another in hurried sentences. Men, women, and children alike flooded the lanes and byways, wide-eyed and alarmed by the looming wrath of their castoff king.

Elaina studied the crowd with curiosity, appalled when she realized how many people were using the chaos as a cover for various crimes. Thefts, beatings, and kidnappings were only a few of the actions being attempted—sometimes achieved—by the swarming citizens of Hebbros. The air was alive with a thousand curses, sung to the mournful tune of the weeping, and by the time they reached the heart of the city and a massive structure of black stone, Elaina could barely see through the tears that blinded her. What was this awful place?

They bypassed the dark structure inscribed with the Mordecai insignia that she had seen on Sir Warin, and turned into an open-air yard that was clearly the slave market. Cage-like prison cells lined the outer edges of the yard, the center of which boasted the infamous auction block. The cages as well as the yard were empty, awaiting Sir Warin's harvest of sixty-one slaves.

She must act now or never.

Casually stretching her stiff muscles, Elaina waited until the weary horse had come to a halt before the auction block. The soldier glanced over his shoulder to check on Adele, and Elaina's instincts propelled her to action. Grabbing the hilt of the man's sword, she quickly drew it from the scabbard and swung her elbow back to connect with his ribs. His cry of surprise was quickly followed by another shout when Elaina threw her weight into a dismount that tossed him from the horse. Landing on her feet, she stumbled momentarily on wobbly legs. Forcing herself to stand upright, she lowered the tip of the sword to point it at the soldier.

She doubted he would understand her words, but she would say them anyway, "Believe me when I say I am acquainted with the use of this weapon. You will permit me to leave by way of the front gate, or suffer the consequences." Her eyes narrowed at his look of suspicion, "I've been told I am most formidable when angry." She held out one hand while steadying the sword with the other, "The key, sir, to unlock my chains."

The soldier glared, "No key." He tensed when she pressed the tip of his blade closer to his chest, and he rambled something about Sir Warin carrying the key.

Elaina resisted the urge to stamp her foot in frustration. She would just have to take the chains with her. The feeling of stability having returned to her legs, she backed away several paces and then turned to dart for the gate. She had almost made it when someone grabbed hold of her hair from behind. Her head jerked back and she was nearly pulled to the cobbled ground.

The soldier growled and spoke a few sarcastic words in

broken Arcrean, "My sword, miss, if you please."

Elaina hissed in pain when he gave another fierce tug to her braid, "I don't please."

Without a second thought she twirled the wrist of her sword arm and brought the blade up between them. The chains binding her wrists slapped the side of her face as the weapon flashed a path behind her, slicing through her long dark plait and leaving it dangling from the startled soldier's hand. Parting company with the majority of her hair, Elaina's head snapped forward and she followed through with the motion and sprang for the gate. Hearing footfalls behind her, she turned and flung the sword low. The soldier cursed and jumped clear of the flying weapon, and Elaina slipped from the slave market and quickly lost herself in the crowd.

Like a swift-moving current the masses pulled her along, sweeping her through dusty streets and past structures of impressive design. Crooked stairways led her up and down a maze of wide thoroughfares, and sandstone archways hid her passage through narrow byways.

Hiding her chains in the folds of her skirt, Elaina walked along, overwhelmed by the sensation of traveling through a foreign city, surrounded by a Mizgalian-prattling throng. The crimes she had witnessed earlier were still fresh in her mind, causing her heart to pound loud in her ears and keeping her fully alert. She noticed several glances aimed her way, filled with suspicion and curiosity, and she glanced down at her Arcrean garb. With the lowering of her head, her short hair fell forward and brushed as low as her chin.

Elaina froze in her tracks. Several people muttered words of annoyance and she was quickly pushed off the street and into the opening of a deserted alley. Standing in the shadows, Elaina stood still as reality struck her.

She had cut her hair! The very hair that her mother had been so proud of!

Her head felt light. The freshly cropped strands brushed against her face and Elaina took a deep breath to steady her whirling emotions. She reached up to finger the dark mane and cringed. It was not customary for a woman to go cropping her hair as short as a man's. What had she been thinking? She hadn't been thinking!

Elaina straightened her arms along her sides and clenched her fists, throwing her head back to gaze up at the visible patch of sky. "It will grow out again," she reminded herself, "and at least I escaped the slave market."

The thought reminded her of Sadie and she turned to look back the way she thought she had come. What would happen to her kindhearted friend now? She shook her head, shivering when dark strands of hair fluttered over her cheek. Even if she thought it wise to return and help Sadie escape, she wouldn't know how to find wherever it was she had come from.

Tucking her hair behind her ears, Elaina stepped to the end of the alley and took in her surroundings. The thoroughfare was still busy, though not nearly as crowded as the streets near the city's heart. The setting sun had dipped behind Desterrar, casting Hebbros in shadow and highlighting the magnificent size of the mountain. The dragons she had spotted earlier now dropped from the slopes to float above the city, and numerous fire towers were lit here and there like giant torches to keep them at bay. Elaina wondered briefly if the royal army, camped outside of the walls, would create a beast-deterrent of its own.

Her eyes shifted to the street. Most of the establishments along this row were still open for business, though the presence of Cronin's army as well as the dragons seemed to be driving many to their homes. Elaina looked to the left and noticed that the place of business directly beside her seemed to be attracting more attention than the rest. A wooden sign hung over the door, creaking softly in the breeze, with a line in Mizgalian painted above the picture of a tankard wearing a squire's cap. A tavern.

A thunderous noise vibrated through the city and Elaina gave a start. Screams in the distance accompanied the sight of flaming arcs in the sky and then more pandemonium as Cronin's army began an assault on Hebbros's eastern region. As catapults tossed their burdens of flame and destruction, wreaking havoc closer to the walls, the few citizens still out on the streets quickly rushed for cover. Elaina was prepared to follow their lead when an unearthly shriek halted her in place and pulled her gaze to the sky.

Overhead, a dragon had caught sight of the activity and made a daring dive for the street. Elaina screamed and ducked against the tavern wall as the creature gave a mighty cry and crashed into a nearby merchant's stall. The contents of the abandoned booth scattered in an unforgiving mess and the canopy that had provided its shade fell within reach of Elaina. The young woman grabbed the length of brown canvas and pulled it over her head in an attempt to disappear from sight. The irritated dragon grappled for prey as it thrashed against the unfamiliar confines of cobblestone and wood, and then quickly retreated to the skies.

Heart pounding, Elaina pulled the canvas closer about her and darted from the alley, joining a group of men and women taking refuge in the tavern. Her breath came in ragged gasps as she pondered what twist of fate had landed her in a dragon-laden Mizgalian city at war with their own monarch.

Elaina slid along the wall and huddled in the corner of the warm room, where she pushed the short strands of her hair out of her eyes and looked around. She scanned the tavern's patrons and took note of the nervous expressions of many as the catapults continued to thunder in the east.

At a table by the far wall, one man seemed indifferent to the danger his city was facing. His face hidden behind a tankard, he tipped his head back and drained the mug of its contents. When he had finished the last drop, he sat forward and slammed the tankard onto the table, calling to the taverner for another round of ale. Elaina froze in horror and her eyes rounded with shock.

It was Sir Warin!

Still shrouded in the dark garb of his Order, the Mordecai waited for the taverner and cast a dark glance around the room. His green eyes narrowed as they took in the sight of the fearful crowd who had just entered, and then shifted to Elaina's corner.

Elaina quickly ducked her head and shifted so that she was behind another woman. Casually drawing the canvas up over her head like the hood of a cloak, she edged her way toward the door. Dragons and catapults or no, she refused to be dragged back to the slave market by the infuriating knight. Especially having sacrificed her hair for the cause of liberation.

Elaina stepped up to the threshold but was crowded back again when a young man entered from outside. Ignoring the young woman he had shoved out of the way, the newcomer's eyes caught sight of someone and he called out.

"Wulf!" He shoved past her, and Elaina looked over her shoulder to see him crossing to where Sir Warin sat. Her brow furrowed and she took a closer look.

The knight watched the other man approach through the

crowd and nodded a casual greeting, "Marley."

Elaina blinked and slowly moved closer along the wall. This Mordecai's voice was different, his hair was longer, and when he ran a hand through the unruly locks she caught sight of a terrible white scar tracing the ridge above his left eyebrow. This was not Sir Warin.

The two men exchanged words in their native tongue and then altered the course of their speech. The jumble of syllables began to make sense, and Elaina realized they were speaking in Arcrean. Shielding herself behind a group moving to a nearby table, Elaina caught the blessedly familiar words amidst the sea of strange voices that surrounded her.

"Marley, you know we've trained to discuss these things in any language but our own. This way the blame will be pointed at anyone but our leader."

"Wulf, I've been looking everywhere for you."

Warin's look-alike rolled his eyes, "Where would I be, if not here, when Valden isn't working me like a dog?"

Marley waved the words aside and lowered his voice, "The Order of Haman is on the move. Cronin's army has positioned itself before the eastern walls and we're to gather for a sortie that will lay waist to the army's southern flank."

A small smile pulled at Wulf's mouth, "At last." He drained his second mug of ale since Elaina's arrival and rose, scraping the legs of his bench against the floor, "Let's get to it then."

Elaina backed away and slipped through the door, ducking around the corner to the same alley where she had taken refuge before. A moment later, shadows stretched across the road as the men called Wulf and Marley emerged from the tavern, speaking Mizgalian once again. They turned to the left, heading south to mischief, when another voice hailed them from the north. Instinctively, Elaina shrank deeper into the shadows and stilled the chains at her wrists. Alarm raced through her. This voice she knew for certain.

Warin slowed his horse just inside the ring of light being cast by the Squire's Tavern. The street boasted the signs of a recent dragon attack, as well as the emptiness due to fear of Cronin's army. Regardless, his brother and another young man were heading south along the dark road. Warin dismounted and led his animal forward as Wulf turned and stepped his way, leaving the stranger behind.

"I figured you'd be coming to find me when I saw you enter the city a few hours ago." Wulf stopped several yards away and smirked, "But as you were in the company of a fair maid, I thought I'd have time for a tankard or two before you turned up."

Warin did not smile, "You smell like more than a tankard or two. Wulf, the city is in chaos, the eastern region is being evacuated, and Roland has called for retaliation on the catapults, yet you decided it was time to leave Sir Valden for a few drinks?"

"It was a stop along the way." Wulf shrugged and tilted his head back toward his friend, "I'm on Valden's business now."

A muscle twitched in Warin's face and he studied his twin, unsure whether he should believe his brother's words.

"Wulf." The stranger called from the shadows beyond the tavern's light.

Wulf glanced over his shoulder and then lifted his brow at Warin, "Can't stay."

Suspicion curled up Warin's spine and he took a step closer, lowering his voice, "Wulf, tell me where you're going."

Wulf's lip curled with irritation, "I just did. I'm on Valden's business, and I'll be late if you don't let me go."

Warin glanced at the stranger over Wulf's shoulder and then studied his brother's face, "Secret business? Questionable friends? Please tell me you're not a part of that Haman Order."

Wulf rolled his eyes, "And what if I am?"

"Wulf, it's dangerous! Sir Valden has been tracking their actions for years, and it's only a matter of time before he discovers all he needs to know in order to crush them. What do you think will happen if he finds out you're one of them?"

"He won't. At least not until it's too late. The Order of Haman will take the city, Warin, and then Valden will be in our service for a change. You ought to join—"

"Wulf, you're speaking madness," Warin shook his head. "Valden trusts you, and his trust is the most hard-earned in the province. You need to cut your ties with this undisciplined faction before you get yourself killed for treachery."

"I can't do that," Wulf scoffed. "Leaving the Order now

would be a death worse than anything Valden could do to me." He cut off Warin's response before his brother could begin, "Warin, don't lecture me. You, who have always lived by the words 'do whatever it takes.' Roland promised greatness, and it never happened. Haman promised war, and it has come. Sometimes we have to take matters into our own hands. You know that. If you hadn't taken the place as Master Slaver, you'd still be one of Valden's lackeys."

"But this is…this is more than just a promotion, Wulf. This is desertion, and as a Mordecai I'm bound to—"

"To what? Report me?" Wulf held his arms out in question, "You would report your own brother, your twin, for joining a movement that has grown so no garrison could contain its numbers?" His brow quirked with amusement, "Your face is identical to mine. If you cast blame on me, who's to say your words wouldn't turn and condemn you instead? We're brothers, Warin. Brothers watch out for each other."

"They also point out defects in one another's behavior. I never thought you'd turn on the one who rescued us from a life in Monty's shadow."

Wulf's head slowly began to shake, "You're so naïve." He shifted with exasperation and grinned at his twin, "Oh come, Warin, I'm teasing you. Valden already knows—he set me up to it. I joined their ranks as his informant to keep abreast of their plans. As soon as Valden has all he wants, he'll pull me from the pack and destroy the rest of the faction. Simple."

Warin stared at his brother, his brow furrowed with confusion.

Wulf shrugged and turned to go, "I'll see you tomorrow. You can tell me all about your new lady friend over a tankard at Squire's."

His tongue tied, Warin watched until Wulf and the stranger had disappeared from sight. Slowly, he turned and mounted his horse, shaking his head over his twin's scattered conversation and that last ridiculous suggestion. Enjoy a mug of ale and some easy conversation?

"Not with the province at war, you empty-headed simpleton."

50
To Keep a Promise

The inhabitants of Exile gazed down on the city of Hebbros with mixed emotions. Luke took in the relief over the army's arrival, as well as the anxiety over what was to come, and then let his own gaze shift to the numerous divisions of armed men camped in the valley beyond Hebbros. A voice spoke from beside him.

"The king's army has arrived."

"Obvious, Elbert. I mean…really?" Ned stood with his arm about Charlotte's waist. Their wedding had barely concluded before the army's catapults had begun their assault below. The couple now stood at the lookout with the rest of the village, watching with some amazement as the rebellious city of Hebbros was at last rebuked for her actions.

Beyond Charlotte stood Pavia, dressed as the bride's attendant and struggling to keep her hem from trailing in the dirt. Luke's mother rested one hand on the redhead's shoulder, and with the other hand covered her mouth in concern. Althar stood at Mariah's other side, looking up when he felt Luke's eyes on him. He held his son's gaze for a long moment and then nodded once.

Luke turned his head to look the other way. Among other villagers, Chris stood nearby, his gaze filled with sadness. To his twin's far side stood Bradley, Sarah, and their four children, along with a grim-faced Lillian and her tenderhearted parents. As Luke watched, Lillian's mother slid an arm around her daughter's shoulders and the young woman quickly pulled away to stalk back toward the village.

"I hate to think that my sister is down there." Bradley's voice drew Luke's attention away from Lillian's angry retreat, and back to the fires that were a result of the catapults. The former nobleman adjusted the weight of his four-year-old daughter on one arm and shook his head, "Regardless of Rosalynn's past behavior toward me, she is still my sister. I wish it were possible to know that she is well."

"There is a way," Sedgwick's voice spoke from behind them, and the cluster of those nearest to him turned to look at the village elder. Luke met the man's gaze and remembered their conversation of a week before. Silently praying for wisdom, he turned to glance at Bradley.

"You're welcome to accompany me down to Hebbros. I'll be leaving at midnight."

"Tonight?" Several voices chorused in unison as the group turned to eye Luke with surprise.

Luke turned back to the scene of war on the valley floor, "The city is nearing its destruction. I must fulfill my promise and complete my mission before the remnant of the Faithful is destroyed with the rest of Hebbros."

"I thought you were waiting for a signal from the remnant." Chris turned, his expression serious, "I was not aware that you had received one."

"Did it come?" Ned came closer, "Have we heard from below?"

Elbert sighed, "There might not be a remnant."

Luke held up a hand, "Several of us have asked God to show us when the time is right, and we are in agreement that the time is now. The city is under siege and Cronin's men will show no mercy if they penetrate the walls. This may be our last opportunity to rescue the Faithful who remain."

Elbert shook his head, "Our banishment may have been the end of the Faithful."

"Our God is always faithful," Luke spoke with assurance, "and I will trust that He has heard my prayers for a remnant." He glanced at Bradley, "If you wish to accompany me, be at the head of the Banishment Path at midnight."

Bradley nodded solemnly and turned to lead his family back into the village.

Charlotte approached and tearfully embraced her brother, "God be with you, Luke. I'll be praying."

"As will the rest of us," an elderly man called out.

"Thank you."

The banished of Exile filed past on their way back to the village, offering words of encouragement and wisdom. Luke heard each and nodded his thanks until only several people remained on the ledge.

Pavia approached and wiped away a tear, "Be safe, and don't let anything surprise you on your journey." She twisted her braid between both hands and shrugged, "Lillian has been acting strange of late."

"Thank you, Pavia," Luke nodded. "With Charlotte no longer at home, see that my mother doesn't fret," a mischievous grin pulled at his face and sparked in his eyes, "and take care of Chris for me."

Pavia scooped Trig into her arms with a sound that was either a laugh or a sob, "I try."

Chris stepped up and glanced after the retreating girl and her catawyld before feigning an incredulous scowl at his twin, "I heard that." Luke smiled, but then grew serious as his brother gripped both of his shoulders and took a deep breath, "I should be going with you."

"No," Luke shook his head. "As the guardian of Exile, you need to be preparing the village. If something goes wrong, the Faithful will need someone here to show them what to do."

Chris clenched his jaw, "You told me you're prepared to—" his words came to a halt and he shook his head, unable to continue. Finally, he pulled his brother into a firm embrace, "You promised that merchant you'd come back. I expect you to do the same for me."

When his twin released him, Mariah drew near and held her son close, unashamed of the tears that wet her face. Luke returned her fierce embrace and squeezed his eyes shut as tears of his own began to fall.

"Oh God," his mother wept against his chest, "please bring

my son safely home to me again."

Althar approached and wrapped his arms around them both. He pressed Luke's head to his shoulder, and Luke felt his father's chin quiver against his hair. The magnitude of his mission suddenly loomed before him, and Luke inhaled deeply.

God, please let there be a remnant, in answer to our prayers. Let them be ready to escape from Hebbros. Use me to get them out, and if it be Your will…please let me live to return to Exile.

Holding one hand aloft while the other clutched his staff, Sedgwick suddenly spoke from beside the group, "My friends, let us pray."

Sarah walked through the village in silence. Beside her, Bradley too kept thoughtfully quiet as he carried a sleeping Rebecca toward home. Myla and Colin, their two eldest children, scampered back and forth on the path ahead, chattering about the events of the day. Sarah looked down at little William, toddling beside her, and smiled.

God had been so good to her. She had been wrapped in peace for many years now, enjoying a life of innumerable blessings, and the Lord had taught her to be grateful. Even while she had known this day would come. Had to come.

"I think you should go with Luke."

Bradley halted and turned to face her, his expression a mask of astonishment, "You do?"

She smiled tremulously and placed her hands along either side of his face, "I think God has been preparing me for this day. While I don't want you t' go and put yourself in danger, m' heart has perfect peace with the fact that you must." She blinked back tears, "Bradley, when we were banished, the chains of m' former slavery were cut away, while yours were merely lengthened." He started to speak, but Sarah put a finger to his lips, "You are still tied t' Hebbros by the bonds of bitterness, and you will remain so until the day certain matters are settled in your heart."

Bradley heaved a deep sigh and glanced up at the heavens, "I admit, I had not thought you would want me to go. Truth be told, I'm not so sure I want to go myself. However, I feel… How would Luke say it? Called to go."

A smile lit Sarah's face and tears brightened her eyes to mirror the stars, "I'll be waiting for you to return, just as I did the last time we were parted. Go to Hebbros, Bradley, and let God remove the collar of your bondage."

The gifted young man positioned himself in a low crouch. Perched as he was on a ledge of stone several thousand feet in the air, the view was magnificent. His slate-blue eyes shifted downward and memories assailed him. Straightening, he continued to stare down on the point where he knew a darkened gate blended with the wall of a city. Would his gift prove to be a help or hindrance in the days ahead? With thousands of faces to be read and one goal in mind, would his deep perception be insightful or overwhelming?

His right thumb and forefinger moved habitually to toy with his bowstring as he shifted his gaze to survey the rest of the city. Fire towers, hovering dragons, and the blockade of an attacking army completed a picture of complete chaos in his mind.

Instinctively, Luke scanned the starry sky and then turned from his vantage point. Deserting the stone ledge, he began to move through the shadows toward his destination. He climbed back to the summit and walked through the village of Exile. His eyes studied the details of his home, glowing in the warm light of the lone fire tower. Would he ever see this place again?

He turned off of the main path and moved beyond the cottages and across a clearing toward the edge of the peak. A small crowd had gathered at the edge of the village to watch him take his leave. Chris waited at the head of the Banishment Path, as did Bradley. The three men exchanged nods, and each broke into a grin when Bradley presented the bag of supplies prepared by his wife.

"She said we'd be prepared for anything, and judging by the weight alone I'm inclined to believe her."

"Master Paul used to say we should be prepared for anything." Luke adjusted the strap of his quiver, "Remember, Chris?"

"Yes, but that was usually when you complained about learning the basics of the Arcrean language."

"I remember those lessons," Bradley made a face. "Never once have I put them to use. My father insisted, though, and to this day the strange sounds of Arcrean words rattle about in my brain like useless bits of rusted knowledge. I say, we should be on our way before my courage shrivels and I turn tail to run home. Let's make this descent in record time."

Luke nodded. He clasped his brother firmly by the wrist in a final farewell, waved to the small gathering by the edge of the village, and then disappeared over the first steep ledge on the path to Hebbros.

Please, God, prepare the remnant, he glanced over his shoulder at the nobleman following in his steps, *and let this be the time when You draw Bradley to Yourself.*

51
Courses of Action

It was the second morning since the start of Cronin's assault and the catapults had fallen silent for a time. The sun had barely risen. In the strange quiet, Sir Valden entered the structure that had once housed the great Peers and quickly strode to the inner meeting hall. Scribes and slaves scurried about, obeying the commands of a number of knights. Sir Fraser stood to one side of the room, hearing and reading reports from various posts throughout the city.

Valden approached the large table at the center of the hall, where Roland had unfurled the plans of the city, and bowed. "You sent for me, my lord?" His eyes took in the detailed diagram of Hebbros on the table between them.

"Yes, I sent for you." Roland straightened and glared at the new Mordecai chief, "Explain to me why, two nights ago, you decided to send out a company of your knights to attack Cronin's southern flank without informing anyone of your intentions."

Valden stiffened, "My lord, they were not—"

"Sir Fraser is in command of all armed movements," Roland interrupted and Valden ground his teeth together. "From now on you will report to him *before* you make any further attempts at heroism. We are at war, Sir Valden, and in the end, rushing headlong into stupidity is not going to win the day."

"But my lord, they were—"

"It makes no difference that your men succeeded in wiping out an entire division of Cronin's men, because another company nearly managed to follow the Mordecais back into Hebbros. Had they reached the gate, the city's southern region would have been decimated before Fraser was even aware that anything was amiss."

"My lord!" Valden's shout brought a momentary stillness to the hall. Every head turned and every eye studied the scene at the center of the room. Roland sent them back to their business with a harsh word, and then glared at the knight across the table.

"Do not dare to raise your voice to me again."

Valden inhaled slowly, "My lord, you have been misinformed. The men who sallied out two nights ago were no company of mine. I heard of the event just this morning. My aide was assisting with the ordered retaliation that night and found himself near the gate in question when the miscreants were returning from their sortie."

Roland's fierce gaze never wavered, "And?"

"He saw them returning with Cronin's men hard on their heels, and so rushed to close the gate before the enemy could gain entrance."

"Were any Hebbros men left outside the walls?"

"None, my lord," Valden shook his head. "Though my aide was not aware of the fact until after the gate was shut."

Roland's jaw worked back and forth, "I was told by a witness that this was the work of the Mordecai Order. If not your men, then whose?"

"My first guess would be Haman."

"The elusive troublemaker." Roland leaned his fists on the surface of the table, "Find him, Valden, or more will be at stake than your position as Mordecai Chief."

Jaw clenched, Valden executed a stiff bow and then turned to leave the rounded hall. His angry stride carried him next door to the Mordecai garrison and into the Reestablishment room in record time. He slammed the door behind him and Wulf turned from the wall of records.

"These have been alphabetized, and I was just about to double-check the master list, unless you…"

"Leave it for now," Valden waved an agitated hand and moved around the table to the padded chair.

Wulf eyed the older man for a moment and then crossed to the window, "I gather it didn't go well."

"Hardly." Valden barked, adding in a lower tone, "I've had enough of his assumptions and condescension. Forget this Haman, it's high time Roland was put in his place."

Wulf looked over his shoulder at the menacing words, "Sir?"

Valden looked up, a determined glint in his eyes, "How many guards are posted at the palace temple?"

Wulf rolled his eyes upward in thought, "Two, sir, outside the doors."

"And there are pillars inside," Valden thought aloud. "Six pillars. And the nine deities." He rose from his chair, his fiery gaze never wavering from his aide, "I want eight Mordecais who would follow my command even to the point of death."

"Done."

"Have two trade places with the guards tomorrow evening. Twenty-four hours should give you plenty of time," the words were laced with scorn. Valden took up a quill pen and twirled it in his fingers, "I will have a note penned in Lady Rosalynn's hand and delivered to Lord Roland, asking him to pray with her in the temple after the evening meal."

"While Hebbros is under siege?" Wulf asked incredulously.

Valden scowled, "His lordship has two weaknesses; his love for the Lady Rosalynn, and his desire to appear utterly devoted to the gods. I can guarantee he will be delighted by a request to exercise his religious fervor in the company of his wife."

"Yes, sir, of course." Wulf lowered his head sheepishly and then glanced up, his eye framed by the distinctive white scar, "And then what?"

Valden answered with a slow grin, "Leave the rest to me."

Sadie sat against the wall of her cage-like cell and hugged her knees to her chest. Her arrival in Hebbros two nights before had thrown her into a whirlwind of exhausting events.

Sir Warin had not brought his horse to a complete stop in the slave market before one of his men rushed forward with the news that Elaina had escaped and was now roaming the streets of this terrifying city. Another had brought word that the soldier in charge of Epic had not returned, but had fled and taken the boy when the army cut off their access to Hebbros. Soon after that, the army's attack had begun and Sadie had spent the next few hours comforting a number of hysterical slaves.

When the catapults had eventually paused their work of destruction, Sadie had been escorted to the cell where she now sat, to help bring another woman's baby into the world. Hours later, with the new mother weak after a difficult delivery, Sadie had begged a blanket from one of the soldiers and then rocked the premature little one in her arms until the sky had shown the first signs of morning. The rest of that day and the night following had been a blur of caring for mother and child.

Sadie shivered in the chill of this new predawn and massaged her tender wrists. Thankfully, Sir Warin had taken pity on her during the first night and removed her chains. Caring for the newborn would have been much more difficult otherwise.

A noise startled her and Sadie lifted her head to find that she had fallen asleep. In high contrast to the terror of before, golden light bathed the market in a warm glow, and somewhere a lone bird ventured a song of hope. The catapults were silent. Across the cell, the new mother and her babe slept peacefully. Sadie reached to adjust the infant's blanket and then rose to her feet to stretch her sore muscles.

"How are you this morning, Little Mouse?"

Sadie pressed her fingers against the back of her aching neck and answered without turning, "Tired."

"I'm indebted to you for your services since our arrival. Because of your willingness to help here, most of my men were free to offer Sir Fraser their assistance elsewhere in the city."

Sadie turned then and studied Sir Warin through the bars of the slave pen. Had the Master Slaver just offered his thanks to a member of his human cargo? She had sensed a gradual change in his demeanor since she had mentioned praying for him. Keeping these thoughts to herself, she replied simply, "You're welcome."

Warin unlocked the door and motioned for her to leave the cell. Sadie obeyed, glancing back at the two other occupants as the door was closed and locked again. What would happen to them? Would the mother be separated from her infant?

Warin turned toward the auction block, grabbing Sadie's arm as he walked by. At the block, he lifted her onto his horse and then leapt into the saddle behind her. Turning the animal toward the gate he nodded to a soldier, who quickly moved to let them out.

"Where are we going?" Sadie asked, but he ignored the question and they rode in silence.

It was not long before they turned into the courtyard of a palace. Sadie gazed at her surroundings in awe as Warin directed his horse to stop before a waiting slave.

"Hold the horse for me," Warin dismounted and tossed the reins to the collared boy. "I won't be long."

He helped Sadie down and took her arm again, leading her up the wide set of stone steps and into the palace. Their quick tread echoed in the torch-lit corridors and stairwells until they came to a broad oak door. Warin knocked and a moment later an elderly woman opened the panel.

Warin motioned with his head to Sadie, "The attendant for Lady Rosalynn."

The slave opened the door wider and Warin gently pushed Sadie across the threshold. Inside the lavishly decorated chamber, her eyes immediately landed on an elegant woman in her late-thirties, seated on a gray divan by the hearth. The velvety folds of her green dress pooled about her and draped to the floor, and bejeweled fingers rested easily in her lap. Bright red hair hung in a braid over one shoulder, with several loose curls framing her face, and large brown eyes studied the young woman at the door with curious intensity.

"Thank you, Sir Warin, that will be all." Her voice was rich and cultured.

Sadie looked over her shoulder as Warin bowed to the lady and then took a step back from the threshold. His green eyes shifted to meet hers with an unreadable expression until the door had closed between them, leaving Sadie's questions unanswered.

"Welcome to Hebbros, Sadie."

She turned back to see the noblewoman watching her with a gentle smile. The lady motioned to a chair across from her and Sadie sat obediently with her eyes lowered to the thick rug on the floor.

"I imagine you are confused," the woman spoke softly. "I am Lady Rosalynn, wife of Roland, the lord of Hebbros. Some time ago, my husband charged the city's Master Slaver with the task of finding a young female slave who could act as my personal attendant." She colored slightly, embarrassed by her own words, "I have many slaves, you see, but few friends. I desired a companion."

Sadie offered a small nod and waited for Lady Rosalynn to continue.

"When the catapults ceased earlier this morning, Sir Warin came to inform me that he wished to deliver my attendant before the work of collaring the other slaves began. Imagine my surprise when I realized I would have no choice regarding who the young woman would be. Nevertheless, Sir Warin insists you are more than qualified for the position." Rosalynn sat back in her divan and studied the younger woman anew, "Personally, I've come to my own conclusions about why you were chosen."

Sadie's eyes lifted at the woman's tone of amusement, and Rosalynn met her gaze with a warm smile, "Did you know that this palace is the most fortified structure in Hebbros?"

"I… No, my lady," Sadie shook her head, confused.

"It is," Rosalynn nodded matter-of-factly. "You will find it is the safest place to be during this siege."

She seemed to be waiting for Sadie to comment, and so the younger woman cast about in her mind for something to say. "Your husband must care for you very much to ensure your utmost safety. Do you have any children?"

"Seven," Lady Rosalynn smiled. "My eldest son is fourteen, and my youngest daughter three months."

"I look forward to meeting them, if I may." Sadie offered a timid smile of her own, "Children are one of God's greatest blessings."

A slow smile crossed the elegant lady's face, "I couldn't agree more."

Sadie blinked, surprised after Warin's warning that this woman had not argued her remark, "I had the privilege to help bring a little one into the world two nights ago."

"During the attack?" Rosalynn sat forward, "You poor girl. No wonder you look exhausted."

Sadie tucked a strand of hair behind her ear, "I was glad to be of assistance, my lady. The mother was so frightened and the other slaves were just as nervous as she."

Rosalynn met and held Sadie's gaze for a long moment. "He was right," she murmured thoughtfully, seeming pleased.

"I beg your pardon, my lady?"

"Sadie, you are the sweetest creature I have ever met."

Sadie ducked her head, uncomfortable with the praise, while Rosalynn suddenly stood from the divan and called to the older slave woman.

"Bring those garments from the chair by the window." The woman returned with a gown of indigo blue, trimmed in soft gray, and an assortment of other necessities. Rosalynn turned to Sadie, "My slave will help you to put these on. As my companion you must maintain a neat appearance. You will wash your face and brush your hair daily, and see that your garments are kept tidy."

Sadie nodded and Rosalynn reached out, almost touching her sleeve, "I can't tell you how glad I am to have a friend at last. We have much to discuss. But first," she turned to cross toward the window, "when you are refreshed I will send for the children."

Sadie blinked and exchanged glances with the elderly slave, "Yes, my lady."

On a busy street in western Hebbros a blacksmith's hammer pounded a steady rhythm. The smith blinked and shook his head when a wave of heat washed over him, and he turned when movement caught his eye. He blinked again.

Standing at the open-air side of his shop was a young woman dressed in the garments of a foreigner. Not so very different from Mizgalian garb, but dissimilar enough to catch a native's eye. Without a word, she shook a thatch of cropped hair out of her eyes and stepped forward, wincing at the heat within the close quarters. Wearing an expression of pitiful desperation and with a touch of wide-eyed innocence she stretched out both of her arms, revealing a chain that dangled between her wrists.

The smith threw his head back in a deep laugh and then feigned a look of sober curiosity, "Run off, have you?"

She licked her lips in apprehension, waiting to see if he would grant her silent request. The blacksmith inhaled and cast a swift glance over her shoulder, and then motioned her forward with his head. "Over here, girl," he moved to a shelf along the wall and selected several tools. "If a slave's got enough pluck to actually make a go if it, I'll not refuse their freedom." He shifted her a glance, "But if I hear you've told 'em it was me what freed you, I'll be calling you a liar."

Elaina gave a vague nod as she laid her forearms on a high worktable and watched with wide eyes as the smith began. She sighed with relief when the chains fell away from each wrist. The iron links met the table with a clatter and the smith quickly tossed them into a basket of scraps in the corner.

She smiled her thanks at the man. She had not understood but three words of what he had said, nevertheless he had obviously grasped her plight immediately. In a city of crooks and perversion, it had finally dawned on her that someone would be willing to help an escaped slave.

Now she rubbed her sore but free wrists while the smith chattered what must be advice regarding the chafed skin. She nodded and the man's gaze moved beyond her. He walked to the door and picked up two empty buckets. Holding them out with one hand, he pointed up the street with the other, clearly asking her to return the favor of his services. Elaina refrained from sighing and took the buckets, deciding it would be safer to fetch the man's water than risk having him tell Sir Warin of her whereabouts.

She stepped outside and was immediately jostled by the crowd. The streets were packed today, the citizens of Hebbros relieved that Cronin's first assault had ended, but anxious to gather needed supplies before the next attack began.

Elaina craned her neck and peered up the street, trying to remember where she had seen a well. When at last she came upon one in the middle of a square, she took her place as fifteenth in line and waited her turn to draw water. She thought of the countless times she had complained about this same task while living in Balgo, and considered the irony of how she longed to be back there now.

"Move along," the woman behind her spoke the familiar words of the slavers when at last it was her turn at the well. Elaina quickly complied, blowing the unfamiliar length of her hair out of her face.

On her return to the smith's shop, Elaina paused at the corner to wipe her brow on her sleeve. She grimaced at the mark of perspiration and self-consciously wiped her dirty sleeve against her filthy red vest.

A voice that was not the blacksmith's drifted from the shop. Elaina inched forward to see another man standing beside the forge in conversation with its owner. Her breath caught when she thought it was Sir Warin, but then she noticed the scar and recognized his look-alike from the tavern. The two men had to be twins.

What was he doing here? Elaina gently set the buckets at the base of the outer wall and crept around the corner to a window in the back. Quieting her labored breathing, she tilted her ear and listened as the familiar strain of Arcrean words once again drifted to her hearing.

"…tomorrow night in the palace temple. Haman's orders."

"And Roland will die?" The smith queried with a voice of fevered excitement.

"Haman will see to Roland. Your job is to be ready for anything. I'm to find eight men who will follow to the point of death. Can I count you among them?"

"I took the oath," the smith sounded affronted by the question of loyalty.

There was movement and then the Mordecai spoke from farther away, "You're to report outside the garrison at sundown tomorrow."

"I'll be there."

The two men reverted to their native tongue and seemed to be exchanging casual pleasantries as they moved toward the street that fronted the shop. The smith exclaimed loudly when he discovered the abandoned water buckets, and with a gasp Elaina lurched away from the back wall and raced down another side street. Her heart pounded erratically and her breath came in shaky gasps as the words of the two men echoed in her head.

They were plotting someone's death! Someone at the palace! They had used the man's name, Roland, as if he were a well-known citizen.

You are no better than they are. The thought whispered in her ear like the hiss of an ignispat. *You plotted against Druet when he searched for Arcrea's heart, and would have led him to his death if you could. Now you stand appalled when you see the same actions in others?*

"No!" Elaina shook her head, trying to dislodge the condemning voice, "That was different, I… I did it for my father."

You lie to yourself. The voice mocked her as she pushed through the crowds along one street and then another. *You know the truth. Everyone knows the truth. You wanted Druet to die because you feared the loss of power.*

"Stop it!" Elaina cried out and several people turned to frown at the crazy young foreigner. Tears filled her eyes as the weight of her sins pressed down on her from all sides.

It was true. Whether or not she had done it to please her father, her goals as Lord Frederick's daughter had been no more honest than the plans overheard at the blacksmith's. When had she come to scorn the underhanded dealings that she had once enjoyed? Had the events of the last two weeks overturned her ideals and caused her to see how insignificant she truly was? Perhaps the time spent with Sadie had taught her the true meaning of goodness.

Elaina stumbled when someone shoved her from behind, and she moved to sit beneath the window of a small shop. She leaned her head back and thought of the years spent at her father's knee, gleaning information and supporting his cause with advice that she had known would be appreciated—striking out at the clans, taxing the merchants, chastising the peasants. Anything to assert his authority.

Her eyes slid shut and she shook her head. She was a farce. She had let her love for her father, though a wonderful thing, lead her down a path of destructive habits. When her father had settled peacefully in Balgo, in essence implying he no longer appreciated those practices that had drawn them together, Elaina had been at a loss. Who was she anymore, if not the mischievous aide to all of Frederick's plans?

You are hopeless. A failure. Tears slipped beneath her lashes and spilled down her face as each admission pierced her heart. Ignored by the passing throng, she pulled her knees up and sobbed against the rough fabric of her dress.

"Oh God, what am I to do?"

The impulsive cry surprised her. Never before had she called on God when in distress. Elaina's eyes darted back and forth in thought. She remembered Sadie's assertion that God still showed compassion, though no one deserved it. Could that be her answer? Would the Creator of all things show her mercy and forgive the sins of her past? Would He let her start over if she asked for such a chance?

"I don't know," she spoke softly. "I don't know how. God, if You can hear me, You must show me the way." Her eyes closed with a painful squeeze, releasing another tear along with the burning admission, "I am lost."

The shop's door opened to her right and the proprietor stepped out to gaze at the young woman seated beneath his window. Elaina opened her mouth to offer some explanation and then remembered she spoke only Arcrean. The merchant's eyes scanned her foreign apparel and then rose to meet her gaze. He smiled and uttered several Mizgalian phrases, spoken with a tentative lisp.

Elaina blinked, catching only a few of the words. Hebbros. Danger. Door. Closed. Her eyes lifted to the darkening sky and then darted to consider the shop's open door. Was he offering her shelter from the dangerous streets? She had spent the previous night huddled in the corner of an alley, fearful for her life. Shelter would be welcome. Perhaps he would give her food, something other than the meager scraps she had stolen the day before. Her eyes returned to the man's kind expression, beckoning her to enter while his door was still open.

Elaina leaned forward and rose to her feet, "I suppose I should come in, then, before it is closed for good."

52
Daughter of a King

Elaina pulled the borrowed cloak tighter about her and tucked the edge under her chin. Her head lay pillowed on a silk overdress, which had been pulled from a trunk and rolled into a lump for the purpose. Above her, a small table was draped in some thick material, creating a tent where she would sleep by the wall of the mercer's back room.

After ushering her into his shop, the kindly old man had continued to babble in his native tongue. He was aware she understood nothing, but apparently hoped she might catch the meaning of a few words. He had led her to the second room where crates and trunks of fine goods were stored in towering stacks, and located fresh garments for her to wear until her own could be cleaned. The mercer had then brought a bucket of water and departed from the storage room, prattling a string of words that Elaina was sure had included "food."

Dressed in the mercer's generous offering of clean apparel, Elaina had scrubbed the dirt of Hebbros from her face and arms, and then combed wet fingers through her short hair. Dropping her own filthy garments into the bucket, she had let them soak while she ate the food produced by her host.

Lying now beneath the table-tent, Elaina rolled over and

looked up at her clean garments, hung up to dry. In the light of her lone candle they looked as fresh as she felt. Wrapped in borrowed robes of soft cashmere and a heavy cloak to fend off the night's chill, she felt like a new person.

Blowing out the candle, she took a moment to close her eyes and enjoy one relaxed breath. Here was a safe place. Here was peace. She couldn't explain how, but Elaina knew without a doubt that bringing her to this gentle haven was the first step God had taken in answering her prayer for guidance. She had admitted that she was lost, and He had shown He knew exactly where she was. There had been no place to turn, and He had opened a door. The filth of this evil city had covered her, and He had provided a way to be clean.

Elaina touched her face and marveled as the truth became clear. The wicked deeds that burdened her heart were like the dirt that had clung to her skin. Uncomfortable. Tiring. Affecting her mentally and emotionally, as well as physically. If washing away the tangible grime had brought such relief, what must it feel like to be cleansed of the spiritual stains?

Sin. Elaina sighed. She must call it what it was. Her life as a young noblewoman had been fraught and framed by sinful motives, which had led to corrupt actions. She had put herself before all others, and sought the downfall of any who stood in her way. She had plotted against the innocent alongside her father and inspired campaigns that resulted in a number of deaths. She had stolen from her mother, cheated and lied when it suited her, and been a shameless flirt whenever she needed the least bit of attention.

Elaina's head began to pound with the knowledge of her wretchedness. Yes, she would call it sin. She could admit her own wrongdoing. But what could she do about it now? How could such filth be cleansed from the garment called Soul, so that her heart could be made to feel new again?

"God's grace is sufficient." Elaina whispered the words that Sadie had said with such confidence on their trek north. She thought of her sweet friend and wondered what had become of her. Had Sadie reached the city before the army's attack had begun? And how did one obtain the grace that she had spoken of?

Elaina gave a weary sigh. So many questions. Where were the answers?

She fell into a fitful sleep that gradually grew deeper as weariness overtook the restless activity of her mind. It was near midnight when a noise across the moonlit room woke her with a start. Soft at first, a sound like stone-against-stone escalated until it came to a sudden stop. Elaina remained frozen in terror. Whatever the noise had been, it had come from beyond the far wall—the city's outer wall—where Mount Desterrar sheltered a multitude of wild beasts.

The noise came again and Elaina stifled a squeal as she threw the cloak over her head. It sounded as if something or someone was pulling stones from the outside of the wall, working their way into the very room where she had taken shelter! Could it be members of the invading army? Or was it a pack of catawylds?

The grating noise began again, sounding closer. They had reached the wall's inner layer of stones.

Elaina peeked from beneath the cloak and her wild gaze fell on the hilt of a sword, half-hidden behind a stack of folded materials in the corner. A determined glint lit her eye. Having done so much for her earlier in the evening, the dear mercer was probably sound asleep in his upper room and unaware of the danger that threatened his shop. In return for his kindness, she would do her best to stop this invasion…or at least slow it down.

Setting her jaw, Elaina sat up and promptly bumped the underside of the table with her head. Hissing against the pain, she crawled from her makeshift tent and scrambled across the room. In the moon's silver light, she could just make out the place where one stone was sliding from its place near the base of the outer wall. Keeping silent, Elaina shrouded herself in the mercer's dark cloak, lifted the hood over her head, and then slowly reached to grasp the hilt of the hidden weapon.

The large stone was at last freed from its proper place, revealing a space as black as pitch behind it. Elaina swallowed, waiting, as a second stone began to move directly beside the first. What felt like hours passed as the second stone was released and the outer stones were pulled back into place from within. The sound of the shifting wall grated like sand on Elaina's ears until finally it ceased altogether. Whatever had entered, it had closed itself inside.

A moment of silence followed, and then Elaina saw a figure slip from the dark space in the wall. The shadowy form of a man straightened and seemed to scan the room, and Elaina felt her instincts take over.

With a stealth learned in the corridors of her father's palace and honed by Leo's tutelage, Elaina crossed the room and swung her sword at the intruder. At the last second, the man whirled and dropped from the path of her blade. His startled cry was echoed by a comrade still hidden within the crevice, and Elaina retreated a step to assess the altered situation. Two against one.

The first man somehow managed to regain his feet with a deadly arrow already fitted to his taut bowstring. He hissed in Mizgalian and Elaina was certain of two things. She had just been threatened, and the intruder was young. Perhaps "young" meant he was as inexperienced as she in the art of combat. With a sudden deft movement, Elaina delivered a low lunge and swept her sword in a wide arc toward the archer's legs. With a quick jump the man easily avoided the blow, but failed to release his arrow.

Behind her, Elaina heard the second intruder crawl into the room. She whirled when her ear caught the faint sound of steel slicing air, and her sword met that of her newest opponent in a fascinating clash. Determination on both sides produced several more exchanges before Elaina whirled and ducked away from the fight, catching a moment's breath before the next bout began.

Out of the corner of her eye, Elaina saw the archer readying his stance and she quickly maneuvered so that his cohort stood between her and the arrow that he so desperately wanted to release. Returning her focus to the second man, she successfully parried several blows and offered an offensive of her own.

Suddenly, her opponent delivered a rapid combination that took all of Elaina's concentration to survive. Step by step she was backed into a corner, until finally their swords locked at the cross-guards and Elaina knew she was done for.

The image flashed. The memory assailed. The loss of the picture's happy ending crushed her. When had her father ceased the old habit of tapping the end of her nose? Didn't he know it was the only sign of affection that had ever been constant in her life?

With a shattered cry, Elaina faltered and her opponent slapped the sword from her grasp. He shoved her against the wall with an arm to her collarbone and lifted his blade at a threatening angle, aimed at her heart.

There's no need, sir, Elaina thought, but couldn't speak the words aloud, *my heart is already broken.*

"Bradley, wait!" Luke barked the low command in the sudden quiet of the fight's aftermath. Breathing heavily, he shouldered his bow and replaced the arrow. His heart raced with adrenaline and fear as he wondered over the reason for this surprise attack. Had something happened to Liam? Had the mercer been forced to give up his shop?

Luke reached for a shelf near the ceiling, where he remembered a stash of candles had always been kept. At first he had been sure they faced a Mordecai, planted in Liam's shop to await their return, but then Bradley had backed the attacker into the corner and the cloaked individual had given a cry of defeat.

A feminine cry.

Luke used flint and steel to light the wick and then turned to hold the candle high. The flame cut a soft sphere from the darkness and shifted over the room's two other occupants. Luke stepped nearer and pushed the stranger's hood back, revealing the pretty face of a young woman. Bradley quickly retreated from his defensive position and stood gaping alongside Luke. The three stood staring at one another in shock, their labored breathing and pounding hearts slowly returning to normal, until Bradley broke the silence.

"By my quaking nerves, what is this?"

Luke remained silent, confronted by a gaze that was almost unreadable for the many facets that swirled within. This was a soul in torment.

"If this is Liam's idea of a jest, I'm going to have to explain to him the difference between our definitions of the word." Bradley was clearly shaken, "I might have killed the girl!" He shook his head at her, "Why didn't you say something? Who are you? Why are you here?"

Her eyes clouded with confusion and Luke's brow furrowed, "She doesn't understand you, Bradley."

"What do you mean, she doesn't understand me? Is she mute?"

"Being mute means you can't speak."

"Is she deaf?"

The candlelight caught the edge of a garment hanging nearby, and Luke shifted to study the apparel. The dark blue gown and vest of red leather had been stitched and fashioned in a foreign style. Luke blinked in disbelief as the puzzle came together. Master Paul's advice to be prepared for anything rang in his ears. Could it be? He turned back to study the young woman over Bradley's head as the nobleman rambled on about the fright she had given him.

"I've not been so startled since the day my eldest son attempted to take flight from the lookout rock!"

Even when terrified by a frenzied redhead, the lines of her face showed a familiarity with fierceness. Her dark eyes were intense as they watched Bradley pace, occasionally darting to the spot where her sword had landed by the wall. Her hand lifted to brush nearly-black hair from her eyes; an impatient movement that suggested she was unaccustomed to the short length. Luke frowned when the cloak slid from her wrist to reveal a patch of raw skin.

He had opened his mouth to speak when another light illuminated the doorway behind him and he turned to see Liam entering with a look of surprise and pleasure on his face.

"I thought I heard *th*omething. Welcome, welcome! Thi*th* day ha*th* been long in coming. It i*th* good that the hole in the wall wa*th* made bigger, for you both have grown!" He came forward with outstretched arms and then paused when his gaze fell on the girl in the corner, "Oh! I did not think… I forgot… I*th* everyone all right?" He turned to Luke and explained how the stranger had come to be there, "The poor girl doe*th* not *th*peak our language, and would have been at the mer*th*y of the *th*treet*th*."

Luke nodded. He took a step toward the young woman and addressed her in what he hoped was her native tongue, "You are Arcrean? A slave?"

At the sound of the familiar words, a shock of recognition flashed through her eyes, "Arcrean, yes. A slave, no."

The challenge in her tone told him she *had* been one. Luke's brow quirked with amusement, "You don't have to be afraid. My friend and I will cause you no harm."

"That's a relief." Her eyes bounced to Bradley and back, flaring with suspicion, "From the sound of his greeting, the mercer obviously knows you. May I ask why he entertains guests at midnight, and why they don't use the door like normal people?"

"You may ask," Luke shrugged, "but that doesn't mean I'll

give you an answer."

Her eyes narrowed and she muttered something about "more questions" just as Bradley appeared beside Luke.

"What's being said, friend? My skills in Arcrean are terribly rusty. Am I missing anything important?"

"She's an escaped Arcrean slave taking shelter with Liam."

"Oh is that all? Is she one of us?" Bradley directed the latter question to Liam and the mercer shrugged helplessly.

Luke waved the nobleman away, "Ask Liam about the remnant. I'll see if there's anything we can do to help her." He shifted his attention back to the girl, "What's your name?"

"Elaina, if you must know. What's yours?"

He grinned at her attempt to pry information from him, "Luke. Is there anything my friends and I can do to help you?"

Several responses leapt to her mind, causing Elaina to pause. Here was someone who, miraculously, spoke Arcrean passably well and who was offering to help her. Which of her many problems was most urgent? Requests tumbled through her head, trying to form themselves into words, until one finally left her mouth.

"Can you get me back to Arcrea?"

"No," Luke crossed his arms, "but I might be able to get you out of Hebbros."

Elaina glared at his refusal, "I need to go home."

Was the woman insane? "Ordinary people don't just uproot themselves to travel kingdom-to-kingdom."

"I'm not ordinary."

"I can see that."

"So find a way to get me home."

"Sorry, I've already been assigned to another mission for the time being." Luke lifted one shoulder, trying to state the truth as gently as possible, "Most slaves who manage to escape make a life for themselves near the region where they were set free. Extensive travel is hard, dangerous, and costly, and quite frankly no one has time for it. It's quite probable you'll never see your homeland again."

Sudden tears pricked her eyes, but she quickly blinked them away and ground out the words, "I. Have. To."

"Why?" The question was out before Luke could call it back—the urge to draw out the puzzling components he was reading to examine their deeper meaning. He couldn't remember the last time he'd read a gaze that held so many compelling dynamics, and his impulsive nature was urging him to solve the mystery of this Arcrean.

Elaina crossed her arms defiantly and shifted her gaze to where Liam and Bradley stood talking across the room.

Luke asked again, "Why is returning to Arcrea so important to you?"

"I…" Her gaze darted about, searching for an answer, and finally touched briefly on the red vest. The words slipped easily off of her tongue, "There's a young man waiting for me."

"No, there isn't."

Her jaw dropped, "Are you calling me a liar?"

"Yes."

"How dare you! I have never before been treated with such disregard," she moved close enough to wave a finger in his face, "and I'll have you know I've experienced plenty of social disrespect during the last few weeks. Your example has surpassed all the others."

Her speech had shifted to include the practiced hauteur of the nobles and Luke figured he was dealing with a lady of some sort. He decided to ignore this fact, as her Arcrean status would do nothing for her here in Mizgalia, and instead returned to the issue in question.

"You and I both know that whoever the vest reminded you of is not waiting for you, and neither are they the reason you wish to return."

Elaina gave three quick blinks and then scowled, "I'm Arcrean! Great goose eggs, why wouldn't I wish to return to my home? Why would I want to stay here, among my enemies, for the rest of my life? I had a life. I have family…"

"Family! Now we're getting somewhere." Luke leaned his shoulder against the wall, "You have regrets that need to be dealt with. You don't really want to go home as much as you want your problems to be solved. Am I right?"

She took a step back, startled, and then turned away, "Leave me alone. You're an unfeeling young man who is far too nosy for anyone's good." She crossed her arms, "I'll go to the docks tomorrow and find passage on a southbound ship. Now, if you'll excuse me and return to whatever mischief brought you crawling through the wall, I should get some sleep."

Luke's brow pinched as he read the sorrow and confusion that could not be hidden by her façade of annoyance. A gentle pressure on his heart compelled him to humble himself, and he sighed, "I'm sorry I pressed you." She paused in her retreat but did not turn to face him, "I've always attacked problems head-on, and my brother isn't here to stop me. I'm still recovering from the surprise of your attack, and I'm sure you're still shocked by our sudden appearance in your place of safety. Forgive me for speaking out of turn."

Elaina remained silent. Luke glanced over his shoulder and found the others watching with curious expressions. The very air seemed to be holding its breath, waiting for something. But what?

Luke sighed. He had come to Hebbros to rally the remnant and remove them from danger. It was not encouraging that his first encounter had been with a foreigner who longed for him to perform the impossible. Like Bradley, Elaina spouted what she believed she wanted, thinking that returning to Arcrea would fill the void in her heart. She couldn't see the deeper issue.

Or else she was afraid to address it.

"Elaina," Luke's voice ventured into the stillness, "returning to your home won't bring you the peace you seek."

She turned then, fear and hope warring in her eyes. She waited for him to continue, and Luke was suddenly faced with the realization of why God had called him to return on the night this foreigner had taken refuge in Liam's shop. Whether or not any Faithful awaited him elsewhere in the city, here was one soul searching for the mercy of God. Here was a remnant.

Luke straightened away from the wall and met the young woman's gaze intently, hoping she would understand the great importance of his next words.

"Have you ever been introduced to Jesus?"

Elaina trembled at the name and then shook with a sob. Covering her face with her hands, she fell to her knees and crumpled into a tearful heap on the floor.

Luke's eyes widened and he watched, uncertain what he should do, as glistening tears dripped into the plush rug that carpeted the hard-packed floor. He tossed a helpless glance over his shoulder and found the other two men in a similar state of indecision. Luke glared at Bradley. The man was married, for pity's sake! He should know what to do when a woman cried.

Taking a lone step forward, Luke crouched down and

stretched out his hand, uncertain whether she would accept the comfort of a friend or if he should not offer it at all.

Inexplicable joy coursed through Elaina. God had heard her cry! Not only had He provided for her safety and comfort, He had sent an Arcrean-speaking believer in Christ at the moment she realized her soul needed cleansing and redemption. Such events were too great to be mere coincidence. They had to be the fingerprints of God upon her shattered life. Truly, He was King over all things.

Still weeping uncontrollably, Elaina raised herself from the floor enough to clutch Luke's outstretched fingers in desperation. "I've lost everything! My home, my wealth, my freedom, and even my hair, have all been taken away." Speaking the words aloud lifted a burden from her aching heart, and she saw compassion in Luke's eyes as he listened and then responded.

"Sometimes God takes us down to nothing so that He can give us all we need. Often we try to hold on to everything anyway, creating idols that mean more to us than God does. We don't realize that our grip is actually crushing the things we love. Our stubbornness does more damage than good."

Elaina sniffed and wiped away a pair of tears, "But why did it have to happen this way? Why didn't God just send someone to tell me while I was still in Arcrea?"

"Would you have listened?"

Elaina thought of how she had erected a wall of bitterness and hatred to surround her life in Balgo, refusing to receive any sort of goodness, pity, or charity. Only when she had been frightened by the prospect of slavery, and humbled by Sadie's kindness, had she allowed a glimmer of the truth in.

"No," she shook her head, "I would not have listened."

"God knew that," Luke helped Elaina to stand. "He also knows what you need to fill the emptiness in your heart."

Elaina was silent for a moment as another round of tears begged for release. The emptiness in her heart. The longing for peace, fulfillment, purpose, love, and forgiveness. She had endured the vacant space for so long, it had eventually become like a natural part of her being. And now she saw that only one thing could satisfy it.

She glanced at the mercer and the man called Bradley, and then returned her gaze to the one who could understand her foreign speech. "Tell me, please," she spoke with a sob, "how to receive the grace of God."

53
Lord Bradley

Into the gray hours of morning, Luke listened closely while Liam told of eleven years filled with secrecy and near-discoveries. On several occasions, the mercer had been certain the Mordecais were coming to arrest him, only to be pleasantly surprised when days would pass with no hint that his connection to the Faithful had been found out. Luke was instantly suspicious that perhaps Liam had been spared for a purpose. He glanced across the table where he sat with the mercer and Bradley, and met the nobleman's wary gaze. Bradley gave a slight nod of agreement before Luke addressed Liam once more.

"We must work quickly before our return is discovered by the wrong people. I mean to spend the day locating children of the exiled and seeing whether they are open to the truth. With the city under siege, we should leave at midnight tonight. How many Faithful are in the city to begin with?"

Liam's brows drew together and then unfolded in an attempt to appear hopeful, but Luke read his gaze and his heart froze in dread, "Are there *any* Faithful in the city?"

"Ye*th*," Liam answered quickly and then sighed, "but only a very few, and they are afraid to let their faith be known."

Luke unconsciously ran his finger along a groove in the table's surface. His mind raced along a path of confusion and despair, "But I prayed for a remnant."

Bradley leaned back in his chair, "Luke, 'a few' *is* a remnant."

"I know, but—"

"Perhap*th* God *th*ent you to gather them together, not merely lead them out." Liam spoke softly, with a glance to the back room where Elaina had fallen into a peaceful sleep.

When Luke did not reply, Bradley spoke again, "Did you expect to return to an utterly reformed city?" He shook his head in answer to his own question, "The evil of this place is not just a hobby, it's a lifestyle. The people are not only ignorant of a better way to live, they don't *want* to know. Now the roots of wickedness have dug too deep to be pulled up without great damage. They would not hear the reasoning of good men like Sedgwick and yourself, so now they must answer to God."

Luke blinked and stared at Bradley in disbelief, and the young lord dipped his head sheepishly, "Terribly hypocritical, is it not? Coming from someone who has exhibited the same stubbornness while living in the very midst of your people."

Bradley's eyes studied the flat surface before him, darting corner to corner, and his two companions waited in silence, sensing that he had more to say.

"On our trek down the mountain, I began to think of what awaited us in Hebbros. I knew your plans were to lead out a remnant, and that I was hoping to see my sister, but more than that I knew that what Sarah told me was right." He looked up at Luke, "There are some things that need to be resolved. Bonds that tie me to Hebbros, from which I must be released. The thought occurred to me that, though I may see this truth, deep down I'm not willing or able to do this thing. I've harbored a bitterness in my soul until it has consumed my every thought and dream." He shook his head as anguish warred in his indigo eyes, turning them black, "Even if the desire for revenge no longer burns inside me as it used to, I can't let go of something that I've spent a lifetime nurturing and protecting."

Liam reached out to place a gentle hand on Bradley's, "*Th*uch an act cannot be done apart from God."

Bradley nodded, and then cradled his head in his hands, "That same thought was impressed upon me as Luke and I descended Desterrar, but I argued."

Luke propped his elbow on the table, listening carefully. Bradley stood and began to pace as he continued to speak.

"I argued that if God had truly wanted me to follow Him, and to surrender these faults in my life, then He should have granted those three requests long ago." He glanced at Luke and saw him nod, "You remember them. I said I wanted my home, my inheritance, and my father, but you knew differently and told me as much. God knew too, for as I struggled He spoke to my heart and said that if I had truly wanted those things, I would have seen that He…" Bradley found his chair again and shook with a soul-deep sob, "He has already granted my requests!"

Luke remained motionless as tears filled his own eyes and guilt pricked his heart. How could he have been so focused on himself that he had failed to notice Bradley's turmoil over the last two days?

Bradley looked up, "It became so clear to me. I said I wanted my home, thinking of Villenfeld, but what I truly desired was a place where I belonged. For eleven years I have lived in a place of peace, surrounded by people who have shown me grace and kindness. I belong in Exile."

"Second," a light slowly beginning to shine in his eyes as his excitement mounted, "I said I wanted my inheritance, but what I truly desired was the purpose and standing that comes with wealth. God gave me the equivalent of these when he blessed me with a wife and children, and a promise of the ultimate inheritance if only I accept His gift of salvation."

"Third," Bradley paused, "I wanted my father. What I truly desired was someone to fill the void caused by his death. I needed a man whom I could look up to and respect, whose example I could follow with a clear conscience." He glanced at Luke, "Your father, Sedgwick, so many men in Exile have been this and more. They have prayed for me, taught me, and lived a life in accordance to the lessons they gave." Bradley splayed his hands across the table, "You told me that night, when we met, that you would pray for me. That God would provide these things in such a way…"

"…That you could no longer deny His existence," Luke finished for him.

Bradley nodded, "He has done that. When I came to realize this yesterday, I saw that I had been faced with these truths for many years, but I was afraid. What if I could not let go of my past?

What if I made a decision to follow Christ and then failed Him when the time came to forgive and forget?" He sighed, "Seeing Elaina's burden lifted last night helped me to see that God is able to save any soul. She told you her story, how she plotted to kill the man who became Arcrea's king, and yet she was able to move beyond this when the grace of God was poured into her heart."

"What are you saying, Bradley?"

"Luke, I want my first day back in Hebbros to be my first day spent for Christ. Whether I see my sister or not, I want to know that I harbor no ill feelings toward her or her husband. It's high time I let go of the chains that bind me to Hebbros, and lay hold on the lifeline of God instead."

During the next moments Bradley wept a prayer of repentance and humility. Luke wiped his sleeve across his eyes more than once, overwhelmed by this answer to the prayers of many and feeling his own faith grow as he witnessed the foundation of another's being built. When Bradley had finished, the others lifted their heads and offered the nobleman heartfelt congratulations.

"I say," he leaned back with a sigh, "I should have done that ages ago. Why is it, do you think, pride never looks so grotesque until you've learned the lesson of humility?" He smiled at nothing in particular, "I feel such…relief." A spark of determination suddenly appeared in his eyes, "I need to speak with Roland while we're here."

"Bradley, that's madness! You know what will happen if you let our presence in the city be known to the man who threatened us not to return. Roland will have us killed before we can rescue the remnant."

"There are things which need to be said. By me. I'll wait until you and the others are prepared to leave in the case something should go wrong, but it must be done." Bradley's eyes begged for understanding, and his voice dropped with raw emotion, "I need to speak with Roland."

"Roland?" A feminine voice pulled their gazes to the doorway of the back room. Restored to her own garments of darkest-blue and red, Elaina stood on the threshold and stared at them with wide eyes. Her face showed surprise, and when she looked at Luke he read a measure of intensity that was borne of purpose.

"Good morning, child." Liam waved, hoping she would

understand the gesture if not the words.

Elaina stepped forward and looked at Bradley, repeating Roland's name with a note of inquiry and then adding a string of words in her native tongue.

"Ahh…" Bradley looked to Luke, at a loss, "I really must refresh my Arcrean. The only thing I understood was 'Roland'."

Luke grinned, "She asked if you know the man."

"Does *she*?" Bradley turned a look of surprise to the young woman.

Luke looked up at Elaina and reminded his tongue to form the words in Arcrean, "Bradley's sister, Lady Rosalynn, is married to Lord Roland."

"*Lord* Roland?"

"He is the ruler of Hebbros." Luke studied her wide-eyed expression, "What is it? What's wrong?"

Startled by this connection to the plans she had overheard the day before, Elaina gathered her thoughts. "There is something you should know."

By midmorning the royal army had begun their second attack on the city of Hebbros. Catapults hurtled burdens of destruction, and attempts were made to scale the walls. Lord Roland's army succeeded in thwarting the worst of the assaults, but many homes were destroyed and streets became littered with the debris of entire rows of structures that had become heaps of stone, tile, and thatch.

The people grew nervous, wondering how long their defenses would be able to stand if Cronin's soldiers refused to give up. The priests posted themselves at constant vigil in the temples of their favorite gods, begging for relief. The citizens of Hebbros added prayers of their own, seeking an explanation for the terror that was upon them. But the idols remained silent. No answer was given at the altars of the sacred shrines.

"It looks like it's going to rain." Rosalynn sat on her divan, clutching Sadie's hand and listening to the noise of the siege outside. She swept a lock of red hair out of her face and tried to still her trembling fingers, "I always tell people that the palace is the safest place to be, however I believe I'm the one who most needs the reassurance."

Sadie smiled and gently squeezed the noblewoman's hand, "God will not let us perish, my lady, until it is our time to join Him in heaven."

"I'm so glad you speak Mizgalian," Rosalynn started when another catapult released its burden, "and your accent is charming. Were you born in Arcrea, or were you a slave there as well?"

"Born," Sadie lowered her head, "but I am content to be wherever the Lord can best use me for His glory."

Rosalynn met the young slave's gaze, "You are very strong for one so young."

"No, Lady Rosalynn. When I am weak, God is strong."

The lady nodded and looked away, "I must learn to exercise His strength. Day after day I think that I should tell my husband of my newfound faith in Christ, but my fear of his response overcomes my sense of urgency." She lifted a hand to her face, and pressed her fingers to her temples, "I know he will be angry, but my heart aches to think that my children will be trapped in this city when the remnant are taken out."

Sadie turned to look at her mistress, "Taken out?"

Rosalynn nodded, "The few Faithful in Hebbros speak of a promise that was made eleven years ago. One who was known as Luke the Terror swore that he would return to lead out any who remained and were willing." Her hand dropped back to her lap, "How could I flee to safety with my children, when my husband does not share my faith? And yet how can I intentionally remain, allowing my children to become the type of people I've learned to despise?"

Sadie was silent for a moment. She whispered a prayer for guidance and then laid a hand on Roslaynn's shoulder, "God will provide a way."

A knock sounded at the door and a slave entered, bowing low. "My lady, there is a merchant in the Great Hall who wishes to speak with you. He says he comes to settle your order of business with a local mercer."

Rosalynn appeared confused, "In the midst of a siege? Is the man insane? I have no unsettled business with a… A mercer?" She suddenly rose from her seat, pulling Sadie up with her, "I will see him directly. You may go."

Lady Rosalynn pulled Sadie from her chambers and through the palace corridors, hurrying along while trying to maintain a dignified speed. Outside, the sounds of conflict pounded over the city, a constant rumble that would not let her forget the peril they were in.

As they neared the entrance to the Great Hall, Rosalynn pulled her attendant closer and whispered as if afraid to be overheard, "The mercer from the western wall is of the Faithful. I dread to think what urgent news would bring him here in the midst of an assault." Composing herself and nodding once to a nearby guard, the noblewoman held her head erect as she pushed open the door and swept inside.

Sadie followed close behind and cast a quick glance around the deserted hall. The slaves had been put to work elsewhere, as the midday meal would not be served at the banquet tables during the siege. The massive hearth was void of its usual cheerful flame, leaving the rest of the room in a dismal pallor of doom-colored gray.

A man stood before the empty hearth, gazing at the cold stones. His apparel said that he was a merchant, but his bearing and stance suggested much more. As the door closed behind the two women, the man turned to face them and his eyes quickly rested on Lady Rosalynn. Already crossing the hall, Rosalynn suddenly gasped and froze in shock. She stared in disbelief as the man smiled and pulled the massive hat and a wig of curly gray hair from his head. He took several steps in their direction and then paused uncertainly when Rosalynn made no move.

"Rosalynn?"

She began to tremble and Sadie stepped nearer to take her hand, "My lady?"

Rosalynn's expression crumpled as her body doubled over and a cry escaped her lips. She quickly straightened and ran forward to embrace the man who had advanced to meet her. "You're alive! And you're here. I thought I'd never see you again." Rosalynn pulled back to smile up into his face, "What are you doing here? Where is Sarah?"

His smiled warmed at the mention of his wife, "Sarah remained in Exile with our four children. I came with Luke to gather the remnant," he took her hands, "and to see you. I heard only this morning that you have joined the Faithful. I was told just after I myself joined the faith."

Rosalynn quirked a brow, "It took you that long?"

Bradley looked sheepish, "Father always said I have a hard head." His gaze sharpened, "Is it true you have seven children? By my poorly-thatched roof, Rosalynn, that is a shock! A pleasant one, mind you, but a shock nonetheless." He smiled, "Someday our children will all play together. Yours will teach their cousins to be polite and gracious, and mine will teach yours to roll in the dirt and terrify everyone with their love of unthinkable heights."

Rosalynn laughed, set at ease by her brother's relaxed manner, "My youngest is three months old now." She lowered her head, "Her name is Sarah."

They were silent for a moment as Bradley lifted her chin and smiled down at her. When he spoke, his voice was low and filled with respect for the struggle such a decision must have cost her. "Sarah will be honored. As am I."

Rosalynn blinked back tears and turned to glance at her attendant, "Sadie, this is my brother, Lord Bradley."

Bradley tipped his head in greeting, "Just Bradley."

Rosalynn smiled knowingly, "The noble nobody." Suddenly, she stepped away and pulled him toward the door, "We must hide you! If Roland sees you, he'll be furious."

Bradley stopped and shook his head, "I want him to see me, Rosalynn."

"But…"

"There is something I must say to him, and also a warning I must deliver to you both."

The door suddenly opened and Roland himself strode into hall, followed by two guards. His gaze immediately found the group halfway between the door and the hearth, and he froze, forcing the two soldiers to halt with him. Shock and anger warred for dominance on the ruler's face as he stared at the man in merchant's garb.

"Roland." Bradley nodded a greeting.

Roland's eyes narrowed, "When I was told a merchant had dared to ask for an audience with my wife in the midst of a siege, I thought I would come and have him thrown out for his insolence." He advanced slowly, "Now, however, I believe I'll have him thrown in…to prison."

"Roland, no!" Rosalynn stepped between them. She opened her mouth to speak, but stopped when she glanced at a point beyond his shoulder, "Send the soldiers out. Please. For a moment."

Roland studied her warily, and then finally motioned with one hand for the guards to leave, "Just outside the door. And tell no one," he growled, "what you've seen here."

The sound of the door closing echoed in the empty hall. Sadie shrank back, feeling out of place, as Roland settled a venomous glare on his wife's brother. Lord Bradley seemed unaffected by the show of hostility, and took a step forward.

"It's good to see you, too, Roland."

"Enough of that," Roland's hand sliced the air in a warning. Bradley stood still as the lord of Hebbros thrust a condemning finger into the space that separated them, "I want to know what you're doing here, and why you dared defy my order to never come back."

Bradley inhaled deeply, breathing a prayer for strength as he met Roland's irate gaze.

Yesterday, this moment would have been impossible.

"First," Bradley heard himself speak, "I'm here to say…I'm sorry."

Roland's face was a mask of confusion as he stared at Bradley for a long moment. Rosalynn's jaw went slack, and she quickly covered her mouth with one hand. Sadie remained a silent witness, standing uncertainly in the background.

Roland's brow finally twitched and his expression turned incredulous. He must have misunderstood. "What?"

"I'm sorry," Bradley repeated. "As my brother, my ruler, and especially as my guardian, I should have treated you with more respect. I did not have to agree with you in every matter, but I should have responded with humility and," he swallowed, "love."

Roland jolted as if he had been struck. The confusion and anger had been drained from his face, replaced by a look that resembled alarm. Bradley took a step closer.

"You opened your home to me when I had no other place to go. You provided for all of my physical needs. You even attempted to offer advice and guidance—" Bradley stopped short when he heard his own words and the truth washed over him. A home. Wealth. A father figure. The requests had been answered twofold. His chest heaved with emotion and he looked down, shaking his head over the willful blindness of his youth. Tears gathered in his eyes as he lifted his head and once again sought Roland's wide-eyed gaze. The younger man searched for the right words and then held his hands out in defeat. "I have been ungrateful all my life. Forgive me."

The last words were spoken in a whisper, yet they reached every ear.

No one moved.

Finally, Bradley gathered himself and took a deep breath, releasing it on a sigh, "I say, you have no idea how freeing that was. Now, as to the second order of business," he looked at Roland, still frozen with shock, "I did not come alone. Luke is also in the city, and is willing for you to know that he intends to seek out any Faithful who yet remain within the walls of Hebbros and lead them out to Exile."

Rosalynn gave a slight intake of breath that caught Roland's attention for only a moment before his eyes returned to Bradley. The younger lord was still speaking.

"We thought it right to warn you, Roland, that a plot is in motion to take your life tonight." His sister gasped louder this time, "With the city in chaos and treason flowing rampant through the streets, Luke said that I was to offer you our assistance. We are willing to give your wife and children shelter in the village of Exile until Hebbros is no longer at war. Luke also asks if you would allow him to aid in disrupting the plans of your would-be assassins."

As he listened, Roland's face grew slack and void of any emotion. Like a torrent of unexpected rain, Bradley's words pummeled him until he felt heavy and dysfunctional. He searched for the anger he had felt only moments ago, but could no longer produce even an ounce of wrath.

Shaking his head slightly, he interrupted whatever his brother-in-law was saying and asked in a tone that sought clarity, "You traveled down the mountain and into a city under siege to offer me an apology and spare my life?"

"I admit this was not our original intent, as I explained a moment ago. However, I believe it was God's intent all along. He has done marvelous things, including sparing us from a pack of catawylds on the journey down." Bradley grinned at the memory, "I was sure we were done for, but Luke proved his skills with the bow have mightily improved while I distracted the lot of ugly felines with my sword. You remember little Pavia? She keeps one for a pet."

Roland did not smile. With an absent expression he walked to the hearth and gripped the mantel with both hands until his knuckles turned white with his firm grip. He had sensed the threat to his life increasing with each passing day, and he had been helpless. Daily visits to the temple, begging the gods to spare his life and grant him wisdom to identify even one in Hebbros whom he could trust, had proven fruitless endeavors. Everywhere he went, he felt traitorous eyes on his back, watching his every move.

Now Bradley had returned. Changed. Humble. But was it a farce? No, Roland shook his head, everything about Bradley's speech and manner shouted that he was sincere. But how could Roland accept him now? He would be the ultimate traitor to his own laws if he admitted that the God whose name he had outlawed from Hebbros had been the one to answer his prayers. He would be laughed at as the world's greatest fool.

Roland exhaled slowly through his nostrils and forced his voice to remain low and controlled, "Get out."

No one moved. The atmosphere shifted on a wave of uncertainty, and so Roland shoved away from the hearth to set them straight with a shout that rang in his own ears.

"I said *get out*! All of you!" His venomous gaze shifted to his wife and he took a step in her direction, startling her into taking a step back, "Thanks to my spies, I am aware—and have been—of your decision to join the Faithful."

Rosalynn's shock increased and she found herself speechless. She shrank away as Roland continued to draw closer to where she stood, the insecurities of her past rising up to mock her as her husband spoke.

"If you wish to consort with the rebels, so be it." Roland's eyes narrowed, "But you will not do it within the safety of these walls."

Rosalynn gasped, "Roland, please! I was going to tell you—"

"But you didn't!" Roland's shriek caused the others to wince. He stared at Rosalynn and shook his head, "You're just like everyone else in this condemned city. I can't trust you."

"Roland, that's a lie," Bradley interjected.

Rosalynn's voice turned pleading, "You know I'd do anything for you."

"Except stay away from the Faithful." Roland grit his teeth,

"Get out, all of you, before I have the guards escort you."

"No!" Rosalynn caught his hand between hers and sobbed, "Your enemies are planning to kill you!"

"My enemies," Roland shook himself free of her grasp, "are those who willfully disobey me."

Rosalynn froze in shock. "Roland," his name escaped on a whisper before she added volume to her words, "what are you saying?"

He turned away from her, "I cannot trust the Faithful. I never have. Now you are one of them." His eyes shifted to meet hers, like shards of ice piercing her soul, "I want you to leave," he shifted to include Bradley, "and this time don't come back."

Another sob shook Rosalynn and she took a single step forward before suddenly turning and fleeing from the hall in tears. She raced through the corridors, intent on gathering her children to take to safety, even as she felt her heart breaking into pieces.

No matter how hard she had tried, she would never be good enough. Rosalynn clasped her hands over her aching heart, grimacing as bitter tears scalded her face. The one decision she had been so certain of, that had brought her such peace and joy, had been the undoing of their bond.

"Please, God," she stuttered between sobs, "cause him to give his life to you so that we might be restored to one another."

When Sadie finally caught up to her, Rosalynn had gathered her seven children and handed them their cloaks. Taking little Sarah from the babe's nurse, she quickly dismissed the puzzled slaves and turned to her companion. "Where is Bradley?"

"Waiting in the courtyard, my lady, in disguise again."

Rosalynn nodded, "We must hasten there and out of this place before Roland decides the children must stay. I'll not have them remain within these walls so long as danger is imminent."

Once in the courtyard, they found that Bradley had brought Liam's donkey cart as a part of his disguise. Placing the children in the back, with a warning to remain silent, they covered the space with a canvas tarp and were soon on their way through the gates and away from the palace.

Wedged between her brother and her slave on the seat of the cart, Rosalynn gazed up at the towering smoke from several burning buildings and listened as shouts and screams filled the air to the east. She turned to look at Bradley, "Tell me of this plot to take my husband's life."

Bradley summarized what Elaina had told them at the table in Liam's shop. When he had finished explaining the details as well as repeating Luke's desire to help, Rosalynn nodded.

"There must be something that can be done, but how? According to Roland, there is no guarantee that anyone in Hebbros is trustworthy. How can we find someone and be ready by nightfall?"

"My lady," Sadie touched a gentle hand to her arm, "I know someone you can trust."

Roland watched from a window in his west turret as Rosalynn took the children and departed from the palace with Bradley. He still could not overcome his shock at seeing his brother-in-law once again in the Great Hall. As if nothing had ever changed.

Roland turned from the window and shook his head. Everything had changed.

He couldn't say what had possessed him to send his dear Rosalynn away, but he wondered if it had anything to do with knowing she would take the children with her. He wanted them to go to safety, but could not sacrifice his pride to accomplish such a feat. Let her think that he hated her. Perhaps it would be for the best.

Roland supported one elbow with the other arm and pinched the bridge of his nose, "I suddenly find myself without allies in a city that has so quickly turned against me."

Looking up, he stared absently at his parchment-littered table. So many plans, so many possibilities, but what were they worth when those who must carry out his orders were already planning to stab him in the back?

Roland sank into his chair, a sense of defeat washing over him, "I feel as if I've raised a child to bring me honor, only to discover I have trained my greatest enemy."

54

The Fueller's Plight

Luke led Elaina through the maze of streets that had formed the backdrop of his younger years. Heading north, he did his best to steer them clear of the regions where flying debris and burning structures had become a common threat.

The people of Hebbros scurried through the streets with their heads down. Only occasionally did Luke catch a glimpse of the hostility and rebellion that lurked within each gaze. They believed they were in the right, and that Cronin's army should be crushed for dealing harshly with the massive sin-sick city.

Luke's eyes swept the scene of dust-brown and hopeless-gray. He took note of the city's latest fashions, a depressing blend of black and gray, and then glanced over his shoulder to ensure that Elaina was following close behind. He faced forward again, a grin pulling at his lips as he shook his head, "Why on earth are you wearing such an outlandish color?"

Elaina huffed as she raced to match his long-legged stride. Their fast pace was making her hair billow out like a pair of wings, "Red is not outlandish."

"In a city that's doing it's best to blend into the shadows it is."

"Well then, perhaps I prefer outlandish to drab," she glanced at his own apparel of brown and washed-out green.

Luke quirked his brow, "And I prefer stealth to standing out like a beacon."

"Your wrist guards are red."

"My wrist guards are very faded red," Luke slanted her a telling glance. "In fact, they're almost brown."

"They don't look like normal wrists guards."

"They were made from a collar."

"You mean like a slave's collar? Was it yours?"

"Possibly."

"It was," Elaina decided. "Where did you learn to speak Arcrean so well?"

"The city-appointed schoolrooms. I speak it well because I have a good memory and remember what I learned."

"Where are we going?"

Luke took a deep breath and nearly choked on the gritty air, "Do you always ask so many questions?"

"Only when I want the answers. Do you always set out without a plan?"

"Only when I want the adventure."

"And how often is that?"

"Always," Luke's grin broadened.

She sent him a rueful glare, "I hate not having a plan."

Elaina fell silent for several minutes. Occasionally she released a heavy sigh that Luke was certain did not result from the excursion of walking. Luke kept his eyes on the thoroughfares ahead, straining to keep a laugh in check. Eventually she would voice whatever was bothering her, but he was in no hurry to invite more questions. He could wait.

Elaina tried to focus on taking the next step and keeping up with Luke's longer stride. The burdens that had weighed on her heart no longer condemned her, and she was finally at peace with God. She had decided to pray for an opportunity to someday ask forgiveness of her father and mother, but until that day she would enter wholeheartedly into the work of the Faithful in Hebbros.

She was relieved beyond expression to have found someone who spoke her language. She had been reluctant to stay with Liam all day, in the company of someone who was unable to converse freely with her, and was grateful that Luke had allowed her to accompany him for that reason.

Nevertheless, he was driving her mad. She gave another gusty sigh and tapped her fingers against the skirt of her dress, "I very much dislike feeling unprepared."

Luke's brows shot upward at her well-bred speech, "Unprepared for what?"

"Exactly my point! We can't be prepared for what we're headed for, because we don't know where we're headed to."

"Nonsense. Liam let you hide his sword beneath your cloak, and I've got my bow. You can rest assured knowing that we are well-armed and both quite capable with our weapons of choice."

"You see, that's what concerns me. I'm supposed to be grateful for the fact we are both armed?"

"No," Luke held one finger aloft as he pointed out, "you're supposed to be grateful that we are prepared."

Before she could respond, he took her arm and turned them onto a broad lane. Elaina exhaled, blowing hair out of her face, and pulled her elbow from his grasp, "I pity the woman who raised you."

"She pities anyone who has to deal with how she raised me." She sent him a scowl and he laughed, "Don't worry, I know where we're going."

"But you just said—"

"That we're prepared."

"You told me—"

"Not to worry. I didn't say anything about where we're going."

"I… You…" her eyes glazed over in thought, and he could tell she was trying to retrace the steps of their conversation in order to prove him wrong. He would spare her the headache. And the disappointment.

"Where did you live in Arcrea?"

She blinked. "Balgo, a village in the region of Ranulf. All of the former lords were sent to live there when Druet was crowned king."

"Was it your mother or your father you most wished to return to?"

"Both. Particularly my father." Elaina shifted her gaze to the road ahead, "We've grown apart these last few years. I fear I've lost his love, but it's my own fault."

"A father doesn't stop loving his child." Luke glanced at the scattering of people on the street, all of whom made this heartless city their home, "Denial of such love is only fear that they will not love enough."

Elaina's brow creased, "But he no longer shows the signs of his affection. It's as if he forgot I existed in the midst of his sorrow."

Luke paused after they turned into a narrow lane, and looked down at her, "People show their love in different ways at different times. A change in your father's circumstances may have altered the way he sees life. If his entire perspective has changed, that will include the way he thinks of affection and how he chooses to show it."

Elaina's mind raced back to the image of herself as a child. She danced the sword reel with her father and their swords locked at the cross-guards. An impish grin stole across her face and Lord Frederick tapped the end of her nose. His love for her was evident in his tender gaze.

Elaina turned to follow Luke up the lane as her thoughts sped forward to more recent years.

In Balgo, Frederick had dedicated himself to learning the work of an artillator. His hands had grown bloody and calloused as he crafted weaponry in the effort to support his wife and daughter. He had returned to their cottage at the end of each day, choosing to sit by his own fire instead of gathering with friends to commiserate over their fallen lot. Her father had done his best to create a happy life in their new world. He had moved on when she would not, and her mother had been trapped between their conflicting desires to live in the past and forge a new future.

"So," Luke's voice drew her from her reminiscing, "was it your father who gave you the red vest?"

"No," Elaina glanced down and fingered the soft leather, trying to refocus her thoughts. "It was from…a friend. Sort of."

Luke glanced at her over his shoulder and then faced forward again as a commotion erupted in the square ahead. Rushing forward, they halted at the end of the narrow lane and studied the scene of chaos before them.

In the entrance of a fueller's booth across the square, a young man of lean build brandished a staff as five brutes attempted to force their way into his stand. The scowling rogues each flaunted a weapon of their own, from daggers to clubs, and it was clear they would hesitate at nothing to gain their objective. The young fueller was in a fight for his life.

"You want wood or coal, you pay for it!" The young man swung his staff at a man who ventured too close.

The brigand growled, "Times be hard, boy, and I'll not pay those prices."

"'Times be hard' is right," the fueller barked. "I'll not let the fuel go for no price at all."

"'Tisn't letting it go if we take it, now is it?"

"Stand down, lad, or we'll run ye through!"

"Back away!"

The few stands that were open around the square held a scant offering of standard supplies. The merchants who ran the booths had backed away in fear, their jumbled carts obviously ransacked by the fiends who now threatened the fueller.

"Luke, what are they saying?" Elaina tugged at his sleeve.

Distracted, Luke pulled his bow from his shoulder, "For pitiful sake, it's wood and coal."

Elaina cast a glance his way, "Pitiful sake? I don't think that's a—"

"We've found our man." Luke drew an arrow as he continued to survey the scene, "Ready your sword and stand by that crate of apples. Wait for my signal."

"Signal? Signal for what?"

The arrow fit itself to his bowstring like the action was second nature. "We're going to defend the square."

Elaina stared at Luke as if he'd lost his mind, "The square? The city's entire eastern border is being harassed by an army, and you want to defend one small square?"

"All right, we'll *take* the square. Does that sound better?" Luke's eyes were glued to the scene across the way, "I need to talk to the fueller, but I can't very well engage him in a friendly chat while his life is being threatened by a bunch of thieves, now can I? Now stand by the crate and make ready."

Bewildered, Elaina moved behind a merchant's stand to position herself by the crate of yellow apples. She pushed her cloak over her shoulders and drew her sword, listening to the foreign shouts of the five brutes.

"Luke, we need a plan."

The fueller bellowed as his staff beat the air in a threatening circle over his head. The thieves continued to snarl and snap like a pack of angry catawylds. Her companion pulled his bowstring taut and Elaina saw the cowering merchants rush from the square, fearful for their lives enough that they would desert whatever goods had been left in their stalls.

Elaina rolled her eyes and adjusted her hold on the sword's grip, "Luke?"

Luke eyed the shot, his gaze as steady as his powerfully trained arms, and then his eyes met hers for a brief moment and a grin split his face, "This'll be fun."

In an instant the arrow had zipped across the square and struck the beam over the booth's entrance, picking up a brute's hat along the way and dangling the cap from its slender shaft. Six heads turned to search for the newcomer, and six men immediately ducked for cover as a volley of arrows followed the first. Two brigands found their capes pinned to the fueller's stall, while another man lost his bag of stolen wares to a flying dart. The two thieves who were not otherwise distracted quickly jumped to their feet, and together with the man not pinned to the fueller's lintel they lunged toward Luke, daggers poised.

In what felt like an eternity, but must have only a few seconds, the young archer watched their swift advance and reached for another arrow. Habitually, he spoke in Mizgalian, "Get ready, Elaina…"

Petrified that she had only understood her name, the young woman's eyes widened, "What do I do?!?"

Luke fit the arrow to the string, oblivious to the reason for her panic as his own tension mounted with her lack of action, "Apples, use the apples—Elaina, the apples!"

Apples. Elaina heard the word three times and remembered the crate at her feet. Dropping the sword beside her, she hefted the crate with both hands.

In the next moment the three rushing brigands cried out as a wave of golden fruit attacked their flank and suddenly they were flat on their backs, having tripped over a number of apples that rolled underfoot. With another flash of motion and three solid whacks, the bloodthirsty fiends were rendered unconscious and the fueller stood just beyond them with his staff balanced in both hands.

In the silence that followed, Luke stood over the prone three with his bow at the ready. He glanced at an apple as it rolled by,

"Well, to be honest, that wasn't what I had expected. But it was magnificent, whatever it was."

Elaina appeared at his side with her sword in hand, grateful that he had remembered to use Arcrean this time. She pushed her fingers through her cropped mop and blew one stubborn strand off of her nose, "What do you need me to do now?"

Luke glanced up and saw that the two fellows he had pinned to the stall beams were also unconscious. His eyes shifted once more and met the surprised gaze of the fueller.

"Great turnips, are you Arcreans?"

The words slammed against Luke's senses, stirring a painful memory and confirming what he had known since they had come upon the square. He studied the many emotions and traits that lurked in the eyes of the young merchant, and willed away the emotions that sought to overwhelm him. How often he had stood on the lookout rock, pleading for one more chance to rescue the little boy in the upper window.

Please, God, soften his heart.

Clouds began to cover the sky, draping the square in shadows. Luke hesitated. What if he said no? Clearing his throat and glancing once at the prone thieves, Luke reverted to his native tongue, "Joel. There's not much time. I'm here to lead you out to Exile if you're willing to go."

The young fueller's eyes grew round and then narrowed as he peered closer, "Luke?"

His answer was a quick nod.

Joel suddenly reared back, eyes and mouth wide as he gave a single whoop and then laughed loudly. He moved forward again and clapped Luke on the shoulder, "About time you came back, brother! Let's go."

Without even a backward glance for the booth he had nearly given his life to protect, Joel marched past Luke and started back the way they had come.

Elaina stepped closer, "What did I miss? Did he just call you brother?"

Luke stood in dumbfounded silence, unable to comprehend how simple it had been this time. He had seen hope and determination and an element of goodness when he read Joel's gaze, but had not expected such eager reception.

"Coming?" Joel called out from the other end of the narrow

lane.

Elaina tugged on Luke's sleeve and they moved after him. Luke replaced his bow and shook his head to clear his thoughts, managing to smile at his old friend as they approached the spot where he waited, "I can't tell you how glad I am, Joel."

The younger man shook his head in wonder, "Nor I. I can't believe I didn't recognize you." He brushed at his brown hair with one hand and then turned to look at Elaina, "Is this your wife?"

"Friend. Sort of." Luke scratched the back of neck, relieved beyond words to know Elaina couldn't understand what they were saying. "She attacked Bradley and I when we entered through the wall, and afterwards joined the faith. She's Arcrean."

Joel scratched his own head, "I see."

Clearly, he didn't.

Elaina appeared even more confused than Joel.

Shrugging, the fueller turned back to Elaina and employed his best grin, "How do you ask for someone's name in Arcrean?"

Luke crossed his arms, "Elaina."

Elaina glanced up when Luke said her name firmly, and then frowned in confusion when Joel repeated it as a question.

Luke rolled his eyes at the misunderstanding, "That wasn't an Arcrean phrase, Joel. Her *name* is Elaina."

"Oh." Joel chuckled, "I was going to ask her myself." His smile turned sheepish, earning a dimpled grin from Elaina, "I guess I didn't pay much attention to the language instructors."

Luke sidestepped into the space between them. "Stay focused. We have other matters that need our attention for now."

"Right." Joel tapped one end of his staff on the cobbled street, "What do we do first?"

"Luke," Elaina turned him by the arm to look back at the square. The five brutes were beginning to stir, and would soon be conscious enough to give chase.

Luke gave Joel a mild shove and grabbed Elaina's arm, urging them forward and around the corner at a fast trot. "Keep going," he nodded when Joel sent him a questioning look. "We need to be as far away as possible if they decide to search the area."

As storm clouds gathered overhead and catapults thundered to the east, the three fugitives sped through the city, away from certain danger and into the unknown. Elaina marveled at the impressive sights they passed, grateful for the guidance and protection of two who knew the city and its thoroughfares, as well as its shadows. She glanced over her shoulder to ensure they were not being followed and then looked forward again, half-running and half-flying as Luke pulled her along at the pace he had set.

Suddenly a company of dark-armored knights appeared on the street ahead. Luke swerved to the left, giving a short whistle for Joel and quickly slipping into a dark lane. Narrow stone steps climbed the building to their right, and to the left a wall of empty crates had been stacked. Hurrying between the two, they ducked behind the crates and waited breathlessly for the knights to pass by.

"I can't risk being recognized yet," Luke peered toward the street, "especially by the Mordecais."

Forcing her breathing to return to normal, Elaina glanced at her companions to gauge their stamina. The sight of Joel, his profile cut from the sunlight on the street, caused her brow to crease with a recollection of moments before. How inconsiderate these two had been to stand talking about her in the street, knowing she was in their company and unable to understand what they said.

Most of it. Leaning slightly to the left and wearing a disconcerted expression, Elaina looked to her only language advocate and whispered, "Did he say wife?"

Luke suddenly leaned away from the wall and surged to his feet, "Time to go."

55
To the Temple

Roland stared at the short message, just delivered by his guard. He blinked and read it again.

Rosalynn was requesting that he meet her in the temple to pray.

Roland frowned and rubbed the sleep from his eyes. He had only closed them for a moment, planning to review the battle plans sent over earlier by Sir Fraser, but his weary sleep-depraved body had had other ideas. When the guard knocked and entered with the message, Roland had been shocked to discover how long he had been sleeping.

Now he looked down at the flowery script of Rosalynn's note and scratched his head. He thought he had he sent her away this morning. Hadn't he seen her leave with her brother? Or had it all been a dream?

Roland rose and moved to the western window, squinting into the setting sun. There was something he was forgetting. Something he had planned to say or do… Or was it something that had been said to him? A yawn overtook him and Roland shook his head. He would think of it later, when his mind was no longer foggy and after he had been to pray with his wife.

He smiled as he left the west turret. What a perfect way to

clear his head.

Valden couldn't keep the sinister grin from his face as he stood in the shadows cast by the nine deities. He glanced up and imagined he saw approval on their stone faces. Tonight he would finally rid the province of the fool who had been in command for far too long. He, the neglected orphan from Lork who had risen from the dust to be chief of the Mordecai Order, would surely be given possession of the city in return for his faithfulness to Cronin. Who better to rule these Mizgalian swine than the man who had systematically inspired them to fear?

Valden stepped from behind the dais to check the positions of his men one last time. Two at the door and one behind each of the six pillars that ran the length of the room. Each had taken his place in silence and stood at the ready with a brooding intensity that Valden could feel. Wulf had done well, he admitted to himself.

The message had been delivered. All they could do now was wait.

Valden hated waiting.

"I can't believe this is happening," Warin shook his head as he scanned the street.

The man to his right shifted to peer around the hood of his cloak, "You never suspected a plot against Roland?"

"That I can understand. It's working alongside you that has me baffled." Warin looked down at Luke, some seven inches shorter than his height of nearly seven feet, "It makes our years of animosity seem like a waste of time."

Luke smirked, "That's exactly what they were." He glanced down at his disguise, "I think it ironic that I'll be entering the palace with a childhood foe, dressed as one of my worst enemies and attempting to rescue another old adversary."

Warin smiled briefly and then glanced over his shoulder at the three others who followed close behind them, also dressed as Mordecai knights. "And I think it ironic that I'll be gaining entrance to the palace *for* my childhood foe, as well as an escaped slave."

"All in God's plan, Warin. It's because she escaped that Elaina was able to overhear your brother's words to the blacksmith."

Warin's jaw tensed, "Wulf is thoughtless and imprudent." He cast a sidelong glance at Luke, "I always thought the two of you had much in common. My brother would do anything for a promotion, but he needs to learn that a promotion is not worth everything. He is first and foremost the reason why I agreed to help you."

"Mmm," Luke nodded, hiding a grin in the shelter of his black hood. "Yes, I'm sure your decision to join us had nothing to do with the desperate young woman who came to the slave market seeking your help."

Luke laughed when he felt Warin's fist collide with his shoulder.

"I'm loyal to Roland," the knight countered, but with little conviction.

"My friend," Luke tripped briefly over the words, marveling that he could be using them to address one of the evil twins; he peeked around his hood with a twinkle in his eye, "you have obviously forgotten my ability to read a man's gaze like an open scroll."

Warin's expression went from startled to annoyed as he purposely turned his eyes forward.

Luke suppressed another bout of laughter, "Yours, sir, is rather telling."

They turned a corner and Warin cleared his throat, effectually changing the course of their conversation, "Are they ready?"

Suddenly serious, Luke fell back several paces and quietly addressed the other three, "We're approaching the palace. You know the orders. Sir Warin will speak for us and lead us in, and once inside we'll head straight for the temple."

Bradley and Joel nodded silently.

"And then what?" Elaina pinned him with an impatient glare, obviously annoyed by the lack of a solid plan.

"We can't know until we learn whether the traitors' plans are already in motion."

Elaina sighed and reached up to shift the chainmail cap that was hiding her hair beneath her hood. It was an attempt to delay anyone's discovery that she was a girl. However, the frame of links around her face only served to emphasize her feminine face, and Luke considered the cap an utter failure.

Shifting into two columns, the four Faithful stepped in time to Warin's stride. They followed in absolute silence as the Mordecai led them toward the gates of Roland's palace, three praying that he would not betray them, and one certain that he would not.

Luke tipped his head forward just enough so he could peer up at the gate. Once inside, they would be outnumbered and friendless. According to Lady Rosalynn's account earlier that day, even the man they were intent on rescuing did not want them here. Luke adjusted his cloak and lowered his head as Warin approached the guard.

God, help us.

Candlelight flickered to either side of the dais and incense burned on the small altar, creating a warm effect that lured Roland closer. The doors closed behind him, leaving him to worship in private, and his gaze quickly bounced back and forth in search of his wife.

"Rosalynn?" His call echoed back to him from the stone walls, and the candles flickered gently. Roland approached the nine deities, staring up at their unresponsive faces and breathing deeply of the fragrant air.

Something was wrong.

Instinctively Roland turned for the door, but froze when he saw a man standing between the dais and the candles on the right. Roland's heart pounded a rhythm of terror and he recalled with startling clarity the warning that he had received from Bradley.

A plot to take his life.

Roland quickly lurched for the door, but found his way blocked by six shadows flanking the center aisle. He turned back to face the dais and the man waiting calmly before it.

"Who are you?" He demanded. His answer was a raspy chuckle, dry and humorless, and Roland's eyes widened with disbelief, "Valden? You?"

"Yes, me." Valden strolled forward, "It has always been me. Since the day I first entered this wretched city I knew you and Kenrick would be easy to remove from power if only I was patient.

And I have been patient," he growled, "You have trampled me, misused me, threatened me, and more, but tonight…" the candlelight highlighted his sickening grin and glinted off of his sword, "tonight it is my turn."

Roland's chest tightened with fear and he struggled to take a breath. The muscles in his hand quivered, longing to draw his own blade, but the knowledge that he was surrounded kept him from doing so.

Then, through the shadows and incense, another voice came.

"You…simpletons…"

Prolonging each syllable with a snakelike hiss, the raspy voice was the same that Roland remembered hearing so many years ago. The voice of the gods. A shiver raced up his spine as he turned to face the dais and dropped to his knees in uncertainty.

Valden's eyes widened and he took a step away from the nine statues. In confusion he scanned the stone figures. Where had the voice come from? A thread of fear mingled with the anger rising in his chest. This was not what he had planned. He turned to signal one of his men forward, but no one moved. Valden's fear grew stronger. These were either the most incapable soldiers of his Order…or they were not of his Order at all.

Laying hold on the grip of his sword, Valden whirled about, simultaneously drawing his weapon with a deadly ring of steel against scabbard. Holding the blade aloft, he gave a cry of rage and leapt toward Roland, who was still on his knees.

Confused by the multitude of unexpected events, Roland could only cower against the dais and throw his arms up in defense. He waited helplessly for the fatal strike, but Valden's cry suddenly changed from one of fury to one of surprise, and Roland looked up to see a look of blank shock on the knight's face. The shock melted away into pain, and then Valden went pale and collapsed at the feet of an unsympathetic statue, his sword clattering harmlessly to the floor.

His breathing ragged and unsteady, Roland stared at the motionless form of the Mordecai and then lifted his gaze to the man who had attacked Valden from behind. Realization dawned, and his eyes widened and then narrowed in disbelief.

Twirling the hilt of a dagger in his hand, the black-clad figure stared back as he bent to retrieve the Order's ring from Valden's hand. Straightening again, he pocketed the golden signet and then drew his sword. Only then did Roland realize that his troubles this night were far from over.

Suddenly, and apparently to the surprise of everyone present, the doors burst open, clapping noisily against the stone walls and flooding the temple in a wash of torchlight from the corridor.

Luke pressed his back against the wall and slowly leaned over to peer around the corner. Studying the positions of the two men who guarded the temple doors for Roland's assassin, he drew back slowly and adjusted his hold on the string-set arrow. If he could help it, he would shoot to wound and not kill. It was possible they would need someone who could tell them more about this Haman.

Drawing the bowstring as taut as his posture would allow, Luke turned his head and gave a single nod. Warin nodded in return and motioned him forward with one hand. Luke turned back to the corner, counted to three, and then launched himself into the open.

His first arrow struck one guard in the right shoulder, debilitating the man's sword arm. Luke drew another and let the dart fly before the second man had drawn his weapon. Aiming for the same spot as on the first, he succeeded, and Joel quickly rushed around the corner to bind and gag the guards.

Luke raced forward, followed closely by Warin, Bradley, and Elaina. Setting a third arrow to his bowstring as he ran, he did not pause when he reached the doors, but instead leapt forward and delivered a kick that forced both panels open at once.

The doors clapped noisily against the walls as the five disguised as Mordecais arranged themselves on the threshold and beheld a cluster of like-dressed figures that stared back in shock. Beyond the six by the pillars, a seventh man stood with sword and dagger poised for use. At his feet, Roland cowered against the dais of nine stone statues, while behind him another man lay bleeding and still.

A look of shock registered on the assassin's face as he stared at the five intruders. His gaze quickly found Luke and rested there a moment, his eyes alight with bitterness and rage, "You!"

Warin took a commanding step forward, "Wulf, stop this madness now. I don't know what that Haman promised you, but it can't be worth throwing your life away to be hunted as a nobleman's murderer."

A strange light shifted in Wulf's eyes as his anger burned anew. "Idiots!" He hissed a string of curses and they echoed in the stone chamber. "Simpletons! You have always—*always!*—treated me as the subordinate. You have all thought of me as the coward, the lout, the fool. You thought wrong!" Wulf roared and spat each word with venomous rage, "It is *you* who are the fools, not me!" His gaze shifted to Warin and his lip curled with contempt, "I do not serve Haman. I am Haman."

Elaina blinked. Something of great significance had just been said, she was certain. Warin's twin had spewed ugly words into the space between them, and judging by the grimaces on several faces, Elaina was glad she couldn't interpret all of them. She had, however, understood the last three words.

I am Haman. Elaina's brow furrowed in confusion. *I thought he was Wulf…?*

Roland suddenly drew his sword. In a flash, Wulf—or Haman—spun and jumped, knocking the blade out of the ruler's hand with a deft kick and raising his own weapon to deliver a fatal blow. At the last second Roland rolled to the right, avoiding the deadly slice and scrambling into the shadows behind a pillar.

Meanwhile, bedlam erupted in the temple when the six guards rushed the door. Luke's bow quickly felled one and Warin's sword another, leaving one opponent each for Elaina and the others while Luke ducked out of reach and circled around toward the dais.

Elaina felt her instincts take over as she met her attacker's powerful strikes. One by one she parried the combinations and cuts of his sword and finally shifted to the offensive herself. Putting to practice one of the sets she had learned from Leo, she backed her opponent several steps toward a pillar. Without warning, Elaina's cap slipped to one side and the sudden distraction caused her to falter. The rebel soldier lurched forward, hoping to take advantage of her confusion, and Elaina blocked his overhead just in time. The two swords ground together with a terrible scraping sound, and then locked at the cross-guards.

Elaina kept her sword steady while inwardly she cringed,

waiting for the onslaught of painful memories to overcome her. Immediately an image did appear before her mind's eye, but not the montage she had expected. Instead it was a picture of her father's face, smiling as he tapped the end of her nose and winked an eye that was so filled with love Elaina wondered how she had ever doubted his affection.

Looking up past the locked swords, Elaina met the vicious gaze of her opponent, so unlike the one of affection in her mental image that she shuddered. Fueled by a sudden rush of determination, she quickly pulled back and ducked, sending the startled guard forward to the floor while simultaneously slipping the chainmail from her head. Straightening, she flung the metal cap into the face of Bradley's nearby opponent. In a fluid motion that proved his capabilities, Bradley delivered a fatal lunge that dropped his adversary, and then whirled about to do the same to hers. Elaina turned her face away from the sight and searched the temple for Luke.

Wulf's sword had obviously connected with Roland's arm in the nobleman's attempt to escape, for the ruler now sat clutching his left limb where the sleeve had turned dark red. Wincing, he cried out as the once-elusive Haman prepared to finish him off.

"Wulf!" Luke called out, hoping to distract Warin's twin. When that failed he lifted his bow and took aim, releasing the arrow just as Wulf's sword began to fall.

Wulf cried out when the dart struck his leg. His sword arm went wide, striking the wall, and he quickly retreated to hide behind a pillar before another arrow could be let loose. Luke raced forward to help Roland to his feet, and they turned just as the rest of the temple fell silent. The others had brought an end to their own combat and stood guard across the aisle.

Realizing he was trapped and without aid, Wulf glared at each individual and then growled like a cornered beast as he grabbed a candle from beside the dais. Pulling something from a small pouch at his waist, Wulf threw both the substance and the candle into the basin and quickly jumped back.

With a flash of light and an ear-splitting blast, the temple filled with smoke.

56
Signs of a Storm

Coughing and sputtering, Elaina opened her eyes and wiped a layer of powdery residue from her face. She spat against the gritty feeling in her mouth and looked up to see Sir Warin kneeling beside her. "You all right?" He asked in broken Arcrean, and then Luke appeared beside him, repeating the question fluidly in her native tongue.

Elaina nodded and then spat again, gagging over the film on her tongue, "What was that?"

Luke waved a hand in front of his face, clearing a path through the floating powder and incense, "Some of it looks like Death Chalk, a defensive product found in the spittle or nostrils of dragons and used to numb their prey."

Elaina's face slackened with a look of revulsion. "That's disgusting!" She wiped a hand over her face again, "Ugh. I think I've heard of it before… Why am I wet?"

"Water causes it to disintegrate. Thankfully Warin recognized the signs and washed his own face before he lost consciousness."

Elaina glanced at the Mordecai, who clutched a water pouch in his hand, "Am I to understand you've experienced a dragon's sneeze before?"

Muttering something about "too many questions," Warin rose

to check on Bradley and Joel. Luke helped Elaina to her feet and she slowly scanned the temple. Roland sat clutching his arm by the doors.

"Is he injured badly?"

"The wound is deep, but he'll heal well if he cooperates." Luke wiped at a spot where the nobleman's blood had stained his vest, "We need to leave immediately, before the palace guards come to investigate."

Elaina followed him toward the doors, where he bent to help the city's pale ruler to his feet. The nobleman was near to losing consciousness due to the loss of blood.

"I must…stay." Roland made a feeble attempt to resist Luke's help, "I'll defend…my place in…Hebbros."

Luke settled a firm hold around the man's waist and draped Roland's uninjured arm over his shoulder, "Hebbros is lost to you, my lord. Let us take you to safety."

Leaving the two guards in the corridor, Warin led the way out of the temple. Elaina and Joel fell into step close behind him and Luke came next, half-carrying Lord Roland. Bradley brought up the rear, moving to help Luke when Roland eventually lost consciousness. They traversed a set of fairly unused halls and corridors, finally crossing the gardens and exiting through a hidden door in the wall. No one spoke.

As sounds of the continued siege pounded in the east, the company of six turned west. Elaina pulled her hood up over her head and studied the darkened streets, aware of the unspoken bond that had united their group. Still, an unsettling knowledge throbbed in each of their minds and pulsed in time to their pounding hearts, for when the dust had settled and the air cleared, one fact had become apparent.

Wulf, or Haman, or whatever his name was, had managed to slip away.

An armored guard appeared at the door of the commander's tent, silhouetted by the torchlight within, "Sir Hugo will see you now."

Wulf traced the scar over his left eyebrow and ignored the suspicious gazes of the watchmen posted outside. Holding his head at a confident angle, perfected after so many years of ignoring the disdain of others, he entered the lavishly equipped pavilion.

Sir Hugo, the newly appointed captain of King Cronin's vast forces, sat on the far side of a table in the center of the canopied space. His unblinking gaze tracked Wulf's approach with a hardness crafted in battle. The two guards who flanked his position, though half-a-foot shorter than Wulf, emanated the unmistakable air of power. Sir Hugo rose from his hand-carved chair and the three stood like a solid wall. The knight gave the barest nod to indicate a chair, "You may sit."

Wulf did so, grimacing when his weight shifted and pain shot through his leg.

Sir Hugo's scrutiny was thorough, "You are injured?"

Wulf shrugged, "A petty wound. Happened during my first attempt to leave the city," the lie slipped easily off of his tongue, as had a thousand others before.

Outwardly Wulf remained calm as he leaned forward and dropped a stolen diagram onto Hugo's table. Inwardly he raged, cursing that scoundrel Luke for interfering once again with his well-laid plans. The rebel scum had been in exile for eleven years! How he had managed to learn of Haman's plot was more than Wulf could fathom.

And Warin. Mentally, Wulf swore. His own brother had been in league with the banished swine. After years of loathing little Luk-Luk and letting their hatred grow to be widely acknowledged and all-consuming, Warin had had the gall to lead the Faithful rabble to Roland's rescue, disguised as none other than a band of Mordecais.

How utterly low.

Sir Hugo's eyes studied the diagram and then shifted to consider the rogue knight across the table. "You say that you will open for us the gates of Hebbros, and grant us access to take the city…"

Wulf dipped his head in a single nod.

"And yet," the skin around the captain's eyes twitched, "I must question the wisdom of placing my trust in you. You think nothing of deceiving the ruling forces of Hebbros. How can I be sure you will not deceive me?"

"My loyalties lie with the king," Wulf's tone turned the words into a jab of logic, as if no one but a fool would question his actions. "Cronin's enemies are mine. Therefore, I do not betray a ruler but a rebel."

Hugo acknowledged the words with a slight raising of his brows, "Very well." He released the diagram of Hebbros and it fluttered to the table, "My men will cease their assault on the walls and receive orders to remain at rest. You have until tomorrow evening, sir, to remove your family from the city and report to me with the plan of attack." He lowered a finger to the map, "If you fail to show yourself before the appointed time, I will use this diagram to search out the weakest point of Hebbros and attack there forthwith. I could then make no promises for your safety."

Wulf paused. He had planned to have Warin spared, though even the Order of Haman, once they had opened the gates to Hugo's men, would largely be left to their own survival. An image of Warin bursting through the temple doors with Luke at his side flashed through Wulf's mind and he flinched. His eyes narrowed. Each twin had made his choice, and now they must live by those decisions. If Warin could so easily disregard him, then Wulf would do the same.

"I have no family," he met Sir Hugo's gaze steadily, "but I thank you for offering their protection anyway."

Sir Hugo leaned one arm on the surface between them, "Surely there must be something you would ask in return for your services. King Cronin will have no matters unsettled. When my men pull out from Hebbros, His Majesty would be done with the affair altogether."

Wulf understood. If he had a favor to ask, it must be presented now or never. He leaned forward to match Sir Hugo's posture and crafted his voice to adopt a tone of humility, "Sir, I am honored simply to serve my sovereign in a noteworthy act of loyalty. However, if the king would grant a favor, there is a boon I would ask."

Sir Hugo reached for a quill and parchment to make a note of Wulf's words, "Say on."

Wulf took a slow breath. This was the moment he had been waiting for. Plotting for. Killing for. Now he would find out if the gods approved of his passion by showing favor.

"All my life I have fought and struggled to better myself. I have proven my loyalty time and again in hopes of earning greater responsibilities, only to be betrayed by everyone I held in high regard. I have been mocked, scorned, and misused until I have lost hope in my fellow men." Wulf's gaze grew intense, "Here is what I ask. If my service is pleasing to the king, then let me further prove my loyalty to him by being considered for the position of building up the new and conquered Hebbros for his glory."

A spark of admiration lit Hugo's eye, and his lips quirked in a small smile of approval at the younger man's daring, "You wish to rule Hebbros?"

Wulf did not answer audibly, but the fire of determination in his gaze responded for him.

Sir Hugo rose and held out his hand, "I will take your request into consideration, and we will see how you perform in the time being." They clasped wrists in a silent pact and Hugo spoke again, "And what name shall I call you by, our lonely ally?"

Wulf smirked. The only reason they were allies was because Hugo was a means to the end Wulf sought for himself. It mattered little to him who lived or died through this ordeal, so long as Cronin received word of Wulf's act of loyalty. Masking these thoughts behind a pleasant smile, he took a step back away from the table and prepared to take his leave.

"Haman," he offered a reply. "I am called Haman."

Stepping out into the shadows, Wulf paused to gaze on the impressive sight of Hebbros. His men would receive their orders to overpower Sir Fraser's gatekeepers and let Hugo's army through the walls. The city would be reclaimed in the king's name and Wulf would be seated as Lord Haman. Once that had been accomplished, Wulf would at last be free to execute a long-overdue piece of business. Fingering the Mordecai signet on his finger, Wulf shifted his focus beyond the city to the peak of Mount Desterrar, and a slow smile creased his face.

The catapults fell silent during the night. The people of Hebbros breathed a sigh of relief, offered a chant of praise to their false gods, and then slipped out into the night by the hundreds to partake in their usual pleasures. As if three days of taking shelter had left them starved for a dose of sin, the streets quickly became alive with ne'er-do-wells and rogues. Crimes became the order of the dark night, and sinister plots flowed freely, woven together by deception and cruelty.

The hour of midnight approached and a distant peal of thunder rolled low and threatening, like an initial warning. God's eye was on the city of Hebbros, and He was not pleased.

The wind blew stronger and whistled through the streets. The noise of the people—men, women, and even children—grew louder and more insistent. Ignoring the signs in the lowering heavens, they fell to their wickedness with a relish that said they wished to block out the symptoms of the coming storm.

The warning went unheeded. Judgment was nigh.

Then, like the tears of God, the rains began to fall.

57
Sacrifice

Warin stood by the door, feeling entirely out of place.

Outside, the relentless storm would not lift. Torrents of rain flowed through the streets and lightning webbed angry paths across the black sky. Sharp cracks of thunder shook the mercer's shop, but did not erase the feeling of peace that seemed to fill every corner. The inhabitants of this place knew for a fact that their God was in control.

Across the room that was crowded with wares, Lord Roland lay on the mercer's table being examined by a physician who looked old enough to have been personally acquainted with the ancients. Fine wisps of white hair floated aimlessly about the man's head as he turned one way and then another, applying a salve and bandaging the ruler's arm.

Holding tightly to Roland's other hand, Lady Rosalynn watched and listened as the physician explained the wound and its probable process of healing. His lordship's two eldest children, Lord Jerem and Lady Celia, stood nearby with a concerned Liam, eyeing their father with anxious expressions and looking almost as misplaced as Warin felt.

The Master Slaver of Hebbros finally relinquished the position he had kept since entering the mercer's shop the night before. Stepping into the back room he slid to the left and leaned against the wall, his gaze making a slow circuit of the storage space.

Several trunks of finery had been opened and offered up for the enjoyment of Roland's other children. Four blond- and auburn-haired youngsters aged two to ten had draped themselves in fine silks and embroidered linens, creating a gaily-dressed parade. Shrieking and laughing with carefree glee, the pack of little ones romped about the room, oblivious to the danger and anxiety that pressed in on all sides. Heedless of the storm.

Warin envied their untroubled state. Never in all his life had he experienced even a moment that was free from care. Tearing his gaze away from the bright eyes and joyful smiles, he continued his survey of the room.

Sadie sat in one corner, holding the infant Sarah and watching the other children with a tender smile. Beside her were the slave woman and her newborn that Sadie had assisted in the slave market.

On their journey from the palace the night before, Roland's rescue party had passed by the slave market and found it destroyed by the work of catapults and fire. The slaves had escaped and were nowhere to be seen. Only this woman had remained cowering nearby, trying to protect her child, and Warin had brought the lone slave along to the mercer's. He hadn't understood the decision, but seeing Sadie's joyful surprise upon their arrival had been reward enough for his confusion.

Warin blinked. In another corner three nameless Faithful whom Liam had summoned sat huddled together, waiting to be told what to do. Standing together by the back wall, Bradley, Elaina, and Joel listened intently as Luke presumably outlined their plans for leaving the city, which had been delayed by Roland's need for a physician.

Warin looked down at the floor as thunder crashed overhead. He had no place among these people. And yet…

"What will you do now?" Luke leaned against the wall beside him and watched as a little boy with fiery-red hair raced by, trailing a length of airy material. The undersized lad ran whooping across the room until a collision with the wall brought a stop to his momentum and he collapsed in a fit of laughter.

Warin inhaled deeply and crossed his arms, focusing his gaze on the far wall, "I'll return to the slave market and eventually report to Sir Fraser. He may be in need of my services."

"Why?"

Warin turned, one brow cocked, "Why? The city is at war and I'm an able—"

"No." Luke waved a hand between them as if to wipe the air free of excuses, "Why do you need to go back?"

Warin sighed impatiently, "Luke, I'm a Mordecai and a slave trader."

"Yes, I know," a grin tugged at Luke's mouth. "For an Order that has no chief and a city whose ruler is about to flee for his life." He raised his brow in a meaningful look, "And don't tell me you'd stay for your brother's sake. We both know that would be pointless."

Warin dragged a weary gaze up to meet the spirited one that stared back, "What is it you want, Luke?"

The other man tilted his head, "I want you to go with us."

Warin's head was already shaking in denial, "I don't belong with the Faithful, Luke."

"A week ago I would have agreed." Luke righted a child that had tripped and fallen in front of where they stood, and then turned a probing gaze back to Warin, "Now I'm not so sure."

"No, you would've been right. I've spent my life stirring terror and pain into the lives of others. I'm not good like the rest of you. Good-intentioned, maybe, but not good."

"God does not ask us to be good, but repentant. Christ covers the past, and God sees only the redemptive work of His Son. The fruit of true goodness comes when our lives are filled with Him." Luke reached out and clapped a hand against Warin's shoulder, "Speaking of goodness, I haven't thanked you for your help rescuing Lord Roland. I never thought I'd see the day when two from our sets would work together. You see? God is already at work in your life."

Warin shook his head at Luke's optimism. "I will admit, a few days ago I would have said that in my case compassion was nonexistent. However," he ducked his head briefly, "someone believed that my opinion was wrong, and I found that I had a capacity for kindness after all. It taught me a lesson in faith. I've been taught all my life that your God does not exist. However, you and your comrades believe otherwise, and in your faith I see evidence of His reality."

Luke was silent and Warin could see that he was restraining himself from pressuring the Mordecai. The young firebrand had matured and strengthened in character during his absence from Hebbros.

Finally another clap of thunder sounded and Luke leaned away from the wall. "I'll leave you with this thought." He took a step forward and looked back at Warin, "With Lord Roland injured, three women in the company, two elderly men, and seven children to keep watch over, we'll need all the help we can get to reach Exile in safety. Perhaps you would consider joining us as his lordship's escort. With the task complete, no one would argue your choice to return. If you chose to."

Warin watched as Luke disappeared through the doorway into the front room. It amazed him that he could no longer stir up the hatred he had once harbored toward the young man, and that the feeling of truce seemed to be mutual. When had he let go of his childish enmities?

Luke's words echoed in his mind. The offer had been wholly sincere and yet, in tune with Luke's character, half-challenge. Why shouldn't he accept? His work as a slaver would be put on hold until the war had ceased, and he was not strictly bound to offer his services to Sir Fraser. Why not ensure that Lord Roland's escort included someone that had remained loyal to him?

Warin looked up when he heard the gentle strains of a song. The four children had ceased their games and sat down in full regalia to listen while Sadie sang their youngest sister an Arcrean melody. Smiling down at them, the young slave sang the words in Mizgalian as her voice wrapped the hearers in a compelling sense of security.

"Place of peace, rest, and ease;
My soul longs to know these things.
In Jesus alone true rest will come;
My soul longs to know this home.
Darkness is poured, mixed with the sword.
My soul longs to know Thee, Lord.
Night slips away, then comes the day.
My soul longs in Thee to stay."

Suddenly the door burst inward with a crash, splintering into pieces and scattering against the floor. Startled screams filled the shop as the candles fluttered out and five intruders filled the doorway. Silhouetted by the occasional flash of lightning, they stood glaring at the shop's inhabitants while rainwater flowed from their cloaks and flooded the immediate area in seconds.

Though it was mid-morning, the storm had blocked out the sun as if it had not risen. Using the darkness and the sudden commotion to disguise their actions, Luke and Bradley quickly lowered Roland to the floor by the wall and covered him with piles of Liam's costly wares.

From the doorway between the two rooms, Warin caught glimpses of the insignia worn by several of the men. Mordecais. Another was a foot soldier, and the last a squire near the end of his term. Warin glanced about to see fear on several faces, and he realized with a pang of irony that he was experiencing the receiving end of a raid so like those he had participated in many times before.

"Shut the brats up before I do it for you," one of the men shouted toward the storage room.

Sadie rose from her chair and clutched the baby protectively, while the other four whimpered and shrank out of sight behind her.

The spokesman grunted, "We have orders to arrest those called Faithful, charged with treason and sedition against his lordship."

"But he—" one child pointed a small finger toward their lord father, but Sadie quickly clapped a hand over his mouth.

"Whose orders?" Luke called from the shadows.

The spokesman gave a dry chuckle, "His lordship's, of course."

"But he—" Sadie dropped to one knee and whispered in the persistent child's ear.

Luke's tone turned suspicious, matching Warin's thoughts, "Who is 'his lordship'?"

"Lord Haman, savior of Hebbros."

Warin gaped as a wave of shock turned to nausea in the pit of his stomach. Had his brother gone mad?

A loud clap of thunder prevented any response to the man's words. Not that anyone had any response to make. Uneasiness settled over the shop and Roland's two-year-old began to cry. Rosalynn cast a longing glance toward the back room, but feared moving from the shadows might betray her identity. Warin understood her dilemma. Responding to a sympathy he did not understand, he retreated from the doorway and scooped the small boy into his arms.

"What are you waiting for?" The spokesman barked, "Form a line, all of you. We've a trip to make through the rain."

His comrades laughed. Luke stepped forward, separating himself from the group, and brought a halt to their merriment with a firmly spoken, "Wait."

The spokesman glared, "What did you say?"

"I know this Haman, and he is an old enemy of mine. I will take full responsibility for the charges and go with you now if you let these others go free."

"Luke, no." Bradley moved forward, but Liam placed a hand on the nobleman's arm even as Luke held up a hand for silence.

The spokesman laughed, "Why would I accept your offer when I could take all of you instead? Do you take me for a simpleton?"

"Only if you fail to accept my bargain." The soldier's eyes narrowed as Luke continued, "You are five men against nine or more who can wield a weapon, let alone those who would do anything in a desperate fight for their lives. Take me, and let the others go on their way."

The spokesman was considering the facts, taking in the size and probable ability of everyone in the shop. Would it be worth a fight?

Warin stared at Luke, unable to comprehend such sacrifice. Didn't he know what Wulf would do to him? "Luke," he spoke quietly, but the young man still turned and met his gaze, "don't do this."

Luke's face was a mask of determination, but there was a glimpse of sadness, "I have to."

"We can fight." Warin spoke louder, not caring that everyone could hear. This was injustice! "We can take them, Luke. Think."

Luke's gaze grew intense, undoubtedly reading his, "Will it satisfy him?"

Warin knew what he meant. He shook his head, "One sacrifice will make him thirst for another."

Luke turned to face him in the darkness, raising his voice when the sound of wind and rain escalated, "I came to free the remnant, Warin. Will this satisfy him long enough to accomplish that?"

Probably. Warin thought the word, but couldn't bear to say it. He stared at Luke, barely containing his rage toward Wulf, and knew his former enemy had found an answer in whatever had passed through his gaze. Luke turned and spoke in a tone that left no room for argument from anyone.

"Take me to Haman."

58

In His Hands

Elaina sat huddled in a corner of the back room, hugging her knees to her chest and feeling like a lost child. Voices swirled around her. Panicked voices. Tearful voices. Mizgalian voices. They spoke so quickly, tension rushing their speech, that she understood only one word being repeated again and again.

Luke…Luke…Luke…Luke…

He was gone. Had been gone for about an hour now. The followers of Warin's brother, Wulf-called-Haman, had dragged him away without another word or backward glance. Where were they taking him? What would they do to him? Elaina glanced up at the faces around her. Those who knew this Haman clearly thought Luke was doomed.

A single tear traced a path down Elaina's cheek. In the day-and-a-half since she had become a follower of Christ, her faith had grown deeper just watching Luke's example. God had sent this Mizgalian across her path and now he was gone. What was she supposed to do? How could she continue to grow confident in Christ when her instructor had been taken from her so abruptly?

She glanced up at Sadie. Her fellow Arcrean had adopted the Mizgalian tongue so easily in this moment of alarm. Luke had been her lifeline in this foreign place. Now she felt far removed from everything that was happening around her.

Suddenly the sound of stone-against-stone, the same noise that had announced Luke and Bradley's arrival, seeped through the wall behind her. The others remained oblivious, the noise of the storm overpowering everything else, until Elaina jumped up and away from the wall with a startled expression.

"Elaina?" Sadie asked tentatively, "What is it?"

Elaina wiped at her tears and pointed toward the groaning wall. The others came closer and hovered around her, watching and listening, as the two loose stones along the inner wall began to move. Bradley and Joel suddenly jumped forward to aid in the wall's disassembly, and a moment later Warin and Jerem joined them. The large stones were pulled from place, revealing the man-sized cavity used by the Faithful for supplies and refugees.

Liam and the physician who had tended Roland's wound brought new candles and held them high, casting a soft glow over the storm-darkened recesses of the storage room. The four helpers pulled back and a man slipped through from outside. Dripping wet and bone-weary, the newcomer lifted his head and Elaina started in shock.

"Luke!?" He looked her way and Elaina instantly realized her error. This was not Luke. The face was familiar, but broader and with different eyes. The man himself was broader and taller than Luke.

Panting with exertion, he spoke a few words in reply to Elaina's mistake and then quickly scanned the gathered crowd with increasing concern.

"He says he is Luke's twin, Christopher." Sadie supplied the Arcrean over Elaina's shoulder. Elaina nodded vaguely, marveling at the difference between two people who shared such a close likeness.

With quick, purposeful movements, Christopher turned back to the wall and quickly helped to pull a young woman through the hole. The petite redhead landed on her feet and slapped at her soaked skirts before plucking a small creature from the floor beside her and tucking its head under her chin. Elaina instinctively took a step back when she saw it was a young catawyld. A miserably wet catawyld, but one of the beasts nonetheless.

Following the young woman, a tall blond fellow slipped into

the room and all three stood staring at their unsuspecting hosts. Then Christopher spoke again, directing his words to Bradley, and Sadie continued to translate.

"Where is Luke?" There was a pause and he stepped forward, "Where is he, Bradley?"

Bradley swallowed and wouldn't meet Christopher's gaze, "Taken. An hour ago."

A stricken look crossed Christopher's features, "By whom?" His eyes shifted and he spotted Warin, "What is he doing here?"

"He has been of great service to us, Chris," Bradley quickly intervened, "and you might as well know now that Roland is in the next room. It's Wulf who has turned everything upside-down and inside-out. Calls himself Haman now and intends to rule Hebbros in Roland's stead. His men took your brother."

"Wulf will kill Luke!" The redhead interjected and the second man muttered about something being obvious.

"Pavia, Ned, please," Bradley pleaded. "We have already considered the dreadful possibilities, and our anguish has reached its maximum."

But the damage had been done. Chris clenched his jaw and fought a threatening wave of emotion, "We need to find him. We might make it in time to rescue him before—"

"No, Chris." Bradley shook his head, "He wouldn't want that."

"Don't say that!" Chris shouted and everyone froze. Elaina could tell by their shock that he was usually a quiet man. Roughly scrubbing agitated fingers through his hair, Chris began to pace. "Luke always went after those who needed help. He always went to someone else's rescue. The least we can do is try to help him."

"Chris, Wulf has an army." Warin spoke hesitantly, "They're everywhere, they're disguised as any other commoner, and they've sworn to obey his every bidding."

Chris shook his head and turned to pound his fists against the wall, wishing to deny what was clearly true. He lowered his head between his arms, "He knew this would happen. He was prepared for it. I was not."

The elderly physician spoke next, "Luke wished to satisfy that fiend Haman long enough for the remnant to escape the city." His voice rang with certainty, "He would want us to leave. Now."

Chris was quiet for several moments, and then finally he

forced himself to give a single nod. "My brother's desires will be accomplished. His sacrifice will not be in vain. Ned, Pavia, and I would be grateful for something to eat and a moment's rest, and then we'll accompany you all back to Exile."

Liam scurried from the room to fetch the provisions. As the mercer disappeared over the threshold, Joel suddenly spoke up, "What brought you down the mount, anyway?"

Chris glanced his way, "We came as soon as we realized there would be trouble. It was no coincidence Wulf knew how to locate you here in Liam's shop." His gaze shifted to Bradley, "The day after you left Exile with Luke we discovered that another member had vanished as well."

"A secret follower of *Haman* all along," Pavia mumbled with disgust.

Bradley looked at one and then the other, "Lillian."

"No, Bradley." Ned sadly shook his head, "It was not so obvious."

"Luke. Can you hear me, Luke?"

His ears worked fine, but the rest of him screamed against making a response. He didn't know how long it had been since the beating, but even before he had fully regained consciousness, Luke could feel the pain beginning to escalate throughout his entire being. Taking a shallow breath, because anything more would have been torment to his lungs, he opened his right eye—the one not swollen shut—and looked up into the face that hovered above him.

Immediately the gut-wrenching agony washed over him anew and he closed his eye, wishing he could turn his head without causing further pain. "Please…go away."

"I brought you water."

A laugh of irony tried to escape Luke, but sounded more like a pitiful sob, "Why, Elbert?"

Elbert looked away, knowing Luke's question was not about the water. He set the goblet down and spoke with hushed intensity, "I was afraid, Luke. My parents didn't teach me of their faith as yours did, so when the soldiers came and took them away, I was thrown into shock and never recovered." He took a shaky breath, "I still hear their cries when I go to sleep at night, and see their anguish when I wake up in the morning. I was afraid."

Luke opened his one good eye again, but Elbert lowered his head and refused to meet his gaze.

"When Wulf approached me one day at the ropemaker's, demanding my allegiance to him, he threatened me with so many terrible things my mind could not comprehend the horror. I felt myself lock up, and heard myself agree. To this day I believe him capable of carrying out those threats, and so I keep my end of the bargain."

"Bargain?" Luke croaked the question, "Elbert, you're his slave."

Solemnly, Elbert dipped a cloth into the goblet and brought the cool water to Luke's lips. Luke waited until the moisture had dripped down his throat, and then looked up to study the other man's gaze.

"How did you hide it?"

Elbert looked away again, "I knew of your gift, and that it would be my ruin. I practiced and learned to create a façade that would conceal my true thoughts. I buried my fears beneath an imitation of your faith during the day, and at night wept over my lack of strength to make it real."

"But, why—"

Elbert's head came up fast and he tilted his ear to a sound in the outer corridor. Looking down at Luke, his eyes grew wide, "Don't tell him that we've spoken, or that I brought the water."

"You're asking me not to betray you?"

Ignoring Luke's words, Elbert sprang to his feet and tossed the goblet clattering out of sight as he moved to resume his post as guard several yards away. Luke watched the traitor stand at attention and then listened as the door opened and a small group of armed men entered. A clap of thunder shook the room.

Luke looked up at the vaulted ceiling. He was lying on the floor in the corner of the Great Hall in Roland's palace. The candlelight showed a large hearth in the wall to his right, and several chairs had been overturned and shoved farther away to his left. A rug covered the floor beneath him, but offered little comfort. His wrists and ankles had been bound by chains, but no further measures had been taken to keep him from wandering away.

None except the battering he had taken, and that had been

enough.

"Awake at last," Wulf's voice rasped with cruel pleasure. "I was beginning to think you'd sleep the entire day away."

Mentally Luke quirked a brow, but he doubted his muscles followed through with the action.

"Marley, get him up," Wulf growled, and one of the men jumped forward to obey.

With the help of another soldier, Marley grabbed Luke's arms and roughly pulled him to his feet. Both the contact and the sudden movement sent tremors of pain coursing through Luke and a cry rose unbidden from his chest. Relying entirely on the support of Wulf's men to keep him upright, he focused instead on breathing evenly and not letting himself heave.

"Feeling any better?" Wulf's tone mocked him, "Or ready for death?" He chuckled as he came closer and stopped in front of Luke, "That will come soon enough."

With great effort, Luke lifted his head to meet the gaze of Haman and swallowed against a wave of nausea, "My life is in God's hands, Wulf."

The Mordecai's green eyes narrowed with evident hatred, "Well then, apparently He let go."

Luke's knees buckled and the two guards jerked him upright again.

"As I was saying," Wulf smirked, "you will die. First, however, I must see that Cronin's army successfully enters and reclaims the city. Then, when I'm named Lord of Hebbros, I will personally escort you back up your precious mountain."

Luke's startled gaze darted upward to peer at Wulf.

"That's right," Wulf exhaled a laugh, "I had planned all along for my men to take only you from the mercer's shop. The others are free to go for now, but I knew if I wanted to ensure your capture, I would have to convince you that you were sacrificing yourself for them." He sneered and leaned closer, "What a waste."

Smiling at his own cunning, Wulf cocked his head to one side and backed away several paces, "Tomorrow the Order of Haman will make ready to congratulate my success, and the following day I will lead them out on a celebratory crusade. You see, I've decided to build a high place of worship in honor of the Mizgalian gods, and your little village of Exile is in the way." His grin turned sinister, "I want you to be there, Luk-Luk, to watch the whole thing. You'll be my witness as the Faithful are finally brought to an end, and then, my friend, you will die with them."

Abruptly, Wulf nodded and the soldiers released Luke's arms. Collapsing to his knees, Luke lowered himself the rest of the way to the floor and closed his eyes.

"Rest well, O faithful one," Wulf's mockery echoed as he turned to leave the hall. "We have a long journey ahead of us."

The door slammed shut and Luke remained still. Lightning flashed. He listened to the rain, still coming down in torrents over Hebbros, and the constant rolling of thunder.

Call unto me.

The words were whispered on his heart and Luke felt a tear drip from beneath his lashes. Doubts assailed him. Could he call upon his God this time? Was there anything that could be done?

Call unto me.

"Oh God!" The desperate prayer was hauled from deep within him. Startled, Elbert glanced his way and then averted his gaze in shame. "God, please," in his pain, Luke wasn't sure if he had shouted the words or merely whispered, "please rescue the Faithful and put an end to this evil."

Another flash cast the hall in white light, and the answering peal of thunder shook the foundations of the palace.

Luke felt a sense of peace wash over him. His life was indeed in God's hands, and even in death his Savior would never let go.

Luke waited and listened, his only news of the outside coming with the change of his guard every six hours. The Order of Haman had opened the gates to Sir Hugo's men, and the army had swept through the city like a conquering wave in spite of the unrelenting weather. Sir Fraser had been forced to surrender, and Hugo had named Haman as the city's ruling lord. The storm continued to build, abating now and then for several hours at a time, only to resume with greater ferocity than before.

Still Luke waited and listened, stretching out on the floor or sitting against the wall in the corner. Gradually the pain in his body lessened, or else Luke had grown accustomed to it, and yet he continued to sit in silence. By all appearances, numb and defeated. His strength was slowly returning, but he would bide his time.

Finally, two days after he had been dragged from Liam's shop, Wulf sent for him.

Luke allowed himself to be led outside. Squinting against the driving rain, he peered up at the churning skies and then shook his head as he turned to shout over the noise of the wind, "Wulf, you're mad to set out now! This is no ordinary storm."

"Silence!" Wulf spat.

Luke ducked his head and marched forward when someone shoved him from behind. He followed blindly through the streets until they came to a stop and he looked up at the massive gate in the western wall.

Drawing his sword and thrusting it into the air, Wulf gave the order, "Open the Thirteenth!"

59
Battle for Exile

Elaina stood on the ledge of stone high above Hebbros. Below her, wrapped like a cloak around the slopes of Desterrar, storm clouds continued to hover relentlessly over the city. Behind her, along the mountain's peak, the village of Exile sat nestled in safety and clear weather.

"It's as if we're in the eye of the storm," Sadie appeared to stand on her right, "and the winds are keeping the storm in place. I can't tell which direction they're blowing from."

Elaina nodded in agreement. She felt a hand slip into her left palm and turned to see the twins' sister, Charlotte, beside her. The young woman smiled and Elaina responded in kind. Neither of them could truly understand the other, but as soon as Chris had led the group into Exile the day before, an inexplicable bond had drawn the two women together in sweet friendship.

Charlotte asked her a question, nodding for Sadie to translate, "She asks if you are well."

Elaina's brow creased as she thought how to answer, "I am relieved to be here, out of Hebbros, but I am still trying to understand the ways of God."

Charlotte nodded her understanding and bit her lip. It had been hard for her to learn of her brother's capture. Now, four days after Haman's men had dragged Luke away, no one doubted that he had made the ultimate sacrifice and forfeited his life for their safety.

"God's ways are not our own, but we can always trust that He is good." Sadie spoke softly, laying a hand on Elaina's shoulder, "I'm grateful that God saw fit to spare Luke long enough for him to lead you to Christ. God knew ahead of time what Luke's fate would be. You must trust that there is a purpose, and that God will use it for good. You must trust Him, Elaina. Don't let this trial destroy your newborn faith."

Elaina nodded and prayed that God would strengthen her faith in Him. The three turned from the lookout and started up the path toward the village, Sadie translating for both of the others.

Charlotte waved when they approached another young woman headed their way. Lillian was a girl of delicate beauty, with pale hair and skin, and an almost sickly appearance. She paused on the path and waited for them to reach her, and then turned to walk with them.

"Is it still storming down there?"

"It is." Charlotte smiled and linked arms with Lillian, "I'm so glad to see you restored to your parents. These last few days have been happy ones for them."

Lillian looked appreciative. "I've been blessed by their forgiveness after all these years. I tried for so long to hold on to my anger at being brought here against my will. When I saw the king's army lay siege to Hebbros, I recognized the grace of God in removing me from danger before it was too late. I could no longer be mad that He chose to spare me in answer to my parents' prayers."

"And the prayers of the entire village," Charlotte added.

They entered the outskirts of Exile and Sadie left them in order to help Rosalynn prepare the midday meal for her household. Elaina continued on with the others, content to swing hands with Charlotte in girlish fashion while she listened to their mild-toned Mizgalian chatter. Eventually Ned appeared, having finished a door for Roland's temporary cottage, and Charlotte waved as she turned to walk home with him. Lillian offered Elaina a tentative smile and spoke an Arcrean farewell before heading home herself.

Elaina stood in the middle of the dirt path that wound its way through the quiet village. She looked toward the spot where the

Faithful had constructed a sturdy home for the nobleman who had banished them from Hebbros. Warin stood as if on guard outside Roland's cottage, leaning against the lintel and staring up at the sky. Elaina wondered if he would leave when the storm finally abated, or if his pensive demeanor these last days meant that Sadie's prayers for the Mordecai would be answered.

Closing her eyes, Elaina breathed deeply of the sharp, clear air and began to hum the melody that Sadie always sang to Rosalynn's children.

Place of peace, rest, and ease…

The sudden blare of a horn tore through the village and gripped Elaina's heart. Whirling toward the sound, she quickly raced toward the head of the Banishment Path. Behind her she heard the pounding of feet as others joined her.

Chris stood at his post, staring down over the edge of the path and occasionally lifting his horn to his lips to give the sound of alarm. Beside him, Pavia stood with one hand resting on the hilt of her sword. A cluster of villagers had already scattered along the perimeter of Desterrar's peak, their gazes turned down as well.

"What's wrong? What's happening?" Elaina called out, and then remembered no one could understand her. Skidding to a halt beside Pavia, she looked down the path to see for herself and gasped.

The cloak of storm clouds appeared to be climbing the slopes of Desterrar, moving upward like a formidable wall. The swirling mass of lightning and torrential rain ascended toward the group of Faithful, who saw with horror that it was accompanied by an army. Crawling their way toward Exile, the mass of armored figures would be preceded by yet another force of vicious creatures.

Pavia pointed, "Catawylds. The army is scaring them from their nests, and they won't fight so many people at once. They're heading this way."

Chris turned to address the crowd, "We don't have much time. Ready yourselves with weapons and prepare for battle."

A few raced back to the village to collect their weapons and Elaina followed their lead, unsure what the exact instructions had been.

Chris turned back to eye the advancing hordes, "It has to be Wulf. Haman." He clenched his jaw. "Luke sacrificed himself for nothing."

Pavia placed a hand on his arm, "He bought us time to escape the city. It will be easier to defend the peak than fight on the streets of Hebbros." She faced the perimeter and put her fisted hands on her hips, "All we have to do is keep the dirty scoundrels from scaling the ridge."

Chris turned to reclaim the group's attention. Bowing their heads, he led them in a prayer for safety and strength, "Defend us this day, Lord. Fight for us, please, and give us victory."

The pack of catawylds came first, swarming over the ridge in overwhelming numbers and with speed that made it impossible to keep all of them back. Swords flashed and beasts shrieked, clicking their tongues in warning as the entire pack sped across the meadow toward the far side of the mountain. Though some were killed, it quickly became apparent that the catawylds were uninterested in battling the inhabitants of Exile.

Pavia was grateful that Trig had learned to remain hidden when told, else he might have been swept along by the herd. She kept a ready stance and watched as one beast darted past her, ignoring her presence altogether. "The storm," She shouted over the noise of the stampede and the rising wind, "They're running from the storm!"

The last of the horde disappeared over the edge of the steeper side of Desterrar. The group of warriors turned from the incredible sight just as the tempest spilled up and over the ridge in a wall of mist. A strong wind instantly pushed them back from the edge, and a flash of lightning charged the air. The clouds swirled upward, churning into a towering pile of black fury that hovered over Desterrar. The rain hit them like a solid wall, unrelenting and penetrating.

Thunder pounded overhead, bringing Trig out from hiding to cower at Pavia's feet. Grabbing him by the scruff of his neck, the redhead quickly tossed him onto her back, where he stayed put by clinging to her thick vest.

On the other side of the group, Ned thought with a wave of sadness that Elbert should be telling him about now that it was raining. A noise drew his attention from the sight of the angry clouds, and he looked with the others to see that the first line of soldiers had formed at the head of the Banishment Path. Their leader stood before them.

Wulf. The newly appointed Lord Haman scanned Exile's

motley force of fifty or so able-bodied combatants, until his gaze came to rest on his brother. A laugh erupted from the core of his being, and his face twisted with scorn, "You fools! You think you have a chance against such insurmountable odds? Where is your God now?"

Standing ready with her sword, Elaina didn't understand a word of what Haman had said, but in the next instant she became fairly certain he had just angered the Almighty.

Luke's eyes widened when Wulf's challenge was followed by a tremor under his fingers. He tightened his grip on a ledge in the side of the mountain and exchanged a startled look with his guard when Desterrar rumbled and shuddered beneath their feet.

"We need to climb," Elbert grabbed his arm and shoved him forward, up the path.

"Obvious, Elbert," Luke tossed the words over his shoulder.

Drifting down on the wind, Luke heard Wulf's order to advance and he cringed to know that the fight had begun. How he wished he could be up there, helping to defend the village. He heard what must have been Chris's answering shout and longed for his full strength to return. Though improved from his condition of four days ago, his weakened body had been taxed by the rations, conditions, and journey that he had been forced to endure since then.

The earth quaked again and Luke doubled his pace, grappling for any solid hold he could find. The company on the slope above them reached the head of the path and swarmed over the ridge to the flatter ground of Desterrar's summit. Luke and Elbert scurried after them, anxious to reach the peak before the shaking mountain tossed them off.

From behind them came the sound of a man's shout, followed by another. Elbert glanced over his shoulder and his eyes widened. "Some have fallen, Luke. They can't hold on tight enough." His eyes swept the path ahead of them and he pointed to a spot several yards up and to the right, "There, beyond that boulder. Head there."

Luke was already on his way. Grateful that his ankles were no longer bound, he climbed against rain and tremors alike, until he reached the place that Elbert had indicated. Using the chains that still held his wrists, he looped them over a protruding root and hauled himself off the path and onto a shelf of rock half-sheltered by an overhang above and the boulder beneath.

Sounds from the battle on the summit were clearer here, begging for Luke's attention. Forcing his mind back to the current situation, he braced himself on the ledge and leaned down to help Elbert climb up.

Just then, Desterrar gave a mighty groan and the entire mountain shook. As if appalled by the wickedness that had invaded its slopes the mount shuddered from base to peak, causing the majority of Haman's men to lose their footing on the path and fall backwards over the numerous crags. In a matter of moments, Wulf's army was dwindled down to the two companies that had already made it to the top.

Luke's face was frozen in a look of shock as he watched the army getting tossed from the steep inclines. Suddenly his body lurched forward when Elbert was nearly pitched from the path and his flailing arms caught hold of the chains dangling over the shelf from Luke's wrists. Luke gave a cry of pain when the metal clasps dug into his flesh, and he scrambled to secure his foothold on the wet stones.

"Luke, I'm slipping! Help me!" Elbert's panicked voice cut through the multitude of other sounds that surrounded them.

Luke finally wedged his foot between two solid objects and looked down to see Elbert's full weight suspending from his bonds as the earth tilted and shifted beneath them. Shaking uncontrollably, due to the earthquake and the cold rain, Luke readied himself and then gave a mighty roar as he hauled Elbert upward. His weary body screamed against the effort, but in a moment the danger was past and Elbert sat beside him on the wide shelf. The young man immediately shrank beneath the overhang, his black hair falling over his face, and he began to weep.

Luke sank back against a patch of earth, trying to catch his breath and his depleted strength as the sounds of conflict intensified on the summit just above him. Shouts, the clash of swords, and the shriek of Pavia's catawyld, all blended with the sounds of the storm to create a fearsome effect. And then, carried on the wind to his listening ear, came the sound of a woman's scream and a man's desperate shout.

"Wulf, *no!!*"

The earth's tremors ceased, at least for the moment, and Luke could no longer remain a bystander. His hand struck a loose object, and he looked down to see an arrow lying on the shelf beside him. Whether a stray of his own or that of a soldier, Luke smiled as he swept the shaft into his palm and turned to his terrified companion.

"Elbert." The young man slowly looked up and Luke read a world of confusion in his gaze. He clapped a hand to Elbert's shoulder and spoke in a direct tone that would reach beyond the fear, "I need a bow."

Wulf gave the order and his men surged forward, entering into combat with Christopher's paltry force. He himself hung back, waiting, as another company of Haman rushed by. Soon the combatants were occupied with their individual opponents, and he made his move.

The earth trembled and shook with every step he took, but Wulf ignored the deterrents of his environment and reveled instead in the sense of power that came with overcoming them. Making a path directly through the center of the scene of battle, he smirked when he caught sight of Warin engaged in combat, and then continued across the small meadow and into the village of Exile.

Elaina struggled to keep her balance as the mountain shifted beneath her feet. Never had she experienced the frightening tremors of an earthquake, and she had certainly never practiced the use of a sword in such conditions. All around her, invading warriors fell to their knees, unable to hold themselves upright between the blinding rain and unstable ground. Miraculously, the Faithful remained on their feet, determined to wipe the murderous Order of Haman from the summit of Desterrar.

Bringing her sword up to block an incoming blow, Elaina ducked beneath her sword arm and shoved against her opponent. As the two blades raced to outmaneuver each other, her mind fought to keep track of what was happening around her. Blinking rain from her eyes and trying to ignore the annoyance of short hair clinging to her face and neck in wet strands, she sent up a silent prayer with every breath.

Please, God, lift this storm.

The battle waged on. Pavia ducked beneath her opponent's swing and Trig leapt at the man with a terrible shriek. Leaving the catawyld to protect her from the soldier's wrath, she turned and added a lunge to the skirmish between Bradley and his opponent. The distracted fiend quickly fell and Bradley jumped to block Pavia from another brigand's sword.

Deflecting another blow to her right, Pavia felt Trig return to her back and she grinned. The poor thing was miserable in this rain. She glanced down at her hem, brown and sluggish in the mud, and shrugged.

"Pavia, down!"

Without a second thought she dropped obediently to the trembling earth, covering the rest of her in thick mud to match her hem. In the next instant Chris leapt over her, landing just in time to deliver a fatal blow to an attacker who had been advancing from behind. The invader fell and Chris offered Pavia a hand up, grinning slightly at her casing of mud. Trig moaned pitifully over her shoulder.

Pavia retrieved her sword and swiped a strand of hair from her face, leaving a thicker trail of mud across her cheek. "Lovely. Now I blend in." She huffed and spun the grip of her blade as she turned back to the fight, "They'll never see me coming."

Time dragged slowly by. The skirmishes seemed endless. The weather and the earthquake were distracting. Chris, Bradley, Ned, and Warin carried much of the fight, having the most experience in combat. Moving quickly from place to place, they helped first one comrade and then another in bringing an end to their savage opponents.

Warin gave a cry of exertion as he shoved one of his brother's followers to the ground and finished the man off. Standing on the outskirts of the battle, he took a moment to catch his breath. He was relieved to see that no more soldiers had scaled the summit, and wondered briefly what had become of the rest of Wulf's army.

A scream suddenly rent the air, sending a chill up his spine, and Warin whirled to face the nearby village. His mind froze at what he saw. Surely his brother would not be so cruel.

Standing by the cottage closest to the meadow, Wulf stared back at him with a knowing smirk on his vengeful face. In one hand he held a drawn sword, and with the other he gripped a terrified Sadie by the arm.

"Wulf, *no!!*"

The earth ceased its tremors.

Wulf laughed, a crazed sound that twisted a sickening knot in Warin's middle. Shoving Sadie to the ground, he stomped on the hem of her dress to keep her from running and held his arms out in a dare, "Save her, Warin. Come and rescue the damsel in distress. Isn't that what you're good at?"

"Wulf, these people only want to live in peace. Go back to your city and your power, and let them be."

Wulf looked incredulous, "Do my ears deceive me? Is the great slaver actually defending the Faithful? What's happened to you, Warin? You're a Mordecai!"

The noise of battle was lessening behind him. Warin remained silent as he took several cautious steps closer.

Wulf sneered, "You always taught me to do whatever it takes. So fight me. Save your Faithful scum and fight me."

"Wulf, I have no wish to fight with you. You're my brother."

A spark of hatred glinted in Wulf's eye, "Not anymore."

He turned and lifted his sword over Sadie, and Warin threw himself forward. Wulf's sword flew from his grasp and the two brothers tumbled to the ground.

With a deafening clap of thunder the rain suddenly ceased to fall. Every eye turned to the heavens in astonishment as the mists were swept upward and the swirling, churning tower of clouds dissipated and vanished. The black sky lightened to gray and in the next moment Desterrar gave a final tremor that started from deep within the mountain.

A noise of terrible magnitude reached them from below, compelling everyone—even Wulf—to look down on the city of Hebbros.

Crowds of people were swarming through the gates, rushing from the city as fast as they could. Dragons floated overhead, desperate for prey, as the confusion intensified. All at once, unable to withstand the force that had shaken its foundation, the western wall crumbled and collapsed. With this far-reaching barrier gone, the restless and swollen Delfron Sea spilled from its boundaries. Still tossing in the aftermath of the violent storm, the turbulent waters tumbled past the broken walls and flooded the sin-stained streets.

No sooner had it begun, then it was over. The small number of citizens who had escaped—perhaps two hundred, mainly women and children—reached the trees that framed the wide valley and turned to gaze back on the shocking scene. Floodwaters had rushed into the expansive city and toppled the remaining walls, forging a path of watery destruction and decimating everything that stood in the way.

Now a stunning silence enveloped everything. Here and there stone spires rose from the unassuming waves, the only indication that a city had only just stood where a placid lake now filled the valley.

The vile city of Hebbros was no more.

"No!" Wulf shrank from the sight and twisted away from Warin's grip on his arm, "No! No! No! My city!"

"Wulf, please," Warin matched his brother's retreating steps with forward motion, "hear me out."

"No," Wulf snarled, "I've heard enough! I've seen enough! I don't need your help. I'll still be the victor this day." His darting gaze saw that his army had been defeated, and he bellowed with fury, "I took the city and I can take you all too. I am lord of Hebbros! I am the great Haman!" His eyes locked with Warin's gaze and he shrieked, "You're a coward!"

Wulf flicked his wrist and a dagger slipped into his palm.

"Warin, look out!" Chris jumped forward and several others cried out when Warin stumbled in his attempt to evade his twin. He fell to the ground and the weapon flashed, grazing his shoulder, and then came the unexpected thud of an arrow finding its target.

Warin rolled over as Wulf froze, stunned by the swift end to his attack. With a moan that sounded more frustrated than alarmed, the great Haman sank to his knees and fell forward.

"Wulf," Warin crawled forward and looked down at his

brother's pale face. Wulf opened his eyes for a moment and Warin was shocked when his concerned gaze was met by a hostile glare.

"Traitor," Wulf whispered on his last breath, and then closed his eyes and died.

Stunned that he had been so blind to the depths of his brother's cruelty, Warin lifted his gaze and found the archer who had put an end to Wulf's violence. Somehow he was not surprised to see that it was Luke who stood at the head of the Banishment Path, bow still poised as he searched Warin's gaze.

Fighting a wave of emotion, Warin slowly nodded in answer to Luke's silent query.

He had done the right thing.

"Luke!" The cry went up from a dozen lips, and the exiled moved to embrace the return of one they'd thought dead. Warin was grateful to be left alone for a moment, kneeling beside his brother's still form. He studied the lines of Wulf's face and wondered how they two had come to be desensitized to a life of anger and brutality.

Another moment passed and Warin felt a hand gently touch the shoulder that was not bleeding. Sadie knelt beside him in silent consolation and Warin felt shamed by the kindness of one who should have hated him.

Every one of them should have hated him, and yet they did not. They would not. Because they knew that their God did not. And that was a mystery in and of itself.

Warin took a shuddering breath, and then covered his face with his hands and wept.

60

Shores of Refuge

With Hebbros and the adjoining valley under water, Mount Desterrar was completely cut off from Mizgalian soil. The waters of the Delfron had enveloped the lower slopes of the mountain, and now lapped at the base on all sides.

Gazing down from the lookout the day following the battle of Exile, Elaina tucked her hair behind her ears and sighed, "What a sad way for so many to die."

Standing to her left, Charlotte heard her mournful tone and squeezed her hand when Sadie translated the words. From Charlotte's other side, Chris responded with thoughts of his own and Luke interpreted.

"What is sad is that those who did escape will move on to another city, another village, and there they'll resume the same wretched lifestyle they knew in Hebbros." He shook his head slightly, "I'm still in awe over the display of God's power that we witnessed yesterday."

To Elaina's right, Pavia exhaled heavily and crossed her arms, "What do we do now?"

Elaina heard Sadie's translation and grinned. She liked the redheaded spitfire and her need for a plan. The discussion continued, with interpretations adding a lilting flavor to the conversation.

"Pavia's right," Charlotte said. "Will we remain here in Exile forever?"

"Where else can we go?" Ned called as he arrived with a subdued Elbert in tow. Ned had volunteered to take charge of his friend in the moments following the battle. He longed to bring the fearful traitor to a true knowledge of the faith, and had taken Elbert under his wing with the steadfastness of a brother. Elbert followed him like a shadow, not even caring to respond to Ned's question by pointing out that they obviously had no boats with which to reach the Mizgalian shore.

"Really we could go anywhere," Chris spoke up, "once we find a way to leave the mountain. We've stayed until now because the western cliffs are treacherous, and to gain access to the sea we needed to go east, down by the walls of Hebbros, and then around. Besides that, the Faithful were not entirely assembled until yesterday. Now we're free to go wherever we wish."

"I would like that," Charlotte spoke softly. "I do love the village of Exile, but I wouldn't enjoy looking daily on the destruction of Hebbros."

"Too many painful memories," Lillian added quietly, as if to herself.

"We could build boats," Ned suggested. He came to a halt beside Charlotte and wrapped an arm around her shoulders.

"We would still have a problem," Luke ran a hand through his hair. Still weary from the exertion of the last few days, he had slept through most of the previous twenty-four hours.

"You're right," Bradley nodded, his eyes resting on the waters below, "I haven't the slightest notion how to build an adequate piece of watercraft, and as far as I know," he glanced about, "neither does anyone else here. We would most definitely run into the possibility of sinking before we reached the other side."

Luke smiled and shook his head, "That's not the problem I was suggesting. Say we did learn to build a boat, or several boats, and were able to leave the mountain. Where would we go? Who would give us shelter? We've already experienced the hatred of our fellow-Mizgalians because of our faith."

"Luke is right." Everyone turned to see Sedgwick standing on the grassy slope just above the ledge. His soft gaze studied their faces, and he smiled to see so many who were dedicated to the safekeeping of their faith.

"What do you suggest, sir?" It was Warin who posed this question, and Sedgwick's heart warmed when he remembered the young man's eagerness to learn of God's mercy the day before. The old man thought back to the day of his exile, some fifteen years past, and tears came to his eyes when he reflected on the work God had accomplished since that time. He focused his gray eyes on the group once again and nodded as he answered Warin's query.

"As we did in times of trouble, so we must do in times of peace. We must pray."

Rosalynn approached her small cottage with a bucket of water, collected from the rains, in her hand. Sadie had served more than her fair share these last days, and Rosalynn felt it her duty to do something in the way of work. This place, these people, inspired her.

She smiled at her children, playing with their cousins, and then paused when she caught sight of her husband sitting on the front stoop. His shoulders were bowed in a defeated posture and his vacant gaze stared at nothing. Rosalynn hurried forward, set the bucket down, and sat beside him.

"Roland?" She wrapped her arms around one of his and laid her chin against his shoulder. At first it seemed he had not heard her, and then Roland slowly began to shake his head.

"What will we do? Everything…lost."

"No," Rosalynn spoke with conviction. "Everything is not lost. We are safe, your children are alive, we are all together… Don't you see?" She turned his face toward hers with one hand, "Those things which truly mattered in your life have been spared."

A single tear marked his face, "I should not have sent you away. I sought your safety, but would not humble myself enough to admit that you were right, and instead became angry. Forgive me."

Rosalynn wiped away his tear as a slow smile appeared on her face, "All is forgiven, and God has answered my prayers. We are together again."

He winced as if in pain, "But what will we do now?"

"We will live, Roland." She turned her head to watch their

children playing in the dirt as Bradley had predicted, "We will learn, and grow, and we will live."

Another two days passed and Luke was growing restless. His preferred method of "action first, plan later" would not work out in this situation. Even he could see that it would be foolish to build a fleet of boats to set sail with no destination in mind. Floating aimlessly about the Delfron would quickly lose its appeal for an entire village seeking to settle down.

Luke heaved a sigh as he walked with his father along the southern perimeter of Desterrar's peak. Althar cast his son a questioning glance and then looked away with a knowing smile. He looked down at young Jerem, walking to his left, and attempted to once again engage Lord Roland's son in conversation.

The boy had been wrapped in grief since the day of battle, confused by the destruction of Hebbros, and guilty that he had hidden from conflict when Wulf appeared at their cottage to take Sadie. Roland had gathered enough strength to defend his family, but the intruder had still managed to drag Rosalynn's attendant away for the purpose of taunting his brother.

Luke listened as his father drew the boy from his shell of insecurity. He recognized and valued his father's ability to minister to others with gentleness and patience. Luke sighed again. He wanted to live in patience as the others in Exile seemed to do, but his desire for answers warred with his need to improve his character, and for once he understood Elaina's preference to plan ahead.

He grinned at the thought. Their Arcrean friend had indeed set about planning for her future, and was preparing for the likelihood that she would never again see her distant home. Elaina had asked Sadie to teach her the Mizgalian language, and was devoting herself to conquering it as quickly as she could. Luke figured if she mastered it as proficiently as she had the sword, she might end up speaking his native language better than he did.

When they caught sight of Sadie and her student up ahead, Althar called out a greeting and they moved toward the spot where the two sat with Pavia and Rosalynn's daughter, Celia, in the shade of a tree by the summit's edge. The four young women laughed as the three wanderers approached and Pavia returned Althar's greeting with a humorous twinkle in her eye.

"Sadie asked us to help Elaina practice."

Elaina scowled and crossed her arms. Celia giggled and Pavia laughed outright as Sadie glanced from one to another and then explained, "She asked if Pavia's Trig likes to hunt quill pens and scrolls."

Celia rolled backward in a fit of merriment. Althar chuckled and Luke fought to control a smile when Jerem suddenly doubled over with laughter. Elaina glared up at him, but the humor in her gaze finally overwhelmed her frustration and she allowed a small grin. She leaned against the tree's trunk and spoke in a mixture of the two languages that Sadie kindly untangled for the others.

"This is so much harder than I thought. I'll never learn to tell the difference between your animals and your household goods."

"You have only just begun," Althar spoke good-naturedly. "It will come."

"Certainly," Pavia agreed, failing to suppress another laugh. "However, I will pity the man you marry when he requests a side of venison, and is served a silver candlestick instead."

Another wave of mirth overtook them, and Sadie reached out to pat Elaina's arm, "Don't worry." Her shoulders shook with laughter, "Give yourself time. You can't learn it all in two days."

"Father! Luke!" Luke glanced up as Chris came running from the west. He stumbled to a halt and grabbed his twin's arm, pulling him back the way he had come and motioning for his father and the others to follow. "Come and see, all of you. There is a ship on the southern horizon, headed this way." He pointed forward, "You can see it best from the western ridge."

The group quickly gained their feet and ran after him.

A crowd was gathering as the village emptied and the Faithful were drawn to the sounds of excitement. If the vessel proved friendly, they could ask for transportation from the mountain-turned-island, and make a home for themselves elsewhere. They watched for several hours as the ship sailed closer, until finally Elaina gasped and grabbed Luke's sleeve where he stood beside her.

"What is it?" He asked, continuing to peer into the afternoon sun.

A smile broke out on Elaina's face as she pointed, "That

vessel is Arcrean, and their flag bears King Druet's royal crest!"

The fire tower was made to smoke in an attempt to catch the eye of the vessel's crew. Discussions were held and the decision made for a small group of ambassadors to descend the mount in advance of the whole village, in hopes that they would have the chance to beg transportation of the captain.

"The Arcreans would be the ideal choice of an escort," Althar spoke to the group. "Their land does not deal in slavery, and therefore we would have no need to fear being betrayed by the captain."

Sedgwick nodded, "We are their greatest enemies. It is a miracle they have sailed a vessel this far north of their border."

Althar and Luke were chosen to leave first, and Chris would lead the rest of the Faithful down half-a-day behind them. The villagers quickly began to gather the few belongings they would need for the journey, and all were ready to leave an hour ahead of the expected time.

Elaina could hardly contain her excitement and impatience. One of the king's own ships was sailing this way on the Delfron! Dare she hope that they had learned of the slave raid and come looking for her and the others?

She glanced at the crowd of eighty or so people, all different ages and backgrounds, and saw their anticipation in the way they worked to help one another down the Banishment Path. The smiles and chatter of all were filled with a hope that bound them together for the journey.

She looked for Sadie and saw the young woman helping with Rosalynn's children, one at each hand and a third tucked in the sling over her shoulder. Sadie smiled and laughed with the noblewoman as if they were old friends, and behind them Warin helped to support Roland down the more dangerous slopes. Elaina marveled at the changes that had taken place among these people, and in such a short time.

Tears sprang to her eyes and she blinked them quickly away. Since the moment she had entered the city of Hebbros eight days before, the thread of her life had somehow become entwined in the tapestry of this people's existence. She longed to return to her home, but suddenly feared that pulling away from the Faithful might tear something precious that had been woven by a divine hand.

As she moved to help an elderly woman through a narrow place on the path, an idea began to form in her head and she smiled. Some might call it selfish, but she would hope that perhaps it was the will of God. The Faithful needed a safe place to go, as well as transportation to get there. If she was correct in her assumptions, then Elaina did have a safe place to go, as well as the transportation to get there. Why couldn't she share those provisions with her friends?

They reached the base of Desterrar three days later and traveled around to the southwestern side of the mountain. Excitement coursed through the Faithful when they saw that the ship had not left, but sat at anchor some distance out to sea. Elaina began to quicken her pace, craning her neck in an attempt to search for signs that a smaller boat had come ashore.

Finally a small group of men came into view. They had obviously heard the approach of the exiled, and were now heading their way across the sloping ground. Elaina recognized Luke and his father, and saw that several others were sailors, and then her eyes fell on a familiar face and she quickened her pace.

Falconer? Elaina bit her lip to contain her pleasure. If he was responsible for bringing the royal vessel into enemy territory, it was a sure sign that Druet had sent his chief informant to locate the Arcreans sold into slavery. She could be certain that Talgus's treachery had been found out, and their trail to Knavesmire followed.

Elaina smiled. The Arcrean spy knew the king's generous heart well, and was sure to agree with her petition to offer the Faithful a home in her native land.

Then Falconer shifted to one side and another man came into view, causing Elaina to halt in place. The man's steps became hurried and he scanned the oncoming crowd, searching. His gaze collided with hers and a smile lit his face. He shouted her name and surged forward.

Tears blurred her vision as Elaina felt her feet move and she rushed forward, letting out a cry of elation when at last she reached her father's open arms. Joyful sobs took hold of them both as she buried her face in his shoulder and held tightly to his neck. Her feet left the ground when he spun them in a circle, and then Frederick spoke in his daughter's ear.

"I thought I had lost you." His voice shook with emotion and he tightened his hold as if he would never let go, "I kept thinking of that last night when we quarreled…"

"I'm so sorry," Elaina's voice wavered and she sobbed again. "I was wrong."

There was a moment's silence, and then, "My child, it is all forgiven." Frederick's chin quivered, "It is I who have felt a deep regret, for there was something which I left unsaid that day, and feared I would never be able to say again." He laid a trembling hand against her hair and squeezed his eyes shut over falling tears, "I love you."

Elaina's heart sang even as her face crumpled with tears.

"I love you, too," she whispered, and then her joy was made complete when her father pulled back, smiled into her eyes, and with one finger tapped the end of her nose.

Epilogue
Home Again

On a quiet Mizgalian road, a lone figure plodded east to the sullen tempo of his thoughts. His clothes and shoes were worn and covered in filth, and his beard had grown ragged and unkempt. His dark eyes remained focused on some unseen point ahead as his feet carried him onward toward an undetermined destination.

Gradually the sound of an approaching cart grew louder, and the traveler slowed to look back over his shoulder. The driver reined in his mule and the cart came to a halt in the road. The driver looked the bedraggled figure up and down with a curious gaze.

"Been through hard times, have ye?"

The traveler gave a single nod.

"I can offer you a ride as far as the city of Gersham, if ye've a mind to keep company with the lad and me potatoes," he jerked a thumb over his shoulder to indicate his load of produce.

"That will be fine." The wayfarer moved to the back of the cart with an uneven gait.

"Been injured, have ye?" The driver eyed him intently.

"Several days ago," his passenger confirmed, "in the city of Hebbros."

"Hebbros!" The driver's eyes grew as round as his head, and

he leaned over the back of the seat, "What a tale! Was it as fierce as they say? The destruction? Is it all true?"

The vagabond stiffened and glared at the other man, "Drive on, sir."

The words were delivered as a fierce command and a look of uncertainty crossed the driver's face. He quickly turned to face forward, called to the mule, and urged the animal up the road at a steady pace. Neither man spoke to the other again as they made their way to Gersham.

Sitting at the back, the weary traveler made himself comfortable for the ride and then hissed in pain when the cart bounced in a deep rut. Gritting his teeth, he felt with his left hand to ensure that the bandage was still in place, wrapped around his middle and covering the wound in his right side.

Turning his head, he looked back the way he had come. Memories of those last few days sped through his mind—the attack, the blast, the rain that had leaked through the roof and washed the Death Chalk from his face, the confusion, the escape from the city—and he grimaced. How could he have been so blind? How had he missed the signs of his aide's rebellion?

As he gazed on the passing countryside from the back of an eastbound cart, Sir Valden of Lork determined that the honor of his name would one day be avenged.

Sensing that he was being watched, Valden turned to meet a gaze of troubled blue in the face of a boy some sixteen years of age—the lad whom the driver had spoken of. Tucked against the side of the cart, behind the load of vegetables, the boy sat in silence and watched him with a mournful expression. Valden's brow suddenly creased.

"I've seen you before, boy." His eyes slipped to the leather collar at the youth's throat.

A slight nod of the blond head, almost imperceptible, and then the lad acknowledged Valden's words, "Yes, master, in Hebbros. I am called Epic."

Elaina filled the first of her buckets with well water and then turned to draw more.

"Can I help you?" Luke reached to take the bucket before she could respond, and quickly lowered it into the well at the center of Balgo's square.

"Thank you." Elaina swept back a strand of hair that had escaped her ribbon. In the six months since her return to Arcrea, the dark locks had finally grown long enough to be tied out of her face.

While Luke drew the full bucket back up again, she turned in a full circle and gazed on the quaint village she had once despised. Where she had once seen the surrounding cottages as a prison, she now saw a safe haven.

Her gaze moved beyond the square to the rows of newer cottages that had been erected for the use of the Faithful. She had been right to suppose that Arcrea's king would take pity on the banished of Hebbros. The village of Balgo had been expanded and the varied group of Mizgalians welcomed with graciousness and goodwill.

Then, two months ago, a courier had arrived bearing word that King Druet requested Lord Roland's presence at Castle Eubank. King Cronin of Mizgalia demanded that Druet relinquish the nobleman who had taken refuge within his borders, so that he might mete out a fair trial regarding Roland's rebellion against the crown. The Arcrean king wished to know how the Mizgalian nobleman would have him respond, and whether he believed himself guilty of the charges set against him. A humbled Roland replied that he did.

At Roland's agreement, Druet had replied to Cronin's orders, stating that he would comply and a contingent of Arcrean soldiers would escort Roland to the city of Mockmor within a month's time. However, Druet had included a condition that his ambassador be permitted to contend for Roland, asking that the reformed nobleman be sent back to Arcrea to lead a quiet life, exiled from his native land.

Lady Rosalynn had insisted that she and her children would accompany her husband. After all that they had been through, and fearing that Cronin would deny the Arcreans' request, she refused to be separated from Roland during what may prove to be his last days.

So the foreign lord, his lady, and their seven children had been escorted from Balgo on horseback, led by Druet's ambassador, Nathaniel, and a company of Arcrean soldiers. Warin had gone too, having become a close and trusted friend of Roland's, and Elaina had not been surprised when she learned that Sadie would be leaving as well.

"I'll miss my homeland, and hope to return with Roland's life spared," Sadie had smiled peacefully when she hugged Elaina goodbye. "I was glad to see my father when we returned to Arcrea by of Filliger, but I knew my time there had come to an end. I believe God has placed me with this family for a reason." She looked over to the cluster of anxious children, "Lady Rosalynn will need help and comfort during this difficult time, and I'm content to be her friend. I know God will use this journey to further His greater plans for my life."

Luke's voice broke through Elaina's thoughts, "You miss Sadie, don't you?" She turned as he lifted a full bucket in each hand and met her gaze, "You always stare toward the northeast when you're thinking of her, and then your eyes glaze over with one of those feminine emotions that make you women choke up and cry." He gave her a look of feigned bewilderment, "I confess, possessing this gift is frightening at times."

Elaina laughed as they started up the street toward her home. "I do miss Sadie. Though her peace at leaving made it easier to say goodbye, and I have hope that they will all return."

"Bradley's children are missing their cousins." Luke smiled, "Bradley, though… His lighthearted nature hasn't let him mourn the departure of his sister for very long, especially with the excitement of his fifth child on the way."

Elaina grinned and stepped aside to let another woman pass toward the square. "I was happy to hear that Chris and Pavia are to be married soon."

Luke let out a gusty sigh, "Finally! You wouldn't believe how many hints it took to help my brother see the truth. I had to take him by the shoulders and force him to look me in the eye, whereupon I kindly informed him that he loves the girl."

"You didn't," Elaina chuckled. "What did he say?"

Luke rolled his eyes, "He already knew."

They stopped before her family's cottage and Luke set the buckets down by the door.

"Thank you," Elaina nodded. "It was kind of you to stop and help me, though I'm sorry it took you away from your other work this evening."

"Actually," he ducked his head with an awkward grin, "I came here first to see if you'd care to take a stroll, and your mother hinted that you *might* be drawing water in the square."

"Oh." Her face flushed slightly, and she glanced away.

"And now," Luke took a step back, "as we've already taken that stroll, and your father will expect me at the shop bright and early tomorrow, I'll be heading home and letting you do the same."

Elaina nodded and for a brief moment met his gaze. Luke gave a small smile and tipped his head in farewell, backing away a few more steps and then turning to walk back down the street.

Elaina stood on the front stoop, hearing the quiet murmur of conversation from the other side of the door and the untroubled tune that Luke was whistling as he made his way home. She closed her eyes and let the spring breeze caress her face, and then looked up at the darkening sky overhead. A song of praise rose in her heart, and soon found its way to her lips.

Place of peace, rest, and ease… Truly, her soul had found these things.

"Mine eyes shall be upon the faithful of the land, that they may dwell with me: he that walketh in a perfect way, he shall serve me."

Psalm 101:6

About the Author

Nicole Sager is a homeschool graduate and an avid reader. She lives with her wonderful parents and has five awesome siblings. Nicole enjoys a number of hobbies, but especially reading and writing (and always with a cup of coffee). *Hebbros* is Nicole's fourth published book, and the first outside of *The Arcrean Conquest* Series.

"In writing each book, I pray that it will bring honor and glory to God, and that He will use it as a tool to bring at least one person to the saving knowledge of Jesus Christ. I pray that my books would be a blessing to readers (individuals & families alike) as they search for wholesome yet exciting reading material for all ages."

~ *N.S.*

Author Fun Facts!

Desterrar is Spanish for Banish,
and the name Sedgwick means Village of Victory.

Online!

Look for quotes, trivia, and reviews for Nicole's books on **Goodreads**, and don't forget to like her on **Facebook** for news, updates, and more fun!

www.facebook.com/arcreabooks

Made in the USA
Thornton, CO
08/13/23 08:52:17

b79f16b4-500e-415b-8a45-ea7e435e2765R01